Seelöwe Nord

To Chris,
With very best wishes

Andy Johnson
March 2010

Seelöwe Nord

The Germans are Coming

Andy Johnson

Spiderwize

Seelöwe Nord

Spiderwize
Mews Cottage
The Causeway, Kennoway
Kingdom of Fife
KY8 5JU
Scotland UK

www.spiderwize.com

ISBN: 978-1-907294-38-9

This book is dedicated to the officers and soldiers of every nationality, who have served with Task Force Helmand.

The tyrant rents his power with blood; the free man must purchase his liberty with the same currency

The author would like to thank Professor Tim Bean from the Royal Military Academy Sandhurst and Mr Simon Whittaker for their assistance in researching this novel.

The author has undertaken to donate a percentage of the profits from this book to British military charities.

The cover illustration is courtesy of the US National Archive and Research Agency (NARA) via Joe McCary at photoresponse.com

Foreword

This is not an academic work. It is essentially a story of men at war, set against a historical background; one which I have seen fit to tinker with in order to facilitate the plot. It is *not* a nostalgic trip down memory lane. It is a warts and all story of men in battle. Those who have served in the armed forces of their nation will understand the descriptions of combat better than most. For the civilian, it may give you an inkling of the horror, the adrenalin-fuelled thrill, and sometimes the complete absurdity of war.

I have tried to stay faithful to the characters of the well known historical figures within the book. The many fictional characters, I hope, typify the diverse nature of all armies from time immemorial. All the historical figures mentioned in this book were extraordinary men, asked to do extraordinary things during the greatest conflict this planet has ever seen. I hope I have reflected that within this fictional novel. No offence is intended or implied to any character, living or dead.

This novel is fiction of course, although Operation Sealion was, to some degree, a reality in 1940. For those with a deep interest in Sealion, or the early part of World War Two in general, there are some excellent works on the subject such as *Blitzkrieg*, by Len Deighton; *Invasion*, by Kenneth Macksey; *Finest Hour*, by Tim Clayton and Phil Craig; and *Dunkirk-Fight to the last man*, by Hugh Sebag-Montefiore. In addition, the *War Diaries of Field Marshal Lord Alanbrooke,* edited by Alex Danchev and Daniel Todman, were invaluable in establishing the nature of relationships between members of the British High Command in 1940, and much of the behaviour ascribed to Churchill in this novel is based on historical precedent.

In no way does this novel attempt to argue a case for the possibility of Operation Sealion ever having been practicable, either on the south coast of England or further north. I have, for the purpose of this book, simply assumed that it was. Any inaccuracies, continuity errors or bad examples of grammar and spelling are mine, and mine alone. I would suggest that if you are unfamiliar with the North and East Ridings of Yorkshire that you have a standard road atlas of Great Britain to hand. Finally, I ask the reader to take the book for what it is; a story of fighting men.

Andy Johnson
November 2009

Contents

PART ONE

Seelöwe

'S' DAY
H -5

STAVANGER AIRFIELD – NORWAY
FRIDAY 20TH SEPTEMBER 1940 – 2330 HOURS

The air was cold, the night was dark; the waning half moon not yet visible. Standing in the doorway of the hanger, Lieutenant Heinz Gerring listened to the subdued murmur of the ground crews as they prepared the five squadrons of Heinkel 111 bombers for the imminent operation. Nearly fifty aircraft, on top of those already stationed here, had been flown in from France over the last three days; hopping from airfield to airfield on their long route to this, their secret destination. Each phase of their route had been shrouded in mystery until the last safe moment. Now they were here in Norway and assigned to the new Air Fleet.

The cause of their unexpected redeployment had been the subject of much debate. If they were being pulled away from the north coast of France, then surely that meant that the invasion of England was off? Now based in Norway, such a concentration of force could only mean that there was an impending offensive against Russia, surely? Some however, said nobody in Berlin would be stupid enough to invade Russia, certainly not at this time of year. They must be going into Sweden or Finland, regardless of the neutral stance of those countries.

The briefing they had just received, however, had revealed the true purpose of this sudden upheaval and left even the most dedicated National Socialists amongst them speechless. Operation Sealion was on alright, but the invasion of Britain was not going to be quite what had been expected. The whole of the summer had been one great deception plan. Even now, Gerring found it hard to believe that the General Staff had been able to put together such a bold and detailed plan in just three months and at the same time, pull off such an enormous ruse. The magnitude of the whole situation was still sinking in. By turns, Gerring was feeling both exultant and terrified.

Only the new, Greater Germany, could have possibly followed up the swift conquest of Europe with the extraordinary venture that was only hours away from becoming reality; a venture that was bold, daring and entirely in keeping with the ethos of aggressive confidence prevalent throughout the armed forces of the Fatherland at this moment. Despite this, Gerring felt uneasy. The knowledge that the success of the operation rested on such critical timings and sweeping assumptions daunted even the most confident young warriors of Nazi Germany. The scale of the plan was vast; with only a narrow margin separating absolute victory and the greatest prize of the war from total disaster. He shuddered involuntarily at the thought.

"Shouldn't you be asleep now, Heinz?"

The voice snapped Gerring out of his reverie. Turning, he found himself in the company of his Squadron Leader, Major Otto Grueman.

"Sorry Sir, I was miles away there!" He smiled. "I was just getting some fresh air; trying to clear my mind."

Grueman smiled too; a thin, half-hearted smile.

"Don't worry yourself Heini." Grueman said, switching to Gerring's nickname and affecting a less formal air. "I've bumped into nearly every member of the Squadron over the last half hour; all trying to find their own little private space so that they can be alone with their thoughts."

The Major came closer and stood beside Gerring, sweeping his gaze across the darkened airfield. The night was fairly clear. There was some broken cloud, quite high up, but behind them countless stars twinkled brilliantly in the great dark void of the night sky.

"I know what you're thinking Heini; much the same as the rest of us. The German in you is proud; unbelievably proud of this magnificent plan and the tasks that have been entrusted to us. But the airman in you; the military man; he's shitting bricks at the thought of what tomorrow will bring. It's a bold plan; some would say crazy. It may just work. But it's going to be our biggest test yet. Worse than Poland. much worse than France and the Low Countries. Worse even than the sorties over London last month or the daylight raids on the British airfields."

For a while, Gerring didn't reply.

"Can it work, do you think?" He asked hesitantly.

Grueman shrugged.

"The cloud's finally breaking up. Good bombing weather…"

"But the fleet?" Gerring said. "They'll be wide open come daylight."

"Doesn't matter now." Grueman kicked at a nearby pebble. "They'll be heading across the German Sea already. The cloud and fog has given them sufficient cover to creep down the Danish Coast and strike west during the daylight. Now they've just got to sail straight across the sea as fast as they can to be off the English coast before dawn. The big ships from Bremerhaven will be with them already. We need the clear weather now; lots of it."

Grueman looked at his watch.

"The Dornier squadrons in France and Holland will be airborne now. Very soon, London, Brighton, Dover Ashford, Maidstone and Canterbury will all be ablaze. The old Rhine barges will be getting herded into the channel. And at dawn, every Stuka and 109 will be hitting the airfields and military camps as far north as Suffolk. And while they're keeping the Tommies busy, we'll be taking off and heading for glory."

Gerring looked across at his Squadron Leader.

"Or death?" He suggested.

Grueman gave a wry smile and nodded.

"Death or glory; indeed."

The Major clapped Gerring on the shoulder.

"Come Heini, let's go and get something to eat before we kit-up; it's going to be a long day."

And with that, the two Luftwaffe officers wandered back over towards the small huts that served as the air-crew accommodation. As they did so, the clock ticked steadily towards midnight and into the new day.

TROOPSHIP BERLINER – SOMEWHERE IN THE NORTH SEA
FRIDAY 20TH SEPTEMBER 1940 – 2335 HOURS

Sergeant Johann Saltz needed a piss. He had been drinking water all night, mainly from habit but partly because he couldn't sleep. Nobody had slept. Ever since they had been given the briefing that morning after their departure from Aalborg, the entire Battalion had been speculating incessantly. At first they had thought it was some kind of joke, but very quickly they had realised there was nothing remotely humorous about what was to come. The issue of the additional ammunition had been routine for large scale exercises. Even the grappling hooks and scaling ladders hadn't alarmed them too much, but when the pioneers had begun putting together live satchel charges in the hold of the vessel, Saltz and his companions had looked on in shock, before descending into a renewed frenzy of debate. Surely, this could be no drill? Live satchel charges in a packed hold? It was unheard of during exercises.

"What is this village called? Saltz?"

The sudden question brought the young squad sergeant back to the present. He looked up at the dimly lit map and saw Captain Dullman pointing at a small collection of buildings.

"Er…Shpee-ton, Captain?" He ventured, struggling with the pronunciation of the unfamiliar English name.

The company commander nodded curtly.

"That's right, Speeton village. And why is it important? Schultz?" He flicked his gaze to another squad sergeant from Second Platoon.

"Because it sits on a ridge that dominates all of the exits from the beach in our sector, Captain."

"Good." Dullman nodded. "Why Else? Bachman?"

"Because the fire control headquarters for the coastal battery is situated on the same ridge, Sir."

"That's correct." Dullman declared again, apparently satisfied that everyone had been taking notice at the brief he had given earlier. "And that's our main objective of the day. Remember, even if we can't get into the gun battery straight away, we exploit eastwards and capture this ridge. We need to secure our foothold in order for the pioneers to deal with that battery and allow the second and third waves to muster without any interference. Once we've got it, we hold onto it until the Second Battalion exploit through us. Then, we wait for further orders. But be prepared to move inland quickly. We need depth in this bridgehead, in order to get the panzers ashore; then we can really get cracking. Do not expect to sleep for at least seventy two hours."

Behind Saltz, Corporal Martin Nuemark, swore quietly. "Fuck my old boots, Jo'. This is gonna be a right old carve-up!"

THE LEWIS GUN TRENCH – HUNMANBY GAP, FILEY BAY, ENGLAND.
FRIDAY 20TH SEPTEMBER 1940 – 2345 HOURS

Both the cloud and the sea mist were clearing now. Myriad stars were sparkling between the broken clouds which sauntered idly through the night sky. The sea was calm and quiet; the surf rolling gently. High tide had been and gone and low tide would be in about another four hours. The mist lingered on the horizon but would soon clear.

George Harper rubbed his gloved hands together, then, for the hundredth time that night, ran his hands lovingly over the newly issued Lewis Gun. He had been a Lewis Gunner before, twenty three years ago in the First War. He had carried it through that long grim winter of 1917, and then on through the glorious offensives of 1918 that had almost broken the stalemate of the trenches, just before the German surrender. Now here he was again, a full corporal in the Filey Bay Home Guard, and the only man in the Platoon who could use the Lewis Gun proficiently. They had received it just a week ago; on account of the new importance that their sector had acquired with the construction of the heavy gun battery just south of this current position, a few hundred yards away at Reighton Gap. The other two platoons had also received one each, resulting in a Christmas-like atmosphere amongst the enthusiastic members of the Home Guard company.

Most of the platoon had been given some rudimentary training on the gun, but it was immediately obvious that Harper was the real expert, and like everything in these dark days, it was expediency that reigned. Therefore, despite being a section commander, he had relinquished his Canadian P17 rifle and taken on responsibility for the platoon's most powerful weapon. Now, at just past midnight, he was staring into the black expanse of the North Sea from the comfort of the new trench. He was proud of the trench; almost as much as he was the gun. Their Regular Army instructor, a tall imposing Sergeant from the Coldstream Guards, had insisted on building a succession of properly constructed fire trenches and strong-points from which to use the newly arrived machine guns.

Harper's thoughts were interrupted by an urgent whisper from Tom Martlesham, the seventeen year old farmhand who was his No.2 on the gun.

"George! There's somebody coming up behind us!"

Harper placed his hand underneath the barrel sleeve and lifted the gun, swinging it around and placing the bipod legs down on the rear parapet, so that the weapon pointed inland, towards Hunmanby village.

"Where?" He demanded in a whisper.

Tom leaned in close and pointed. Following the indication, Harper raised his eyes slightly, using his peripheral vision to pick up the movement. There; he could see it. Just one person, moving fast, but not in a particularly suspicious manner.

Harper knew what looked suspicious and what didn't. One of his other tasks in the First War was trench-raiding. As a former bare-knuckle boxer in his youth, Harper had been first choice for raiding parties back in Flanders.

"Keep him covered, but don't fire unless I say so." He instructed his young companion quietly. "And Tom…"

The young man peered at Harper through the dark, expectantly.

"Keep your finger off the trigger; just leave it on the trigger guard."

Martlesham nodded and turned back to look down the sights of his rifle.

The figure was closing on them now. It was someone who knew where they were going and what they were looking for. Harper watched until the dark figure was barely fifteen yards away and silhouetted against the dark blue sky before he issued the challenge.

"Halt!" He barked in a firm, clear voice, and the approaching person did exactly that, coming to a stand-still and making no attempt to hide or take cover.

"Who comes there?" Harper barked again.

"Sergeant Jackson." Replied the dark figure in a crisp voice.

"Advance one, and be recognised." Harper ordered.

The man stepped forward slowly and Harper could see the distinctive outline of the British pattern steel helmet and the Lee Enfield rifle that the man carried, which he held out to one side in a non-threatening manner.

"Halt." Harper ordered again, feeling sure of his visitor's identity now. "What's your regimental motto?"

There was a slight pause, and then the man replied. "Nulli Secundus; that's 'Second to None' in English."

Harper relaxed.

"Pass friend; all's well."

Harper lifted the Lewis Gun and swung it back round onto its primary arc of fire, covering the beach, and threw a meaningful glance at young Tom. Even in the dark, Harper could see the sudden look of worry on the boy's face. Harper grinned.

"Evening Sergeant." He greeted the newcomer, who dropped down into the trench, between the two sentries.

"Evening lads. All quiet?" Replied Sergeant Davey Jackson of the Coldstream Guards.

Harper regarded their Regular Army instructor with an admiration he'd held for the Brigade of Guards since the Somme. Jackson had arrived in the company some three weeks before, with only a days notice. According to Lieutenant Wainwright, their platoon commander, the Coldstream Guardsman had been sent to assist in training the whole Company for a period of several weeks whilst he recovered from his injuries. The sergeant had been at Dunkirk by all accounts, fighting with the rearguard, when he had been concussed by a bomb-blast. As a result, he had nearly gone blind, but had somehow managed to carry his wounded officer back to the Company Aid Post before collapsing himself. Since then, he had been dogged by poor eyesight and after several months of rest, his eyesight was only slowly returning to anywhere near normal.

And so, temporarily unfit for front-line duties, it had been decided to send him on some leave, after which he would conduct training for local Home Guard units. So here he was. A Goole lad by birth, Jackson was now billeted in Hunmanby and responsible for training all three Platoons from the Filey Bay Company. And what a transformation he had made in his short time with them. He had brought the Company on leaps and bounds these last couple of weeks. Physically imposing, ruthless in pursuit of excellence, yet surprisingly mild mannered, Jackson had quickly won over the Home Guard officers and allowed them to learn without fear of being embarrassed in front of their men. Weapon training and fitness training had been relentless; but it was the constant barrage of tactical advice that had been the most absorbing for all of the Home Guard volunteers.

Jackson had brought back stories from France and Belgium that dismissed much of the public hype and allowed them to focus on the harsh realities of potential invasion.

"The Germans are bloody good at fighting, and don't let anyone tell you different." Those had been his very first words in his initial briefing on minor tactics. "Don't think you can sit in a pill-box or behind a barricade and take pot-shots at him all day long because you can't. A pill-box is fine for the first half-hour at the most, while you plug the bastards as they come off the boats, but once they've got their jack-boots on terra firma then you need to get your arse moving. Jerry uses mobility. He infiltrates and uses cover, no matter how small it is. He'll outflank you time and again. You've got to do the same. Keep him guessing. Take him from a different angle every time. Confuse him. And most importantly; when you kill your first German, take his bloody weapons, because he'll be carrying a shed-load more ammunition than you've got."

Sound advice indeed. To Harper, a veteran infantryman of the First War, all of the sergeant's advice rang true. Just having the chap around imbued everyone with confidence, although it also caused them to sharpen up their act too, for despite his dodgy eyesight, Jackson missed nothing. He could almost smell a dirty rifle and would quickly produce his spectacles in order to conduct closer inspections when he suspected that standards had lapsed. Jackson had personally supervised the construction of the new trenches, ensuring that they were built and then camouflaged to the very highest specifications. Yes, thought Harper, thank God for the Guards.

Jackson was wearing his spectacles Harper noted. He obviously didn't like wearing them but was professional enough to understand when he needed them.

"A calm night again by the looks; and the skies clearing too." Observed Jackson.

"Aye Sarge… sorry, *Sergeant*." Replied Martlesham, nervously. "Do you think they'll come now? There's been rumours of it for a fortnight, ever since 'Cromwell' night."

"Hmm." Jackson puckered his mouth, thoughtfully. "Could do lad. Conditions are good for boats I reckon. Clear skies for bombers, within reason. And time's running out. If they don't come soon they'll have a right old job trying to pull it off in the winter. They'll probably wait until spring if they can't do it before October. And we'll be stronger then; much stronger."

"No news is good news, eh, Sergeant?"

"Normally lad, but don't count your chickens just yet. Remember what I told you about the buggers. They're risk takers by nature. They'll always try something once, no matter how bloody hair-brained it seems. So keep your eyes peeled; you just never know."

"By the way," continued Jackson, turning to Harper, "I got you some more ammunition. Here." He unslung two canvas bandoliers from his shoulder and passed them to the old corporal. "There's another hundred rounds there."

Harper looked down in surprise.

"Crikey! Where did you get those from?"

Jackson's face cracked into a smile.

"The officer commanding that coastal battery down there squared it away with his battery sergeant major. They were more than happy to hear we've dug new positions along this stretch. Makes them feel more comfortable knowing they've got someone covering the back door and the flanks, especially with the big flap on just recently. I would have liked a bit more, but beggars can't be choosers, eh?"

Harper slung the two bandoliers over his head and shoulder.

"That they can't." He agreed happily. "And this little lot doubles my load. Shame we can't get anymore of the rifle ammo, mind you."

Jackson grunted.

"Mmm. That'll prove much more difficult. The .30 ammunition isn't standard issue for the Regular Army, so we've only got what's been shipped in with the rifles. But like I said before; first German you kill, nick his rifle and webbing, you'll be able to get your hands on their bullets easier than you will this Canadian stuff. Keep hold of that Lewis Gun though; there'll be plenty of .303 about if the balloon goes up."

"So what's the take on all this from the Gunners at Reighton Gap?" Harper asked, interested to know more about the sergeant's visit there.

Jackson sucked his teeth for moment.

"They're all a bit bored to be honest. The excitement seems to have died down. I can understand it to a degree; we've been standing-to for a fortnight and still nothing. Their headquarters people reckon that 'Cromwell' is going to get cancelled pretty soon."

The Coldstream sergeant paused briefly, before adding, "But like I say; don't switch off just yet. You know the Jerries as well as me, if not better. The bastards are full of surprises."

He fumbled in one of his pouches and produced something small and round which he held up for Harper to see.

"Got a couple of my own little treats mind you! Just in case the Jerries do appear!"

Harper gasped in surprise.

"A Mills Bomb!"

Again, he saw the white slash in the dark as Jackson grinned at him.

"No.36 Grenades; the updated version of the Mills." He corrected the older soldier. "Another present from the Gunners. They loaned me two of them. They want them back though and I had to sign for them; tight buggers."

"What about these then?" Harper asked tapping the bandoliers.

"Oh, they're ok. We can hold onto them. They'll just write them off against a range practice or something."

The sergeant hauled himself up the rear off the trench. "Anyway, I'm off to check on No.3 Section. Keep warm and stay sharp lads."

Harper nodded at the silhouette of the young Coldstream Guardsman.

"We will Sergeant. Watch how you go. And thanks for the ammo."

"My pleasure George."

And with that, Jackson disappeared back up the re-entrant towards the rear section's trenches.

Harper turned back to stare out at the dark sea.

"Hope he's right." Mumbled young Martlesham. "Hope we do get stood down soon."

"Aye." Harper concurred. "But all that depends on Mr Hitler, doesn't it?"

NAVAL AND MILITARY CLUB – LONDON
FRIDAY 20TH SEPTEMBER 1940 – 2350 HOURS

General Alan Brooke, Commander-in Chief British Home Forces, removed his spectacles and rubbed his eyes. He stared blankly across the room, his mind elsewhere. It had been another long day, with a good, useful visit to see Oliver Leese and his 29th Independent Brigade, followed by a tedious afternoon with Prince Henry. Then, leaving the headquarters at 8 pm for dinner, he had retired here. He placed his journal down on the table beside him, his entry for the day complete. He should go to bed now, yet his sharp, intelligent brain was still whirring with ideas and thoughts.

Still no invasion. Would they ever come, he wondered? Probably not, if they didn't come tonight. The Channel was reported as being perfect for a seaborne operation and the mist and cloud from earlier in the day was predicted to clear overnight. Nothing out of the ordinary so far, though. He had put the entire country on stand-by for an imminent invasion nearly two weeks ago, using the codeword 'Cromwell'. That decision had been based on predicted weather conditions and information passed from Military Intelligence. The two week bracket given for the German operation had now run its course and Brooke was beginning to hope that Hitler had decided to wait for the spring before making an attempt. If that was the case then Brooke would be happy.

Having taken over this appointment in July, Brooke had spent the last two months working tirelessly to improve the anti-invasion defences of Britain, touring hundreds of miles of coastline and visiting dozens of strong-points and fortifications. At the same time he had been trying to revitalise his under-equipped forces; in effect trying to exorcise the demons of Belgium and France. For many British Generals, and certainly for the public, the Germans had become something akin to bogeymen. The Army's confidence was shaken badly. It lacked confidence in its soldiers, its commanders and its equipment. But Brooke knew that people were missing the point. The Germans weren't super-human, nor was their equipment necessarily that much better than that of the British Army. But what the Germans did do well was *think*. They paid attention to detail. They trained their staffs well, and they wargamed and experimented with new ideas. That's what had beaten the British Army in France; not tanks or dive-bombers or parachutists dressed as nuns, but ideas.

If only the Germans held off, Brooke would have a chance. During the winter, the Government could do its bit and re-equip the Army, whilst Brooke trained it. He would get rid of the Army's fortress mentality and teach it to think more flexibly; teach it to fight not just with fire-power, but with manoeuvre too. He would have to remove some commanders from post and promote others. Some would have to stay for a lack of suitable substitutes, and those would need to have their mind-sets changed beyond recognition. If Britain was to survive, never mind win this war, it needed a new kind of Army.

Brooke suddenly thought about the tanks he had been ordered to send out to the Middle-East. He supposed they must be half-way to Egypt by now, and cursed inwardly. Another of Churchill's demands, via the Secretary of State. Here was Britain, fighting for its very survival, and out of the blue, Churchill decides to send three regiments of valuable armoured vehicles to Egypt to help defend a sandy corner of the Empire! A thought occurred to Brooke and he grunted with amusement. Hitler and Churchill were not that different really, allowing for the fact that Hitler was a humourless upstart who sought to deny freedom to millions of people and impose harsh, totalitarian rule across the whole of Europe in order to further his own perverse policies.

Other than that, they were very similar though. Both gifted orators, inspirational and loved by the masses. Both of them too, military amateurs; arm-chair strategists with narrow minds and prone to random decision making. That is what he had heard of Hitler anyway; and with Churchill he had first hand experience. How strange fate was he thought, to bring me to this place, this time, this predicament. He should probably pray at some point. His recent work routine had left him little time for it. A pang of guilt nagged at him, but he couldn't settle his mind enough for prayer. It seemed relatively quiet tonight, but not unusually so. Surely they wouldn't come now? Despite the calm weather predicted over the next couple of days, it would be October soon and the channel was not a nice place to be in winter, even for proper ships, never mind invasion barges.

He glanced down at a well thumbed book on birds of the British Isles and allowed himself a half-smile. Another of his penchants that he had been neglecting recently. Perhaps when this terrible business was over he could go away with his family and spend some time in the country? Scotland perhaps? But now it was time for sleep. He stood with a groan and stretched off, raising his arms above his head and yawning. He needed to sleep, no matter how much was going on inside his mind. Even the greatest military thinkers could be transformed into dull-witted fools through lack of sleep.

He remembered with distaste, watching a number of senior officers suffer nervous breakdowns during the retreat to Dunkirk. Strange, he thought, that he was able to feel both pity and disgust towards those individuals simultaneously. Two emotions that were diametrically opposed, yet he remembered feeling both when confronted with those poor, broken men. But not me, he thought with a sudden flash of resolve. Not me. I *will* rise to this great challenge that God has set before me. I will prevail. But I need to sleep if I am to do so. And tomorrow, he thought as he began to unhitch his braces from his shoulders, if the Germans haven't come, I will cancel the Cromwell alert.

U-47 – 45 MILES SOUTH-EAST OF THE ORKNEY ISLANDS SATURDAY 21ST SEPTEMBER 1940 – 0025 HOURS

It was a surprisingly calm sea for this time of year in the ocean surrounding the Orkney's. A calm sea and clear skies, observed Lieutenant Commander Gunther Prein, national hero of Nazi Germany and submarine ace. There had been thick cloud and a persistent sea-mist earlier in the evening but it was clearing now. There wouldn't be any cover on the surface when the dawn came. He looked around him, turning full circle in the conning tower, squinting into the darkness as he did so. Nothing; just the dark void and the sound of the sea. Just how he liked it. Prein loved the solitude, the feeling of challenge, not just against the enemy but against the forces of nature too.

The sense of isolation was deceptive of course, for this mission was unusual for Prein, in that he was most definitely not alone. Somewhere, out in the darkness were another seventeen U-Boats, much like his own. They were already split into their packs; three flotillas of five each with a fourth, smaller flotilla of just three boats. Prein was the overall commander of the entire force, an honour conferred upon him in the wake of his raid on Scapa Flow last year, when he had sunk the Royal Oak, and also because of his recent, successful raid into the North Atlantic, where he had sent eight merchantmen to the bottom in just one patrol. His was the task of bottling up the British Home Fleet in Scapa Flow for as long as possible. Leading the centre of the three large flotillas, he was responsible for sealing the southernmost exit from the flow; the one used by the battleships and aircraft carriers.

The other two would be responsible for keeping the cruiser and destroyer channels sealed up tight, whilst the small flotilla of three boats was tasked with covering the tiny exits on the eastern side of the Flow, including the channel that Prein had used himself to get U-47 in amongst the British fleet and strike a headline blow against the Royal Navy, just six weeks after the outbreak of war. The plan was simple enough in theory, but much more difficult in practice. His air cover would be minimal; a handful of Condors if he was lucky, and the odd re-supply boat or additional submarine, but that was about it. In short, the German High Command was asking him to stop the mightiest Navy on the face of the earth for at least four days with less than 900 men in just eighteen boats. Most men would have baulked at such a task, but not Gunther Prein. He loved this kind of challenge; lived for it in fact. The sheer enormity of the task and its potential historical implications were not lost on him, and he was resolved to do his level best.

It wouldn't be easy though. They were in range of allied aircraft and would be vulnerable during their battery charging sessions on the surface, never mind the systematic depth charge dispersal that would surely be used against them when the British realised exactly what was going on. The plan rested on two essential points. He and the other flotillas would need to plug the exits from Scapa Flow at all costs, whilst a separate force of some eight U-Boats would need to watch their backs and try to hold off any destroyers coming out of mainland British ports to try and break the Scapa Flow block.

If the British Home Fleet managed to break out in force, Operation Sealion would be dead in the water.

Prein checked his watch. It had started. Hard to believe it, standing up here in the conning tower, staring out across the calm, dark, ocean. But soon the calm would be gone. These waters would become a killing ground, a nameless place in the middle of the German Sea that would decide the fate of nations. And further south, there would be even more killing. Prein thought he should be feeling something. A profound sense of fate perhaps? A sense of foreboding maybe? Jubilation? In fact he felt nothing other than the icy professional calm that had allowed him to achieve his formidable reputation. His mind was alive with the mass of detail that he would need to tap into, minute by minute, over the course of the next few days. He knew how difficult his task was, yet at the same time knew he could do it.

It was all about professionalism; keeping cool under pressure and thinking straight. He had asked for and been given the pick of the U-Boat Captains. Many of them were old friends; all of them had proved themselves in action. None of them were under any illusion about what would happen if the Royal Navy broke out of Scapa Flow and closed with the invasion force. The German capital ships like Gneisnau and Deutschland were powerful in their own right, but there simply weren't enough of them to hold off squadron after squadron of British battle-cruisers. No; the success of Sealion depended on Prein and his submarines. There was no room for error. It was all or nothing; the last, and the biggest gamble of the war. They must succeed.

"Captain?"

Prein looked around at the voice, his thoughts suddenly interrupted.

"We are 45 miles from the south coast of Orkney."

Prein nodded at the First lieutenant who had brought him the news.

"Very well." He acknowledged the information quietly; without emotion. "It is time then?"

"Yes Captain. We are ready to dive when you give the order."

Prein took one last look out across the black void and sucked in a long breath of salty air.

"Let's get to it then." He smiled at the lieutenant. "History awaits us. Take her down."

The Lieutenant saluted and disappeared inside the submarine, followed shortly afterwards by a lookout, and then Prein himself.

"Yes," thought Prein as he watched the hatch being sealed behind him, "history awaits alright. And how many ships will be sunk, and how many men will die before this page is written?"

Outside, the clouds were rapidly fading, revealing more stars and just a sliver of moonlight. Moments later, the water around the submarine began to bubble and froth, and then, as if it had never been there, U-47 slipped silently beneath the cold, dark waves.

'S' DAY
H -3

CHURCH OF ST MARY AND ST EADBURGA – LYMINGE, KENT SATURDAY 21ST SEPTEMBER 1940 – 0210 HOURS

"Bloody hell, Frank!" Breathed Lieutenant Ronald Farlston, a history teacher by day and currently on duty as the platoon commander of the Lyminge Platoon of the Home Guard. " It's like a scene from the Bible!"

Next to him, his Sergeant, Frank Detling, was also gazing southwards, as rapt by the nightmare vision as his officer. To his left, the other two sentries were also staring open mouthed. The Church of St Mary and St Eadburga was one of only a handful in this part of Kent that had a crenulated tower and flat roof, rather than the pointed, Norman tiled canopy, and therefore offered one of the best vantage points around. Now, the command group of the Lyminge Home Guard were staring in awe at the spectacle around them.

The night sky to the south was bright red, and the sound of explosions could be clearly heard. Every now and then, a bright orange flash in the distance showed where the latest bomb had detonated. Behind the distant drone of aircraft and the sound of exploding bombs, the sharper report of anti-aircraft fire could be distinguished.

"The whole of Dover and Folkestone must be on fire!" Farlston marvelled.

"Looks like everything along the coast has copped it." Detling added.

Farlston traversed his gaze, following the line of the coast. Indeed, it seemed as if the entire coast-line was on fire. He looked back eastwards and saw that there were flames coming from the direction of Hawkinge. The airfield had received a short but savage pounding, almost as soon as the raid had begun. He wondered if the airfield had taken the hits or whether it was the village that had suffered the damage. Whichever, there were several large fires burning, so some poor bugger had been on the receiving end.

He turned about and moved to the other side of the tower, looking north-west now. Another expansive red glow lit up the sky just a few miles away.

Ashford. That too had received a pounding. Farlston turned back towards the others and found Detling regarding him with a concerned look.

"This is the worst ever, by a long way." He said. "It doesn't seem right. Why not London, or just the harbours? Even the airfields perhaps? But all of it in one go, and the whole coastline too…" His voice tailed off.

Farlston nodded, equally lost for words at the scale of the destruction. It seemed to him that from up here on the church tower, that Lyminge was an island. It was as if the village was invisible to German bombers, and amongst all the flames and fire and destruction, Lyminge was the one little parish that had been completely untouched.

Just then, the anti-aircraft guns at Hawkinge began firing again.

"Sweet Jesus!" Swore Detling. "Not again?"

Hurriedly, the four men on top of the tower donned their steel helmets again and knelt down against the crenulations of the tower, peeking through the gaps in order to observe the next stage of this vicious aerial onslaught.

"Do you think we should go down to the shelter?" Asked one of the two privates, a young farm lad. "Maybe, they'll be coming here next?"

"We'll stay put for now." Farlston managed to say, despite having exactly the same thoughts himself. Was it duty that had forced him to say that, he wondered? Perhaps? But there was something else that was keeping him there. He wasn't sure what. Some kind of feeling of dread? Or was it expectation?

"Just keep your eyes peeled chaps. Let's see what the hell Jerry is up to."

It was then that he heard the first aircraft. A low, droning noise, surprisingly loud; as if the aircraft was very low. The anti-aircraft batteries on the airfield at Hawkinge were now banging away at the rapid rate. He caught several bright flashes high up in the night sky, which wasn't all that dark now, due to the preponderance of burning towns and villages in the area. The sound of the enemy aircraft was louder now, a deep throbbing noise, obviously a heavy bomber by the sound of it. Still no whistling though; no explosions.

A sudden flash of terror ran through him. Perhaps the youngster was right? Maybe it was their turn? The plane must have passed over Hawkinge by now, surely? Perhaps it was Lyminge's turn to get flattened. He crouched there as the noise of the plane grew deeper and louder and every part of his brain was screaming at him to run for cover and get off this exposed church tower.

"Keep in against the wall, lads!" He heard himself call, and cursed his own stupidity once more.

"Oh, my sainted bloody aunt!" Cursed Detling. "He's coming straight for us!"

One of the young privates began swearing uncontrollably.

"Oh, fuck! Fuck, fuck, fuck..."

The other lad began whispering the Lord's Prayer as the noise of the engine drowned out the distant explosions of anti-aircraft fire.

A dark shadow passed momentarily overhead and Farlston held his breath, listening for the tell-tale whistle of imminent death. Nothing. And then the engine noise was diminishing. He heard everyone sigh with momentary relief.

"Oh, fuck!" The swearing private cursed again.

More engine noises. Not over head but passing nearby. Two, three, four... five and six. Where were they heading? Ashford again? Or further west perhaps? Maybe north, to Maidstone?

"Parachute!"

Detling's sudden exclamation made Farlston jump.

"What?"

"There look; parachute! One of the bastards has baled out! We must have hit one of the buggers!"

Farlston followed Detling's outstretched arm and instantly spotted the large pale canopy descending through the semi-illuminated night sky. It was dropping to the west of them, out in the big open stretch of fields.

"There's another, look!" Called the praying private.

There it was, slightly off to the north, but unmistakeable.

"The whole crew must have baled out. There'll be at least three of them." Farlston reasoned.

"Five if it's a Heinkel." Detling said.

"Where's the plane? I didn't see it go down."

"Me, neither." Detling frowned. "Didn't hear it go down either; did you?"

Farlston shook his head, scanning the countryside to the east for burning wreckage or more parachutes.

"Oh, God!" Uttered the swearing private. " Mr Farlston! Mr Farlston!"

Farlston and Detling turned around to look at the young man. The school master in Farlston was tempted to reprimand the young private for his unbelievable profanity, but instead, Farlston's jaw dropped open at the sight before him. The two privates were standing against the eastern side of the tower, staring out towards Hawkinge. Beyond them, littering the night sky, were dozens of parachutes. They descended slowly, almost gracefully, silhouetted by the illumination thrown up from the burning towns and villages of Kent.

"Bloody hell!" Farlston breathed.

That aint no crashed Heinkel." Detling stated the obvious.

"They're going for the airfield." Farlston realised out loud. "Ring the bell."

"What?" Detling asked, caught off guard.

Farlston felt a deep, sinking feeling in the pit of his stomach, as if he was on the verge of toppling into a big, black, hole from which there would be no escape.

"It's an invasion, Frank! Ring the bloody bell! The Germans are coming!"

NAVAL AND MILITARY CLUB – LONDON
SATURDAY 21ST SEPTEMBER 1940 – 0240 HOURS

Brooke rolled over and sat up with a start.

"Sir! Sir!"

The sound of Captain Barney Charlesworth's agitated voice was unmistakeable.

"It's me, Sir!"

Instantly, Brooke was wide awake. Barney Charlesworth was his unflappable Aide De Camp and the sound of his agitated voice in the middle of the night was enough to send a thrill of alarm through the Commander Home Forces.

Brooke groped for the lamp.

"Come in Barney!" He shouted. "Come in!"

He found the switch and the lamp came on. He fumbled for his glasses as the door opened.

Dropping his glasses into place and blinking, Brooke looked up to see Charlesworth standing in the doorway dressed in pyjamas and slippers, his face flushed with excitement and a plain manila envelope in his hand.

"Barney? What is it?" Brooke forced himself to sound calm.

Charlesworth took a deep breath.

"A message has come through from CIGS, Sir. You are to report to the Cabinet War Rooms at Storey's Gate immediately. Your driver has just arrived from St Paul's. He has a similar message and orders to take you directly there. He also brought this note from the watchkeeper."

Brooke blinked again, then held out his hand.

Brooke's ADC walked into the room, his gait awkward and unsettled. He came to a halt by the bed and handed the envelope across. Taking it, Brooke noted that it was addressed 'C in C Home Forces, By Hand, SECRET'. He broke the seal and removed the single piece of paper within, then held it up to the light of the lamp and focussed on the bold, type-written script.

SECRET. Unusually heavy bombing of all coastal areas from Ramsgate to Eastbourne. Dover and Folkestone in flames. Dover Castle badly damaged. Airfields in Kent, Sussex and London area bombed. Large assembly of unknown craft in channel coming north out of Dunkirk, Calais, Boulogne and Le Havre. Large numbers of parachutists reported in vicinity of Hawkinge. Invasion anticipated. SECRET.

Brooke felt his heart lurch with foreboding. He read the message again; slowly. Then he looked up.

"It's begun." He said simply.

Charlesworth merely nodded.

"Barney, make a call to our headquarters at St Paul's please. I want the skeleton planning staff that we nominated, to assemble and then proceed to Storey's Gate. The remainder of the headquarters is to stand-to and start processing all reports. I want formal situation reports every half hour from 0330. Critical information as it comes, straight to our watchkeeper in the map room at Storey's Gate"

"Very well, Sir." His ADC nodded his understanding.

Brooke smiled wanly at his ADC.

"Then get dressed Barney. I want to be away in fifteen minutes. We have work to do."

Charlesworth returned the smile.

"Indeed, Sir. I'll meet you out front, presently."

He left the room, closing the door behind him.

Brooke swung his legs out of bed. He ran a hand through his dark, slightly greying hair and took a deep breath. He read the message one more time. Then, for the first time in several days, he knelt down beside the bed and prayed.

GLIDER VALKYRIE ONE – SOMEWHERE OVER THE NORTH SEA
SATURDAY 21ST SEPTEMBER 1940 – 0245 HOURS

Major Walter Koch was nervous. This wasn't going to be like Eben Emael. For a start off, he was going to be hundreds of miles from his start point with no guarantee that his relief force would even get onto the same piece of the continent as his own men. The target was bigger. Not as well protected mind you, but much bigger. And of course, there was the sea. Their target was a narrow strip of land that was several miles long and projected into the river estuary. A tiny margin of error that, even for the superb pilots of the glider force. He would be glad when they were on the ground. At least then he would be in control of his own destiny.

Still, he reflected, no anti-aircraft fire yet. They hadn't been seen. There was some fire over to the south-east of course, just as there should have been, targeting the decoy force. He looked at his watch. 0245 hours. Just fifteen minutes to the scheduled touch down time. He reckoned they were going to be a few minutes late. Just at that point, the co-pilot tapped him on the shoulder.

"There's the estuary up ahead Major. About twenty miles. We're going to cast off very shortly."

Koch gave a thumbs-up. Looking around the cabin, he gave the signal for 'Fifteen minutes from target'. His squad acknowledged the signal and began adjusting their positions, ready for the final descent.

Koch began checking his own equipment, but his mind was elsewhere. Once again he went through the plan in his mind. There were more gliders this time; a total of sixty, carrying seven hundred men. Two groups of twenty five gliders each would land in two locations. The first at the southern tip off the spit off land that projected into the estuary, their target the gun batteries and fortifications located there. Koch himself would lead that group. The other group, led by Captain Witzig, would land on the northern end of that same spit of land, at a place called Kilnsea, where his target was the heavy guns of the Godwin Battery. The final group of just fifteen gliders would land centrally on the spit and capture the signal station, before linking up with both of the other groups, clearing the narrow peninsula as they went.

All the artillery boys were with Koch and Witzig. Their job was to capture those big guns and get them ready for use against their former owners. No destroying the guns this time; capture them intact, in order to help secure the southern flank. Christ almighty, thought Koch. You couldn't make this up! The plan was entirely crazy; and this time they would be fighting the Tommies, not Belgians. It was going to be hard and bloody, he was sure. But they must succeed. They must. The lives of over eighty thousand German troops were depending on it. And if anyone could do it, then it was his boys. Nearly two thirds of them had been at Eben Emael or the bridges back in May, and the rest had all dropped by parachute as part of the wider operation. They were as ready for this as anyone could be.

"Line's away, Major." Said the co-pilot suddenly, snapping Koch out of his private reverie. "We're in the lap of the Gods now."

Koch nodded, wordlessly. For some reason he could hear a piece of music in his mind. Opera; Siegfried's Funeral March by Wagner.

"For fuck's sake!" Koch murmured out loud.

"What was that Major?" Asked Sergeant Major Linden who was sitting next to him.

"Nothing." Koch replied quickly. "Just mumbling away to myself. First sign of madness that, you know?"

Linden grinned broadly, his teeth showing bright in the dark of the glider's cabin.

"OK, Major Koch; we're at 7,000 feet and dipping for the target." The co-pilot's voice sounded again.

Koch looked towards the cockpit and saw, through the glass screen, the narrow spit of land clearly visible against the river estuary and the sea. Far beyond, miles inland, he could see fires and high altitude explosions from enemy flak. The glider curled around in a wide arc, first south, then west, then north again, until the nose was head-on to the long, thin stretch of land. And then the nose dipped, and Valkyrie One dived toward its landing zone on Spurn Point.

MOTOR TORPEDO BOAT 13 – OFF THE COAST OF SUSSEX SATURDAY 21st SEPTEMBER 1940 – 0255 HOURS

The engine hummed gently as MTB 13 crept along the friendly side of the minefield. She was making no more than ten knots, the coxswain ensuring that they didn't stray too far south and into the minefield itself. Out of Portsmouth just over an hour ago, they were now on station, and treading carefully. They were far enough out for the light from the fires on shore to be of little use, and so they chugged along, keeping their eyes fixed on the dark surface of the water. Lieutenant Rob Stevens glanced back toward the shore of England briefly, then ran his eyes over the night sky.

"I can still hear them. The bastards just keep coming."

"Aye, Skipper." Grunted Leading Seaman Arthur Middleton, as he nudged at the wheel. "But it's the buggers down here I'm more worried about."

"I'm with you on that one Middleton." Agreed Stevens, raising his binoculars and scanning the darkness off to starboard.

Stevens snatched them away from his eyes after just a few seconds and raised his eyes, trying to use his peripheral vision to scan the water. They were covering the sector opposite Le Havre and, apparently, one of their sister boats had bumped into a sizeable flotilla of enemy ships of various types earlier in the night. The details remained sketchy, other than that she had come under intense fire from several directions at once and had been forced to make a rapid withdrawal.

"Could have been a pack of E-Boats out to catch merchantmen?" Suggested the coxswain.

"Possibly?" Stevens allowed. "But Fleet want us to have a good dig around and see if we can get more detail. And we need to be prepared to hit opportunity targets if presented."

"Well by my reckoning, Skipper," continued the coxswain, "the safe lane in the minefield should be just up here a little way."

"Good. Let's keep our eyes peeled."

The Vosper 70 footer continued its steady patrol north and east along the British side of the minefield, its crew standing ready by its small compliment of weaponry. After a short while, a message was passed back from the bow lookout, via one of the sailors manning the starboard Lewis Gun.

"Message from up front, Skipper. There's something on the surface not far in front. Distance unknown."

Stevens frowned.

"What kind of something? A buoy? Or a boat?"

"Not a buoy, Skipper." Replied the gunner. "Some kind of boat by the looks."

Stevens nodded to the coxswain. "Drop the power; but stand-by to put her right up if I give the word."

The sound of their engine died off to a low hum, but Stevens still couldn't hear anything else. He went along the deck, ducking under the barrel of the starboard Lewis Gun, then forward to the bow. A young seaman was leaning against the front wire straining his eyes into the dark.

"What is it?" Stevens demanded.

"Something big, Skipper. Hard to tell. Looks huge, anyway, unless we're close up to it. You'll get a better view looking up from the deck."

Stevens crouched low, copying the young seaman, and tried to fix his eyes on the gap between horizon and sea. Bloody cloud, he thought. If only it would clear completely.

He followed the line of the sailor's arm and quickly caught sight of the dark blob; indistinct, but obviously sizeable. Steven's heart began thumping.

"Power off!" He whispered urgently back towards the nearest gunner, and moments later, the sound of their engine died off completely.

They didn't have long. The boat would start to drift, so the engine would have to go back on shortly. Stevens strained to pick up any noise he could. There! Water being parted, but not too fast. A slow moving vessel.

"Stand-by weapons and engines!" He whispered the orders back. "I'm going to put up a Very Light."

He reached into his holster and pulled out the Very Pistol. Breaking the weapon open, he rummaged for a cartridge.

It was then someone shouted. A distant shout, but one that carried across the water. His blood went icy cold. Then, shattering the night, two similar sounds, one after the other, in rapid succession. Plonk, plonk. Suddenly, there was a crackling noise, and the whole surface of the water around them was illuminated, throwing a garish light onto a scene that took Steven's breath away. He could hear more distant shouting now. He turned back towards the wheel-house and literally screamed the next order.

"Power up! For God's sake get us moving!"

The crew were ahead of him, for the boat's three powerful engines roared into life, just as the first tracer came flying through the night air towards them.

As the boat reared like an unruly stallion, protesting at the sudden surge in revs, Stevens held on grimly to the bow-sprit and stared in disbelief around him. Over to port, between their boat and the English coast, a German destroyer was executing a wide turn, as if attempting to hem them in against the edge of the minefield. There was no mistaking the vessel. A large Z-4 was painted on its funnel and bow, whilst a Kreigsmarine standard fluttered from the ship's mast. And in front of them, emerging from the minefield through a cleared lane, was a fleet of smaller ships; trawlers, barges and merchantmen of varying designs, all carrying the Kreigsmarine flag.

"Bloody hell!" Stevens swore out loud.

A line of tracer stitched the water nearby and more passed overhead with a high pitched series of cracks. Then, something much heavier began engaging them from the destroyer. He jumped as their own 0.5 inch Vickers machine guns rattled into life.

"Back to the wheelhouse!" He snapped at the young seaman.

The two of them staggered back across the lurching boat, holding onto anything they could reach to steady themselves.

"Which way Skipper?" Middleton's voice came over the noise of the engine and the gunfire.

"Straight on!" Stevens hollered back.

"What?" Came the coxswain's voice, registering disbelief.

"Straight on!" Stevens roared. "Full ahead! All guns at that destroyer! Ready torpedoes! We're going straight through them!"

"Bloody hell-fire!" Stevens heard someone swear.

A heavy calibre shell cracked overhead, narrowly missing them, but deafening Stevens momentarily. "Christ! Swing her about a bit and make them work for it!"

Almost instantly, the boat veered off to port, then back again, forcing Stevens to hang on for dear life, lest he topple overboard. With an effort, he managed to duck under the nearest Lewis Gun which was firing away, and tumble over the spray shield into the wheelhouse.

"Fuck, fuck, fuck!" He swore, clawing at the back of his collar.

A red hot empty cartridge case from the Lewis had fallen down the back of his neck and inside his clothing. He felt the small brass case slip further down inside his clothes to the area near the small of his back. "Oh, fuck it!" He swore again.

"What's that Skipper?" The coxswain shouted.

"Nothing!" Stevens snapped. He lurched forward to grab hold of the spray shield and stared out across the water. The convoy of assorted transports was looming closer now. All around him, the crack of passing bullets or cannon shells assailed his ears, making it difficult to hear the voices of the crew. They were already past the enemy destroyer which was still executing its turn, and to his satisfaction, he saw tracer from the MTBs guns ricocheting skywards off the superstructure of the German vessel.

"Get further over to port, then straighten up again!" He shouted over the noise. "That'll give them less chance to use all their guns against us."

"What about the torpedoes Sir?" The boat's chief petty officer called from behind him.

Stevens looked forward again, surveying the black silhouettes of the enemy transports. The star-shell was fading now, but he still had his Very Pistol in his hand.

"Stand-by to let them go, Chief!" He answered. "On my order."

More gunfire was coming towards them from starboard. The gunners on the transports had spotted them. A sudden impact just in front of him made Stevens duck as shards of wood splintered viciously from the spray shield. Fighting to stay calm, he snapped the Very Pistol

"Stand-by torpedoes!"

Half-crouched, he raised the pistol to a forty five degree angle and fired. The flare arced into the sky, adding its limited light to the flickering scene on the water. It was enough.

"A point and a half to starboard!" He ordered.

Instantly, the boat swung across.

"Steady! Straight on! Stand-by! Stand-by!"

A merchantman was right in front of them, barely four hundred yards by Steven's reckoning.

"Launch torpedoes!"

There was a loud 'plonk', followed by another, as both torpedoes were released.

"Hard to port! Steady! Now go! Get the hell out of here!"

The MTB pulled sharply away from its torpedo run as the two seaborne missiles raced toward their target. Stevens looked back. The destroyer was almost side onto them again and the enemy tracer continued to churn up the sea behind their speeding boat. There was a sudden flash in his peripheral vision and a deafening crack. He looked round and saw that a chunk of the wheel house had been blown away. Miraculously, both Middleton and the coxswain were still at their posts, though the pair of them looked shocked to the core.

"Get amongst the transports, then go like hell for the coast!" Roared Stevens.

Middleton shouted a reply, but Stevens didn't here it, as two huge explosions in succession drowned the words out. Turning his head to starboard-stern, he saw that the two torpedoes had found their mark.

"Bang on, Skipper!" Cried out the starboard Lewis gunner. "What a peach!"

"Just keep firing!" Stevens yelled. "Fire at everything as we pass!"

The gunner responded wordlessly and opened up on the silhouette of a low, barge-like vessel to their starboard, some two hundred yards away. There seemed to be less fire coming their way now, and Stevens thought he could see open sea beyond the two small craft they were about to pass between.

"Give it everything she's got!" He encouraged the wheelhouse crew, clapping Middleton on the shoulder and pointing directly ahead. "Straight through there. Then turn for the coast and don't stop until we get to Portsmouth."

Middleton nodded and set his face as he steered the MTB between the boats.

"Give me everything, gunners!" Stevens roared, hastily ejecting the spent cartridge from the Very Pistol. Fitting a new cartridge, he snapped the gun shut and turned to face the stern. Glancing to either side, he saw the two dark bulks of enemy transports as their boat sped by.

"All clear ahead, Skipper!" Called the coxswain.

"Go on then; all the way to Portsmouth. Full speed." Stevens replied.

He raised the pistol once more and fired. Again, the small flare rose lazily into the night sky behind them. As it reached its zenith, the garish light that it threw across the water revealed once more the surface of the water, crammed with boats and ships, including the heavily listing transport they had just torpedoed, whilst the destroyer was hidden from them by the mass of other craft.

"Stop firing!" Stevens ordered above the rattle of the boat's four guns. "Stop firing! Stop firing! Let's disappear before that destroyer gets us!"

The MTB's guns fell silent and Stevens realised there was no more incoming fire. Hopefully, other friendly ships would have seen the gunfire and flares. He had done all he could do; one enemy transport was on its way to the bottom, and he had shot up several others. Now it was time to get back and report what he'd seen.

"Hammond!" He called to the other officer on the boat.

"Here!" Came the reply.

"Get those signal rockets up; sharpish. England needs to know what's coming!"

Over a mile and a half behind them, on the bridge of Z-4, the young Kreigsmarine lieutenant turned to his captain. "They're still in range Sir. Shall we keep firing?"

The captain shook his head slowly.

"No Willi. Let them go. We have done what we needed to. If that doesn't get the Tommies jumping, then I don't know what will. Pull alongside that transport and get its crew aboard as quick as we can. Then let's cut the other transports loose and get back through the minefield. It will be daylight in less than two hours and I don't want to be here when the English Bombers come out to play."

'S' DAY
H -2

THE CABINET WAR ROOMS – STOREY'S GATE, LONDON
SATURDAY 21ST SEPTEMBER 1940 – 0320 HOURS

Brooke strode into the Chiefs of Staff planning room and found a scene of frenzied activity. Staff officers from all three services were moving urgently around the tiny room, whispering messages into the ears of senior officers and placing new, large scale maps of Britain over the existing maps of the world. He stood for a moment, taking it in. Everything had looked different on his one and only visit prior to this. He spotted his immediate superior at the far side of the room, who caught his eye at exactly the same time. General Dill, Chief of the Imperial General Staff gave a friendly smile and beckoned to Brooke. Quickly threading his way around the room, Brooke approached his old friend and colleague, noting that he was in the company of the two other men who, with Dill, constituted the Joint Chiefs of Staff.

Admiral Sir Dudley Pound, the First Sea Lord, looked his debonaire, measured self. Cyril Newall, Chief of the Air Staff, looked agitated.

"Alan. Good Morning." Dill greeted him in his typically congenial manner. "It seems we are about to be put to the greatest of tests after all. You know the First Sea Lord and the Chief of the Air Staff ?"

Brooke nodded his greetings, and received curt nods back in return.

"So it's true then?" He asked. "They're coming?"

"It would seem so. We are about to go and brief the Prime Minister. I would like you to come too; if you have no objections gentlemen?" Dill raised a questioning eyebrow at the other two Chiefs. There was no objection.

Brooke turned to Charlesworth, who had followed him in.

"Barney, go to our cell and see if the staff have arrived yet. As soon as they are settled, I want every Regional Command brought to immediate notice to move. All Commands are to report when they are fully stood-to, and send full details of any enemy activity within their boundaries."

Charlesworth nodded his understanding amd turned away to locate the Home Forces Staff, taking Brooke's satchel from him as he went.

"Right then, gentlemen, shall we go and see the Prime Minister?"

"This will be entertaining!" Newall observed dryly.

They left the room, turned left and then right down a corridor, passing the BBC wireless rooms, the map room and Brooke's own office. He was pleased to see that his staff were all in place and looked thoroughly busy. The group of senior officers stopped at one of the doors further on. Pound knocked.

"Come in." The deep, rumbling voice from within was familiar and sent a small ripple of excitement through Brooke. The feeling surprised Brooke, but his expression remained impassive and together, the group of four senior officers passed through the doorway and into the small room beyond.

The Prime Minister was sitting at a small writing bureau, dressed in his air force blue battle-dress style suit which he often wore. Next to him, General 'Pug' Ismay, his Military Attache, was standing attentively by. The room was heavy with cigar smoke, which Brooke found irritating. Winston Churchill, the new, inspirational, and in Brooke's opinion, slightly eccentric Prime Minister, turned to face them. He studied their faces with dark, searching eyes, from underneath that heavy, bull-dog like brow of his.

"Gentlemen?" rumbled Churchill in his deep, rich voice. "What news?"

"The air situation, Prime Minister, is this." Began Newall. "As you are aware, there have been huge raids on the south coast this evening. The targets are a thin strip of coastal belt from Margate at one end, down to Portsmouth in the west. Just inland from the coastal strip, there has been some depth bombing. All major airfields in Kent and East Sussex have been attacked, and several towns sited at prominent rail-heads have been hit. Dover Castle has been heavily bombed, and the town itself, along with neighbouring Folkestone, is on fire from end to end. Eastbourne has been heavily bombed, along with Portsmouth, Hastings, Brighton, Worthing, Deal, Cantebury and Ashford."

Newall paused only long enough to draw breath, then continued.

"Both of 11 Group's night-fighter squadrons are up. They are flying circuits over the coastal areas. I am currently aware of two German aircraft that have been shot down by night-fighters, and I believe that CIGS may have information about others brought down by anti-aircraft batteries."

"Only two?" Churchill interrupted with a grunt.

"Two *confirmed* kills at present Prime Minister, bearing in mind that the Blenheims are still up."

Churchill nodded curtly, without comment, and Newall went on again.

"We have just had reports that a long stream of bombers has been identified heading north-west from Holland, skirting East-Anglia. A report has also arrived stating that Hull is being bombed. Night-fighters from 12 Group have been scrambled to investigate, but only a single flight. The remainder have been stood by to come south once 11 Group's aircraft need to disengage for refuelling and rearmament. Finally, fighter command is fully stood-to and ready to launch at first light, along with all the squadrons from bomber command, given what the First Sea-Lord is about to brief you on."

Newall looked at Pound, handing over the reins.

The First Sea Lord, began describing the naval situation. "There has been heavy damage to the harbour at Dover and at Folkestone. One of our destroyers has been hit astern and badly damaged. Flag Officer Dover confirms what the Chief Air has just said. Dover Castle is in ruins, but the underground operations rooms are all fine. Portsmouth harbour has also been hit, although not as badly as the others. Two steam gun boats have been damaged there. However…"

At this point, Pound fixed the Prime Minister with a grim look.

"There have been two contacts this evening with enemy vessels. One of our motor torpedo boats, off the coast opposite Eastbourne, clashed with a flotilla of enemy craft of various types, a couple of hours ago. The report claims at least two transports were spotted, and that the MTB was engaged by several E-Boats and another vessel, substantially bigger. Then, within the hour, there has been an urgent signal from Flag Officer Portsmouth. There have been reports of a short but heavy sea-battle taking place some fifteen miles or so off the coast of Brighton. A number of invasion signal rockets have been sighted; the same signal flares that all of our patrol vessels carry. In addition to that, coastal command has now confirmed that there are three distinct enemy fleets gathering in the channel. One is assembling mid-channel out of Calais, a second out of Bolougne, and a third out of Le Havre. Given the several contacts that have already occurred, and their locations, it is certain that these fleets are attempting to breach the mine-belt off the south-coast. I have despatched all the destroyers in the southern ports to picquet the belt, with MTBs in support. The cruiser and destroyer flotilla at Harwich has been brought to full steam and is leaving port now."

At this point, Pound took a pause for breath, but Churchill did not interrupt. He was staring fixedly at the First Sea Lord, his face sombre. Pound went on.

"The cruisers and their escorts in Hull, the Tyne and Rosythe have been stood-to, but will not raise full steam until we deliver firm orders. They are a potent force, but must be concentrated in order to deliver a sledgehammer blow against any invasion fleet. The same applies to the Battle Squadrons at Scapa Flow. Once we know how the enemy has deployed his capital ships, we will over-match him at the decisive point.

Churchill was frowning.

"Do you, First Sea Lord, believe that the dreaded moment has come?"

Pound nodded.

"In view of the evidence, Prime Minister, I think there can be no doubt that the enemy is about to attempt a landing operation on the south coast of England."

Dill stirred at this point and added his own information.

"There have also been reports of parachutists across Kent and Sussex, in particular around key airfields. I would like to believe that we have shot down lots of German aircraft and that these parachutes belong to their unfortunate crews, however, I would err on the side of caution. All installations are on full alert, and the local commanders are conducting wide sweeps to try and locate these parachutists before they can concentrate in any great strength."

Slowly, Churchill stood. He took several ponderous steps forward, then glared at the group of officers.

"Gentlemen," he began, "the day we have feared these last few months seems to have arrived. Today, Britain will fight for her very existence against a most ruthless foe. Our very survival and that of the free world rests upon the outcome of the next few days. I encourage you now to spare no measure, regardless of its extremity, that will ensure the defeat of the Nazi armada which is now approaching our shores. We must ensure that the English Channel flows red with German blood and that the entire width of it is transformed into a graveyard for German ships. This day must become Germany's Gotterdammerung."

There was silence in the room as Churchill's fiery words sank into the minds of the four officers.

"How long," Churchill broke the silence again, "before you can turn Berlin into a pile of ashes, Chief of the Air Staff?"

Newall reacted with surprise.

"Not today Prime Minister." He replied, in a bemused voice. "Nor tomorrow. The fate of Britain will not be decided over the skies of Berlin, but over the English Channel; as you have said yourself. Every aircraft is sitting ready to attack the invasion fleet at first light, Sir."

Well said, Brooke thought. Churchill laughed; a loud, volcanic rumble.

"Ha! I tease you at the most inopportune moments Chief Air! As you say, let us first sink every damned rust-bucket that the Germans have put to sea. But then…"

Again, Churchill's face went suddenly serious and he waved a pudgy finger at Newall.

"But then Chief Air, once we have repelled this invasion, I want Berlin flattened! I want it ruined entirely; not a building left standing! I want it in ashes from end to end! And then, you can photograph it for me from the air. And we will give a copy to every citizen of Dover."

Brooke raised an eyebrow in mild surprise. It sounded like a jest, but the look on Churchill's face suggested that he was deadly serious.

"And now gentlemen," Churchill stood as straight as he could. "It is time to be about it. I will let you get on with your business. If it is fine with you, we shall convene for ten minutes each hour for an update? In the map room?"

Dill cleared his throat. "If you don't mind Prime Minister, we are preparing the Chiefs of Staff conference room as a joint briefing cell. I am keen to avoid cluttering the map room. Along with General Brooke's office, it will be the operational hub."

Churchill glanced round the faces in the room, then nodded agreement.

"The first briefing to be at 0400 hours then, Sir?" Dill suggested. "We are due more reports. I believe we should have more clarity then."

"Indeed CIGS. That will be fine."

With that, the Joint Chiefs nodded to the Prime Minister and began to leave. As they did, Churchill called to both Dill and Brooke. They paused just inside the doorway and turned back to face him.

"The Army is ready to play its part CIGS?" Asked Churchill in a low voice.

"The Army is as ready as it can be, Prime Minister." Dill replied simply. "We are where we are. Our resources must suffice. The key now is to stop him in the water. But if we can't, then we must quickly work out his intentions once he lands; and then we must move quickly to deal him a fatal blow; before he can get tanks and artillery ashore. The C in C Home Forces and I have fought this enemy before. We know his measure now. He will not win Britain as easily as he won Belgium and France."

"He must not win it at all." Churchill replied in a low, thoughtful voice.

He looked up, directly at Brooke. "General Brooke. I am sorry that fate has put you in this terrible position. You must fight the Nazi invader for us, if he does manage to land. You will have my complete support. You must put every gun to him."

Brooke, fixeded by Churchill's intense gaze, returned it impassively.

"Indeed I will, Prime Minister." He replied, his tone clipped and business-like. "Provided that you grant me something with immediate effect."

Churchill's brow furrowed with suspicion.

"Anything within my power that helps is yours."

Brooke glanced at Dill, who made no objection.

"I appreciate that this request would normally come through CIGS, however, since we are here together, I will ask now in order to save time. I need complete authority over the railway system from this moment. If we are to out-manoeuvre the Germans when they do land, I must get my reserves to the crucial point in good time. I need the railways Prime Minister, without caveat. Otherwise, he will get past us as he did on the continent. And then all will be lost."

Churchill nodded.

"The railways are yours General Brooke. I will inform Bevin immediately. He'll sort it for you. General Ismay, could you ask my Private Secretary to come and see me immediately please?"

Ismay nodded acknowledgement and left.

"Thank you, Prime Minister." Brooke said. "God-willing, we have a fighting chance."

"God?" Churchill barked suddenly. "We'll be needing Him alright! Make no mistake, we are fighting against the Devil himself!"

HQ NORTHEN COMMAND – YORK
SATURDAY 21ST SEPTEMBER 1940 – 0340 HOURS

General Sir Ronald Adam looked in the mirror to check the line of his jaw and, seeing that he had missed a couple of whiskers, brought his razor up and carefully removed the offending bit of stubble. It was early for a shave; but he was not the kind of person to be seen unshaven in the headquarters, regardless of the time of day or night. He had been woken with a message from C in C Home Forces just ten minutes ago, stating that it looked as though the invasion was about to happen in the south, as expected. All commands were to stand-to and concentrate reserves, in anticipation of a move south in due course.

Hopefully, the landings wouldn't actually get anywhere. If the Home Fleet could intercept the invasion force in mid-channel then the Germans wouldn't even set foot on British soil. But, he reflected, the Germans were no ordinary enemy. They were a different nation to the one they had fought back in 1914. This Germany was radical, bold, and enlightened, at least from a military perspective. It wouldn't do to take chances; otherwise, there could be a repetition of the debacle in France and the Low Countries. Brooke wouldn't take chances, he knew. They had served together as young officers, and Adam respected his peer's logical, clear-minded approach to military matters. Brooke had a formidable brain, and given the peril the country now found itself in, he was undoubtedly the right man for the job.

He heard the air raid siren begin, some distance away. Unsurprising, he thought. Hull was already being bombed. York wasn't a million miles away and so it followed that there would be some overspill; either bombers wandering off course, or a whole batch being despatched to try and locate the numerous airfields in the area. Finishing his shave, he wiped himself clean and pulled on his shirt. Walking back through to the bedroom, Adam found his batman waiting patiently. Without a word, Corporal Stokes handed Adam his tie. Within minutes, the general was fully dressed, including Sam Browne belt and cross-strap. As he made one final check of his appearance in the mirror, Corporal Stokes handed him his gas mask satchel and steel helmet.

"I may be some time." Adam explained. "I'll let you know what's going on once I've been briefed at the headquarters."

"Right, Sir." The corporal acknowledged with a smile. "A strange hour of the night to be up Sir, eh?"

Adam laughed. "Indeed. Bloody Germans. They couldn't be civilised enough to invade in the daylight could they?"

"Bunch of heathens, Sir." The corporal agreed.

Adam left the small flat that occupied a corner of the barracks, then set out at a brisk pace towards the headquarters building. The sirens were still going, and he was barely halfway across the camp when he heard the first anti-aircraft guns fire. He stopped and looked up into the night sky, judging the direction of the ack-ack guns. He thought it must be the battery on the Knavesmire; York's distinguished racecourse.

He turned and hurried towards the headquarters. Then he heard the drone, followed only seconds later by the whistle. He looked back, just in time to see the first in a series of blinding flashes, which were followed by a tremor under his feet and a sickening, dull 'crump'.

"Bloody hell!" He exclaimed. The bombs were being dropped across the river on the western side of the town, towards Dringhouses. "The railway." He said to himself. "The buggers are after the railway."

By the time he arrived in his operations room, the noise of bombs in the distance was relentless. The HQ was coming alive, with lots of staff cutting about the place.

"Looks like a big raid, everyone." He said loudly as he entered the room, effectively announcing his arrival. "Best don our helmets for now."

He exchanged his cap for his helmet, setting the example, and the entire staff followed suit. With the chin-strap in position, he walked calmly over to his office door.

"Tom." He called out to Thomas Cartwright, his Brigadier General Staff. "I'm going to drop my things. Have a brief ready in two minutes please?"

"Right, Sir." Acknowledged the staff officer and instantly began rattling off instructions.

Within less than two minutes, the entire planning staff was gathered around the map table in the centre of the room.

"Right, then." Adam began calmly. "Let's start with that message from C in C Home Forces. Remind me of it again."

Cartwright, shuffled some papers then began.

"SECRET. All indications suggest enemy will attempt invasion of mainland Britain before 0900 hours, 21st September 1940. Likely landing areas on south coast between Ramsgate and Portsmouth. Heavy bombing of all coastal areas and ports in target areas, in addition to inland rail-heads. Reports of parachutet drops in Kent. Dozens of enemy ships crossing the channel towards south coast area as outlined above. All Commands to assume enemy landing is imminent. All reserve formations to be brought to one hours notice to move in support of Southern Command. All Commands to remain alert for Fifth Column. SECRET."

"Hmm. Well, there we have it. Have all subordinate headquarters been given the notice to move order?"

"Yes, Sir." Replied Cartwright.

"Good. Let's have the detailed intelligence picture then shall we?"

A young major cleared his throat, stepping forward.

"The overall situation in the south is exactly as described in the C in C's signal. Regionally, Hull has been hit by a heavy bombing raid, within the last half hour. We're just getting reports that the ports on Teeside and the Tyne are also suffering raids. As you can hear, York also is under attack. I've spoken to Headquarters 13 Group, Fighter Command, and they say there are large streams of bombers coming up from Holland. In addition to that, they have picked up streams coming across from Denmark and Norway, so it looks like Jerry is planning a long night of it. 13 Group are putting up some night-fighters to try and disrupt the enemy raiders over the coast. All fighters south of the Humber have been directed southwards in anticipation of being used against the landings."

Adam rubbed at his chin thoughtfully.

"Hmm. So what's your assessment of all that then, James?" He asked the young major.

"Well, Sir," began the intelligence officer hesitantly, "it seems to indicate an attempt by the Germans to divert RAF resources away from the south coast by conducting extensive diversionary attacks in the north. We should also be on the alert for Fifth Columnists, who will undoubtedly try to damage the rail network in order to prevent us from moving reserves south."

Adam nodded, thoughtfully.

"Sounds about right. I want more detail though. Get me SITREPs from every Divisional Sector, and speak to RAF Coastal Command too."

The young intelligence officer nodded.

"In addition," Adam went on, "I want all static defence units and all Home Guard on their tip-toes until further notice. If the Fifth Column is operating in our area, I want every key point properly secured. Every telephone exchange, every bridge, every rail-head. And not just static sentries; I want roving patrols up and down railway lines and in the areas around bridges. The communications and transport network must be maintained. Once the C in C knows the full extent of German intentions, he will call for reserves, and I want to be able to despatch them rapidly when the call comes."

Across the table, Cartwright was scribbling down the instructions with rapid strokes of his pencil. Next to him, a young ATS Sergeant passed a signal to the intelligence officer. Adam watched the young officer scan the document and turn pale.

"What's that you have there, James?" He asked calmly. "An update?"

The major looked up to stare at his superior, his face registering disbelief.

"There..., there is a signal, Sir; from the Hull Sector. It says Spurn Point is under attack."

Adam pulled a bemused face.

"Not surprising that, surely? If the enemy is bombing the major ports and arterial routes, he is also likely to attack obvious military targets, would you not think?"

"No, sorry Sir..., I wasn't clear. Spurn Head isn't being bombed by German aircraft. It is under attack from the ground. There are German troops on Spurn Head!"

SPURN HEAD – HUMBER ESTUARY
SATURDAY 21ST SEPTEMBER 1940 – 0345 HOURS

"Fucking Hell! Where did that come from?"

Koch threw himself down as the bullets cracked over head. Beside him, one of his men started screaming.

"My fucking arm! Fuck, fuck, fuck!" The young soldier was gripping his right arm and writhing in agony.

"Eichman, get a dressing on his arm, quickly!" Shouted Koch above the crack of small arms fire.

"They're behind us, Major!" One of his soldiers called.

"I thought we'd destroyed both of those bunkers?" Called another.

This was chaos, thought Koch. Absolute bloody chaos. He had expected both the confusion and casualties, but this was a complete and utter nightmare. The Tommies had been well prepared. That the headland had been dotted with bunkers and barbed wire he knew from air photographs. That was to be expected. He had even expected to lose gliders into the sea, due to the narrowness of the peninsula. But it was much worse than that. The Tommies had planted thick wooden stakes or metal posts, ten feet high, across the open length and breadth of Spurn Head, and these stakes had taken a devastating toll on the German gliders as they landed. Iin some places, Spurn Head was barely a hundred and fifty metres wide. As a result it had been easy for the Tommies to sew the belt of anti-glider obstacles without leaving any gaps.

Koch's own glider had lost a wing on landing. It had been torn off with a gut-wrenching crash, the force of the strike spinning the glider round, until it had smashed up against another post and come to a halt. They had lost three men to broken limbs just on landing, so that from the very beginning, and including the two pilots, only seven of the ten men had climbed from the glider in any condition to fight. Shortly after landing, they had come under fire from a bunker, and as they moved to attack it, they had come across the wreck of another glider which had struck one of the stakes belly on. The stake had ripped through the aircraft like a knife through butter, splitting the fuselage wide open, straight down the middle, killing and injuring half of its occupants in one fell swoop. He knew too, that some gliders had hit the water, whilst others had skidded off the firm ground onto the mined areas by the beach, detonating several devices. All this he had watched in numb horror during those first few minutes.

They destroyed the bunker eventually. One of the pioneers from another crew had appeared out of the dark and asked for covering fire. He had crawled rapidly forward, cut the wire, and crept right up to the base of the concrete fortification. The bunkers weren't like Eben Emael; the slits here were wider. The sergeant had decided to use his grenades instead of the satchel charges or shaped charges, and within seconds, the occupants of the small bunker were dead. A heart-beat later, so too was the brave pioneer sergeant, as he went down in a hail of fire from a bunker sited in depth of the first. They had captured that too, using the same tactics, although it had taken longer. By the time the second position was destroyed, Koch had managed to gather together nineteen men from several crews and the whole of Spurn Point had come alive, like a giant ant-hill. Flares drifted to and fro' over the peninsula, explosions reverberated, heavy guns fired, and tracer cut through the night. There was a constant high pitched crack as bullets passed over head, and it seemed to be raining shrapnel as bullets or debris from spent anti-aircraft fire dropped from the sky.

Now it was getting worse. There were people moving around behind them and opening fire. The chances were it was friendly fire. There would be German troops all over Spurn Point tonight, and although he had lectured his men extensively on identifying targets before engaging them, in the heat of battle it was entirely possible to make mistakes.

"This is Valkyrie One!" Koch bellowed across the undulating grass hummocks. "Valkyrie One!"

Several single shots cracked over his head in reply, followed by a short burst of automatic fire; an unusually slow burst of fire he noted, and certainly not German.

"Stand by to engage when the light goes up!" He ordered the nearest group of men.

Quickly fitting a white light cartridge, he raised the flare pistol and fired it high over the piece of ground where he could see muzzle-flashes.

For a few moments, the bare landscape was bathed in a sickly light and Koch spotted a figure ducking for cover some forty metres away. If the strange soup-bowl shaped helmet wasn't enough to convince him, the unmistakable silhouette of the long broad-bladed bayonet on the man's rifle was.

"Tommies!" He screamed, as one of his men let rip with a machine-pistol. "Get some fucking fire down!"

He ducked his head again as several more single shots cracked by, one of them hitting the ground to his front and spraying him with sandy-soil and grass. His own men were blasting away now, and Koch began racking his brains to come up with a solution. Bloody Tommies, he cursed inwardly. Why couldn't they just be sleeping in their bunkers like the Belgians? This was either a small local counter attack or a routine clearance patrol. Either way, it complicated matters hugely. No fixed enemy meant a long and bitter fight. Bollocks.

As he wrestled with options, he raised his head to look for a suitable route in order to sweep the enemy up from a flank. As he did so, and in the dying light of a flare, something small caught his eye, sailing through the air just off to his forward-right.

"Grenade!" He roared, attempting to bury himself into the soil.

Crump! The grenade detonated with a hollow thump that shook his entire body. A split second later, he heard a pitiful moan from the far side of the hollow he was in.

"For fucks sake!" Koch snarled, anger rising inside him. He yanked out one of his own stick-grenades, quickly prepared it, then yanked the cord and lobbed it back towards the enemy.

"You lot!" He snapped as his own grenade exploded some distance away. "Come with me now; we're going to flank those bastards! Deiter!"

"Sir?" Replied the nearby squad corporal.

"I'm going left to flank these bastards. You and your men cover me, and don't throw any more grenades. Leave that to us."

"Right, Sir." The corporal acknowledged.

Koch beckoned to his own group. Pulling back from the lip of the depression they began to skirt to the left. At first, they had to keep on all fours, but then they came to a reasonably deep scar in the dune that allowed them to move at a crouch. There was still an exchange of fire taking place, and that allowed Koch to keep a fix on the enemy position. Just as he judged they were about in the right place to strike the enemy patrol from the flank, he caught a movement to his front, barely ten metres away. Dropping to one knee quickly, he brought up his MP-40 machine pistol ready to fire, then froze at the last moment. The person he had seen was also kneeling, and something about the man's silhouette looked familiar.

"Valkyrie One!" Koch hissed as loud as he dared.

"Valkyrie Two Six!" Came the reply in German.

Sighing with relief, Koch held his MP-40 up so that it could be clearly seen. The other man did like-wise, and seconds later, they were scrabbling towards each other on all fours. As they met, he saw the man smile broadly.

"Major Koch, thank God we've found you! There are Tommies all over the fucking place! It's like they were ready for us!"

Koch thought he recognised the man's face in the gloom but couldn't put a name to it.

"Who's that?" He said, pushing his face closer.

"Corporal Braun, Sir; from Valkyrie Two Six. I've got seven men with me. We lost one of the pilots and the sergeant to a bunker back there. I saw another glider smack straight into the water."

"Never mind that now." Koch said, trying not to tally the increasing number of casualties in his mind. "There's a squad of Tommies over this rise, about twenty metres or so. I've got five men with me. Get your boys ready. You and me will both throw grenades, then we're going over the top, nice and fast. Kill everything as soon as you see it; the bastards have got bayonets on."

Corporal Braun grinned madly.

"Amen to that. About time we got to shoot back!"

They fanned out quickly, briefing their men. Then, working together, Koch and Braun lobbed their stick-grenades simultaneously.

"Down!" Hissed Koch, and they all pressed themselves against the low bank.

Crump! Crump! The two grenades went off with a sharp report.

"Go!" Koch bellowed.

He stumbled over the lip of the small depression, bringing his MP-40 up and tucking it against his hip as he staggered forward over the grassy tufts.

He could hear moaning from somewhere in front and headed for it, Braun and his men coming up with him on the left, and his own men hard over his right shoulder. A figure loomed up barely metres in front of him. Instantly, Koch pressed the trigger of his machine-pistol and it rattled into life. Two other men saw the British soldier at the same time and fired their own weapons. The lone Tommy span around madly as he was stitched across the torso with heavy 9 mm slugs.

Koch suddenly found himself on the edge of a ditch and half-jumped, half-fell into it, landing heavily and biting his tongue in the process.

"Ah, fuck!" He swore, then, seeing something writhing on the floor and moaning, he emptied a short burst into the figure. Just to his left there was an ear splitting scream and he whirled around, his heart hammering with fright. In a split second, he recognised the figure of Corporal Braun leaning back against the side of the ditch as a Tommy soldier drove his bayonet deep into the German's guts. Even as Koch brought his machine-pistol up, the Tommy fired his rifle into Braun at point blank range. Braun jerked wildly for a brief second then sagged. Before Koch could fire, another German soldier loomed out of the darkness, armed only with a Sauer Pistol and shot the Tommy in the side of the head. Something wet and jelly-like splashed across Koch's face, as the Tommy collapsed heavily onto the floor of the ditch.

It was over in moments. There had been perhaps half a dozen Tommies in the ditch, including a machine-gunner armed with an archaic looking light machine gun with a top fitted circular ammunition magazine. Now they were all dead, but so were several Germans.

"Valkyrie One!" Koch shouted, back down the spit of land. "Valkyrie One! Position clear! Deiter! Close in!"

He could taste something metallic dripping down his face and onto his lips and wiped at the sticky goo with irritation. He suddenly realised it was the dead Tommy's brains and gave a startled cry. Using his sleeve, he wiped furiously at the side of his face and spat several times.

A group of men appeared above him and tumbled into the ditch.

"Major Koch?" It was Deiter's voice.

"I'm here, Deiter." Koch called out, searching for the corporal amongst the crowd of dark figures. Deiter pushed his way through the other soldiers until he found his commanding officer.

"Alright Sir?" Deiter asked, sounding ridiculously happy.

"Fine." Koch replied, jealous of the young soldier's high spirits. "We've got half a dozen men here from two-six. Corporal Braun was with them but he's just been killed."

"What? Lucky Erich?" Deiter asked, sounding genuinely surprised. "That's a bit of a shitter."

"Never mind that now." Koch snapped. "Let's do a head count, then split the group up into new squads and platoons."

"What's that?" Deiter asked, cocking his head to one side.

"I said…" Began Koch, starting to get irritated, then broke off as Deiter put a hand on his chest and pushed him roughly backwards.

"Down!" Bawled the corporal as he forced the major onto the floor and landed heavily on top of him.

For a second, Koch lay there stunned, wondering if Deiter had gone mad, when suddenly, a huge menacing shadow of darkest black appeared over the top of them. A heartbeat later there was a deafening crash as something heavy smashed into the ground above them.

"What the fuck was that?" Koch heard himself shouting.

"Glider." Deiter spoke nonchalantly into his ear, then levered himself up.

Once on his feet, Deiter grabbed Koch's hand and helped him upright. Together, they peered over the top of the ditch and saw the unmistakable outline of a glider's tail-plane sticking up from the earth, just a little way down the causeway.

"Bloody late-comers!" Deiter said casually and began changing the magazine on his machine pistol.

Koch stared at Deiter for a moment, then at the glider, then back at Deiter. This is bloody crazy, he thought to himself.

"Get someone over to that glider." Koch managed to say, his voice a little unsteady. "Anyone fit to fight is to rally over here with us. Then let's get organised and do what we came here to do. It'll be daylight soon, and if we haven't got the guns by then, we'll find ourselves right in the middle of a proper shit-sandwich!"

SOMEWHERE OVER THE NORTH SEA
SATURDAY 21ST SEPTEMBER 1940 – 0355 HOURS

"Keep your eyes peeled for night-fighters." Gerring warned his crew over the intercom. "They'll know we're coming from their radar."

"Hopefully they'll be too busy tackling the other groups over the Humber and Tyne, eh, Lieutenant?"

"Don't kid yourself Gunther." Gerring smiled at the pilot. "Once they realise what's going on, they'll be round us like flies. We need to drop our load and be on our way before it's light enough for Spitfires."

"Amen to that." Murmured the dorsal gunner.

"There's the coastline." The pilot nodded.

Gerring studied the dark line of the English coast then glanced down at his map. Over to their left was a short, needle like spit of land, and beyond that a wide curving bay that ended at a much larger, prominent headland. Further on, the coast appeared to run smoothly southwards.

"That's Flamborough Head over there." Gerring pointed through the cockpit window. The Heinkel's cockpit was great for observation and navigation, but by God it made Gerring feel vulnerable. In the very far distance, he could make out anti-aircraft fire.

"That'll be the Hull raid going in. Stand-by to turn for our bombing run."

The words were barely out of his mouth when the explosions began. They were a little high, and too far to port. A search-light beam suddenly cut the air to starboard.

"OK, let's start to turn now." Gerring prompted. "We don't want to get caught in that."

The pilot acknowledged and turned his steering column. The Heinkel banked gently to port, away from the search-light.

"Straight on now," instructed Gerring, "until we cut the coast-line, then turn again."

They were almost there now. The flak was a little closer but still too high.

"OK, Gunther. Bring her round and follow the coast south."

Again, the plane banked gently round.

Gerring was looking straight down now through the glass and could see the pale sea against the darker land.

"That's Filey Brigg coming up. Ready bombs."

"Ready bombs." The bomb-aimer repeated.

"About two thirds of the way down the bay, remember?"

"Yes, Lieutenant. No worries." Replied the bomb-aimer calmly.

"A little to starboard, Gunther…steady." Gerring murmured.

The flak was much closer now.

Suddenly, another search-light stabbed into the night sky, this time right in front of them, from the direction of Flamborough Head. It shot straight up to their left, aiming where the flak was currently exploding, but then, just as suddenly, it swung straight towards them.

"Fucking hell!" Swore the pilot as the light swept over the aircraft, temporarily dazzling them.

"Keep her steady! Keep her steady!" Gerring called out. "Nearly there. Stand-by bombs. Stand-by…anytime now."

"Right Sir." Came the bomb-aimers relaxed voice again. "Bombs away."

The searchlight beam flicked back again, searching for them. In a moment they were caught in its glare. This time it stayed on them.

"Oh, fuck!" Breathed the pilot.

Gerring saw the man's arm reflex and he reached out his own hand, placing it over the pilot's. "Steady Gunther, just a moment more." Gerring soothed the nervous man.

"Bombs gone!" Called the bomb-aimer, his voice suddenly urgent.

"Dive to port out of the beam, then back up again!" Snapped Gerring.

The pilot needed no urging and he instantly flopped the aircraft hard over to port, just as a brace of anti-aircraft shells exploded close by, peppering the fuselage with splinters.

"Lose more height!" Gerring ordered. The plane roared as it made a steep dive to escape the beam.

They were out of the light, but they were not clear yet. The beam would follow.

"Pull her up!" Gerring said, then as the pilot struggled to bring her nose up, "And hard to starboard! Level her out."

The pilot reacted and the plane twisted sickeningly as he brought the great machine around again.

Gerring allowed the plane to cruise for a few more seconds, before ordering the pilot to bank hard to port again; then drop low and put on a spurt across the German Sea. Towards the east, the sky was just starting to brighten. They needed to be well clear before the Tommies got their single-seater fighters up. Behind them, the first German bombs began to explode in Filey Bay. Operation Sealion North had begun.

'S' DAY
H -1

CABINET WAR ROOMS – STOREY'S GATE, LONDON
SATURDAY 21ST SEPTEMBER 1940 – 0405 HOURS

Churchill stared at the First Sea Lord seriously. Eventually he spoke. "So, we are engaging them mid-channel, and thus far it appears that only one of the three German Fleets is through the minefield?"

"That is correct." Pound replied. "The Dover flotilla is holding the enemy at the minefield, and the joint cruiser and destroyer flotilla is steaming out of Harwich now to give them some more punch. I would expect to see engagements with their bigger ships developing over the next hour or so. As for the break-through south of Brighton, the Portsmouth Flotilla is steaming towards it now. I expect contact before 0500 hours."

"What about their capital ships?" Asked Churchill, gruffly.

"We haven't had any engagements yet." The First Sea Lord replied. "In fact, we believe they are probably somewhere off the coast of Belgium or Holland, having steamed south from Germany overnight. We expect them on our eastern flank presently."

"And then it'll get bloody." Churchill observed.

"Potentially, Sir." Pound allowed. "But there again, they will be sailing into narrow waters, within close range of our bombers and fighters. We have submarines inbound to the area as we speak, and they'll be penned in by some of our bigger ships once the flotillas from the Humber and Tyne rendezvous in the North Sea and form a battle-squadron. I am fairly confident that within the constrained arena of the English Channel, we can more than match them, and still have the battle-squadrons from Scapa Flow in strategic reserve."

"Good." Churchill murmured. "But perhaps it may be prudent to bring out the entire Home Fleet from Scapa Flow and simply overwhelm them from the outset?"

Pound drew breath.

"By concentrating our ships from the east coast ports, we can hit them hard enough, and the ships out of Portsmouth will serve as the anvil to their hammer. But, like all things in war; we must assume that we have not yet discovered the enemy's full intentions. We must have that reserve. It will be at sea shortly, but we will hold it back from the channel until we have confirmed exactly where our targets lie."

Behind Pound, Brooke nodded sagely, agreeing with the logic. Churchill made a strange rumbling noise, like a bull-terrier growling, but he made no further comment.

Newall used the opportunity to interrupt.

"Bomber Command is in the air, Sir. Fortunately there was no bombing last night over Europe so our crews are well rested. The southern groups are taking off now and will be over the channel by daybreak. Fighter Command is ready to go too. In addition to the night-fighter squadrons, we've just put two hurricane squadrons up to try and get any late-running German bombers. The remainder of 11 Group is launching now to give depth protection to our bombers over the channel, and we're starting to ferry 12 Group Squadrons southwards in anticipation of heavy commitment over the channel."

"Excellent!" Churchill snapped. "We must have a never ending stream to throw against him, all day long, so that not one invasion barge touches an English beach."

"We are set up for exactly that Prime Minister." Newall assured him.

Churchill gave his desk a little thump with his clenched fist and nodded to himself, approving of some private thought, it seemed. He was enjoying this, thought Brooke; like a schoolboy would enjoy an adventure story.

"CIGS?" Churchill turned his attention to Dill. What of the Army? Have we killed any German paratroopers yet?"

"The anti-invasion forces remain poised Prime Minister. The Army reserve has been stood-to and rolling stock is being moved to the designated loading points, ready to move our strategic reserve when required. As for enemy parachutists, the reports remain sketchy. None of the headquarters report any attacks as yet.

Churchill pulled a face; his large bottom lip jutting out belligerently.

"The reserve is 'stood-to?' Should we not be moving them, straight towards the south coast? Even if the enemy does not land from the sea, there will be plenty of these paratroopers to deal with. And why have we not yet caught or killed any? They were spotted landing some two hours ago were they not?"

Dill exchanged a knowing look with Brooke.

"For very much the same reason as the First Sea Lord has given, we intend to hold the reserve until we can give it a definite target to hit. We don't want to punch and find ourselves swinging into thin air. That is what the BEF did in Belgium, and we are all aware of how the Germans wrong-footed us."

Churchill absorbed the answer quickly, then countered.

"But the paratroopers, General Dill? What about them? I am expecting a carpet of dead German paratroopers by breakfast! What is the Home Guard doing? Why haven't we heard anything? Surely the reserve can be used to sweep the whole of the Home Counties clear of these marauders?"

Dill paused to formulate his argument, but Brooke, forcing himself to maintain a calm voice despite the temptation to laugh out loud in derision, stepped in.

"Prime Minister. The Army reserve is the most powerful force available to us, and is designed to counter the enemy's main thrust, which will undoubtedly include tanks and mechanised forces. Trying to flush out small handfuls of paratroopers with an armoured division is inappropriate. As for the Home Guard, they are largely static forces, so until the enemy attacks them, they are unlikely to be engaged. Besides, trying to organise a thorough sweep of several counties, in the dark, in the middle of heavy bombing raids, is hardly practicable. Suffice to say, we have a clear and robust plan to deal with the paratroopers in due course, but for now, we must posture ourselves according to the developing threat, rather go hunting for ghosts."

Dill, having allowed Brooke to talk, nodded his agreement and looked back to Churchill. "Precisely the case, Prime Minister."

Churchill growled like some moody terrier. After a moment or two of pouting, he allowed the corner of his mouth to curl into a hint of a smile.

"That is your diplomatic way General Brooke, of telling me to shut up and stop interfering!"

Brooke maintained his neutral expression. "I merely wished to inform you of the logic behind our thoughts, Sir." He said.

Churchill laughed.

"Very well; I consider myself informed and chastened!"

Churchill stood and walked over to the map which was marked with the details of this latest brief. He studied it for a moment, before turning back to the Chiefs of Staff.

"Well Gentlemen, it seems that battle is about to be joined, and that we shall see the enemy's intentions soon enough. For the time being, I think we have no choice but to let the First Sea Lord and the Chief of the Air Staff get about their business. You both, jointly, have the privilege of being the first to put a spanner in Herr Hitler's works. Meanwhile, Generals Dill and Brooke, please feel free to continue to posture as you see fit. But if the enemy should land, I want you to give him a punch on the nose he'll never forget!"

Despite himself, Brooke smiled. It was hard not to admire the Prime Minister's fighting spirit.

"Orders have gone out to that effect, Prime Minister." Brooke confirmed.

Just as he was making his reply, there was a knock at the door. Pound, who was the nearest, opened it. A naval staff officer was in the doorway, his face betraying a slightly alarmed look.

"Yes, Jenkins?" Pound asked quietly.

"My apologies, Sir." He began, his eyes darting around the high ranking group of individuals within. "There are some urgent signals that I thought you might wish to see straight away. Also, on my way in, I was asked if I could pass on signals to the other two Chiefs of Staff from their respective operations rooms."

"Thank you, Jenkins." Pound said, taking the sheaf of paper from his subordinate. "Very kind."

The Lieutenant Commander gave a small bow in salute and turned away. Pound closed the door and looked at the small collection of secret signals.

"Now then, what have we here?"

"Why don't you just read them all out yourself, First Sea Lord?" Suggested Churchill. "The contents of those messages affect us all."

"Very well, Prime Minister." Pound said, and looked back to the sheaf of documents in his hand. He was still for a moment; silent as he read the first signal. Then, in a low, grave sounding voice, he began reading the reports. "The first signal is from Flag Officer Dover. Dover and Portsmouth Flotillas are both heavily engaged with enemy transport ships and E-Boats mid-channel. Shelling of Folkestone and Dover continues from enemy long range guns on French coast. Still no evidence of enemy capital ships. Enemy invasion fleets making heavy smoke. Request that no friendly aircraft drop bombs on vessels within ten miles of English coast. All friendly ships are engaging enemy fleet from stand-off positions."

Pound looked up at Newall, who nodded acknowledgement.

"Crews have been briefed on target identification procedures before take off. They've been told to concentrate on transports and leave warships to the Navy."

Pound moved on to the next signal. "The next from the Humber Squadron." Again, he paused. He appeared to read the note several times before reading it aloud. "The Humber Squadron has attempted to deploy, however, HMS Pendragon has been torpedoed as she came out of the estuary. She is reported as sinking fast. The remainder of the squadron is holding back until first light, and is requesting a sweep by Coastal Command prior to the next attempt to come out."

"U-Boats at the mouth of the Humber?" Churchill growled. "Are they trying to box us in?"

"It would appear so Prime Minister." Pound replied quietly. "However, given the current situation in the channel, the Humber Squadron isn't under too much time pressure just yet. I am hoping that we can cause enough disruption to the invasion force without having to deploy too many of our bigger ships into the constrained waters of the Channel. I would prefer to leave the squadron in the safety of the Humber while we conduct an anti-submarine sweep at first light. By the time we have completed that and got the squadron out, we should know where the enemy is concentrating his big ships."

Churchill considered the argument for a moment, then nodded.

"Very well; if you think that is best. And the squadron in the Tyne? Have they come out?"

Pound shuffled through the signals.

"They have been told to make steam and deploy to their rendezvous off the Wash…"

He came to the signal he was looking for.

"Here we are. One of the destroyers in the Tyne has received minor damage from a near miss during an air-raid. Other than that, they have started to manoeuvre out of the estuary. They should be out in their entirety by 0600 hours."

Churchill growled again, a noise that sounded like grudging approval.

"Anything else?" He asked.

"Yes Sir." Pound continued, looking back to the signals. "There is a signal from GOC Northern Command in York. Message reads…" Pound checked himself for a moment. "Message reads… dismounted attack taking place against gun emplacements on Spurn Head. Local troops conducting clearance of area. Heavy bombing taking place on coastal areas and a number of major towns, including York, Doncaster, Middlesbrough, Hull, Newcastle and Sunderland."

Pound looked up at Dill and Brooke.

"Dismounted attack?" He raised an eyebrow.

Brooke and Dill exchanged a look of surprise. Brooke responded.

"We had expected attacks by the Fifth Column country-wide. A warning to all regional commands was sent out an hour ago. This is just the first instance. I fully expect there to be more. We can expect attacks on military installations and centres of communications or transportation."

There was silence in the room for a while. Eventually, Churchill spoke.

"Indeed gentlemen. I think General Brooke has summed up the situation neatly. The situation is already complicated, and the enemy will seek to make it even more so. From what I have gleaned from those who fought in France, the enemy will seek to disorient and dislocate us constantly. We must remain focussed on our main objective, rather than be led a merry dance by the enemy. And I remember well, a conversation I had with the commander of the Guards Brigade that fought the rear-guard action at Boulogne. They were harassed by Fifth Columnists right up until the moment they boarded the ships. Our static forces and Home Guard must deal with this whilst the Regular Army poises itself for the great struggle ahead."

It never ceased to amaze Brooke how Churchill could switch from the realms of fantasy to the cold, succinct reality of a situation in a matter of seconds. The Prime Minister was right on the money this time.

"I am with you on that, Prime Minister." He said. "The orders to the regional commands were quite thorough, and we will evaluate each new piece of information as it comes."

"Good." Churchill grunted. "Is that it, First Sea Lord?"

"No Sir." Pound said, glancing down at one last signal. "There is a signal from HQ 145 Infantry Brigade in the Folkestone area."

Churchill nodded, indicating that he should proceed.

"It says," Pound went on, "that a number of fighting patrols have been deployed in sweeps against the parachutists that were reported earlier."

"Ha!" Churchill barked suddenly and slapped the desk with his hand. "That's more like it! Hunt them down! Good aggressive tactics."

Pound threw a nervous glance around the room at the other military men, before finishing the message.

"The report says that over two dozen parachutes have been located thus far, and in every case, they were attached to dummies."

"Dummies?" Churchill's eyes bulged. "Dummies? Have they not killed or captured *any* Germans?"

Pound shook his head. "It merely states that all the parachutes recovered were attached to dummies."

"That does rather bear out what we've just been saying of course, gentlemen." Brooke interjected calmly. "Dummy parachutists are just one of many tricks the enemy will be seeking to employ."

"Quite, so." Dill spoke up. "I think our next step Alan, is to obtain more detailed information and then plot everything we know onto the map. Then perhaps we might start to see a clear pattern?"

He was interrupted by another knock on the door. Pound grabbed the door handle and yanked it open, impatiently. Jenkins was there again, another piece of paper in his hand.

"I'm sorry, Sir." He stammered apologetically. "But this has just come in from the RAF; I said I would bring it straight away. I think it might be of immediate interest."

Pound took the piece of paper from the staff officer and began to close the door straight away.

"Thank you Jenkins." He said, taking the paper.

Turning back to face the others, Pound lifted the despatch and scanned it quickly.

"This signal is from 13 Group, Fighter Command." He spoke quickly. "Night-fighter squadrons are returning from engagement of enemy bomber formations over the Yorkshire Coast and Hull. So far, three enemy aircraft reported shot down. Also..." Pound stopped in mid-sentence. He was a man of pallid complexion by any standards, yet any colour that had been in his face suddenly drained from it.

"Also..." He continued hesitantly. There are reports from several returning aircraft that a large fleet of ships has been spotted approximately thirty miles off the Yorkshire coast, almost directly east of Bridlington. There appear to be dozens of vessels, including several large ships. They are sailing west...towards the coast."

He looked up at the others. There was absolute silence in the room. This time, nobody broke it.

RAF DRIFFIELD – EAST YORKSHIRE
SATURDAY 21ST SEPTEMBER 1940 – 0410 HOURS

Leading Air Craftsman Billy Scotton stood by the pill-box and looked out across the darkened airfield. It was getting lighter. He could see the silhouettes of the hangars and the aircraft quite clearly now. In the distance, he could hear the sound of explosions. That had been going on for a good ten minutes or more now, and by his reckoning, it was all over towards Bridlington way. He supposed it was only a matter of time before the German raids crept this far north. Bloody Germans. He cursed them silently. They had raided this airfield just a month ago, catching everyone by surprise, destroying a number of bombers and damaging four of the five hangars. As a photographic analyst, he had spent the last 36 hours developing pictures and scrutinizing them in order to establish the results of the latest raid over Germany. He had fallen into bed the night before completely exhausted, but cheered by the knowledge that he could enjoy a lie-in, as there was no bombing planned for the next day.

That had changed at 0300 hours when he had been kicked out of bed and told that he had been fast-balled for sentry duty. Until the raid last month, it was the Army who did all the guard duty; the men of the East Yorkshire Regiment who were assigned to the ground defence of RAF Driffield. After the raid however, the soldiers from the East Yorkshires had been re-tasked to bolster the insufficient anti-aircraft defences, and thus the RAF personnel were required to assist with the day to day sentry duties too. So now, he was standing on the edge of the bomber base at Driffield, cursing his choice of clothing as well as the Germans.

In this last hour before dawn, the temperature had dropped considerably and he was regretting not donning his greatcoat before reporting for duty. He was no happier for being stood next to Leading Air Craftsman Austin Bevan, a West Countryman like himself, who had been wise enough to grab his greatcoat before reporting in.

"Sounds busy, eh?" Bevan murmured. He wasn't referring to the distant sound of bombing, but rather the excited buzz that could be heard across the airfield as the ground crews armed the big Whitley bombers.

Scotton shivered.

"They could have bloody planned it a bit better, couldn't they?" He replied grumpily. "Fancy pulling us out of bed at the last minute!"

Bevan shrugged.

"That's war though isn't it Billy?" He said philosophically. "Don't think this was down to anyone's fault at our end. I heard a WAAF from the ops room saying she'd been called in because there's a big flap on. Something down south apparently. The whole group's been stood-to. She said Command HQ wants all squadrons ready for take-off before dawn."

Scotton simply grunted and shuffled his feet in an attempt to keep warm. Bevan noticed his friend's discomfort and jerked his head towards the perimeter fence.

"Come on, Billy, let's go patrol our beat; it'll keep us warm and help pass the time."

Still shivering, Scotton nodded his agreement and the two men wheeled off to their right and began pacing towards the perimeter fence, their bayonet-tipped Lee Enfield rifles slung over their shoulders. A heavy dew was beginning to form on the grass and it was clear that dawn wasn't far away.

"Wonder if it's anything to do with this invasion alert that's been going on for the last fortnight?" Bevan speculated.

"God knows." Observed Scotton tiredly. "All I know is that yesterday, I wasted Christ knows how many hours developing photographs of targets in Germany, only to find out that our crews had hardly hit a bloody thing!"

Bevan chuckled.

"You're in a proper foul mood Billy, aren't you? Well, not to worry mate. An hour and a quarter and we'll be done; then you can get back to your bed."

"Roll on!" Scotton murmured.

From across the airfield came a new sound. It started out as a low moan, then slowly built up to a high pitched wail.

"Air-raid siren!" Bevan commented unnecessarily. He stared up at the sky, which was slowly starting to lighten.

"Maybe it's an overspill from that business out towards the coast?" Scotton said. "They're leaving it late to come this far inland. Our fighters will be up soon; it's probably light enough for them now."

"Aye." Bevan replied, still gazing up at the sky. "Still, we'd best get back to the pill-box, just in case."

They set off, without hurry, but they had barely gone twenty yards when they heard the station's anti-aircraft guns open up. The two men stopped and looked up at the sky again, worried now. Somewhere in the night sky, amongst the little orange explosions, there were aircraft. Both of them could hear the engines.

"Come on, Austin." Scotton nudged his friend. "Let's get a move on."

They began hurrying towards the pill-box.

"They crept up on us quickly." Bevan said as they marched briskly across the grass.

"No bombs yet though. Maybe they're just passing over; towards York or Doncaster or somewhere?" Scotton observed.

"Maybe?" Bevan shrugged. "But we'd better get ourselves under cover before the debris from that ack-ack starts falling out of the…"

Bevan came to a sudden standstill.

Scotton, now a couple of paces in front of him, stopped and turned back to face his friend.

"Austin? What's the…"

"Bloody hell-fire!" Bevan exclaimed, staring up at the sky beyond Scotton.

"What?" Scotton asked his comrade, feeling slightly bemused.

"There look!" Bevan pointed.

Scotton followed the indication and, involuntarily, took a step backwards.

"Sweet Jesus!" He swore, for there, not far above them and descending fast, was a broad, pale coloured parachute.

"They must have got one!" Bevan shouted excitedly. "The crew's baled out!"

Scotton watched the parachutist descending through the semi-darkness, tracing his path. The figure was drifting towards the runway.

"Come on Billy!" Bevan called out, racing past him, his greatcoat tails flapping behind him. "Let's get him as he comes down!"

Scotton leapt after his friend, yanking his rifle off his shoulder as he went. Bevan was fiddling with his weapon and as Scotton ran, he heard the unmistakable sound of a rifle bolt clicking shut.

"Bloody hell, Austin! Don't shoot him. Take him prisoner!"

"I'm going to!" Bevan called back. "But make sure you've made ready. You can't trust these Nazis!"

Scotton groaned aloud. Bevan was far too keen for his liking. He should've joined the Army instead of the RAF. Never-the-less, Scotton followed Bevan's lead and worked the bolt of his rifle, sliding a round into the chamber.

The parachutist had drifted over a hundred yards from them and was lower than they realised. They were still some fifty yards off when he landed, tumbling over heavily, his parachute silk collapsing over him. They were about twenty five yards away, just a few feet apart, when they saw the figure stagger to his feet and throw off the silk. The dark figure of the man looked about him, apparently trying to get his bearings.

"Oi!" Shouted Bevan, slowing to a fast walk and levelling his rifle and bayonet at the man. "Stand still! Get your hands up! Come on matey, hande hoch…"

Bang!

Bevan and Scotton literally jumped apart as the man fired at them with some kind of weapon, the bullet cracking between them.

Bang! Bevan's rifle barked as he fired at the man from the hip. His shot went wide of the man, who fired back again…and again.

Bevan was running to the right, circling towards the enemy, and Scotton could hear him working the bolt of his rifle again. His heart thumping, Scotton copied his friend, going out to the left. To his amazement, it seemed to be doing the trick, because the enemy was still firing at Bevan, who was weaving wildly across the grass, making himself a difficult target. With his heart feeling like it was in his mouth, Scotton advanced quickly towards the parachutist from the left, gripping his Lee Enfield tightly now, the heavy brass butt wedged into his shoulder. It was still too dark to use the sights and so he was looking along the stock, as if he was using a shotgun. He was barely ten paces away now and couldn't believe that the enemy hadn't noticed him. Perhaps he could end this quickly without any more shooting.

"Drop your weapon!" Scotton heard himself shouting. "Hande hoch!"

The man whirled around, his hands out in front of him, obviously gripping a small firearm of some kind. Even as he turned, Scotton knew the man wasn't going to surrender. He saw the man's body swing fully round. He saw the silhouette of a round helmet and the glint of the man's eyes beneath the helmet's rim. In that split-second, Scotton saw the grimness behind those eyes and realised that here indeed was one of those much-feared Nazis; one of those ruthless Teutonic warmongers who would stop at nothing in the pursuit of total victory. In that split second, and much to his surprise, everything seemed so clear to Scotton. Everything seemed so natural. He was a Royal Air Force photographic clerk, yet he felt perfectly in control as he took up the first, and then second pressure on the trigger and squeezed off a perfectly controlled shot.

The Lee Enfield bucked in his shoulder and made a ferocious noise as it fired, and Scotton was rewarded by the sight of his enemy flopping backwards with his arms flailing. Without even realising it, Scotton was working the bolt on his rifle, and even before his ears had stopped ringing from the sound of the first shot, he had stepped several paces closer and fired a second round into the spread-eagled enemy parachutist. He worked the bolt again, still pointing his rifle at the figure, but didn't fire a third time.

"Austin? You alright?" Scotton heard his own voice and was surprised at how confident and authoritative he sounded.

"I'm okay, Billy." Came Bevan's voice, and a moment later, his dim figure stepped cautiously forward toward the body on the floor.

"Good shot mate!" Bevan breathed. "Keep him covered while I take a look."

Bevan stepped up to the figure and poked it with his bayonet. When the figure didn't react, he leaned in and stared down at the man on the floor.

"Bloody hell, Billy! You got him right through the head! And another through the chest! Oh, bugger me, what a mess!"

Scotton suddenly felt his body start shaking. Hesitantly, he stepped forward to look down at the man he had just killed. He deliberately tried not to look at the face.

"Hold on mate, this ain't right!" Bevan's Bristol accent was more noticeable now he was excited. "This chap doesn't look like a pilot to me. What do you think, Billy?"

Reluctantly, Scotton leaned forward to examine the dead man. To be sure, he wasn't dressed in any pilot rig that would be found in the RAF. He wore a rounded, rimless helmet and a large, padded smock, with baggy trousers of a similar design. His belt and equipment was more like a soldier's than a pilot's, and there was a badge on his chest that looked like a pair of wings.

Scotton's inspection was interupted by the sound of more gunfire. Not the ack-ack from across the airfield, but the sound of small arms fire. The two airmen stood straight and scanned around them, trying to judge the direction of the gunfire. The ack-ack was still pounding away, but there were no bomb-blasts. They heard distant voices now, shouting urgently. The two men cocked their ears to the night air. A second later, they looked directly at each other, their eyes saying everything. In a quiet voice, heavy with dread, Bevan said. "That's no English accent that I've ever heard Billy."

Then, with a jerk, he looked up and swore.

"There's another one of them!" Bevan cried out.

Scotton swung around and brought his rifle up, the adrenalin suddenly surging through his veins again.

He glanced up and saw another parachute descending; and another.

"There's more of 'em!" Bevan was hysterical now. "Bloody hell, Billy! They're everywhere!"

As Scotten swung his gaze around, he could see more and more pale coloured blobs, descending like ghosts out of the sky.

"They're bloody paratroopers!" He shouted to Bevan, and pulled his rifle into the shoulder. "Blow the whistle, Austin! Blow the bloody whistle!"

Scotton tracked the nearest parachute down, picked out the dark blob that hung underneath it and pulled the trigger of his rifle. Bang! He worked the bolt feverishly and looked for the target again.

Off to his right, Bevan blew his whistle. The shrill blast rang out across the open meadow of the airfield.

"Stand-to!" Bevan roared after several blasts. "Stand-to!"

Almost immediately, there was a clatter of automatic fire from beyond the perimeter fence. Glowing orange blobs of tracer ammunition arced towards them, then passed off to their left with an ear-shattering 'crack, crack, crack'.

"Come on!" Bevan yelled, loping off towards Scotton's previous target. "Get the bastards as they hit the deck! Use the bayonet!"

It was an hour before dawn, and the Germans were coming.

TROOPSHIP BERLINER – 10 MILES OFF THE YORKSHIRE COAST SATURDAY 21ST SEPTEMBER 1940 – 0420 HOURS

"For fucks sake Bachman, come on!" Hissed Saltz, glaring up at the young private hanging from the scramble net above. "The sea doesn't get any calmer than this!"

Bachman stared down at his Squad Sergeant through the pre-dawn gloom.

"Just a moment Sergeant, I'll be ready in a moment." He whispered nervously as his guts churned at the thought of the jump onto the landing barge. Just one slight misjudgement and he would be over his head in the freezing depths of the German Sea, being crushed between the barge and the ship.

"Hurry up Bachman, you cabbage-crunching idiot!" Snarled Schmidt, a private from the second squad of their platoon.

"Shut the fuck up Schmidt, we'll sort this!" Saltz bit back at the boorish private, whom he had detested ever since he had joined the platoon.

Looking up, Saltz saw that Nuemark had climbed down beside Bachman, bringing up the rear of the squad.

"I've got him Jo', don't worry." Whispered the veteran corporal who was Saltz's second in command. The NCO, a pre-war soldier like Saltz, slung his machine-pistol over his shoulder and took Bachman's KAR98 rifle from him and passed it down to Saltz. "Grab that Jo' will you?"

Having handed the weapon down, Nuemark grabbed hold of Bachman's arm and gave him a reassuring grin.

"Right then, Bachman, you Westphalian cow-fucker; on my word we're gonna jump, and don't you go hanging onto the net when I say 'go', or we'll both be going for a swim before breakfast, ok?"

"Yes, Corporal." Bachman replied, nervously.

"Here we go then." Nuemark said. "Eyes on the barge. When it comes back on the next swell… stand-by… go!"

The two soldiers leapt down towards the barge as it bumped the side of the troopship's hull, Bachman giving a small cry as he jumped. They landed heavily amongst the remainder of their squad, but safely on the deck, all the same.

"There we go, big lad," whispered Nuemark to the relieved private, "nothing to it. No need to say thanks; just make sure I get first hump on any big-titted English bitch you come across!"

"Come on," Saltz snapped quietly, thrusting Bachman's rifle into his hands, "let's move out the way for Second Platoon."

He turned toward the ladder that led into the open hold. As he did so, Lieutenant Hagen's head appeared at the top of it.

"Saltz? Is that you?"

"Yes Lieutenant."

"Have you got all your squad yet? We need to get moving?"

"They're all here, Sir."

"Good. Get yourselves to the front. The company commander wants to speak to all platoon and squad leaders as soon as we're all on."

The officer disappeared back into the darkness of the hold, which was already filling with men from the other platoons.

Saltz led his men down into the hold, and having counted all of them below, he then began making his way towards the prow where the modified ramp had been fitted. It was slow going, pushing past the other infantrymen, all loaded down with weapons, equipment and a double scale of ammunition. Halfway along the hold, Saltz's squad had to edge their way past a squad of pioneers, weighed down with back-packs full of explosives and one of them with a flame thrower. Finally, he found his way to the front of the vessel, where there was a small space left for his squad's form-up position. He turned and whispered to Nuemark to get the men queued up in order, then moved across to a huddle of men standing by the exit ramp. In the gloom he saw the white braid on epaulettes and rank flashes on jacket sleeves.

"That you, Saltz?" Captain Dullman's sharp voice came from the front of the group.

"Here Sir." Saltz replied, feeling slightly sheepish.

"Good." Dullman snapped. "Right then, listen in, because this is the last time you're going to get orders off me until we're over the beach and up the cliffs."

He paused briefly and the group of officers and NCOs exchanged grim looks. Even now, it didn't seem real. Were they really about to invade England?

"As you can hear," Dullman went on, "the Luftwaffe has begun its preparatory bombardment. We haven't had any contact at sea, which means that the Kreigsmarine and the fly-boys have done a top job with the diversion and by keeping the Tommy fleet in port. There's another half an hour or so of the bombing left. At exactly 0500 hours, when we're just five miles from the beach, the Luftwaffe bombing will move inland to strategic targets and the naval guns will take over. They will continue to fire until the first barges hit the beach. As soon as the spotters see us on the beach, the guns will switch fire. That means we need to get our arses across the sand as quickly as we can. Do not drop onto your bellies as soon as you hear the first shots. There's nowhere to hide on the beach, so make this the fastest three hundred yard sprint you've ever done! Understand?"

"Yes, Captain." The group of commanders chorused.

"Finally…" Dullman said, his voice taking on a warning tone. "remember what we've got to do. Ignore the gun battery. Leave that for the Second Battalion. Our job is to blast our way through the beach defences, by-pass the gun position, then clear our way across that open ground and take the fire-control centre up on that ridge by Speeton village. Hopefully, the paras landed on time and on target and our job may already be done for us. But if not, we need to clear that ground and secure that ridge as soon as we can. If we fuck about and take our time, and the Tommies get their reserves or their armour up onto that ridge before us, then we are properly fucked! You know what happened to the 7th Panzer Division at Arras when they got careless? So, let's move fast and secure the beachhead in short order. The sooner we can get our panzers ashore, the better. These island-monkeys don't know how to deal with panzers, so once the tanks are ashore, the Tommies will shit their pants and run away!"

Again, Dullman paused to let his words take effect.

"Right, I won't bore you any longer. Get back to your men and brief them up. Fight hard and move fast and I'll see you all in Speeton for breakfast."

The group broke up among a smattering of subdued laughter.

As Saltz turned, he saw that he had been standing next to Schulz, one of the squad sergeants from 2nd Platoon. The big man chuckled as he caught Saltz's eye.

"Did you hear that? Island-monkeys!"

Saltz grimaced.

"Monkeys with their backs against the wall." He murmured. "I hope you've brought some nuts Sculzi!"

'S' DAY
H – HOUR

BRIDLINGTON HARBOUR – EAST COAST OF YORKSHIRE
SATURDAY 21ST SPTEMBER 1940 – 0440 HOURS

Dickie Holme looked up from where he lay on the fore-deck of his small fishing trawler. The sky seemed to be clear of aircraft now, thank God. He and his crew had been up early, anticipating that the long awaited 'stand-down' would be given by dawn that day. Ever since the nationwide alert had begun, a fortnight earlier, the fishing fleet had been confined to harbour. Not only was that inconvenient for men trying to make a living, it also reduced the contribution to the country's food supply. He had been told the night before by the harbour master, that it was likely there would be a stand-down today if the Jerries didn't come. His friend, Burt Billingsworth, another trawler skipper, had also heard a similar story from a separate, military acquaintance. As a result, even before the grey light of pre-dawn began to filter across the harbour, virtually every crew in Bridlington were on their boats, preparing for the long awaited chance to put to sea.

Then, an hour ago, the bombing had begun. Not a very long raid, nor very accurate either, but it had been terrifying all the same. They had heard the bombing going on to the south as they prepared their boats at half-past three that morning. Then the air raid siren had gone off in the town and they had sat, mesmerised, as they watched the dark silhouettes of dozens of aircraft pass high over-head. The ack-ack had begun, which although noisy, wasn't too alarming. But just before four o'clock, the first bombs had begun to drop on Bridlington itself. Or at least, the Germans had tried to hit the town.

Very few of their bombs had come down amongst the built up area, with only one landing in the harbour, and that had caught the seaward side of the north pier, knocking a large chunk of masonry out of it, but causing no damage to any of the boats that were at anchor. It had been enough to worry the fishermen of course. As they lay there on the decks of their boats, they worried about their families in the town, where the other bombs had landed. Most of the bombs however, seemed to be going wide. From his position on the southern side of the harbour, Holme had seen explosion after explosion up the coast along the North Beach as it ran towards Flamborough Head. The headland itself had taken a number of hits too, but by far, the majority of explosions seemed to be south of the town, all along the sea front for several miles.

The last bombs had dropped about five minutes ago, and now there was a strange silence over the town and harbour. Holme looked around in the half-light of early dawn. There was a pall of smoke from well inland at the western edge of town and, along the south beach, there were several fires and more plumes of smoke.

"What now?" Asked Davey Simpson, the youngest lad in his crew.

"I reckon we ought to go and check on our families. Maybe see if the ARPs or Home Guard need any help. There could be people injured."

"Do you think?" Asked Simpson, his eyes wide.

"Possibly." Holme replied, climbing to his feet with a grunt. He shivered at the light breeze that was blowing off the sea.

From behind the cabin, a large, hulking figure appeared.

"Jerry bastards!" Cursed Mal Chaloner. "Fancy bombing Brid'! What have we ever done to Mr bloody Hitler?"

"I've no idea, but I'm just glad they're bloody rubbish at hitting the target." Holme grunted.

As he twisted, loosening his stiff muscles, he caught sight of Burt Billingsworth rushing down the quay-side.

"Don't think they'll let us out now Burt?" Holme offered as the veteran trawlerman came level with his vessel. Billingsworth looked grey and shocked, thought Holme.

"I'm going back home." Billingsworth said in an unsteady voice. "Our Mam lives up that end of town."

Holme followed Billingsworth's outstretched arm and saw he was pointing towards the pall of smoke that was thick in the air over the old part of town, just beyond the station.

"Hold on Burt; I'll come with you." He shouted up to his fellow skipper. Turning to Chaloner, he said. "We'll not be going out before mid-morning now Mal. I'd get back home for a brew and make sure the missus is alright. You too, Davey lad. I'll see you both back here about elevenish."

"Right you are, Dickie. I need to warm up, any road. Lying on a cold deck all that time isn't good for a man of my age"

Chaloner lumbered back towards the cabin, grumbling away to himself.

Leaving his crew-mates to themselves, Holme grabbed hold of the ladder that ran up the quay-side and quickly climbed up, stepping out in front of Billingworth, who was looking agitated. As soon as Holme was on the quay-side, the older man set off walking in a rush, talking as he went.

"She always ignores the siren does our Mam." He worried. "I've told her God-knows how many times that she has to use the shelter, but she won't listen; you know what old-folk are like? 'No German's making me sleep in the scullery' she's always saying."

Holme glanced at Billingsworth and gave him a reassuring pat on the arm.

"She'll be alright, Burt; you'll see. That smoke's well over towards Priory Church. I reckon it's well away from your Mam's house."

They were on the main quay of the harbour now, and suddenly, Billingsworth stopped dead in his tracks.

"What's that?" He said.

Holme stopped and looked at him.

"What's what?" He asked, bemused.

Billingsworth was staring over his shoulder.

"That, there." He replied, pointing across the harbour, towards Flamborough Head.

Holme turned, looking northwards across the harbour and north bay, and took a sharp intake of breath. Little orange blobs were arcing through the murky sky, whilst yet more were racing upwards at all kinds of angles. Holme cocked his ear to the breeze and picked up the distant sound of gunfire.

"What are they firing at?" Asked Billingsworth, puzzled.

Holme didn't answer. Then, another noise sounded which made them both jump.

"Christ almighty!" Swore Billingsworth as he swung around and stared up into the town towards the junction of Windsor Crescent and West Street. It was gunfire. To be precise, machine gun fire; and close. It was so loud that it must have come from within the town. There were shouts now; some distant, some closer. Then they both heard the bell. The sole surviving church bell in the Priory Church, ringing out with urgency, time and again.

The two skippers looked at each other aghast.

"That can't be right?" Wondered Billingsworth out loud.

Holme didn't have time to answer. A small group of men whom he knew came clattering into the harbour. Dressed in the baggy denims of the Home

Guard, the group of locals turned sharply at the bottom of Windsor Crescent where it met South Cliff Road and began manhandling a pile of crates into the road way.

"What the bloody hell is going on there?" Holme finally managed to say. He began running down the side of the harbour towards the group of Home Guardsmen, conscious that there was more gunfire coming from within the town now.

"Hey, fellas! What's going on? Fellas!"

Two of the Home Guardsmen turned to look at Holme, whilst the others continued piling obstacles in the centre of the narrow road. A fifth man knelt on the corner, his rifle held at the ready.

"Give us a hand! Quickly!" One of the uniformed men shouted back.

"What's happening?" Holme repeated himself as he drew near the group.

Before he could get an answer, the sound of squealing brakes made all of them stop what they were doing. Behind them, a green Army staff car was turning sharply round the corner of Bridge Street, rocking dangerously to one side as it took the bend far too fast. Miraculously, the driver managed to keep control of the vehicle and having straightened up, roared towards the group of Home Guardsmen and civilians standing by junction. They group jumped back several paces as the driver slammed the brakes on and the large staff car screeched to a halt barely feet away from the improvised barricade.

Even before the vehicle had stopped, the passenger door burst open and a tall soldier jumped out. He was an officer by the looks of him, wearing a great-coat and steel helmet and brandishing a revolver.

"Wilkinson." He snapped at his driver. "Manoeuvre the car into the junction here and then disable the engine. We'll use it to bolster this barricade."

"Right, Sir." The driver answered crisply and began doing as he was ordered. Meanwhile, the army officer came around the vehicle and confronted the group of locals.

"You men." He addressed the Home Guardsmen. "Who's the senior one amongst you?"

An older looking man with a number of medal ribbons sewn onto his jacket raised his hand.

"It's me, Sir. I'm the section commander."

"What are you orders?" Demanded the officer.

"Mr Dempsey told me to get the lads back here and start barricading this road. He's sent another group to do the next one along. I think he's going to do the far-side himself, Sir."

The officer gave a brisk nod of approval.

"Good. Get a move on. And get some of these harbour labourers to help you." He jerked a thumb at Holme and Billingsworth. "I've got two sections of my own men coming across. They'll be here in a minute. I'll get a Bren Gun in that pill-box on the corner and seal this side of the harbour with another barricade."

"Yes, Sir." Replied the Home Guard veteran.

The officer looked directly at Holme and Billingsworth.

"Can either of you find me someone with a boat?"

"We've both got our own trawlers tied up to the South Pier." Replied Holme, still utterly bemused.

"Perfect." Snapped the officer. "Both of you, get back to your boats. I want you to move them into the harbour entrance and scuttle them."

"You what?" Spluttered Holme. "You want us to scuttle our boats? What the hell is going on round here?"

Surprisingly, the officer smiled; a slightly devilish smile, Holme thought.

"Invasion is what's happening, gentlemen." He replied. "And my name is Major Holdham, the Garrison Second in Command, and I want you to block the harbour entrance with your boats, immediately."

The two trawler skippers looked at each other agape, then looked back at Holdham.

"Invasion?" Breathed Billingsworth.

"Yes, invasion. There are German paratroopers all over the place and they'll be here before you can blink. We're going to hold this harbour to the last man, and you two are going to block it for me, before their invasion fleet appears. Any questions?"

For a moment, neither Holme nor Billingsworth spoke. They just stared at the officer, blinking stupidly. In the background, the sound of small arms fire was intensifying. Finally, Holme spoke.

"What invasion fleet?" He managed to ask; his voice barely a whisper.

Before the officer had a chance to answer, there was a sound like an express train which made them all look southwards in surprise. Something slammed into the sea-wall barely two hundred yards from the harbour and the huge explosion sent a shockwave through the air which made them all stagger.

Major Holdham smiled indulgently once more and nodded towards the horizon.

"*That* invasion fleet." He said. "Now then. Let's start making life unpleasant for the Germans shall we? Go and scuttle your boats in the harbour."

He made to turn away, but stopped, looking back.

"Oh, and then I suggest you take cover."

THE LEWIS GUN TRENCH – HUNMANBY GAP, FILEY BAY, ENGLAND.
SATURDAY 21ST SEPTEMBER 1940 – 0445 HOURS

Jackson literally tumbled into the trench, gasping for breath, having sprinted across the fields from where the other section was entrenched, his breath fogging in the cold dawn air. Harper and Martlesham were crouching in the bottom of their trench and had to jump aside quickly as the tall Coldstream Guardsman dropped in on them unexpectedly.

"Bloody hell!" Martlesham yelped as he managed to move his hand just before the Sergeant's hobnailed boot landed on it.

"Sergeant Jackson?" Harper eyed the regular soldier with unease, recognising the look in the younger man's face. "Are you alright?"

Jackson leaned against the parapet of the trench and looked down at Harper, then yanked his spectacles off in irritation as they began steaming up.

"I'm fucking bollocksed!" He gasped.

The sergeant dropped down into a crouch beside the two Home Guardsmen.

"You both okay?" He asked, fighting hard to regain his composure after the mad dash across the cliff tops.

"We're fine Tom, aren't we?" Harper looked over at the younger man meaningfully.

Martlesham nodded. "Aye, fine." He replied, his face still white with shock from the earlier bombing. "My ears are bloody ringing though!"

"What's going on, Sergeant?" Harper asked. "Those bombs came bloody close. It's like they knew exactly where we were."

Jackson shook his head slightly as he wiped his spectacles on a handkerchief which, Harper noticed with distracted amusement, was clean, white and immaculately pressed in a neat square.

"They weren't after us." Jackson said, his voice slowly settling back to normal. "They were after the gun battery down the way." He jerked his thumb southwards, towards the coastal gun battery sited on the cliff-face at Reighton Gap. "They've been bombing all along the coastline, right up past Filey and over towards Brid' as well. Lots of stuff landing on the beach and cliffs. Nothing really in-land, just the odd stray. It's just the preliminary bombardment; they're trying not to cause damage to the bits they need. Lots of aircraft going well in-land though, towards York; bombing in depth I suppose?"

Harper felt his heart go heavy with apprehension. It was a feeling that he had not felt since the last time he had gone over the top in the First War.

"What do you think's happening?" He gave the sergeant a serious look.

Jackson placed his glasses back on, and through the dim light of the grey pre-dawn, he gave Harper a knowing look.

"They're here George." Jackson said, so matter of factly that Harper though he must have misheard.

"Did you hear that small arms fire over at Flamborough? And the explosions?" Jackson asked him.

Harper exchanged a quick glance with Martlesham.

"We heard a bit. I assumed it was our ack-ack going up."

Jackson shook his head.

"No mate. I was watching it from back there, during a break in the bombing. There's a gun battle going on up on Flamborough Head, towards the radar station." Jackson paused to give Martlesham a quick glance.

"The invasion has begun. The Germans are here."

Harper stared at him for long moments.

"Are you sure?" He asked at length.

As if in answer, there was a sound of machine-gun fire in the distance, carrying clearly in the chill morning air. All three of them listened to it for a few seconds. "Aye." Jackson replied at last. "I'm sure. Take a look over the top." He nodded at the parapet above them.

Stiffly, they rose to their feet and, keeping as low as they could, peered over the top of the trench. Hunmanby Gap was right below them, still looking very much the same as an hour earlier, although some of the cliff-face had collapsed as a result of the bombing, the rich, red-brown earth lying in huge heaps on the beach, and in one case, forming a ramp over the barbed wire entanglement that blocked Hunmanby Gap.

Across the Gap, high on the cliff and set back in a defile, was one of the hastily constructed pillboxes, with its small Hotchkiss 6 Pounder gun pointing right past them and up the bay towards Filey. Jackson however was pointing hard over to the left, right out to sea.

"There you go fellas." He said quietly. "Who do you reckon they are then?"

The heavy feeling in Harper's stomach and heart suddenly became so intense that he thought he would collapse. For a second or two, he thought he was back on the Somme, waiting for the whistle to blow. Right in front of them, still only ill-defined blobs in the half-light, and littering the horizon across the breadth of the wide bay, were dozens of ships. They were still a long way out. Even so, there was no mistaking that a vast fleet had arrived on their doorstep during the dark night.

"Here." Jackson picked up the pair of old naval binoculars that rested on the parapet and passed them to Harper. "Have a look."

Harper took the proffered binoculars and put them to his eyes. He took a while to adjust them for focus, but then swept them steadily from left to right. He brought the binoculars down and took a deep breath. He was not a naval man, but he knew an invasion fleet when he saw one. There was something menacing about the way the distant dark blobs just seemed to be sitting there on the horizon, as if relishing their power and destructive potential. So this was it? The Germans really had come. Of a sudden, he remembered young Tom was with them and felt a pang of guilt. Harper was a veteran of the trenches, and he was feeling non-too-good, so how must poor young Tom be coping? He looked across at the youngster and forced a grin.

"Well there you go Tom. At last; your chance to give the Jerries a good seeing to."

The seventeen year-old attempted to smile, but instead he looked as if he might burst into tears.

"There'll be more bombs and shelling I imagine." Jackson said, his voice grim "And hopefully, our guns will be all over them, along with the RAF. But if they reach the shore, we won't be able to hold them for long." He looked quickly from Harper to Martlesham. "So, you take as many of the buggers down as you can. Try and get your shots in while they are still bunched up, coming off the boats. Once you've used up your ammunition, we'll pull back to our secondary positions and see if we can scrounge some from the regular army boys. If we can't, then we head back to the village and reconstitute as a platoon there. Happy?"

Harper felt the tension beginning to melt away. That old sense of fatalism was creeping back into his mind, a feeling that had lain dormant for over twenty years.

"Oh, yes." He said, taking hold of his Lewis Gun and giving it a check over. "Happy as Larry."

Just at that point, there were a number of tiny pin-pricks of light on the horizon.

"What was that?" Martlesham frowned.

"Get down!" Harper growled, understanding exactly what the flashing orange lights were. He ducked, dragging Jackson and Martlesham down into the trench with him.

As they thumped to the cold earthen floor, they heard the great whoosh, and instinctively opened their mouths to prevent their ear-drums from bursting.

The ground shook violently and a split-second later, their ears were assailed by a huge thunder-clap of an explosion. It was followed closely by two more. Only moments after the first impacts, did the dull, distant rumble of big guns firing reach their ears.

"No doubt about it now!" Harper shouted. "Here they come!"

The German bombardment of Filey Bay had begun.

CABINET WAR ROOMS – STOREY'S GATE LONDON SATURDAY 21ST SEPTEMBER 1940 – 0455 HOURS

The room was quiet. Churchill stood glowering at the map. Eventually he turned and looked towards the group of officers.

"Go on then Gentlemen; tell me what you have."

Pound cleared his throat and stepped forward.

"Prime Minister, the situation remains very confused. I will give you a brief in as logical a sequence as possible, and then I will ask each of the Chiefs of Staff to give you their appraisal of the situation."

Churchill nodded and sat down heavily in his chair.

Pound moved across to the wall-mounted map of the United Kingdom and Europe. He jabbed a pencil at the English Channel.

"Flag Officer Dover reports that the enemy fleet has been successfully engaged at three points. Only at the most westerly point, opposite Brighton and Eastbourne, did the enemy get through our minefield. Even then, they were spotted early. The destroyer flotillas from Dover and Portsmouth, along with all available MTBs and gunboats have been engaging the enemy for around three hours. Over forty enemy vessels are reported sunk with more damaged and on fire. RAF bombing runs against the invasion fleet began about half an hour ago. Reports suggest that the enemy fleets are pulling back towards the French Coast and a number of enemy fighting ships have been spotted heading northwards out of the channel. It is possible they have been sent to try and intercept the Harwich Flotilla. It is assessed that the enemy is unlikely to make landfall on the south-coast. The Army and RAF Chiefs may have additional points for you."

Pound looked across at his colleagues in invitation.

Dill cleared his throat and spoke briefly.

"We remain poised Prime Minister. There have been many more reports of dummy parachutists over the last hour, but no sightings of the real thing; not in the South of England anyway."

Dill looked at Newall.

Newall waited a moment, gathering his thoughts.

"Fighter Command and Bomber Command are over the channel as we speak Prime Minister. No.2 Bomber Group, and No.11 Fighter Group are up in their entirety. I will have a more detailed report of their missions by six. I have No.3 Bomber Group taking off now as a second wave. No.12 Fighter Group are acting as the back-stop for London. The remaining Bomber Groups are being made ready, but will not be committed unless necessary."

Newall looked back to Pound.

"That Sir," Said the First Sea Lord, "is the situation in Southern England at the moment. However, in the North of England, we have cause for concern. We have just received confirmation from all three services that a large enemy naval force is currently off the coast of Yorkshire. The RAF is planning a strike against the fleet as we speak. The destroyer flotillas from the Tyne and Humber will break out at dawn, after a surface sweep by aircraft. The cruiser squadron will also come out of the Humber and engage the enemy ships off the coast of Yorkshire. The destroyer flotilla from Harwich is being told to hold back from the channel, should we need to flick them northwards. The main battle squadrons in Scapa Flow are making ready to depart at first light, although Scapa Flow itself has been under air-attack for the last two hours. There has been heavy bombing of the Tyne-Tees cities, Hull, Immingham, Grimsby, York, RAF Leaconfield and RAF Church Fenton overnight, and in the last hour, there has been heavy bombing of the coastal strip between Scarborough and Hornsea."

Pound had been pointing at the map with his pencil throughout, and now he paused for a moment, allowing the Prime Minister to absorb the detail.

"In addition to this," he continued, "it seems that an attack has been made by enemy parachutists on the coastal batteries at Spurn Head. Chief of the Air Staff has also received reports of enemy parachutists in the area of RAF Driffield. GOC Northern Command has reported that many of the communication links with the east coast are down. Finally, despite a successful night for the RAF's night-fighters over the North Sea, the radar station at Flamborough Head has gone off-line. There has been no contact with it for over an hour and consequently, we now have a gap in our radar picture over the North Sea. Do you have anything else to add, gentlemen?" He cast his eye round the small audience once more. They all shook their heads.

Churchill spoke in his customary deep growl.

"Where does that leave us at the moment, gentlemen? Are we saying that we have defeated the German invasion, but still have an enemy diversionary force to contend with?"

The Chiefs of Staff exchanged worried looks. Pound shook his head slowly.

"No, Prime Minister. We believe we might be seeing the opposite. There is a possibility that the channel operations were the diversion and that the enemy intends to make his main landing on the east coast of Yorkshire; as hard to believe as that is."

"Yorkshire?" Rumbled Churchill. "Yorkshire? I know that in July we thought East Anglia might be an option for them, but Yorkshire? In September? The North Sea can be very unforgiving this time of year."

Pound gave a wan smile.

"I am inclined to agree with you that a German attempt at landing on our east coast would be madness on their part, however, the fact remains that there has been no serious threat of a landing in the south yet, whereas we now have a substantial German force off Yorkshire, with reports of paratroopers in two places. We do need more information, and communications with that part of England have been difficult, but there does seem to be something brewing."

Churchill grunted something unintelligible, then rose to his feet and stared closely at the map.

"Is it possible?" He asked looking back at the Joint Chiefs of Staff. "To get an invasion force across the North Sea? How far is it? Two hundred and fifty miles?"

"About two hundred Prime Minister," answered Newall, "at its closest point. It would be a difficult prospect for their air force, I have to admit. They can conduct long range bombing raids of course, as they have been for months, but trying to support a land-force at a distance of two hundred miles? I'm not sure that it's possible. It's well out of the combat radius of their fighters and Stukas."

"Unless they capture an airfield." Dill added. "Like Driffield."

Newall looked at him and nodded thoughtfully. Pound gave a sigh.

"It's a mad notion I'll warrant you, but the reality is that they have managed to get a substantial naval force off the east coast without being compromised, regardless of whether it is meant to be a diversion or not. If it is an invasion force, then they'll be in trouble when we get the Home Fleet concentrated. I can't believe they can possibly hope to hold a sea-lane open for long. If it's just a diversion force however, they can be back in German ports before the squadrons from Scapa Flow get near them. I'm trying to put myself in Raeder's shoes. The prospect of holding a sea lane in the North Sea against the Royal Navy wouldn't be a pleasant one. He'd need every submarine, every torpedo boat and destroyer, every capital ship the Kreigsmarine has."

"And lots of luck." Newall observed. "And why Yorkshire? What's he going to gain by landing so far up north. York isn't that important. He needs a quick win if he invades and he'll be miles from London or the West Midlands."

Pound shrugged. "Going for Hull perhaps? A major port?"

"Coal." Brooke said from the back of the room.

Everyone turned to look at the C in C Home Forces.

"Coal, General Brooke?" The Prime Minister gazed at him over the top of his glasses.

"Yes, Prime Minister." Brooke answered. He walked across to the map and both Churchill and Pound moved aside for him. He turned and looked at his small audience and, like Pound, jabbed his pencil at the English Channel.

"What does Hitler get from landing here on the south coast? High cliffs, dense forests, undulating terrain. A couple of ports; maybe some bigger ones if he pushes west. Lots of empty fields with the harvest almost done. A close stab at London perhaps? A city with the bulk of the British Army ready to throw itself in there and turn it into a death trap, that will soak up thousands of German troops. A difficult run to the industrial Midlands, through the Weald, the South and North Downs, the Marlborough Downs and Salisbury Plain, and several major British Garrisons."

Brooke paused and looked around.

"So." He continued. "If I was Hitler, would I cross here, where the water is narrow and the enemy is strongest, and where he expects me? No. I wouldn't do that, because I am German and I have revolutionised war. I land here."

He circled the east coast of Yorkshire with his pencil.

"A long crossing, yes. But assuming the Kreigsmarine and Luftwaffe do their bit and get me on the ground, I land here. Long sandy beaches, with headlands like Filey Brigg and Flamborough Head to act as bulwarks. Small but useful harbours here at Bridlington, Scarborough and Whitby. A clear run to airfields east of York, so I can fly in reserves and stores. But above all," and he fixed his audience with an expansive gaze, "I get a clear run of barely forty miles, maybe fifty at the most, to the South Yorkshire coal fields. Selby, Doncaster, Rotherham, all providing coal to fuel the war effort. Coal, which powers ships, powers factories, fires power stations. And not only that,

I get to isolate the Humber ports. Even if I don't land on both flanks of the Humber, possession of one bank prevents the use of ports on the other. And then there's Sheffield, with its steel industry, or Leeds and Bradford with their mills. Give me a week, and a clear run over this excellent tank country here," His pencil circled the Yorkshire Wolds. "and I will cause havoc in Britain. If I was Hitler, and if the Navy could pull it off for me, that is what I would do."

Churchill emitted a deep purr like a lion stirring from slumber, and regarded Brooke with twinkling eyes. "I am glad you were not born in Germany General Brooke."

Just at that point, there was a knock on the door. Pound answered it briefly, taking a sheaf of reports from a young Army officer. He came back over to the group.

"I asked for all flash signals to be sent straight in Prime Minister." He said. "The situation is moving quickly and we must stay abreast."

He glanced at the messages quickly and began to read.

"Message from Fighter Command. Heavy enemy fighter concentrations over the Channel. Fighter Command losing significant number of planes. Request that bombing attacks over Channel aborted if not essential in order for Fighter Command not to over extend. Better to fight on its own terms over Britain."

Newall frowned, but Pound moved on quickly.

"Message from AOC No.2 Bomber Group. First wave has attacked enemy invasion fleet and returning to base. Heavy losses expected due to heavy fighter concentrations. Request reappraisal of situation over Channel before repeating mission."

He flicked to the next message.

"Radar reports show enemy aircraft concentrations heading towards Thames Estuary. Still no contact with Flamborough Head. Bomber Streams from Holland heading north-west towards Humber Estuary. Bomber Streams heading for Yorkshire from Norway."

He flicked again.

"From Flag Dover. Enemy has broken off action in the Channel. Many transports adrift or burning. Enemy fighting ships heading north at speed. Heavy dive-bombing attacks have begun on Royal Navy ships in the Channel. Dover suffering renewed bombardment from cross-channel guns."

Pound flicked to another message.

"From GOC Northern Command. Enemy paratroopers confirmed at Driffield and Glider troops at Spurn Head. Local Brigade is counter-attacking. Large enemy fleet off Scarborough, same off Bridlington. Naval bombardment of coastal areas underway. This command proceeding on assumption that invasion is imminent. Recommend all RAF aircraft pulled back west of River Ouse in Yorkshire. Request land-line discussion with C in C Home Forces urgently. Request that No.4 Bomber Group and No.13 Fighter Group are allocated to this command for tactical co-ordination. Comms with east coast garrisons tenuous."

He turned to the last message.

"From AOC No.4 Bomber Group. Driffield under attack from parachute troops. Attempting to evacuate aircraft to Leeming. Local troops attempting to secure area. Request permission to crater runway...."

SPURN HEAD – HUMBER ESTUARY
SATURDAY 21ST SEPTEMBER 1940 – 0500 HOURS

"What have you managed to scrape together Baden?" Koch fixed the pioneer lieutenant with a grim look.

"Two flame throwers Major, about a dozen satchel charges, and three shaped charges." The young officer was wet through and shivering, having waded out into the water just fifteen minutes ago to recover what he could from one of the aircraft that had overshot the peninsula.

Koch nodded.

"That'll do. It'll have to. Heiss? How many of your gunners have you got?"

The artillery captain rapped out a reply.

"Twenty three of us left who are fit for anything, Major. Enough to use two of the bigger guns I reckon. Three if some of your men can help with the ammunition. Possibly four at a stretch."

Koch murmured acknowledgement.

"Well done so far." He said to the artilleryman. "You and your boys have done a good job. But I want you to stay back now. I can't afford to lose any more of you. When we capture the battery, we need as many of you to work those guns as we can; so no more stubble-hopping for you!"

He looked around his small command group. Following the chaotic battle of the last few hours, Koch was finally left with one hundred and thirteen men fit to fight, but almost twenty percent of them were the valuable gunners. He was tired and on edge, but at last they were almost within reach of their final objective. They had fought a ferocious running battle during the darkness against the Tommies, who, unlike the Belgians, had come out of their fortifications and engaged them at close quarters. It had been a costly, bloody affair, but now the entire headland was in German hands, except the heavy battery of guns on the point itself. And this of course, was the real prize.

"Listen in." Koch began. "We have about thirty minutes at the most until full daylight. At that point, if we don't have the battery, we'll be stuck out here like spots on a baby's arse; perfect targets for Tommy aircraft or ships. More importantly, the enemy ships that are down the estuary there, will be trying to get out again soon. Our Messerschmitt 110's are keeping them busy for now, but it won't last for ever, and we need to have Heiss' boys manning those big guns before the Tommy ships try to break out again. We must stop those ships from getting out. Understand?"

"Jawhol!" The group of dirty faced officers and NCOs chorused back at him.

"Good." Koch nodded. "Right, you all know the plan. Big diversion on the eastern side, then in with the flame throwers and the satchel charges from the West, as quick as you like; no fucking around. We need to be in there before the Tommies realise what's happening otherwise they'll spike the guns."

He looked at his watch.

"Now, get back to your men and shake them out. Let's get this right first time. I make it 0503 now. H-Hour will be…0515. Any questions?"

Silence. Koch nodded to them in dismissal.

"Let's do it."

RAF DRIFFIELD – EAST YORKSHIRE
SATURDAY 21ST SEPTEMBER 1940 – 0510 HOURS

"Christ almighty!" Scotton cursed as he surveyed the burning offices and body-strewn tarmac.

He and Bevan had managed to kill three more German parachutists as they landed on the airfield, before they had been targeted by a large group of enemy attacking the airfield from the ground. Neither he nor Bevan had actually seen their assailants, but the heavy volume of automatic fire that had erupted from just outside the perimeter fence had been enough to send them running for the cover of the station's administrative buildings. It was a bad move. The main gate of the camp was under heavy attack. The guardroom was on fire, as was station HQ. Several blue uniformed airmen and a WAAF lay dead on the tarmac in front of the blazing buildings. Among them lay the bodies of several soldiers from the East Yorkshires. Scotton, an educated, intellectual kind of man, was already in a state of shock at having being forced to kill another human being, and now his senses were being overwhelmed by the unfamiliar sights of battle, which he had never expected to witness here on the peaceful lawns of RAF Driffield. He had hoped that the previous month's air-raid would prove to be his first and last taste of death. It wasn't to be.

Rat-tat-tat-tat! Scotton ducked back around the corner of the barrack block.

"Bloody hell Bev', they're all over the place!"

Crack! Crack! Two rifle shots whizzed past them from behind. They swung round, rifles up in their shoulders, and saw there was another airman across the road, firing from the far corner of another barrack block towards the main gate. He paused after firing the shots, pulling back behind the corner, working the bolt on his Lee Enfield feverishly. He shouted across at them.

"Get over here! They're all over the bottom edge of camp! We're all collecting over by Hangar 3. I'll cover you."

Bevan looked around at Scotton.

"We're going to have to leg it over there Billy." He nodded towards the other airman.

Scotton just nodded.

"Come on; let's make a dash for it?" Bevan said, turning back towards the other barrack block and waving to the airman. "Oi! Stand-by! We're coming over!"

The other man gave a thumbs-up and swung back around the corner, bringing his rifle up into the aim and firing again.

"Come on Billy!" Bevan yelled and leapt off across the gap between the buildings.

Cursing under his breath, Scotton followed him. As they ran, he noted that Bevan was running in a zig-zag manner, and Scotton, appalled at how his mild mannered friend, a steward from the Officers' Mess, appeared to be relishing the morning's apocalyptic chaos, decided that it was probably a good idea and copied him. His body was already aching from the physical exertion and shock of the last hour, but fear kept him moving. He watched with fascination as the airman by the far corner of the next block fired shot after shot towards the main gate, working the bolt of the rifle feverishly between shots.

Half way across, a rattle of shots cracked past them. Scotton almost danced with fright as one of the bullets hit the tarmac nearby and ricocheted off with a deadly sounding 'ping'. They were almost there and he couldn't help taking one last look over his shoulder. As he did so, he caught his breath; the heavy, sick feeling in his stomach becoming immediately worse.

Through the dim light of early dawn and the billowing smoke from the burning HQ building, he saw them. Grey, ghost-like figures in baggy trousers and smocks and distinctive rimless helmets were streaming across the gap between the guardroom and station HQ. Perhaps a dozen of them, he thought? Crouching low, with weapons and grenades hanging off them, the Germans were moving quickly, confidently, like-professionals; like killers.

His backwards glance was nearly his undoing as his foot caught on something small, sticking up from the grass. With a surprised yelp he tumbled forward, landing painfully on his chest. As he hit the ground, the impact catapulted his face forward onto the working parts of his Lee-Enfield and the rear sight smashed painfully into his face. Instantly he caught the metallic taste of blood in his mouth and he groaned aloud at the pain that shot through him

"Billy!"

Scotton looked up and saw Bevan, breathing heavily, crouched behind the cover of the wall.

"Are you alright? Come on!"

"I'm okay." Scotton called pitifully and raised himself onto all fours, still feeling winded.

Bevan, kneeling down by the side of the other airman, swung round the corner with his rifle up in the aim, to help give covering fire.

Scotton half-scrambled, half-crawled the last few yards, spurred on by several more shots that cracked overhead. He tumbled into cover behind the building, Bevan grabbing his arm to pull him out of the enemy's sight. As the two men fell back into cover, the other airman pulled back around the corner, the bolt of his rifle hanging to the rear.

"Let's get moving." He snapped at Bevan and Scotton. "You must be the last ones from this side of the airfield? We need to get to Hanger 3; that's where the Station Warrant Officer's forming a rally-point."

He reached into his ammunition pouch, pulling out a clip of five rounds and pushed them down into the rifle's magazine.

"That's my last five." He frowned, glancing back at the other two. "You got any ammo spare?"

Bevan nodded. "Here, matey." He replied, handing up three clips.

"You okay to move Billy?" Bevan asked, looking back to his friend with concern.

Scotton, his mouth dripping blood from several cuts, nodded breathlessly.

"Yeah!" He gasped. "Let's get the fuck out of here."

He began to stagger to his feet.

Blam!

"Watch out!" Yelled the third airman, working the bolt of his rifle, having just fired another shot. "Enemy in the top window!"

He raised his rifle towards the top floor of the barrack block that Scotton and Bevan had just run from. As he did so, a white blur appeared at the window, and a bright orange flash followed a split second later. Several bullets smashed into the wall above them, showering all three with shards of brick.

"Jesus!" Swore Bevan, ducking.

Blam! The third airman fired again.

"Let's go!" He screamed. "Move!"

Before they had chance to respond, something whooshed past them with terrific speed and smashed into the barrack block that was occupied by the enemy. A split-second later there was a thunderclap, followed by a shock-wave that made all three of them stagger. It came again; then again.

"Bofors!" Shouted the unknown airman. "Thank God! They've turned the ack-ack guns on them!"

Whoosh-bang! Whoosh-bang! The top floor of the barrack block was billowing smoke now.

"Let's go!" The third airman grabbed Bevan by the shoulder and shoved him in the direction of Hanger 3. "Move, move, move!" He used the flat of his rifle to push Scotton.

The three of them ran flat out, their muscles protesting at the unexpected burst of physical exertion so early in the day. Scotton reflected that, in hindsight, he was glad he had forgotten his heavy greatcoat after all. It was getting lighter now, and above the background noise of gunfire, explosions and the crackling of flames, Scotton thought he heard a new noise. It seemed familiar, yet due to his exhaustion and the ringing in his ears, he couldn't quite place it. Then, with a jolt, he realised what it was.

"Plane!" He gasped.

"What?" Bevan puffed, looking over his shoulder at Scotton.

"Plane." Scotton repeated.

"Where?"

Before Scotton could reply, the noise of the aircraft engine grew suddenly louder and deeper, then, out of the grey dawn-light, a huge dark object came hurtling past them, just a hundred yards away across the field. The long, ungainly Whitley bomber had its nose up, and seconds later, its rear wheel left the ground, and with a roar of its powerful engines, it climbed lazily into the sky like a huge sleepy dragon.

As the bomber soared upwards into the grey dawn light, tracer rounds reached up towards it from various directions, yet the goliath of the RAF continued on its inexorable path upwards, climbing ever higher.

"There's another!" Bevan said, and sure enough, rumbling down the runway, was another of the station's resident Whitleys.

"That's it!" Snarled Scotton, feeling suddenly enraged. "Bomb the bastards!"

"They're not bombing anyone!" Shouted the unknown airman. "They're evacuating."

"Evacuating?" Scotton yelled in amazement.

"Yeah! They're getting the planes away. And if we don't get moving, we'll be stuck here on our own with the bloody Jerries!"

Scotton rolled his eyes in disbelief.

"Oh, my good God!" He breathed to himself as he stumbled onwards.

Bevan started laughing suddenly.

"What's so funny?" Scotton demanded, looking angrily across to his friend, who was sweating profusely under the thick greatcoat.

The sturdy Bristolian glanced sideways, a broad grin on his face.

"I was just thinking." He said, his teeth showing bright in the dawn's half-light.

"That sign you tripped over back there…"

Scotton frowned at his colleague, completely nonplussed.

"It said… 'keep off the grass'!" Bevan chuckled.

To his left, the other airman began to laugh too.

Scotton shook his head.

"Mad-men!" He muttered. "I'm surrounded by bloody mad-men!"

ST HILDA STREET – BRIDLINGTON, EAST YORKSHIRE
SATURDAY 21ST SEPTEMBER 1940 – 0515 HOURS

Major Schulz, commanding officer of the 3rd Battalion, 1st Regiment, 7th Parachute Division, pounded down the road, swearing at the top of his voice.

"Bloody, fucking Tommies! They've taken down all the street signs!"

He pulled up abruptly and threw himself against a doorway. Behind him, the young lieutenant did the same. The thirty other men automatically melted into cover on either side of the street.

"This town's a fucking maze! Where the fuck are we?"

He dropped into a squat and pulled the map out of his smock. Squinting in the dull morning light, he stared at the document, trying to get his bearings. The lieutenant looked over his shoulder.

"That's the train station back up there, Sir, which puts us about here?" The young man jabbed his finger at the map.

Schulz squinted even more.

"Hilda Street? Hmm. Yes; I think you're right. That means we're not far from the harbour."

Schulz traced the route with his finger.

"So, down here and left at the end, into Torp Street."

"Thorpe Street." The lieutenant pronounced the name in the English way.

"Stupid fucking language!" Schulz muttered. "It's a choice of two roads then? Both of them dog-leg and lead onto the harbour and the sea-front. Here look, they both meet at the same junction; Windsor Crescent and West Street."

"I reckon that's it, Major. We'll be there in minutes."

"Thank fuck. We need to secure that harbour as quickly as possible. The first-waves will be hitting the beach in fifteen minutes. As soon as the Tommies realise what's going on they'll try to block the harbour. They've probably got barricades up already thanks to that racket back there!"

Schulz jerked his head back towards the small train station where he'd left two full squads trying to clear out an enemy strongpoint. The Tommy position had shot up his lead squad badly as they infiltrated into the town and now the cat was well and truly out of the bag. He could only hope there were other groups from his battalion converging on the harbour simultaneously. He jabbed his thumb at the map.

"When we reach this dog-leg here, I'll take one squad with all the heavy weapons and follow this row of buildings along. We'll break into them and get eyes on the harbour. Once we're set up, I'll send you in with the others, hard and fast. Happy?"

"Happy, Sir." The lieutenant replied. "Just give me the nod when you want me to launch."

Schulz stuffed the map back into his smock. "Let's go then."

They stood, and the lieutenant gave a low whistle and pumped his hand up and down several times. The paratroopers emerged from the doorways and small front gardens, ready to follow. It was just then that a dark figure popped up from behind one of the low garden walls, barely fifteen feet away. Schulz saw the figure appear but before he could react, there was a loud bang, a bright flash, and the young lieutenant was being thrown backwards by the blast of the shotgun. He landed with an unceremonious thud on the paving slabs, his arms and legs flopping loosely, dead before he hit the ground.

Schulz threw himself into the doorway, just as the surprise attacker fired the second barrel at him. The major swore foully, loose chippings of brick and mortar showering his face as he forced his body into the tiny alcove.

There was a sudden burst of automatic fire from across the road as one of his men reacted to the sudden ambush. The 9mm slugs rattled across the narrow street and thudded into the garden wall where the enemy was hiding. There was a scrabbling sound from the direction of the Tommy position and Schulz pointed his pistol around the corner of the doorway, firing several shots towards the noise, blindly.

"Stay back Major!" A burly paratrooper vaulted over a garden wall behind him, and pushed past his commanding officer, firing a pistol as he went.

In his other hand he held a grenade. The enemy with the shotgun had escaped back into the house and the paratrooper fired a couple of shots into the open doorway, then tugged the firing cord on the stick grenade and tossed it into the dark interior of the building.

"Grenade!" He warned the others and ducked low behind the wall.

Crump! Blam, blam, blam!

The paratrooper fired through the doorway repeatedly after the grenade exploded and then made to go inside the house.

"Straight past!" Schulz ordered. "Leave the bastards! Push on! Head for the harbour!"

The scratch platoon of German paratroopers began running downhill towards the next junction and the harbour beyond. Schulz reached down and grabbed the dead lieutenant's MP40 and some spare magazines, then lurched after his men, leaving the dead officer, the burning building, and the fighting at the train station behind him.

THE LEWIS GUN TRENCH – HUNMANBY GAP, FILEY BAY, ENGLAND
SATURDAY 21ST SEPTEMBER 1940 – 0520 HOURS

Whoosh…crump! Whoosh crump!

Shell after shell slammed into the cliffs. Many were falling to the south, towards the Reighton Gap battery, but enough were coming very close to their own trench. Martlesham, once again, thanked heaven that Sergeant Jackson had been so insistent that their trench had been properly revetted. The interlocking wooden planks and solid posts that had been hammered into position were holding the trench together even though it felt like the cliff was heaving and falling. His jaw was aching. Harper and Jackson had advised him to keep his mouth open during bombardments, in order to prevent his ear-drums from bursting. So far, it seemed to be working, but his jaw was stiff from the effort.

Next to him, Jackson fidgeted.

"What's that smell?" He asked of no one in particular, and sniffed at the chilly dawn air.

Martlesham watched him for a second, then caught a whiff of something acrid himself. His heart leapt with renewed fear.

"Gas!" He whispered incredulously, and made to reach for his gas-mask in its satchel.

"No." Jackson frowned dismissively. The tall Guards sergeant stood up and peered carefully over the parapet. Martlesham watched as he scanned around the cliff-top, his eyes squinting.

"Smoke." Said Jackson calmly after a moment or two. "It's all along the beach and cliffs. That's why the barrage seems to have slackened; they're mixing smoke with the HE."

He glanced down at Martlesham and Harper, crouching together in the left hand side of the fire-trench.

"Get ready lads." He said, gravely. "They're coming."

Instantly, Martlesham's pulse began racing again. As if reading his mind, Jackson said. "If you need a piss, go now. Then take post. We'll see them soon enough."

Immediately, the sergeant set the example and began urinating in the corner of the trench. Harper too, climbed into a crouch and began to relieve himself in the opposite corner. Martlesham stared at the two veterans in amazement. Catching his look, Jackson smiled at him.

"Don't worry young fellah, you'll be too busy to notice the smell soon enough."

Nodding dumbly, Martlesham succumbed and emptied his own bladder. It was a blessed relief when he did, though he thought at one point he would never stop. Steam rose, hot and pungent in the cold morning air. Despite the foul stink in the trench, Martlesham felt instantly better. As he was doing up his buttons, he heard a new sound join the cacophony around them. Explosions of some kind obviously, yet some how different from the impact of the German shells.

"That's our guns opening up." Jackson observed staring southwards across Hunmanby Gap. "They're on the way. Stand-to."

Harper dragged his Lewis Gun up onto the parapet and Martlesham hurried to place the spare drum and bandolier next to it. Jackson meanwhile had picked up the binoculars and was scanning the distant grey ocean for enemy. That in itself was difficult, as Martlesham found when he popped his head over the parapet. Much of the beach was obscured by thick white-grey smoke, as was much of the cliff-top to their left and right. Martlesham could see clearly down into Hunmanby Gap and noticed that more dark clay had fallen away from the cliff and collapsed onto the beach below.

A different feeling pulsed through Martlesham now; more excitement than fear. He was surprised to realise he was smiling. He noticed Jackson glance at him.

"The waiting's over now lad." Said the big sergeant with a grin. "Time for the fun to start."

Martlesham smiled wanly back at the Coldstreamer. Even with spectacles, there was something frightening about the Guardsman; as if there was something explosive and terrible contained behind his tight-lipped and disciplined façade. Martlesham switched his gaze to Harper, who was staring calmly out to sea. He too, caught the young man's eye and returned his gaze with a wink. The tide was about three quarters out but on the rise. He could only just see the breaking waves through the dense artificial fog. Very few shells were falling in their area now. Instead they seemed to be falling behind them by several hundred yards.

"Remember lads," Jackson spoke without hurry. "Short, accurate bursts with the Lewis Gun, at tight groups of enemy, when they're trying to get off the boats, when they're wading ashore, or when they take cover together in a huddle. When each magazine is empty, young man, you fire your rifle to cover Corporal Harper as he changes magazine. Then, use the bandolier to fill the empty magazine. Understand?"

The seventeen year-old nodded eagerly.

"Yes, Sarge…I mean Sergeant."

"Good." Jackson snapped. "Because the bastards are here."

Martlesham swung his gaze back over the parapet and looked down at the shore line. For a second, he could see nothing more than the vague pattern of white froth amid the smoke screen. Then, almost right in front of him, barely three hundred yards away, something dark and sinister nosed its way through the skeins of smoke, creating a large white tumble of surf before it. Long, narrow, dark, with a square shaped board protruding upwards at the bow, the boat nudged forward. Martlesham held his breath. Along the cliff-top, he heard small arms fire erupt, along with other, heavier weapons. Orange tracer ammunition suddenly curved out of the artificial mist on the shoreline towards the cliff-top and the heavy calibre machine gun bullets cracked sharply overhead.

"Ready." Jackson ordered in a curt voice.

Next to Martlesham, there was a harsh ratchet-like noise as Harper dragged back the cocking handle on the Lewis Gun.

Then, as he stared in awe at the dark, ominous vessel to his front, he saw that it had come to a halt, and suddenly, the large square object at the front began to fall forwards. The ramp of the first landing craft was coming down on British soil. The Germans had come.

INVASION BARGE PARSIFAL 5 – 1 MILE OFF HUNMANBY GAP SATURDAY 21ST SEPTEMBER 1940 – 0520 HOURS

"Oh, my fucking God!" Saltz groaned. The barge heaved as a shell landed in the water close by, with a loud plunging noise that came clearly through the hull of the vessel. He was feeling nauseous in the extreme. The barge was making perhaps seven or eight knots at the most, and although the sailors on board insisted that the sea was calm and the conditions 'as good as they get in the German Sea', his stomach had continued to churn as the vessel bobbed slowly towards the coast. The sound of the German fleet opening fire had initially taken his mind off his sea-sickness, though not for long. Looking around the dark hold, he saw that he was not alone in his suffering. There were plenty of pale faces and the smell of vomit hung rank in the humid confines of the vessel. Saltz found himself praying for the barge to hit the beach. All he wanted to do was get his feet on dry land, even if the Tommies *had* spotted them approaching.

The sound of several loud bangs made him jump momentarily. He looked around and saw worried faces staring up towards the ceiling of the barge.

"Don't worry." He reassured his squad. "That's just our 88's on the Seibels opening up. We've got plenty of close support for the landings."

"Uurghp!" Next to him, Corporal Nuemark threw up noisily.

"Fucking hell, Martin!" Exclaimed Saltz looking down. "That's gone all over my fucking boots!"

Nuemark looked up, a bitter grin on his face as he wiped his sleeve across his mouth.

"Sorry, Jo'." He grunted. "Look on the bright side though; you'll be able to wash it off in the sea in a couple of minutes."

"Terrific!" Saltz grimaced.

Next to Nuemark, Bachman was staring at the ramp, his face white as a ghost and a thin sheen of sweat coating his cheeks. Next to him was his friend Halder, another Catholic boy from Munster, who was praying in Latin. Hearing the fervent prayer, Nuemark turned to Halder with an irritated growl.

"Will you shut the fuck up, Halder? That's all we need; a nervous Catholic on the fucking boat!"

Nuemark turned back to Saltz and rolled his eyes. Behind him, Halder fell silent, though Saltz noticed his lips were still moving rapidly as he finished off his prayer. This was the way of it, thought Saltz. It all seemed so familiar; this waiting before a battle. He had seen it in Poland and then again in France. Every soldier had his own little ritual. As he reflected on that, he slipped his hand inside his collar and felt for the little leather photograph locket that hung around his neck. He had taken the precaution of wrapping it in several layers of waxed paper, so there was no point in pulling it out; he would not be able to see Luci's face. Instead he just gripped the little package for a moment, before withdrawing his hand.

A new sound erupted just then; a rapid, heart shuddering series of bangs. It was the 20mm cannon fitted by the wheelhouse of the barge, Saltz realized. If it was firing, then they were almost at the beach.

"Get ready!" He warned his men and pulled his machine pistol from his shoulder.

"Stand-by!" Captain Dullman shouted and slid down the ramp into the hold again. The company commander had been sitting on the main deck, staring through a small gap in the raised drop-ramp, trying to get a glimpse of the enemy shore.

"Twenty metres!" Dullman warned them. "Lots of smoke. Don't worry about it. Just run like fuck for the cliffs."

Halder had started praying aloud once more. Nuemark ignored him this time; he was too busy staring up at the drop-ramp, his fingers flexing repeatedly around the stock of his rifle, pre-occupied with his own private thoughts. From behind their squad came a harsh, boorish voice.

"Hey, Bachman. Don't you seize up on the ramp like you did on the net or I'll kick your arse into the water." It was the unpleasant Schmidt again, one of the privates in Second Squad.

Saltz turned to give the loud-mouthed private a blast, but Heyman, Schmidt's own squad sergeant, beat him to it.

"Shut the fuck up, Schmidt! Concentrate on your own job."

There was a loud, repeated, knocking sound on the wooden hull of the barge and Saltz realized with a start that it was the sound of bullets hitting the vessel's side.

"Oh, fuck." He breathed quietly to himself. "Oh, fuck, fuck, fucking fuck!"

There was a sudden judder that ran through the very structure of the boat and for a heartbeat, Saltz worried that they had been hit by something bigger and he waited, frozen in fear, expecting the side of the barge to suddenly implode as an enemy shell broke through in an explosive orgy of death. It didn't happen, and then a second later he heard a metallic squealing noise. He glanced upwards and saw the drop-ramp toppling forwards out of view. Christ almighty, this was it!

"Okay men," called Dullman over his shoulder, "let's go kill some fucking Tommies!"

There was the sound of a loud splash from above. The Navy marshal, who was crouching at the top of the exit-ramp, turned, gave the thumbs-up to Dullman, and slid down into the hold, out of the way. Saltz watched Dullman take a stride up the ramp and shout back over his shoulder.

"Gooo….!"

THE LEWIS GUN TRENCH – HUNMANBY GAP, FILEY BAY, ENGLAND
SATURDAY 21ST SEPTEMBER 1940 – 0525 HOURS

"Fire!"

Rat-tat-tat-tat-tat! Harper responded instantly to Jackson's command, with a well disciplined five round burst.

He paused slightly, jerking his head to the left to observe the fall of shot.

"Too low!" Jackson called. "Add one hundred! Go on!"

Harper quickly adjusted the rear-sight and put the weapon back in the aim. The first Germans were already off the boat and into the water, scurrying like little black beetles. He brought the foresight blade down onto the dark opening at the top of the ramp again and saw that it was still crammed with men. He pulled the trigger. Rat-tat-tat-tat-tat-tat!

He caught a glimpse of a tracer round arcing through the air and dropping onto the target.

"You're on! Fire!" Jackson screamed.

Harper's finger was already depressing the trigger. He could see bodies falling at the top of the ramp and knew he had the range. A smile suddenly crept onto his face. Just like old times, he thought grimly.

Rat-tat-tat-tat-tat! A pause. More bodies falling; into the water this time. Rat-tat-tat-tat-tat-tat!

Blam! Jackson was firing his rifle towards a second barge that had beached about a hundred yards to the right of the first one. Harper left the sergeant to it and continued to rake the enemy vessel in front of him. Click.

"Magazine!" Bellowed Harper.

He ducked down slightly and cocked the weapon. Martlesham was already scrabbling at the magazine. He dragged it off the gun, then fumbled and dropped it on the trench floor.

"Leave it!" Snapped Harper. "Get the other one on, sharpish!"

Martlesham reached onto the parapet and grabbed the other large, drum magazine. He slid it onto the magazine post, pushed down hard and rotated it clockwise. Click.

"Okay!" Harper shouted and pushed himself fully upright, forcing the gun back into its firing position.

"Get that magazine bombed up!" He shouted as he looked for his next target.

Jackson was working the bolt of his rifle furiously and releasing shot after shot towards the ramp of the invasion barge over to their right. Harper looked between the two barges. His original target had a number of bodies strewn across the ramp or laid in the surf around it, but the knot of enemy soldiers had disappeared from its bow. Instead, the surviving enemy were well spaced out and sprinting towards them over the flat beach.

A line of tracer cut across the beach from far off to the left and Harper saw an enemy soldier spin round, then fall. To the right, however, there were still men on the ramp of the second barge, which he saw had 'P-4' painted on its hull. He swung the gun over to the right and took aim on the ramp.

"George! Take over!" Jackson shouted, dropping down behind the lip of the trench with his rifle bolt fully to the rear. "Get that second barge. Aim for the ramp."

Harper was already firing as Jackson spoke. He cursed as he noted sand spurting upwards in front of the barge. Uttering a string of profanities he ratcheted the sights up another hundred yards.

Down in the bottom of the trench, Martlesham was fumbling with the heavy .303 inch rounds, forcing them into the drum magazine as quickly as he could. The young man watched in awe as Jackson smoothly pushed two full clips into his Lee-Enfield and slammed the bolt shut.

"Back in!" Jackson called, popping back up into a firing position. "Hold on George." He tapped Harper on the arm.

The Home Guard Corporal released the trigger and the Lewis Gun fell silent.

"That's them all out. They're too spread out now."

Jackson pointed down the cliff-face in front of them.

"Keep those buggers suppressed down there, mate."

Harper glanced down and saw that some of the Germans from the first barge had reached the base of the cliff beneath them. Most had disappeared from sight, either behind the large piles of clay that had fallen away from the cliffs, or behind the contours of the crumbling edifice itself. Some however, were already flitting between the anti-tank cubes that were set in position to block Hunmanby Gap.

"Just go for groups of two or three, George. I'll do the individuals."

Crack, crack, crack!

"Fuck me!" Harper fell sideways as something smashed into the parapet just to his right hand side. Jackson too, threw himself away from the sudden explosion of dirt and wood. The two men, their ears ringing, looked at each other in shock. Between them, in the bottom of the trench, Martlesham looked up in surprise, his helmet and shoulders covered in soil, grass and splintered wood.

"They've seen us then?" Harper was the first to recover.

"I reckon so." Jackson gasped. "That was something heavy calibre I reckon; from the boats maybe?"

"Best keep low then?" Harper raised his eyebrows.

Jackson nodded silently. He glanced down at Martlesham.

"Come on Tom, lad." He said in a surprisingly mellow voice. "Get that magazine filled."

Without another word, he and Harper cautiously raised their heads above the parapet again.

They saw that the enemy barge to their front was pulling back from the shore, as was the other vessel to the right, and with the smoke screen almost dissipated, they could see too, the host of other craft coming toward them. Another entire wave of vessels was barely three hundred yards from the shore, which meant even more German troops would soon swarm across the beaches. There was a sudden flash of bright light over to the right by the shoreline and, from his eye-corner, Jackson saw the right hand enemy barge rear up at its stern as its bows erupted in a large explosion, replaced an instant later with a broiling black cloud.

"Machine-gun!" Harper called.

Looking down, Jackson saw the two man crew of a light machine-gun setting up their weapon behind an anti-tank cube, directly below them. They appeared to be setting their sights on the pill-box at the other side of Hunmanby Gap. The pill-box boasted a stubby Hotchkiss 6 Pounder, which was firing steadily across their front at targets further down the beach.

"Take 'em out, George." Jackson ordered.

Several deafening cracks passed overhead, making both Harper and Jackson wince, though they remained in their positions.

Rat-tat-tat-tat-tat-tat-tat! Harper opened fire on the enemy machine-gun crew. There was a high pitched whine from below as chippings and dust erupted around the pair of Germans. Several of the bullets ricocheted off the anti-tank cubes at wild angles, but at least one of the rounds found its mark, for one of the Germans span around and collapsed out of sight. His partner jerked backwards, ducking into cover behind another cube.

"Got him!" Harper said with quiet satisfaction.

Whoosh…boom! The 6 Pounder in the pill-box fired across their front, its shell hitting the face of the cliff barely a hundred yards over to their left. Jackson saw the clods of brown clay fly high into the air above the gorse that lined the cliff-top.

"That was close." Harper observed, looking in the direction of the explosion.

"They're firing at the front of the cliff." Jackson replied. "The Jerries must be trying to scale it."

"They'll walk right into the rest of our section if they do." Harper commented.

Jackson pulled a face.

"Four men with rifles, and ten rounds each? That won't hold them for long."

"Over there!" Harper called suddenly, swinging his gun over at a wide angle towards the based of the cliff at the far side of Hunmanby Gap.

Jackson turned and saw that a group of over a dozen Germans had come around the base of the cliff and were peering cautiously into the Gap itself. One of them was having a shouted conversation with another enemy, who was somewhere below them at the base of the cliff. At the same time, a group of half a dozen enemy were climbing the steep bluff in an attempt to assault the 6 Pounder position from its blind-side. They were already beyond the first barbed wire, having crossed the entanglement where the cliff had collapsed onto it. They were dangerously close to the second set of wire and moving fast.

"Take those buggers out, George!" Jackson ordered, pointing at the small assault group. "Martlesham, get that magazine up here and then start using your rifle."

Martlesham popped up almost immediately, placing the re-filled magazine next to Harper, who was already firing again.

The young man winced as the gun blasted noisily away, close by his ear.

"There, look." Jackson leaned in close to Martlesham and pointed out the enemy soldier shouting across the gap to his unseen comrades.

"Try and take that bastard out, and some of the others too. Take your time; well aimed shots only. Keep their heads down, okay? I'll be back shortly."

Martlesham regarded the Sergeant with a worried look.

"Where are you going?"

Jackson turned and prepared to haul himself out of the trench over the rear parapet.

"I'm going over to the left to visit the rifle group; there's something going on over there. I'm going to find out what."

With that cryptic explanation, Jackson slid over the rear lip of the trench and crawled away on his belly. Martlesham turned back towards the Gap and laid his P17 Rifle over the front parapet. He laid his foresight onto the German shouting the orders and fired his first ever shot in anger.

THE BEACH – HUNMANBY GAP, FILEY BAY, ENGLAND SATURDAY 21ST SEPTEMBER 1940 – 0525 HOURS

"Go, go, go!" Saltz screamed, imitating the company commander, and threw himself up the ramp

With a roar, the two platoons of German infantry launched themselves toward the barge's exit, led by Dullman, the company staff sergeant, Hagen, Saltz and Nuemark. Saltz emerged from the dim interior of the hold and stepped onto the lip of the drop-ramp. The noise of battle increased sharply without the boat's hull to muffle it. Saltz's first impression was of a dream world. There was artificial smoke sweeping across the front of the boat, which seemed to have stopped a worryingly long way from the sand. White frothy surf swirled around the drop-ramp and, through the shifting skeins of smoke, he registered a huge brown and green blob that extended to his left and right in an endless curve, as he pounded down the ramp. The sergeant paused for just a heartbeat as he wondered how deep the water was, but then he saw Dullman and Staff Sergeant Hilfziger splash into the sea up to their waists, so he followed their example.

Saltz leapt off the ramp, trying to get as far forward as possible. Even as he flew through the air, he caught the sight of wet sand splattering upwards just to his front. He landed with a huge 'kersplosh' and took a sharp intake of breath.

"Fuck me!" He gasped.

The water was freezing and he felt his jack-boots fill up immediately. Nuemark splashed down next to him, along with Hagen.

"Machine-gun's seen us!" Saltz gasped, lifting a heavy foot and staggering forward a pace. "Get moving!"

Behind him, he heard the voice of Schmidt.

"Come on, you lame arses!" The unpleasant private growled in his thick Hamburg accent. "Get fucking moving!"

There was a shout of alarm, and Saltz glanced back just in time to see Schmidt push the rear man of his squad. The young man tumbled down the ramp, smashing into the rest of the squad and sending them tumbling in all directions, into the water.

One of the soldiers slid down sideways and went under the water at the bottom of the ramp. Another went head first into the surf at the other side.

"For fuck's sake, you idiot!" Saltz snarled at Schmidt.

The big Hamburger never heard him, because at precisely that point, the Tommy machine-gunner fired again and this time did not misjudge the range. Saltz saw a bright orange flash whiz close by him and heard the deafening crack of bullets flying past only inches over his head. A split second later, Schmidt's head seemed to explode as a bullet hit him square in the face; another going straight through his chest. Next to him another soldier went down like a dead weight, whilst the squad corporal of Second Squad span around with a curse, holding onto his arm. Schmidt's body toppled backwards into the hold, collapsing heavily onto the soldiers behind who were already drenched in the blood and brains of the dead man. Another burst of fire followed quickly after, and one of the bullets ricocheted off the metal fittings with a high pitched whine.

"Get off the fucking ramp!" Saltz heard Heyman screaming, and saw his fellow sergeant jump sideways into the water as the burst of fire hit the bows of the boat. Tearing his eyes away from the plight of Second Squad, he reached back and grabbed the arm of his squad member who was floundering in the water at the bottom of the ramp. Nuemark was there too, and between them they brought the young soldier up to the surface, coughing and spluttering, his eyes bulging in shock and fear.

"Fucking come-on!" Saltz cried in exasperation, and both he and Nuemark began hauling the soldier through the water with them. Saltz glanced over to his right and saw Bachman, the young farm-boy, dragging the other floundering squad member along by his equipment braces.

"Come on you fuckers!" Came a familiar voice. "Get a fucking move on!"

It was Dullman, on the sand now, and beckoning them with his arm as he swore and cursed. The sodden private had found his feet now, and was capable of staggering forward unaided, so Saltz and Nuemark released their grip and splashed forward, the water becoming steadily shallower.

"Come on First Squad!" Saltz roared. "Let's fucking go!"

Something slammed into the beach about twenty yards away and exploded in a black cloud. Saltz staggered sideways as the shock-wave hit him, and cursed as a wall of wet sand slapped him in the face, half-filling his mouth with sludge. He regained his footing and staggered on, forcing his legs to move faster, despite the weight of water in his boots. He spat as he ran, trying to clear his mouth of the cloying sand. It was as noisy as hell. The Tommy machine-gunner was having the time of his life. Short, professional bursts came one after the other, cracking dangerously low over Saltz's head as they sped towards the ramp of the barge. He watched as a line of tracer rounds came from somewhere well off to their right and slammed into the sand, just behind Dullman and Hilfsziger. The bullets stitched a line across the sand and then sliced through the only other person between Saltz and the company headquarter staff. The soldier span around violently as if having a fit, and just before he dropped, Saltz recognized him as the company clerk, who was acting as Dullman's runner.

Saltz was nearly half-way across the beach now. He couldn't have gone more than one hundred and fifty metres from the barge, but it felt like kilometres. His thighs felt heavy and they seared with pain at the effort required to propel him across the sand, whilst his lungs felt as though they would burst; providing of course, that he didn't choke on the wet sand that still clogged his mouth. Next to him, Nuemark was keeping abreast, his face contorted with the sheer physical effort. He had both hands on his rifle and was pumping the weapon in a diagonal motion, reminding Saltz of an Olympic pole-vaulter making his final run-up. Another figure began to overhaul the two of them. To his surprise, it was young Bachman. The slightly built soldier was sprinting, apparently without effort, across the beach, despite being weighed down with ammunition. As the No.2 on the MG34 light machine-gun, he had three belts of ammunition slung around his body, along with his own rifle and a metal box containing another belt of machine gun rounds. He carried those last two items one in either hand, though he appeared not to notice their weight as he pumped his arms franticly in his dash to get across the beach.

"Fuck me!" Gulped Nuemark, fighting for breath. "Look at that bastard go!"

Saltz didn't reply. Instead, he bent his head and staggered forward with renewed energy as another burst of cross-fire clattered past them, once more kicking the sand up just metres away. Strangely, as they got closer to the cliffs, the fire seemed to slacken. After what seemed like an age, Saltz and Nuemark collapsed into the shelter of a mound of red-clay at the base of the escarpment, having negotiated a stretch of badly shredded barbed wire entanglement, torn apart by the preliminary barrage. They dropped to the ground exhausted, fighting for breath, and waved franticly at the remainder of their squad. Nearby, Dullman was pouring water out of his jackboots.

"Saltz, where's Lieutenant Hagen?" He demanded.

Saltz scanned the beach behind him, trying to identify the officer amongst the spread of individuals tottering up the beach towards the shelter of the cliffs.

"He was right behind us, Captain. God knows where he's gone."

"No matter." The company commander shrugged, pulling his boot back on. "We need to make some elbow room on this cliff. Get your squad set up here and start suppressing that pill-box at the other side of the draw. Use your whole platoon, come to think of it. Tell Hagen when he arrives. I'm going to send Second Platoon up the cliff. We'll feed Third Platoon through them once they get here. Just keep those enemy quiet on this flank. Got that?"

"Yes, Captain." Saltz acknowledged, his mouth still thick with sand.

Around him, the rest of his squad were flopping onto their knees, their chests heaving after the mad dash. They were all soaking wet, their field grey uniforms matted with sand.

Blam!

Saltz looked over towards the draw and saw Bachman firing his rifle towards a pill-box, which sat high up on the cliff at the other side of the ravine. He turned back to his other squad members.

"Come on you lazy swine; the new-boy is already fighting the Tommies! Get your arses over onto this shoulder of land and start helping him! Schumann, get that machine gun set up; move!"

One by one, his men forced themselves upright and began creeping over the piles of thick red earth that had fallen onto the beach.

Private Schumann, carrying the powerful MG34 light machine-gun, staggered towards Bachmann, unwinding the belt of ammunition from around his gun. Coming alongside the young man who carried the bulk of his spare ammunition, he gave him a nudge.

"Come on Hans; let's get set up and start giving some back. Over here." He nodded at the large concrete cubes just in front of them and began creeping forward. Bachman followed him. Schumann unlocked the bipod legs of the machine gun and positioned it on top of the nearest cube, allowing the belt of ammunition to hang down over the side. Bachman came in alongside him and bent down slightly to open the spare box of ammunition he was carrying. Schumann looked through the sight and aligned onto the pill-box made from red brick that he could see high up the cliff and tucked well back behind a natural bulge in the terrain.

Just at that point, the concrete block seemed to erupt in a cloud of dust and loose chippings. Something slapped Schumann hard in the face and he span around violently with the impact, losing his balance and collapsing heavily onto the sand, his MG34 clattering noisily onto the beach. Bachman let out a small yelp and ducked in close behind another cube. Schumann groaned, his head was spinning and his ears roared with a loud rushing noise, as if he had waves crashing inside his ear drums. He felt a harsh, wet, metallic taste in his mouth and tried to speak. The action made him groan in agony. An unbelievable pain shot through his mouth and face. Bachman was pulling at his leg.

"Jochim! Jochim! Are you all right?"

With an effort, Schumann forced himself up onto an elbow and crawled into the cover of the concrete block. As he did so, Bachman stared in horror at his friend's bloodied face. A bullet had caught him squarely in the cheek and gone straight through his mouth. His cheeks were a mass of tattered flesh and his mouth was gushing with blood and broken teeth. Bachman had a sudden memory of a horror story he had been told as a boy, where a man had turned into a wild, murderous wolf-like beast. He tore his eyes away from the injured Schumann and reached out for the machine gun that lay nearby. As the young private dragged the gun closer to him, Saltz dropped down next to him.

"Where did that come from?"

Bachman pointed vaguely up the slope of the cliff, directly above them.

"Up there somewhere, Sergeant. They got us from the side."

Saltz whirled around and shouted towards Heyman, who was crouching some way back.

"Willi! Whatever's left of your boys, get 'em over here, mate. Get them up on this slope. There's a Tommy position somewhere up there; see if you can pin it down."

Saltz turned to Bachman again.

"Second Squad got minced on the ramp." He explained quickly. "Lieutenant Hagen's missing. Now, get that gun set up and keep low this time."

He glanced at Schumann.

"Hold on there, Schumann lad. We'll get you fixed up in a moment."

The injured machine-gunner nodded dumbly.

Just then there was an ear-shattering crack.

"Fucking hell!" Swore Saltz, clamping his hands over his ears. "That Tommy artillery is firing straight over our heads. Get that gun into action, Bachman. Now!"

"Third Company! Third Company!" The voice carried to Saltz above the noise of the gunfire.

He popped his head around the concrete block and saw, just thirty metres away, a group of men from Second Company at the other side of the draw, crouching in the limited shelter of the cliff's base.

"Yes? Over here!" Saltz called, waving an arm.

A man spotted him and waved back.

"There's a Tommy trench fifty metres above you, right on top of the cliff!" Yelled the Second Company soldier.

"Yes, got that." Saltz acknowledged. "You've got a bunker on your side, tucked behind the face of the cliff. It's got a big gun in it. We'll give you cover from this side."

"Got that." The Second Company man replied. "We're going to get moving straight away. First Company have landed right in front of the enemy gun battery; they're getting cut to pieces!"

Next to Saltz, Bachman pulled the trigger on the MG34 and a long burst of 7.92mm rounds rattled off towards the enemy pill-box that housed the artillery piece. Saltz turned and looked back along the base of the cliff, and across the wide, open beach. The entire stretch of sand was covered in bodies, and crowds of men were gathered under the high, clay bluffs. There were invasion craft beached all along the wide, curving bay, some of them on fire.

"Christ almighty!" Saltz murmured to himself. "Nuemark was right. This is going to be a proper carve up!"

GUN CASEMATE 'B', GREEN BATTERY – SPURN HEAD SATURDAY 21ST SEPTEMBER 1940 – 0530 HOURS

Twenty two year old Lance Bombardier David Sandler of the Royal Artillery was scared. Scared and angry. He raised the medium weight sledgehammer and brought it down with a crash on the telescopic sight of the six-inch gun. On this, his fifth blow, the sight shattered completely. What a waste, he thought. He had been sat here at Spurn Head for weeks, just itching for a chance to have a go at a German ship or U-Boat that might be stupid enough to nose its way into the estuary, yet here he was now, rendering his gun useless as they prepared to surrender to the Germans who had somehow managed to attack them from behind. Their big coastal-defence guns were useless against the enemy glider-borne troops who had slowly but surely fought their way closer to the battery during the night. Now, virtually out of small arms ammunition, and pushed back to the concrete casemates of the guns themselves, the battery commander had ordered the guns to be spiked. Sandler suspected that the order had been hastily issued as soon as the enemy flamethrower had come into action, just fifteen minutes ago.

They had watched in horror as their two outlying pill-boxes were swallowed by a long burning tongue of orange flame in the early dawn light and the screams of the occupants still rang through Sandler's ears. After the flames, the enemy had rushed them. The perimeter had collapsed, and, armed mainly with rifles and the odd Bren Gun, the survivors of the battery had retreated back to their precious six inch guns. After all, thought Sandler, they were not trained infantrymen, and they were fighting against German storm troopers armed with machine guns, flamethrowers and, it seemed, an endless supply of grenades. He watched two members of his crew man-handle the breech-blocks across to the firing port of the casemate and topple it out, where it fell heavily to the sand below. Outside, another pair of gunners would retrieve it and carry it out to the waterline, before throwing it as far as they could; in probability just a few feet.

"Bom' Sandler, is that gun disabled yet?"

The well spoken voice snapped Sandler out of his private thoughts. He looked over to the doorway and saw Lieutenant Shaw peering into the gloomy interior.

"Two minutes and we're done, Sir." He replied crisply. "I'll send the boys out onto the beach when we're good to go."

"Okay." Replied the young subaltern. "Quick as you can. We're losing people here unnecessarily. As soon as the guns are spiked the BC's going to show a white flag. We don't want them using that bloody flamethrower again!"

The fear in the young officer's voice was obvious. He disappeared outside again.

"All done, Bom'." Said the nearest gunner, staring out of the gun port. That's the other two coming back round to the door now."

Sandler nodded with satisfaction. "Good. Now get yourselves outside lads and report to Mr Shaw. Tell him 'B' sub-section is spiked and the casemate clear."

"Yes Bom'." Nodded the gunner and nudged his mate. The two of them left the casemate, moving with urgency. Sandler noted how suddenly the battery's morale had plummeted when it had witnessed the flame-thrower's power. As soon as the officers' had made the suggestion that they should spike the guns, the men had followed like eager puppies. The thought made Sandler angry again. There was however, another reason why Sandler, a professional soldier, was both angry and frightened. He was Jewish.

Born into a family of tailors in the East-End of London, he had decided against joining the family firm and enlisted in the Army in 1936. The wages were modest, yet regular, and he enjoyed the camaraderie. As a bright lad, quick to learn, he had found rapid promotion to lance bombardier, and his officers' thought well of him. It was during conversations with the public-school educated officers that he had learned so much about Adolf Hitler and this new Nazi Germany. And then, whilst home on leave in 1938, he had found out a whole lot more about that country and its leader.

His grandma on his mother's side, and one of his aunts, had arrived in London with three of his young cousins. They were destitute, and carrying what was left of their world in three small suitcases. He had listened with horror as Grandma Feldman had told the terrible story of how his grandfather and uncle had been beaten to death by Nazi thugs. The Nazis had come just before closing time at the small solicitors' office where they both practiced. The exact purpose of the visit had been a mystery to the family. All they ever knew was that the authorities had claimed that his relatives had assaulted 'policemen' whilst they were conducting an investigation. In the ensuing scuffle, both Grandpa Feldman and Uncle Hugo had been clubbed to death.

Shattered, the women of the family had just managed to arrange a burial before they received word from friends in the legal profession that the Nazis were planning to arrest the whole family for 'anti-government activity'. They had fled. It was a testament to the strength of his bereaved aunt and grandma that they had managed to evade the Nazi authorities and cross the Dutch border. From there, they obtained passage to Britain where they threw themselves on the charity of their distant relatives. The story still angered him now. He felt the rage and frustration rise inside him. When would someone show these bastards that they couldn't just bully the whole world and get away with it. The Nazi war machine had run both his mother's family and the British Army out of Europe, and now they were here, in England, ready to bully and torture and murder his own branch of the family, along with anyone else unlucky enough to attract the Nazis' displeasure. How could he surrender? A Jew in a German prison! He wouldn't last long. And what of his family if England fell?

Sandler stood silently for a while, thinking. He realised that the shooting had stopped on the edge of the beach. He could hear voices shouting now; German voices, not English. He walked quietly to the rear of the casemate and glanced out through a narrow slit. The battery had surrendered. He could see the bulk of his comrades standing in the centre of the beach in the grey dawn light, their hands raised. Out in front was the battery commander, talking to a wary looking German. There were Germans emerging from the scrub and gorse now and filtering down onto the beach. Some of them pushed other prisoners in front of them where they had flushed them out of their positions. He saw a German striding across the sand, a sub-machine gun clasped in one hand and gesticulating with the other. He was rattling off a string of orders in a harsh, guttural language. In response, several groups of Germans broke away from their comrades and began doubling across the sand towards the concrete casemates.

Suddenly, Sandler knew that he was going to do it; the idea had been going through his mind for an hour now. The fear was gone, he found to his surprise. All that remained was the cold, restless anger that he always felt when he thought about his murdered grandfather and uncle. He saw a group of four Germans come running towards his casemate. There was no time to worry now. It had to be done. He was not going to let these Nazi scum walk all over Britain as they had done to the rest of Europe. Moving quickly, he walked across to the far side of the dark casemate, reaching into his pouches as he did so, and withdrawing the two No.36 Grenades. He turned to face the door as he side-stepped amongst the five up-ended artillery shells on the floor. As he did so, he carefully removed the safety pins from both grenades, ensuring that their fly-off levers remained secure in the web of both hands. Then, with a deep breath, he placed both hands behind his back and focussed on the doorway.

The boots clattered on the concrete steps. He heard the urgent German voices. The muzzle of a machine-gun poked through the door, then a face. He saw the eyes of the German glittering; he was looking straight towards the six inch gun with a look of excitement. Sandler realised in that moment that the Germans wanted the guns intact, and why. He chuckled. The German whirled around, eyes narrowing, his sub-machine gun pointing straight at Sandler.

"Hands up!" Yelled the German in broken English. "Quickly! Hands up!"

Several more Germans pushed past the first, levelling their weapons at Sandler. With a smile, he opened his hands, releasing the grenades. He raised his arms above his head, looking the first German in the eyes as the two grenades clunked onto the concrete floor. He heard the small pop as the two fly-off levers came free and the striker hit the percussion cap, lighting the fuses in turn.

"One for Grandpa, and one for Uncle Hugo." Sandler laughed.

The Germans frowned at him. Then, one of them suddenly realised the danger, and in the last second of Sandler's life, he had the pleasure of seeing a look of complete fear run across the German faces.

Cruump – Kaboom!

The two grenades detonated simultaneously inside the close confines of the casemate and amongst the ready to use artillery shells. The dull thud of the exploding grenades was followed a split second later by the most enormous, mind numbing explosion that could be imagined. The force of the huge blast actually stripped the concrete from the roof of the steel-reinforced casemate, sending it hundreds of feet into the air. The gun disintegrated into a thousand steel fragments which were propelled out of the gun port and observation slits. A huge black cloud billowed out of the concrete bunker and the shock wave that came with it knocked everyone over, German and British alike, who was standing within a hundred and fifty yards.

As the echo of the huge explosion rolled off across the wave-tops of the North Sea and Humber Estuary, an eerie silence descended across the beach at Spurn Point. Casemate 'B' of Green Battery had ceased to exist.

'S' DAY
H +1

THE CLIFF TOP – HUNMANBY GAP, FILEY BAY, ENGLAND
SATURDAY 21ST SEPTEMBER 1940 – 0540 HOURS

Ducking low, Jackson threw himself down behind the rear lip of the trench.

"Fellas, what's going on? Why have you got your bayonets fixed?"

The group of four Home Guardsmen looked over their shoulders with a look of relief.

"Sergeant Jackson, thank God you're here!" Began the grey-haired lance corporal. "We're out of ammo for the rifles and the Jerries are coming up the cliff! They're making slow progress because of the machine-gun in the pill-box over to the left, and that 6 Pounder over your side, but they'll get up here eventually."

"What about the Boys?" Jackson asked, indicating the long, ungainly anti-tank rifle.

"Still got all five rounds." Replied the lance corporal. "No tanks to fire at yet."

Jackson nodded and looked around.

"No sign of that regular platoon yet?" He asked.

"No Sergeant; none at all. We'll be overrun soon."

Jackson looked at the old lance corporal's face and experienced a pang of admiration at the determined, fatalistic expression that he saw on it. These men would die here, fighting bullets with bayonets if that was what their duty required. But Jackson was a pragmatist, and he knew how to fight Germans. He would not leave his men to die here on the cliff-top.

"No we won't." He said quickly. "Prepare to pull back to the secondary positions at the other side of the field. We'll regroup there and see what we can do. If the regulars haven't turned up, it means there's a problem elsewhere. Get ready to move, whilst I have a look."

The four Home Guardsmen nodded and, keeping as low as possible, crawled over the rear lip of their trench. Jackson crawled forwards and off to the side, right up to the edge of the cliff. It was properly light now, the sky over-cast and grey. Out to sea was a bank of black smoke, being deliberately produced by the enemy ships. Closer to shore, he could clearly see enemy barges and boats from the first wave backing away from the water line and heading back out to the troopships, whilst a fresh wave of landing craft brought in the second and third waves. He glanced to his left and took in the sight across Filey Bay. He felt his heart thud at the sight of the vast armada that filled the wide, picturesque seascape. There were hundreds of enemy soldiers, like little ants, running across the beach towards Filey town, which was on fire from end to end.

Reaching the edge of the cliff, Jackson peered over and caught his breath.

"Bloody hell!" He whispered quietly, dropping his head even lower. There must have been a couple of dozen German infantrymen clambering up the steep, grass-tufted bluffs, the nearest ones being only thirty yards away. He edged his rifle forwards and lined up on the closest enemy soldier. The German was breathing hard, his face red underneath the helmet. Blam! Jackson fired and the German seemed to lift off his feet and was thrown backwards down the slope. Jackson heard a cry of alarm and some of the enemy went to ground. Several of them began firing blindly up at the cliff-top, saturating it with fire. Jackson grimaced as a bullet cracked over his head, but he stayed in position and swung his rifle onto another target as he worked the bolt. His next target was carrying one of the short sub-machine guns that the enemy's NCOs and officers tended to use. Jackson steadied his breathing and lined up the foresight blade on the man. Just as Jackson took up the first pressure, he saw his target produce a small pair of binoculars.

"Commander." Jackson murmured to himself, holding his breath and pulling the trigger.

Blam! The German catapulted backwards.

"Dead commander." Jackson said, feeding another round into the breech of his Lee Enfield.

Then they spotted him. He heard the frantic shouting of enemy voices and realised they had seen him. That was confirmed when, seconds later, a number of shots slammed into the earth nearby, far too close for comfort. Jackson rolled back out of view behind the crest and delved inside his pouches for a grenade. Pulling one out he quickly removed the pin and rolled back over, ready to throw. The big sergeant paused for just a moment as he mentally tried to place the enemy below him. He remembered a small knot of them, slightly over to the left, half-way up the slope, and threw the grenade over the edge in that direction. For a second, there was nothing, but then came the sound of alarm; a German voice shouting a warning. Crump! The grenade exploded and moments later he heard moaning and frantic screaming. Bingo.

Shuffling back slightly, Jackson moved over to the right several yards and popped his head over the edge again. Most of the enemy had gone to ground, but one of them spotted him and fired. The bullet cracked past his left ear, just inches away. He pulled his head out of sight quickly once more. The enemy had usefully given his own position away, so he would inherit the second grenade, thought Jackson. He quickly removed the grenade from his pouch and prepared it, then, judging his target's position, tossed it over the cliff's edge. This time, he didn't hang around. He rolled back away from the cliff and began running at a low crouch towards the Lewis Gun trench. It was time to go. As he ran, he heard the satisfying crump of the exploding grenade. God only knew, it felt good to be giving Jerry one back for Dunkirk.

As he sprinted across the cliff top, stray rounds cracked by him. He glanced inland and saw the four Home Guardsmen disappearing through the far hedgerow towards their fall back positions. He saw nothing else beyond that. There should have been at least a platoon of regular infantry manning this spot with them. They were part of the reserve unit set slightly back from the coast towards the village of Hunmanby. Their task was to shore-up the most threatened area of coast once the enemy landings had been identified, but there was no sign of them at all. He was starting to get a sinking feeling. They had already taken care of a good few Germans without suffering casualties, but soon, the German weight of numbers would tell. His little section could not plug all the gaps in the three hundred yard stretch of cliff between the 6 Pounder position and the machine-gun pill box further north.

He dropped into the Lewis Gun trench heavily, as a whole volley of shots cracked through the air beside him. As he steadied himself, Martlesham turned to him with a worried look.

"I'm out of ammunition, Sergeant, and George's got the last full magazine on. This one's only half full!" He indicated the circular drum magazine that he clasped in his hands.

Rat-tat-tat-tat-tat! Harper fired another burst at the enemy trying to scale the cliffs at the far side of the Gap. For his pains, a flurry of rifle shots cracked through the air, several of them smacking into the soil just yards in front of the trench.

"Bastards know where we are now!" Harper growled, ducking away from lip of the trench as a German bullet ricocheted off a nearby rock with a deadly whine. "They're hitting us from both sides of the Gap!"

Jackson nodded.

"We can't hold 'em without more ammo and grenades. I've just pulled the rest of the section back to the fall-back positions. There's a whole load of Jerries coming up the bluffs to our left. We're going to have to pull back from here too, before we get outflanked."

"What about those regulars that we've had here recently?" Harper frowned "I thought they were meant to stand-to at dawn?"

Jackson shook his head dismissively.

"Not seen. Something must have gone wrong elsewhere. Either way, we need to pull back now and try to cadge some more ammunition. The pill-box up to the left is slowing them slightly, along with this 6 Pounder up here, but they won't hold 'em for long."

Another flurry of shots cracked overhead, followed by a burst of machine-gun fire.

"How are we going to get out of here, then?" Harper raised a questioning eyebrow at the Guards Sergeant.

Jackson's reply was instant.

"Fire and movement, George. You and Martlesham move first whilst I give you covering fire. Get back to the first hedgerow, then cover the cliff-top over to the left. Then I'll pull back to you. We'll pick the others up and take it from there."

Harper nodded and gave Martlesham a nudge.

"Get ready to run, lad. Shove that drum in your haversack and don't forget to bring those binos."

The old soldier turned back to Jackson who was fishing two more clips out of his ammunition pouch.

"Sure you don't want me to give the covering fire, Sergeant?"

Jackson gave him a silent look of appreciation, but shook his head.

"No mate. Thank you for offering, but you need to get Tom out of here along with the Lewis Gun. Right now it's our only real asset. Okay, stand-by..."

Harper and Martlesham poised themselves against the rear of the trench.

"Now!" Snapped Jackson, and in a flash, popped up at the parapet and levelled his Lee-Enfield towards the far side of the Gap and fired a shot. He worked the bolt quickly and fired again, before throwing himself to the left hand side of the trench, working the bolt again as he did so. Blam! His third shot was directed towards the enemy below. The two Home Guardsmen were already out of the trench and throwing themselves towards the crest that would remove them from the sight of the Germans on the beach. A burst of automatic fire came up at them, followed by numerous rifle shots. The air around the trench filled with the sharp crack of passing bullets and Jackson worked his bolt ever faster, releasing shot after shot towards the base of the cliffs.

Just as Harper and Martlesham scrambled safely over the edge of the cliff-top, Jackson worked his bolt to see that both the chamber and magazine were empty. With practiced ease, he dropped into a crouch, grabbing two spare clips, and rammed one after the other into the charger guide, pushing down on the big brass bullets to force them into the magazine. Have done so with both sets of five rounds, discarding the empty clips in the bottom of the trench at the same time, the Coldstream Guardsman took a deep breath and prepared to pop back up, but this time with the intention of following Harper and Martlesham back over the top of the cliff.

As he crouched there, gathering himself for the dash, he picked up a new noise amongst the cacophony of battle that resounded across the wide bay. A deep noise, it seemed, like a powerful engine, along with a dramatic increase in small arms fire. Jackson frowned a moment, trying to read the noise of the battle. Then, with a jolt, he recognised the sound. Aircraft. Almost at once, the noise of the aircraft engine increased and he realised that there was at least one plane overhead and by the sound of its engine, diving fast. He glanced up from the bottom of the trench, but could see nothing, so he edged upwards and peered over the top of the trench. Instantly, he saw tracer rounds going skyward, both from down below him on the beach, and from the enemy vessels out on the water.

With a flash of movement, an aircraft suddenly appeared at the right of his field of vision and for a brief moment, he felt the rising sense of panic, worrying that somehow it would be one of the dreaded Stuka dive-bombers. To his relief and amazement, he saw a brown and green camouflaged aircraft with distinctive blue, white and red roundels of the RAF, flying at an unbelievably low height across the bay in front of him, heading towards Filey Brigg. His aircraft recognition was not brilliant, but it was one of the sturdy looking planes with a prominent dome-shaped turret behind the cockpit that sported four machine-guns. He saw the plane trundle past, seeming oblivious to the mass of tracer whipping up towards it. Then he saw that the turret was facing towards him, and a second later, there was a series of bright flashes as the RAF gunner opened fire. Jackson ducked instinctively, but was surprised not to hear the sound of bullets cracking through the air.

He looked over the lip of the trench to see that the aircraft was gone, but just at that point, another aircraft, and then another, buzzed straight across the bay, following the first, and this time Jackson saw what they were doing. They were machine-gunning the face of the cliff; or at least one of the machines was. The third aircraft, slightly further out to sea, was directing its fire at the invasion barges as it passed by them. He heard the clatter of the quadruple mounted machine guns spitting their deadly offering towards the Germans, and noticed with joy that there was a huge cloud of sand and dust being kicked up right below him by the anti-tank cubes where the Germans had gathered. He heard the high-pitched whine as the bullets bounced off the concrete cubes, and he was sure he could hear men screaming. Now was his chance! The RAF had finally joined the battle and he didn't have long to take advantage of it. With a heave, he pulled himself out of the trench and stumbled upwards, over the edge of the cliff, ducking low.

He glanced backwards once and got an awe-inspiring sight of the whole bay. Ships and boats as far as the eye could see, were spitting orange tracer in all directions as a whole squadron of the strange looking British aircraft dived in towards the beaches that were already swarming with German infantry. Here and there, a German boat was on fire, or lay heeled over in the rolling surf. Tearing his eyes away from the scene of mayhem, he pounded across the meadow towards the gap in the hedge, just beyond the concrete blocks that sealed the exit from Hunmanby Gap for vehicles. Harper and Martlesham were already there, and he saw them look back towards him.

"Keep going!" He hollered. "The RAF are strafing the beach and the cliffs! Keep going up the lane…tell the others to get moving!"

He was panting heavily now.

"We need to get clear of the cliff-top as quick as we can; get bloody moving!"

He saw Harper give a thumbs-up, then wave towards the far hedgerow where the remainder of their section had already gathered. They needed to move quickly whilst the RAF gave them breathing space. He knew they would be leaving the Gap wide open for the enemy to outflank the Reighton Battery, but without ammunition there was little they could do. The Home Guard rifles fired .30 inch ammunition, which was difficult to come by, and the section had already expended everything they had. Between Jackson's rifle and Harper's Lewis Gun they probably had about seventy to eighty rounds of .303 inch ammunition. It wouldn't last long. Jackson's mind raced. He was determined to pay the Jerries back for Dunkirk, but he needed ammunition to do it. They had to keep fighting, but not from static positions; the Germans were too good at soldiering to be held up for long by positional defence. He had his breathing space to redeploy, courtesy of the RAF, but where the hell was he going to get the bullets?

GREEN BATTERY – SPURN HEAD
SATURDAY 21ST SEPTEMBER 1940 – 0540 HOURS

"Oh, my fucking God!" Koch sat upright then fell sideways onto his elbow, his head swimming. He tried to focus his eyes but couldn't, and there was a tremendous rushing noise in his ears, like water pouring through a giant drain. A strange, sickly smell came to his nostrils and along with his disorientation, it overpowered his senses. With a loud retch, he fell forward onto all fours and vomited onto the sand. He hadn't eaten for hours, and so the vomit was watery and acidic. It gushed over his forearms and down his nostrils, burning the back of his nasal passage. Having emptied his stomach, he fought to steady his breathing. Bringing it under control, he opened his eyes and, to his relief, found that he could focus properly at last.

He pushed himself up into a sitting position and gazed around him at the scene of devastation. The remains of the casemate were pouring with thick black smoke which smelled of rotten eggs, whilst the sand around the shattered bunker was covered with lumps of concrete and pieces of twisted metal. The debris was strewn amongst the dead bodies that littered the beach; some whole, others ripped apart. Above the noise in his ears, Koch could hear shouting. He turned, as if in a dream, and saw some of his men running onto the beach from the dunes. They were waving their hands excitedly, gesturing and shouting. He saw one of them run up to a Tommy prisoner who was standing around looking dazed. The German paratrooper was armed with a machine pistol and he emptied the magazine into the Tommy from a dozen paces.

As the Tommy span around, collapsing into the sand, Koch's mind seemed to catch up with reality.

"Stop!" He shouted, surprised at how weak and hoarse his voice was. With an effort, he forced himself upright. He wobbled slightly, finding his feet. His body felt as though it was made of lead; every movement heavy and slow.

"Stop it!" He shouted again, his voice gathering some of its original force. "Stop firing! Don't shoot anyone!"

The man who had shot the Tommy looked around at him in surprise. From another direction, he heard a familiar voice.

"It's the Major! He's alive!"

Koch turned toward the voice and saw one of his staff sergeants running towards him.

The NCO slowed as he approached his commanding officer, taking in Koch's torn clothing, scorched face and the blood trickling down his face from his nostrils and ears.

"Sir? You're alive; thank fuck! What happened?"

"Fuck knows!" Koch growled. "Something went bang. Just tell everyone to stop shooting. Nobody kills anyone unless I say so. See to the wounded…and find me the officer in charge of the Tommies; if he's still alive."

"Yes, Sir!" Snapped the staff sergeant and ran across the beach, barking out a string of orders in rapid succession.

Koch turned back to survey the scene of destruction once more, and suddenly felt completely and utterly drained. He pulled off his helmet and let it drop to the sand, next to his machine-pistol, then sat down on top of the helmet and ran his blackened, grimy hands through his hair.

Somewhere nearby, he could hear the sound of gulls crying as they swooped above the waves, looking for their next meal. He grimaced; it was the nearest to a smile he could manage. Not quite like the old days at the beach when he was a boy, he reflected. The sound of tramping feet on the wet sand made him look up. The staff sergeant was frog-marching a dishevelled looking young Tommy towards him. Koch rose painfully to his feet. The Tommy was young, he noticed, and had a single brass diamond shaped badge on his epaulettes. His steel helmet was dented and scratched, and his face and clothes matched Koch's own for raggedness.

"Their commander is dead, Sir." Said the staff sergeant, coming to a halt in front of him. "Killed in the blast. This is the only officer left among them."

The young man's eyes were hollow, sunken into their sockets. He was clearly in as much shock as the rest of them.

"I am Major Koch, commanding officer of the Storm Battalion." Koch began in his thickly accented English. The young British officer blinked.

"Good morning, Sir." Replied the young man politely.

Koch almost laughed. Good morning? How ludicrous! These Tommies were completely mad.

"Are there any more demolitions prepared?" Koch asked directly.

The Tommy looked puzzled.

"There are no demolitions at all, Sir." He replied earnestly.

Koch's eyes narrowed.

"And I suppose that explosion was in my fucking imagination, was it!" He growled, swearing expertly in English.

"I have no idea how that happened, Sir." Protested the young officer. "We didn't set demolitions…just smashed the sights and threw the breech blocks into the sea. I checked that casemate myself…"

The young man's voice tailed off, but he held Koch's gaze, his eyes innocent and bemused. He was telling the truth. Koch could see it.

"If there are any more explosions, you will all be shot. Do you understand?"

The Tommy officer nodded.

"Where did you throw the bits for the guns?" Koch demanded.

"Oh, good Lord, no!" The Tommy breathed suddenly.

"What?" Demanded Koch.

The British second lieutenant was looking beyond Koch now, across the open water of the Humber Estuary. Koch, feeling a returning sense of dread, whirled around and stared out into the wide mouth of the River Humber, where it ran into the North Sea.

There were ships; lots of them. Koch counted. …Seven, eight, nine. Some were bigger than others but all of them were moving at speed towards the open sea, their funnels pouring smoke as they steamed boldly for the deep water. One of the smaller ships, he noticed absently, was producing more smoke than the others. His heart sank. He had failed. His entire mission was a disaster. His sole aim had been to capture these guns intact and get his gunners to use them against the Tommy ships and maul them as they tried to exit the estuary. But he had failed. Dozens of his men were dead, yet the Tommy ships were sailing past unmolested, on their way to engage the invasion fleet. Koch could only hope that the Kreigsmarine would be ready for them, with their U-Boats and some of their own big ships. Koch felt his heart sink into complete and utter despair. He was a failure.

"I'd put your helmet on if I were you, Sir." The young British officer commented behind him. Koch, not sure if he had heard the Tommy properly, screwed his face up in exasperation and gazed at the dark grey warships sliding past the headland. Then, his mind suddenly catching up again, Koch realised what the Tommy had said; just as the sides of the first British ships erupted in numerous balls of orange flame. Koch caught his breath, feeling as if his heart were about to jump into his mouth. Then he heard it – the sound of something terrible, like a freight train hurtling towards him at terrific speed. With a terrified yell, he whirled around, snatching up his helmet as he began running for the nearby dunes, shouting the warning at the top of his voice.

"Incoming!"

BRIDLINGTON HARBOUR
SATURDAY 21ST SEPTEMBER 1940 – 0545 HOURS

"Go, go, go!" Schulz hollered from the window of the end house in the terrace. "Fire!" He went on, turning back towards the paratroopers sharing the room with him. "Everything you've got!"

Instantly, they opened fire, and from the other rooms of the house, he heard the remainder of his fire support group open up. He was going earlier than intended. Heiden, the sergeant now in charge of the assault group, had only just moved his men into position against the garden wall, but circumstances had suddenly played to their advantage.

To Schulz's delight, just as he was making his final preparations to storm the harbour, a huge fire-fight had erupted at its northern side. One of the other companies must have got into the town from the far side and were launching their own attack. At the same time, the barges of the first wave were hitting the beaches all along the coast to the south. This was the perfect distraction; now he could take advantage and make up time. Seizing the initiative, he just rolled his men straight through the forming up point and hurled them at the barricade.

The enemy were waiting for them, but hadn't seen them infiltrate into the nearest house. The barricade itself was poor. A lorry, a civilian van and an assortment of barrels and crates. Not only that, the defenders, barely a couple of squads at the most, were immediately distracted by the separate attack at the north side of the harbour, and so his assault group were over the wall and sprinting across the open grass towards the barricade before the Tommies realised what was happening. The intense fire from Schulz's group rained down onto the Tommies behind the barricade and they scuttled into cover behind the immobilised vehicles. Suddenly, the enemy realised they were being charged at the same time, and opened fire on the German assault group.

The defensive fire was not especially fierce. The Tommies only managed to get off half a dozen single shots and a short burst of automatic fire before the twelve Germans in the assault group piled into them. Schulz saw one of his men smash to the ground and another spin around, then stagger, but the others were amongst the defenders, their automatic pistols and machine-pistols chattering harshly as they sprayed their enemies. Schulz turned away from the window.

"You!" He pointed to the paratrooper who was blazing away on the light machine-gun. "And you!" He indicated the No.2 on the gun. "Stay here and continue to suppress any Tommies you can see inside the harbour. Start by neutralising that pill-box on the nearest pier."

The two soldiers nodded their understanding.

"The rest of you, follow me!"

Schulz stormed out of the small bedroom and clattered down the stairs, followed by three more of his men. As they stepped into the hallway at the foot of the stairs, Schulz glanced left into the rear parlour and noticed another of his paratroopers standing guard over an old man and woman; the occupants of the house.

"Leave them and follow us!" He snapped, stepping out of the rear door and into the garden.

Following the same route as his assault group, his heart pounding with the thrill of the battle, Schulz led his men over the garden wall and across the grass towards the road block, which was now firmly in German hands. As they neared the obstacle, a rattle of machine-gun fire sounded from the other side of it, and an orange tracer round bounced off the nearest truck with a whine and flew skywards. Realising that there was yet more opposition, he closed the gap quickly and threw himself in against the side of the vehicle.

The assault group were all there; some firing around the vehicles at the enemy beyond and others taking cover behind the large wheels of the trucks as they reloaded their weapons.

"Keep down Major!" Heiden shouted. "There's a machine-gun in that pill-box beyond the barricade."

Schulz twisted round to see the sergeant peering at him from behind the next vehicle in the barricade. All around the vehicles were bodies; mainly Tommies, but several Germans too. Right next to where Heiden crouched, one of his men lay slumped with a long pole protruding from his belly.

"What the fuck happened to him?" Schulz, demanded, frowning at the dead man.

"Those fucking Tommies are mad!" Heiden cursed. "They had their bayonets fixed and one of the bastards had a medieval pike of some kind! Poor Reinherd got skewered by the old fucker!"

Schulz, keeping low, moved gingerly along the rear of the road-block so that he could kneel next to Heiden. The tarmac was thick with blood and slippery, and when he knelt down, Schulz felt his knee touch something wet.

"How many did you lose?"

"Four dead and one badly wounded." Frowned Heiden. "Four as we took the barricade and one to that machine-gun in the pill-box."

"Show me." Schulz ordered.

Nodding, Heiden eased himself backwards and pointed through the open cab of the nearest truck.

"There look; right on the end of the pier. There's at least two people in there. The machine-gun is keeping us fixed here, but there's a rifle too, firing across the harbour at the other assault force. Did you see them, Major? There's a fair few of them got into the town over there. Looks like they're making short work of the Tommies on the northern pier."

Schulz looked through the cab and grunted.

"That's the pill-box we spotted from the house. The MG34 team are still up there and will cover us. We need to neutralise it quickly and get onto the pier itself."

Heiden frowned.

"He's not asleep, Major, that Tommy gunner, and he can't miss at this range. We'll need to try and go wide."

Schulz gave a dismissive snort.

"There's no time to fuck around; our boys are already hitting the beaches, look." He jerked his head southwards.

Heiden peered along the sea-front, and although his view wasn't entirely clear, he could see enough to realise that the main amphibious assault force was touching down on the beaches as they spoke.

"Use grenades." Schulz ordered without further hesitation. "Four or five, right in front of the pill-box. Shake him up a bit and draw his attention; then send your two fastest men around to the right and get up against the bunker itself. Then use more grenades. Move."

Heiden nodded his understanding and began shouting instructions to his men. As he went about organising the storming party, Schulz took another look across the harbour. There were a couple of burning buildings at the north side of the small port, and thick black smoke billowed across the quay-side. He could see another barricade, a couple of hundred metres north of their current position. It too had been captured and he could see the blue-green figures in their distinctive parachutist uniform, as they buzzed around the bullet riddled car and heaps of boxes and barrels. He could feel the excitement rising to fever pitch. The climax of the battle was rapidly approaching and the great prize was almost within their grasp. He had already lost too many good men, but his mission was almost complete.

"Grenade!" The chorus of voices snapped Schulz back to reality and he saw that the assault on the pill-box was beginning. To his left, several paratroopers were hurling stick grenades over the obstacle towards the front of the pill-box where the enemy machine-gunner had his primary arcs.

Crump! Crump! Crump! Crump!

Four loud, sharp explosions punched the dawn air, leaving a haze of shifting smoke in front of the pill-box. He heard the clatter of boots and knew that the assault pair was already moving. Around him, the remaining paratroopers opened up on the bunker with every weapon they had. Above his head, the bullets from their own MG34 in the house came cracking over.

The enemy gunner was slow to react, stunned perhaps, by the four explosions in front of his aperture, but he opened up again now, and Schulz ducked behind a wheel as heavy calibre bullets slammed into the metal chassis of the truck and shattered the windows of the driver's cab.

"They made it!" Heiden's excited voice came to his ears.

Schulz knelt on all fours and peered underneath the truck. He saw the two paratroopers straight away, keeping low, pressed in against the side of the pill-box. With practiced ease, one of them pulled a stick grenade from his belt, primed it and stood-up quickly, pushing it through the firing slit of the small bunker. Schulz watched as the man dropped down again into a crouch, and, with his partner, began edging towards the rear door of the strong-point.

There was a slightly muffled crump, and then dark grey smoke billowed out of the narrow slits of the bunker. Seconds later, there was the sound of a machine pistol firing from within the confines of the concrete position. The shots died away with an echo and all was quiet for a moment. A pale coloured blob of a face appeared at the firing slit, and a voice with a distinctive Bavarian twang shouted.

"Position clear!"

Schulz stood quickly, shouting new orders as he straightened.

"Heiden! You and three men stay here to hold this roadblock. Remainder, follow me!"

He trotted around the obstacle then pelted across the open tarmac towards the pill-box. The sound of booted feet told him that the others followed.

Reaching the pill-box, he crouched down in its lee and looked behind him. Four paratroopers had followed him across the road.

"You two in there!" He shouted. "Stay put and watch the southern approaches along the sea wall."

"Got it, Major." Came the reply from within the newly captured strongpoint. "We can see the whole stretch of beach. Our boys are all over the place; ships and landing craft as far as the eye can see. The Tommies can't stop us now!"

Schulz grinned at the sound of the paratrooper's boyish enthusiasm, but he forced himself to stay focussed.

"Don't gawp at our boys! Keep your eyes peeled down the promenade and make sure you sing out if there's any sign of a Tommy counter-attack brewing! I'm going down the pier to check the rest of it."

The soldiers inside the pill-box shouted their understanding, and Schulz waved at his small group of men.

"Come-on, let's go." He said.

They broke cover and clattered down the south pier, their boots hammering noisily on the stone flags. As he ran, Schulz looked across the harbour and saw men in paratrooper uniforms swarming along the north pier. Then, from the furthest end of it, a green signal flare sailed lazily into the grey morning air, followed several moments later by another, then another. His heart soared. They had done it. They had captured the harbour! The whole of the northern side must be secure. All he had to do now was get to the end of this, the southern one, and make sure that there were no nasty surprises in the two large wooden buildings at the end of it. He pulled his flare pistol out of his smock as he ran, keeping one eye on the pier to his front, the other scanning the harbour. He was conscious of heavy guns firing out to sea, and somewhere on the cliffs to the north and south of the harbour. There was a constant crackle of small arms fire some distance away, and up in the air, the drone of aircraft engines could be heard. The great battle for Britain was raging all around him, and now he was so close to achieving the most important of objectives on this momentous grey September morning.

It was just then that something caught his eye. Schulz, still running at full tilt down the lengthy pier, turned his head to look at the small movement that had caught his attention. There was somebody in the water, right in the middle of the harbour. He stared at the small figure, puzzled at why there should be a swimmer in the middle of the water at this time of the day. Suspicious, Schulz slowed to a halt and waved his men in against the side of the pier wall. His eyes followed the swimmer, who was making his way towards the centre pier; the wooden one that protruded into the middle of the harbour. There were several men standing underneath that pier, clinging onto the wooden struts and supports. A sense of foreboding rose inside Schulz and he scanned the harbour quickly. There were dozens of fishing boats moored against the various piers. Some of the smaller ones, closest to the shore, were grounded, and Schulz remembered that at low tide, much of the harbour was drained of water, except at the far ends of the main piers where the deep water began. Suddenly, with a sense of panic erupting inside his stomach, Schulz leapt to his feet and began hurtling down the pier once more.

"Come on!" He yelled at the others.

Ignoring the large wooden structures, and anything or anybody that might be hidden within them, Schulze pounded the last thirty metres to the end of the stone pier and stared down in disbelief at the harbour entrance. He had seen the masts as he approached; or at least, he had seen the faintest glimpse of the masts anyway, with barely a metre or two of the thick white poles showing above the stone. The harbour entrance was blocked. Two good sized fishing boats were side by side in the water, their decks submerged, and the roofs of their cabins occasionally showing beneath the gentle roll of the waves that broke against the harbour's walls. Out to sea, a vast fleet filled the grey vista. Orange balls of flame showed where the warships fired their huge shells towards the Tommy defences up on the cliffs. Huge geysers of water erupted amongst the myriad little ships and barges of the landing force as the second and third waves followed up the first. And right in front of him, in the narrow entrance to Bridlington harbour, two block ships sat firmly on the bottom, preventing both entry and exit. Schulz looked up at the grey sky and roared in despair.

"Bollocks!"

THE MORTAR PITS – SCARBOROUGH CASTLE
SATURDAY 21ST SEPTEMBER 1940 – 0550 HOURS

"Range, one five hundred! Direction, one eight seven, lay barrels on!"

The voice of Sergeant Willows, mortar section commander, rang out above the din of battle as he relayed the orders from the observation post on the southern cliff. Behind him, the junior non commissioned officers commanding each mortar team repeated the orders, and their crews, trained endlessly in the drills these last two months, threw themselves at the task. One by one, they reported in, having double checked the bearing and elevation of the mortars.

"Two on!"

"One on!"

"Three on!"

The NCOs raised their arms as they looked into Willows.

"One round, ranging. Fire!"

In the pits, the NCOs nodded to the No.2s on the big, 3 inch mortars. Having checked that the bombs had been set with the correct charge, The No.2s went into action. The mortar barrels swallowed the squat, ugly bombs, one by one and the crews ducked aside, covering their ears.

Thump! Thump! Thump!

The three bombs sailed high into the air at a steep angle, passing over the castle wall, before reaching their culminating point high over Scarborough harbour, and then diving down again at an equally steep angle towards the beach below. Back in the pits, the crews waited, their tense faces betraying their eagerness to get into action against the invader. This battalion hadn't been in France, but its sister battalion had, and was decimated during the fighting withdrawal to Dunkirk. Many of its survivors were amongst them now, passing on their experience, and the desire to give pay-back was running high amongst the Teesiders who made up the lion's share of the regiment.

Far below, on the beaches of the South Bay, the three bombs fell about one hundred and fifty metres short of the large knot of German soldiers now huddling against the sea wall, as they tried to cut their way through the endless wire entanglements, and escape from the killing area of the open beach. One of the bombs landed on the promenade itself, whilst the other two hit the hard shingle and rough sand that constituted Scarborough's beach. Although the blast was too far away to be of real danger, shards of red-hot shrapnel along with hard pebbles were propelled through the air at terrific speed, and three of the tough German soldiers from the 1st Mountain Division went down instantly. Crouching there, in front of the Great Eastern Hotel, the huge silhouette of which dominated the hillside before them, the German troops felt as though they had been tipped into a cauldron of fire. The preliminary air-raids and naval bombardment hadn't achieved anything. The wire on the shore was thick along the entire length of the bay, whilst fire raked them from every direction. At the water's edge, a full nine of the barges from the first wave lay broken and burning in the rolling surf, whilst the beach itself was littered with the bodies of Germany's elite troops.

"Add two hundred! Report when ready!" Willows yelled.

Again, the NCOs relayed the orders and signalled the section commander when all was done.

"Fire!"

Once more the three wide barrels spat their stubby bombs upwards. This time, the three bombs landed in a perfect belt, right across the stretch of beach in front of the Great Eastern Hotel. There were screams, and cries of terror, as German soldiers were tossed through the air or decapitated in the blink of an eye by the deadly shrapnel from the blasts.

"Get that fucking wire cut!" Yelled one of the German sergeant majors. "Get fucking moving or we're all dead!"

The German assault on Scarborough was going badly. It had been a risk of course, going for such a wide extension to the beach-head, but the planners at OKW had believed that it was worth the risk in order to capture another harbour. Sitting as it did at the bottom corner of the Yorkshire Moors, the town was also meant to act as the hard shoulder of the German right flank. It was a great theory, but harder to achieve in practice, because Scarborough was a death trap. Heavily garrisoned by the Home Guard and regular units, the town had been turned into a fortress. The regular troops had been training on the local moors, but, in keeping with the recent Cromwell alert, they had continued to stand-to at last light and first light in their allocated positions.

The brigade commander was new, his predecessor being dismissed by the C in C himself. This new brigadier had commanded a company in France during the Great War and was a real fire-breather. In the course of just one month he had worked the brigade into the ground, hammering them with early morning PT, night exercises, construction of strong-points, weapon training twice a day, and endless battle drills and rehearsals. He had incorporated the local Home Guard into the programme and thus, the defenders of Scarborough knew exactly what they were about, now that the moment of destiny had arrived.

The air raid had damaged parts of the town, but hadn't caused any real breach in the defences. If anything, the bombing had strengthened them. The regulars were already in their positions, so the collapsed buildings simply helped to create additional anti-tank obstacles. The naval guns too, although terrifying, had achieved little of real value. The Great Eastern Hotel was on fire, as were several other large and easily identifiable buildings, and the derelict castle was now even more ruinous. Despite this, the three battalions of regular infantry, along with the hundred and fifty Home Guardsmen, were dug in, well supplied and ready to fight.

The German barges had been spotted well out to sea, and so by the time they chugged into range, every gun was trained on them. The observation posts on the castle headland and Oliver's Mount had already identified targets and relayed fire orders to the mortars and the assorted medium guns that had been built into the coastal defences. Thus, when the brigade commander had given authority to open fire, the German assault force had been rocked by a wave of fire, unbelievable in its intensity. And so the killing had begun. The only advantage for the Germans was that, unlike Filey Bay to the south, the low water mark at Scarborough was much closer to the promenade, and so the dash for cover was much shorter. Even so, the first wave was being cut to pieces, with the survivors cringing against the small sea wall as they strove to get through the wire entanglements. Coming up behind them, right into the lion's mouth, came the second wave.

In the mortar pits at Scarborough Castle, the three NCOs looked expectantly at Willows, who lay against the stone wall with the field telephone jammed firmly against his ear. They heard the buzz as the telephone rang, saw his face twitch as a voice began talking at the other end, then held their breaths as he raised his eyebrows and turned to them with a grim look etched on his features.

"You're on! Ten rounds HE, fire for effect! Go on!"

And so more explosive death rained down upon the beleaguered troops of the German 1st Mountain Division, and the British gave truth to that defiant pledge made by their leader only recently on the radio. The Germans had come, and today, the British would fight them on the beaches.

500 YARDS INLAND FROM HUNMANBY GAP – FILEY BAY, ENGLAND
SATURDAY 21st SEPTEMBER 1940 – 0555 HOURS

"Whoaa! Steady on! We're British!"

Jackson held his arms out to either side of his body, showing his Lee-Enfield to the startled young private soldier who was levelling his own rifle towards the Coldstream Guards sergeant. Jackson watched the young man blink, and then sigh with relief as he lowered his weapon.

"I'm with the Home Guard, sonny. We just pulled out of Hunmanby Gap."

The young soldier gawped at him for a moment, then looked back over his shoulder and hollered down the hedgerow.

"Sarge! We've got some of our lads coming back towards us."

Jackson walked slowly forward and knelt down by the private, who turned to look at him with a worried expression. Jackson towered over the young soldier, who was almost cowering away from the grim-faced and bespectacled Coldstreamer. Another British soldier came loping up the hedgerow, his rifle at the short trail, and Jackson spotted the chevrons on the man's sleeves instantly. The sergeant slid down next to the private and he too gave Jackson an appraising look.

Jackson noted that both the sergeant and the private had their top buttons undone, but he forced himself to ignore the sloppiness and concentrate on more pressing matters.

"Hello, mate." Jackson said, offering his hand. "Davey Jackson, Coldstream Guards; attached to the local Home Guard."

The other sergeant took his hand and shook it, firmly.

"Tom Barker, mate; 3rd Hambeldon and Moorlanders. What's going on?"

Jackson's mind jumped in recognition for a moment. Hambeldon and Moorlanders? Where had he heard that name before? They were a Territorial Army crew as far as he knew. Why did that name ring such a bell?

Jackson pushed the question out of his mind and began briefing his fellow sergeant. He had to raise his voice slightly due to the noise overhead, where more RAF planes were racing towards the sea, and twin-engined German fighters wheeled overhead like menacing vultures.

"I've got a section of Home Guard with me. We've been holding this side of Hunmanby Gap, but they're all out of ammunition for their Canadian rifles, and the Lewis Gun is down to its last half a mag'. We're going to fall back on the village and see if we can get some more ammo or change these rifles for .303's somehow. If you're the reinforcement platoon, you'd best get moving. There are Jerries all over the beach and cliffs. We managed to pin 'em down and kill a good few before we ran out of ammo. As you can see, the RAF have made an appearance and they're brassing them up along the beach. It won't hold them long mind you, and there's more boats coming in. If you move fast enough, you might just catch 'em before they're up on the top of the cliff."

Barker shook his head, frowning.

"Bloody hell, mate, this is chaos! We were getting ready to move back to Driffield this morning. Then the Jerry paratroopers started landing all over the place. We've had a proper dust up already and lost a couple of blokes. Killed some of the Jerry bastards though!"

Jackson caught his breath.

"Paratroopers?"

Barker nodded.

"Aye, mate. The buggers started dropping just before first light. A whole bunch dropped right on top of us, and there's even more dropped over towards Hunmanby village. I don't know if you'll get into the place now, mate; there's a proper scrap going on. Mr Patterson took a section with him to help out the Home Guard, and told me to bring the rest of the boys to the stand-to positions."

Jackson grimaced, taking in the new information.

"Roger." He grunted. "In that case, you'd better get going. We'll see what we can do up at the village. We can't do anything here without ammo. As soon as we're bombed up again we'll get back down here and help out, if we don't end up fighting paratroopers that is. Good luck, mate."

Barker gave a wry smile. Turning, he jerked his head at the young private beside him.

"Come on then, Atkinson lad. Get moving. There's Jerries waiting for us down there."

The young private blew out his cheeks, the apprehension starkly obvious on his face. He rose and began moving along the hedgerow once more. Barker waved his arm and the rest of his men began filing past. As a full corporal went past them, Barker gave Jackson a brief nod of farewell and moved off.

"Good hunting." He murmured.

Jackson watched as the half-platoon filed passed him. The faces were a mix of young and older men; some nervous, others looking set and determined. They were not in particularly good order he noted, with their buttons unfastened and equipment worn in an untidy fashion. He forgave them their sloppiness however, understanding that they had been thrown into a confusing battle without notice. They were here, and they were ready to fight, and that was all that mattered. As the last of the regular soldiers filed past him, Harper came up alongside Jackson and knelt down.

"Is that the lot?" He asked, sounding disappointed.

Jackson nodded.

"It is, mate. The rest of their platoon is up in the village, trying to fight through to the rest of our platoon. Apparently there are Germans everywhere; paratroopers."

Harper raised his eyebrows.

"Paratroopers? That's going to be interesting! Never come across them before."

"Me neither." Jackson admitted. "But they'll die just the same as normal Germans, so let's go see if we can bag a few, shall we?"

Harper gave the rest of their section an appraising look.

"A bunch of old men and teenagers with hardly any ammunition against Nazi paratroopers? Not the best odds in the world!"

"No." Jackson agreed. "But we've got something on our side the Germans don't like."

Harper gave Jackson a quizzical look. The sergeant's face hardened, a gleam appearing in the big Coldstreamer's eye as he dragged the seventeen inch blade at his waist from its scabbard.

"Tell the men to fix bayonets again." He growled.

HMS ELEKTRA – TWO MILES OUT OF THE HUMBER ESTUARY SATURDAY 21ST SEPTEMBER 1940 – 0600 HOURS

"Two enemy ships, green ten, 25,000 yards; big ones!"

Captain Jeremy Bulstrode tore his eyes away from the heavily listing HMS Veteran, which had been rocked by two huge explosions just moments before. Mine or torpedo, it was hard to tell, but his money was on torpedoes. HMS Wild Swan had been hit in a similar manner just several hours earlier, when the flotilla had first tried to deploy. They were supposed to be coming out with air cover, but the last few hours had become chaotic. First they had pulled back into the estuary, having picked up survivors from Wild Swann. Then they had watched the distant fighting on Spurn Head, whilst suffering a low level attack by German fighter-bombers. Then, finally, the order to break-out had come, along with the instruction to bombard Spurn Head on the way past. They had done exactly that, just minutes after the Spurn Point battery had erupted with a huge explosion. Now the whole flotilla was surging forward, out of the Humber and into the open waters of the North Sea. The invasion was on, and everybody wanted to get stuck in. Now they were about to.

"Relay that to the cruisers." He ordered the first lieutenant who had just informed him of the sighting. "And tell the engine room to give us everything. Full ahead, straight towards them. Warn the gunnery officer to engage when in range."

"Aye, aye, Sir." Replied the first lieutenant, and turned to pass on the orders.

Bulstrode looked back towards HMS Veteran.

"She's going down." He observed dispassionately. "She won't survive that. Definitely torpedoes, he thought. Surely you wouldn't get two mines that close together? And how would the Germans get in that close to lay mines, anyway?"

"ASDIC contact, wait!" The first lieutenant suddenly called out from his place by the communication tube.

"Get me a fix on that, straight away!" Bulstrode barked, looking round.

"Bearing red four nine! Large contact!" The first lieutenant relayed the information from the ASDIC operator.

Bulstrode looked out from the bridge and made the calculation in his mind.

"That's the bugger!" He snapped. "It all fits. Bring us hard over to port, and signal Venomous to do the same. Let's sandwich him and sink the bastard. That'll give the cruisers a clear run! Copy our intentions to the cruisers and warn the rest of the flotilla to cover the southern flank."

"Aye, aye, Sir." Came the reply.

Around Bulstrode, the bridge was alive with activity.

"Tell Venomous that we'll ring the contact with depth charges, and then they can do the cross over." He rapped out more instructions.

Glancing up, he saw a stream of small aircraft passing overhead. Probably the fighters which had chased off the German fighter-bombers, he supposed. A thrill went through him. Action at last, and a clear enemy to attack. It was just how Bulstrode liked it. He was an aggressively minded Captain, in the finest tradition of the service, and had distinguished himself in the Norwegian campaign. Since then, he had been frustrated by the mundane convoy and mine-laying work, especially when he heard the reports of how Admiral Cunningham's ships were getting stuck into the Italians in the Mediterranean. But now it was their turn. The Germans were on the doorstep and HMS Elektra was coming out to fight. This was the kind of day that Nelson had lived for, reflected Bulstrode, and the thought made him smile.

"Enemy ships have opened fire!" One of the ratings called out the warning.

"Ignore them." Bulstrode said, his attention now fixed on the main threat from the U-Boat they had detected. "Leave them for the cruisers. We'll deal with this submarine first."

The ship was already turning sharply to close in on the ASDIC contact, when a loud howl came clearly over the water. A moment later, a series of huge splashes erupted in front of them, just a quarter of a mile away. Great columns of water rose upwards as the eleven inch shells from the Admiral Scheer slammed into the sea.

"Cruisers acknowledge, Sir." The first lieutenant said, calmly. "Commodore Cruisers wants us to give them plenty of space to deploy. Flotilla Commander instructs us to deal with the submarine, then break north up the coast with Venomous and the sloops. Remainder of the flotilla will stay with the cruisers."

"Acknowledge." Bulstrode ordered. "And prepare to lay depth charges. Get a target depth estimation from the ASDIC and stand-by to drop. If we can't get a depth, then set the usual detonation sequence on the charges."

"Aye, aye, Sir." Snapped the first lieutenant, turning once more to the communication tubes.

Bulstrode looked over to port. They were passing the Veteran now. She was going down fast, with men already in the water. Beyond the sinking ship, he could see that Venomous was also turning sharply to the attack.

Bulstrode looked at the small bobbing heads in the water around Veteran and felt a pang of regret at not being able to stop for them. But then he checked himself, as he always did, for this was the reality of war at sea. The enemy was at hand and the chase was on. There was business to be done. He looked around and saw the first lieutenant watching him expectantly.

Bulstrode gave him a wink.

"Right then, Mr Welch; let's go sink us a U-Boat, shall we?"

CABINET WAR ROOMS – STOREY'S GATE, LONDON
SATURDAY 21ST SEPTEMBER 1940 – 0605 HOURS

"You can't just have bombers like that!" Newall said defensively, looking at Brooke. "We've got a thousand and one things to deal with at the moment and we need to prioritise."

Brooke didn't blink as he returned the gaze of the commander of the Royal Air Force. When he spoke, it was in his usual, measured voice.

"I understand that, Sir." He said. "But there is a large German fleet anchored off the east coast of Yorkshire, and by all accounts, hundreds, if not thousands of German troops are landing on the beaches there. Surely that must be classed as a priority? Charles Portal and I did discuss this some weeks ago."

Newall's face reddened. He was visibly under pressure.

"Everybody thinks they are a priority at the moment!" The Chief of Air Staff retorted acidly. "I've got No.11 Group shot to pieces over the Channel and trying to refuel and re-arm. No.12 Group is trying to cover London and the South East while they do so, as well as trying to bale out the Harwich Flotilla which is under heavy attack off Margate. No.13 Group are tackling aircraft streams over the North Sea and trying to cover the Tyne and Humber Squadrons as they come out. On top of that, No.2 Bomber Group has been hammered over the Channel, along with 11 Group. No.4 Group is busy trying to evacuate Driffield. We've already got Battle and Defiant squadrons up in the air over the east coast, but until I have a clear picture of what's going on, I am not going to commit any of our medium or heavy bombers and risk getting them shot out of the sky for nothing."

Brooke stared back at Newall with his owl-like eyes for several moments, then, in a mild voice, he said. "Of course, Sir. I understand the frictions entirely. I fully appreciate that there is much to be put in order and that you are heavily engaged on all fronts. However, the sooner I am able to have a striking force working directly through General Adam's Headquarters in York, then the sooner I can leave you and your staff to concentrate on running the strategic battle. All I need is a few squadrons, suitable for ground attack. But you are right, Sir. You have much to sort out. I will remain patient until you have reorganised."

Newall seemed placated. The red-flush in his face was subsiding.

"Thank you, Alan." He said, more evenly this time. "I understand your desire to strike quickly against the beach heads, but I just need some time to sort out the commitments versus resources. You will have your planes, I promise you. I have my staff putting together a temporary force with a skeleton staff for you as we speak. I'll have details within the next couple of hours."

Before the discussion could go any further, Pound reappeared from the Prime Minister's room.

"The Prime Minister is free now, gentlemen." He announced, and ushered in the other three officers. Dill led the way, followed by Newall and Brooke.

On entering, they found Churchill glaring at the map of the United Kingdom, which was covered in symbols and coloured hatching. He continued to frown at the map for a few moments more, before turning around and sweeping his small council of war with a serious look.

"I have been thinking, Gentlemen." He began. Brooke stifled a groan. When Winston Churchill began thinking about strategy and tactics, you could end up down all sorts of rabbit holes.

"Are we sure this business off the Yorkshire coast is the *real* invasion site? Could this not be an enormous double bluff by the Germans? There are reports, I believe, of new fleets gathering in Dutch ports, and of their Channel fleets re-assembling off Calais?"

For a moment or two, the three Chiefs of Staff and Brooke exchanged knowing looks. It was Pound, the chairman of the Chiefs of Staff Committee, who answered.

"I believe it is unlikely that the Germans are launching not one, but two diversionary attacks, Prime Minister. His naval assets must already be stretched very thinly, as you will gather shortly from the updates we have for you. I have also seen those reports about the Channel fleets, Sir, and there can be any number of rational explanations as to why the surviving craft from the Channel operation are reforming off Calais. Given that we now have some major engagements taking place on the very coast of Yorkshire itself, I am inclined to believe that the invasion site is there; unbelievable as it might seem. I have already spoken on the difficulties facing the enemy should this east coast situation really be their main landing, but it must be remembered that we are dealing with Nazi Germany here. They are re-writing the practice of war, almost on a daily basis. Despite the apparent over-boldness of this move, I think we must view it as their main thrust. All our evidence thus far points that way."

"Mmm." Churchill growled and stared back up at his map. "But why would the Germans land here on this section of coast line? This colour coding here tells us that this entire stretch is unsuitable for landing tanks. South of the Humber, fine, but not here. How can they invade without tanks? Perhaps it is just a raid in strength? A large scale diversion perhaps?"

He turned his face back towards the military men, one eye-brow arched in a questioning manner.

"That area of coast-line is more than suitable for tanks, Prime Minister." Came Brooke's calm reply.

Churchill turned to face him.

"This map says not! General Ironside had it produced for me by his Intelligence Branch in late June. Are you telling me it is wrong, General Brooke?"

The Prime Minister regarded the Commander in Chief Home Forces with a challenging look.

Brooke remained unflustered. His voice, when he replied, was clipped and precise; the voice of a man who knew his business.

"Not wrong Prime Minister, but misleading. I have never seen that map before until just a few hours ago, however, I have recently toured that entire stretch of coast-line with General Adam and his corps commanders. Although the Scarborough sector is a difficult landing area, the whole of Filey Bay and Bridlington Bay are fine for landing tanks. The probable reason for that stretch of coast-line being designated as poor for tanks, is that there are high cliffs lining the shore for miles. *However*, the sand itself will certainly take the smaller German tanks and armoured vehicles. There are also plenty of exits off the beaches, such as natural draws and re-entrants, not to mention the purpose-built ramps at Filey for the fishing cobbles. At high tide, the enemy can bring his landing craft right up to those ramps and drive his heavier tanks straight up them. As long as the enemy infantry secure a beach-head, the Germans will get their tanks ashore alright. After all, the Germans have outstanding engineer units within their divisions. If need be, they'll build a tank landing ramp."

Churchill allowed a grim smile to cross his features.

"Sometimes, General Brooke, your logic scares me! You could never be accused of optimism."

Brooke's expression did not change.

"I will tell you what you *need* to hear Prime Minister; not what you *want* to here. We will get nowhere without being honest with ourselves. The situation is far too serious for that."

Churchill chuckled.

"Well said, C in C! Well said! I will be quiet now and allow the briefing to continue."

With that admission of intellectual defeat, the stout politician moved across to his chair and sat. As he did so, from the corner of the room, Lieutenant General Pug Ismay, Churchill's military advisor, caught Brooke's eye and smiled, winking his approval. Brooke suppressed a smile.

Pound waited for Churchill to settle himself then continued his brief.

"You are aware of the situation over the Channel, Prime Minister. Our own ships have pulled back to within three miles of the coast and the RAF are patrolling as best as possible over the coast-line itself, without pushing too far out to sea. The surviving ships from the enemy fleets are reported as reassembling between Calais and Dunkirk, whilst a number of German fighting ships are reported as moving north along the coast of Belgium. German fighters continue their sweeps across the Channel whilst there is a huge concentration of dive-bombers currently attacking the Harwich Flotilla. I'm afraid we've already lost one destroyer, and another is so badly damaged that she's having to limp into the Thames. The remainder are making best speed North by nor-east in order to get out of range of the Stukas. Fighter Command now has an umbrella over our ships and the attacks appear to be tailing off slightly."

Churchill sucked heavily on his cigar.

"Go on." He nodded at Pound.

"The RAF has switched to a defensive stance over the south coast, having suffered heavily over the Channel during the last couple of hours." Pound paused, seeing the Prime Minister's eye-brows rise.

"How badly have they suffered?" He grunted.

"Full details are still awaited," Newall cut in, "but at the moment it looks like thirty percent losses amongst the bombers, and a similar figure for the fighter squadrons. If we continue like that, No.2 and No.11 Groups will cease to exist within twenty four hours. Now that there is doubt about the exact nature of the Channel operation, I see no point in taking unnecessary casualties. Portal and Dowding are of the same opinion."

"Hmm?" Churchill rubbed his ear thoughtfully. "So are we going to accept German air superiority over the south coast?"

"Over the *Channel*, yes." Newall replied. "Over the *coast*, no. We will continue to guard London and our airfields in the south, without being drawn into a pointless and costly battle over the English Channel. That said, if this landing on the east coast turns out to be the main event, then we will have no choice but to strip the defences of southern England to a minimum in order to over-match the Germans where it matters."

Churchill turned the information over in his mind for a moment or two. During the pause, Dill spoke.

"General Brooke is of the opinion, Prime Minister, that this Channel operation was a deliberate attempt by the Germans to draw out our naval and air strength into a suitable target area, where they could be ambushed by superior enemy assets. Looking at what has happened to our aircraft this morning, along with the ongoing attacks against the Harwich Flotilla, I am tempted to agree with him."

Newall looked across at the Chief of the Imperial General Staff, then to Brooke, and nodded slowly.

"Yes." He agreed. "It does seem as though there has been a deliberate attempt to cause attrition here, as well as causing a suitable diversion. That is why I have ordered the switch to defensive operations only, south of the Thames. We need the breathing space to assess the threat in the north and reorganise. Over half of our assets have responded with commendable speed to the perceived threat, however, that means that we now have over fifty percent of our fighter strength and a large part of our bomber strength on the ground rearming and refuelling. Added to that, is the chaos currently reigning in No.4 Group due to the parachute landings around Driffield."

Churchill nodded, his face creased in a deep frown.

"Which brings us onto the situation in the North of England." Pound took up the thread again. "It probably makes more sense for CIGS to take the lead to start with, as much of the reporting is coming via HQ Northern Command in York. The Chief of the Air Staff will then fill-in the remaining detail."

He nodded to Dill, who moved across to the map on the wall. Lifting his pencil, Dill began to draw imaginary lines over the map as he spoke.

"The parachute landings around Driffield have been confirmed by the local infantry brigade and by the RAF station itself, which is under direct attack from the ground. The exact strength of the landings is unknown, but they are certainly widespread. The local brigade is currently heavily engaged against these landings, as well as moving a battalion towards Bridlington to reinforce the town, where there have been reports of more paratroopers. There is fighting in the town, and the garrison commander has signalled his intent to sink the block ships in the harbour and fortify it."

Dill allowed his pencil to drift southwards.

"At Spurn Head, all communication with the garrison there has ceased, however, reports from all three services confirm that the battery at Spurn Point has blown up; cause unknown. We have assumed that the whole of Spurn Head has fallen to enemy storm troopers, and accordingly, the Humber naval forces are bombarding the entire length of the headland as they break out into the North Sea. The infantry brigade based in the Beverley area has sent a battalion to Spurn Head to try and seal off the enemy landing there. Fort Paull, just a little further up the estuary, is still in our hands and will attempt to bombard Spurn Head, should there be a further requirement."

Churchill had stopped nodding now. He was simply watching the CIGS, a grim expression set on his face. Dill's pencil traced the coastline northwards again.

"Enemy troops were reported as approaching the beaches in landing craft about forty minutes ago. Communications remain difficult, however, reports received from the garrison commander of Bridlington confirm that enemy troops have landed on the beaches at either side of the town. Thanks to the RAF, we also know that the enemy has troops ashore here, in Filey Bay. The RAF have reported that the whole area of ground behind these two landing sites is littered with parachutes, for several miles inland, so we must assume that the enemy has launched a simultaneous attack in-depth."

The CIGS barely paused for breath, as he went on relentlessly.

"We know from the RAF that there is heavy fighting in the Filey Bay area, but there are no reports yet from the area ground commander. At Scarborough, the picture is much clearer. The local infantry brigade closed on the coast last night as part of a training and readiness scheme organised by their commander, so they are manning all of their positions and have good communications with General Adam in York. They report that the enemy has attempted to land troops in both the North and South Bays, and possibly in a smaller bay just to the south of the town. The brigade and its artillery units, along with the Home Guard, are engaging the enemy with every weapon at their disposal."

"Good!" Churchill barked suddenly. "That is exactly what I want!"

Dill cleared his throat and continued.

"Several RAF squadrons have attacked both the landing beaches and the enemy fleet, though I believe Chief Air is currently planning a more co-ordinated attack. There have been several more bombing raids against York, Leconfield, Hull, Newcastle, Church Fenton, Doncaster and Selby. The enemy continues to target major rail-heads, transport choke-points and airfields."

Dill lowered his pencil and gave the Prime Minister a serious look.

"Given all of this, I believe there can be no doubt that the enemy main thrust is indeed falling on the east coast of Yorkshire and that we must focus our main effort on defeating this operation. The defensive stance ordered by the Navy and RAF in the South of England makes absolute sense if we are not to fritter away our scant resources on less pressing threats."

Dill paused and looked back over towards Pound and Newall.

"Gentlemen, over to you."

Pound stepped forward again and began pointing to the wall-map.

"The Humber forces are deploying as we speak, Prime Minister. They were attacked in the Estuary by a large force of ME110 fighter-bombers, but the RAF have kindly seen them off for us. One destroyer received a direct hit and has suffered some damage, but is still fit to fight. The entire force are breaking out now, and bombarding Spurn Head as they pass. The intention is for the cruiser squadron with half of the destroyers to break out due east, through our minefields and then wheel northwards where they can intercept the invasion fleet from the rear. They will be joined by the Harwich Flotilla in due course. The remaining destroyers, along with several minesweepers and armed trawlers, will peel off north as soon as they exit the estuary and hug the coastline towards Bridlington. Their task is to attack the enemy fleet from the southern flank, close to shore, in order to get in amongst the troop carriers and smaller craft."

Churchill was nodding vigorously, the talk of offensive action a perfect fuel for his aggressive spirit.

"Simultaneously," Pound continued, "the destroyer force in the Tyne is coming out. They will move as a complete force and attack from the north, probably just inside our own mine-field. We have just received a signal however, stating that one of the Tyne destroyers has suffered an explosion, but it doesn't say what caused it. The main issue we're going to have is U-Boats. I have no doubt that the enemy has relied heavily on U-Boat concentrations, covering the areas of main threat. We've already lost two destroyers through torpedo hits, possibly a third one now, so we know there are submarines in the area. In addition to that, we can see from the sudden reduction in shipping losses over the last two weeks that Raeder must have recalled the vast majority of his U-Boats from the Atlantic in order to bolster this operation. At first we thought our convoy system was starting to bear fruit, but it would seem that the Germans were merely concentrating their forces."

"Indeed. Indeed." Churchill rumbled throatily. "But now that our destroyers are at sea, they will be able to manoeuvre more freely and deal with these submarines, will they not?"

"They will certainly be better able to defend themselves, that's a fact." Pound nodded. "But, we should be prepared for an initially high loss rate amongst the destroyer flotillas, as it is they who must break the assumed German blockade of our ports. Also, they will be outgunned initially by the bigger German surface units. We must hope that the sheer numbers of our destroyers, combined with their speed and agility in coastal waters, will give them an advantage over the bigger enemy vessels. We learned some valuable lessons from Norway, which will be put to good use. That includes working with the RAF in order to achieve a two dimensional offensive capability."

At this point, Pound glanced over at Newall for a confirmatory nod, which would signal they were sticking to the strategy both of them had jointly discussed fifteen minutes before. Newall however, was at the door, holding it slightly open and taking a piece of paper from a staff officer.

Seeing that Newall was otherwise engaged, Pound continued.

"We are about to see the results of the first major surface action. RAF fighters have reported two large enemy cruisers some eighteen miles off the Humber Estuary. It is obvious that they are there to contain our own cruiser squadron. We expect an exchange of fire to take place imminently. In fact, I suspect it is happening as we speak."

"Good!" Churchill barked again. "The sooner we have our superior fleet in action, the better. I look forward to announcing the sinking of two German battle-cruisers by lunch time. Now, what about the main Battle Squadrons at Scapa Flow?"

Pound took a deep breath.

"They have not deployed yet Prime Minister, nor will they for another twenty four hours."

"What? Why not?" Churchill demanded, looking outraged.

"Because Prime Minister, I have no doubt that the enemy will have applied the same measures to Scapa Flow and our heavy surface units as they have done to our estuary based flotillas. I expect that there is a sizeable pack of U-Boats just waiting to pick off our big ships as they come out…"

Churchill exploded.

"But they *must* come out, First Sea Lord! They must! Now is not the time to spare the rod with the Germans! I want Royal Navy battleships pounding the German fleet into oblivion! I want the Hood and her companions running amok through burning Nazi ships and landing craft!"

Churchill's face was redder than normal, his jowls wobbling with excitement. Looking on, Brooke couldn't help thinking that the Prime Minister's little outburst had resembled a spoiled child deprived of some treat or other. Pound however, remained calm, and his tone was firm and precise when he spoke again.

"As we all do, Prime Minister. But we must be clear on one thing. We *will* win this battle; of that I have no doubt. It is simply a case of how complete or how costly the victory. Make no mistake, this war will not be won once we have beaten back the invader. It will damage him. It will hurt him. It will embarrass him. But it will not win the war. Europe will still be occupied by Germany, U-Boats will continue to haunt our convoys, and the Italians will continue to cause problems in the Mediterranean. Therefore, we cannot afford to waste our ships in hastily planned operations that have not been sufficiently thought through. I have no intention of sacrificing the Home Fleet in a knee-jerk reaction. The Home Fleet *will* come out, but it will do so safely, and in good order, ready to take the offensive, rather than running scared through a gauntlet of submarines, losing ships every few miles until there are none left."

Brooke was impressed with the First Sea Lord's riposte. He had thought Pound to be a somewhat lazes-faire individual at first; urbane and slightly disinterested. However, over the course of the last few hours, he had begun to change his opinion of Britain's senior naval officer. Pound was thinking about the bigger picture; thinking strategically. More importantly, he wasn't allowing Churchill to bully him. Churchill glowered at the First Sea Lord for several moments, and Brooke held his breath, expecting the Prime Minister to challenge the rationale. Churchill however, suddenly relented, his voice calming.

"When and how exactly, First Sea Lord, will the Home Fleet come out?" He grumbled.

Having regained the advantage, Pound once more drew breath and began to explain.

"Early yesterday, a strike force from the Home Fleet was despatched to Norwegian waters, something that Admiral Forbes has been doing regularly over recent months. Its mission was to launch an air attack against Trondheim and disrupt any German naval activity in the area. That force consists of the aircraft carrier Furious, the cruisers Berwick and Norfolk, and the destroyers Eskimo, Matabele and Somali. They have been ordered to turn about and steam back towards Scapa Flow. My intention is for this force to conduct an anti submarine sweep to the south of the Orkneys during the dark hours tonight. The sweep will coincide with the break out by the remainder of the Home Fleet. They will have an advantage in the dark and hopefully any German submarines will be caught between the Furious Group and the Home Fleet. Once free, the entire fleet will be joined by remaining ships from the Tyne, Humber and Harwich and then deploy against the enemy fleet off the Yorkshire coast."

"So, what you are telling me then," Churchill murmured, "is that for the next twenty four hours, our destroyer flotillas and the Humber cruisers will be doing their best to disrupt the enemy landings, with the possibility that we may lose some ships to U-Boats. But then, in twenty four hours, we will have the entire Home Fleet in the North Sea, ready to deliver a knock out blow against the German invasion fleet?"

Pound nodded.

"In essence Prime Minister, yes, although it will be more like thirty six to forty eight hours before the Home Fleet is in position to have full effect. That said, once they are fully deployed, I expect them to be decisive. And of course, whilst we make these moves, we also have some of our own submarines being deployed to the area. The intention is to lay a gauntlet of friendly submarines between Bridlington and the German and Dutch ports."

Churchill stared at Pound long and hard, his eyes scrutinising the First Sea Lord intently. After a while, the Prime Minister nodded slowly.

"Alright, you have forty eight hours to execute your plan. I only hope that the RAF and the Army can hold on that long."

"We will." Brooke said assuredly. After a pause, Newall, having finished at the door, said that the RAF likewise, would give everything it had for the next two days.

"Anything else from you, First Sea Lord?" Churchill asked.

"Just one more thing, Sir." Pound replied. "Assuming that almost every U-Boat is now supporting the invasion force, it is my intention to run as many convoys across the Atlantic as possible over the next week or so. The amount of escorts will be limited for obvious reasons, but there has never been a better time since the start of the year to get shipping across the Atlantic. As I've already said, as serious as this invasion might be, we must look forward to our ability to maintain the advantage once we have repelled the Germans."

Churchill nodded, silently. After a short while, he looked across to Newall.

"Chief of the Air Staff? What news do you have for us?"

Newall glanced down at his notes briefly, then began his summary.

"The situation in the south is essentially a holding action now. As soon as No.11 Group are back in play, they will assume all defensive responsibilities south of Hertford. No.12 Group will then reorganise and begin to interdict air movement from mainland Europe towards the Yorkshire coast. Additionally, all night fighters are being ordered to No.12 Group airfields, in order that they can continue to interdict over-night. No.13 Group has already begun engaging the enemy, along with several light and medium bomber squadrons which have acted semi-independently in response to the invasion. We are now currently trying to reorganise our forces in the north in order to provide a more co-ordinated response. Our intention is for the Hurricane and Spitfire Squadrons of No.13 Group to concentrate on interdiction of enemy aircraft formations, whilst the bomber groups concentrate on enemy ships."

Newall turned a page, then glanced up at Brooke as he continued.

"I have just received confirmation from my staff that an Air Striking Group is to be put together for co-operation with the Army. It will consist of five Blenheim Squadrons, three Battle Squadrons and two Defiant Squadrons. We are also moving a Squadron of Fulmars across from Coastal Command at Castletown to join that force. The Blenheims will be working out of the new airfield at Topcliffe, whilst the fighters are all being assembled at Catterick. A small liaison team and an Air Officer Commanding the force are being despatched to General Adam's HQ in York as we speak, although it is estimated that the striking force will not be fully ready to operate under the new arrangement until mid afternoon. In order to cover that, I have ordered the remaining bombers from No.4 Group to stand-by to attack the Filey and Bridlington beach heads from high level, on request from HQ Northern Command."

Newall glanced at Brooke, who nodded his grateful acknowledgement.

"Finally, Sir," Newall continued, looking back to Churchill, "I have ordered the evacuation of Leconfield. With immediate effect, all aircraft from that station will land at Church Fenton on return from sortie. The station is packing up and moving at best speed. They have been told to destroy all fuel that can't be moved and crater the runway before the base is finally abandoned. If there are paratroopers all over Driffield, and landings south of Bridlington, then I am not prepared to take any chances. I have no desire to sacrifice valuable Spitfires by leaving them exposed to ground attack."

Newall finished and looked at the Prime Minister, expecting a cross-examination. Churchill however, remained silent for a while, before heaving himself out of his chair and pacing the small room. After a moment or two, he stopped and glared up at his wall-map of national defences. He grunted once, then turned to look directly at Brooke.

"So then, C in C? What are we going to do?"

Brooke blinked several times, before walking across to join Churchill at the map. The three Chiefs of Staff, along with General Ismay, crowded in behind him where they could see. Brooke took a few seconds to gather his thoughts, then began.

"I have spoken with the Head of Military Intelligence, and with the Brigadier General Staff at Northern Command. I have arranged to speak to General Adam in about half an hour on a secure line. I am assuming that the German landings will be successful, at least as far as achieving a beach-head."

At this point, he used his pencil and drew a number of small interlocking semi-circles that began at Scarborough and went as far south as Skipsea, just below Bridlington. He then drew two small bubbles; one over Driffield and the other over Spurn Head.

"Our main reserves," he continued, "are in the South of England, although we have the 2nd Armoured Division slightly nearer, here in Cambridgeshire. I have ordered Fourth Corps complete to entrain. They will be given orders in due course, but I expect it will be twenty four hours at least before they have arrived in the York area. The 2nd Armoured will be instructed to move by road shortly, once I have spoken with General Adam, but again, it will be at least night-fall before they are anywhere near concentrated enough to be of any use in the Yorkshire area. I will now go through the possible German intentions, followed my proposed responses."

Brooke paused in order to allow for objections or questions, but nobody, not even Churchill, interrupted. Every man in the room was watching him intently.

"Option one for the Germans." Brooke pressed on. "A two pronged advance on York; the first from the Scarborough-Filey bridgehead, using the axis Staxton – Malton. The other, a thrust through Driffield, then Stamford Bridge. They capture York, a major city of historical significance, with a small manufacturing base and a major railhead, and they breach the GHQ line. They come close to the Great North Road and threaten more of our airfields that lie to the west of the River Ouse."

The Commander in Chief Home Forces paused just long enough to let the possibilities sink in, then moved his pencil down to Bridlington.

"Option two. A powerful thrust to link up with the paratroopers at Driffield, then straight on through Market Weighton, to cross the Ouse somewhere between Selby and Goole. Once over, they can strike on southwards into the coal-fields and industrial areas of South Yorkshire and the East Midlands, or they can turn sharply in order to roll up the south bank of the Humber, thereby securing major ports, along with thousands of tons of supplies. They could even turn north to isolate and capture York."

Brooke's pencil retraced the route back to Bridlington.

"Option three. He goes straight for Hull. Link up with Driffield to get the airfield, then drops down through Leconfield and Beverley. Another column comes off the beach here at Skipsea and sweeps south, rolling up Hornsea as it goes. Meanwhile, the enemy force at Spurn Head breaks out west. He captures Hull, with all its resources, then expands his bridgeheads in any direction he chooses."

Brooke lowered his pencil, inviting comment.

"He could break out north too, perhaps?" Offered Churchill.

"He could, but what for?" Brooke shrugged as he answered the Prime Minister with another question. "A twenty five mile slog over the Yorkshire Moors, before he even gets close to Middlesbrough? I'm not sure that even the Germans would go for that?"

"They got through the Ardennes." Churchill observed, and Brooke nodded, acknowledging the point.

"What do *you* think, General Brooke?" Churchill asked.

The Commander in Chief looked over the map once more then tapped his pencil over the Yorkshire Wolds.

"I think it could be York or somewhere to the south, which means them coming over the Wolds. Hills they might be, but gentle hills with wide open fields. Although Hull is a tempting target, I can't see what use Hull is without the south bank of the Humber being in their hands too."

"What if they conduct another landing in the near future?" Cut in Newall. "Down there near Grimsby maybe?"

Dill shook his head.

"I don't think so Cyril. To split your invasion force in two with such a huge obstacle like the Humber would be madness, even for the Germans. And as far as we can see, they are probably very near their naval capacity already with their current deployment."

"So," Rumbled Churchill, impatiently, "what do you propose, General Brooke?"

Brooke lifted his pencil again and drew a straight line, running approximately north to south, parallel with the Yorkshire coast, and cutting straight through Driffield.

"All our troops east of this line are already committed. For better or worse, we cannot hope to give them useful orders. They must do what they can, and we will know exactly what that amounts to by dusk this evening. They will have either repelled the landings, or died trying." He paused and looked around his audience, his eyes hard. Churchill, he noted, was rapt.

"If we manage to hold Scarborough, then we reinforce it immediately. We use the town as an anchor point to lock down the northern extremity of the

German landing. If we lose it; we recapture it, quickly, with the reserves that will be coming down the coast from the Tyne-Tees area shortly. We pull back the Beverley Garrison on Hull and fortify the city. If it is the enemy objective, then we deny it to him. If it is not his primary objective, then it gives us a lodgement on his flank. We try to hold onto Driffield. If we can't…" Brooke gave a long sigh. "If we can't, then it gets complicated. We need to delay the enemy and keep him away from the Ouse as long as possible. We strip the entire North of England of troops and seal off the whole of East Yorkshire. And then? Then it is a race against time to get our reserves into a position to counter-attack before he makes his thrust."

Brooke lowered his pencil and stepped back from the map slightly.

"We will not learn anything significant for several hours now. It will take that long for HQ Northern Command to establish enough detail for us to make more concrete plans. I will speak with Adam shortly to discuss the options with him. To that end, I suggest we delay the next update until 0830 hours, and also that we hold it in the conference room. We all need the time to get to grips with the situation before we meet again."

"Agreed." Newall said. "I need to get everything untangled and back in some sort of order."

"And we'll know if our Humber and Tyne assets are safely out by then." Pound added.

Churchill nodded.

"That sounds fine, Gentlemen. I am to broadcast to the nation at eight."

The military staff exchanged looks.

"What will you tell the nation?" Dill asked in his quiet voice. "What will you tell the world?"

Churchill's face hardened.

"I will tell them the truth." He murmured. "I will tell them that we are fighting for our lives.

THE FILEY TO BRIDLINGTON ROAD – BY HUNMANBY
SATURDAY 21ST SEPTEMBER 1940 – 0610 HOURS

"Down!" Jackson waved the section of Home Guardsmen into cover.

One by one, they tottered across to the drainage ditch and slid down the bank into the ankle deep sludge. They were breathing hard, not used to such sudden bursts of physical activity. Eldridge, a private in his fifties, set down the heavy Boys Anti-Tank Rifle with a loud groan.

"Shh!" Hissed Jackson.

He beckoned Harper, who had been bringing up the rear. The rumble of artillery shells and mortars continued around them, albeit at a good distance, whilst the chatter of small arms fire provided a continuous back-drop of noise. Somewhere overhead, an aircraft engine whined painfully as a pilot threw his machine around the grey skies. Every few minutes, stray bullets would crack or buzz overhead, depending on how spent their velocity was.

"Look at this!" Jackson hissed into Harper's ear as the older man sank down next to him, breathing heavily.

Cradling his Lewis Gun, the First World War veteran looked through the hawthorn hedge in the direction indicated by the younger Coldstream sergeant.

The old-soldier's eyes took in the scene readily. There was a huge pillar of thick black smoke coming from Hunmanby village, whilst in the distance, dust and smoke rose up into the air where the enemy's naval guns were engaging unseen targets far inland. Across the fields to their right, they could see more smoke rising from the direction of Filey. Most significantly however, there was the sound of heavy gunfire coming from Hunmanby village.

"Looks like they got the petrol pumps at the garage?" Harper murmured, nodding towards the oily black smoke rising above the hedgerow across the road.

"Or our boys have blown them?" Jackson added. "Either way, there's a proper dust-up going on in the village by the sounds of it. We need to try and find our way in and link up with the rest of the platoon."

Harper pulled a face.

"Sounds like we'll have to fight our way in. That'll be interesting with hardly any ammunition between the two of us, and all the lads' rifles useless!"

Jackson nodded glumly, his face betraying frustration.

"We need to find some more ammo, or some different weapons, and sharpish. We're just wasting our…"

Harper clamped a hand over the sergeant's mouth suddenly and gave him a warning nod.

As Harper took his hand away, Jackson slowly turned his head, following the corporal's line of sight. He caught his breath. Barely twenty five yards away, a group of figures at the other side of the road were crouching behind the hedgerow near a gate. It was hard to see them clearly, but they were in a bunched file, all closed up as if getting ready to dash across the road. The thought had just crossed Jackson's mind, when the line of figures began to shuffle closer towards the gateway, taking care to keep low as they went.

Jackson found his glasses were steaming up slightly, so quickly pulled his handkerchief out of his cuff and rubbed them quickly, before staring back towards the unidentified group.

"Fucking hell!" He heard Harper swear.

He quickly understood why. As the group of figures shuffled warily past a slight gap in the far hedge, Jackson saw the distinctive pot shaped helmets and the green-blue baggy smocks that they wore. Jackson nodded to Harper and the Home Guardsman immediately understood what was required. As quickly and as silently as he could, Harper slid the barrel of the Lewis Gun over the lip of the ditch and under the lowest branches of the hawthorn. At the same time, Jackson sank down lower in the ditch and began waving at the others franticly with one hand, whilst he placed the fore-finger of his other hand over his lips.

The five part-time soldiers looked at him, their faces betraying concern, which only deepened when he gave them the field signal for 'enemy seen'. Beckoning them closer, he whispered his orders urgently.

"Enemy paratoopers at the other side of the road. George is going to shoot them when they try to cross. Get ready to follow me with your bayonets. Kill them all."

His blunt words left them aghast, and Jackson was faced with more than one pair of bulging eyes.

"Get ready!" He hissed. "Move fast and kill everyone!"

He turned back towards the road and moved in close against Harper's shoulder. The old soldier was tracing the movement of the Germans with his gun and Jackson saw that they had come to a halt, right by the gateway, although they were still partially obscured by the hedge.

"No ditch at their side?" He whispered in Harper's ear.

Harper, a local man, shook his head.

"No ditch." He confirmed.

"We'll come at them from the left." Jackson said, and Harper nodded his understanding.

"Tell me when you're ready."

"Okay. But if they start crossing the road, shoot them anyway."

Jackson turned away, picking up is rifle as he did so. The section were waiting for him, nervous faces looking pale beneath their helmets, their knuckles white as they gripped their empty Canadian rifles. He pointed at Eldridge first.

"You stay here with the Boys Rifle."

Then he pointed at Martlesham.

"You come right behind me."

The young man nodded, his eyes like those of an obedient dog.

Without another word, Jackson led his group left, along the ditch, towards a gateway in the hedge on their side. Arriving at the culvert, he was relieved to see that the gate was open. The half-platoon of regulars they had passed a while ago must have left it open. Thank God for small mercies, Jackson thought. Carefully raising his head above the ditch, he checked there were no other enemy in addition to the ones they had already spotted, and then glanced back at Martlesham.

"Come on." He mouthed at the younger man, and began to climb out of the ditch. As he crawled up the bank, Jackson's heart began to thump. Shooting at people was one thing, but engaging them at close quarters was another, and he remembered with distaste the grim hand to hand struggle with a German patrol on the banks of the Escaut just a few months earlier. That had been his first taste of close quarter fighting and as his mind relived the details of it, his stomach felt suddenly hollow and his limbs heavy.

Jackson's thoughts were shattered an instant later as Harper's Lewis gun blasted into life. Despite the background gunfire, the sudden burst, close by, made the Coldstreamer jump. Half out of the ditch, he leaned through the gateway and looked right. He saw two figures laying flat on their backs in the middle of the road, another on all fours, and a fourth crawling back towards the other gate. There was shouting from behind the far hedge. Another burst of Lewis Gun fire shattered the air, and Jackson saw the hawthorn hedge in front of the Germans quiver as the heavy .303 inch slugs ripped through it.

"Come on!" He screamed, dragging himself out of the ditch and throwing himself across the road.

The hedge at the other side of the road was probably chest high, and Jackson, a tall man, threw himself at it like a professional high-jumper. He felt the prickle of thorns on his hands and a painful scratch across his face as he tumbled sideways over the hedge, landing heavily on his right knee. He didn't even pause to worry about the pain, as Harper's gun rattled once more, then cut out abruptly as the breech block closed on an empty chamber. Jackson was on his feet instantly and lurched down the back of the hedgerow towards the enemy. He spotted a line of green-blue figures lying prone, and saw a huge cloud of dust and smoke rise up around one of them, as the German paratrooper opened fire with his machine pistol. The bullets were not aimed at Jackson however, they were going back through the hedge towards Harper at the far side of the road.

Jackson stumbled on and saw the enemy paratrooper glance up in surprise. The prone man shouted something and began to bring his machine pistol round towards Jackson. Between Jackson and the enemy soldier, was a second paratrooper. That man twisted round to look over his shoulder, alerted by his friend's shout, but Jackson was already there, stamping down on his back with a heavy ammunition boot. He heard the man grunt as he was forced down into the dirt and saw the momentary look of terror in the other paratrooper's eyes as Jackson swung his right leg toward him. Jackson's studded boot smashed into the face of the paratrooper with the machine pistol, and the German flipped over onto his back with a piteous cry as his nose, teeth and jaw splintered. The big Guards sergeant didn't hesitate; he simply thrust his rifle forwards and down in a powerful but controlled thrust. The long bayonet sliced straight through the German's throat, causing a thin spurt of blood to gush upwards, covering Jackson's hands.

Even as he heard the dying man's gurgling death rattle, the German that he'd trampled on gave an agonised scream, and Jackson realized with relief that the others had followed him and settled for the other enemy paratrooper. Just at that point however, there was a sharp bark of a weapon firing, and a bullet cracked past Jackson's right ear, deafening him. He jerked backwards instinctively, pulling his bayonet free as he did so. As he stepped back, he saw a third German, tucked right in by the gate-post, a carbine-style rifle in his hand. As the German worked the bolt of his rifle, Jackson levelled his own weapon and pulled the trigger. The German slammed back against the post violently as the large calibre round hit him squarely in the chest at just five yards range. As a dark stain began spreading across the man's baggy smock, he slumped sideways into the bushes, dead.

Automatically, Jackson worked the bolt of his rifle, ready to fire again, but the enemy soldier was obviously no more of a threat. Gingerly, the sergeant stepped sideways, and then towards the gateway, bringing the butt of the Lee-Enfield into his shoulder as he did so.

"George! It's me!" He called, eyes focussed on the gateway. "I'm coming into the gap. Are there any more left on the road?"

From across the road and beyond the hedges, Jackson heard Harper's broad Yorkshire accent pipe up.

"None of 'em standing." Harper shouted back. "There's one nearest the gate who might still be alive though."

Carefully, Jackson stepped around the gate-post so that he could see the road. In front of him, bearing testament to Harper's accuracy with the Lewis Gun, were four German bodies. Three of them lay sprawled across the centre of the road, arms and legs flung wide, and dark pools of blood forming under them. Nearest to Jackson however, was a fourth German, face down, his arms bent inwards as if he had been trying to crawl. The enemy paratrooper gave a slight wheezing noise, as if air was escaping from his body somewhere, and so Jackson poked the man's shoulder with his bayonet tipped rifle. Again, the German didn't move, but another wheezing noise came from underneath him. Jackson noted grimly that there was a large exit wound in the centre of the German's back, the baggy smock soaked with thick blood, whilst behind him on the tarmac, there was a short bloody trail of sticky red fluid that showed he had attempted to get back into the cover of the hedgerow.

Forcing his breathing to slow to something like normal, Jackson reversed his rifle and held it in his right hand, with the heavy brass butt plate hovering just above the German's helmeted head. With the other hand, the sergeant grabbed hold of the paratrooper's smock and heaved him over onto his back. The man was heavy, his limbs floppy and powerless. Having turned him, Jackson stepped back quickly, bringing his rifle and bayonet back into the thrusting stance. After a moment or two, Jackson relaxed. The German was nearly dead. He had been shot through the right hand side of his chest, missing the heart and spine, but ripping through his lung by the look of it. The wounded paratrooper's breathing was shallow and slow, yet every time he breathed, the torn material around the bullet hole seemed to get sucked in, then flutter again as the wheezing wound leaked more air out than it had taken in.

The man's eyes were glazed and there was blood everywhere. He would be dead within a couple of minutes. There was nothing to be done. As Jackson stared down at the dying German, Harper appeared on the road and came across, followed by Eldridge, both of them hefting their bulky weapons. The old soldier came to stand next to Jackson and stared down at the paratrooper.

"Sucking chest wound." Harper stated bleakly. "Poor bastard's a gonner."

Jackson nodded and looked up. Eldridge, cradling his Boys rifle, was staring around him in shock at the bloodied tarmac and the dead bodies.

"Strip them of weapons and ammunition" Jackson ordered. "Food and water too. Anything we can use; and that includes grenades."

Harper nodded and began ushering Eldridge towards the furthest enemy body.

Meanwhile, Jackson moved back through the gateway. He found the others standing by the row of dead bodies along the hedgerow, and like Eldridge, they were staring around their feet in horror. Jackson realised that there was one too many bodies and one less Home Guardsman than there should have been. He spotted the old man instantly, his green shade of khaki denims obvious amongst the German uniforms. Quietly, he walked over to where Martlesham was staring alternately at the dead body of Private Fred

Dean, a shop-keeper by trade, and the body of the German that he had bayoneted several times in the back.

Dean had been shot once; straight through the face. He lay flat on his back, half of his face a welter of blood, bone and teeth. Jackson remembered the single shot that the German by the gate had fired; the one that had cracked past his ear, barely inches away. He looked left into Martlesham's young face. The seventeen year old had a blank expression on his face, as if he had suddenly woken up and found himself in a different world. The bayonet on the end of his rifle was slick with blood.

"Is the German dead?" Jackson asked quietly.

Martlesham blinked in surprise.

"What? Oh! Yes…I think so."

Jackson nodded.

"Good lad. Well done." He said matter of factly.

Several feet away, one of the other Home Guardsmen vomited in the hedge bottom.

Jackson gave him a couple of moments to void his stomach and then spoke to them all in a firm, even voice.

"Well done, fellas. You see now that the Nazi's aren't supermen and that they *can* be killed? Make no mistake, we're going to kill a whole lot more of them. Don't worry about it. Forget your conscience. Don't stop to think about these people as human beings. Just kill every one of the bastards who gets in your way. The more you kill, the faster this nightmare will be over. Once it's over, we can say our prayers for Fred Dean and mourn him properly. But now's not the time. Accept it. We're here to fight. We're here to kill Germans. It's them or us. Understand?"

The small group of Home Guardsmen stared back at him, their faces betraying a range of conflicting emotions.

"Understand?" Jackson repeated the question, his voice harder now.

"Yes, Sarge." The others chorused, in quiet, shaky voices.

"It's Sergeant, gentlemen; not Sarge." He corrected them out of habit. "Now strip the Jerries of everything that's useful. Every gun, every grenade, every bullet. And take their water too."

He turned as Harper appeared in the gateway behind him.

"Dean's been killed." Jackson told him simply.

Harper's eyes flicked across the bodies on the ground only briefly.

"We'll need a hand over this side, there's loads of stuff on 'em." Said the corporal.

"No dramas, George. We'll be round there in a moment."

A sudden, deep whine made them look up. For a second, Jackson's heart leapt into his mouth as he remembered the sound of the Stukas over the beach at Dunkirk. He had a brief mental image of the big, ugly looking planes pulling up, their angular frames silhouetted against the blue sky, and the small, black blobs of the bombs coming down towards him. But then both the feeling and the image vanished as a burning aircraft plummeted diagonally across the front of his vision, probably no more than half a mile away. He caught the brown and green camouflage on the aircraft fuselage and a quick glimpse of the RAF roundel on the underside of a wing, just before the aircraft smashed into the ground, over by Hunmanby village, and exploded in a ball of flame and black smoke. He watched in fascination as bits of the aircraft wheeled lazily through the air, scattering across the open fields.

"Come on." Jackson heard himself saying with renewed urgency. "Let's strip these bastards and get going. "There's a battle to fight."

THE CLIFF TOP – HUNMANBY GAP
SATURDAY 21ST SEPTEMBER 1940 – 0615 HOURS

"Expended belt!" Bachman roared, as the working parts of the gun slammed back and came to a sudden stop with a metallic 'clunk'.

Feverishly, he threw open the top cover of the MG34 and allowed his No.2 to slam a new belt of ammunition across the feed-tray. As soon as it was done he slammed the top cover down, tapped it once to ensure it was locked, then realigned his sights onto the hedgerow and pulled the trigger once more. Rat-tat-tat-tat-tat-tat-tat! The weapon lurched in his shoulder like a wild beast as it spat the heavy 7.92mm bullets towards the enemy position across the field.

Behind him, Corporal Nuemark was still swearing.

"Fuck, fuck, fuck, fuck!" Cursed the squad's second in command. The blood was pouring down his sleeve from underneath the dressing that he was trying desperately to fasten in place with his good arm. "Fucking Tommy planes! Where the fuck is the Luftwaffe?"

"Don't worry about the bloody planes, Martin!" Saltz answered, noting that even for Nuemark, the corporal's profanity was reaching an impressive tempo. "Just keep your head down, and let me tie that off for you, before the Tommies knock your ugly turnip off!"

They had been hit from the front and rear simultaneously. Having sensed that the resistance was slackening above them, the entire company, or at least what remained of it, had stormed up the steep bluffs to reach the cliff-tops.

Despite losing several men to grenades and cross fire, they had succeeded on reaching the high ground, and were now lining the cliff-top and preparing to thrust inland. It had happened suddenly. From their front, a large squad of Tommy infantry had opened fire on them from a position in the far hedgerow, about a hundred metres inland. At the same time, a Tommy aircraft had flown up the line of the beach, at cliff-top height, its rear-turret gunner spraying the length of the cliffs with machine gun fire; the latest in a swarm of attacking aircraft.

Two more men in the platoon had died in that burst, and Nuemark had taken a flesh wound in his right arm. Although not too serious, his arm was pissing blood and causing the corporal to use an even larger selection of expletives than was normal.

"Right," Said Saltz, yanking the two ends of the dressing tight and tying them in a firm knot, "that'll do you nicely."

"Aagh! Fucking hell Jo'! You nearly cut my arm off!" Nuemark complained.

"Stop whinging, Martin! It's only a scratch. Now get along the edge of this cliff and start collecting some more ammo belts for Bachman. I'm going to collect as many riflemen as I can and take them left flanking up the side of the draw. Give me your grenades."

Clumsily, Nuemark yanked the two stick grenades out of his belt and passed them to Saltz, who was already shouting orders to the others lining the cliff-top. As he was doing so, Heyman appeared next to him.

"Saltzi, I've only got four lads left. How about you?"

"I've got six left in action, eight counting Nuemark and Schumann. Have you still got your machine-gun?"

"Yeah, still got it, but half the spare ammo is wrapped around dead bodies on the beach."

"Not to worry." Saltz replied, quickly doing the maths. "I'm going to go left flanking with some riflemen. I'm going to leave Nuemark and Schumann here with Bachman on the gun. Can you bring your gun up too, and control the covering fire? I'll take any of your spare riflemen with me and we'll clear those Tommies out of that hedgerow there."

Heyman squinted across the field, keeping his head as far below the line of the cliffs as he could.

"No problem, I'll give you three guys. Any sign of Hagen yet?"

"None." Saltz confirmed. "What about Third Squad?"

"Not seen Weimer." Heyman replied. "I think he copped one on the ramp. Seen some of his boys though, just down there." He jerked his thumb back towards the bottom of the cliffs.

Saltz nodded.

"Okay. Try and sweep up any of Weimer's squad and bolt them on to your cover group. We'll reorganise the platoon once we've taken care of this position across the field."

"Got that." Heyman acknowledged. "Give me a minute to sort out these guns, then you can get moving."

With that, Heyman ducked away and began shouting orders to his surviving squad members. Around Saltz, his own squad members were assembling, grenades and rifles in hands. Whilst he waited, Saltz removed the half empty magazine from his machine pistol and swapped it for a full one. He glanced out across the beach and out to sea and felt a sudden surge of awe rise up inside him. The panorama of battle from this vantage point was huge. Ships and boats and barges filled the wide bay, some giving off smoke, others on fire or sinking. Bodies littered the sand, left and right as far as the eye could see, especially over the far side of the draw where some of their battalion had landed right in front of the enemy coastal battery. Overhead meanwhile, aircraft roared past at low level, their guns chattering. They were mainly British, diving in to the attack through a huge curtain of anti-aircraft fire, the lethal residue of which continually showered down onto the beach and cliff-tops. Higher up, he saw the unmistakable silhouettes of their own ME 110 fighters, as they fought desperately to keep the RAF from attacking the beaches.

The battle was well and truly in the balance, he thought. Yet they were ashore and up the cliffs nevertheless, whilst the second wave of infantry was already storming across the wide beach below.

Crump!

He twisted over to his right and looked across to the south side of the ravine, where a large cloud of smoke was rising from the seat of the explosion. It was the pill-box with the small Tommy artillery piece. It looked as though Second Company had taken the bunker out at last. That was good, he thought; his left flanking assault against the Tommies in the hedgerow would be less vulnerable now.

"Ready when you are Saltzi!"

Saltz twisted back round to see Heyman giving him the thumbs-up. There were now two gun teams set up on the cliff's edge, with Schumann and Nuemark helping to organise the ammunition. Eight riflemen, a mix from the First and Second Squads, crouched precariously against the edge of the cliff, watching him with eager eyes.

He scanned their young faces and saw that they were still full of fight, and once more he felt a surge of pride at what fine young soldiers the German army continued to produce. Suddenly, he knew that they would win this battle. The worst was over. There were German soldiers on English soil…and Britain was finished.

"Okay, lads." He beamed at the men of the ad hoc assault group. "Let's go take this battle by the bollocks, shall we? Follow me!"

PART TWO

BEACH-HEAD

'S' DAY
H +2

FIRE CONTROL TOWER – KREIGSMARINE SHIP ADMIRAL SCHEER
SATURDAY 21ST SEPTEMBER 1940 – 0620 HOURS

'Fire!' The gunnery officer of the Admiral Scheer snapped the command.

He heard his voice echo down the communication pipe, where it was acknowledged in the fire control room. Moments later, the ship began to shake and the low growl turned into a roar, as the two batteries of big eleven inch guns blasted off another salvo towards the British Cruisers that were turning side on to them, ready to release their own broadsides.

'Three and five batteries, Fire!"

The assistant gunnery officer repeated the commands to the batteries containing the battle-cruiser's secondary armament.

Another roar, not quite as loud as before, caused the big ship to shudder again as the 5.9 inch and 4.1 inch guns on the port side spat out their shells towards the centre of the three British cruisers.

The two gunnery officers raised their powerful binoculars to watch the fall of shot whilst they awaited the reloaded signal from the fire control room.

"Ach! Almost!" The gunnery officer tutted as he saw the big towers of water erupt around the distant Tommy ship. "Shells straddling the left hand cruiser! He's turned side on now. We'll get him with the next salvo."

"Short!" Cursed the junior lieutenant. "But only just. Add four hundred!"

He paused before bringing his binoculars down, listening to his orders as they were relayed down in the fire control room.

"Tommy ships returning fire." He commented conversationally.

"Hmm." Mumbled the senior of the two lieutenants. "They'll miss first time, and probably the second and third. They always do. Hold on, what's that?"

The junior lieutenant raised his binoculars again.

"Explosion against the middle cruiser." Said the gunnery officer. "Just one; big one too."

His companion pulled a face.

"Can't be us. I didn't hear any late firers. Mine perhaps?"

"Probably." Agreed the senior lieutenant. " Or one of the U-Boats? That'll give them something extra to think about."

"Five battery ready." Came a voice from the fire control room. Then, a second later. "Three battery ready."

The smaller guns were faster to reload than the big eleven inchers.

"Fire!" Barked the assistant gunnery officer.

As the ship rocked again under the salvo, the voice from fire control reported that One and Two Batteries were ready again.

"Fire!"

As the two officers raised their binoculars once more, the first British shells plunged into the water nearly a quarter of a mile away.

"Told you." Murmured the gunnery officer.

Seconds later, another British salvo crashed into the water, but this time much closer, by at least two hundred yards.

"That one was better." He muttered.

The two Kreigsmarine officers remained glued to their binoculars as they waited for their own salvos to land and were rewarded moments later as huge geysers of water erupted around the centre and left hand ships of the trio. A bright orange flame erupted from the centre ship, followed by the same on the other one just seconds later.

"Hit!" Cried out the junior lieutenant, excitedly.

"And here!" His senior laughed. "Fire control, you're on for range against both targets. Reload and fire when ready, all batteries."

Having given his orders, the gunnery officer turned to his companion.

"We have them now Hans! They'll be lucky to get us with their next one, but ours should tear holes in them!"

What about those destroyers they've got with them?"

The gunnery officer pulled a face.

One's been hit already according to the bridge; mine or torpedo. Hopefully the rest will be too busy trying to keep the U-Boats off the cruisers' backs to get involved."

His second in command nodded thoughtfully.

"Besides," Said the senior lieutenant, brightly, "once we've taken care of the cruisers, we can pick off the destroyers at our leisure, so if they've got any sense they'll scuttle back into the estuary."

Before his assistant could reply, another British salvo smacked into the water, barely a hundred yards away.

"Christ on a cross!" Swore the senior lieutenant. "They seem to be wide awake today!"

Before they had time to make any more comments, a siren began sounding loud from the bridge, and seconds later, the light anti-aircraft batteries began banging away. The two officers twisted around to look upwards and saw a formation of around nine or ten aircraft approaching them from the south-west. They had been flying at a medium altitude, but appeared to be climbing as the Scheer's anti-aircraft ordnance began to pepper the sky in front of their flight path.

"Tommy planes, small ones!" Came the warning from the anti-aircraft lookout.

The officers brought their binoculars up to study the swarm of climbing aircraft that were probably three miles distant now. They appeared to be peeling to starboard, adopting a line astern formation as they gained height.

"Single engines." Murmured the assistant gunnery officer. "Fighters?"

"Yes." Agreed the senior lieutenant. "Probably gaining height in order to avoid us and go past towards the landing beaches. Either that or they're another batch of those fighters we saw chasing our ME 110's.They're no danger to us. They'll save their machine guns for something more suitable. Ugly looking things too, must be Hurricanes. Tell the anti-aircraft batteries to save their ammunition. I'll brief the Captain."

The gunnery officer had his hand on the communication pipe already, but he stopped in his tracks and looked skywards again as the distant drone of the aircraft engines changed in tone. His eyes widened as he watched in disbelief. The lead aircraft, having reached a considerable height almost directly above, suddenly dipped his nose and dived straight towards them.

"What the hell…? Are they mad?"

"Are you *sure* they're fighters Heini?" The assistant gunnery officer queried.

They weren't fighters. They were Fairey Battle light bombers heading towards Bridlington at 15,000 feet. The squadron had spotted two major German warships and decided that they were a target that just couldn't be passed up, and so, with the same suicidal bravery that they had displayed in France, they gained height in preparation for a steep attack run against the enemy ships. As the first aircraft dipped its nose, the Scheer rocked; once, then twice, as the whole array of batteries on the port side of the ship opened fire on the British cruisers once more. The two officers should have brought up their binoculars to watch the fall of shot, but instead they just stared upwards in amazement as the Tommy aircraft hurtled down towards them, despite the heavy curtain of black explosions that filled the air, high above the ship.

"Fucking hell!" Swore the gunnery officer, suddenly allowing his alarm to break through his professional detachment. "He's going to crash into us!"

Instead, the aircraft suddenly pulled upwards, groaning like an angry beast, and as it did so, four small, dark, sinister looking items fell from beneath its wings and came sailing, almost lazily, through the air towards the ship.

"Bombers!" The assistant gunnery officer shouted pointlessly as the dark shadow of the aircraft roared overhead and began climbing upwards again.

The ship suddenly turned sharply.

"Steindorf!" Came the voice of the Captain through the communication tube. "Get every gun onto those bloody planes, man! Less the main armament!"

"At once, Captain!" Replied the gunnery officer, but even as he turned to his companion, the four bombs landed.

Three of them missed the ship by only a few metres, but the fourth one clipped the port deck and the ship trembled as the bomb exploded with a loud crump.

Steindorf felt a wave of hot air sweep across the top of the open-decked fire control tower, and was aware of lumps of metal, flying past them and bouncing off the other parts of the super-structure. His hat disappeared over the side in the blast.

"Hard a-port and full ahead!" The Captain's muffled voice came to them through the tubes, which showed how loud he must be shouting.

Next to Steindorf, the assistant gunnery officer was shouting into the tubes himself, ordering all of the secondary gun batteries to switch fire to the aircraft. The fire control room acknowledged the order, but then sent a request up for confirmed fire direction data for the main batteries. The sudden evasive action of the Scheer had created an unaccounted-for error in the calculations.

"I'll do it!" Steindorf snapped at his assistant. "You concentrate on the aircraft!"

Another deep whine was coming from above them and the sound of small arms fire and light anti-aircraft fire had become continuous and deafening. As Steindorf glanced up briefly, the sky above them was black with smoke from dozens of exploding shells. The sound of the Tommy light bombers was turning his blood cold and making it difficult for him to concentrate on his calculations as he reset the bearing towards the left hand Tommy cruiser. His view was obscured momentarily as two spouts of water shot up right next to the ship. He forced himself to remain calm and, having checked the information and added the variables, he shouted the information down to fire control. It seemed like an age before the response came, saying that One and Two batteries were ready, during which he noted with relief that a Tommy aircraft was weaving away from the ship trailing lots of smoke.

"Fire!" He bellowed as soon as he had the word that the guns were laid on.

Crump! The six big guns of the Scheer's main armament shook the battle-cruiser once more, and Steindorf forced the binoculars to his eyes, desperately trying to ignore the ongoing bombing around him. He first laid eyes on the centre of the three big Tommy ships and saw that it appeared to be turning away. Their was a single plume of unnecessary smoke coming from the left hand ship, but even as he watched, he saw the tiny sparks of flame that indicated it was returning fire at them once more. Then, his heart leapt as he spotted two larger flashes against the ship's side.

"Two hits!" He cried out excitedly, but then cursed as he felt the Scheer heel over in another tight evasive manoeuvre. That would mean more calculations and corrections. He might not be as lucky as to get two hits from an un-ranged first salvo again.

"Three battery's gone!" The assistant gunnery officer shouted suddenly as he strained to hear the voices from the fire control room above the sound of their own anti-aircraft barrage. "That bomb hit them square on!"

"No time to worry, now!" Steindorf shouted above the din. "Just keep the others firing and get those Tommies off our arse!"

Steindorf's mind was racing now. Trying to calculate fire control information was awkward enough, without the added annoyance of an air attack and the ship making unexpected turns. He jumped as an aircraft engine suddenly whined in his ears with such intensity that he thought the plane was about to land on him, but instead, the flaming aircraft plummeted past their tower and smashed into the water by the starboard side of the ship. Water splashed into Steindorf's face, which he wiped away with his sleeve irritably as he continued trying to plot the information for his next salvo.

Barely had the fountain of water from the doomed plane subsided, when a high pitched whistling noise suddenly filled the air around them. The two officers looked up in fear, realising that the unusual sound of the enemy shells meant that they had found the range, more or less. They felt a small rush of wind and then two enemy shells slammed into the water behind them to the starboard side of the ship. Once again, Steindorf found himself sprayed with sea water.

"That was bloody close!" He cursed, his face betraying surprise at the accuracy of the British guns.

Focussing on the enemy cruisers once more, he began to work out the new information for the main batteries, passing it down through the fire control room as he went along. In the seemingly endless minutes that it took to reload and re-lay the guns, another two enemy aircraft dived down at the Scheer, and on both occasions, it was only through swift manoeuvring that the bombs missed the big ship, literally by inches each time.

"Fire!" Yelled Steindorf, once he received the ready signal from down below.

Once again, the big guns boomed loudly, shaking the ship in the water. The gunnery officer watched the distant target for the fall of shot, and cursed when he saw the shells go over the enemy ship and hit the water behind it.

"Damn!" He swore, striking his hand of the shelf in front of him. "All this bloody twisting and turning is putting us off. "Drop five hundred!"

He looked up into the air and saw that several enemy aircraft were circling at a distance, very high up, whilst the remaining enemy aircraft appeared to be concentrating on the Admiral Hipper, which was busy using all of its guns against a single target. Steindorf understood why. The enemy cruiser, the right hand one of the three, had pulled away from the firing line of its companions and was making good speed towards the Hipper, only its front batteries engaging as it chopped through the calm grey sea. It must still be a good 15,000 metres away thought Steindorf as he watched the big enemy cruiser emerge from behind a curtain of water spouts. They were closing the range to improve accuracy, he realised. But that was dangerous. Why would they come in so close and make themselves a bigger target?

Steindorf moved his glasses to the left and saw that the centre enemy cruiser appeared to be withdrawing back towards the estuary, an unusual amount of smoke coming from her. The third cruiser, the target of their own main batteries, was also smoking heavily, but still firing too. He saw the tiny pin-pricks of light as the cruiser fired at them again.

"Incoming!" He warned his second in command.

"Steindorf! This is the Captain. Watch those destroyers trying to come round to aft! Start engaging them with your secondary armament."

The assistant gunnery officer jumped in surprise as the crisp order came through the tube.

"Destroyers?" He raised his binoculars once more, panning well to the left.

And there they were. Three small ships had broken away from the rear of the cruiser group, abandoning their flank protection role. Instead, they were ploughing through the ocean; much like the third cruiser was, trying to close the range desperately.

"It's a pincer operation!" Steindorf thought aloud. "They're trying to sandwich us! That air attack is just a distraction!"

He glared at the three enemy destroyers in the far distance. Two of them were well ahead of the third, which was making excessive smoke as it trailed the other two.

Crash! Steindorf was thrown sideways as a large shell slammed into the side of the ship's hull.

"Fuck me!" He stammered, as he picked himself up from the deck and stood once more, albeit shakily, to stare out across the sea.

Next to him, the assistant gunnery officer pulled himself upright, his eyes wide with shock.

"Christ almighty, Heini!" Stammered the junior lieutenant. "This is getting a bit hairy!"

"Tell me about it!" Retorted Steindorf.

"One and Two batteries ready!" Came the call from below.

"Fire!" Steindorf croaked into the tube, his throat suddenly dry as a bone. "Hans, get the secondary batteries onto those destroyers now!" He turned to look at his assistant, who still looked pale and half stunned from the recent blast. "Before this goes horribly wrong…"

BRIDLINGTON HARBOUR
SATURDAY 21ST SEPTEMBER 1940 – 0625 HOURS

"How many men have you got with you?"

Schulz fixed Captain Hausman with an eager look.

"Thirty seven including myself, Major." Gasped the company commander breathlessly, having dashed across the broad promenade to gain the shelter of the harbour wall. "I left a squad of eight at the railway station, with the men you left there. They've captured the place now, but needed more men to secure it properly."

"Excellent, Hausman; well done!" Schulz's temper was improving. With these reinforcements he could make a real difference to the battle. He looked towards Sergeant Heiden, his second in command up until now.

"What's the story from over there?" He asked the grim faced non-commissioned officer.

"It's Lieutenant Maxse from Third Company." The sergeant replied, jerking his head across the harbour. "He's got about forty men with him. He says he can hold the whole of the northern side for the time being. There's only been a couple of small probes in the last ten minutes. Probably just small groups of enemy falling back to the harbour, then realising it's in our hands anyway."

Schulz thought for a moment.

"Right Hauseman, I want you to give a squad of ten to Heiden, in order to bolster his strength at this side of the harbour. I want another two men to work directly with me, as runners. As for yourself and the remainder, I want you to exploit along the sea front and start rolling up the enemy positions."

The captain from First Company nodded curtly, his face business-like.

"Here, let's take a quick look." Schulz nodded towards the southern beach which was hidden from view by the harbour wall.

Gingerly, the two parachute officers raised their heads just high enough to peer over the top. The strip of beach that ran off into the distance was swarming with men and boats, some of those vessels grounded, on fire, or sinking. Most of the troops from the first wave had reached the foot of the sea wall, less those who were dead and those who were trapped in front of the huge wire entanglement that blocked the slip road to the promenade.

"The second wave is on its way in. They'll just pile up against the first wave by the sea wall if we don't give them a chance to get off the beach. See that pill-box?"

Hausman followed the Major's finger and spotted the squat concrete building that dominated the barricaded slip road to the beach, along with the huge stretch of sand beyond it.

"They've got at least one machine gun in there. It's cutting up those boys as they try to get through the wire. And it's mutually supported by a strongpoint in that row of houses beyond. Seen?"

"Yes, Major." Nodded Hauseman.

Ping!

The two officers dropped back behind the wall quickly as the bullet ricocheted of it, only feet away.

"I need you to take your group and double back into the town slightly, then get in behind that row of houses. Clear it out, then destroy that pill-box. Once you've done that, we can bring those boys off the beach by the ramp and pump them into the town that way. Plus, we'll have an exit for armour. The sooner we get some tanks ashore, the sooner we'll have the Tommies on the run. Got that?"

"Got it, Sir." Hausman nodded. "It'll be nice to get stuck in at last! I've spent half the night wandering around the bloody fields."

"Well, no more wandering now. Shake your men out and get moving; as fast as you can. The men you leave with Heiden can assist in giving you some fire support while you work your way round.

"At once, Major." Hausman nodded his understanding and turned away to begin reorganising his men.

"Are those nets here yet?" Schulz demanded, turning back to face Heiden.

"On their way right now, Sir." The sergeant jerked a thumb down the quayside.

Schulz peered past him and saw a group of the Tommy civilians who had been hiding under the jetty. Overseen by two paratroopers wielding machine-pistols, the civilians were dragging fishing nets along the inside of the harbour wall. It had been Heiden's own idea that; to use the fishing nets as scramble nets by securing them at this side and then throwing them over the other side of the harbour wall. The entrance to the harbour might be blocked, but the troop barges could haul in alongside the outer face of the stone pier and offload their infantry up the nets and into the harbour that way.

It would be slow initially, but it was another way of getting extra fighting power into the town all the same. The more men they could pump through the harbour, then the quicker the coastal defences could be rolled up to allow a mass exodus off the beaches. Time was the key factor. They had to get ashore and establish a beach-head before the Tommies could get their reserves to the coast. Most importantly, they had to get armour moving inland quickly, in order to relieve their sister regiment that had been dropped nearly fifteen miles behind the coast over the town of Driffield. It was all down to speed.

"How long before those nets are in place?"

"Ten minutes maximum, I reckon."

"Good." Schulze nodded, checking his watch. "0628 hours."

The battalion commander looked back up at Heiden, feeling his confidence and fighting spirit return, thanks to the sudden improvement in his tactical situation.

"Send the signal now. Keep on sending the signal until it's acknowledged or until you see the barges heading this way."

Heiden raised an eyebrow.

"Harbour open?"

"Yes." Schulz replied decisively. "Signal them that the harbour is open."

CAYTON BAY – EAST COAST OF YORKSHIRE
SATURDAY 21ST SEPTEMBER 1940 – 0630 HOURS

"Grenade!"

The voice carried clearly down the slope to where Colonel Willibald Utz was crouching amongst the Gorse bushes his tactical headquarters. Two muffled explosions came moments later, followed shortly afterwards by the sound of machine-pistols firing in a confined space. That was followed by several screams, an aggressive burst of shouting in German, then a lengthy silence. A few more moments passed, during which the commander of the 100th Mountain Infantry Regiment continued to study the map, his brow furrowed in a thoughtful frown.

"Bunker clear!" Came the distant voice again.

Across from him, the three officers watched their commander expectantly. A calm and decisive man, it was not unusual for Utz to be this far forward. He wouldn't interfere, they knew; but he would insist on seeing the battle develop for himself, in order for him to have the fullest appreciation of the situation. They waited patiently as his clear, shrewd eyes, surveyed the detail of his map, on which he had made a number of pencil marks already. As they waited for him to come to a decision, a soldier came sliding down the escarpment in their general direction.

"Captain Kranmer?" The soldier was shouting. "Captain Kranmer, Sir?"

Kranmer, one of the three officers waiting on Utz, knelt up and waved towards the panting soldier who was casting his gaze about in an attempt to locate his battalion's second in command.

"Here, boy!" Shouted the captain. "Over here!"

The soldier heard the voice, looked around quickly, spotted Kranmer, then began sliding across the slope of the steep bluff towards him. A few moments later, the young private slid to a halt next to Kranmer, his breath coming in big gulps.

"Major Schlepp's compliments, Sir. That's the last bunker taken on the cliff-top. A long one, with half a dozen Tommies in; all dead now. He's going to push inland to the first hedgerow; about a hundred and fifty metres beyond the crest. There's a couple of Tommy trenches sited in depth, but all with rifles by the looks of it. Nothing too serious, he says. He asked if you could speak to the colonel and get further direction on the axis of advance?"

Kranmer nodded.

"Just wait there for a minute, lad. The colonel's about to brief us. I'll give you a message to take back shortly."

The soldier nodded his understanding and fell back to a respectful distance.

As he did so, Utz looked up, his eyes alert and his features sharp.

"I assume that the 2nd Battalion's area is now clear?" He said, looking directly at Kranmer?"

The captain nodded back.

"It is, Colonel; as far as the cliff-top is concerned. Major Schlepp has spotted a couple of positions in depth, about a hundred and fifty metres back, which he wants to destroy, so he can push forward off the cliff's edge. But everything dominating the beach is clear of enemy."

"Good." The colonel replied crisply. "Tomas?" He shouted down slope towards a small group of soldiers who constituted his advanced tactical headquarters.

"Yes, Colonel?" His signals officer looked back over his shoulder at his commanding officer.

"Signal the ships. Gudrun is clear of enemy. We are exploiting inland. The beach is open. Tell them that; and repeat it. Happy?"

"Happy, Colonel. Sending it now. Do you want us to use the flares too?"

"Absolutely." Utz agreed. "Make sure there is no mistaking the message."

The signals officer nodded, turned away and began briefing the soldier holding the flash-lamp.

"Right gentlemen." Utz turned his gaze back to the three officers next to him, reversing his map so that they could look at it from a proper orientation, rather than upside down. "Let's get down to business, shall we?"

The colonel of mountain troops jabbed his pencil towards the map.

"We're bang on target and almost on time." He stated, indicating the small bay on the map marked 'Cayton'. "Thank God the Kreigsmarine gave way and allowed us to use those motor launches. These rocks would have caused chaos if we'd tried to land here using the barges. Imagine trying to manoeuvre those beasts in a bay this small?"

The three officers murmured agreement with their commander.

"So, we are ashore, with somewhere around ten percent casualties by the sounds of your reports?"

He paused, raising a questioning eyebrow at the officers. Kranmer, along with the major commanding the 1st Battalion murmured their confirmation that those were indeed the accurate casualty figures.

"And you Peter? Your battalion is fully intact, less a couple of losses as you cleared the beach."

"That's correct, Colonel." Confirmed the major commanding the 3rd Battalion. They had landed barely ten minutes ago as the regiment's second wave.

"Excellent. That's good work so, gentlemen. Please pass on my thanks to your men and keep them going at full tilt. There's no time for complacency. We must move quickly before the Tommies can muster a suitable force for a counter attack. We shouldn't under estimate them. They put up a good fight here; right to the bitter end. If they had been equipped with more machine-guns and some better artillery or heavy mortars, we might not have got off the beach. However, we've done it, and now we must exploit. So, 1st

Battalion, you are to clear inland and expand the perimeter until we have troops covering from this point here…Os-god-by…" He traced his pencil in an arc west and then southwards. "…to this village here, called Cayton." He looked up at the major commanding the 1st Battalion who nodded his understanding.

"Max," He looked now to Kranmer. "I want you to brief Major Schlepp to keep on pushing inland. Your battalion is to establish a perimeter running from this southern point of the bay, across to this village here, called Lebberston, then up to the village of Cayton, where you are to link up. Arrange the boundary between yourselves, but make it something obvious, like a church, and then let me know. As soon as you've got that far, both battalions are to dig in and prepare for a counter-attack. Understand?"

Both Kranmer and the commanding officer of the 1st Battalion voiced their understanding and began sketching diagrams on their own maps, copying from Utz's.

"Peter," Utz turned to the commander of the 3rd Battalion. "you are to come up in reserve and be prepared to attack through the other two battalions and into this other village of Eastfield. Your limit of exploitation is the railway line. You may seize the bridge over the line, but do not exploit beyond it just yet. Depending on the level of resistance, there are a couple of alternatives thereafter. Potentially, we might have a hard fight through these built up areas and suffer counter-attacks as we go along. In that case, the main effort will be to establish that perimeter that I've outlined and await the next wave. On the other hand, if we can establish this quite quickly, and there is no immediate threat from the south or west, then I may flick one of the battalions, or a portion of it, northwards to attack up this spur of land and capture this high feature here…Oliver's Mount. This high feature dominates the town of Scarborough, so it's essential that we capture it as soon as possible. It will help take some pressure off the 98th who are landing in the town itself. Does that all make sense?"

All three of the officers nodded vigorously, looks of eager anticipation on all their faces. Utz smiled. They were good boys; a good regiment with good leaders, thirsting for action. Whatever they came up against, they would fight like lions.

"Message from the flagship, Colonel!"

The signals officer's voice made Utz look sharply in his direction.

"Have they acknowledged beach open?"

"Yes, Colonel. They say that Brunhild is not open, repeat, not open. 98th are stalled on the beach and taking heavy casualties. Stand-by for 99th to land on Gudrun for exploitation north, followed by artillery and anti-tank units."

Utz was silent for a moment. He gazed northwards, listening to the sound of distant gunfire.

"Okay, Tomas." He said at last, his voice still calm and precise. "Acknowledge the message. Seb?"

Another officer from his tactical headquarters looked up at him from amongst the knot of men.

"Yes, Colonel?"

"I'll brief you in a moment on the plan for us. In the meantime, start organising some guides on the beach for the 99th. I want you to mark out marshalling areas for troops and a rendezvous point for the regimental commander to meet me for a face to face. Get the engineers working on it straight away; and get them to start clearing some proper paths up this slope so we can get the guns off the beach when they arrive."

The officer gave a thumbs-up and began rattling out instructions to the remainder of the headquarters group.

"There you go, gentlemen." Utz said, turning back to the three battalion representatives. "The makes it nice and clear for us. It sounds as though the poor old 98th are getting minced on Brunhild, so let's bust out of this beachhead and give the 99th room to swing round and bale them out. No time for caution I'm afraid. Go at it hard and fast before the Tommies get themselves organised."

As if to add emphasis to his words, there was a sudden 'whoosh' in the air above them and a moment later the ground shook, as a mortar bomb landed just a hundred and fifty metres away with a dull 'crump'.

The four officers ducked their heads instinctively as clods of soil and gorse pattered down around them. They stayed low as the first bomb was followed by two more.

"I suppose that means the Tommies up on Oliver's Mount have seen us then and realised we've broken through?" Utz gave a toothy smile to the other three. They laughed at that.

"Any questions at all, men?"

"No, Sir." The three officers chorused.

"Good stuff! Off you go then. Move out straight away and remind your boys that if we don't do this quickly, there won't be anything left of the 98th. Our own boys are depending on us. Now, go."

The three officers jumped to their feet and began doubling away towards their respective units. As they did so, Utz was vaguely aware of a distant rumble of artillery fire somewhere. He though little of it for a moment or two, watching instead as his operations officer clambered up the slope to speak to him.

"I think we'd best move into one of the captured bunkers, Sir; now that the Tommies have got their mortars into action. There's a big one just along the cliff there, overlooking the natural draw. I reckon it'll be big enough to get the 99th's headquarters in too, once they've landed..."

The captain broke off and looked upwards suddenly as a high pitched moan turned into a whoosh.

Crump! Crump! Crump! Crump! Crump! Crump!

The shells slammed into the cliff-top one after the other, shaking the ground violently and loosening sizeable chunks of clay and rock. One of the shells passed over the cliff top and exploded below them on the sand and shingle of the beach. Utz and his operations officer pressed themselves flat against the slope as bits of red hot metal shrapnel and stones whizzed dangerously past their heads. The acrid smell of burnt explosives assailed their nostrils. Around them, a number of voices had begun screaming.

"Medic!"

"Incoming!"

"Stay down!"

"Those aren't mortars!" Croaked the operations officer. "Those are field guns; big ones!"

Utz grimaced. Field artillery. That must mean they were facing a major enemy formation. Either that or the area had been established as a strongpoint with fixed heavy artillery.

"That bunker, Seb?" Utz looked sideways at his operations officer through the long grass.

"Yes, Sir?"

"I think perhaps, it's a good idea!"

WHITE ROSE FARM – BY HUNMANBY, EAST YORKSHIRE SATURDAY 21ST SEPTEMBER 1940 – 0635 HOURS

"The bastards are everywhere!" Harper whispered quietly to Jackson.

The Colstream sergeant nodded silently as he surveyed the view to the south from their position behind the cattle trough. All along the ridge towards Reighton, and beyond to Speeton, there were tell-tale signs of close combat; small explosions, tracer rounds ricocheting into the air, the sound of whistles, shouts and small arms fire. Several plumes of smoke rose from amongst the trees and cottages that marked the location of the nearer village. Jackson lowered the old pair of binoculars that he had brought from the Lewis Gun trench and stuffed them back into his gas-mask haversack.

"Looks like it." He agreed, as he fastened the haversack. "I reckon they must have dropped paratroopers right across the back of us, from Brid' up to Filey. I'm guessing that they're after the fire control bunkers up at Speeton from all that fighting over there."

He looked at Harper.

"Just as well we didn't go back towards the coast; I don't think they'll be held for long on the beaches. We'd have been cut-off down by the cliffs in no time at all, I reckon. This way we stay ahead of them, and that means we can pick and choose where to hit them."

"So where do we go from here?" Harper asked quietly, casting an eye over the others who were lying prone against the hedgerow behind them.

Jackson gave a small sigh and glanced around the fields to his right.

"Not back to the coast, or towards Filey. I don't think there's much we can do down at Speeton either. I reckon there must be at least a company's worth of Jerries down there. By the time we get over there; *if* we get there, it'll probably be done and dusted. Besides, we need to join back up with some of our own blokes. We need to concentrate our forces if we're going to stand a chance of putting in any kind of counter-attack."

"So, back to the village?" Harper nodded towards Hunmanby, a sizeable collection of houses just under a mile away across the fields to their right.

"Sort of." Jackson nodded. "But there's been plenty of firing from that direction; and the platoon sergeant of those regulars said that their platoon commander had taken a section into the village to support the rest of our lads. So, we'd best be careful. I reckon we work our way through this farm here; see if the farmer knows what the situation is. Then we move up the hill to the strip wood and try to link up with our observation post. How many lads did we have up there?"

"Two." Harper confirmed.

"Okay. We'll link up with them and see where we go from there. Who's the farmer in this place?"

Harper pulled a face.

"His name's Jim Farley. Bit of miserable bugger to be honest."

Jackson chuckled.

"Well, he'll have plenty to chunter about this morning! Come on; let's go."

The small section of Home Guard volunteers followed on behind the tall Coldstream Guardsman. Martlesham was right behind him, his face still pale with the shock of their recent encounter. Despite this, he wore a determined look on his features and he gripped his newly liberated machine-pistol tightly against his hip; his empty Canadian rifle now slung across his back. The others followed, all carrying fully loaded German weapons, with Harper bringing up the rear, his Lewis Gun also slung. Cautiously, Jackson led them through a gap in the hedge and into the grounds of the farm. They found themselves padding across a long thin stretch of grass that was littered with chicken feed. Several birds clucked noisily at the far end of the strip, by their runs, but other than that, everything seemed quiet. They crossed the open ground quickly until they passed between two barns. At the far end of the gap, both barns were joined by a brick wall that was breached by a single gateway. Against the right hand barn, there was a large dung heap covered with tarpaulin, perhaps chest high, whilst to the left of the gate, a pile of bulging sacks, presumably containing animal feed, were stacked five high.

Jackson looked round at Martlesham and raised a questioning eyebrow. Martlesham closed up on the sergeant and whispered in his ear.

"The farmyard is through there." He pointed at the gate. "You'll see the cattle sheds on the left as you go through. The cottage is directly opposite. To the right, there's nothing; just an open view up the track towards the village."

Jackson nodded and turned back towards the gateway. Unlike the others, he still brandished his own rifle, still having several clips of ammunition left for it. He advanced steadily towards the gateway now, the Lee Enfield raised in the alert position, the bayonet still fixed. Just feet away from the gate, he suddenly froze and waved a hand urgently without looking behind him. To his rear, the five Home Guardsmen halted abruptly, watching the tall sergeant keenly and trying to work out what had caused the sudden halt.

Then they heard it. Their hearts leapt in panic as the German voice shouted out something unintelligible and laughed. A heartbeat later, a soldier appeared in the gateway. Dressed in a strange blue-green smock and trousers, with a pot shaped helmet, the German paratrooper was still laughing and talking as he looked back over his shoulder into the farm yard. Looking back to his front, his face suddenly drained of colour and he stumbled to a halt, right in front of Jackson. The paratrooper's mouth fell open, either in shock or prior to shouting a warning. They never knew which it was, because at precisely that point, Jackson reverse-swung the butt of his Lee-Enfield downwards, then back up in a neat arc, so that the heavy brass butt-plate smashed into the man's jaw with horrific force.

The German never even had a chance to raise the automatic pistol that he carried in his right hand. His head snapped backwards with a distinctive and sickening crack, and then he simply collapsed, heavily, onto the floor, his arms flung wide.

"Bloody hell!" Breathed Martlesham in awe.

Jackson had already recovered the rifle and stood poised to drive his bayonet down into the German, but stopped in mid-movement as he realised that the man was already dead. After a moment, he dropped to one knee and snatched the pistol from between the dead man's lifeless fingers, watched by the stunned Home Guardsmen behind him.

Another German voice came from behind the wall; a questioning voice. A split second later, another German paratrooper appeared in the gateway. Like lightening, Jackson brought up his arm and pulled the trigger of the retrieved pistol once, twice, three times. The German staggered backwards and fell, as the heavy slugs slammed into his chest at almost point blank range. Suddenly, there was urgent shouting from behind the wall and then a rattle of machine-gun fire. Chunks of brickwork flew in all directions as the 9mm slugs cracked into the gateway from an acute angle.

"Take cover!" Jackson yelled, throwing himself towards the stack of feed bags to the left of the gateway, whilst the Home Guardsmen automatically filtered right, into the cover of the dung heap. Even as the British soldiers scattered, another burst of fire smashed into the gateway.

Jackson threw himself behind the sacks, glimpsing several figures in the farmyard beyond the gate as he moved. Without thinking, he raised the pistol and squeezed off several shots as he went past. As soon as he was safely against the wall, he turned about, leaning around the sacks with the pistol up in the aim, expecting the Germans to come piling through the gap any second. Instead, he heard the Germans shout something; a word which sounded vaguely familiar. A moment later, something heavy clanked noisily on the cobbles as it rolled through the gateway. Grenade! Again, acting purely on impulse, Jackson stepped out of cover and, like a footballer taking a penalty, swung his right foot towards the small metallic object with its wooden handle. His foot connected and the grenade lifted off the ground slightly and disappeared back through the gate. He half dived, half fell, back around the pile of sacks, just as the grenade exploded. It was a short, sharp, loud detonation, distinctly different to that of a British grenade. Above the 'crump' of the explosion, he heard an agonised scream, and a moment later, a cloud of grey-black smoke billowed through the gateway.

He heard more shouting, and more shots came through the gateway, and then two more grenades came through the gap; one landing not far away from the gate, the other bouncing well into the space between the two barns.

"Grenades!" Jackson bawled, pressing himself right into the corner where the pile of sacks abutted the wall.

Crump! Crump!

The two explosions were deafening in the gap between the barns, and the whole space was suddenly full of dense smoke. With his ears still ringing, Jackson released his grip on his Lee-Enfield, sank to his knees, then leaned out from behind the sacks, pointing his pistol towards the gateway which was obscured by the smoke.

Several bursts of machine gun fire came cracking through the gateway, and then something moved in the smoke and took on a definite form. A German appeared from the grey smoke, his machine-pistol up, his eyes squinting as he scanned for a target.

Blam! Blam! Blam! Click!

The German was thrown back by the shots, as Jackson looked down at the empty pistol in disbelief.

"Fuck!" He cursed, as a hail of automatic fire ripped into the sacks above his head, and another enemy loomed through the rapidly thinning cloud of smoke.

Dropping the pistol, Jackson rolled back behind the sacks, scrabbling for his rifle as he went. He managed to get his hands on the weapon, rolling once more so that his back was against the wall as he tried to get the long rifle into some kind of firing position.

As he braced himself for the appearance of more enemies, he realised that he was about to die. Just then, there was a sudden, violent eruption of automatic fire at the other side of his small barricade. He held his breath, waiting for at least a brace of Germans to appear, determined to take at least one of them with him. Nobody appeared. The firing stopped and the echoes died away. Then the voice came.

"Are you alright, Sergeant?"

It was Martlesham's voice.

Jackson leaned forward and peered around the sacks.

The smoke had cleared now, and there was a pile of bodies lying just at this side of the gateway. Six German paratroopers lay dead, whilst standing by the dung-pile, were four men in Home Guard uniforms, the muzzles of their captured German weapons smouldering. Harper moved forward gingerly, stepping over the dead Germans and disappeared through the gateway. Martlesham and the others began walking slowly after him, their weapons still up in the aim. One of them, Eldridge, was limping. Jackson blew out his cheeks in a deep sigh, and dragged himself to his feet, feeling slightly unsteady. His spectacles were askew, and he pushed them irritably back into position.

"Agh!" The pained voice made Jackson look back at the Home Guardsmen.

"Mister Eldridge!" Martlesham gasped, grabbing the older man's arm and steadying him. "You're bleeding!"

Jackson, walked across to them.

"Get him sat down, lad. Take a look at it. Do you know any first aid?"

Martlesham nodded as he eased the wounded Eldridge down against the wall.

"A little bit; just what I learned in the Scouts."

"Good." Jackson nodded. "Get a bandage of some kind on that leg. You two…" He turned to the remaining two private soldiers. "One of you against the end of those barns and keep an eye towards the coast, the other there by the gate. Shout out if you spot anything."

At that point, Harper came back through the gateway.

"There's two more that side." He jerked a thumb over his shoulder. "Both dead. Quite messy."

Jackson looked around at the bloody scene about his feet.

"Okay lads, well done. Fucking well done, in fact. We'll take all their ammo and water; grenades too, same as before. Then we need to get out of here."

He looked down at Eldridge and then gestured to Harper to come to one side.

"George," He said, under his breath, once they were a few yards from Eldridge and Martlesham. "I don't think we'll be able to take him with us. He's been hit in the leg and he's losing blood. He won't be able to keep up. He needs rest too, or else he'll bleed to death. We might have to leave him with the farmer, if he's still here."

Harper sucked in his cheeks, thoughtfully, looking across to where Martlesham was doing his best to strap up the wounded man's injury.

"I think it might be best if he comes with me." Said the old soldier. "I don't have far to go."

Jackson frowned at the veteran of the Great War, not understanding.

"Go with you? Go where?"

Harper didn't reply. Instead he undid the flap of the pocket on his denim fatigues and pulled out a small flat package wrapped in a handkerchief. He unfolded the cloth and pulled out a small brown envelope. He opened it and produced a piece of paper which he unfolded and handed to Jackson. Bemused, the regular soldier took the paper and stared down at it. Instantly, he saw that it was type-written on official War Office paper and realised that he was reading a formal instruction. Jackson scanned the document.

To the Officer Commanding Corporal George Stanley Harper of the Local Defence Volunteers:

This soldier is under the direct command of GHQ Home Forces and has been given specific orders. He is not permitted to discuss these orders with anyone. On presentation of this letter of authority he is to be immediately released from all duties, without question. Every assistance is to be granted him. Failure to comply with this order will result in serious disciplinary action.

Jackson glanced further down the page at the signature block.

R F ADAM GCB, DSO, OBE
Lt Gen
GOC Northern Command

The sergeant looked back up at Harper with raised eyebrows.

"Crikey, George!" He said quietly. "You've got some powerful friends, haven't you?"

Harper smiled apologetically. "Sorry Sergeant. I've got to go. I've got things to do."

Jackson nodded.

"What do you need, mate?"

Harper sighed, relieved that there was no dispute.

"Nothing really. I'll leave the Lewis Gun with you; you'll need it, providing you can find some more .303 ammunition. I wouldn't mind keeping this though." He patted the MP40 machine-pistol that he was cradling. "And one of those posh pistols that all the Jerries are carrying."

"Take them." Jackson agreed. "And plenty of ammo too. Once we've stripped this lot we'll have more than we can carry I reckon."

The Coldstreamer looked back across at Eldridge. Martlesham had managed to bind the injured leg, although there were traces of blood starting to seep through it.

"Are you sure you can manage him?"

Harper nodded.

"I'll manage it. I haven't got that far to go. We can't leave him here; not with all these dead Jerries. When their mates turn up, they'll shoot the poor bugger. I know what the bastards are like; I've fought them before."

Jackson grunted his understanding.

"You're right there, mate. Thanks for that. We'll be able to move quicker."

Harper looked up for a moment as the sound of a distant fire-fight erupted somewhere back towards the village. Looking back at Jackson, he asked, "Where will you go?"

Jackson sucked his teeth.

"Not sure." He said. "Up to the observation post initially; see if it's still there. If not, then at least we'll get a better view of what's going on across the whole front. If we can't link up with the rest of the platoon, I'll start working my way south-west, towards Driffield. There's a regular brigade down that way. They should be counter-attacking towards Brid' before long, I reckon. We'll try and link up with them."

The older man nodded.

"Makes sense." He agreed. "You'd best get going though. I reckon the Jerries will be all over this place soon enough."

"Sergeant! Sergeant Jackson!"

Jackson and Harper both looked over to where Private Dutton, a farm labourer by trade, was staring out towards the coast. The two non-commissioned officers moved quickly across to him and peered around the corner of the barn.

"What is it?" Jackson demanded of the twenty year old.

"Over there look." The young man said, pointing northwards, towards Filey town.

The town itself was largely obscured by the undulating terrain and the tree-studded hedgerows, which even this late in September were green and healthy. In the middle distance however, probably no more than a mile away, long lines of men could be seen moving across the fields and along the hedges, closing rapidly on the main Filey to Bridlington road.

"They must have got off the beach at Muston." Harper commented.

Out to sea, although the ocean and the invasion fleet were hidden from view, the constant swoop of distant aircraft and the thud of heavy naval guns told the story that the landings were still being heavily contested.

"There's more that way." Said Dutton, pointing in the opposite direction.

Jackson and Harper looked back towards Reighton and Speeton and, sure enough, the distant black figures filing across the freshly harvested fields were numerous. There were dozens of them; too many to be British, and all moving inland, climbing the slope towards the ridge on which Reighton village rested.

"Sergeant!" Came the call from the man by the gateway. "I can see Jerries over by the village; maybe a dozen or more. Looks like they're coming this way."

Jackson and Harper exchanged dark looks.

"We've probably stirred up a hornets nest with our little battle here!" Harper said.

"Aye." Jackson agreed. "And the Jerries are pouring off the beach in strength. They'll want to secure a foothold on these ridges." He gestured towards the high-ground that lay inland from the coast. "We need to get moving before they're on top of us."

"You take what you need," Said Harper, "then get off. I haven't got much of a trek so I'll soon have old Eldridge out of harm's way. I think Driffield's your best option, by the way."

Jackson looked back at the old soldier, a sombre look on his face.

"I reckon so." He replied, then held out his hand. "Good luck George, and thank you for looking after Eldridge."

Harper shook hands with the Coldstreamer and smiled. A sad smile, like one might see on a man heading for the gallows without hope of reprieve.

"And you Sergeant. Thanks for all you've done. It's been a pleasure fighting alongside the Guards again."

Jackson gave a grunt of embarrassed laughter.

"Take care of young Tom for me won't you? He's a good lad."

"I will George, don't worry. He'll be alright. I'll see to it."

The older man nodded, silently. After a while he jerked his head towards the high ground that lay west of their current location.

"Go on, then. Get off while you can."

Jackson nodded, smiled again, then turned away.

"Dutton, come on. Martlesham, on your feet. It's time to get the fuck out of here!"

NAFFERTON VILLAGE – TWO MILES EAST OF DRIFFIELD SATURDAY 21ST SEPTEMBER 0640 HOURS

The brigade was meant to be heading for the coast at best speed, in order to support the defences around Bridlington and help counter-attack any German footholds. It wasn't happening. Half the brigade was trying to counter-attack the seemingly omni-present German paratroopers who had overrun the airfield in the early hours. Another significant portion of the brigade was busy fortifying the centre of town, following several large attacks by the enemy into the built up area itself. The remainder were split to the four winds. Several platoons had been sent out on clearance-sweeps around the countryside to try and locate the enemy, but as of yet, none of them had returned. To add to the confusion, there was no contact with any of the artillery units, although it had been established that the brigade support group was still at Market Weighton and relatively safe for the moment.

Lieutenant Dickie Smithson looked at his tourist map and studied the detail of the road system around Driffield. He was happy enough with his geographical position now. They had just swung back onto the main road that led from Driffield to Bridlington, having been told to avoid the town itself at all costs. According to Smithson's commanding officer, the brigadier could only spare one battalion to head for the coast; theirs. The colonel himself was having a devil of a job trying to extricate the rifle companies from the sporadic fighting around the town, and so he had told Smithson, commanding the carrier platoon, to start rolling without delay and clear the route. In due course, the rest of the battalion would follow. Smithson was to take his platoon as far as the outskirts of Bridlington, locate the garrison commander and obtain a situation report, before establishing a rendezvous and briefing point, through which the battalion could pass. It sounded good in theory, but something was worrying Smithson. He wasn't sure what it was; he just knew that his stomach was turning over and over. The brigade's situation was pretty confusing and he didn't like it one bit.

Still, there was no point worrying. He had his orders, which were reasonably clear. He would get on with his small part in the operation and let the commanding officer worry about the technical difficulties of extracting a battalion in contact and moving it to another battlefield, with minimal transport. He took one last glance towards Driffield town, where several plumes of smoke were rising high into the grey September sky, and allowed his eyes to sweep across the fields where countless parachutes littered the countryside. The thought of that sudden, shock descent by enemy paratroopers made him shudder. They had been utterly surprised by the landings. Having spent two weeks on constant alert, the brigade had just been stood down and was looking forward to a quiet Saturday, when the enemy's elite shock troops had appeared out of the dark night sky like avenging angels of death.

Smithson had been lucky. Only three enemy paratroopers had landed in the area of his platoon's billets and they had been easily dealt with. Elsewhere however, large groups of enemy had managed to form up and launch concentrated attacks against the dispersed sub-units of the brigade. He had been told that the airfield itself was almost certainly in enemy hands now. Shoving the dark thoughts away from the forefront of his mind, he stuffed his map back into the case.

"Alright, driver." He leaned over and tapped Private Soames on the helmet with his walking stick. "Turn right here, then straight on for Bridlington. Forward."

The engine of the tiny Bren Carrier revved and, a moment later, the vehicle lurched forward and jerked uncomfortably to the right as it negotiated the junction.

The carrier was followed by six more of the small armoured vehicles. There should have been eight, but the platoon sergeant's carrier had broken down before they had even begun to move out, so it had remained where it was, leaving Sergeant Holdcroft and his two men to spread out among the other vehicles. Once he was around the corner and trundling forwards at a good steady twenty miles per hour, Smithson looked back to ensure his platoon were following. He was pleased to see they had remembered his instructions and instead of following him blindly in column, the remaining vehicles were well spread out and staggered, so that each of the carriers was using a different side of the carriageway. That was good. They were thinking tactically, which meant that their limited training had not been entirely wasted.

The training probably saved their lives. As Smithson gazed back at his small mechanised force, he noticed the commander of the third vehicle waving at him furiously. The corporal's voice was lost above the clatter of tracks, but for a moment, Smithson suspected he was trying to make some kind of comment about the route they were taking. Corporal Harris was like that. He had been with one of their sister battalions in France and never tired of playing the old soldier. He always thought he knew best. Just then, Harris' carrier veered sharply to the left and pulled in against a high hedgerow. Further back, the other vehicles also began swerving off the road.

Smithson frowned. He was about to order the driver to halt, when he heard Soames yell a sudden profanity, after which the carrier veered sharply to the right, almost taking them into a deep, water-logged ditch.

"What the hell? Soames…"

Smithson's protests stopped abruptly as a new engine noise overwhelmed that of the carrier and a large, dark shadow passed overhead. The lieutenant commanding the carrier platoon looked up in surprise and caught a glimpse of a grey aircraft undercarriage, with a gaping black hatch in the centre of its belly. He also glimpsed the unmistakable insignia of the small, symmetrical black crosses; one on either wing.

Then came the whistle.

"Get down!" Someone yelled franticly as the Junkers 88 bomber roared overhead.

Something in Smithson's head told him that now was not the time to remind everybody that he was supposed to be in charge, and he followed the wise advice, ducking down below the lip of the carrier's twelve millimetre armoured wall, just a split second before the first bomb exploded with an unbelievably deafening 'crump'.

Smithson gasped as the shock wave ripped past the carrier, causing it to rock and sway as if it were nothing more than a child's pram. He could feel the oxygen being literally dragged out of his lungs and he howled in pain as the thunder-clap of the explosion burst one of his ear-drums. The raw power of the tremor was terrifying and it felt to Smithson that the huge blast had actually taken place in his stomach, such was the sudden feeling of nausea inside him. The worst bit of it all was that he didn't suffer this terrible feeling just once. Instead, several more explosions of equal force rocked his world, leaving him feeling numb, winded, and completely shattered.

As the aircraft roared westwards, climbing rapidly, the Junkers' tail gunner couldn't resist the temptation, and a long burst of machine-gun fire raked the length of road where the British carriers stood helpless. Smithson crouched there for long moments, trembling, and then something tapped him on the helmet.

"Sir? Mr Smithson, Sir? Are you alright?"

Smithson forced himself up onto his knees and stared at Soames, his driver, who was staring back at him wide-eyed. The young man's nose was bleeding, two red trails of bloody snot running down into his mouth.

"That was a bit close, eh?" The young private commented excitedly in his harsh Teesside accent.

Typical Soames, thought Smithson, bewildered by the boyish glee in the soldier's face. The man had always been the master of under-statement within the platoon.

Private Knowles, the gunner, was also up from his cockpit.

"Crikey, Sir! Look at that!" He nodded back down the road.

Smithson turned to stare back towards the rest of the platoon.

The carrier behind him, from No.1 Section, was on its side in the middle of the road, the three crew members sitting on the tarmac, staring about them in shock. To the other side of the carrier, about fifteen yards away, a huge chunk of hedgerow was missing. In its place, there was a large smouldering crater, the earth from which was spread liberally across the road. Tentatively, his head reeling and his limbs feeling drained of all energy, Smithson clambered over the side of the carrier and onto the road. His legs felt slightly unsteady, and he remembered his walking stick was in the carrier. He looked into the rear compartment for the long, polished yew stave, which had been a present from his grandfather, but he couldn't see it. Instead, he pulled out the driver's rifle and held it by the muzzle, using it to steady himself.

Using the rifle for support, Smithson tottered back down the road towards the overturned carrier. As he did so, he saw a squat, powerful looking figure loping up the road towards him, the man's rifle at the short trail. He recognised the bulldog-like figure of his platoon sergeant instantly. They met up at the overturned carrier.

"You alright, Sir?" Sergeant Holdcroft asked, looking at his pale-faced platoon commander anxiously.

"Yes, thank you." Croaked Smithson.

He cleared his throat.

"What about you chaps?" He looked down at the three soldiers on the road.

All three of them looked how he felt; absolutely stunned. Like Soames, all of them had nose bleeds, along with what looked like flash burns to their cheeks and hands.

"I…I think we'll be alright, Sir; in a mo'…" Stammered Lance Corporal Percy, rubbing his left arm.

"Thank God those other three landed over there!" Holdcroft breathed.

Smithson followed his gaze and saw there were similar craters in the field at the opposite side of the road, the nearest about twenty five yards away.

"Is everyone else alright?" Smithson asked Holdcroft. "Down there?"

"Aye, Sir." The sergeant confirmed, then threw a glance behind him, up at the sky.

Of the German aircraft, there was no sign.

"Bloody lone raiders; they're always the ones to watch for." Holdcroft observed, shaking his head. "The RAF will be too busy chasing the big formations, you see?"

"Quite." Smithson replied distractedly, noticing that his hearing wasn't what it should be. His ears were ringing and Holdcroft's voice sounded muffled, as if he was talking through a cloth.

"Well, this one's a write-off." The sergeant continued, gazing at the overturned Bren Carrier in dismay.

Smithson looked at the vehicle and saw that the left hand side of the vehicle, which was uppermost, was badly dented, its dark gloss green paint completely stripped off, whilst large chunks of steel bomb casing were embedded in the contorted armour plate. More critically, one of the road wheels and the rear-idler were completely missing, and the track was split in two places.

"I assume we'll be carrying on, Sir? Towards Brid'?"

The young lieutenant looked at his platoon sergeant for a second, trying to order his thoughts.

"Yes…" He said at last. "I suppose. Those are the orders."

Holdcroft nodded curtly.

"Right then, Corporal Percy, get your boys spread among the other carriers. Retrieve everything you can; Bren, spare ammo, the lot. You'll have to see to those cuts and bruises on the way. Look lively now."

Lance Corporal Percy nodded phlegmatically.

"Yes, Sarge." He said, levering himself up with a grunt.

Holdcroft looked back at Smithson.

"You still okay to lead, Sir?"

"Yes.., yes I think so. I'll be fine."

Holdcroft nodded again.

"Five minutes then, eh, Sir? I'll tell the others."

Smithson turned away and began walking back towards his own carrier, glad that he had brought the rifle with him to lean on. Their orders were indeed still the same; head to Bridlington. But what they were going to find when they got there, God only knew!"

SOMEWHERE ON SPURN HEAD
SATURDAY 21ST SEPTEMBER 1940 – 0645 HOURS

Koch picked himself up and brushed the sand off his smock in irritation. This whole operation was turning into his worst nightmare. They had been forced to evacuate Spurn Point for two main reasons. Firstly, the battery of heavy guns had been effectively put out of action by the defenders before they surrendered. Thus the guns were useless when it came to keeping the British ships bottled up in the Humber Estuary. Secondly, and more pressingly, the British ships had bombarded the point heavily on their way out to sea. At first, Koch had thought that the Tommy bombardment, although fierce, would not last very long. But then, as the last of the Tommy ships had sailed past them, a fresh bombardment had begun to rain down on them.

It was only then that Koch had remembered the presence in the estuary of the two forts. Raised on steel platforms that had been sunk into natural sandbanks, the two metal islands were bristling with weaponry, and, as soon as their own ships were clear, the gunners in those forts had opened fire upon

Koch's depleted storm-group with everything they had. Lacking the guns to fire back, Koch had been forced to withdraw northwards, up the peninsula towards the neck of Spurn Head, where Witzig and the rest of the storm-group had landed. And so they had reluctantly abandoned the ruined battery that they had fought so hard to capture. Accompanied by over seventy prisoners of war, Koch and his men had moved onto the eastern side of the headland as they marched northwards, to keep themselves out of sight of the estuary forts.

After half an hour or so, they had succeeded in extracting from the danger area, and their forced march had slowed to a more leisurely pace, as side by side with their prisoners, they had watched the developing naval engagements with fascination. And that was when they were bumped by the enemy aircraft. Two ugly, ungainly little planes; Hurricanes, Koch believed was their designation. The aircraft had presumably been involved in the hectic dog-fighting over the estuary with their own ME 110's earlier and spotted a target of opportunity. Whatever their original task, the fighters had almost finished off Koch, his men, and the prisoners too. Only at the last moment did any of them spot the two low flying machines, racing up the peninsula's eastern shore-line at barely a hundred feet.

All discipline had evaporated instantaneously and every man on the beach, German and British, had gone sprinting for the cover of the gorse bushes and dunes as the first aircraft had opened fire with its eight .303 inch calibre machine guns. The burst had been a long one, raking up huge spurts of sand over a stretch of about three hundred metres, and the second aircraft had subsequently duplicated the strafe pattern of the first. Thankfully, both aircraft had pulled up immediately after their attack, and continued on their northerly course.

As Koch finished dusting himself down, the only surviving staff sergeant of the group, Schwarz, came pushing through the gorse, down onto the beach, breathing heavily.

"Fucking hell, Major! I think I want a transfer to the Tank Corps!"

"You can get in the queue behind me, Schwarz!" Koch retorted.

In his mind, he was beginning to feel like a victim of fate. Were the Gods playing some cruel game with him?

"Any casualties?"

Schwarz shook his head, pulling a tangle of prickly gorse from his sleeve as he did so.

"No Sir; none of ours anyway, but two of the Tommies got caught in that first burst. They're both dead."

Koch sighed and glanced up at the grey skies, which were just starting to show a feint sliver of blue, here and there.

"Well," He said. "there'll be even more enemy fighters about before long. That sky's starting to clear, I reckon. The Tommies must have woken up now, so it won't be long before they throw everything they've got at us."

Schwarz nodded out to sea.

"They're already having a good go, eh, Sir?"

Koch looked out across the rolling grey ocean and took another look at the sea battle that was still raging. The biggest of the Tommy ships were well out to sea now, and two of them were firing at targets on the horizon, their big guns flashing orange and growling like mythical beasts. The third of the big ships however, looked as though it had turned back towards the estuary. There was a trail of smoke coming from the vessel and it looked odd; as if the front of the ship was sloping downwards at an acute angle.

Scattered all over the surface of the ocean, were the smaller enemy ships; the destroyers. Koch's men had cheered when one of those destroyers had suddenly been rocked by explosions and started to sink. Two other enemy ships had turned sharply away from their flotilla at that point and were now circling around a patch of ocean several miles out. From the regular fountains of water that kept erupting in their wakes, Koch assumed they must be laying depth charges. Despite all of these exciting spectacles however, it was the other procession of ships that was fixing his attention more than anything else.

Coming out in a separate group behind the cruisers and destroyers, the group of seven vessels had quite literally taken a short cut around Spurn Head, coming relatively close inshore, their shallow draughts meaning they were not restricted to the deep water channel. At first, Koch had wondered what the strange collection of vessels was, but after studying them with his binoculars, it became apparent enough. Although most of them resembled civilian trawlers or small merchantmen, their flat, grey paint schemes and improvised armament showed that they had been pressed into Royal Navy service. A mixture of patrol boats and minesweepers, normally used for keeping the Humber Estuary clear of mines or marauding U-Boats, this small flotilla was the hidden threat to the landings. With the Kreigsmarine fully focussed on the enemy's capital ships and destroyers, these small craft were being fed up the coast line, making use of the shallow waters, where they could then fall on the flank of the invasion fleet at its most vulnerable point. By the look of the vessels, they were armed with little more than a hotch-potch collection of small calibre guns, cannon and machine guns; but that was all they would need against barges, Seibel ferries and the myriad small landing craft that had been pressed into service to get the invasion force ashore. Those seven ships could cause chaos once they got amongst the German landing fleet.

"If only we had something to engage these smaller ships with," Koch spat in frustration. "instead of just sitting here as targets for the Tommy air force!"

He watched the small flotilla of patrol vessels sail boldly past them, perhaps a mile out to sea at the most. They may as well have been at the other side of the German Sea for all he could do about it.

"Come on, Sir." Schwarz said gently. "We'd best get moving. We don't want to get caught on this beach again when the Tommy planes come back."

Koch nodded, feeling the sense of helplessness on his shoulders like a lead weight.

It was as he stood there, trying to find the resolve to get on with making the best of his situation, that the first gun fired.

Koch snapped is head up and glared northwards along the beach. A moment later, a fountain of water erupted not far from where the small British ships were ploughing through the coastal waters. The sound of another gun firing rolled down the beach through the morning air. Moments later, there was another splash in the sea, this one a bit too far beyond the British boats.

"Is that what I think it is?" Schwarz raised an eyebrow at his commanding officer.

Koch looked from the British flotilla back towards the northern end of the narrow peninsula where it joined the mainland, just in time to see a feint whisp of smoke rise into the air above the gorse. Boom…

The echo of the gun came to his ears a second later.

"They've done it!" Koch said, his tone almost disbelieving. "Witzig's done it! He's captured the Kilnsea Battery intact and got it into action! Thank fuck for that!"

Schwarz grinned at his commanding officer.

"He bloody-well has done, hasn't he?"

Despite his fatigue, pain and generally despondent mood, Koch laughed suddenly.

The little bastard's gone and done it alright! Let's just hope those gunners can hit something now. If nothing else, we can push those Tommy boats further out to sea where the Kreigsmarine's big ships can deal with them."

He laughed again.

"Good old Witzig! The little fucker's after another medal isn't he?"

The Major, his spirits lifting at last, slapped his staff sergeant on the arm.

"Come on Schwarz, you ugly sod, let's get moving and join up with Witzig's group. Then we can get back into this bloody battle, good and proper!"

Without another word, the two men began jogging up the dunes towards the reassembling formation of German storm-troopers and British prisoners. Off to the south-east, the big ships of the Kreigsmarine and Royal Navy continued their duel to the death.

THE CLIFF TOP – HUNMANBY GAP
SATURDAY 21ST SEPTEMBER 1940 – 0650 HOURS

"Okay Schumann, take these three to the staff sergeant for questioning. Once you've handed them over, find the company medic and get him to take a proper look at that face of yours."

Saltz was standing by the hedgerow where the three Tommy prisoners, all of them young men, knelt in the grass with their hands on their heads. Their dead comrades were strewn along the base of the hedge over a thirty metre stretch; more than a dozen of them. He looked at his wounded squad member for a moment to gauge if he had understood the order.

Schumann looked back at his squad sergeant and nodded several times, to confirm he had got the message. The private had no other way of communicating at the moment, his mouth being stuffed full of wadding from a ripped open field dressing. Bizarrely, Saltz could see the wadding through the holes in Schumann's face, even though the man's mouth was clamped tightly shut. He looked as though he was in immense pain, but in fairness to him, he had continued to fight on during the battle to clear the cliffs, despite receiving his injury early on. The sergeant jerked his head in dismissal and Schumann went across to the three Tommies where, using only hand gestures and an occasional jerk of his bayonet tipped rifle, he signalled them to get to their feet and start walking towards the cliff edge.

Saltz turned away and briefly watched Second Platoon advancing quickly towards the first low ridge that lay perhaps two hundred metres further inland. Away to his left, the Second Company was fanning out quickly at the other side of the deep gulley which the Tommies called Hunmanby Gap. The small pill-box that had been cleverly hidden in a defilade position, high up on the far side of that gulley, was now a smouldering ruin. Second Company was being reinforced by the survivors of First Company, who had landed right in front of the enemy coastal battery suffering heavily as a result. The machine-gun company was also now ashore, and one of its platoons was following on behind the other two infantry companies as they began their flank and rear assault on the coastal battery.

"Saltz!"

He turned at the sound of his name to see Captain Dullman striding across the field towards him, with none other than Lieutenant Hagen in tow. The latter was panting heavily and looking slightly shame-faced. Saltz noted that the lieutenant was draped with hundreds of rounds of ammunition for the MG34.

"Look who I found!" Dullman barked. "I'm afraid your delusions of grandeur end here Saltz. You'll have to go back to being a squad sergeant. And while we're on the subject, can you please try not to lose your platoon commander again? They're bloody expensive to train, you know?"

Saltz grinned at his platoon commander, who had gone red with embarrassment. He was a good lad, young Hagen; not bad at all, as junior officers went, but he was still wet behind the ears and easily hurt.

"Tell him what happened, Henri; go on!" Dullman nudged the young officer.

With a sigh, the blushing platoon commander told his tale in a low murmur.

"I got caught in a shell-blast halfway up the beach. It must have knocked me out for a couple of moments. When I came to, I was confused. I made my way up towards the cliffs, but ended up amongst the Third Battalion."

"Had a dizzy spell in other words!" Dullman barked again and slapped the hapless young officer on the back, making him stagger. "Still, he comes bearing gifts. Look at all this ammo he's picked up on his travels! Now that's why he's an officer Saltz; he always thinks several steps ahead of you peasants!"

"Good to have you back, Sir." Saltz commented neutrally, not wanting to prolong Hagen's embarrassment.

The lieutenant gave a wan smile of thanks.

"Anyway," Dullman went on, "while I've got you two together, you may as well pin your ears back. I've just been talking to the Major and there's a slight change of plan. We're only going to go as far as that first little ridge, and then we're going to secure it. Because the rest of the battalion got cut up quite badly, they've had to cobble First and Second Companies together for the assault onto the battery, and we don't want to get too dispersed and leave ourselves open to another, larger counter-attack."

At this point, Dullman looked down at the dead British bodies in the hedgerow and jerked his thumb in their general direction.

"This bunch held us up for nearly half an hour, and there were only twenty of them. We're going to hold a reduced perimeter along this small ridge here, on both sides of the gulley. Second Platoon will hold the right hand side, whilst you need to take your boys across the gulley and up onto their left. I've snaffled a section of machine guns for each of you; they'll be up here shortly. Third Platoon is in a bit of a state, so I'm going to keep them with me in reserve. The Second Battalion has already landed and they're shaking out at the bottom of the cliff. They're going to pass through us shortly and exploit up to the main ridge, then peel around to the left and secure the main village. After that, who knows?" He shrugged, smiling happily.

Saltz had to admire Dullman. He was a natural soldier who lived for battle. He didn't seem to know fear like other men, and despite having been through the same horror as the rest of them, he appeared to be none the worse for wear.

"Once you're in position, take a look at your organisation. If you've lost too many men, then feel free to amalgamate as you see fit. Go down to two strong squads if necessary. Happy?"

Both Saltz and Hagen nodded their understanding. As they did so, the staff sergeant's voice came drifting across the morning air.

"Captain Dullman, Sir!"

All three of them turned towards the voice. The staff sergeant was waving at them from his vantage point on the edge of the cliff.

"Get down Sir, please? They're about to blow!"

"Aha!" Dullman commented and dropped to his belly.

Following their commander's lead, Hagen and Saltz dropped to the ground alongside him.

"Blow what?" Saltz asked Dullman, but his voice was swallowed up by the sound of the enormous explosion that followed.

They felt the ground shaking first, and it trembled with such ferocity that Saltz imagined there to be a mythological beast under the ground that was raging to be out in the open air. Then came the ear-shattering thunderclap of a huge amount of explosives, detonating simultaneously. The air turned momentarily hot and an acrid smell assailed Saltz's nose.

"Ha, ha!" Dullman was laughing, his face full of glee like an excited child on his birthday. "Those engineers know how to make a big fucking bang, don't they?"

Bits of soil, grass, concrete and barbed wire thumped down onto the cliff-top around them like rain. As the hail of detritus subsided, Dullman knelt up and stared at the huge billowing black cloud that was rising from within the gulley.

"That's the way! Now we can get everyone off this beach faster and really make some progress."

From far below them, a green flare rose into the air above the level of the cliff and arced gracefully, before descending again. Moments later, another green light repeated the trail of the first, and then another. The signal was being sent to the fleet. Hunmanby Gap was open.

HEADQUARTERS 92ND INFANTRY BRIGADE – SCARBOROUGH CASTLE
SATURDAY 21ST SEPTEMBER 1940 – 0655 HOURS

Brigadier James Southerby-Sacks, commander of the 92nd (South Teesside) Infantry Brigade, glared at his battle-map from under his bushy grey eye-brows. He was unusually old for a brigade commander, but he had been brought out of retirement and mobilised to command this Territorial Brigade after the disaster in France. With the threat of invasion rife, every spare man and every spare weapon had been brought into use, and so it was that he had found himself commanding an active brigade once more.

A veteran of the first war, he had won his Distinguished Service Order on the Somme as a young lieutenant, and then won the bar for it during the infamous Ludendorf Offensive as a captain in temporary command of a company. It was his fierce, and some would say ruthless, pursuit of military efficiency that had turned this brigade from a lack-lustre, untrained rabble, into a confident, motivated, and reasonably well trained fighting formation. Southerby-Sacks, or 'Sulky-Slacks' as he was fondly known by his men, had wanted more time. He knew his men had a long way to go before they would be the highly trained masters of war that he desired them to be, but fate had decided otherwise. The time had run out and the Germans were here.

That said, he was fairly happy, even if he didn't look it. Outside, the guns of the big German warship on the horizon continued to pump shell after shell into the ruins of Scarborough Castle. He had supposed that the castle would inevitably become a target, which was why he had arranged for this solidly constructed underground bunker to be built over the summer. He had always known that if the Germans were ever foolish enough to come here whilst he was in charge of the local brigade, that he would dominate the battlefield from two main features; here, and Oliver's Mount. So far, touch wood, he was indeed dominating the battle. It was however, starting to get difficult.

He had been up-top several times to see for himself the truth of what the reports were telling him. He had seen the South Bay full of burning and sinking enemy landing craft, and the beach covered with bodies. He had watched with approval as the mortars from one of his battalions had adjusted their precious mortar bombs onto the killing area, quickly and efficiently. He had shuddered at the rush of distant memories as he witnessed his own brigade's machine guns cutting through the ranks of the enemy infantry as they fought vainly to disembark and fight their way off the beach. He had also seen the second enemy invasion flotilla pull away from its course that had originally seen it heading for the North Bay. The Germans had realised early on that the landings here had become a massacre and it was obvious that they did not intend to throw good money after bad. What he couldn't see however, was the events taking place well to south, towards Osgodby and Cayton.

But now he had the reports. The radio relay station on Oliver's Mount was still working well, despite the fact that the Germans were bombarding that position heavily too. It seemed that the Germans had achieved some success at Cayton Bay. Inwardly, he cursed himself for paying too much attention to local fishermen, who claimed that the bay was highly dangerous because of its rock ledges and submerged hazards. He was fighting against the Germans, who of course would take their time to conduct reconnaissance. That had paid off handsomely for them, and Brigadier 'Sulky' had nodded silently at the news that the Germans had approached Cayton Bay in fast boats, storming ashore in small groups, quickly outflanking and clearing the pill-boxes and trenches there. The observers on Oliver's Mount had said that the British garrison at Cayton Bay appeared to have fought to the end, but the simple fact was, the Germans were ashore and reinforcing their toe-hold quickly. So, now it was time to get pro-active. The initial phase was drawing to a close, and Sulky needed to make some decisions, and fast.

He looked up at his chief of staff.

"What are the latest reports from the South Bay? How many do we think actually got off the beach?"

The chief of staff used his cane to indicate a point halfway along the sea-front in the South Bay.

"2nd Moorlanders estimate that perhaps a platoon-plus has managed to infiltrate across the promenade. Perhaps a company-minus even? They seem to be focussing their attacks against the Great Eastern Hotel, but the company commander there insists he can hold out indefinitely. The top floors of the hotel have collapsed following the bombardment, but other than that, the position itself appears solid. There was also a report of an enemy section in this area, just at the bottom of Valley Road.

"Hmm." Sulky stroked his greying moustache. "And what about the German foothold at Cayton? What's their progress so far? Is Oliver's Mount in danger?"

The chief of staff pointed once more at the large scale map of the town and outlying villages.

"The enemy appear to be expanding to create a 'bubble' of sorts around the bay. It's really a matter of debate, what they do after that. They might sit tight and await reinforcements; the OP's say that the redirected flotilla is definitely heading for Cayton and will be there within the hour. Alternatively, they might go for the obvious choice and head straight up the spur of Oliver's Mount in order to secure a decent vantage point for themselves; bags of smoke and straight up the middle, so to speak. They could always turn south to link up with the Filey beach-head. The OPs say that there are definitely enemy ashore at Filey and that heavy fighting continues to the south. And then of course, they could ignore Oliver's Mount and start infiltrating around the flanks of it and into the town. That would cause us real problems with co-ordination, if we had numerous small groups of enemy roaming around the town."

Sulky listened to his chief of staff's appraisal in contemplative silence. At length, he took his hands away from his chin and moustache and placed them flat on the table, indicating that he had reached a decision.

"We will proceed on the assumption that Cayton Bay is thus far, their only success, and that they will seek to exploit it. To that end, we will thin out our forces in the North Bay and re-deploy them. Take the following down…"

He paused whilst the chief of staff beckoned the operations officer across. The young captain stood poised with his pencil and notebook.

Sulky set his face and began talking; his voice powerful and precise, the rhythm and pitch calm.

"The Home Guard Platoon in reserve at the railway station is to conduct a sweep down Valley Road, and then northwards towards this location, and attempt to winkle out those few enemy who have escaped from the beach in the South Bay. The Home Guard Platoon in the North Bay is to move immediately to our gun line at Hatterboard Hill and reinforce the platoon that is already there. I want our only field artillery asset well protected. I then want a full company from 1st South Teeside to move as quickly as possible from the North Bay, via the station and along the railway line, until they reach Seamer Station. They are then to counter-attack through Eastfield with the intention of securing the village and replacing the elements of 2nd South Teesside lost in the coastal defensive positions. H-Hour to be as soon as possible. The company commander of the reinforcement company is to give the signal when he is in position. The mortars on Oliver's Mount and the remainder of 2nd South Teesside are to give fire support as they attack. Ensure that all parties are clear about what's happening. Understand?"

The brigadier lifted his eyes to scrutinise the young captain, who nodded back to show that he did indeed understand the intention.

"Read it back to me, young fellow." Sulky rumbled.

The captain did as he was told. As he listened, Sulky nodded away to himself, mentally ticking off the plan in his mind as he heard it once more. When all was done, he stood and nodded at the operations officer.

"Good. Get those orders out straight away; and make sure they are transmitted in plain English, not gobbledy-gook!"

"Yes, Sir." Replied the captain, and backed away from the table.

Sulky turned back to his chief of staff.

"Is that situation report ready to go off to division yet?"

The chief of staff confirmed that it was indeed ready to send.

"Okay. Those orders I've just given; have them added onto the situation report as my future intentions. Also, put in the following recommendations for the GOC. I suggest that the division concentrates east of Pickering soonest and launches a strong divisional counter-attack through Seamer and then turning south onto Filey."

"At once, Sir." Replied the chief of staff. "Anything else at all, Sir?"

Sulky glowered at the map on the table for a few seconds.

"Yes." He said eventually, turning around and grabbing his steel helmet. "Hold the fort for a while. I'm going back up top to have another look."

DRIFFIELD TO BRIDLINGTON ROAD – BY RUSTON PARVA SATURDAY 21ST SEPTEMBER 1940 – 0700 HOURS

"Good God almighty! What now!"

Smithson threw himself flat in the bottom of the carrier as the bullets clanged into the left hand side of the vehicle, several of them ricocheting off with a loud whine. They had barely travelled more than half a mile after their earlier incident with the German bomber, and that particular near-death experience had taken place over quarter of an hour ago. Now, Smithson's carrier was being peppered with bullets from an unseen enemy.

"Ambush left!" Called out the gunner, Private Knowles.

Soames, the driver, swung the Bren Carrier to the left slightly, driving it right up to the nearby hedge and then slammed on the brakes, causing Smithson to crunch up against the front of the compartment.

"Ow! What are you doing?" Demanded Smithson from the back of the vehicle.

"Enemy left, Sir." Knowles called out. "Just trying to spot the buggers."

Another burst of fire came their way, although this time, only one of the rounds pinged off the carrier's armour plate; the others going high overhead with a vicious crack.

"Over there, Dan!" Soames was shouting above the noisy engine fan, which was inconveniently situated between him and the gunner. "In that copse! Just there look!"

"Seen!" Knowles cried out excitedly, and a second later, the Bren gun chattered into life.

It was happening again. He was supposed to be in charge, but the situation was chaotic and his simple orders were proving difficult to execute. It was as if the whole German war machine was going out to stop him from achieving his task. Yet again, he was in another life-threatening situation without a clue what was happening, whilst his men were doing their own thing. He had to do something; this was bonkers!

Forcing himself up, he peered over the lip of his compartment. Soames had driven the vehicle right up against the edge of the drainage ditch that ran alongside the hedgerow. Beyond it was a wide meadow, where the crops had been recently harvested, and in the middle of that field, perhaps two hundred yards away at the most, was a sizeable copse. Rat-tat-tat-tat-tat! The Bren Gun chattered again.

"Where are they?" Smithson shouted.

"In the copse, Sir!" Soames shouted back over the noise of the engine and the Bren Gun. "And I'm sure I saw one in the field somewhere, amongst the stubble."

Smithson squinted towards the distant clump of trees. Several bullets cracked past the vehicle, which he tried to ignore. He was rewarded by the sight of a small, barely noticeable whisp of smoke, which rose out of the stubble just off to the left of the copse as he looked at it.

"Seen him! I've seen him!" He cried in what he suddenly realised sounded like a very childish voice.

Trying to fight down his sense of awkwardness and confusion, Smithson decided that he needed to do something that would not just look the part, but make him feel like he was in control of the situation.

He looked down and saw Soames' rifle on the floor of the compartment. He grabbed it, and saw that it wasn't cocked, so he opened the bolt and was surprised to see that the magazine was full of rounds. Soames must have loaded the magazine separately without feeding them in through the top slide. Smithson rammed the bolt shut and locked it down, then slid the rifle over the front of the compartment and took aim on the approximate spot where he had seen the enemy soldier. It was a long while since he had used a rifle back at Sandhurst, but he remembered the sighting system well enough and took careful aim. Bang! He squeezed off the first shot.

"Ah! Fucking hell, Sir!"

Smithson looked down in surprise and realised that Soames' head was just inches below the muzzle of his rifle.

"Sorry, Soames." Smithson apologised. "Keep your head down."

"Magazine!" Knowles shouted suddenly, and began going through the drill of changing his empty magazine for a full one.

Smithson took this as his chance to get properly involved and took aim again.

Bang! This time he fired into the copse.

"Soames! Refill that empty magazine for Knowles!"

Bang!

"Pass us the bandolier, Sir!"

Smithson reached down and grabbed the small set of canvas pouches and slung them over the lip of his compartment and into the driver's cab. As he did so, Knowles threw his empty magazine across the top of the engine fan and into Soames' lap. Bang! Smithson fired into the copse once more, worked the bolt, then fired again.

"Back in!" Roared Knowles.

Rat-tat-tat-tat-tat! His Bren Gun opened fire again.

"Sir!"

Smithson didn't register the voice at first. His adrenalin was just starting to kick in and he was enjoying himself enormously with the rifle.

"Sir!" The voice came again. "For fuck's sake! Mr Smithson, Sir!"

The mention of his name suddenly registered with Smithson. He looked around in surprise and saw that the rest of the platoon's carriers had also pulled in against the hedgerow, where they too had begun to engage the enemy. More pressingly, Sergeant Holdcroft was crouching behind Smithson's carrier and shouting at him over the noise of the gunfire.

"For Christ's sake, Sir! Stop fucking about with that rifle and come here, will you?"

Holdcroft's typically no-nonsense manner immediately brought Smithson back down to earth. Still holding onto the rifle, he slid along the compartment and clambered over the back of the vehicle. He dropped onto the tarmac next to Holdcroft who was crouching below the lip of the carrier's hull.

"Right, Sir." Holdcroft began, getting straight down to business. "What do you reckon we've got? So far I've seen a couple in the copse and at least three amongst that stubble. Don't think there's much more than a section of them, but they've got themselves a decent machine-gun. I've got one of the carriers watching the other side of the road, just in case there's some over by that farm."

Smithson nodded.

"Yes…I think that sounds about right. We should be able to take them on I reckon, don't you think?"

"We can certainly give 'em a good seeing to alright. But it's a case of how long do we want to chase a bunch of parachutists around a field for? If our main mission is to get to Bridlington, we could just drive right on through. Doesn't look like they've got anything that'll take out the carriers; some grenades perhaps? As long as we don't get too close, we should be okay."

Smithson thought on the sergeant's words for a moment. Holdcroft was thinking logically, sensibly, just as Smithson should be. The young lieutenant rubbed his face, scratching at his morning stubble as he forced himself to think straight. He was sweating already and glad for the slight breeze.

"I agree." Smithson said. "We can't waste too much time here. But we shouldn't just leave them to shoot up anything that goes past. There'll be buses full of infantry coming along here in due course. That machine-gun of theirs will cause chaos against a packed bus or lorry."

Holdcroft nodded, seeing the danger in by-passing the group of enemy.

"I can take Two Section around the flank if you want; round to the left there? There's a track we can follow and then turn into the field. They'll have to split their fire if we do that. We can come across the field and beat them out like pheasants. You can stay here with One Section and pick them off as they pull back."

Smithson returned the nod.

"Yes. That makes sense. Let's do it."

Just as he spoke, there was a loud 'crump' behind them, about forty yards back down the road. The two British commanders ducked instinctively as shards of red hot shrapnel and lumps of tarmac cut through the air around.

As the noise faded, Holdcroft turned and looked towards the seat of the explosion. There was a cloud of grey smoke by the verge, right by the carrier that was covering the other flank.

"Where the fuck did that come from?" He swore.

A moment later, he heard a panic-stricken voice.

"Sarge! Sarge! We've got casualties! The driver of the carrier appeared out of his cockpit, crouching low as he slid over the side.

"Where did that grenade come from?" Holdcroft bellowed down the road, fearing a flank attack from a separate group of enemy.

"It was a mortar!" Came a voice from somewhere amongst the other vehicles. "I saw it fire from the front edge of the copse!"

"Oh, bloody marvellous!" Holdcroft looked back at Smithson and rolled his eyes. "We need to wrap this up quickly, or else they'll take us to pieces! I'll see to those casualties, Sir; you get Two Section moving!"

Smithson's mind began racing.

"Okay, but…"

His voice tailed off. Holdcroft was already on his feet and doubling back down towards the area of the blast at a low crouch. The young lieutenant took a deep breath and forced himself to stay calm. This was it. He was in command now and he needed to deal with this situation, and sharpish. It was time to earn his officer's pay. He reached over into the back of his carrier, ignoring the crack of enemy bullets as they raced past, and grabbed a second bandolier of rifle ammunition which he slipped over his shoulder. And it was as he did so that he saw the jerry-can of petrol…

FIRE CONTROL TOWER – KREIGSMARINE SHIP ADMIRAL SCHEER
SATURDAY 21ST SEPTEMBER 1940 – 0710 HOURS

"Good shooting!" The gunnery officer called as he saw the foredeck of the second British destroyer erupt, in a series of bright, orange explosions.

The first British destroyer had got to within just two miles of them before she had finally heeled over and begun to sink, her entire superstructure an inferno of flame and smoke. This second destroyer had come on in similar style, until it too had been riddled with fire from the Scheer's secondary armament. The Tommy destroyer had slowed considerably and, with the latest salvo, come to a virtual standstill, almost exactly in line with her sister ship. Neither of the two destroyers had managed to inflict any damage on the Scheer, either from their small guns or with torpedoes. Somewhere in the back of his mind, the gunnery officer was feeling a mixture of pity and admiration for the British sailors who had sacrificed themselves so willingly in such a hopeless attack.

He kept those thoughts well to the back of his mind however, because two of the enemy cruisers were still in action, despite the third having withdrawn from the firing line. Both of the remaining British cruisers had suffered multiple hits but most of their guns remained intact and continued to fire back at the German ships. Moreover, the Tommy fire was surprisingly accurate and the Scheer had already taken several hits herself, losing another secondary gun turret and suffering two punctures to the hull. So far, the damage was manageable, but the Tommies were still going at it hammer and tong. The Hipper too, just a couple of miles north of them, had taken two hits from its British opponent.

With this sudden, suicidal diversion by the British destroyers nearly dealt with, it wouldn't be long before the Scheer could turn every gun on the enemy cruiser and finish this business. Thankfully, there had been no more air attacks to complicate matters, and the Captain was eager to deal with the British cruisers before the Royal Air Force returned in greater strength.

"Now keep your eyes peeled for that third destroyer." He warned the assistant gunnery officer. She's well behind the other two, and trailing smoke. I think she's already damaged but it's hard to tell."

The two men looked across the waves at the bank of thick smoke that was pouring from the two stricken destroyers. It was effectively acting as a smoke screen, hiding the third, slower destroyer from their view.

"Get every one of your guns to lay onto the gap between those two burning wrecks so that when the other ship appears, we can give her everything we've got in an instant."

The junior lieutenant snapped an acknowledgement and relayed the instructions to the fire control room.

As he did so, the by-now familiar noise of the incoming British shells came clearly to the two Kreigsmarine officers.

"Those are going over by the sound of them." The gunnery officer said, looking up. His face betrayed that the words were spoken more in hope, than in certainty. A moment later, six huge columns of water erupted a quarter of a mile to the starboard side of the Scheer, and the gunnery officer heaved a sigh of relief.

"One and Two Batteries ready." Came the voice from fire control.

"Fire." The senior lieutenant responded automatically.

A few heartbeats later, the big eleven inch guns roared once more and spat their huge shells towards the British cruiser, rocking the ship as they did so.

The gunnery officer raised his binoculars and watched the distant target. The long seconds seemed interminable, but then he saw the tell-tale splashes in front of the enemy ship, and a bright flash against its grey silhouette.

"One hit!" He cried in delight. "Against the superstructure."

Quickly, he informed the fire control room to reload the main batteries and repeat the broadside using the same data. It was just then that his companion in the fire control tower let out a yelp like a puppy-dog. The gunnery officer looked sideways at the other man in surprise, and saw that he was staring towards the burning destroyers with a look of shock. Before the gunnery officer was able to question his assistant, the younger man grabbed hold of the communication tube and yelled into it.

"Torpedoes! Half-left!"

The lieutenant's shout made his companion flick a horrified gaze towards the two sinking enemy destroyers. For a moment he didn't understand what he was looking at, but then the realisation hit him. The third enemy destroyer had chugged right up towards them using the smoke from the doomed ships as cover, and then launched two torpedoes blindly from behind the artificial smog. Now he saw the two feint trails, straight as arrows, coming towards them through the grey sea. The Captain must have already spotted the two deadly water-borne missiles because the Scheer was turning sharply, trying to bring its stern around and present a narrower target.

The two officers stared with open-mouthed anticipation as their view of the battle changed with the alteration of course.

"One and Two Batteries ready. Confirm no change to gunnery data?" The voice came up from the fire control room.

"Wait!" Snapped the gunnery officer down the tube, realising that he would have to revise the bearings once more.

The two silver trails in the water were so close now that the two officers had to lean over the balcony of the fire control tower to follow their path.

"Oh, my God!" Breathed the assistant gunnery officer. "I think they're going to hit us!"

There was nothing they could do other than watch. The furthest of the two torpedoes raced past them in the water below, appearing to be almost parallel to the ship, and they saw that it would indeed go clean past the bow of the Scheer, but as they searched for the second torpedo, the ship suddenly lurched, and a split second later, the sound of the detonation came to them, as a huge plume of water erupted against the forward, port side of the bow. The two men staggered under the impact and grabbed hold of the balcony rail to steady themselves.

"The bastard's hit us!" Yelled the junior lieutenant.

"It was only one," The gunnery officer reassured his companion, "and only a glancing blow. We'll be alright. The old Scheer's a tough one. Now bring all the guns round astern and find that third destroyer! We don't want any more torpedoes up our arse!"

They both threw themselves towards the rear of the tower and looked back towards the sinking destroyers which were half-way under now. To their surprise, the third enemy destroyer had pulled away from the gap between the other two and swung around them, emerging through the left hand side of the bank of smoke. Now however, she was turning straight on to the Scheer's stern and dipping her bow as she picked up speed. There was a small flash from the front of the destroyer as her two forward guns opened fire. The gunnery officer ducked as the pair of four inch shells slammed into the stern deck of the Scheer. Small but lethal pieces of razor sharp steel flew overhead and many more slammed into the wall of the fire control tower with angry metallic clangs, as the two officers sheltered behind it.

They both raised their heads and saw that some of the secondary armament on both sides of the Scheer was swinging round onto the defiant enemy destroyer that was now closing on their stern at a worrying rate. Many of the anti-aircraft batteries were already engaging the Tommy ship of their own accord, and the small vessel was taking a constant hail of fire, little red tracer rounds bouncing off her superstructure in all directions. The Scheer was starting to turn again, in an attempt to come side on to the destroyer, and at first, the senior of the two gunnery officer's couldn't understand why. But then, with a growing sense of disbelief, he realised what the Captain of the Scheer already understood.

The gunnery officer looked down at the tiny destroyer ploughing stolidly towards them through the hail of incoming fire, and he shook his head in admiration for the enemy captain.

"Oh, my good God!" He exclaimed, remembering the story of the Admiral Hipper's experience in Norway at the hands of HMS Glowworm.

"She's going to ram us!"

'S' DAY
H +3

CABINET WAR ROOMS – STOREY'S GATE, LONDON
SATURDAY 21ST SEPTEMBER 1940 – 0830 HOURS

The Chiefs of Staff conference room had been transformed. The sprawling maps of the various continents had been covered over using army issue bed-sheets, and those in turn had been overlaid with several large scale maps of Britain and the northern coastline of Europe. There were several maps of even larger scale showing the Yorkshire and North-East Midlands, and all of these maps had been marked over the last couple of hours to show airfields and military headquarters, with the various units marked by coloured pin-flags.

Around the table sat the three Chiefs of Staff, Brooke, the Head of Military Intelligence and several note-takers. A young woman from the Auxiliary Territorial Service stood ready by the maps, ready to move any of the unit flags if required. Surprisingly, the room was extremely quiet, with no one talking. Most of those present were lost in their own thoughts, staring broodingly at the maps before them. Brooke, however, flicked through his notes, busily making small manuscript amendments in pencil as he went. It was onto this subdued stage that Churchill stepped, just a little after the half-hour.

The military men stood briefly, in respect for the Prime Minister's appointment, then took their seats again after he had taken his own place at the head of the table. For a couple of moments he fumbled for his spectacles, then, having placed them on, he looked around the table at the assembly, his face sombre.

"Well, gentlemen," He began in his deep voice. "the people of Britain now know of the hideous spectre that presents itself before us, this autumn morning. They will, I am sure, rise to the challenge in every way asked of them. But now, let us discuss the exact nature of our peril, shall we?"

He sat back and looked at the First Sea Lord. Pound stood and moved around the table to the map. He took the proffered pointer from the ATS girl and turned to face his audience.

"The naval situation is as follows. There has been no major change to the situation in the Channel, although the re-assembled enemy transport fleet off Calais has begun moving north, along the coast of Europe. The Tyne destroyer flotilla has broken out into the North Sea, but at a cost. Three destroyers have been lost upon exiting the mouth of the Tyne. Two were sunk my mines early on. It seems that the Germans mined the area heavily during last night's raids. A third destroyer was sunk by a U-Boat shortly after reaching open water. Despite this, we now have eight destroyers at sea, north of the enemy landings. This force has been ordered to mount a two pronged attack on the northern flank of the landings. Half of the force will turn due south and attack down the coastal strip, whilst the remainder will conduct a wide sweep east and then south west to hit the invasion force from behind. They have been instructed to avoid engagements with enemy capital ships and conduct hit and run attacks against enemy transports and small fighting ships."

The First Sea Lord paused to give Churchill time to digest the information, but Churchill nodded his understanding and gave a flick of his fingers, indicating that Pound should continue.

"The Humber force has had a rough time of it. As the joint force of cruisers and destroyers broke out, they lost a destroyer to a U-Boat strike and one of the cruisers has lost a large portion of her bow to a mine. The cruiser has limped back into Immingham, as she was taking on lots of water. At about the same time, two large enemy warships were identified some fifteen miles out to sea. At 0620 hours, our cruisers engaged the enemy ships, which have since been identified as the pocket-battleships Admiral Hipper and Admiral Scheer. During the ensuing battle, both of our remaining cruisers were damaged by enemy gunfire and a further three destroyers were lost."

He paused again, seeing the look of alarm in Churchill's face and noting the raised eyebrows around the table.

"However," Pound went on quickly. "There is good news. One of the destroyers was lost whilst conducting a torpedo run against the Scheer, achieving one hit in the process. Following this, the destroyer then rammed the Scheer in its stern, after which the destroyer sank. Both the Hipper and Scheer have received multiple hits from our cruisers, and a squadron of passing Fairey Battles kindly dive-bombed both enemy ships, achieving at least one hit."

He saw Churchill's face brighten slightly, a look of anticipation creeping across his features.

"Unfortunately, neither of the German ships was damaged seriously enough to sink them…"

The Prime Minister's face dropped again.

"But," Pound hurried on, "we have received a report that the two enemy ships have disengaged and fallen back on the main invasion fleet. As a result, we now have two cruisers at large in the North Sea. The remaining destroyers managed to locate and destroy the U-Boat that I mentioned earlier. Those two destroyers have now joined a force of around half a dozen minesweepers and armed trawlers that are, as we speak, attacking the invasion fleet from the south along the coastal strip. This group of ships was bombarded by the Kilnsea battery at Spurn Head as it passed by, resulting in the loss of one mine sweeper and some damage to the destroyer, HMS Venomous. We must therefore assume that the enemy has full control of the Kilnsea battery, and I would recommend either a dismounted attack to recapture it, or a heavy bombing raid against it. As for the two cruisers, they are now executing anti-submarine manoeuvres in the open sea, with the plan of linking up with the Harwich flotilla just before last light. They will then attack the German invasion fleet from the south-east during the hours of darkness."

"Well, that's something at least." Churchill mumbled. "We have paid a heavy price to get our ships out of port, have we not?"

"We have indeed Prime Minister." Agreed Pound, which is precisely why I have opted for a more deliberate operation to get the Home Fleet out of Scapa Flow."

Churchill understood that the First Sea Lord was politely saying 'I told you so!' and with that in mind, he changed the subject.

"What news of the Harwich flotilla?"

"They are clear of air attacks now, Sir, though they were under constant attack for over two hours and lost another ship. However, they are picking up the monitor HMS Erebus on their move north. We estimate that they will RV with the Humber cruisers around dusk tonight."

"Erebus?" Churchill raised an eyebrow. "She's an old ship isn't she?"

"Yes, Sir. She is of little use in action against modern ships, but her big guns will be useful in bombarding the landing beaches."

Churchill nodded, silently.

"Other than that Prime Minister, we are in the process of deploying. The Furious Group will be in position to help the Home Fleet break out just before first light tomorrow, whilst the first of our submarines will be off Kiel tonight. I will give you the results of the Tyne flotilla's attacks as soon as I have them, Sir."

Churchill's bottom lip jutted out, even more than it was prone to.

"Well, it's a start." He rumbled. "But I will be happier when we have the first German capital ship at the bottom of the North Sea!"

Pound ignored the Prime Minister's waspish comment and offered his pointer to Newall.

"The Chief of the Air Staff will now brief you on the air situation, Sir." Pound said flatly.

Newall came round the desk and spent a couple of moments gathering his thoughts. He began by laying his pointer against the Kent coastline.

"No.11 Group is refuelled, rearmed and once more covering the south coast. The concentrated Stuka attacks against the Harwich flotilla, although costly for the Navy, were also costly for the Luftwaffe. No.12 Group are claiming 17 kills from this engagement alone. There have also been Stuka attacks against our radar chain, which No.12 Group has also been dealing with. There was more attrition against the enemy on these occasions too, although we have suffered some losses ourselves, as these attacks came with heavy fighter escorts. There have also been wide-ranging enemy fighter sweeps against ground targets across the South of England over the last couple of hours."

Newall turned away from the map and looked the Prime Minister in the eye.

"It is my firm opinion now, that the enemy operation in the south is indeed a feint, with the sole intention of drawing off as much of our combat power as possible away from the north. To that end, I have ordered three squadrons of fighters to be transferred from No.11 to No.13 Group. I have also ordered a fourth squadron to move from No.11 Group to No.12 Group. Having spoken with Dowding at length, we have decided upon the following course of action. No.11 Group will cover everything from Northampton southwards and concentrate solely on large bomber formations. No.12 Group will still engage enemy aircraft as far north as the Humber and protect the industrial midlands, but more importantly, they will be used to intercept the enemy formations cutting across from Holland and Belgium, towards Yorkshire. I suspect that the enemy is trying to establish an 'air-bridge', for want of a better term, and so No.12 Group will concentrate on interdicting this. Accordingly, we are moving every available night-fighter squadron into No.12 Group as soon as we can."

Newall paused to see if there were questions, but there were none.

"As for No.13 Group?" He continued. "They will obviously become the key players in all this. They will also receive more squadrons from Coastal Command and No.10 Group. Their sole task is to intercept the air-bridges coming straight from Germany and Scandinavia, although we will detach two squadrons to the Air Striking Force that is working with Northern Command. As for the bomber groups, No.1 and No.2 Groups will now be employed to conduct strategic bombing against enemy ports and airfields in Europe, whilst No.3 and No.4 Groups will be employed in concentrated raids against the enemy beach-head and invasion fleet. No.5 Group will remain in reserve and be used to plug gaps in capability or to maintain the momentum when squadrons need to rest their crews."

He took a deep breath.

"As for the present? Well, No.4 Group is slowly getting itself sorted following the chaos at Driffield. We know that the airfield *has* indeed fallen, and four Whitleys have arrived at Leeming after making a swift departure from Driffield when the attack began. It is my intention to bomb Driffield this evening, once the situation is clearer. Orders have been given to evacuate Leconfield and crater the runway. As far as enemy intentions are concerned, we have a real mixture of enemy activity at the moment in this area. There are squadrons of enemy twin-engined long range fighters, apparently working in relay, circling over the invasion beaches and making the odd strafing run against opportunity targets. Even these long range fighters will have a limited time over the coast and so I suspect that the enemy may not be able to keep this level of cover up for long. There are several massed formations of bombers heading for the coast, and we've also had a significant number of lone-raiders coming in low across the North Sea and trying to interdict targets across Yorkshire, especially in depth of the landing zones. All in all, it seems that the enemy is trying to over-face us by conducting a wide range of operations simultaneously."

Churchill stirred at last.

"And is it working?"

"We are struggling to cope Prime Minister." Newall admitted. "But as our squadrons are redeployed, we will be able to deal with the enemy's incursions with increasing effectiveness, whilst *he* will start to suffer from fatigue. His crews are flying long missions, and suffering every time they get to their targets. It is simply a case of how long can the Germans sustain their efforts under such pressure. If we accept that the South of England must become the poor relation in fighter cover, then I believe we will be able to hold our own."

Churchill grimaced.

"Then suffer the South of England must!"

Newall nodded in agreement. He accepted Churchill's terse comment as a blessing on his strategy.

"Finally, we have already had squadrons in action against the landing grounds, although admittedly, without co-ordination. Most of these squadrons were the light and medium bomber units who were quick to respond, along with the local fighter squadrons, mainly from Church Fenton, Leconfield and Catterick. The next wave of attacks against the enemy invasion fleet will be a high level raid at around midday by No.3 Group, with fighter cover from No.13 Group. Whilst that happens, the Air-Striking Group will be put together and briefed."

He looked across at Brooke for acknowledgement and was rewarded with a smile and a nod. Newall went on.

"The temporary AOC of the Group is now at HQ Northern Command. All squadrons in the group have been ordered to work directly to him for mission-tasking until further notice. They will be ready for initial strikes, we estimate, by about 1130 hours today. Any questions, gentlemen?"

Newall laid the pointer across the table as he waited for a response. It came from Churchill.

"You sound fairly confident, Chief Air?"

Newall grimaced.

"At the moment, Sir, despite initial confusion, I think we can hold our own and, God willing, gain an advantage over the next 48 hours. The only thing that worries me is whether the Germans somehow manage to get aircraft onto British soil. If they can get fighters onto a captured airfield, along with the fuel and ammunition to replenish them, then we could be in trouble."

Churchill nodded.

"And the picture from the air? What do we think is happening? There have been several mentions of a 'beach-head' already."

Newall looked across at the two senior officers in Army uniform.

"I think perhaps you may wish to explain that, gentlemen?"

Dill nodded acceptance and relieved Newall of his place by the map.

"According to the latest reports, which we have drawn from all three services, this is how the situation looks at the moment, Prime Minister."

Dill lifted the pointer and jabbed it at the map.

"Spurn Head is in German hands, captured in the early hours by glider-borne troops. They have destroyed Green Battery on the point, and captured the Kilnsea Battery here, the guns of which they have turned on our own ships. German paratroopers have captured RAF Driffield, although the town has not yet fallen. The enemy has attempted to land in three distinct areas. Firstly, they have landed here at Scarborough. Reports state that the enemy have suffered heavy casualties attempting a seaborne assault against the town itself, however, a smaller landing just a couple of miles to the south has been successful and they are trying to attack northwards to capture the town from the landward approach. Fortunately, the local brigade is in a strong position, so at the moment, we appear to be containing this particular beach-head. Reserves are moving to the area now, as the C in C will mention shortly.

However, it seems that the Germans have successfully landed here in Filey Bay, and here in Bridlington Bay. Communications with both garrisons have been lost and friendly aircraft report large scale troop landings across a broad front of some fifteen miles. The landings run from Filey Brigg, here, right through Flamborough Head, and down through Bridlington to the area of Skipsea."

Dill looked up and saw that Churchill was staring at the map, a deep frown on his face.

"I will now ask the C in C Home Forces to go through the fine detail with you, as he has just spoken to General Adam at Northern Command."

Dill looked at his subordinate and friend.

"Allan? All yours…"

Brooke pushed back his chair, gathered his notes and walked round to take his position by the map. Turning to face his audience, he pushed his spectacles a little further up his nose, and began.

"Firstly, the Scarborough situation. It seems that the enemy has attempted to take the town and the port by storm, without any kind of action in depth from parachutists. General Adam is in touch with the brigade commander there, and what is clear is that the enemy has been repulsed from the sea front of the town with heavy losses. As you have heard, they have managed to get a foothold just to the south, here in Cayton Bay. It seems that the enemy is now pushing his second and third waves through this small beach head and doing several things. Firstly, he is trying to link up with the Filey landings, which he is almost certain to do without interference. Secondly, he is pushing west towards the east-coast railway; presumably to establish a firm defensive perimeter. At the same time, he is mounting attacks against a high feature to the south of the town. It is clear that the enemy is keen to get Scarborough, for whatever reason; possibly the harbour, possibly its geographical position at the foot of the Yorkshire Moors. The local brigade has launched a counter attack and at the moment, has managed to contain the enemy on the eastern side of the railway line. Adam has ordered the remainder of 59th Infantry Division to close up on the town from the west in order to contain the beach-head. They'll leave a battalion at Malton, in order to block any German rush for York down this natural defile. Initially, this particular area appears most ripe for a successful counter-attack."

Churchill unexpectedly thumped the table in front of him.

"Exactly! That's what we need! Throw the invader back into the sea!"

Brooke raised one eyebrow at the Prime Minister's little outburst before continuing.

"We must however, not get blinded by our success here," he warned, "as the main battle is really being fought down here at either side of Flamborough Head. We are fairly sure now that the Germans are well ashore from Filey down to Bridlington. To be honest, that is no surprise. We always knew our coastal defences were nothing more than a thin crust and that the real battle would be fought inland. What we are now seeking to do then, is rationalise the battlefield, and, rather than let the enemy shape it to his own design, shape it to our own."

He looked at the Prime Minister briefly and saw his nostrils flare impatiently. Churchill was a man who loved action and loathed hesitation.

"So to that end," Brooke went on, "I have spoken with Adam and agreed the following. It will take at least twenty four hours to get our reserves anywhere near in position to launch a decisive counter-attack. Our forces currently engaged, the best part of two infantry divisions, must do what they can until then. With the exception of the Scarborough sector, which is holding together nicely so far, we must assume that anything east of Driffield is lost to us from a command point of view. Any unit between Driffield and the coast is already in contact with the enemy and they will either hold them, or be over-run; fact."

Brooke paused and looked up to see if there would be any challenge to his logic, but all he saw was a sea of expectant faces.

"We must leave these forces to do their best, whilst we move troops up to contain the battlefield. Once it is contained, we can then shape it, as we start to get an idea of the enemy's intentions. Bearing in mind that York lies only forty miles from the coast, and that many of our reserves are twice that distance away, we are essentially engaged in a race to the River Ouse. Therefore, in addition to 59th Infantry Division closing up on Scarborough and the foot of the Yorkshire Moors, the Catterick Garrison and 24th Army Tank Brigade will move to close the gap between Malton and York, with the 24th Tank Brigade being prepared to support a major counter-attack against the Scarborough sector if required. Much of the 2nd Infantry Division is already engaged. One of its brigades is already in the thick of it along the Filey and Bridlington sectors and around Driffield. Another is currently in the Beverley area. That brigade has a battalion trying to deal with the incursion on Spurn Head, another protecting Leconfield, and another, we believe, trying to counter-attack towards Skipsea. That brigade is being ordered to pull back and concentrate around Beverley and Leconfield. Once the airfield has been put out of action and we have got an idea of the enemy's intent, we can manoeuvre that brigade as required. If need be, it will form a brigade sized anti-tank island around Beverley, or it may even fall back on Hull to protect it as required."

Brooke paused once more and consulted his notes. He studied them for a moment, then moved his pointer again, moving further inland.

"What remains of 2nd Infantry Division will fall back on York and defend it. Meanwhile, the 44th Infantry Division will move up from the East Midlands and secure the Ouse between York and Goole. At the same time, 1st Infantry Division will close up on the south bank of the Humber to guard against an incursion there. In order to support this containment line, the 37th Infantry Brigade is being moved up to reinforce 2nd Infantry Division from Norfolk, and a whole collection of machine-gun and anti-tank units are being stripped out of divisions and brigades in the west and sent across to bolster the containment divisions. The final, and slightly controversial move in securing the area, is the mobilisation of Home Guard units outside their normal areas. I have authorised Adam to concentrate them where we are establishing nodal-points, or anti-tank islands; call them what you will. These will give depth to the containment line."

He took a deep breath after his lengthy explanation of troop movements. Churchill used the opportunity to interrupt.

"So, we are going to rush our troops to Yorkshire and then...dig in? Rather than attack?"

Brooke shot the Prime Minister a schoolmaster-like glare.

"No, Sir. We are going to rush our infantry and anti-tank forces to Yorkshire in order to contain the battlefield and start shaping it. Whilst that is happening, we will be concentrating our most powerful formations ready for a properly executed counter-attack. Very much like the Home Fleet, we cannot afford to sacrifice our most powerful assets in dribs and drabs. We have a chance here to fight the Germans on our terms and we must not waste the opportunity."

"But I thought you were in favour of immediate counter-attack?" Churchill challenged him, remembering their conversation several months ago at the time of Ironside's retirement.

"I am in favour of rapid counter-attack at the critical point, at the critical time and with critical mass." Brooke replied firmly. "Thus, whilst we seal the Germans into this pocket of ground between the Humber, the Ouse and the Yorkshire Moors, we will be moving our strategic reserves into position for an overwhelming counter-stroke. My intention is to field at least two corps, if not three, to operate together under a single commander."

He looked down at his notes momentarily, having thus dismissed Churchill's challenge.

"Seventh Corps is moving as we speak, via Birmingham, Manchester and Leeds, to rendezvous at Wetherby, near York. As a reminder, this corps currently comprises 1st Armoured Division, 1st Canadian Division, elements of 2nd Canadian Division, with the deficit made up by the New Zealand Brigade and the Australian Brigade. I am also bringing Fourth Corps together with a few amendments to their order of battle. They will concentrate at Selby, with 2nd Armoured Division moving via Nottingham and Sheffield"

He looked up, and scanned the faces in the room. Their attention was complete, and Brooke got the feeling that these senior men were finally starting to accept him and more importantly, accept his intellect.

"My final bit of reorganisation, is to put together a large, powerful division, to act in concert with the two main corps from the strategic reserve. My intention, if there is time and sufficient space and resource, is to develop this into a full corps, but for now it will remain as a Divisional Group. It will consist of 21st and 23rd Army Tank Brigades and the 20th and 24th Guards Brigades. For want of a suitable number, and due to lack of time to worry about such niceties, I will simply call this formation, the Guards Armoured Division. It will concentrate just north of York at Strensall Garrison. It will receive all of the Divisional Support Troops from 35th Infantry Division, currently located in Cheshire."

From the corner of his eye, Brooke saw Churchill's mouth curl upwards slightly.

"Guards Armoured Division, eh?" Murmured Churchill. "I rather like the sound of that."

"My intention," Brooke continued, is to get the Fourth Corps into position by first light tomorrow, should the enemy make a mad dash for the Ouse or the Humber. If need be, elements of this Corps will act as a delaying force whilst I await the arrival of Seventh Corps. I estimate that Seventh Corps will be largely complete by last light tomorrow and ready for *planned* offensive operations in exactly two days from now. Our ideal solution is to launch these two corps at the enemy simultaneously. I would also like to hold them back until I have assembled the Guards Armoured Division, but that may be too much to hope for."

Brooke placed the pointer on the table along with his notes.

"Are there any questions, gentlemen?"

There was silence in the room. Even Churchill, desperate to be at the Germans' throats, managed to hold back any impulsive comments that might have been on the tip of his tongue. Reassured by the absence of criticism, Brooke decided to seal his proposed plan in concrete.

"I appreciate that for everybody this will be a long and frustrating forty eight hours whilst we balance ourselves for a counter-stroke, however, we must not allow ourselves to be rushed into making any costly mistakes. On this occasion, we are fighting on home ground. There is nowhere to run to and, in my opinion, the Germans may well have unwittingly created a strategic trap for themselves. It is up to us to exploit the situation fully, in order to inflict upon them a crushing defeat that will demonstrate to the rest of the world that Britain has what it takes to defeat Hitler, with or without allies."

A polite cough interrupted Brooke's hard-sell of his plan. He turned towards the door and saw that a tall, elegant and bespectacled civilian had entered the room, clutching what appeared to be a telegram. Brooke instantly recognised Brendan Bracken, Churchill's Private Secretary and the most faithful of his followers.

"My apologies, Prime Minister," Bracken murmured, "but we have just received a message from President Roosevelt via their Embassy. I thought you would want to see it straight away."

Churchill beckoned his Private Secretary across with a quick hand gesture. Brooke stepped aside to let the civil servant past. Churchill took the telegram and slumped back in his chair studying the document with a characteristic pout. He scanned the telegram several times in silence, before grunting and looking over the top of his spectacles at the assembled military and naval men.

"President Roosevelt has received word that the Germans have landed in force on British soil. He says that German sources are claiming that panzer divisions are already running riot across large portions of the country and that the defeat of Britain is inevitable. Those same sources are asking him to put pressure on us to surrender with immediate effect, in order to save large scale casualties amongst our population. He therefore wishes us the very best of luck in our hour of need!"

Churchill smiled as he spoke the last sentence.

There was cynical laughter from around the table.

"How very kind of him!" Newall commented sourly.

Churchill gave a grunt of laughter too.

"We should remember of course, that President Roosevelt is barely a month away from a Presidential election, and a contentious one at that. He is in a very difficult position."

"Not as difficult as *your* current position, Prime Minister." Pound commented in his laconic way.

Churchill laughed, a wry smile etched on his face.

"Brendan, could you please draft a reply for me? I will look at it directly after this conference has closed."

The Prime Minister took a deep breath.

"Thank President Roosevelt for his message of support and remind him that if Britain falls, then the free world falls also. Tell him that I will be unable to reply in full for several days as I am extremely busy."

Churchill paused a moment, turning over the proposed reply in his head.

"And tell him that should he not hear from me by the 1st October, then all future correspondence concerning Great Britain should be addressed to Herr Hitler in Berlin."

SEALION HEADQUARTERS – THE HAGUE, HOLLAND
SATURDAY 21ST SEPTEMBER – 0835 HOURS

Keitel paced up and down the polished floor of the big room. Kesselring and Raeder continued to discuss the arrangements for air cover in hushed, but heated voices. Brauchitsch remained rooted to the spot in front of the map-board, as he had been for several minutes, his eyes running over the features of the map continuously, obviously deep in thought. They were three hours into the critical phase of the main operation now and during those three hours, they had received only one, rather vague report. This latest message from the commander of the amphibious landings had started to come in just as they had settled down to discuss their probable courses of action. Now they waited expectantly. Jodl himself was standing over the de-coder in the intelligence cell, waiting to bring the despatch straight to the conference.

Keitel glanced at his watch as he paced. Just after half past eight. Fat Herman would be on the phone soon, wanting to know the details so that he could be the first one to tell the Fuhrer the great news when he awoke. If it wasn't going to be Reichsmarshal Goering who rang first, then it would be Himmler, demanding to know if his SS unit had been disembarked yet. Keitel, the head of German Supreme Headquarters, snorted in annoyance at the thought. They both wanted to be the first to show Hitler that they had taken a leading role in the great plan. Unless of course it went disastrously wrong, in which case they would suddenly disappear into the background and pretend that they were mere spectators to the event.

The door opened and Jodl strode into the map room, a piece of paper in his hand and an excited look on his face. Keitel stopped pacing and looked up at Jodl as he came across the floor towards him. Even Brauchitsch turned to eye the chief of operations as he entered. Raeder and Kesselring too, went silent and turned their attention towards him. As Jodl caught Kesselring's eyes, he couldn't resist a flicker of a smile and a confirmatory nod. Kesselring immediately gave a sigh of relief and turned to face the others.

"Alright gentlemen, gather round please?"

The senior officers of the Sealion staff gathered in front of the map board, whilst from around the edge of the room, their aides shuffled forward, clip-boards and pencils in hand.

"Kesselring. You first please?" Keitel invited the head of the newly formed Sealion Air Fleet to take centre stage. Kesselring, though relatively junior, was a thoroughly competent Luftwaffe officer, and possessed a sharp intellect. It was for this reason that Goering had virtually stripped out Air Fleet One and given the squadrons to Kesselring's Air Fleet Two, renaming it Air Fleet Sealion in the process. Goering had gone further in fact. Disinterested in the detail, the Reichsmarshal had decreed that Kesselring would write the Luftwaffe plan for Sealion, which essentially involved the Air Fleet Commander giving orders to his peers. Fortunately, Kesselring was also a diplomat, and thus far, the Luftwaffe plan was going like clockwork.

"Gentlemen," He began, "first of all, I would like to give a quick run down of the air operation in support of Sealion South. You are already aware that the diversionary raids last night proved highly effective. Apart from keeping the enemy's attention focussed southwards and convincing them that the air offensive was being conducted in advance of a landing operation, we have successfully drawn out a large portion of his air force and caused considerable attrition. As far as our losses are concerned, during last night's raids, only seven bombers failed to return out of nearly one hundred and forty employed. Every major city, town and harbour between Dover and Portsmouth was left in flames."

He glanced down at a small piece of card that he was holding, and after a brief pause, continued.

"Once the enemy's air force took the bait and came out in strength over the Channel, just before full dawn this morning, we were able to pounce with ninety percent of our fighter strength. Current reports indicate thirty four enemy bombers and some twenty six enemy fighters destroyed, for the loss of just nine of our own fighters. We also bombed airfields across the South of England during the night, so it's likely that more aircraft were destroyed on the ground. Our remaining fighters conducted a sweep across the enemy coastline an hour after dawn and reported mass confusion and destruction on the ground, with only limited interference by enemy aircraft. At the same time, several radar stations were attacked by Stuka squadrons, who lost three aircraft. Over towards the Thames Estuary, our main Stuka force was launched against the large enemy naval flotilla that had been spotted heading towards the Channel. At least two of the enemy destroyers have been sunk, with a third seriously damaged. Unfortunately, enemy fighters did arrive on the scene in some strength and eleven Stukas were lost."

Kesselring paused, allowing the numbers to sink in, and he noticed Raeder's nod of approval at the mention of the enemy ships being sunk.

"Finally," Kesselring went on, "It is my intention to launch further fighter sweeps over the English coast throughout the day in order to keep the pressure on their own fighters. Also, tonight, the Dornier squadrons from Air Fleet One will raid against London with incendiaries, with the sole intention of burning the place to the ground. Hopefully, the threat of major destruction will keep RAF fighters in the south, and reduce their strength in the area of the main operation. In addition to the Dorniers, the Condor squadrons will launch raids deep inland against major railheads, particularly those running north from London."

He paused once more, consulting his card, and then slapped his cane against the map, right over the port of Hull.

"Sealion North, then." He began. "The preliminary raids went according to plan, with Hull, Immingham, Grimsby, the Tyne and Rosythe all being heavily bombed, and mines being dropped into the major estuaries. Raids also went inland, with the major rail junctions at York and Doncaster being bombed. The airfield at Church Fenton was also bombed. Further north, a bombing attack was launched against Scapa Flow, in order to divert attention from the insertion of the U-Boat screen. Additionally, the coastal defences from Scarborough to Skipsea were given the planned, short preparation of just one hours bombing. All targets appear to have been found and the Heinkel squadrons were able to do a good job with little interference. Only three bombers failed to return from the northern raids, with an additional aircraft being lost over Scapa Flow."

Kesselring moved his stick back towards the bulge of coastline around Flamborough Head.

"The paratroop drop and glider drop also appear to have been successful. In total, five Junkers transports failed to return, however, all others returned empty and are currently being prepared for the move of the air-landing division. Currently, we have several squadrons of JU-88s conducting solo bombing and strafing runs along the major avenues of advance in depth of the beaches. Additionally, there are four major formations flying in to target York, Selby, Doncaster and Darlington. Each of these is under escort from ME-110 squadrons. We also have our remaining squadrons of 110s rotating over the landing beaches as top cover. Although losses so far are minimal, I expect the next 24 hours to become more expensive in terms of aircraft losses, unless we are able to secure several suitable airstrips on English soil, in order for me to send across some flying artillery in the form of Stukas, along with some fighters that can spend longer on station over the beaches."

Kesselring flicked a quick look in Raeder's direction.

"Finally, in consultation with the Grand Admiral, I have agreed to commit a large bomber force against the enemy Home Fleet, should it break out of Scapa Flow, and provided we are able to keep a track of its course."

He looked around the room, searching the faces there for any signs of disquiet. He saw none.

"That is all from me, gentlemen."

The commander of Air Fleet Sealion walked back towards the large, highly polished conference table and perched himself upon it, taking a huge breath as he did so. The plan was complicated, with the missions worked out in minute detail, right down to the last aircraft, and took into consideration the performance of each aircraft type. The targets were many and varied, and the need to keep pressure on the British would mean almost round the clock flying; all of this conducted at long range. Kesselring had assured the planners that he could keep the Luftwaffe hard at it for twenty four hours a day, over the first four days. After that, the intensity of Luftwaffe operations would have to reduce significantly due to crew fatigue. He was sure that he could give the Army and Navy the breathing space to get ashore, but then they had to get moving. By his reckoning, the Army had four good days. Four days to force a surrender from Britain, or even inflict a comprehensive defeat against her field army. After that? They would be in the lap of the Gods.

Even as these thoughts were going through Kesselring's mind, Raeder was taking the hot-spot. Raeder, even more than Kesselring, had been horrified at the thought of an amphibious landing operation against the defended coast-line of Britain, but knowing that Hitler and his cronies would not be swayed once they had the bit between their teeth, he had spent months finalising the naval plan in exhaustive detail, much as Kesselring had with the air plan. Raeder had pressed into service anything that would float and could mount a gun, in addition to modifying hundreds of civilian craft. Even before the offensive in the West had begun back in May, suspecting that Hitler might be tempted to order the near impossible, Raeder had begun the construction of hastily designed landing craft that would be capable of transporting the heavy, mechanised forces of the Army.

The infantry would make do with transport ships and trawlers, before transferring to barges and motor-boats at the last moment, but the tanks and guns would have to be transported in decent craft, capable of sailing across two hundred miles of sea and then landing their cargoes on a shallow beach. He had done so against a certain amount of opposition, but being the political animal that he was, Raeder had sensed that Hitler would not be satisfied with just a victory on the continent, and he had sensed equally that Britain was unlikely to give up easily. History went against that particular theory, and the appointment of the pugnacious Winston Churchill as British Prime Minister earlier in the year had simply confirmed Raeder's suspicions.

Now, the Commander in Chief of the German Navy stood before the entire German High Command, wearing his characteristic sharp expression. With his winged shirt collar and naval cravat, he looked like a dour school master.

"From a naval point of view, Sealion South has been a resounding success. Losses to the escorts were minimal; just two S-Boats and some minor damage to a couple of the destroyers. As we had hoped, the dummy invasion fleet brought all of the Royal Navy's assets out into the Channel, from Portsmouth, right round to Harwich. We currently believe that a total of thirty seven redundant craft were sunk from our skeleton fleet, with many of the crews being able to abandon ship as planned. There is no doubt that the enemy took this force seriously, judging by their swift and heavy response. Although no enemy fighting ships were sunk in the *Channel*, a number of them have been damaged, and my congratulations go to the Luftwaffe for their very effective ambush against the enemy destroyer flotilla coming out of Harwich. All in all, a successful first step."

Raeder turned to the map and, using a set of naval dividers, indicated a route from the area of Calais, cutting across the North Sea, past the coast of East Anglia, towards the Humber.

"The remainder of the skeleton fleet will now conduct its second diversion, heading towards the area of Sealion North, in an attempt to fool the British into thinking this is a follow up wave bringing reinforcements. Hopefully, this will suck away enemy air and naval strength from the main landing force. The Luftwaffe have agreed to give the skeleton fleet a certain degree of fighter cover for the first hundred mile stretch, partly to make the force look credible, and partly to help cause attrition against any enemy naval or air units that attempt an interception. As already discussed, regardless of losses to this fleet of rust-buckets, the force will continue towards the mouth of the Humber where it will be anchored in order to give the Tommies food for thought. Meanwhile the fighting ships, having removed the crews from the skeleton fleet, will then proceed to join up with the Sealion North landing force and assist with our main effort."

The Grand Admiral looked directly at Keitel who nodded his understanding. Jodl, standing beside him, had been scribbling furiously throughout the brief thus far. Raeder continued.

"In the north, our U-Boats and mine fields appear to have been effective. Enemy naval forces breaking out of the Humber and Tyne have suffered heavily. Half of the destroyers from the Humber have been sunk and all three of their cruisers damaged. One of the cruisers has limped back into the estuary, apparently badly damaged. Having said this, both the Hipper and Scheer have been slightly damaged; the Scheer suffering slight damage to its rudder after being rammed by a sinking British destroyer. Ramming battle-cruisers appears to be something of a habit for Tommy destroyer captains!"

The assembled officers chuckled, remembering the Hipper's experience in Norway.

Raeder allowed himself a brief smirk at his own dry humour, then sobered and went on.

"In the face of the suicidal destroyer, and the British cruisers attempting to close the range, along with a renewed air attack, Hipper and Scheer have peeled back round to rejoin the main landing force. The Tommy cruisers have gone out into the sea and are being followed by a U-Boat as we speak. We do believe that some of the surviving Tommy destroyers, just a handful, have managed to destroy one of our submarines near the mouth of the Humber and turn north, heading along this coastal strip. If the Army's storm-battalion has done its job, the Tommy ships might take some fire from the Spurn Head batteries as they pass, however, the Hipper has signalled that the enemy were able to break out of the estuary without any apparent obstruction from shore-based artillery. I think we should therefore presume that Koch's force has failed in its mission."

He saw Von Brauchitsch wince at the suggestion of an Army failure, but didn't give him time to raise an objection.

"Regardless of that," Raeder pushed on, "the Tommy destroyers will come up hard against our newly laid mines off Hornsea, and be subjected to attacks from the joint S-Boat and destroyer force guarding the southern flank. In addition to that, the bombardment ships will be able to target them easily enough. Initial reports suggest that the requirement for naval gunfire support may be diminishing quickly?"

He flicked a glance over at Jodl, who looked up, nodded curtly in agreement, then continued scribbling notes.

"Likewise, the surviving enemy destroyers from the Tyne will hit our hard shoulder on the northern flank, just off Scarborough. There will be a few losses, I'm sure, but as of yet, the enemy hasn't committed enough resources to spoil the landing operation completely, or disrupt it to any serious degree. The landing fleet has suffered some air attacks, which are getting heavier by the hour, but at the same time, our shore based anti-aircraft screen increases in potency at the same rate. Unless there is anything hugely upsetting in the signal we are about to hear, then my intention is for the second echelon to set sail at midday. This will allow them to begin landing in England a little after midnight, in order that they can be committed to the land battle at first light tomorrow."

Raeder took a deep breath.

"Which brings us to the sleeping giant; the British Home Fleet at Scapa Flow. As of 0800 hours this morning, there had been no attempt at breaking out. Given the experience of their forces in the Tyne and Humber, they may well be exercising some caution, which is not entirely unexpected. Our submarine force is in place and ranged in depth, so we are ready for them when they finally do make an attempt. I must once again, publicly, remind everyone that in order to have maximum attrition against the British Home Fleet, the submarine force will need backing up by air power at the decisive moment. If we can catch the enemy as he is tightly bunched and manoeuvring in confined waters, then we have a good chance of dealing him a catastrophic blow."

The Grand Admiral lowered his stick and scanned the audience.

"Are there any questions, gentlemen?"

There was nothing but the shaking of heads, and Raeder returned to his original spot by the table. Jodl, still scribbling furiously, walked over to the map board. After a moment or two, he looked up and caught the eyes of the senior officers in the room.

"Gentlemen, I will firstly give an update on information received from the Landing Force Commander, then I will hand over to the Chief of Army Staff for his 'options' brief."

He glanced over at Keitel who gave his nod of approval. Having being given the signal to proceed, Jodl lifted his cane and began briefing in his usual rapid, yet precise manner.

"Signal from Landing Force Commander regarding situation of Sea-lion North as at 0830 hours, 'S' Day. The northernmost landings have encountered some problems. The 1st Mountain Division's first wave against the seafront of Scarborough sustained heavy casualties and the beach there is impractical. However, the second regiment of the first wave made a successful landing just south of Scarborough, here at Cayton, and are extending the beachhead rapidly. The 1st Mountain Division are now landing all subsequent waves here, with the intention of swinging around and attacking Scarborough from the south, by land. That said, given the initial set-back, and the heavy enemy resistance, it is anticipated that the town will not be secured before nightfall."

Jodl barely paused; waiting just long enough to flick the tip of his cane to another spot on the map before continuing. The senior officers present were anxious to know what Jodl had discovered from the recently arrived signal, and listened to the operations chief intently.

"Elsewhere, the news is good." Jodl snapped. "The 7th and 17th Infantry Divisions have landed successfully in Filey Bay. Despite fierce initial resistance, the enemy defences were thin, and both Divisions are more than a kilometre inland. In some places, they are up to three kilometres inland and several units have linked up with elements of 7th Parachute Division. Filey Town is secure, as is Flamborough Head. The radar station is disabled, as is the large enemy gun battery in Filey Bay. Bridlington is more or less secure, just some mopping up to be done, the town being captured almost entirely by the paras. Unfortunately, the enemy did manage to block the harbour entrance, although the paras have improvised an unloading system for the landing force. 35th Infantry Division has landed from Bridlington to Skipsea, with resistance being similar to that in Filey Bay. The Division is now more than a kilometre inland in all places and has linked up with elements of the paras."

From around the room, there was a collective release of breath, and for the first time that morning, the assembled cream of the German General Staff allowed their faces to crack into smiles, the tension lifting from their careworn faces. They were ashore. Jodl paused slightly, allowing the audience to have its brief moment of release before going on, raising his voice slightly to indicate that there was still business to be done.

"The second wave has begun landing in the Filey and Bridlington sectors, with 12th Infantry coming ashore at Skipsea, and 8th Panzer Division coming shore at Bridlington and Hunmanby. It is estimated that the combat elements of both divisions will be ashore by 1500 hours. During the remainder of the day, 30th Infantry Division and SS Totenkopf Division will set sail with the intention of beginning landing operations around midnight. They will move forward to their start lines by 0800 hours tomorrow."

Jodl flicked his cane inland now.

"As for our depth operations? The Second Regiment of the Parachute Division was dropped on time and on target. We know little else other than that, however, thus far, there appears to be no major British thrust towards the beachheads from the direction of Driffield, with the Luftwaffe reporting only minor enemy units in close proximity to the landing areas. At Spurn

Head, we have no clear picture of what is happening. There has been gunfire reported from this location, so we know that at least some of Koch's men have found their target, even if they were unable to achieve their mission. As planned, 12th Infantry will push hard to relieve the storm battalion within twenty four hours whilst probing towards Beverley and Leconfield, with the intention of securing them by tomorrow morning."

Jodl lowered his cane and sighed.

"That gentlemen, is the situation on the beaches thus far."

He looked across at Von Brauchitsch.

"Sir? Over to you."

Jodl took up his original position next to Keitel. As he did so, he noticed that Reader was having an urgent whispered conversation with a naval staff officer who had just entered the room. The Grand Admiral's face was darker than normal and he looked irritated. He whispered something furiously at the staff officer and waved him away. Jodl saw that Keitel too had witnessed the exchange, and resolved to tackle Raeder straight afterwards, to see if there was a problem.

"So far gentlemen, the entire operation has gone unbelievably well." Von Brauchitsch began. "And I offer both my thanks and congratulations to the Luftwaffe and Kreigsmarine for playing their parts so admirably. Now it is time for the Army to make use of this wonderful opportunity. At the moment, I have no intention of changing the plan too much. We will support 1st Mountain Division's new plan of attack against Scarborough. At the same time, we will slowly expand the beachhead westwards in the Filey Bay area in order to give depth. But, as planned, the main effort for the rest of today is to get our panzer division ashore and get it moving towards their limit of exploitation immediately. We must have those airfields, and we must scare the enemy into thinking we are about to capture his major port and city in the area. Then, tomorrow, we break out as planned, with the reinforcements provided by SS Totenkopf, and we rip through the heart of Britain. If the Kreigsmarine can hold the sea lanes open for a further 48 hours, we will further reinforce with 10th Panzer, in order to cause as much confusion and collateral damage as possible by S+5. And then, maybe, the Fuhrer will have his British surrender."

Von Brauchitsch looked across at Keitel.

"At the moment, I can offer nothing further than that. We go with the plan."

Keitel nodded.

"That is fine. The detailed planning that we conducted for this operation has paid off already, for which I thank all three branches of the forces.

Undoubtedly, the Tommies will retaliate at some point, depending on how quickly they can respond. We must be ready for the warning signs and be prepared to react accordingly. However, for the time being, we continue to make every effort to support the current plan and drive it forward."

He glanced across at Raeder, who had just been handed some photographs by the same staff officer with whom he had been whispering just minutes before. The Grand Admiral was staring at the large square prints in consternation, his eyebrows pointing downwards in a deep frown.

"Is there a problem Raeder?" He asked evenly.

Raeder looked up, his face perplexed. He thought for a moment before speaking.

"It's the British Home Fleet." He said. "These photographs were taken over Scapa Flow at first light this morning. They have just been developed."

Keitel remained impassive.

"And what do they show? Has the Home Fleet begun to move?"

Raeder shook his head.

"No, the fleet is still there, at anchor; most of it anyway."

"Most of it?" Keitel's voice suddenly became sharp. "What do you mean?"

"It's their aircraft carrier." Raeder said, shaking his head, nonplussed. "It's missing…"

THE SECRET BUNKER – NOT FAR FROM HUNMANBY
SATURDAY 21ST SEPTEMBER 1940 – 0840 HOURS

"You shouldn't have brought him George."

Tommy McGinn, long time local tramp of the Filey area, and more recently, a member of Churchill's secret army, looked down at the wounded man on the bunk bed. Harper, pulling the camouflage back into place, closed the two trap doors to the hidden bunker and turned back to face his associate in the murky, subterranean hideout.

"I couldn't leave him for the Hun, Tommy. If he didn't bleed to death in the mean time, they'd have just shot him on the spot. Those German bastards are like that. I've seen it before in the First War."

McGinn pulled a face, his weathered features crinkling up like an old newspaper.

"Well, he's here now, and he doesn't look like he's going anywhere in a hurry. As long as he doesn't cry out whilst he's unconscious. If he turns delirious and starts shouting his mouth off, we'll have to kill him."

Harper regarded the old tramp with renewed interest. He'd known 'Tommy the Tinker' for over fifteen years, but still knew virtually nothing of the man's past. He judged him to be of a similar age to himself, and knew that he had once lived in Cheshire, but other than that, Tommy was a mystery.

Harper had always thought of him as a loveable rogue, fond of a drink and anything poached from local farmers, with nothing more to worry about than where he would make his bed for the night. But with the onset of fighting in France earlier in the year, Harper had seen a new side to the old tramp. McGinn had seemed amazingly well informed about events in Europe and would often give very profound opinions as to where the world was headed. Of course, McGinn claimed his knowledge came from reading so many discarded newspapers, but Harper suspected that before his wandering days, Tommy McGinn had been a man of some respectability.

And then, with the fall of France splashed all over the front page of the papers, it was McGinn who had approached Harper with the offer. At first, he had thought that the tramp was drunk, or out of his wits, but it had soon become clear that McGinn was deadly serious. And so Harper, to his own surprise, had become a member of an organisation so secret that it didn't even have a name. He looked at McGinn now; heard the words spoken in such a matter of fact way, and suddenly shivered. There was much more to Tommy the Tinker than met the eye.

"Anyway." McGinn continued. "Let's hope poor Mr Eldridge can keep his tongue still? And let's take a look at this leg of his, shall we?"

Eldridge was unconscious. He had been for the last ten minutes, his strength giving out through loss of blood and shock just a short distance from the bunker. The trip from the farm to the organisation's hidden operating base was relatively short in real terms, but with an injured man to assist, and the danger of bumping into German paratroopers in every hedgerow, the going had proved to be slow and frustrating. Along with the sleepless night and intense fighting of the last few hours, the experience had left even Harper, a robust countryman, feeling exhausted and washed out. McGinn knelt beside the supine Eldridge and, producing a penknife, ripped open the material of his trouser leg and tore it completely away from the garment.

"Do me a favour, George, will you? Put that kettle on and make us both a brew. You must be buggered? Do some extra hot water so we can wash this wound out too. We don't want him catching gangrene. If he does, then he's finished."

Obediently, Harper moved across to the small cooking area and followed McGinn's instructions, suddenly aware how ravenous he was. He eyed the tins of corned beef and processed cheese and felt his stomach churn with hunger. As he began to boil the water, McGinn rummaged in the first aid satchel, producing some clean dressings and bandages.

"Any sign of Freddie or Sam yet?" Harper asked, rubbing his eyes and removing his helmet.

"Aye." McGinn murmured, placing the bandages down on the bed and then filling the wash bowl with a small amount of water from the Jerry Can. "They've both been here a few hours now. I sent them up top about half an hour since to see what they could fathom out. What's it like up there?"

Harper sat down on a spare bunk and watched the tramp rubbing soap into his careworn hands.

"Bloody chaos, mate. There's Jerries everywhere. Looks like they've dropped paratroopers behind the coastline just before dawn. Me and the boys bumped into a couple of groups after we pulled back from the coast, but we finished the buggers off pretty quickly."

McGinn looked up from his ablutions.

"So they're on the beaches too?"

"Oh aye!" Harper grunted. "Thousands of 'em Tommy. I've never seen so many boats in my life. We held 'em up for a while, but then we ran out of ammo. There was nothing else to do but pull back. We should have had more ammo, mate. If we'd had some more ammo we could have still been down there, killing the sausage-munching bastards."

McGinn smiled.

"Such are the fortunes of war, George. But we'll be able to really spoil their day soon enough, eh?"

He finished drying his hands on a towel.

"What about the rest of the lads you were with?"

Harper looked up.

"Fred Dean's dead." He said quietly.

"Poor Fred." McGinn murmured, placing the towel back on the hook. "What about the others?"

Harper made a vague gesture as if pointing over his shoulder.

"Sergeant Jackson's taking them towards Driffield, across country; trying to join up with the infantry brigade that's based down there. They've got a load of captured German weapons and ammo, so they'll be alright."

"Jackson?" McGinn raised an eyebrow. "The big Guardsman who's been doing all the training?"

"Aye." Harper nodded. "Christ Tommy, you ought to see the bastard fight! I pity any German who gets in his way."

McGinn chuckled.

"Oh yes! I can imagine. Good boys, the Guards. I reckon GHQ will be sending the whole damn lot of them in this direction pretty quickly. Then the Jerries'll be in for a bloody nose! I fought alongside the Irish Guards in the First War; by God those boys loved a scrap. Good old Micks!"

Harper looked up in surprise.

"You fought in the First War, Tommy?"

McGinn didn't reply. He had frozen at the sound of a knock from outside the bunker. Swiftly he leaned across to the nearby ammo box and scooped up the Thompson sub-machine gun that was laid across the lid. Moving towards the ladder he pointed the muzzle of the weapon upwards and waited. The knock came again, but this time a series of them, beating out in a pre-arranged rhythm. From his seat, Harper recognised the pattern of knocks easily, having practiced them religiously over the last couple of months. McGinn carefully opened the inner door, then called out the password challenge. Just a moment later, the correct response filtered down to them, the voice familiar. McGinn gave the 'clear to enter' signal, and there was a sudden but brief surge of natural light within the chamber. The light was cut off just seconds later as Freddie and Sam dropped down the ladder and into the bunker.

The two men blinked, adjusting their eyes to the gloom of the underground lair, which was illuminated by a lone hurricane lamp. They were both breathing heavily. After a couple of moments they noticed Harper sitting on the bunk bed and Eldridge's unconscious figure on the bed opposite. Freddie Bowyer frowned at the sight of the unexpected guest and looked up at McGinn with a questioning look on his face.

"I'll tell you in a minute." The old tramp pre-empted the inevitable question. "First of all, tell me what you've seen up top."

Harper noticed that McGinn's voice, normally so care-free and jovial, was now possessed of a sharpness and precision that surprised him. It reminded him of an officer's voice, but one with a country twang.

It was Sam Holderness who replied.

"The Jerries are everywhere!" He gasped, trying to calm his breathing. "Hundreds of them moving inland from the beaches. There are discarded parachutes all over the place. Hunmanby looks like it's in German hands. We saw dozens of Jerries moving about in the village all relaxed, as if there wasn't any danger. They must have over-run the Home Guard strongpoint. There were some big explosions from over near Reighton and Speeton too. We think the Reighton Battery's been destroyed. The Jerries are moving inland, mainly down towards Bridlington and Flamborough. There's an air battle going on over the coast, but it's calming down a bit now."

McGinn listened to the report in silence, then nodded his head.

"Right then, it looks as though we shall have some work to do in the very near future..."

Bowyer interrupted.

"There's tanks as well."

"Tanks?" McGinn's eyes narrowed.

"Aye. Only small ones mind you; and some armoured cars and motorbikes with sidecars on. Looks as though they've managed to get up the draw from the beach, over by Muston."

McGinn pondered that information for a moment.

"What are they doing once they get off the beach?" The old tramp asked.

Holderness took a deep breath, exchanging a look with Bowyer.

"Driving like hell towards Bridlington." He said.

BURTON FLEMING – 3 MILES SOUTH OF HUNMANBY SATURDAY 21ST SEPTEMBER 1940 – 0845 HOURS

They approached the village with caution. At first, they were suspicious of the peaceful scene that met them as they reached the outskirts. In the background, the noise of distant battle continued. It was almost as if the entire village had somehow managed to sleep through the invasion without realising what was happening just a few miles away. When they reached the crossroads by the church, they realised how wrong they had been. On their journey south from Hunmanby, Jackson and his three men had travelled through a landscape strewn with German parachutes, but miraculously they hadn't come across any of their owners. The enemy were in the area though, as they discovered when they checked on the OP above Hunmanby. There they had found two members of their platoon laid dead among the branches and leaves of their camouflaged shell-scrape. Nearby lay a dead German paratrooper.

Having stripped the .30 inch ammunition from their own men and searched the weaponless German, Jackson and his men had set out almost due south, crossing the railway line and climbing the ridge beyond, before dropping down into Burton Fleming. Standing now on the crossroads in the centre of the village, the reality of the situation was apparent. Perhaps thirty villagers, men and women, young and old, stood gathered round the line of eight bodies that had been covered with blankets. Several of the men, serious faced farmers, cradled shotguns. The vicar from the nearby church was saying a prayer over the corpses. As the clergyman finished the prayer, the crowd turned their attention to the newcomers in khaki, their eyes a mixture of sadness and hostility.

"My name is Sergeant Jackson of the Coldstream Guards." The tall regular soldier announced. "What happened here?"

At first no one replied, but then a surly looking man of middle age with a sun-browned face and shoulders like a bull, grunted a reply.

"The bloody Germans turned up, that's what happened! They appeared in the middle of the night. These boys here were just doing their duty."

He jerked his thumb towards the corpses hidden beneath the blankets.

Jackson looked at the covered bodies for a moment.

"Local Home Guard?" He asked the obvious question.

The middle aged man nodded.

"Heroes." He replied, his voice breaking slightly with emotion.

Jackson took a deep breath, knowing he had to be brief and reasonably blunt, yet suspecting that many of those standing around him were related to the dead men.

"Where are the Germans now?" He asked.

"Gone." Replied the middle aged man simply.

"I saw the bastards go past; towards Flamborough." An old woman of considerable age chirped up. "They went out of the village along the Grindale road."

"So, what's going on then, Sergeant?" The dour man asked. "Is it the invasion?"

Jackson looked the man in the eye.

"Yes, it is. They landed on the beaches at dawn. We fought them until our ammunition ran out. Then we came inland and found some parachutists. We killed them and took their weapons. Then we found some more and killed them too. We lost a couple of our men in the process. Now we're going to find some more to kill."

The middle aged man gave a low growl of approval.

"Well that sounds good to me, lad! I don't suppose I'll have much work on in the fields today, so I suppose I can do my bit now. No doubt the bastards will be back soon enough? Then we'll pay 'em back; the shit-eating Boche bastards!"

Jackson grimaced. The spirit was good but the logic poor.

"You can't fight them here." He said. "You're civilians."

"I can!" Snarled the farmer. "Those German fuckers killed my lad. And when they come back again, I'll take a good few of the bastards with me!"

There was a murmur of agreement amongst the crowd of villagers and Jackson felt a stab of pity for the farmer. So, one of the dead Home

Guardsmen was his son? Jackson thought quickly, needing to stamp his authority on the obviously volatile crowd.

"If you fight the Germans here, then you'll throw away what these boys did for you." He gestured towards the covered bodies. The crowd went silent. There was no response, but he saw the look of doubt cross the farmer's face.

"Your boys died defending this village. If you fight the Germans when they return, they'll flatten this place. I've seen it in France. They'll use mortars or dive-bombers; almost certainly tanks. They'll destroy every house. Every animal will die. Every person will die; whether you're carrying weapons or not. The Germans don't fuck about; they'll clobber you with everything they've got. Besides that, look around you. You're surrounded by high ground. You won't last five minutes. This isn't the place to fight the Germans. If you want to make the sacrifice of these men worth it, then you need to be a bit clever."

The crowd looked back at him wordlessly. It was the farmer who eventually spoke.

"So what are you suggesting? That we run away?"

"No." Jackson replied firmly. "Those who can't fight should stay here. Move into the church if need be. But stay here and don't resist. Those of you who are of fighting age can come with me. We've got weapons you can use, and you take the helmets and equipment from your own dead. I'm going to fight the Germans. I owe them a few debts myself, so believe me when I say that I'm going to make the bastards suffer. But… and it's a big but, I'm going to fight them on my terms, not theirs."

He saw a flicker of interest among some of the men in the crowd.

"What are you going to do, then?" Asked the farmer.

Jackson took a second to scan the faces in the crowd before replying.

"I'm going to do what the Germans don't like. I'm going to use their own tactics against them. I'm going to keep moving. When I find them, I'll kill them. But then I'll disappear and leave them swinging into thin air like a blind boxer. And I'll do that again and again. All of the time, I'll be heading towards our main counter-attack force which is over Driffield way. Then, once we've joined up with our main forces, we'll come back up this road and kick the Nazi bastards back into the North Sea!"

There was a low murmur in the crowd; a positive one. His fighting talk was appealing to them. He saw the farmer look across at a woman of similar age with a tear-stained face. His wife, Jackson presumed. She nodded at the farmer, setting her lips in a firm, thin line. The burly civilian looked back at Jackson.

"Count me in, then."

Several other men murmured their intention to join him.

Jackson took another deep breath, glad that the crowd had swung his way. They could have turned nasty just as easily. These people were angry and bereft; with little control left over their emotions, and the feelings of loss and hatred were a strong combination, he reflected.

"If you come with me, then you'll need to be fit enough to march across country." Jackson declared.

"We've trod this land since we were bairns." The farmer assured him.

"Good." Jackson acknowledged. "Then we need to move quickly. I'll need you to remove the helmets and brassards from your lads." He indicated the row of bodies again. "And their equipment too. You'll be needing it. Where are their weapons?"

The farmer nodded back in the direction of Hunmanby.

"The pond you passed on your way in; the Jerries took the bolts out of the rifles and threw them in the water."

"What about their ammunition?" Jackson queried.

The farmer shrugged.

"Can you check your boys' pouches," Jackson asked him as gently as possible, "and see if they've got any ammunition left? If you want to fight alongside my section then get yourselves kitted out quickly. We need to be moving in the next ten minutes."

The farmer nodded and began summoning together the other men who had volunteered to fight. Meanwhile, Jackson turned to face his three original men, all of them young seventeen year olds. The three youngsters looked tired and pale, and they were eyeing the row of covered bodies with serious faces.

"Fellahs?" Jackson snapped, grabbing their attention. "Everyone alright?"

The three Home Guardsmen nodded vaguely.

"I've got a rare blister coming up on my right foot." Complained Dutton.

Jackson nodded curtly.

"Not to worry. We've got ten minutes. Take your boot off and get your foot padded out with something; a handkerchief or something like that. The good news is that we'll be able to share out some of these weapons in a minute, so you won't be carrying as much weight."

He cocked his wrist, glancing at his watch.

"0850 hours." He commented. "Grab yourselves a drink of water; a good one. It looks like the clouds are breaking up and it's going to be a warm day I reckon. Once you've had a drink, fill your bottles up again; use one of these houses or the church."

Wearily, the three youngsters nodded and began fumbling for their water bottles. It was at that stage that a young boy, perhaps twelve or thirteen years old, came running onto the crossroads from down the Grindale road. As breathless as he was, he only needed to gabble one phrase, which required no elaboration. Stumbling to a stop in front of the milling villagers, he drew breath and called out his news.

"The Germans are coming!"

THE SLIPWAY – BRIDLINGTON PROMENADE
SATURDAY 21ST SEPTEMBER 1940 – 0850 HOURS

"Good morning, General." He snapped to attention. "Major Schulz, Third Battalion of the First Parachute Regiment. Welcome to England!"

Lieutenant General Hans Reinhard returned the salute and extended his hand.

"Morning Schulz. Well done, and thank you. Your boys did a great job. I suspect it's been a pretty busy morning for you?"

"It certainly has, Sir, but worth it to see these boys coming ashore."

The two officers stepped back together as the latest batch of Panzer I light tanks from the 8th Panzer Division clattered up the stone ramp that led from the beach to the promenade.

The assault pioneers of the 35th Division had blown the concrete and steel obstacles out of the way less than an hour before, whilst Schulz's men, alongside the infantry from the 35th, had began fighting through the town and away from the coast, side by side, attempting to establish an initial beachhead. At the same time, the steady stream of British prisoners, along with the large collection of civilians from the harbour, had been pressed into service by the 35th Division's engineering officer. Schulz had been impressed by the man's improvisation. Under German supervision, the British workers had pulled away the thick wooden cladding from the harbour buildings and one of the smaller piers, and laid the wooden planks and posts side by side, in a gradually lengthening causeway that began at the foot of the ramp and extended towards the waterline. The wooden track had then been covered over with heavy fishing nets, which in turn had been secured against the soft sand with hastily improvised steel or wooden pegs. In addition, the prisoners had then been made to carry the large, heavy lumps of concrete from the shattered obstacles and dump them over the top of the nets, along either side of the improvised causeway.

The novel product would not last forever on these shifting sands, especially if the sea state worsened, but the engineering officer reckoned it would survive at least one high tide, enabling the 8th Panzer to make a swift landing in order to join in the battle.

"A shame about the harbour entrance being blocked." Commented Reinard, as a half-track carrying a squad of panzer grenadiers rumbled past them.

"Yes, I'm sorry about that, Sir." Schulz reddened. "The Tommies beat us to it. But I gather that the boats are not proper block-ships, just scuttled fishing boats. The naval engineers tell me that come low tide, half the harbour will be free of water anyway. They reckon they can re-float the two boats and clear the entrance by tonight."

"Excellent." Reinhard nodded. "Don't mistake me Schulz, I'm not picking fault. I know what a shit-sandwich you were given, and if it hadn't been for your boys rolling up this stretch of the promenade, my division would still be fighting its way over this sea wall. You did well."

"Thank you, Sir." Schulz acknowledged the divisional commander's praise.

"Such are the fortunes of war, Schulz, and I suspect that I will become a victim of them myself before the day is over! I reckon we should be able to get the harbour open by the time those black bastards from the SS arrive in the middle of the night. Can't have Himmler's little pets getting their nice clean vehicles wet can we?"

The general laughed, and Schulz laughed with him. There were few in the military that had any real respect for the armed units of the SS, especially the Totenkopf Division. It was generally believed that the majority of people in the Deaths Head formation were nothing more than glorified prison guards with aspirations of military glory. Still, they had the favour of Hitler, and they were one of Germany's most well equipped and mobile field formations, and thus they had earned their place on this great expedition.

"So, what's the situation in the town?" Reinhard asked, changing the subject.

Schulz reached in his smock and took out the air photograph of Bridlington town. He laid it on the wall in front of the general and began to mark it with his wax pencil.

"This whole area here is secure, as far as the railway station. At the northern end of town, we've linked up with our boys from the Second Battalion who have secured Flamborough Head. There's a maze of streets just up here that we're starting to clear through now. Once that's done, the whole central and northern end of town will be properly secured. We'll hold that perimeter and allow your boys to push onwards from there. Down here, your first two regiments have cleared the initial part of the town, and I believe your third regiment is now in the process of exploiting beyond the railway line and through these two small villages here; Bessingby and Carnaby. They may have already reached them. Once there, it's a clear run straight down this highway towards our other regiment at Driffield. At the speed these tank-boys are driving, you might find that 8th Panzer are already pushing through those villages."

They both glanced up as a half-track towing a 37mm anti-tank gun trundled up onto the promenade and turned a sharp left to follow the newly sign-posted route for Driffield. Once it had gone past, Reinhard looked back down at the photograph.

"Okay, in which case I'll get my third regiment to push beyond this road by at least a kilometre and establish an anti-tank screen. I'll then reorganise the other two regiments and start exploiting south, in order to open up the beachhead towards Skipsea and give 12th Division plenty of elbow room to get ashore. Once the Navy boys have assumed full control of the harbour, I want you to concentrate your battalion along this line here, right up to where the railway line cuts due north up the side of the town. No doubt Colonel Brauer will tell you precisely where the boundary with your Second Battalion will be. Have you seen him at all?"

Schulz gave a shake of his head.

"Not yet, Sir. He dropped with the Second Battalion. I believe he was planning to watch the attacks go in against Reighton and Flamborough, then head south to brief me on future intentions."

Reinhard nodded.

"That's fine. For the time being, go with what we've just discussed. If Colonel Brauer wishes to make any alterations when he arrives, he will find me down near the village of Carnaby. Depending on the progress of 8th Panzer, I may even go as far forward as Burton Agnes."

"Yes, Sir. Got that." Schulz nodded.

Their deliberations were interrupted by the sound of heavy gunfire from the south; not just small arms fire, but heavier weapons too. The two officers stared along the line of the beach, where the gently rolling waves were less than a hundred and fifty metres from the sea-wall now.

"What's going on there, then?" Reinhard frowned at the sudden barrage of noise.

The gunfire was getting louder, as weapon systems just a short distance down the sea-front suddenly burst into action. Then they saw them. Banking round sharply, having come in low over the fields, the line of enemy fighters veered onto a course that took them directly up the water line of Bridlington Bay. Howling like demons, the fighters dipped their noses, one after the other, and let rip with their twin banks of .303 inch machine guns, before pulling up sharply and rolling to port and disappearing inland again.

"Down, Sir!" Yelled Schulz, pulling Reinhard sideways into the cover of a half demolished concrete block.

It wasn't a moment too soon. An ear-shattering series of high pitched cracks whipped past the two men as they pressed themselves in against the anti-tank cube, and bullets smashed into the paving slabs of the slipway and promenade all around them. The enemy fighters howled and whined as their pilots threw them about in tight manoeuvres, designed to foil the mass of incoming anti-aircraft fire. Above the deafening chatter of gunfire and the crack of enemy bullets slashing through the air around them, the two officers heard the sound of screaming. The attack seemed to be over in a matter of seconds, although Schulz had the impression they had been strafed by at least half a dozen fighters. The enemy had come and gone in the blink of an eye.

Cautiously, the two officers stood and peered over the top of the mangled cube. On the slipway in front of them, a half-track was slewed across the ramp at an angle, steam pouring out of its bonnet, dead and wounded panzer grenadiers slumped over the side of the vehicle. Two of them lay sprawled on the concrete ramp, rivulets of their blood trickling down the slope. Down on the beach, halfway along the improvised causeway, an open-topped staff car was on fire and more bodies were strewn around about it, including some of the British prisoners. Reinhard let out a deep breath and pushed his cap back on his head.

"So, the Tommies know we've arrived then?"

THE COTTAGE – BY SEAMER BRIDGE, SCARBOROUGH SATURDAY 21ST SEPTEMBER 1940 – 0855 HOURS

Major Peter Stadtman was excited. He hid the excitement behind his impassive features, but secretly, his heart was thumping and every nerve in his body was on edge. The sounds of fighting in the nearby town of Scarborough had diminished; understandable, with the abandonment of the landings on the sea-front there. Instead, the background noise was that of large explosions. Out to sea, the German bombardment ships had begun firing again, once it became apparent that the 98th were getting massacred on the shore line. For the past two hours, the big naval guns had steadily fired round after round into the defiant British town and its defenders. Now, a huge pall of dark smoke hung over place. In the last half an hour, the naval guns had also turned their attention to the high ground in front of him, the place known as Oliver's Mount, from where the Tommy mortars had continued to bombard the landing beach at Cayton. Added to the enemy mortars, there was heavy artillery fire from British guns located somewhere inland. Their observers were doing a fine job and they had suffered regular and accurate artillery fire throughout their move into position.

Fortunately, the division had finally succeeded in getting its own mortars ashore at Cayton, and now they were bringing their own steady barrage down onto Oliver's Mount; a mixture of high explosive and smoke. Other than that, the battlefield had become relatively quiet in terms of manoeuvre. The other battalions had taken over an hour to clear through the villages of Cayton and Lebberston. In addition to a very stubborn strongpoint in the centre of Cayton, manned by a mixture of men and boys from the British militia group, known as the Home Guard, they had also been pestered by a small but evasive group of enemy regular troops, who had fought a cat and mouse battle with them from building to building. The delay was frustrating for Stadtman, who, as commander of the Third Battalion, was eager to conduct the forward passage of lines with his sister battalions and get stuck in.

Finally however, he was here. Kneeling by the upstairs window of a small cottage on the edge of another tiny village, just beyond Cayton, he had a clear view of the ground before him. Directly to his front, northwards, lay the long, steady spur of Oliver's Mount, the entrenched enemy positions currently invisible behind the cloud of artificial smoke and debris from the explosions of the German mortars. The approach up the Spur was wide open, and quite possibly mined. He could certainly see the thick concertinas of barbed wire that blocked the approach to the summit. The only feature that broke up the expanse of bare fields was the farm, over to the left hand side, situated on a small shoulder of the feature. If he could get his machine-guns and possibly some mortars into that farm, he would have a really useful fire support location that could suppress the enemy defences at close quarters.

Stadtman looked left, where the narrow road ran directly towards the village of Seamer. A dark scar that ran north to south betrayed the line of the sunken railway. The roof of the village station was just visible to him through a clump of trees that stood near the bridge, where it crossed over the railway line. He scanned the area of the bridge with his binoculars. All quiet. He thought for a moment, turning the options over in his mind. After a moment, he reached his decision. No time for caution now. If the survivors of the 98th were to be saved, he needed to capture the bridge over the railway line, and possibly Oliver's Mount, as quickly as he could and then allow the 99th Regiment to come through and break into the town proper.

He leaned out of the shattered window and whistled. Below, poised against the garden gate, the company commander of Third Company looked up at him.

"Okay Feisler. Go for it; exactly as we said. Secure the bridge and the station, but go no further than that. I'll feed the First and Second Companies though you and up the railway line, once you're in position. Move out."

By the gate, the captain in charge of Third Company gave a thumbs-up and then shouted a brief instruction to his men nearby. Stadtman watched with satisfaction as the highly trained mountain troopers immediately shook out and began their advance on the bridge, which was little more than two hundred metres away. Sliding back inside the window and dropping onto one knee, Stadtman looked to his operations officer.

"Right, Wolfgang, this is the plan. Third Company is moving now, as we discussed. As soon as they have secured the bridge and station, they will establish a defensive perimeter. We will then feed the rest of the battalion through them; order of march, First Company, Machine Gun Company, then Second Company…"

He paused whilst the young captain jotted down the instructions. When the operations officer looked back up, Stadtman continued.

"First Company are to infiltrate along the edge of the spur, hand-railing the crest of that escarpment, see?"

The captain glanced out of the window and nodded.

"Seen." He confirmed.

"Good. Whilst they do that, I want their mortars, along with the entire Machine-Gun Company, to peel into the farm up on that shoulder of land there. They are to turn the place into a fire-base and will suppress the enemy positions on the summit once First Company begins its attack. Second Company is to hold fast in that small re-entrant, just beyond the farm, and form the reserve. We'll move up to the farm where we can keep a close eye on things. Happy with all that?"

"Happy Major." The captain replied confidently. "I'll send a runner to call the company commander's in. Do you want to brief them, Sir, or are you happy for me to do it?"

"You do it, Wolfgang. You know what I want to happen. As soon as we get the signal from Third Company, step the others off; and send a message back to Regimental HQ that it looks as though we'll be able to take Oliver's Mount under our own steam. That should allow the 99th to just roll through into the town itself."

The operations officer nodded curtly in response, then hurried out of the room.

He was a good lad, that one, reflected Stadtman. Very efficient; calm, precise and diligent. Just what was needed from a battalion operations officer. Stadtman listened to the captain's footsteps descending the stairs of the cottage, then turned back to the window. The men of Third Company were halfway to the bridge and Stadtman felt his stomach lurch with the nervous expectation of the coming assault on Oliver's Mount. He brought his binoculars up to study the farm that he had chosen as his fire support location, traversing them from left to right. There were plenty of suitable locations for his tripod mounted machine-guns, he noted. As he studied the complex of buildings, dung-heaps and hedgerows, something moved slightly at the very base of his field of vision.

Quickly he brought his binoculars down and found himself staring at a substantial and lengthy hedgerow that ran along the base edge of the farm's boundary. He could see only bushes, trees and grass at first, for the long, hot summer had left the hedgerows thick with foliage even at this late stage of September. And then he saw it; just a slight movement, but enough to betray the presence of the man crouching in the hedgerow some five hundred metres away. He felt his heart pick up speed. He blinked several times, adjusted the focus slightly, then stared at what he was sure was a person. The figure moved and he caught his breath.

"Bollocks!"

No mistake. A figure in the khaki battledress of the British Army and wearing one of those unusually shaped helmets that looked like a soup bowl. He followed the figure and cursed again. There were more of them.

"Bollocks!" He cursed a third time and glanced down at his watch. 0859 hours.

"Wolfgang…" He began, then realised that his operations officer had already left.

Then it happened…

He heard the shells coming several seconds before the first one landed almost slap bang amongst the advancing soldiers from Third Company.

Whoosh-crump! Whoosh-crump! Whoosh-crump!

The British artillery fire slammed into the open ground between Stadtman's vantage point and the bridge, instantly shrouding the field in grey smoke. He ducked instinctively as another shell landed nearby, and a split second later, clods of earth and razor sharp metal splinters showered the side of the small cottage. Stadtman raised his head carefully, just enough to look over the ledge of the window. The men of Third Company had disappeared. Most of them were flat on the floor or crouching in the hedgerows and ditches that bordered the Seamer road. They were well and truly caught in the killing ground. Then something else happened.

After several salvoes, the next one came down not on the men of Third Company, but on the small group of cottages where Stadtman and his battalion headquarters were. The enemy were switching fire. Then the machine-guns started. He picked the noise up instantly. A strange sound; much slower than the staccato chatter of German machine-guns. The 'chug-chug-chug' noise came from up slope; from the farm. Stadtman ducked again as several rounds cracked over his head and slammed into the wall of the bedroom, smashing several huge chunks of plaster free. The Tommies were ambushing them! He could scarcely believe it. Suddenly the house shuddered and filled with dust as another salvo of shells landed amongst the group of buildings.

Choking on the dust, he curled up against the corner of the wall as the explosions rocked the house, whilst bullets continued to slap into the walls of the room above his head. And then the shells moved on again. He felt the intensity of the explosions diminish as the British observers switched the next salvo another hundred metres eastwards. The machine-gun bullets however, continued to slam into the building.

"Muller!" He shouted down the stairs, calling to his signals officer. "Muller! Get everyone in headquarters to start returning fire at that fucking farm! And get the Machine-Gun Company up here, fast!"

Stadtman never heard the answer from below, even if one was given, for another noise had come to his ears now; a noise which chilled him to the bone. He could hear whistle blasts, lots of them. Then he heard the cheer. It was a cheer like he had never heard before. Dozens of voices, edged with determination and anger, the sound of desperate men. They cheered as one, a great roar of defiance, and Stadtman suddenly felt as though he had a stone in his stomach. His arms and legs felt suddenly weak, and he had to drag himself upright in order to stare over the window sill. His mouth dropped open.

Emerging from the sunken railway line, as if they were ghouls rising from the dead on judgement day, a long line of Tommies were screaming across the fields on either side of the road, straight into the dispersed, disoriented men of Third Company. With bulging eyes, Stadtman gawped in disbelief as the extended British line hurtled towards his men, their rifles and long bayonets levelled. Suddenly, Stadtman realised that the great tales of German superiority and victory following the defeat of France had been a huge fallacy. Britain was not beaten yet, and her army still knew how to fight.

Now, that army was coming straight for him and the men of Third Company; and they were coming with bayonets fixed and vengeance in their hearts.

Ducking again as more bullets smashed into the wall just below the window, Stadtman realised that he was in danger of being overrun. Raising his head once more, he saw just how close he was to that nightmare scenario. The British were amongst Third Company now. He saw three Tommies go down in a hail of fire, as one of Third Company's MG34 teams caught them with a lengthy burst. A second later however, two more Tommies pushed through the hedge behind the machine-gun crew and Stadtman watched in horror as the khaki-clad figures lifted their rifles high over their heads. He saw the glint of their long, vicious looking bayonets, watched them plummet downwards towards the machine-gun crew, and heard the screams as those deadly steel blades found their victims. He saw the bayonets come back bloody, and the Tommies charged on.

It was at that point that Third Company broke and ran.

"Bloody hell fire!" Stadtman gasped in disbelief.

His men were running for their lives now, making no attempt to stand and fight. They were pounding back across the fields and along the narrow road as fast as their legs could carry them, whilst behind the group of panic stricken mountain troops, roaring their challenge as they scented victory, the Tommies, with their long bayonets, came after them.

"Muller! Get those fucking machine-guns up here now!" Stadtman bellowed, struggling to his feet and fumbling with his machine-pistol. He raised the barrel and let off a burst towards a group of Tommies coming straight towards the cottage and who were barely fifty metres from the little garden now. Not a single Tommy fell. They came on, their faces purple with rage and blood lust, and Stadtman felt as though his legs would give way at any moment.

"First Company too!" He yelled down the stairs. "Get the whole fucking battalion up here, now!"

He had no idea if his tactical headquarters group could hear him above the crack of incoming bullets, the distant crump of explosions, the screaming and shouting, and the bark and chatter of their own weapons. It was chaos. Complete and utter bloody chaos; not like the clear logical wargames that they had been through over and over again in preparation for this invasion. He saw the last survivors of Third Company disappear around the side of the cottage, and then there were just dozens of Tommies in front of him, charging across the fields on either side of the Seamer road or pounding straight down it. In desperation, he aimed his MP40 once more and released a burst. Twenty yards below him, just beyond the garden fence, one of the

Tommies spun around suddenly and collapsed onto all fours. Next to him, another Tommy looked up sharply, spotting Stadtman in the window. The Tommy was armed solely with an old fashioned revolver attached to a long, pale lanyard; an officer. The Tommy raised his arm and fired three shots at Stadtman. The three heavy calibre rounds cracked into the window frame with surprising accuracy, forcing the German commanding officer to twist away as splinters of painted wood flew into his face.

He turned back, raising his machine pistol once more, but the Tommy officer was already sprinting around the side of the cottage, whilst a group of about half a dozen more British infantrymen, all armed with bayonet tipped rifles, followed him. Stadtman whirled around and hollered down the stairs.

"Close the doors! The Tommies are amongst the buildings!"

There was a sudden surge of gunfire from down below. He heard a scream, a crump of a grenade exploding, more screaming, then hysterical voices yelling in both German and English. Then, he heard a loud, distinctive English voice. Stadtman didn't speak much English, but there was no mistaking the words.

"Kill the German bastards! Kill them all!"

Stadtman's blood ran cold. He ran across to the corner of the room and tucked himself into a tight gap behind the large double bed, training his weapon's barrel over the top of the mattress, aiming straight at the doorway.

There was a sudden explosion down below, right outside the cottage by the sound of it, then the unmistakable sound of the door crashing open. Stadtman couldn't breath; his heart was thumping like a crazed drummer at a Nazi Party rally. He wondered how much ammunition he had left in his magazine, then reached down to his belt, yanking a stick grenade free. There was a chatter of machine-gun fire from the hallway below; loud and deafening in the confined space. And then the heavy, urgent footsteps sounded on the staircase; coming up…

THE GRINDALE ROAD – BURTON FLEMING
SATURDAY 21ST SEPTEMBER 1940 – 0900 HOURS

"Just a little more…" Lieutenant Victor Malk prompted, and the driver gunned the engine gently, allowing the four wheeled armoured car to trundle forward. "Just until we're on the bend. So you can see the motorcycles."

The driver applied a few more revs and the Sd Kfz 223 rolled forward onto the bend in the road, giving the crew a perfect view down the broad street of the village.

"That'll do." Malk confirmed. Then, speaking to the radio operator, he said. "Tell them, we think we've come to Burton Fleming. We're going to do a circuit of the village to confirm, then try and find the southern exit towards Driffield. We'll call them forward once we're happy it's all quiet."

The radio operator acknowledged his commander's instructions and began relaying the message. Meanwhile Malk studied the road ahead. The two motorcycle combinations were about eighty to ninety metres in front of him, perhaps twenty yards between the two vehicles, one of them on either side of the road. He could see the men in the sidecars traversing their MG34s around the street ahead, ready for trouble at a moment's notice. The two riders sat astride their bikes, the engines still running, their rifles resting across the handlebars. He saw the lead rider turn back and signal to him. He was indicating a junction on the right and a road straight on. The village was deathly quiet.

Malk held up his own hand, the palm flat, facing towards the lead rider; the signal for 'wait'. He turned around and gave the same indication to the commander of the Panzer 1 light tank behind him. He watched the commander pass the signal back to Sergeant Jaeger who was in the open topped car. Behind Jaeger, tucked into the side of the road some hundred and fifty metres back, was their last vehicle, a similar version of his own armoured car but with a limited radio capacity. The reconnaissance platoon commander leant against the anti-grenade cage that surrounded his turret and studied his map. He then compared it to the air photograph. Neither was perfect, but he was fairly sure that he was at the village known as Burton Fleming. If his map was correct, there was an intersection of roads within the village, one of which would take them southwards, where they could join up with the main thrust on the outskirts of Driffield; providing there were no road blocks of course. Thus far, thankfully, they had come across only two, both of them near the landing beaches, and both of which the assault pioneers had blown to pieces with their usual efficiency.

It seemed that the Tommies had very little left in reserve. Their main strength had been on the beaches. So far, the units on the main effort had only come across major resistance on the south-west side of Bridlington, centred on the main highway to Driffield, as might have been expected. Hence Malk's presence here. This was the new German way of war. Never get sucked in to one point; always put your feelers out. Find a way round, by-pass large enemy positions. Get behind him; dislocate him. It was the way of lightening war, and the 8th Panzer Division did it well.

Malk made his decision. They would take their time to confirm the topography of the village and check it for enemy presence, after which they would identify their new axis and move off again, calling forward the panzer grenadier company that shadowed them. He looked up towards the motorcycle combinations again and saw the lead rider watching him. Stretching out his arm, Malk gave the signal for 'go right'. He watched the lead rider give a thumbs-up and turn back to face his front. He heard the throttle of the bike change tone; and he saw the familiar objects suddenly bounce into the road from the doorways on either side of the combinations. Small objects, like small cans on sticks that rolled across the tarmac with a metallic clink. He saw the riders and machine-gunners suddenly twist round in their seats and shout with alarm. And then the three grenades exploded…

"Fucking hell!" Shouted Malk's driver, watching through his viewing port.

"Fucking hell!" Malk copied him, ducking down inside the turret as the street ahead filled with clouds of grey smoke and the motorcycle crews were thrown from their machines. Then there were gunshots. Not many, perhaps half a dozen in rapid succession. Not the high pitched crack of rifles though; dull thumps, like shotguns going off.

"Hello Gustav Two Zero, this is Fredrick One Two; contact…wait, out!" The radio operator was instant with his response.

"Tommies in the houses, either side of the road!" Roared the driver.

Malk was already on it. He swung the turret round onto the row of houses to the left hand side of the road, and opened fire with the MG34. The machine-gun clattered into life, and he loosed off a long burst towards the nearest house.

His driver began edging the vehicle forward, saving Malk the fuss of traversing the turret. Instead, Malk just fired burst after burst into the row of houses, as the vehicle's movement took his gun barrel conveniently along the length of the buildings. He paused as the gun's ammunition expended.

"Stop! Go back!" He yelled at his driver as the gun clicked on an empty chamber.

Malk yanked away the empty belt and dragged a fresh one out of the rack, working feverishly to get the gun back into action, scraping his knuckles on the weapon's working parts as he did so. He glanced up, keeping as low as possible, as the odd rifle shot came towards him. All four of the men from his motorcycle section were down. Three lay still, whilst the other was crawling along the road, dragging something long and thin behind him. With a rising sense of horror, Malk realised it was the man's entrails, his belly having been ripped wide open by red hot shrapnel.

Something caught Malk's eye, high up in the air to his right, as he dragged back the cocking handle of the machine-gun.

"Grenade!" He roared, pushing himself down inside the tiny turret of the armoured car.

Crump! The grenade exploded near the front right tyre of the vehicle.

"Aagh!" The driver screamed in agony.

"Get back!" Mal yelled. "They're on our flank in the bushes!"

"I can't see! I can't see!" The driver was screaming frantically. "Oh, sweet Jesus! My eyes are bleeding!"

"Grueman! Reverse for fucks sake!" Malk screamed down through the turret towards the crew compartment. "Just go back!"

Amazingly, despite his pain, panic and physical blindness, the driver heard Malk's order and responded to it. The vehicle lurched backwards, throwing Malk's face against the rear sight of the machine gun and cutting his top lip. The metallic taste of his own blood filled Malk's mouth. There was a sudden, gut wrenching crunch as the vehicle came off the tarmac, over the verge and hit a small tree, stopping the vehicle.

Malk was thrown back against the rear of the turret, cracking his head. For a second he was stunned, the pain in his skull immense. As his mind cleared, he made a mental note to wear his helmet from now on.

"Lieutenant, we need to bale out! Grueman's lost his eyes!" The radio operator shouted up through the crew compartment, his voice edged with fear.

Malk opened his mouth to reply, but just then there was a sound of breaking glass, a familiar, sharp smell, and then suddenly a sheet of flame whooshed up above him, enveloping the front of the armoured car and sucking the oxygen from the young lieutenant's lungs. The scream that came from the crew compartment below went through Malk like a thunderbolt. It was a terrible sound of unbelievable suffering and pain; a sound that Malk would never forget. His own professionalism forgotten now, he wailed in terror and scrambled over the rear of the turret, desperately trying to struggle through the gap in the anti-grenade cage. The burning heat he could feel on his back as he threw himself face-first down the rear of the armoured car was unbelievable. He heard the breaking of more glass, and that terrible whooshing noise of yet more petrol igniting spurred him on.

He toppled onto the tarmac behind the rear left wheel of the vehicle, landing heavily on his shoulder.

"Aagh, fuck!"

A loud, hydraulic noise made him roll instinctively sideways onto the verge, and only seconds later, the Panzer 1 raced past the burning armoured car, its two machine-guns chattering angrily.

"No..." He tried to shout, but his voice was nothing more than a painful rasp and there was no way the tank crew was going to hear him.

He lay there for a moment breathing heavily, fighting for breath, gathering his thoughts. Somehow, he managed to get to his knees and peer around the burning armoured car, doing his best to shut out the sound of screaming from within it. There was a terrible sweet smell in the air. He remembered it from the battles on mainland Europe and realised it was the stench of burning human flesh.

He looked up the road to where the Panzer had come to a halt, just before the dead men of the motorcycle combinations. The vehicle's turret was facing half right, raking the wall of a nearby barn with its machine-guns. A cloud of dust and shards of brickwork erupted from the building as the 7.92 mm bullets slammed into it repeatedly. Something caught his eye over to the left of the vehicle, behind the hedgerow. Movement; an enemy petrol-bomber. Then it came, sailing through the air in a high arc, almost gracefully; a glass bottle filled with liquid, a flaming rag stuffed in the bottle neck.

The bottle shattered against the side of the turret and the whole flank of the armoured vehicle erupted in flame. Malk could only watch in horror as another bottle followed, landing on the very top of the Panzer's turret and instantly igniting. He saw that the tanks hatches were battened down; the crew might be alright yet. The screaming had stopped inside his own armoured car, but now individual bullets were exploding inside it from the heat of the burning petrol which was seeping down into the open turret. He knew he had to move before the fuel tank went up, so gathered himself, ready to see if his shaking legs would support him. From up front, He heard a loud metallic clang, followed by a howling whine and he looked round sharply, just in time to see something bright red bounce off the Panzer's hull and rocket skywards. Seconds later, the tank began reversing towards him.

"Sir!"

He heard the shout above all the clamour somehow, and looked back down the Grindale road. The car was pulled into the side of the road and Jaeger was crouching by the front passenger-side bumper. He was shouting something, but Malk couldn't hear what it was. The lieutenant put his hand to his ear.

"What?" He croaked.

The sergeant's face was contorted with frustration.

"For fucks sake! Get back here, now!"

Malk suddenly realised what he was being told. Groaning with the effort, he pushed himself upright, grabbing onto the rear of the armoured car to steady himself as he did so. He looked towards the retreating Panzer and saw that he had room. Taking a huge breath, he lurched away from his burning command vehicle towards the car.

The staff car was barely forty metres away, but it felt like forty *kilometres* to Malk. He was past the bend in the road now and out of sight of the retreating Panzer, and he felt a tremor run through his legs. He stumbled slightly, his legs feeling as if they were about to collapse. Jaeger saw it and charged forward, grabbing his officer's arm just as the young man sagged. Cursing, the sergeant half carried, half dragged Malk to the car, glancing back over his shoulder as the Panzer edged its way carefully back around the bend in the road, the flames on its hull much reduced now, the fuel that fired them almost spent.

To the rear of the staff car, the other armoured car had pulled up against the hedgerow and its machine-gun was rattling out burst after burst, across the top of the hedgerows, to where the Tommy petrol bombers had been hurling their deadly devices from. With a grunt, Jaeger bundled the semi-conscious officer into the back seat of the car.

"Come on, for fucks sake! Get in!"

Having dumped his burden safely into the vehicle, Jaeger clambered into his own seat, next to the driver.

"Go!" He snarled at the driver. "Straight back up the hill; sharpish!"

The driver needed no further prompting, and a moment later, the vehicle leapt backwards, making room for the retreating Panzer 1.

Jaeger looked back at his platoon commander. The young man's neat blond hair was singed and unkempt, his face black with smoke and sweat. The young officer stared back at his platoon sergeant groggily.

"What now?" Was all Malk could manage to say, his voice hoarse and grating.

Jaeger gave him a grim look.

"We get the fuck out of here and call the panzer grenadiers forward; that's what!"

HMS ELEKTRA – 3 MILES OFF HORNSEA
SATURDAY 21ST SEPTEMBER 1940 – 0905 HOURS

"Bloody hell, that was close!"

Welch peered out from the open bridge as the water thrown up by the brace of enemy shells splashed over him. He wiped the water from his face and found himself looking straight down into the sea. The ship was heeling over as it executed a sharp turn to starboard. Under the Captain's orders, the crew continued to hurl the destroyer around in sharp, evasive manoeuvres, as they continued their unequal duel with the enemy ships.

The last three hours had been chaotic and devastating. After breaking out of the Humber, HMS Elektra had peeled off from the main force with its companion, HMS Venomous, and the handful of assorted sloops, minesweepers and patrol boats. Their orders had been quite simple. Destroy the U-Boat and sail like hell up the coast to hit the German invasion fleet in the flank. It sounded simple anyway, though the reality of carrying out those instructions had been much more difficult in practice than in theory.

It had started well enough. The U-Boat waiting at the mouth of the Humber had made a fatal error by getting itself compromised in shallow waters. As soon as the ASDIC contact had been made, the U-Boat was as good as finished. Elektra and Venomous had turned sharply onto their prey, closing on it with speed. Leaving the survivors of HMS Veteran to fend for themselves, the two destroyers had dropped a full pattern of depth charges, before crossing over and repeating the pattern again. With no deep water for refuge, and unable to outrun the destroyers whilst submerged, the U-Boat had been stricken by the concentrated depth charge attack and surfaced within minutes. It hadn't stayed on the surface for long however, for it had suffered fatal damage and it was only through the skill of its crew that the vessel had managed to surface at all. Even as the German submariners began streaming off their vessel, it had begun to slide back under, stern first. The whole episode had taken less than forty minutes, and Elektra's Captain hadn't even paused to recover survivors from either HMS Veteran or the U-Boat. Instead, the two British destroyers had turned their bows northwards and set course as ordered to assault the Nazi armada.

And that was when the trouble had begun. As the destroyers raced to catch up with the smaller vessels in their strike force, they had seen the small craft pulling away from their direct course along the coastline, huge columns of water rising up amongst the assorted vessels. They were being fired on by the Kilnsea Battery. Bulstrode had ordered that the usual recognition signals should be sent; both by flag and by lamp. For their efforts, Elektra received four shells from the Kilnsea Battery, which landed very close by.

"It's the Jerries." Bulstrode had said simply. "They've got the guns at Kilnsea too."

In typical Bulstrode fashion, he had ordered both of their big guns to return fire at the battery as they sailed past. At the same time, they began making smoke in an attempt to obscure the Kilnsea Battery's view of the smaller craft.

The gunners at Kilnsea were worryingly accurate and Elektra was subjected to over a dozen near misses; very near misses indeed. Venomous, less fortunate, took a direct hit and was left with a gaping hole in her port side, amidships. The hole belched acrid black smoke and flames, but their companion destroyer sailed on with them, returning fire from its own guns as they went. Eventually, after half an hour of fierce exchange, the small British flotilla sailed out of range of the big guns, and focussed their energies on the main task ahead. They didn't have long to focus however, for within ten minutes, they were under attack again, this time from the air.

Two pairs of Me 110 fighter-bombers had come screaming at them across the wave-tops from the seaward flank, their 20mm cannons chattering away as they riddled the superstructure of the two destroyers with fire. They had dropped their bombs too, pulling up and veering to starboard suddenly as their deadly black cargos tumbled downwards towards the British ships. Again, Elektra had come close to being hit, but managed to avoid the falling bombs through violent evasive action. Poor old Venomous was not having a lucky day however and took a bomb on its foredeck, resulting in the loss of its main armament. Despite the second explosion and yet more casualties, the courageous men of Venomous had driven their ship on. More than that, as the German twin-engined planes came howling back in for a second pass, it was the anti-aircraft gunners of that ship who had brought one of the aircraft down.

The Messerschmitt had been so badly raked with fire that its starboard engine had exploded, ripping most of the wing off. Almost instantly, the plane had simply arced over and smashed nose first into the sea, its crew still trapped inside it. The other three aircraft had come in against the smaller British craft this time, using their cannon and machine guns against the minesweepers and patrol boats. One of the tiny sloops had taken three long bursts of canon fire and begun to burn, its wheelhouse completely ripped to shreds and its crew decimated. As the three surviving German planes wheeled off eastwards, their attack complete, Bulstrode and Welch had noted that one of the aircraft was trailing a thin stream of smoke.

The British flotilla had ploughed on, and when they reached a point just off Hornsea, the enormity of the German invasion hit them. The horizon to the north was full of ships of every kind. Although still some ten miles distant, there was no mistaking that they were faced with an impossible task. However, this was the Royal Navy, and the small strike force had their orders, and so there was no option but to attack. That was when they hit the minefield.

It wasn't meant to be there, but the Kreigsmarine knew how vulnerable their invasion force was, and how powerful the Royal Navy was, should it choose to concentrate its strength and attack in force. With that in mind, the Germans had layered their defences, and the laying of a hasty minefield to cover the shallow waters of the northern and southern flanks was just a part of that defence. The first the British knew of the mines was when one of the small sloops suddenly, and quite literally, blew up in front of their eyes. The little craft had disintegrated as the huge explosive content of the mine detonated with a resounding 'thump'.

With the minesweepers pushed well forward from then on, the remaining craft in the British force had gone on, piercing the enemy minefield, as the German flank protection flotilla raced southwards to meet them. The odds had always been heavily stacked against Elektra, Venomous, and the handful of smaller craft, but the battle that had raged over the last hour had been far from one-sided. The three German destroyers and the E-Boat flotilla that came out to meet them had launched a two pronged attack against the British intruders. The destroyers had come on together, big guns concentrating on the British destroyers, whilst the fast, heavily armed E-Boats had curled around the landward flank of the British and come racing in towards the small force of sloops and minesweepers.

Within minutes, two of the smaller British ships were going under, but not before their combined firepower had brought one of the E-Boats to a standstill, the boat burning fiercely as its crew hastily abandoned it. Meanwhile, the remaining E-Boats had turned their attention to Elektra. For almost an hour now, the destroyer had been fighting two battles. One had been the close-in, breathtaking fire-fight with the vulture-like E-Boats, as they came in time after time to launch torpedoes or blaze away with their cannon and machine-guns. Thrice, Elektra had come close to being hit by the long, deadly, sub-surface missiles, but thanks to Bulstrode's superb seamanship they had succeeded in turning the ship away from disaster on each occasion. At the same time, Elektra's pair of four inch guns had continued their duel with the enemy destroyers.

Poor, brave old Venomous had lived up to her name. With no main armament and burning fiercely already, the destroyer had seemed like an easy target for the German ships. Two of the enemy destroyers had focussed on the vessel, raining shell after shell down onto the stricken ship. The Captain, understanding that his ship was already doomed, wasted no time with evasive action. The ship seemed to pick up speed as it ploughed head-on towards the enemy, and, once in range, launched a pair of torpedoes at the nearest enemy ship. The German destroyer managed to turn away in time, the torpedoes from Venomous sliding by, just behind the ship's stern; but Venomous wasn't finished with her opponent. The bows of Venomous came around a few points and, seconds later, two more torpedoes were on their way towards the enemy vessel. Once more, the German captain managed to pull his ship out of the path of the torpedoes, whilst the second German destroyer turned side-on, raking Venomous with every bit of firepower it had… and in doing so, fell into the burning British destroyer's trap.

Unbelievably, with its whole deck and superstructure on fire, the Venomous had suddenly heeled sharply to starboard and dipped its bows towards the second of its opponents. The captain of the second German destroyer had realised his predicament too late and Elektra's crew had heard the huge 'clang' as the Venomous had rammed the enemy vessel amidships. Both of the ships went down, the German first. Venomous, defiant to the last and true to its name, finally dipped below the waves after its victim had disappeared from sight, leaving Elektra and just a single minesweeper to fight on.

Unable to get Elektra with torpedoes, the E-Boats had managed to isolate the minesweeper, circling it like wolves closing in on a wounded sheep. The poor old minesweeper didn't stand a chance and was shot to pieces within a minute. However, this did give Elektra's machine gunners the chance they were looking for and they used the opportunity to systematically rake the E-Boats with rapid fire. Seeing their danger, three of the enemy craft pulled away, leaving the stricken British minesweeper to sink, but a fourth German craft, caught by concentrated fire, was going nowhere, its engines shot through. Captain Bulstrode had been in no mood for mercy, having already watched the minesweeper torn to shreds, along with the sacrifice of the Venomous and its brave crew.

"Blow the bastard out of the water!" Bulstrode had ordered Welch, bluntly.

Welch had passed on the order and, seconds later, every gun bar their main armament had opened fire on the crippled German E-Boat. Less than thirty seconds later, the German craft had exploded in a huge orange fireball.

Crash! The violent explosion somewhere to the rear of the ship brought Welch out of his reverie. Bulstrode was shouting.

"They've hit us again, just behind the funnels! Get me a damage report on that Mr Welch; quick as you like."

Bulstrode stood ram-rod straight against the front wall of the bridge, his face as dour and calm as if he was watching a peace-time gunnery drill. Welch grabbed hold of the communications tube and relayed the demand for a damage report, then staggered over to where Bulstrode glared out across the waves.

The scene was one of chaos. Welch imagined that nothing like this had been seen since Jutland, nearly a quarter of a century ago, except perhaps in Norway earlier this year. The surface of the grey water was littered with debris and the remains of burning craft. A constant haze of dirty smoke seemed to be hovering above the waves, whilst a cloud of steam still lingered above the spot where both the Venomous and the German destroyer had gone down. In every direction there were bodies. Some of them were dead, floating grotesquely in the cold murky water, whilst others were alive; some bobbing in the sea, their heads above water, whilst others clung desperately to bits of wreckage or life rafts.

Bulstrode seemed oblivious to it all, and Welch was in awe of him. This must have been what it was like to stand next to Nelson, he thought.

"Damage report, Mr Welch, Sir. Boiler room still intact and able to give full power. The damage from the last shell was superficial, but we've lost one of the anti-aircraft guns."

Welch turned and acknowledged the report from the rating standing by the communication tube. He looked back at Bulstrode who glanced at him. The Captain nodded to signal he had heard the damage report, then looked away again, giving instructions to the gunnery officer. As the lieutenant moved away to execute the Captain's orders, Bulstrode turned back to Welch.

"We won't survive much longer, Mr Welch." He said calmly. "Not if we hang around."

The Captain scanned the scene before him, holding tightly onto the bridge as Elektra's four inch guns roared in anger once more.

"We won't get through to the enemy transports on our own. It's only a matter of time before we take a bad hit. Then we'll be finished."

He looked Welch directly in the eyes.

"I am conscious of the sacrifice made by Venomous and the patrol flotilla, but we still have our guns and our means of propulsion. We can be of use to the fleet still. To sacrifice ourselves here for no gain would be a waste of a valuable ship, Mr Welch."

Welch simply nodded.

"I propose to break off the action, Mr Welch. I do not do this lightly. I am not running scared because I'm worried about casualties. We serve to sacrifice ourselves; that is the Navy way."

The Captain's eyes were intense now, and Welch could see the clash of desires within them. Bulstrode wanted to fight. With all his heart, the Captain wanted to stay here and follow the example of Venomous. But at the same time, Bulstrode was a professional. He understood the bigger picture. He was no coward, but his brain was telling him that to die a heroes death at this time, and at this place, would be a waste. Welch could see the internal conflict that beset his Captain. The man's eyes were the window into his soul, and with a start, Welch realised that Bulstrode needed someone to help him decide. So he did.

"If we break off the action now, Sir, nobody can deny that we did our service here. As you say, there is no chance of us breaking through. We can sacrifice a valuable destroyer for the sake of our own pride, or we can break off the action and join up with another force, where we can fight the Germans again and give an even better account of ourselves. I know what the Admiralty would prefer."

Bulstrode stared at his first officer for a long moment, nodding solemnly.

"I agree Mr Welch." He said "We will break off the action. I have ordered the gunnery officer to concentrate every weapon on the nearest enemy destroyer. We will turn broadside on for just one minute and give them everything we've got. Then we turn away and run like hell, making smoke as we go. We can only hope that they won't follow. Once we're clear, we'll make contact with the cruiser squadron and arrange a rendezvous. Does that make sense?"

"Perfect sense, Sir." Welch assured him.

Bulstrode nodded.

"Good. Give the order then. Hard to port, standby to go full ahead."

Welch saluted.

"Aye, aye, Sir."

'S' DAY
H +4

BY BRACEY BRIDGE – THE DRIFFIELD-BRIDLINGTON ROAD
SATURDAY 21ST SEPTEMBER 1940 – 0930 HOURS

The battle seemed to have taken just minutes, but when Smithson looked at his watch he saw that it had taken in excess of two hours. He sat in the crew compartment of his carrier, staring forwards, his face grim. The little carrier rattled along the tarmac road towards Bridlington, the surviving four carriers spaced out behind in their usual formation. About two hundred yards behind the carriers were the two civilian buses, loaded with two platoons and the tactical headquarters group of 'A' Company from Smithson's battalion.

Smithson scanned the road and fields ahead with bleak, alert eyes. He was a different man to the one who had set out from his billet in the early hours of that morning. Any boyish dreams that he may have had about commanding men in battle were distant memories. He knew now what it was like; how dirty, unpleasant, and downright terrifying battle could be. He had changed sometime over the last couple of hours, he reflected.

The trick with the petrol had worked. He and several other men had crept forwards into the ditch that bordered the road and then poured out their jerry cans of fuel onto the stubble beyond the hedge. It had only taken a petrol soaked handkerchief tied to a twig and thrown over the hedge to ignite the petrol soaked stalks. The subsequent 'whoosh' as the fuel went up had probably scared Smithson as much as it had the Germans, for he had realised too late that he was far too close, and lost his eyebrows as a result. He ran his hand over his singed and smoke blackened face as he went through the turbulent events of the last two hours in his mind, wincing when his dirty fingers ran over one of the small burns on his cheek bone.

The fire had taken quickly, and, as he had predicted, the lively breeze had blown the ever expanding flames inexorably north-eastwards, towards the copse and the Germans hiding amongst the remains of the stubble. For their part, the Germans had reacted instantly, breaking cover and running like hell for the comparative safety of the field behind. That had been his second eye-opener, after his lesson about the volatility of petrol. The Germans had not been the handful they had expected, but nearer two sections-worth, going on for a platoon. They did indeed have a mortar, along with two light machine-guns, and suddenly the field had come alive with enemy paratroopers, firing and manoeuvring with great professionalism as they withdrew hurriedly in front of the wall of flames.

Smithson had led the attack. He had taken No.1 Section right flanking around the edge of the creeping flames, whilst Holdcroft had gone round to the left. They had literally herded the German paratroopers along, mowing them down with their Bren Guns to keep them moving. At first, Smithson had been slightly intimidated by the amount of enemy they had flushed out, and by the sight of their obvious professionalism. He had almost come to the decision that it would be enough to drive them back from the road for just a couple of fields, and then pull back, to get on with his original task. But then the Germans had killed Holdcroft. Two of the enemy, feeling slightly bolder than the rest, had tucked themselves well out of sight against the hedgerow at the far side of the field, where Holdcroft was leading No.2 Section around the flames. The Germans had held their nerve until Holdcroft's carrier was coming right by them, and that was when they leapt out of cover and tossed their grenades into the open topped armoured vehicle.

The carrier had exploded in a cloud of flame of smoke. Even from his position two hundred yards away at the other side of the field, Smithson had watched the bits of vehicle and body parts fly through the air, almost lazily, before thudding down amongst the remains of the harvest. He saw the two Germans die almost immediately as the following carrier tore into them at point blank range with its machine-gun. And that was when he decided to hunt down every last one of the Germans.

Smithson was an educated man. He had studied theology at Cambridge and considered himself a balanced and civilised individual. Revenge was not an emotion with which he was familiar, nor fond of, but out in that burning field of straw, he had resolved to kill every German present. Instead of withdrawing, he drove right into the middle of the Germans, sitting upright in the back of the moving vehicle and picking his targets with the Lee-Enfield, whilst his gunner used magazine after magazine on the vehicle's Bren Gun. Even Soames, caught up in the fury of pursuit, had done his bit, physically chasing down one of the paratroopers and crushing the screaming man beneath their tracks. Smithson should have felt pity for the German, or simply revulsion at the terrible death, but instead he had congratulated Soames on his kill, then ordered him to stop for a moment so that he could retrieve the enemy's machine-pistol.

Then the Germans' discipline had broken. Their rapid, but organised withdrawal turned into a rout. They stopped firing and just ran, not in controlled groups as before, with one group covering the other, but in a pell-mell dash for safety. Smithson didn't let them get away. In theory, now he had time to think about it, had the enemy kept their nerve they could have easily defeated the small platoon of British carriers. But in battle, a man's mind does not always work in a logical manner. And so Smithson and his remaining men had gunned down every last German they could find, until the field was silent except for the sound of flames.

The reorganisation following the hectic battle had been quick through necessity. The flames were spreading rapidly and the smoke was becoming a serious hazard. Any attempt to view what was left of Holdcroft's carrier or its occupants was prevented by the flames which had already engulfed the shattered vehicle. Across the fields, individual rounds went off randomly as the creeping wall of fire reached them. Smithson and his men had looted the dead. Not for trinkets, but for weapons. They left the German rifles, but helped themselves to the very useful looking automatic pistols and machine-pistols which many of them carried. The two light machine-guns were also liberated and thrown into the back of the carriers, along with a small supply of ammunition that was left for them.

As for the enemy mortar, neither Smithson nor any of his men had the faintest idea what to do with the thing, and so they had dumped it in front of the advancing flames and laid its half dozen spare bombs alongside it. By then it was time to get moving. The field was just one big cloud of choking grey smoke and the heat from the burning stubble was becoming unbearable. The copse too, had caught light, the dying leaves on the branches catching fire with a loud crackling noise. Leading his smoke blackened and battle-weary men in a long loop, Smithson had regained the main Driffield to Bridlington road just as the first bus appeared.

He had immediately recognised Major Marcus Hornby, commanding 'A' Company of his own battalion. The company had started late, and only two buses had turned up, instead of three. To that end, Hornby with his small headquarters and two platoons had set out towards Bridlington, whilst the company second in command waited behind with the third platoon; their orders to follow on at the earliest opportunity. Hornby had told them to start marching and that he would send a bus back for them once he and the main body had reached Bridlington. The grimy and newly hardened Smithson had commented that at the present rate of advance, the third platoon of 'A' Company would probably get into Bridlington before them.

Then had come the scare. Six aircraft had appeared out of nowhere, attracted by the rising cloud of smoke and the collection of vehicles on the road. For a moment, Smithson had experienced a surge of panic, remembering the savage impact of the earlier bombing by the German raider. But then, looking up, he saw the distinctive, graceful shape of the small aircraft, their RAF roundels showing bright against the green-brown camouflage paint scheme on their fuselages. For their part, the half dozen Spitfires had circled the convoy of carriers and buses once, probably to satisfy themselves of the owners' identities. Then, with a waggle of his aircraft's wings, the lead pilot had peeled off sharply eastwards and roared away towards the coast at tree-top height, his five companions hurtling after him.

Smithson and 'A' Company had followed. Their original orders stood, and the RAF seemed to know where they were going for sure. The young carrier platoon commander had a growing feeling however, that his day was going to be anything but straight-forward. As Smithson reflected on the chaos in which he had just been involved, he hear a loud 'crump' some distance behind him. Looking back without too much haste, he saw the dark stain of smoke rising above the lighter grey clouds that hung above the burning field. He surmised that the German mortar bombs had finally been caught by the flames. Looking back down the road, he reckoned they had gone perhaps a mile at the most. He noted the junction that they had just passed and realised that they would soon be passing the village of Ruston Parva. The ground was rising slightly on the northern side of the road, and he knew that it would soon drop away again as the road came over the side of the spur. The village would be down to his…

"Whoooa...!"

The driver threw the brakes on so hard that Smithson was propelled forward, thumping painfully into the top end of the cab.

"Aagh!" He cried out, his voice a mixture of pain and anger. "Soames! What the hell do you think you're…"

"Mr Smithson, Sir?" His driver's voice interrupted him. "If those aren't Jerries, then I'm a monkey's fucking uncle!"

Smithson scrambled upright and peered over the front of his compartment, pushing his helmet rim up.

They were on the crest of the spur. Sure enough, the village of Ruston Parva lay down in the low ground, off to their forward left. Directly in front of them, the road dropped away into a shallow valley, before rising up towards the crest of another ridge, perhaps a mile and a half further on. In the bottom of the valley, the road crossed a wide stream by means of a small bridge, although it was hard to see as the line of the stream was edged with a long stretch of woodland. Just before the trees swallowed the road, there was a cross roads, maybe five hundred yards away at the most. Sitting right on that junction was a collection of motorcycles and an armoured car. The armoured car was of a design that Smithson had never seen, and the men standing around it were dressed not in khaki, but a grey-green colour.

For a long, endless moment, Smithson stared towards the crossroads, and he saw the faces of the grey-clad figures turn and stare back. And then the first burst of machine-gun fire bounced off the tarmac thirty yards in front of them, the bullets ricocheting upwards and outwards at acute angles, the deadly metal slugs whining in protest at the sudden deflection.

"Jerries! Open fire!" He roared needlessly as his gunner opened up with the Bren Gun.

More bursts of German fire came towards them, more accurate this time, cracking right past Smithson's ears as he brought up one of the pilfered German light machine-guns.

"Head down, Soames!" He shouted as he balanced the long barrelled weapon over the rim of his compartment, taking aim on the distant vehicles.

He pulled the trigger.

Rat-tat-tat-tat-tat-tat-tat-tat!

The weapon lurched in his shoulder and Smithson released the trigger, surprised at the rate of fire.

"Bloody hell!" He swore, staring in awe at the gun's smoking barrel.

Several enemy bullets bounced off the front of his vehicle, making him duck urgently.

"Jerry bastards!" He yelled, popping back up and realigning himself onto the enemy vehicles.

Rat-tat-tat-tat-tat-tat-tat-tat! He loosed off another long burst of fire.

There was the sudden roar of an engine, then the squeal of tracks and running gears braking sharply. Smithson glanced to his left and saw that the section commander of No.1 Section had driven up abreast of him. Within moments of coming to a halt, the other vehicle's Bren Gun burst into life, whilst the corporal in the rear compartment began loosing off rounds with his Lee-Enfield.

"What have we got, Sir?" The corporal yelled above the noise.

He didn't bother to look at Smithson, concentrating on his aim instead.

"Looks like German recce vehicles!" Smithson hollered back in reply. "I think we can probably take them!"

Just at that point, something moved further down the road, well beyond the cross roads. Smithson caught the movement as he let rip with another long burst towards the armoured car. He released the pressure on the trigger and looked up, squinting into the bright morning light. He heard the distant rev of the engines, which confirmed instantly the initial thoughts that his eyes were passing to his brain. From the shadowed confines of the wood-line, where the road passed over Bracey Bridge, several black shapes emerged, rattling up the slope towards the crossroads. Smithson's mouth dropped open in surprise and a bolt of electrifying fear ran through him.

"Tanks!"

Down by the crossroads, the grey figures had melted away into the hedgerows and a steady fire was coming from them now, the rounds bouncing off the front armour plate of the carriers or slapping against the tarmac. The armoured car had driven forward a short distance, covering the abandoned motorcycles, and it too was firing at them with its turret mounted machine gun. Further back, three other vehicles came clattering onwards in support. The first two vehicles were tanks; Smithson could see that. The vehicle behind was another kind of armoured car or personnel carrier, but he couldn't quite make out the vehicle's exact function.

"Back!" He shouted to the neighbouring carrier. "Get back over the crest! Soames! Reverse! Straight back over the crest!"

Soames was already moving, the mere mention of tanks enough for him. Even before Smithson had got the words out, the carrier jerked backwards, hesitantly at first, but then at speed. Smithson turned, watching the rear of the vehicle and shouting out steering corrections as Soames rapidly withdrew the carrier from enemy sight. Even once they were back on the reverse slope, Soames kept going, and Smithson allowed him to do so, until they were about a hundred yards back from the ridge and in danger of slamming into the rest of their platoon.

"Stop!" Smithson reached over and tapped the young private on the helmet.

The vehicle jerked to a halt and once more Smithson was hurled down the compartment, this time slamming against the rear of the carrier. Ignoring the pain, he struggled upright and turned to face his carrier crews. A small forest of heads had appeared, a dozen sets of eyes watching him in anticipation.

"German armoured column!" He blabbered quickly. "Half a dozen vehicles. At least two tanks! One Section, fan out to the left in that field. Two Section, fan out to the right. Get your Boys Rifles up and loaded. If they come over that hill, give them everything you've got! Concentrate on the tanks! Move!"

Without further prompting, the carriers began peeling left and right off the road.

"What about us, Sir?" Soames shouted up.

"We stay here, Soames. Pull over against the hedgerow there, so we're not too obvious, but leave us nose on to the crest."

"Right, Sir." Soames acknowledged and immediately threw the vehicle into gear.

Smithson reached over and tapped the gunner on the shoulder.

"Knowles, get in the back here and get this Boys Rifle set up. As soon as anything comes over that hill, put a round straight through it; understand?"

"No dramas, Sir." Replied the gunner, struggling out of his tiny cab, as the vehicle lurched over the grass verge.

As Soames pulled the carrier against the hedge, Knowles clambered into the rear compartment. Smithson meanwhile, grabbed the German light machine-gun and a spare belt of ammunition for it, then dropped over the rear of the vehicle. He was met by Hornby and his company sergeant major, who were doubling up the slope from the pair of stationary buses. The two vehicles were now tucked into the side of the road and dozens of khaki-clad infantrymen were disgorging from the cream coloured vehicles. Hornby gave Smithson a worried look.

"Dickie, what's going on, old boy?"

Smithson, his face scorched and dirty, looked the company commander squarely in the eye.

"Marcus," He said, "I'm afraid we're in big trouble!"

STONEGATE – HUNMANBY VILLAGE
SATURDAY 21ST SEPTEMBER 1940 – 0935 HOURS

When the German Army had marched triumphantly through Holland, Belgium and France earlier that year, the civilians had looked frightened. Some of those civilians, the older ones mainly, had looked ashamed and wept openly. So, it was something of a surprise when the first British civilian they encountered spat at them in contempt. He was a boy of perhaps eleven or twelve who stood defiantly on the pavement in his slippers and a pair of blue and red striped pyjamas.

The villages of Reighton and Speeton had fallen quickly, thanks to the paras. The enemy battery on the cliffs had followed soon after, attacked from all sides by the pioneers of the 17th Division with their satchel charges and flame throwers. Now Hunmanby was in German hands too. The paratroopers had been involved in some surprisingly tough fighting around the village, which was of a considerable size, more like a small town.

On their march up to the village, Saltz and his men had passed the bodies of half a dozen dead soldiers from the 7th Parachute Division, sprawled grotesquely in a gateway by the main road, their congealing blood forming large dark stains on the tarmac. As the men of Third Company entered the village itself, they came across a squad of paras manhandling some of their dead comrades towards a collection point, where a senior non commissioned officer was making notes.

Also laid out at the collection point, were the bodies of the British defenders. They were a strange sight; dressed in badly fitting uniforms of cheap denim material, that were more green, rather than khaki-brown, which Saltz usually associated with the British. He noticed also that they wore armbands bearing a title in black letters. Not being an English speaker however, Saltz had no idea what the words meant. The most striking feature of the enemy dead however, was their faces. Most of them were old, their hair silver-grey, or else extremely young; teenagers barely out of school.

"Ha!" Barked Lieutenant Hagen, as they clumped past in column of twos. "See that, Sergeant? Old men and boys! That's all the Tommies have got left to fight us with. England is finished. We'll have them on their knees within days!"

The senior NCO from the paras looked up and glared at Hagen, although the young officer paid no heed. Saltz didn't bother to point out to Hagen that there were more German bodies lined up than there were British. He looked at the lifeless, care-worn faces of the British dead with a sinking feeling. Saltz's earlier elation at being in the thick of battle was disappearing fast. Their company had suffered nearly twenty percent casualties, whilst the other companies had lost maybe thirty percent or more. And was all that suffered at the hands of just a handful of old men and boys? Their victory on the beach and the cliff-tops seemed hollow somehow, when Saltz reflected how inadequate the defences had been. There was no glory to be had there, he decided.

They marched on, directed by guides from the paras, right into the heart of the village and past one of the much discussed Tommy 'pubs', then onwards, up a broad straight avenue, apparently the village high-street. It was there that they saw the boy in his pyjamas. He wasn't alone. He stood on the pavement in front of his house, with his younger sibling, another boy, and their mother. Saltz could see more civilians beyond the first group, all of them eager to see what the dawn had brought. And that was when he noticed the looks on the faces of the Tommy villagers. Far from looking terrified by the might of the Third Reich, the full weight of which had appeared on their doorsteps like a thunder-bolt on this grey morning, the civilians looked grim and recalcitrant.

Marching next to Hagen, Saltz caught the eye of the older boy and gave an involuntary shudder at the look of utter hatred that emanated from him. When they were no more than three paces away, the boy hawked and spat onto the road in front of them. Hagen pulled up sharply.

"You dirty little bastard!" The lieutenant swore at the boy.

"Leave it, Sir." Saltz murmured quietly.

The boy, instead of shying away from the angry German officer, simply stared up at Hagen, and then, yet again, he hawked and added another blob of spittle to the tarmac.

"Why, you little fucking…" Hagen stepped forward, raising his hand.

The woman grabbed her son's shoulder and yanked him back a pace, but still the boy stared defiantly at Hagen. Saltz grabbed his platoon commander's arm and pulled it back. Behind Saltz, one of his men sniggered.

"Leave it!" Snarled Saltz at the young officer. "Don't rise to it, Lieutenant."

Hagen's face was purple with anger as he stared from the boy's face, to his mother's, and back again. The woman was glaring at Hagen with a look that was nothing short of disgust. Hagen lowered his arm reluctantly.

"You're all a bunch of island-monkeys!" He sneered at the family.

They probably didn't understand a word of German, but the woman now followed her eldest son's example and spat on the floor at Hagen's feet. A split second later the youngest boy, who couldn't have been more than nine years old, added his spittle to the pool of mucus.

Hagen exploded.

"You fucking bunch of fucking island-monkeys! Don't you realise you're fucking-well beaten!"

Saltz yanked the officer's arm and pulled him onwards up the street.

"Leave it, Sir; for fuck's sake! Come on!"

Hagen allowed himself to be led, but as Saltz dragged him up the street, the officer threw an angry glare back at the woman and her children.

"You stupid fucking whore! All your men are dead! And you'll be following if you don't change your attitude!"

Watching him get pulled away, the woman spat in his direction once more.

Hagen looked back at Saltz.

"Fucking Tommy bitch! Fucking hell, Saltz, these bastards need teaching a lesson!"

"Ignore them." Saltz grunted, his face growing dark.

"But they're just a bunch of fucking island…"

"Sir!" Saltz snapped loudly, glaring at his platoon commander. "Shut the fuck up and just march!"

Hagen looked shocked at Saltz's reprimand, but then looked away and fell silent. Just as he did so, he passed an old woman standing on her doorstep. She spat on the road in front of him and his jack-boot crunched down into the spittle a moment later. Hagen flung a look at Saltz, but the sergeant was staring grimly ahead. There was nothing Hagen could do but march on and keep quiet.

Behind them, the rest of the platoon had stopped laughing. They had all now passed the furious looking boys and their mother, all three of whom had continued to spit onto the Germans' jack-boots as they passed. And when they tramped by the old lady at the next house, she did the same. And so did every Tommy civilian in the street. For the young German soldiers who had only recently joined the division, the reception was a shock. Their own radio had been telling them for months that the poor British people were just waiting for the Third Reich to free them from the oppressive yoke of their aristocratic King and his fat Prime Minister. Their generals and politicians had been telling them all summer that the British were finished; that they would capitulate soon. Looking at the faces of the British civilians, all of those claims suddenly appeared to be complete and utter nonsense.

For the veterans of the division, the men who had fought through Poland and Western Europe, the reception was even more worrying. They had seen many civilians and refugees over the last year. Most of them had been pathetic, helpless creatures, despairing at the fate that had befallen them. But these Tommy civilians were different. They were unafraid. They looked defiant. Their faces spoke of nothing but utter hatred and contempt for the invaders. Somehow, those civilian faces looked much more intimidating than any counter-attack force the British Army could throw at them. One by one, the German soldiers looked away from the civilians. Some looked at the sky, whilst others looked fixedly at the equipment strapped to the back of the man in front.

And on they marched. The men of the German 17th Infantry Division tramped through the main street of Hunmanby, and through an ever growing sea of phlegm.

THE RAILWAY CUTTING – SEAMER BRIDGE
SATURDAY 21ST SEPTEMBER 1940 – 0940 HOURS

"Christ almighty, Company Sergeant Major!" Swore Major Francis Archibold. "There's a lot more of the buggers than I thought there were!"

Panting heavily, Company Sergeant Major Chris Chillingham nodded back at his company commander.

"You're not wrong there, Sir! I think we must have run into a full battalion of the bastards!"

"Yes..." Archibold replied thoughtfully, placing fresh .38 inch rounds into his revolver as he did so. "We caught that first bunch on the hop alright, but there were hundreds more queuing up beyond those cottages. I reckon they were forming up for an attack on Oliver's Mount."

Leaning on his bayonet-tipped rifle, Chillingham nodded in agreement.

"Yeah; I reckon so. Anyway, Sir, we certainly put a spanner in their works didn't we?"

Archibold chuckled.

"We certainly did, but you can bet your next month's wages they'll be coming back at us shortly. How many did we lose?"

Chillingham pulled a face.

"I think maybe twenty all together. I've called for an ammo and casualty state from the platoons, so I'll have exact numbers shortly, Sir."

Archibold clicked the drum of his revolver shut, then looked up and down the shallow cutting through which the east-coast railway line passed.

"It's a great forming-up point, but not brilliant for defence. I think we'll pull everyone back to this side of the bridge and barricade the gap underneath it. That way we can secure our southern flank somewhat. I'll get Company Headquarters and No.5 Platoon to move into the station and fortify it. No.4 Platoon can stay here and hold the bridge, and No.6 Platoon can stay up there in the farm; it's a brilliant place for enfilade fire. As long as they hold it, the Jerries will be pushed to mount a frontal assault."

"Unless they've got tanks." Chillingham pointed out.

Archibold smiled.

"You love pulling my grand strategy to pieces, don't you Company Sergeant Major?"

"Just didn't want you to miss out the detail, Sir, that's all."

The last forty minutes had been both exhilarating and terrifying. Having been ordered to move rapidly from their original positions in the North Bay of Scarborough town, 'B' Company of the 1st Battalion South Teesside Regiment had found itself in the thick of the fighting. At first, everything had gone surprisingly well. The promised bombardment had not only come down on time, but on target too. The Germans to the front of 'B' Company had been shattered by the sudden barrage, and when the whistles had sounded at H-Hour, the big ex-dockers and steel workers from Middlesbrough, Guisborough and Redcar had driven all before them.

The enemy had reeled backwards, losing men all the time, either shot from the flank by No.6 Platoon in their fire support location, or else skewered from behind by the men of No.4 and 5 Platoons as they charged into the invaders. For ten minutes, it had been pure joy for the Teesiders, wreaking revenge on the Germans in a frenzy of killing that harked back to the berserker antics of their distant Nordic ancestors. But then they had run into the German reserves; lots of them. Not only was the village of Eastfield full of Germans, but most of them seemed to be armed with machine-guns. 'B' Company had run into a hail of withering automatic fire, suffering a number of casualties in the process. At that point, Archibold knew he had reached his limit of exploitation.

As the German fire intensified, and more and more grey-clad figures filtered towards them, the commander of 'B' Company realised that it was time to withdraw to a more defensible location. Slowly, deliberately, and with much difficulty, he had managed to extract his two platoons back to the railway line, where the shallow cutting provided a modicum of cover and where his left flank was protected by the No.6 Platoon fire support position. It wasn't over though; Archibold could see that. In fact, he sensed that the real battle was only just beginning.

A burst of machine-gun fire cracked overhead, having skimmed the top of the cutting. Up on the bank, several riflemen returned fire. In the bottom of the cutting, several figures approached them. The first was Corporal Dickinson from No.5 Platoon. He gave his company commander a grave look.

"Mr Pullyen's dead, Sir. So is Sergeant Stockdale. We've lost three other blokes, and there's a couple of walking wounded too. Other than that we're okay for ammunition and we've still got all our Brens and the Boys Rifle."

Archibold exchanged a quick glance with Chillingham.

"Okay," Archibold sighed, "thanks Corporal 'D'. Well done. I want you to step up as Platoon Commander for the time being. Get your lads formed up and ready to move. You're going to head down to the station and prepare it for defence. Company HQ will be co-located with you as well. Happy enough?"

The young corporal nodded.

"Aye, Sir."

"Good man. Now get your lads sorted. I'll be leading you off shortly.

"What about the prisoner, Sir?"

"You've got a prisoner?" Chillingham spoke.

"Aye, Sir. Wounded he is. Found him in the field over there as we pulled back."

"Bring him to me in the station." Chillingham replied crisply.

Dickinson nodded, did the same to Archibold, then turned on his heel and crunched off back down the gravel bed of the cutting.

As he moved away, a second person approached them; Second Lieutenant Winterton from No.4 Platoon.

"Hello Johnny, are you alright?" Archibold greeted him jovially.

The pale-faced young officer nodded hesitantly.

"Yes, fine thank you Francis..."

"I'm afraid I've got a tad bit of bad news for you, old boy." Archibold remained buoyant in tone. "Poor Billy Pulleyn has bought it."

The young officer's eyes widened, but Archibold went on quickly.

"But his boys did a grand job and we mustn't dwell on the poor chap now. What's the state of your platoon?"

Winterton blinked several times, confused by his company commander's sudden change of tack.

"Er... we're missing seven men... including Corporal Watts. We've got four wounded as well, including Sergeant Shepherd."

Archibold frowned.

"Crikey Johnny, you've been through the mill! How's Sergeant Shepherd? Is it serious?"

"No, just a slight wound to his arm. He and the other three can still fire their weapons."

"Good, good!" Boomed Archibold, larger than life as ever, even in the midst of battle. "Well the good news is you don't have to do any more running around. We're going to hold the bridge and the station until we get reinforced. Your boys will hold the railway cutting at this side of the bridge. I also want you to try and barricade the bottom of the cutting where it goes under the bridge there; no doubt the Jerries will try and outflank us to the south in due course. No.5 Platoon will hold the station and give you mutual support from there. Company HQ will also be in the station. I'm going to leave No.6 Platoon up in the farm because they're already in a good position. Are you alright for ammo?"

Winterton blinked again, then reached into his pocket and produced a small scrap of notepaper.

"Sergeant Shepherd says we're not too bad, with about seventy percent of our first line scale left."

Archibold nodded.

"Right, well, that will have to do for now. I think we'll get a runner back up into town with a situation report and a request for more ammunition."

He glanced at Chillington.

"We'll sort that one out in a moment, Company Sergeant Major."

"Aye, Sir." The warrant officer acknowledged.

"Now then, Johnny." Archibold turned back to Winterton. "Get your boys shaken out and see what you can do about blocking off this wee tunnel here. You should expect a German attack imminently. You might also wish to start digging some shell scrapes into that bank and building up your positions a bit."

"Yes, Francis." Winterton saluted clumsily, rapping his knuckles on the rim of his helmet as he did so. As he turned away, Archibold called after him.

"Oh, and Johnny."

"Yes, Francis?"

"Give a message to Sergeant Shepherd for me, would you please? Tell him that I'm pleased he's not seriously hurt. I can only assume that the

German who shot him was put off his aim by Shepherd's big, ugly cow-head!"

Winterton blinked again, bemused, then turned away and began climbing the embankment.

As the young officer clambered back to the top of the bank, Archibold and Chillington chuckled together.

"That will give Shepherd something to chunter about!" Chillington laughed.

"He'll probably moan the Germans to death!" Archibold agreed. "But on a serious note, I make that about twenty percent casualties? Perhaps a bit more?"

Chillington nodded.

"We can't keep that up for long."

"No…" Mused Archibold, "but I've no intention of making any more bayonet charges. There isn't much we can do without significant reinforcement. Our main effort now is to hold onto this position for as long as possible with minimum casualties. I'll need you to get a work party into the village and start bringing some stuff forward to use as barricades. If the Jerries do bring tanks up, then we're going to have a devil of a job holding them."

"Major Archibold, Sir!"

Both the officer and his company sergeant major looked up at the man hailing them from the western embankment. It was the company clerk, lying prone on the grassy crest as yet more bursts of German fire continued to rattle across the top of the cutting.

"Yes, Perkins? What is it?"

"Armour, Sir, coming this way!"

"What?" Archibold's relaxed manner suddenly evaporated.

"Armour, Sir. Bren Carriers by the looks, coming this way from Pickering."

Archibold gave a huge sigh of relief.

"Bloody hell!" He breathed quietly.

"Perhaps that's the rest of the division moving up, Sir?" Chillingham guessed.

Archibold managed to smile again, the brief panic over.

"I don't care who they are, company sergeant major; as long as they're on our side!"

BEHIND THE COTTAGES – SEAMER BRIDGE SATURDAY 21ST SEPTEMBER 1940 – 0945 HOURS

"What happened Peter?" Utz frowned at the visibly shaken battalion commander.

Stadtman took a breath and jerked his thumb towards the distant bridge.

"The Tommies launched a counter-attack, just as we were going for the bridge. Their artillery came down smack-bang on top of Third Company. Then they shifted the barrage right through the entire battalion. As it went through us, the Tommies came over the top from the railway line and charged right into us; with bayonets fixed, the crazy bastards! Third Company got cut up badly and my headquarters got trapped in the far cottage. We only just managed to barricade ourselves in before the Tommies broke into the built up area."

Stadtman paused, giving an involuntary shudder as he remembered the feeling of absolute terror, crouching there behind the bed, listening to the heavy footsteps pounding up the stairs. He had been poised to empty a full magazine into the Tommies he was expecting to appear in the doorway, but at the last moment, the sound of his signals officer's voice had prevented him from opening fire. The young lieutenant, sweating and bloodied, had called out Stadtman's name, just before he had bowled into the room. For just a couple of awful minutes, Stadtman and his small headquarters had been forced to defend themselves within the cottage as a group of Tommies had tried to force their way in, tossing grenades through the windows and trying their hardest to smash the doors in. Several members of the headquarters had been killed and injured during that short, but terrible fight.

It had been a near run thing, and only the sudden, but welcome arrival of the Machine-Gun Company and First Company had freed them from the attention of their besiegers. Good old Wolfgang. He had brought the remainder of the battalion up in quick time once he realised that the Tommies were on the offensive. The young operations officer was definitely in line for his own company in the near future.

"Fortunately, Colonel," Stadtman went on, "Captain Beck was in the process of bringing the rest of the battalion forward, so he immediately committed them and managed to bring the Tommies to a halt. I reckon there was maybe a company or so of the enemy, and they didn't seem to have any heavy weapons. They've got some light machine-guns up in the farm, but not much more than that. As soon as our Machine-Gun Company got stuck into them, they pulled back to the bridge."

Utz stared long and hard towards the said bridge, some five hundred metres away.

"So, what's the situation now?"

"Well, we've got a company or so of Tommy infantry down by the bridge and hiding in the sunken railway line. They've also got their machine-guns up in the farm, along with their mortars on Oliver's Mount. Their observers, wherever they are, can see every move we make. Their guns have stopped for now, but as soon as we try anything else, they'll come into action."

Utz pulled a worried face.

"Right, well, you'd better just consolidate where you are for now Peter. Don't try and go for the bridge again; just hold this perimeter and use your heavy stuff to keep that bridge and the farm suppressed. The 99th is coming up behind us now, so I'll brief them on what we've got here. I'm going to suggest that they hook south and come up the railway line that way. They might even try and hook right, behind the town, depending on how deep the enemy positions are. The Divisional Commander should be on the ground now, so I'll go and talk the problem through with him and the Colonel of the 99th. I'll ask them to get some more naval gunfire onto that hill too, and anything else we can get into action."

Utz looked back up the road again towards the bridge.

"Is this the first time you've fought the Tommies, Peter?"

"It is, Sir, yes." Replied Stadtman, quietly.

Utz nodded thoughtfully.

"Hmm. Well, Peter, you did well to hold them. It was only a matter of time before they got organised and launched a counter-attack. But I have one top tip for the future…"

Stadtman regarded the Colonel with serious eyes.

"Never let the Tommies get up close, Peter." Said Utz. "They're not the same as the Norwegians, French or the Belgiques, you know? The British are a nation of peasants. They like to drink, they like to fornicate, and more than anything, they like to fight. The Tommies always try to get close to you where they can use their bayonets and their fists. And that's a place you really don't want to be!"

"No, Sir." Stadtman acknowledged, feeling slightly embarrassed by the lecture.

"Keep them at arms distance, Peter." Utz continued. "Clobber them with your big stuff; machine-guns, mortars, grenades, whatever you've got. Their kit is crap compared to ours, so use that advantage to its best; stand-off and whack the bastards!"

"Yes, Sir."

"Now then, get your boys organised and dig in. I'll confirm what the plan is with the 99th as soon as I can. In the mean time, sit tight and clobber them every time they lift their stupid heads!"

"Right, Sir."

Utz pushed himself up off his elbow and prepared to stand. As he did so, a shout of alarm stopped him in mid-movement.

"Major! Major Stadtman, Sir!"

It was Beck, the operations officer. He had been kneeling a discreet distance away by the corner of another building, studying the distant bridge through his binoculars. Now, the energetic young captain was looking over towards both his battalion and regimental commander with a worried look on his face.

"We've got Tommy armour inbound! They're coming towards the bridge on the far side of the railway; maybe a couple of kilometres away. Looks like personnel carriers of some sort."

Utz looked across at Stadtman. As ever, the colonel's expression remained calm and thoughtful, even as he uttered the single word in reaction to the news.

"Bollocks!" He murmured quietly.

BY BRACEY BRIDGE – THE DRIFFIELD-BRIDLINGTON ROAD SATURDAY 21ST SEPTEMBER 1940 – 0950 HOURS

"Come on!" Smithson whispered in frustration, his sweaty finger curled in readiness around the trigger of the German machine-gun. "Where are you, you bastards?"

He was staring along the barrel, which in turn was trained onto the centre of the road where it crested the ridge in front of him, perhaps a hundred yards distant. At the other side of the road from him, his carrier was tucked against the hedge, with Private Knowles crouching over the front of the vehicle with his Boys Anti Tank Rifle at the ready. Ranged either side of him in the fields were the remaining carriers from his platoon, their own gunners training their Brens and Boys Rifles towards the crest of the ridge.

It must have been a quarter of an hour since their initial contact with the German vehicles. What were they waiting for? Did they suspect that the British had tanks at this side of the ridge? Were they being cautious? If only his battalion did have some proper tanks, Smithson thought, they would be in a position to do something. God only knew how long it would take the strategic reserve to reach the area? He glanced back over his shoulder quickly and saw that the men of 'A' Company had made good use of the time. The buses were back on the road now, positioned to block both it, and the side road that branched off towards Ruston Parva, their engines immobilised. The remainder of the company had been spread out in depth of the carriers, the young infantrymen clawing at the soil feverishly with their entrenching tools to improvise a hasty defensive position.

It hadn't taken Hornby or Smithson long to come to the same conclusion. If there were German tanks ahead, then the enemy had obviously landed in strength and any plans of getting through to Bridlington to reinforce the garrison were now irrelevant. The task of the small British force was now depressingly simple. Dig in, defend and delay. Smithson looked back towards the crest.

"Come on you Jerry bastards! Come on! In the name of God, let's get on with it!"

His prayer, snarled through gritted teeth, was answered almost immediately. Above the low hum of his own carrier's engine, which was idling, ready for immediate action, Smithson now heard something more distinct. Revving engines; the deep growl of machines being accelerated or forced up a steep incline.

"Here we go, men!" Smithson called. "Stand-by Soames."

He tucked the butt of the machine-gun into his shoulder and focussed through the sights.

"Please God," Smithson murmured, "don't let this bloody gun have a stoppage?"

He had worked out how to load, cock and fire the strange weapon, but if it were to jam at any stage, Smithson was far from confident that he would be able to deal with the problem.

The engine noises became louder, and he could hear something else now, above the dull roar. It was the squeal of tracks. Smithson's heart was thumping hard, his mouth bone dry, his cracked lips crusted with dried blood. He had rehearsed this moment in his mind over and over again, during the last few months; how it would be when he met the invader for the first time. His dreams and the reality of the situation bore no resemblance whatsoever. He blinked irritably as a trickle of sweat ran down his forehead and into his eye. The squeal of the tanks' tracks was louder than ever now, as was the ominous drone of powerful engines.

And then they appeared; not where Smithson expected them, but off to the flanks, bursting over the sky-line in the middle of the fields on both sides of the road. He heard the shouts of alarm from his flanking sections before he saw the enemy himself. He flung a look to his left and saw a tank ploughing up the earth as it sped towards the two Bren carriers from No.2 Section.

Looking right he saw a similar picture; only on this flank, the tank was backed up by a half track. Before he had a chance to shout orders, the enemy vehicles opened fire. The air was suddenly filled with the constant 'crack-crack-crack' of automatic gunfire, accompanied by the panicked shouts of Smithson's men.

The Germans had caught them out and Smithson cursed his own stupidity. Did he really think that the Germans would be gullible enough to just drive straight up the road and into his killing area? He watched helplessly as his furthest Bren carrier on the right was shot up badly and then rammed by the enemy tank.

"Knowles, take out that bloody tank on your right!" Smithson screamed as he tried to bring his machine-gun around to the left to support the other section. Knowles was already moving, although the hedgerow was proving to be an obstacle to his line of fire.

Just at that point, the Germans showed exactly how coordinated they were, as their third group appeared over the crest, exactly where Smithson had originally expected them. Moving at high speed, a motorcycle and sidecar followed by the wheeled armoured car burst over the ridge and roared towards them along the tarmac.

"Jesus fucking Christ!" Blasphemed Smithson, the former student of theology, and pulled his machine-gun back round again.

He was too late to save poor Knowles. Both the armoured car and passenger of the motorcycle combination swung their guns onto Smithson's carrier and opened fire simultaneously. There was an unholy racket as bullet after bullet slammed into the already battered hull of the carrier with a deafening series of clangs. Knowles was lifted into the air, as if by some giant unseen hand and thrown violently back into the hawthorn hedge behind him.

Smithson watched in horror as Knowles was riddled with bullets. For long seconds, he was unable to move, his mind completely dislocated by the sudden rush of events.

Soames however, safe behind the armoured cab of the carrier, reacted in his typically unpredictable manner. The carrier suddenly lurched forward from its position against the hedgerow, and accelerated straight towards the oncoming Germans. The rider of the enemy motorcycle clearly didn't expect the reaction from the British vehicle and tried to swerve desperately as he saw the small green monster coming for him. He was nowhere near quick enough however, because Soames had anticipated the man's evasive manoeuvre and, in much the same way that he had chased down the German paratrooper earlier, he now rammed the motorcycle combination side on.

Smithson heard the crunch of the machines colliding, followed swiftly by the terrified scream of the motorcycle's rider and passenger as the Bren Carrier's tracks clattered up and over the top of them. In the blink of an eye, the motorcycle combination was on its side, a mangled wreck, and its crew a bloody mess of ground pulp.

Smithson, still overwhelmed by the horror developing around him, could only watch in stunned silence as Knowles reversed the carrier backwards off the wrecked enemy machine, leaving a pool of blood and petrol around the heap of metallic and human debris. As the Bren Carrier reversed backwards, a hail of automatic fire clattered against it once more, and one of the rounds ricocheted off it with a loud 'ping', barely missing Smithson's head as he lay there on the opposite verge. The British lieutenant suddenly came alive and brought the butt of the machine-gun into his shoulder. He stared along the barrel again to see the enemy armoured car bearing down on him, although the turret was still pointing towards Soames in the carrier.

Forgetting the sights, and with both eyes wide open, Smithson pulled the trigger on the weapon and it jumped into life with a deafening clatter. He saw the rounds bouncing off the enemy vehicle, and fired again with a much longer burst this time. The enemy vehicle didn't stop, although it did slow somewhat, and Smithson thought he heard frantic shouting from within the armoured car's turret. Just then, there was a deafening crack by his ear. It was so loud that he cried out and twisted away to his left. His right ear ringing painfully, Smithson looked up and saw that the armoured car had veered left and was hard up against the hedgerow on his side of the road, a mere twenty yards away.

With a surge of relief, Smithson realised that the loud crack had been the sound of a large calibre armour piercing round flying past him. Hornby's men were already making their presence felt with a Boys Rifle and Smithson thanked his lucky stars that he and his platoon were not on their own. He aimed his gun at the vehicle again, this time using the sights on the weapon, and unleashed another burst at the immobile enemy vehicle. As the sound of his burst died away, Smithson heard a strange grating noise. It stopped for a moment, but then he heard it again. His mind suddenly understood that the German vehicle had somehow stalled, and he fired another burst into the armoured car, this time aiming at its forward left tyre.

As his own burst tailed off, another deafening crack rattled Smithson's ear drum, making him wince at the noise once more. Despite this, he was elated to see something strike the armoured car with a bright flash. A split second later, somebody within the vehicle began screaming. Just at that point, he saw his own carrier suddenly appear in his peripheral vision. Soames was launching himself at the enemy vehicle. Smithson wondered what he was hoping to achieve, for there was no way the tiny Bren Carrier would be able to do any serious damage to the bigger German vehicle. To his surprise however, the carrier slammed to a sharp halt, right next to the armoured car. Moments later, Soames appeared from within his cab, standing upright, clearly outlined against the morning sky. The young soldier threw something under-arm towards the German vehicle, before dropping back down into his cab out of sight.

Smithson just caught sight of the small dark object as it landed on top of the wire cage that surrounded the vehicle turret and realised what Soames was doing.

"Christ!" Swore Smithson, realising he was within the grenade's danger area.

He pressed himself flat into the grassy verge. The three seconds it took for the grenade fuse to burn seemed endless, during which he heard the revs of his carrier as Soames attempted to reverse out of the blast area.

Crump!

The grenade exploded above the turret of the vehicle and Smithson held his breath. For a second, he just laid there, wondering if he'd been caught by the shrapnel, but when he realised he could still think and breath, he raised his head cautiously. The enemy vehicle was completely still, wreathed in smoke, and no voices came from within its grey hull. Not far away, Smithson's own carrier was sitting in the middle of the tarmac by the crushed motorcycle combination, stationary.

Shouting and gunfire made him roll onto his left shoulder and stare over toward the field on his right flank. He saw tracer rounds zipping to and fro' across the top of the recently harvested stubble. One of No.1 Section's carriers was on its side. The other was moving about the field, returning fire against the half-track, which was also manoeuvring about the open space, churning up the plough beneath its tracks. The enemy tank, he was amazed to see, was immobile; sort of. The tank was attempting to reverse, but every time it attempted to move backwards, the squat armoured vehicle juddered and veered around to the right.

Smithson frowned, wondering what was wrong with the vehicle, but then caught sight of the flailing track. It was then that he saw the khaki figure leap onto the tank's rear decks. He watched in disbelief as the lone British soldier clambered over the top of the metal beast, holding on tightly as it jerked and shuddered. The figure jumped aside in shock as the machine-gun in the vehicle's turret suddenly chattered into life, firing a stream of bullets towards a group of Hornby's men at the far side of the field. Even as the machine-gun blasted away, the khaki figure crawled with extreme care along the side of the vehicle's hull, right to the very front. He watched the figure raise and then lower an arm, and then roll off the vehicle and begin running away.

Smithson frowned, wondering what on earth the man was doing. Then he heard the screaming. Even from forty yards away, he could hear the terrified screams coming from within the metal monster. And then it exploded. There was a muted metallic thud, and then sparks erupted from the tiny vision slots of the tank, after which, the vehicle began to billow with thick black smoke. Moments later, individual rounds within the burning wreck began to detonate in a never ending series of muffled bangs.

Meanwhile, the half-track was beginning to back away over the crest, its machine-gun still chattering away as it reversed slowly over the ridge. As it went, lines of tracer followed it, either kicking up the earth around it or bouncing off the front of the vehicle's cab. Smithson rolled over, peering through the hedge into the other field. He could see one of his carriers on fire, whilst the other continued to fight on. The other German tank was withdrawing back towards the ridge itself, following the example of the half-track at the other side of the road. It was moving quickly, no apparent damage to its running gear, but the turret of the vehicle was billowing thick grey smoke. Within moments, every serviceable German vehicle had suddenly disappeared back over the crest, and the small arms fire died away.

Feeling completely overwhelmed by events, and somewhat amazed to still be alive, Smithson climbed awkwardly to his feet. He lifted the German machine-gun and walked slowly towards his carrier, making a wide detour in order to avoid walking through the remains of the German motorcycle crew. Coming up to the carrier, he leaned over the steel hull and looked with trepidation into the driver's cab. Soames was leaning against the side of the cab, the whole side of his face covered in blood. Smithson caught his breath for a moment, but then, with a tired groan, Soames moved. The young soldier turned his bloody head towards his platoon commander, and Smithson saw that the private was missing most of his left ear. Despite this, Soames grinned at him.

"Blimey, Sir, my head hurts like buggery!"

Smithson gave a sob of laughter, but wasn't quite sure why. He stared around him at the hellish scene of death and destruction and found it hard to believe that he had just witnessed the awful spectacle. As he cast his eyes about, a noise came to his ears once more. The noise made him look around sharply towards the crest, expecting to see more enemy vehicles. Smithson's eyes widened and his mouth fell open. It wasn't the reappearance of tanks that rendered him stupefied, but something up in the air. The grey skies and patchy cloud of the dawn were giving way to blue skies, with only a handful of fluffy white clouds to spoil the vista. And it was against that backdrop that Smithson now stared upwards at the huge armada of aircraft.

There were dozens of them, flying in groups of four, which in turn formed distinct waves. It was hard to tell what kind of planes they were, for the massed formation was at a considerable altitude, though one thing was obvious; they were heading inland. Smithson had never seen so many aircraft before; not in one place at one time. Over they came, wave after wave, heading roughly westwards. As the first waves disappeared over Driffield, the odd anti-aircraft shell burst amongst them, but there was little else to stand in the way of their inexorable progress. It was just coming up to ten o'clock in the morning…and the Luftwaffe was back.

HEADQUARTERS NORTHERN COMMAND - YORK
SATURDAY 21ST SEPTEMER 1940 – 0955 HOURS

"I need you to get competent officers to all of these points soonest, Jeremy. I don't want any confusion. We haven't got time to mess around. I want the Home Guard ammunition in one place where it's easy to find, with all the other stuff separate. Speak to GHQ and tell them where we want it all dropping. Understand?"

Adam fixed his logistics officer with a searching look.

"Yes, Sir; got all that." The colonel nodded in acknowledgement.

"Good. Once you've sorted that out, start putting together your plan for getting ammunition and supplies forward. Come back to me by midday with a list of what you've got available to move stuff with, and I'll tell you where we're going to need it."

Adam paused slightly, checking himself.

"Sorry, Jeremy; I'm getting in the weeds again aren't I?"

The logistics colonel made no reply.

"I just need everyone to understand that we can't afford to have any loose ends on this occasion. We won't get a second chance. I need every detail checking and double checking; every control measure in place. There is no room for error. You know that don't you?"

"Indeed, Sir." The colonel smiled. "I hear what you're saying. I'll personally dot every 'I' and cross every 'T'. There'll be no mistakes."

Adam nodded, effectively dismissing the officer, who hurried away, beckoning to his own junior staff officers as he went.

"Engineers?" Adam searched the small group of faces looking at him in anticipation.

"Yes, Sir?" Another colonel stepped forward.

"How many field troops can you spare, allowing for the work we've already discussed?"

"I could free up to six full troops, Sir. Any more than that and I couldn't guarantee the other tasks you've given me within the deadlines."

Adam nodded curtly in acknowledgement.

"That'll do. Six will suffice, I think. What about mines?"

The engineer colonel flicked a glance at his notes.

"We've got three hundred in command reserve, ready for immediate use. The 2nd Division has got another five hundred, although we won't be able to get hold of the entire stock as some will already be in use. The other three infantry divisions have similar numbers. In short, there's enough to make a start, but if you still intend to carry out the plan you briefed me on earlier, we'll need thousands more, Sir."

Adam was silent for a moment, nodding to himself repeatedly as his mind turned over. His staff watched him keenly, waiting for a reaction.

"Alright, gentlemen." He said calmly at last. "Let's get the intelligence picture updated, and then I'll tell you what my intentions are afterwards. James? Let's get on with it."

The intelligence officer moved to a central position by the map table and waited for the staff to settle down around it. Once the crowd were in position, he glanced across at the GOC, who nodded for him to begin.

"The situation as at 0945 hours was as follows, Sir. The enemy has conducted large scale parachute landings here over Driffield and here, in depth of Bridlington and Filey. A glider-borne force has also made a precision attack on Spurn Head. In addition to this, the enemy has mounted amphibious landings from Scarborough, right through this coastal strip, including Filey and Bridlington, as far as Skipsea. Driffield airfield has fallen to the enemy and the RAF has abandoned the station. Several aircraft managed to escape to RAF Leeming, but the rest were destroyed in situ before the base was abandoned. The runways themselves remain intact. As far as Driffield town is concerned, we believe that there is still heavy fighting taking place between enemy parachutists and the local brigade, which is currently split to the four winds. The situation in this area is confused and chaotic. We are unable to gain detailed situation reports and we currently have no influence on the battle."

The intelligence major flicked his pointer towards Scarborough.

"There has been a degree of success here, Sir. The local brigade has reported that they successfully repelled an amphibious assault against the town, inflicting heavy losses on German assault troops. South of the town however, the enemy has succeeded in getting ashore in Cayton Bay. They have now formed a beach-head and are reinforcing it rapidly. Our brigade has launched a limited counter attack, but is now waiting for the rest of 59th Division to join them, before they can launch a major assault. Their lead elements should be at Scarborough within the hour. At the moment, it appears to be check-mate in the Scarborough-Cayton area. The enemy are contained, but we aren't strong enough to counter-attack just yet."

The intelligence officer looked across to Adam, who gave the faintest of nods for him to go on.

"In Filey Bay, we have lost all communications with the local forces, including the Reighton coastal battery and the fire-control station. The RAF has lost all contact with its radar station on Flamborough Head too. Initial reports from RAF aircraft indicate that the enemy has been successful in this area, with enemy troops reported as moving inland, and armoured vehicles seen on the beaches. Anti-aircraft fire is getting heavier by the hour, which suggests that the enemy has managed to get his land based anti-aircraft assets ashore."

The major ploughed on.

"In Bridlington, we know that the town was assaulted from the rear by paratroopers during the early hours and that enemy amphibious troops also began landing at dawn across a broad front. We lost communications with Bridlington just over an hour ago and the RAF report enemy vehicles moving inland towards Driffield."

The intelligence major paused, taking a huge breath.

"In short, Sir, I believe that we must assume the Driffield Brigade has been effectively neutralised. We must also assume that the Germans will succeed in holding onto Driffield for at least the remainder of the day and that the German amphibious forces are now in a reasonably strong beach-head. They will undoubtedly try to expand that beach-head and link up with their parachute forces at Driffield, along with the glider-borne troops at Spurn Head."

Adam stared at the map in front of him. The intelligence officer had prepared it faultlessly with green flags indicating friendly units and blue flags indicating enemy forces. The picture it created on the map was as bleak as the verbal report. Adam looked up at the major from his intelligence branch.

"Go on then, James; tell me what they're up to." He said with a grunt. "You've told us the facts, but you're the chap with the big brain around here. What do you think they're playing at? What's their big plan? What's this business at Spurn Point all about?"

The young officer thought for a moment, brushing a lock of hair away from his brow nervously. Eventually, he began to expound some theories.

"Well, Sir, it's obvious that the enemy's first concern was to cause disruption to us in depth. With his various landings and air raids, he's removed our radar cover over a portion of the coast, which will give his air force some breathing space and a real chance of supporting their ground forces on a more even footing. He's also caused some damage to railheads and airfields in the North and South Ridings of Yorkshire, obviously hampering our movement of reserves. We can expect to see more of that. He's removed our coastal batteries through precision attack. The Reighton battery made absolute sense. As for the batteries on Spurn Head? I'm not sure about that. The defences at Sand-le-Mere weren't attacked, and they're much closer to the landing grounds. I can only assume that the Spurn Head operation must have been some kind of diversion, or an attempt to threaten Hull from the east."

The officer's pointer drifted back up the coast.

"He's gone for two harbours, and a third location with good exits off the beach. That will allow him to speed up the offloading of his heavier vehicles and stores, especially if the sea state gets worse. He's got two of them, but we've kept him out of Scarborough. He may decide to fight for Scarborough from the south, or abandon that part of the operation completely in order to focus his available forces on his areas of success. In summary, I believe that Driffield is the key to all of this. If he gets his ground forces to Driffield, which he almost certainly will, he has the perfect start point for his next move."

The intelligence officer threw a gaze around the assembled staff in order to emphasise the importance of his next words.

"He can punch due west towards us here at York. Theoretically, if Driffield falls before lunch, he could be here by nightfall."

There were sharp intakes of breath around the room and an exchange of worried looks.

"Alternatively, he can strike south-west towards the Ouse crossings between Goole and Cawood, in order to penetrate into the industrial heartlands of Yorkshire and the North Midlands. As a third option, he can drop due south, sweeping up Beverley, along with RAF Leconfield, then on into Hull, and capture himself a major port."

The major looked directly across at Adam.

"My personal opinion is that he will concentrate all efforts today on capturing Driffield, and maybe even make a grab for Leconfield and

Beverley. Tomorrow? Well, we can only wait and see what the Germans decide."

He finished his brief and waited for the GOC's response. Adam continued to study the map for a long while, before finally glancing up at his intelligence officer.

"You may be interested to know, James, that your assessment is almost identical to that of the C in C Home Forces."

The major flushed slightly.

"The big question at the moment is, do we reinforce the 59th at Scarborough with the 24th Tank Brigade, in the hope we can score a quick success, or do we bring them down towards York, where they are more central and easier to deploy? Do we throw them in quickly, or wait until the rest of the GHQ reserve arrives so that we can hit the enemy with a sledgehammer?"

The major cleared his throat and ventured his opinion.

"Although we are enjoying some success at Scarborough, Sir, there is still some confusion as to the exact state of play there. The garrison is still suffering heavily from enemy naval gunfire, and moving a Tank Brigade through the Yorkshire Moors will be time consuming. If the Germans do make a thrust for York either this evening or tomorrow morning, we could really do with those tanks here. The 2nd Division has only one infantry brigade uncommitted, besides its divisional support troops It isn't capable of holding York on its own."

Adam nodded silently, weighing up the young officer's words. Then he turned his head and looked at his Brigadier General Staff.

"How long did the C in C tell us it would take the 2nd Armoured Division to get here?"

The colonel pulled a thoughtful face.

"Not before last light, Sir; more likely midnight. Possibly later. They're motoring most of the way too, so they'll need refuelling on arrival before we can commit them to anything."

Adam absorbed the information without reply. After a couple of seconds, he walked slowly around the table, looking over its flags and markers from several angles. Eventually, he came to a halt by the intelligence officer. The general folded his arms, one finger stroking his chin thoughtfully.

"Alright," he said, suddenly looking up and reaching out for the intelligence officer's cane, "this is what we're going to do..."

He took the major's cane and leaned over the map. Looking up, he saw that the eyes of the staff were fixed on him. He allowed himself a brief smile.

"I will not be repeating myself gentlemen, so you may wish to get your notebooks out for this one..."

'S' DAY
H +6

BY BRACEY BRIDGE – THE DRIFFIELD-BRIDLINGTON ROAD SATURDAY 21ST SEPTEMBER 1940 – 1130 HOURS

Smithson hadn't expected the Germans to attack again so quickly. He had watched the waves of enemy bombers heading inland for a moment or two, before remembering that Soames was injured. He had then spent several minutes trying to bandage the private's head and stop the flow of blood from his mangled left ear. It was during that time that the German had crawled out of the wrecked armoured car. The enemy soldier had looked unusually like one of Smithson's men, only that he was dressed in field grey and not khaki. The man, probably the driver or radio operator, had staggered towards a surprised Smithson, holding his right arm and wincing in pain with every step. His face, like Soames', had been a mask of blood.

The shocked and dazed enemy soldier had said something to Smithson which he didn't understand, but it sounded distinctly like an appeal for help. The young lieutenant, slightly flummoxed, had waved vaguely behind him, towards where the men of 'A' Company were positioned.

"Go over there." Smithson had casually told the German. "They'll sort you out."

Clearly not understanding Smithson's words, but getting the jist of them from the gesture, the enemy soldier had staggered off, back down the road towards the immobilised buses.

Smithson had turned his attention back to Soames, finishing off his attempt at first aid.

"We'll get the medic from 'A' Company to do that properly in a moment." Smithson had reassured the stunned young private, surveying his poor effort with the field dressing.

"Sorry, Sir?" Soames had asked loudly, his face one of confusion.

"I think we'd better abandon the vehicle and pull back to the 'A' Company position. Their medic can look at you there." Smithson had explained, assuming the man was still dazed.

Soames frowned at him.

"Sorry, Sir. I can't hear a word your saying." Replied the private, his voice still unusually loud.

"You're as deaf as a post, Soames, aren't you" Smithson had observed needlessly.

"Eh?"

"Come, on. Let's get back down there." Smithson had jerked his head in the direction of 'A' Company.

The young soldier had climbed unsteadily out of the carrier, whereupon Smithson had handed him a rifle and a spare bandolier. The lieutenant had then retrieved the Boys Rifle from beside Knowles' dead body and handed that to the private too. Having loaded up with weapons and ammunition, including the captured German machine-gun, they had begun to totter down the road towards the buses, where several men from 'A' Company had begun searching the injured German. It was at that point that Smithson suddenly remembered he had other men to command, and he had turned to look into the field on the northern side of the road, intending to order the surviving carrier and its crew to join 'A' Company. And it was just then that the main German attack fell on them…

It couldn't have been more than ten minutes since the first German force had withdrawn back over the crest, when the half-tracks burst over the horizon on the northern side of the road once more. Not just a single half track this time, but perhaps ten of them, all bristling with heavily armed infantrymen. The speed and ferocity of the attack had taken Smithson and his surviving men, along with the 'A' Company force, completely unawares. With unbelievable speed and precision, the line of vehicles had roared across the crest, using the side road from Ruston Parva as their axis, and descended the slope towards the British positions like a lightening strike. Within moments of coming over the ridge, the machine-gunners of several German vehicles had spotted the surviving Bren Carrier on that side of the main road and immediately saturated the lone vehicle with fire. As Smithson and Soames had dived for cover into the drainage ditch by the side of the road, they had witnessed the crew of the carrier flop over the sides of the vehicle, riddled by heavy calibre rounds.

By the time Smithson and his driver had managed to get into the ditch and start firing onto the flank of the attacking German armoured vehicles, the half-tracks had disgorged their infantry squads, and the two isolated British soldiers had found themselves in an unequal fire-fight with half a platoon of enemy infantry, whilst another large platoon of Germans had begun to sprint forwards towards the main 'A' Company positions. Smithson had watched several grey clad figures drop like stones as 'A' Company opened up on them, but the Germans were unstoppable, and the menacing looking storm-troopers had ploughed on regardless, whilst the half-tracks had begun moving in a wide hook around north of the 'A' Company defences.

At that point, Smithson had realised that their situation was critical. It was made hopeless just seconds later, when he heard the roar of heavy engines behind him. Whirling round, he had been lost for words at the sight of the four tanks roaring across the field on the other side of the Driffield road, followed by another four, infantry laden half-tracks. One of the tanks had jerked to a halt just yards after cresting the ridge. In the split second before the vehicle fired, Smithson had noticed that although it looked roughly similar to the tanks from the earlier attack, there was something peculiar about this latest metal beast. He had found out what it was a moment later when its gun gave a single, loud bark.

A moment later, his surviving carrier in the southern field was thrown sideways at speed, as if pushed by a giant, invisible hand. At the same time, bits of debris erupted from within the small, open topped vehicle. Seconds later, it burst into flames.

Smithson's heart had sunk. These tanks had more than machine-guns; they were proper battle-tanks. At that point, he had known they were beaten. Soames had tried his best. Bleeding, deaf, and still half-stunned, the young man had fired the Boys Rifle at one of the half-tracks in the northern field. The bullet missed the vehicle, the round flying harmlessly over the top of it. That was when Smithson had been flung backwards against the bank of the ditch.

For a moment, he hadn't been able to understand what had happened, until he had tried to push himself back up with his left arm. He had screamed in agony at the terrible pain that had raced through his shoulder as he put weight on the arm. Looking down, he had seen the thick red blood soaking the blouse of his battle-dress and the dull, white shard of bone sticking out of the hole in his left shoulder. And then he had collapsed, the darkness finally overtaking him.

He was awake now, just. His eyelids felt heavy, his brain even heavier, and every thought that passed through it seemed to take an effort. His shoulder was numb, and it felt as if his entire left arm was somehow encased in rock. He was sitting against a wall in a dirty, cobbled farmyard, staring at a badly damaged civilian bus that was toppled sideways into a ditch. There was muted conversation all around him and the background hum of engines. Something big went past his eyes with a growl. He blinked, managed to focus, and was in time to see another dark object race past in front of him. He was looking out of the farmyard at the road, and he realised that the big, dark objects were tanks. Another vehicle sped past; this time a half-track towing a small artillery piece.

"Hello, Sir. Thank God you're awake!"

The voice took a while to register with Smithson, but for some reason, it made him smile. A moment later, Soames' face appeared right in front of him.

"Thought you were a gonner at first, Sir? You proper scared me, you did."

Smithson stared at the soldier. Underneath the mask of blood and the badly applied dressings, Soames' face was cheerful, his teeth showing white beneath the red-black grime that was smeared across his skin.

"What happened?" Smithson managed to croak.

Soames frowned for a moment, staring at him with a look of intense concentration. After a second, the young private smiled again.

"Oh! What happened? Sorry, Sir, I'm stone deaf. I have to read your lips. You took one in the shoulder, Sir. Made a nasty mess and broke your collar bone too, but the German medic reckons you'll live."

Smithson frowned, feeling bemused.

"German medic?"

Soames nodded.

"We're prisoners, see? The Jerry bastards overran us just after you got hit."

The young man leaned in close to Smithson.

"There's bloody loads of 'em, Sir. Tanks and armoured cars and trucks; you name it. There was no way we could've stopped 'em with just a few Boys Rifles. Hopefully the anti-tank platoon is waiting for the buggers at Driffield with their two-pounders. Then the bastards will get a bloody nose! Major Hornby's still alive, Sir. I'll go fetch him in a mo'."

Smithson felt his head swimming. There was so much to take in yet his brain didn't seem to be working properly.

"Here, Sir. Have a drink of this."

Soames put a water bottle to Smithson's cracked lips and poured a small amount into the officer's mouth. Smithson almost forgot to swallow, and some of the water trickled down his chin. Some of it went down his throat though, and he felt instantly better as the cool liquid washed over his bruised and bloodied mouth. He coughed; a tiny child-like cough.

"You hold on there, Sir. I'll try and find Major Hornby, for you." Soames backed away and disappeared from Smithson's field of vision. The wounded officer felt reasonably comfortable and surprisingly relaxed. He sat there for a while, listening to the nearby murmuring, but not bothering to turn his head. As he stared vacantly towards the gateway of the farmyard, he noticed more tracked vehicles going by. A pair of figures appeared in the gateway, walking slowly, but with weapons at the ready. He noticed they wore German uniforms.

He had no idea how long it took for Soames to return with Hornby, but after a while, he saw the moustachioed face of 'A' Company's commander appear in front of him.

"Hello, old boy." The middle aged major began with a fatherly smile. "Glad to see you're awake. You've been through the mill and back again this morning, haven't you?"

Smithson gave a feint smile.

"Hello, Marcus." He managed to drawl.

"Don't you strain yourself just yet, Dickie." Hornby said. "I think we'll be here for a while. They smashed us up pretty badly. We managed to destroy a couple of their half-tracks and I reckon we did for twenty odd of their foot-sloggers, but their tanks just rolled right over us. We lost nearly half of the boys. It was all a bit one sided. Looks to me like we waltzed right into the middle of a panzer division. Right now the Jerries are keeping the road clear and just pumping more armour towards Driffield. By God, Dickie, these buggers aren't hanging around! I've never seen anything like it."

Smithson took the information in slowly, his mind still clouded.

"So, what now?" He managed to say.

Hornby sighed, and sat back on his haunches.

"God knows. I think they'll just keep us here under guard until they've got most of their spearhead troops past. Then they'll probably move us somewhere towards the coast, where well be out of the way. As for the bigger picture…" He heaved another large sigh. "Hopefully the brigade will manage to hold them at Driffield. We've got two pounders in the town. That'll make the Jerries stop and think; for a while at least. I suppose GHQ will be rushing everything they've got in this direction soon enough."

Hornby looked absently around the farmyard for a moment or two, his face looking drawn and unsure.

"Still," he brightened suddenly. "the flyboys have already been doing their bit. While you were out cold we saw a whole load of those Jerry aircraft coming back this way. They were getting shot to pieces by our fighters. One of their bombers crash landed a little way over towards the village. It cheered the boys up no end!"

He flashed a smile at Smithson, who gave another weak smile.

Hornby had run out of things to say. He smiled at Smithson again, then looked across the farmyard, searching for inspiration; tapping his fingers absently on his shins. As he scanned the area, there was the sound of gunfire not too far away. Hornby looked up sharply at the sound of machine-gun bursts.

"What on earth are they firing at now...?" Hornby began.

Behind him, the two figures in field-grey began shouting excitedly in German. In the yard, the British prisoners started in alarm, suspecting that they were about to be shot. Instead of turning their guns on the prisoners however, the two Germans were running into the yard away from the road, looking anxiously up into the air as they sprinted across the cobbles.

The continuous rattle of sharp, cracking noises came to the ears of the yard's occupants a moment later. A huge cloud of dust and tarmac suddenly erupted on the road in front of the yard, and then, like an avenging angel, the RAF fighter roared over the buildings at rooftop level, making the men below flatten themselves on the cobbles in fear. Smithson could hardly move, but he looked up with difficulty as the dark silhouette passed over them. Barely a heartbeat after the first aircraft had passed over, another plane roared past, preceded by a hail of machine-gun bullets. The roar of aircraft engines was continuous now, adding to the cacophony of gunfire being thrown up from the armoured vehicles and infantry out on the Driffield road.

"Bloody hell!" Hornby shouted above the noise. "Looks like the RAF has turned up mob-handed!"

For reasons that Smithson couldn't fathom, he began laughing.

"About bloody time, too!" He rasped.

He cringed as a large explosion detonated somewhere not far away. Unlike his previous experience of bombing, the shockwave from this explosion was more tolerable. Even in his mind-fuddled state, he understood that the buildings had absorbed some of the blast. More explosions made the ground shudder, and thick smoke began drifting into the yard, as bits of earth and gravel began to patter down on them from above. Smithson just sat there, watching the air raid as if he were watching a newsreel at the Odeon in York. He was laughing still, despite the pain it caused him to do so.

He couldn't stop laughing. A German soldier armed with a rifle came skidding into the yard, looking for cover. He ran towards a stationary tractor and flung himself behind it. Turning to look over the front of the tractor, the German raised his rifle and fired into the air. As the soldier worked the bolt of the weapon, an aircraft howled past, and a second later there was another explosion nearby. Smithson laughed harder. Next to him, laying face down on the cobbles, Hornby began laughing too.

Smithson was convinced he was going mad. Why was he laughing? He was bruised, battered, shot, scorched and mangled. He was a prisoner of war, and now he was being bombed by his own side. It was completely and utterly bonkers; not at all how he imagined war should be. And as he sat there laughing at the preposterous situation in which he found himself this mad, September morning, the RAF's Air Striking Group pressed home the first of its coordinated attacks.

SEALION HEADQUARTERS – THE HAGUE, HOLLAND
SATURDAY 21ST SEPTEMBER – 1140 HOURS

Raeder looked up from his charts as the staff officer came over to him.

"Anything?" He asked, keeping his voice low.

"No, Admiral." Replied the commodore. "None of the U-Boats have answered yet. They are likely to remain submerged for most of the daylight hours. Captain Prein isn't due to make his next broadcast until 1800 hours this evening. We'll keep broadcasting the signal though, until one of the boats acknowledges."

Raeder sighed, irritably. He sat back in his chair and stared down at the chart in front of him.

"That's no good." He said, more to himself than the staff officer. "That carrier could be within striking range of our landings already if she left during the night."

He looked up at the commodore.

"Remind me of the carrier group's details. What did we say was missing from Scapa Flow?"

The commodore didn't need to check the notes. He had personally studied the two sets of air photographs half a dozen times over the last couple of hours and counted the ships that appeared on those images over and over again until he was sure of his maths.

"A carrier, two cruisers and three destroyers, Sir. Without doubt, they have left Scapa Flow over the course of the last twenty four hours."

Raeder was tempted to swear, but resisted the urge. Instead he just slammed his pencil down hard on the table.

Taking a deep breath, he leaned forward, staring hard at the chart again.

"If the enemy goes due south, he will be in a position to launch air strikes against the landing fleet, and then attack it at close range. If that force links up with the surviving destroyers that came out of the Tyne, then they could present a serious threat to the northern and eastern sections of the fleet. Alternatively, if they steer a little south-easterly, they can intercept our corridor across the German Sea. The first wave of empty transports is getting ready to sail back to Bremehaven as we speak. They're due to leave English waters at 1300 hours local time, with just a small escort. And then of course, we've got the second echelon already en route; the entire SS Totenkopf Division along with thousands of tons of supplies and a whole range of administrative units. If that lot gets intercepted we'll have a disaster on our hands."

The commodore looked at Raeder impassively, not bothering to risk an opinion. Raeder rubbed his temples with his fingers, trying to ease the headache that had been developing over the last hour or so. He needed to get a little sleep soon. Kesselring, happy that everything was going to plan thus far for the Luftwaffe, had already been in his bed for an hour following the long night, and Raeder envied him. Brauchitsch had slept for most of the night, unable to contribute anything useful until his first troops began to land, and thus he was fresh and alert. Only Jodl was in the same boat as Raeder, yet the chief of operations was as energetic and active as usual, going about his business like some kind of automaton. That thought only irritated Raeder more. Poor Keitel, just as tired as Raeder, had gone to deal with an ever growing list of callers, most of them hangers-on at the Fuhrer's headquarters, desperate to be the first ones to give the supreme leader any good news. Raeder knew that he needed to sleep if he was to be fit for the next twenty four hours, which could prove to be the decisive phase for naval operations. This damned business of the missing carrier was an unwelcome complication.

He slammed both of his hands down on the map and looked up at the commodore.

"Right. This is what we'll do. Speak to the Luftwaffe. I want every Condor they have. Get them up in the air over the German Sea, looking for this carrier group. They need to be looking well south, around here, given that the enemy ships must have left Scapa Flow in darkness. Also, they need to use some of their shorter range aircraft to sweep down the coast of Denmark, towards the German ports, in case the carrier group has decided to make a dash straight towards us and attack the second echelon as it is leaving our waters. Tell them that they will need to keep several squadrons of bombers in reserve for when we locate the enemy. This enemy force must become a priority target. Understand?"

"Yes, Admiral." The staff officer replied, scribbling notes down as he listened.

Raeder drummed his fingers on the table top, looking back down at the vast expanse of ocean which the British liked to call the North Sea.

"Make sure you draw up a proper set of boundaries for that search; the Luftwaffe needs the detail, otherwise they'll just fly round aimlessly achieving nothing. And get hold of the U-Boats. Tell Kretschmar that I want half of his flotilla pulled away from the landing areas and deployed in a screen sixty miles north of the fleet. Get hold of Prien too. I want to know about this carrier group. How did they get out without being reported? More importantly, he needs to send a third of his units southwards by south-east in pursuit. I want those ships found and sunk as soon as possible."

He looked back at the commodore.

"Speak to Admiral Donitz and pass him my regards. Ask him to see to the detail. And remind him that his submarines are the key to all this. Prein's force has already allowed a carrier and its escorts to break out; the same is not to happen when the enemy's battle squadrons make their dash for open water."

"Of course, Sir." Replied the staff officer, still making notes.

"Finally," Raeder went on, glaring at the chart, "get in touch with Lutjens. Instruct him that he should assume an enemy cruiser and carrier force is to his north and rapidly approaching to within striking distance. He is to ensure he has plenty of major surface units covering the northern sector of the landings."

The commodore finished making his notes then glanced at the admiral, who remained transfixed by the chart on the table.

"Is there anything else, Sir." He asked deferentially.

Raeder was silent for a moment, then grunted.

"Yes." He said. "I'm going to bed for a short while. Have me woken at 1600 hours, unless there is any significant news in the meantime. For now, you have one priority only…find that damned aircraft carrier!"

IN A HEDGEROW – 400 METRES SOUTH OF SEAMER BRIDGE SATURDAY 21ST SEPTEMBER 1940 – 1220 HOURS

"Reloading!"

Private Frederik Wessel shouted the information sideways, towards where his squad mates continued to exchange fire with the mix of enemy infantry and personnel carriers. He shuffled rearwards on his stomach until he was down in the slight fold, pressing himself flat against the cold earth and damp grass. His uniform was soaking wet from the combination of sea water and heavy morning dew. Staying as low as possible, he thrust a hand into his ammunition pouch and produced another clip of ammunition. Working feverishly, he tilted the rifle to the left, slid the clip into place, pushed the rounds down into the magazine, then swept the opening clear and rammed the bolt forward.

It had been one hell of a morning. He had spent over seven hours on an invasion barge after transferring to it from the troopship. The barge had been a conversion, rather than one of the fancy new vessels that he'd seen the 8th Panzer Division loading onto at Bremerhaven. Just thirty minutes after his platoon had boarded, the improvised landing craft was awash with vomit and urine. Bobbing along at a sluggish pace, they had headed for their designated landing beach to the north of Scarborough, the voyage seemingly endless, and he had never been so relieved in his life, as when they had been given the twenty minute warning for landing. That relief had turned to despair just minutes later when the boat began turning back out to sea, and a Kreigsmarine NCO had told them that their original beach landing had been aborted and that they were now being taken to a new landing site.

It had meant another hour and a half on the stinking, rolling barge, and Wessel thought more than once that if he puked anymore he would probably die. He was more than happy to run the gauntlet of fire on an enemy held beach rather than stay on the boat a moment longer. It wasn't his choice to make of course, and so he had been forced to endure the ninety minutes of misery as their flotilla was led by an S-Boat to the new landing site. There had been much cursing amongst the mountain troops, packed below the covered decks, as they had been redirected. Most of it was aimed at the naval personnel, as everyone had assumed that they had probably committed a navigational error. However, after a few minutes, a serious faced officer from their own company had come below and announced that their sister regiment was getting annihilated on landing beach 'Brunhild'; hence the change of plan. Following that announcement, there had been a taught silence on the crowded, reeking landing craft for the remainder of the journey.

It had been with some relief that the Tyrolean and Bavarian born mountain troopers had finally splashed ashore in the small bay, without having to suffer incoming small arms fire. There was artillery of course. The enemy still held the high ground to the north and west, and regular salvos of high explosive rained down on the inlet as the men of the 99th Mountain Regiment had queued, one barge behind the other, to make land fall on the rocky shoreline. It had been a slow process and two of the barges had been hit, but eventually Wessel and his comrades had come running ashore, desperate to feel solid earth under their feet at last.

After nothing more than a short pause to gather themselves, they had been launched on a forced march inland for several kilometres. They had reached a rendezvous point where they had been given a brief set of orders. The Tommies had established a strong-point where the road crossed the railway line, and that railway line was the key infiltration route into the heart of Scarborough town. It would enable them to outflank and isolate the Tommy artillery and mortars. Their regiment had been tasked to make a flanking attack from the south and Wessel's battalion was the spearhead. He had been happy with that. A clear, simple task; and a chance to let off some steam after the long, miserable hours in the puke laden boat.

But now he wasn't so sure. As he crawled back into a fire position, another burst of fire cracked overhead; the bullets passing in a slow, but loud stammer that was characteristic of the Tommy light machine-guns. Even worse, the Tommy mortars had begun firing again, and it seemed to Wessel that the Tommies had a lot more people and firepower than they were letting on. His orders had stated that they were facing a company at the most, who were dug-in by the bridge and railway station, with perhaps half a dozen mortars and a battery of artillery in support. Initially, that wasn't seen as too much of a problem, for the two big Kreigsmarine ships out to sea were busy shelling the enemy positions on the high ground with a continuous barrage. Added to that, the entire complement of mortars and machine-guns from the 100th Regiment were now providing close support against the defenders of the bridge, station, and the farm that lay in depth of them.

It hadn't taken long however, for Wessel and his mates to realise that the Tommies were holding something back. Just as the mountain troops thought they had found the weak spot in the enemy position, another personnel carrier would appear with its Bren Gun coughing away at them, or they would suddenly suffer a mortar stonk, despite the fact that all the Tommy mortars were supposedly out of ammunition or being neutralised by naval gunfire. And that's where Wessel's platoon found itself now; barely two hundred metres from the edge of the village and the station, with the bridge just beyond them. They were pinned down in the last hedgerow that provided any form of cover before one had to enter the wide, open meadow beyond, which formed a perfect killing area for the Tommies. The German mortars mortars had just brought down a heavy bombardment onto the station and the village, whilst Second and Third Companies moved around to the left, slowly edging further westwards beyond the railway line, in an attempt to envelop the position. The Tommies however, seemed to be oblivious to their own predicament. They had obviously decided to stand and fight.

"Expended belt!"

Wessel heard Jurgens, their machine-gunner, shout out the warning. Instantly, there was an increase in rifle fire, as the other members of the squad attempted to cover the gap in suppressive fire from the MG34. Wessel slid his rifle forward and aimed it towards the square green armoured box that was tucked in against a distant cottage. The Tommy carrier was positioned so that only a tiny portion of its hull was exposed; just enough for the machine-gunner inside to use his weapon effectively. Wessel lined up the foresight blade onto the enemy vehicle and squeezed the trigger of his rifle. There was a loud bang, and the muzzle of the rifle reared up as the 7.92 mm bullet streaked out towards the enemy.

"MG link! Anyone got link spare?"

He heard Corporal Seibel yelling the request.

"Yes! Over here Corporal!" Laying his rifle on the grass, Wessel rolled over and began yanking the belt of ammunition over his head, which proved difficult, as the linked cartridges were catching on just about very button and piece of equipment he was wearing. With a curse, Wessel rolled onto his knees and elbows, raising himself higher in order to try and free the ammunition belt. He lifted the linked cartridges and yanked them again. They came free of the obstruction and he kept on pulling. Several loud cracks went right above him and he cried out in surprise. He gave one final pull and the belt of ammunition came free, rattling over his helmet as he dragged it off his shoulders.

Dropping flat on his belly he flung the belt of ammunition over the tangle of long grass and weeds, towards where he judged Corporal Seibel to be.

"Ammo coming over, Corporal Seibel!" He yelled, as he flung the belt with as much force as he could muster in the prone position.

He saw an arm reach up for them. The belt of ammo fell, just a couple of inches short, and the arm dropped, the hand grasping for the link.

"Cheers Freddie!" He heard the squad second in command's voice hail him, above the sound of gunfire.

"Keep it up fellahs!" The squad sergeant's voice cut in. "Just a few more minutes and then the rest of the battalion will be going in from the left to clear the place out. Just stay low and keep firing!"

Wessel glanced at Private Richard Petrowski to his left, an ethnic German from the Danzig province who had somehow found his way into the mountain troops.

"Hear that 'Ski?" He grinned. "Just a few more minutes. Wish the other companies would get a shift on; this place is getting a bit hot for my liking!"

"I'm with you on that one, Freddie boy!" Replied Petrowski, squeezing off another shot.

Nearby, the MG34 crackled back into life. Wessel saw the tracer illuminate after the first hundred metres, and then, just a split second later, bounce of the front plate of the enemy carrier that he had just been engaging. He heard the revving of an engine, and then the enemy vehicle reversed out of sight behind the cottage.

"Go on, you fucker!" Wessel laughed out loud as he saw the carrier withdraw. "Get the fuck out of it!"

Just then, there was a deafening crack, followed by a thud, and Wessel felt something hit the equipment on his back, as if he had been kicked. At the same time, something small and hard hit his left cheek and he was spattered with liquid of some kind.

"Ah, fuck!" He swore, and wiped at his cheek. He glanced down at his hand and was surprised to see blood.

"Oh, Jesus!" He breathed, feeling his heart leap into his mouth. "Oh, Jesus, I've been it!"

In a sudden panic, he ran his hand over his cheek once more. It came away bloody again, covered in a jelly like slime.

"Oh, fuck! What's happened? 'Ski, what's happened? Have I been hit?"

Wessel rolled onto his right arm and looked over at his neighbour.

"'Ski, I've been hit! Is it bad? Can you see? Can you put a…"

Wessel's voice tailed off. Petrowski was collapsed on the ground. What was left of his face and head was a bloody, pulped mass of bone, blood and shredded flesh. A great swathe of bloody jelly and bone fragments lay spread out between the dead soldier and Wessel's fire position. With a gasp of sick realisation, Wessel began rubbing at his face urgently with his sleeve, trying to wipe his dead comrade's blood and gore from his cheek, as he stared in horror at the mutilated corpse that lay barely two metres away.

As he did so, Wessel was vaguely aware of the sudden increase in gunfire, especially over to the left of their position. He could hear whistles and shouting, and it sounded like something big was going on; probably the attack by Second and Third companies his sub-conscious reasoned. But it was the nearer, more urgent shouting in German that snapped him back to reality.

"Enemy left! Enemy left!" There was no mistaking the sound of the company commander's voice. "Second Platoon, switch fire left! We've got

Tommies coming right through the battalion from the west. Fucking hell! Trotman! Get your platoon to swing round! Form a fire base!"

Wessel's heart was racing even faster now. He could hardly see what was going on, so he picked up his rifle and crawled over to the dead body of his friend, ignoring the cadaver's shattered skull, and lifted his own head tentatively. The hedgerow ran away westwards and tailed away to the south slightly. In the middle distance, he could see dozens of his own comrades, presumably the Second and Third Company men. They were milling about in the centre of the wide meadow. Some were kneeling and firing towards the station and the village, whilst others were running back towards the hedgerow at an angle, heading towards the left flank of Wessel's company. Others were backing away slowly and firing towards the distant village over to the west. Then Wessel understood why.

Beyond the mass of field-grey figures in the meadow, came a long line of khaki-clad Tommy infantry. On one end of their line he saw another of the small green carriers trundling forwards. Bullets cracked through the air from several directions now and Wessel's mind began to race.

"Fucking hell!" he swore, confused at the chaotic situation. "Who's outflanking who?"

He had barely finished asking himself the question when a 'whoosh' made him look up sharply into the patchy blue sky. He caught a fleeting glance of something small and black flying past in his peripheral vision, and then he felt himself being lifted into the air as the ground suddenly lurched underneath him. A split second later his ears were shattered by a thunderclap of an explosion and then he was being dumped face-down on the earth again. He lay there for a moment, dizzy and winded by the near miss. The enemy mortars were in action again, and the Tommies had miraculously found yet more infantry from somewhere. The British were indeed still up for a fight and they had no intention of letting the Germans just walk into the suburbs of Scarborough. Wessel's head was spinning and his ears were ringing. Despite that, he heard quite clearly the urgent fire control order from his squad sergeant.

"Seibel! Hard left! Get that gun swung round! Tommies, two hundred metres...rapid...fire!

At that point, Wessel feinted.

'S' DAY
H +12

THE AUCTION ROOM – DRIFFIELD MARKET
SATURDAY 21ST SEPTEMBER 1940 – 1730 HOURS

"Still nothing?"

Brigadier Charles Willard fixed the signaller with a hopeful look. The young lance corporal turned towards the brigade commander and shook his head ruefully.

"Nothing, Sir; sorry."

Willard remained tight lipped. There was no point swearing out loud. To do so would only shake his men even more. He turned away and found his chief of staff waiting nearby. The major from the Moorlanders had a look of resignation on his face.

"I assume that the news is bad, Henry?" Willard asked, casually.

He knew it was bad of course. He could hear the tank fire and mortars for himself, along with the incessant rapid chatter of German machine-guns.

Major Henry Clarke nodded sombrely to his brigadier.

"I'm afraid so, Sir. The 3rd Hallamshires have just lost their last 2 Pounder, and there's a combined column of Jerry armour and infantry smashing their way into town from the east. I've instructed the Hallamshires to fall back to the final defence line immediately; otherwise they'll get cut to pieces. The rest of the brigade, or at least those elements that we managed to scrape together, are already in their final positions. I don't expect that any of the troops from the counter-attack force will make it back here now. They were probably wiped out at the airfield, judging by how many Jerries are filtering in from the western outskirts."

Willard nodded thoughtfully.

"How are we for ammunition?"

The chief of staff shrugged.

"We've got somewhere in the region of a first-line scale per man, although we're getting thin on grenades. Nothing heavy left of course; all the mortar ammunition's gone. We've managed to put together a few dozen petrol bombs however, which will give us an edge in the close confines of the town centre. All in all, Sir, if the Jerries keep at us like this, we can probably last until midnight."

Willard made some silent calculations in his mind. Surely the GHQ reserve would be moving by now? How long would they take to get here?

"What about our wounded and the civilians? Have we got many left in the perimeter?"

The chief of staff shook his head.

"Not that many, Sir. Most of them went into the churches as directed, before we pulled the remnants of the brigade back into the town centre. We left all the seriously wounded there too, along with a couple of medics and the doctor from the Hallamshires. Both churches should now be in German hands, so I'm fairly sure that they're out of immediate danger. We made sure not to conduct any delaying engagements around those two locations."

Willard ran a hand over his tired face, His stubble was beginning to annoy him and he pulled the chin strap loose and removed his helmet. He stared down at the hand drawn map of the immediate battle area which sat on the nearby table and gave a long sigh.

"Right, well... as far as the possibility of continued resistance is concerned, we're in a reasonable position. As we now have enemy tanks and regular infantry in the town, as well as paratroopers, then we must assume that there has been a successful landing on the coast, and that 1st Hallamshires have been defeated. That means that the Germans will only increase in strength as time passes. Likewise, the fact that we still have pressure from the west in the form of parachute troops, suggests that the 1st Wirrals were defeated and that the airfield remains in enemy hands. In any other theatre of war, or on any other battlefield, it would make sense to withdraw; breakout with the men we've got left and make a dash for our own lines, so that we could live to fight another day."

He sighed again, but then looked up at his chief of staff, fixing him with a hard stare.

"However, this situation is an exception. This is the invasion of Britain. There is nowhere left to go. GHQ will be throwing reserves up here from the south just as fast as they can, but the more time we can give them, and the more attrition we can inflict on the Germans, then the greater chance the general reserve will have of arriving in good order and launching a properly coordinated counter-attack."

He paused for a second, gathering his resolve.

"Now is not the time for weakness. As long as we are holding out here, we are causing the Germans delay and casualties; delay and casualties that they can't afford. So, I'm afraid that fate has put us in this unenviable position. For us there can be no retreat and no surrender. We must make our preparations to fight on to the very end; to the last man and the last bullet. What's left of the brigade remains here. We stand or die."

There was a long moment of silence as Willard and Clarke stared at each other, both of them fully aware of what that meant. After a while, the major spoke.

"I'll make the arrangements, Sir, and pass on a formal order to the remaining units and sub-units."

Willard nodded his acknowledgement.

"Tell them to concentrate on the tanks and vehicles, Henry." He said. "The Hun needs his vehicles more than anything. He uses his vehicles and tanks to achieve the speed and surprise that served him so well on the continent. So, we must make our sacrifice worthwhile. Every tank, motorcycle, half-track, or whatever he commits; it must be destroyed or damaged. And make sure that we've have immobilised all transport left within our own perimeter. Clear, Henry?"

"Crystal clear, Sir." The chief of staff replied, a feint smile crossing his tired features.

The brigadier caught the look.

"Why are you smiling?"

The major shrugged.

"It's sort of appropriate, Sir, isn't it? I always fancied myself as a hero; and it's this kind of situation that buys you the immortality. Like the Spartans at Thermopylae, or Harold and his Housecarles at Hastings. Well, now history will be able to remember Willard's last stand at Driffield. The world will never forget us, eh, Sir?"

Willard smiled too.

"No, Henry. I don't suppose they will."

"Sir!"

Willard looked round sharply at the urgency of the signaller's tone. He saw the young man leaning forward over his set, his hands pressed over the ear pieces, his face a mask of concentration.

"What is it?" Willard asked, his breath catching in his throat.

The signaller didn't respond for a moment; he was busy listening intently to something in the ear-pieces. After a while, he let out a breath and looked up at the brigadier.

"It's Div' HQ, Sir. They're acknowledging our Morse. I can't get voice comms, but the Morse has got through. They're asking for a situation report. What shall I tell them, Sir."

Willard exchanged a quick look with his chief of staff, then looked back at the signaller.

"Here, pass me your pencil and paper. I'll write it down for you..."

EAST OF WOLD NEWTON – FOUR MILES FROM THE BEACH SATURDAY 21ST SEPTEMBER 1940 – 1745 HOURS

"Thank fuck we didn't hang around in that shit-hole any longer." Nuemark commented sourly as they trudged along the road that traversed the side of the ridge. Over to their right, the farm that First Company had just attacked was burning fiercely.

Bachman, his MG34 balanced over his left shoulder, gave his squad corporal a sideways glance.

"Yeah, they didn't seem to like us very much, did they Corporal?"

"Fucking cock-sucking, island-monkeys!" The surly corporal observed in his typically irreverent manner.

"So why did they move us south again, after all that digging in?" Bachman asked, ignoring his NCO's profanity.

"Bloody generals, boy! They chop and change their minds like there's no tomorrow. Besides, I heard that the Mountain Division has run into problems up north and the 7th Division needs more elbow room. So we go south and pick up another road. Then we clear it. Going to be a long old slog I reckon. Still, won't be long until dark. We'll probably stop for the night then. Hopefully some other poor fuckers will get the patrol tasks and we can get our heads down. I'm bollocksed."

They tramped past a group of First Company men, who were gathering by the long approach road to the burning farm. There were two friendly wounded soldiers sitting by the roadside, both with arm injuries which were heavily bandaged. A corporal was checking the ammunition states of the remainder of the group, and Nuemark hailed him as they went by.

"Oi, Feltzy! How was that? What were the Tommies like?"

The other corporal turned and scowled.

"They were a pain in the fucking arse, mate. Four of the bastards were holed up in there like rats. We had to winkle the bastards out."

"Just four of 'em?" Nuemark frowned. "You were going at that for over an hour!"

Corporal Feltz shrugged.

"Bastards have got their backs against the wall, Martin. Wait and see when it's your turn. I heard that a recce platoon from 8th Panzer got minced in the next village, so watch your step, mate."

They passed by, staring ahead in silence for a while; watching the remainder of their platoon and company tramping up the road ahead of them. After a few moments, Bachman spoke.

"We'll still beat the Tommies though, won't we Corporal?"

Nuemark glanced sideways at the young private.

"Of course we will, Bachman lad. They've been on the ropes since Dunkirk. It was only the Channel that was keeping them safe. Now we're on their turf, we'll beat them alright. No doubt about that. We proved who the better army was in Belgium and France. It's just a case of how long the buggers will keep fighting, that's all. Stubborn see, the Tommies? My dad told me that; said they were the same in the First War. I don't reckon they've changed much since then, so we'll probably have to really kick the shit out of them before they give in."

Bachman went silent again, mulling over the corporal's answer. After a few moments, he gave a feint smile.

"I hope they give in before we get to York. It's not far from here is it? I'm told they have a great Minster there; the largest of its kind in Europe. It's early-medieval apparently, in the Gothic style. I hope I get the chance to see it, even if it is a Protestant church now. They say the architecture is breath-taking. Now that would be something to write home to the folks in Munster about."

Nuemark rolled his eyes.

"Fuck my old boots! How in the name of Adolf's arse did I get stuck with a God-botherer?"

If he was expecting an answer, Nuemark didn't get one, because at just that point, gunfire sounded some way off, up in front. He cocked his head slightly and frowned. "Hard to tell where that came from." He murmured. "Somewhere round the side of this hill by the sounds…"

They stopped abruptly as they saw the men in front splitting to alternate sides of the road and taking cover in the hedgerows. Bachman and Nuemark followed suit and passed the field signal for 'short halt' back down the line. As they settled down opposite each other in the hedgerows, they heard more gunfire. Nuemark continued to cock his head and listen with a strained expression on his face.

"That's a Tommy machine-gun." He said at length. "You can tell by how slow it is."

A few seconds later, the sound of the Tommy machine-gun was joined by other weapons; a flurry of rifle fire, followed by the rapid chatter of one of their own MG34s.

"Sounds like the point platoon have been bumped. We should find out what the deal is in a moment. There'll be a warning order coming back soon enough."

They sat there patiently, listening to the exchange of fire. After a minute or so, the noise of battle suddenly intensified. As the rate of fire increased between the unseen protagonists, a small tremor came through the air, followed a moment later by the sound of a fairly loud explosion. The blast made the long lines of waiting soldiers sit up and pay more attention.

"Was that our mortars?" Bachman asked.

Nuemark shook his head.

"Don't think so." He said, wafting irritably at a cloud of small midges that were pestering him. "Don't think we've got ours in action yet."

The sound of jackboots clattering on the tarmac made the two of them crane their necks forward and stare up the road. A lone soldier was pelting down the road towards them, his rifle at the trail and a scrap of note-paper clutched in his free hand. Even before he got level with them, they could see he was sweating. The evening was still surprisingly warm and the young soldier's sleeves were pushed up over his elbows. As the soldier drew level with them, Nuemark recognised the company commander's new runner and called out to him.

"Karl? What's up matey?"

The soldier barely glanced at the corporal as he dashed past, his face bright red and his breathing laboured.

"Tommy position up front; big one by the looks. Got some kind of mortar with 'em. Looks like it's going get messy!"

With just those few gasped words, the company runner pounded on past them, back down the slope.

"Bollocks!" Nuemark swore. "Looks like my early night's gone out of the window."

Bachman looked over at his corporal.

"Was it like this in France?"

"Sort of." Grumbled the sour-faced NCO. "But over there we had Stukas in the air, wherever we went. If the Tommies so much as farted in our direction, we just called the fly-boys in. After a visit from the Stukas, the Tommies were never really in the mood for a long scrap."

"How come we haven't seen any today?" Bachman asked puzzled.

"Too far for 'em to come; they haven't got the range. That's why we keep getting strafed by Tommy fighters. We need to capture an airfield sharpish so we can get some proper aircraft forward-based. Then the Tommy air force will be in for a shock."

The corporal looked across at his young gunner with serious eyes.

"But until the clowns at the circus big-top get that organised, we'll be doing it the old fashioned way."

He went quiet then, for the sound of booted feet running along the road had come to him again. This time, there was more than one man. In fact, there were a couple of dozen, and all running upslope towards the front of the column. Nuemark took one look at them and recognised the men from the Machine-Gun Company. The big, strong looking soldiers clattered past, festooned with machine-guns, tripods, sight boxes and ammunition belts. They were even more breathless than the company runner had been, having doubled forward from behind the battalion commander's group.

"Christ almighty!" Nuemark swore, eliciting a disapproving look from his gunner. "This looks like it's going to be a right old punch-up!"

He saw another group of soldiers struggling forwards from the rear of the column, at a fast walking pace. They broke off from the tarmac about twenty metres before they reached Nuemark and moved into the nearby field, where they promptly set about assembling their weapon systems.

"Mortars too." Nuemark commented, his face growing moodier. "Must be a nasty one coming up, then?"

Across the road, Private Bachman crossed himself and began whispering a prayer, quietly.

"Hey, Bachman!" Shouted Nuemark grumpily. "You pack that shit in, right away! Since when was praying an official part of battle procedure? Make yourself useful and get some oil on those working parts!"

The devout young soldier looked up with a hurt expression, but made no reply. Instead, like everyone else lined up along the road, he suddenly dived even further into the hedgerow as a small aircraft appeared out of nowhere from behind the cover of the hill, banked in an unbelievably sharp manoeuvre, then roared over them, rattling it's machine gun bullets off the tarmac as it strafed the entire length of the battalion column, before flipping off over another hill and disappearing from sight.

As the echo of the Tommy fighter's guns and engines faded, Nuemark popped his angry head up from amongst the bed of stinging nettles that he had just rolled into.

"Fucking hell!" He cursed loudly. "Now I am properly pissed off!"

NEAR ELMSWELL WOODS – WEST OF DRIFFIELD
SATURDAY 21ST SEPTEMBER 1940 – 1800 HOURS

Jackson was worried. They had moved towards the sound of the fighting during the late afternoon, getting ever closer to Driffield. The closer they had got to the small market town however, the more they had realised how far behind German lines they were. He should have realised earlier of course. He had been on the receiving end of the new German way of war in France. The Germans were moving fast along a narrow front, in order to dislocate the

British defences and cause chaos within the British command network. Everywhere they had moved that afternoon, Jackson's group had found themselves one step behind the fighting. The only British soldiers they had come across were dead ones. There were dead Germans too of course, but the vast majority of bodies they came across were British. Jackson and his small band had savoured the sight of a dozen burning German vehicles in the area between Ruston Parva and Nafferton, but otherwise their progress had been marked by the signs of British defeat. The only positive side to their long, careful journey along the hedgerows that afternoon had been their opportunity to strip the British dead of ammunition and weapons.

All of the Canadian rifles had been dumped now, and every man carried a Lee-Enfield, along with at least thirty rounds each. They had also managed to fill up both Lewis Gun magazines, as well as collecting another dozen rounds for the Boys Rifle. On top of all that, the group of eight were still in possession of their liberated German weapons and ammunition. An earlier halt for rest, lasting a full hour, had done them all good. Even though Jackson hadn't slept, his three Home Guardsmen had taken the opportunity for a cat-nap, and they were all a liitle brighter for it. Dutton's feet had been well strapped up and Jackson had liberated a pair of ammunition boots from a corpse, which fitted the young man much better than his own farm boots.

Their journey had taken them inexorably towards Driffield, where the sound of gunfire had continued throughout the afternoon. All the while, aircraft had continued to battle with each other in the skies above, and on one occasion, just after three o'clock, another low level air-strike by several dozen RAF aircraft had come roaring in along the Driffield to Bridlington road to their south. Jackson had noticed that, unlike the earlier RAF raid, this one had met with much heavier anti-aircraft fire, and he had seen at least three friendly planes go down in flames, one of which exploded before it even hit the ground.

Arriving by Nafferton a couple of hours ago, Jackson and his cobbled together section had quickly realised that they would not be linking up with the Driffield garrison from the east. From Nafferton village, right the way into the town, was a huge, and ever growing force of German vehicles. There were armoured cars and half-tracks, motorcycle combinations, open-topped cars, trucks, towed anti-tank guns and light tanks. Squatting in the hedge bottom over a mile away to the north, Jackson and his companions had watched the first of the larger tanks arrive from the direction of Bridlington. Even without using the binoculars, it was obvious that the Germans were here in force and that they were on the verge of overwhelming the Driffield garrison.

Thus, the small group of civilians-turned-soldiers had begun to work their way carefully around the northern edge of the town, desperately trying to find a way through to the British troops within. The further west they moved, the more parachutes they found, and it became apparent what the German plan was. Crouching now, in a hedgerow to the north-west of the town, Jackson shook his head in reluctant admiration.

"These Jerry bastards are fucking clever, you know? You can see what they've done. They've laid a carpet of paratroopers all the way from Bridlington to Driffield, and dropped a whole load more of them right on top of the town and the airfield itself. There's no wonder the brigade here never got to the coast; they were too busy fighting off a parachute landing. And all the while the Jerries have been pushing hard along the Driffield road with their armour, racing to link up with their paratroopers. This is how the Jerries fight, you see? They get into your rear areas; cause paralysis. Then, while your headquarters is still trying to work out what's going on, their main force just waltzes up to you and gives you a proper kicking!"

Crouching nearby, Bob Bishop, the surly farmer from Burton Fleming, nodded his understanding.

"I saw 'em try something similar at the back end of the last war; not with parachutes mind you. Took us by surprise they did, with specially trained storm-troopers. They broke right through our front lines and the first I knew about it was when the buggers came over the hill in front of my gun battery. Fortunately, it was your boys that saved the day for us. The Guards Division was just marching back out of the line for a rest period at the time, but when they looked over their shoulders and saw the Hun coming, they just turned about, calm as you like, formed extended line, then counter-attacked and pushed the buggers back. Not sure if I'd be here today to be honest, if it wasn't for the Guards."

Jackson felt a small pinch of pride at the farmer's war story. He didn't have time to savour it though, for there were more pressing matters to attend to. What on earth were they going to do? It looked as though the town was completely isolated. He took the binoculars from his gas mask case and raised them, carefully scanning the village to their forward left.

"I think that's Little Driffield isn't it?"

Bishop grunted his agreement.

"Aye, that's him. And that little cluster of buildings over to the right, beyond the wood line, is Elmswell. That's not a big place mind you; a few houses and a farm. The York road cuts just in front of it. From what I remember, the aerodrome is just beyond those trees."

Jackson was listening intently whilst scanning with the binoculars.

"So, that road takes you through Wetwang and Fri..." He stopped in mid-sentence. "Bollocks!" He murmured.

"What is it?" Bishop sat up and peered in the same direction as Jackson.

"Jerries. In the village; Little Driffield. They're building barricades."

The Coldstream Guardsman lowered his binoculars and looked at the rest of his section lined up behind him in the ditch.

"Looks like they're preparing for a counter-attack. They must have nearly secured the whole town by now. They're probably expecting a counter-attack from up the York road, so I suppose they'll go firm here for the night, and advance again in the morning."

Martlesham blinked sweat out of his eyes and stared tiredly at Jackson.

"What do we do now then, Sergeant?"

Jackson glanced along the line of faces, a mixture of young and old, both tired and reasonably fresh.

"Well, we came here to join up with our own troops, but there's not much chance of that happening now; not round here anyway. We also came to fight some Germans, but we ain't going to be taking on the best part of a panzer division with just a couple of machine-guns. We've got two choices I reckon. We can break off due west and follow the York road over the Wolds, and hope we run into some of our own boys. Alternatively, we can drop south from here, skirt the airfield, and see if there are still some of our troops in the area who aren't cut off inside that town. Does anyone have any particular preference?"

He looked down the line again. Every man either shrugged or shook his head.

"It's a long walk across some wide-open hills if you follow the York road." Bishop said. "I seem to remember that the road down towards Market Weighton and Holme-on-Spalding Moor is a bit more covered. Not much mind you, but a few more trees about than the other way."

Jackson tossed the thought over in his mind.

"Yes; I'm from down that way and your right, the country is a bit closer. It'll still be a dodgy trip though; we'll be hugging the ditches and hedgerows all the way."

He sucked in his breath.

"That said, I know there are definitely friendly forces in that direction. I came up from Goole on the bus when I got sent to Filey, and I remember coming past quite a few units who were based down towards the Market Weighton area. In fact, I remember seeing loads of vehicles parked up all over the place by Holme."

Bishop pulled a face.

"Sounds good to me. If we can find some of our troops, we can get back into the war, can't we?"

Jackson dropped the binos back into the haversack that was strapped to his chest and sucked in his cheeks, thoughtfully. He scanned the countryside around them for a few seconds, then turned back to the expectant line of men.

"Okay, fellahs; we go south-west, towards Market Weighton and Goole. We'll need to get over the York road and then feel our way around the airfield. We might even find some of our boys still holding out on the airfield, but if not, we'll pick up the Goole road and make best speed."

The Sergeant pointed towards the line of trees that ran from the area of Little Driffield towards the partially hidden hamlet of Elmswell.

"We'll follow this ditch and the hedgerow straight down towards the road and try to find a decent place to cross. The trees on the far side come close to the road, so we'll be in cover pretty quickly."

He fixed them with a serious look.

"Those Jerries look like they're the front line of enemy troops. I'm assuming that of course. They may have patrols further this way, towards Elmswell, so keep your heads down and your eyes peeled. Also, given that we're about to head into close country, get your rifles slung over your backs and make sure you've got your Jerry machine-guns and pistols to hand. Everyone happy?"

The seven men remained silent, but nodded their acknowledgement.

"Good." Jackson murmured. "Sort your kit out quickly. We'll move in five minutes."

The sun was starting to drop in the sky now, and the blue skies of mid-afternoon were starting to cloud over again. The autumn was almost upon them, and the days were getting shorter and shorter. The combination of cloud and the waning moon would bring the night on even faster and darker than last night. He slung his Lee-Enfield over his back, adjusting its position for comfort, then picked up and checked the German machine-pistol. They had five of the weapons between them, and Jackson suspected that they would be handy at close range. As an after thought, he re-positioned one of the German stick grenades so that it could be easily retrieved from his right hand ammunition pouch. He was soaking with sweat under his battle-dress, and whilst the others adjusted their equipment and weaponry, he unfastened the top button of the blouson, allowing some air inside the garment.

For a brief moment, he thought of Audrey. He had met the young brunette by sheer coincidence whilst on leave. They had both been waiting for a train at Goole station, and after twenty long minutes of standing together in silence on a deserted platform, it was the attractive young woman who had finally broken the silence. Another fifteen minutes of small talk had revealed them to be of similar outlook and disposition, and Jackson, not a confident man when it came to women, had thanked his lucky stars when it transpired that they were both going to the same village; he to visit his grandfather, and she to return to the family farm, just outside Snaith.

His mind wandered a little more. The train journey although short, had rendered a useful opportunity, and that same evening, by mutual agreement, they had met again at the village pub. She had insisted on seeing him back on the last train to Goole, and during their time on yet another railway platform, they had arranged to go on a visit to York together, once Jackson had finished his secondment to the Filey Home Guard. He was still owed one more week's sick leave before he would have to return to the battalion for an eye-test that would confirm what his future in the Army would be. Audrey loved York, she had said. Jackson admitted that he too, despite being a straight-laced, gruff-voiced NCO from the Guards, loved nothing more than touring the ancient city and exploring its numerous snickets and back-streets that lay in the shadow of the great Minster.

Jackson let out a sigh, much to his own surprise, when he suddenly realised that the trip to York had been planned for the following Wednesday. It would never happen now, he reflected. For a moment, he allowed himself a rare moment of self-pity, but then, just as quickly, his mind flicked back to business, and he felt both his anger and resolve growing inside him once more. If he had it his way, the Germans would never get as far as Goole, or Snaith. They would never be granted the pleasure of destroying the beautiful city of York. This was Britain; *his* Britain, and he would not let the Germans ruin it, nor stop him from seeing the only woman to show an interest in him in years. Suddenly, despite his growing fatigue and a headache induced by wearing his spectacles for too long, Jackson felt a burning desire to go and wreak havoc amongst the enemy.

"Fucking German bastards!" He snarled quietly to himself.

"Sorry Sergeant? Did you say something?"

Jackson looked over his shoulder and saw Martlesham staring at him. He ignored the young man's query.

"Everyone ready to go?"

The group of heavily armed amateurs nodded in response. They looked brighter he thought. The earlier rest had done them good.

"Alright," He snapped curtly, "let's get moving."

CABINET WAR ROOMS – STOREY'S GATE, LONDON
SATURDAY 21ST SEPTEMBER 1940 – 1815 HOURS

"Thank you, Ronald; that all makes sense. I am more than happy with your proposed dispositions. As for the tank-brigade; I will order them as far as Stamford Bridge only, but they must remain in reserve there, until we see what the enemy intends. Launch the counter-attack at Scarborough as planned. If it looks like it's making progress, then I'll reconsider releasing the tanks, but at the moment, our sole aim must be to concentrate enough force in one place in order to defeat the enemy's main effort, once it has been identified."

Brooke paused to hear the GOC Northern Command's response.

"Indeed." Brooke said after a moment. We'll speak again at 1200 hours tomorrow. I suspect that the enemy's intentions will be clearer by then. If you have any concerns in the meantime, don't hesitate to call."

There was another brief pause.

"Okay, Ronald, good night, old boy…Oh, and Ronald…Make sure you get some sleep tonight; that's an order. You'll be good for nothing in the morning if you don't rest."

Brooke placed down the secure telephone link and removed his spectacles, rubbing his eyes and nose with the forefinger and thumb of his free hand.

"I don't suppose you'll be following your own advice, will you Alan?"

Brooke turned in surprise at the voice. Seeing his old friend and immediate superior, John Dill, he smiled.

"I will at some point, John, I promise; but I just need to make sure that the movement plan for our reserves is going without a hitch. Then I want to wargame some options, depending on what the morning brings. I believe we're back in with Winston at eight tonight?"

Dill nodded.

"We are indeed. Hopefully he'll leave you alone after that, so you can get on with business. I suspect that I and the other Chiefs will have a lengthy cabinet meeting to attend afterwards, however."

Brooke winced at the thought of being stuck in a room full of politicians. The Chief of the Imperial General Staff moved across to the map that was pinned to the wall in front of Brooke and sighed.

"I've managed to get Pug to persuade the Prime Minister that he should go on a morale boosting visit to Dover and the south coast tomorrow; lots of press and the like. That will give us all some breathing space during the day, whilst we fathom what Jerry is up to. I'm sorry I haven't been around much these last few hours to support you Alan. I've been dealing with all this business in the Middle East. That's all sorted now though, so feel free to dump anything on me that you need a hand with."

Brooke looked up at his old friend.

"Ah, yes; Egypt. How's all that looking?"

Dill pulled a neutral face.

"Archie Wavell is quite concerned at the strength of the Italian forces involved, but at the same time slightly surprised at their rather leisurely progress. He's got O'Connor out there in the desert with everything that's available and so far he's managed to fight a pretty successful delaying operation. It still remains a dangerous situation of course, but given that we now have several thousand German troops on British soil, Archie understands that our priorities lay elsewhere at the moment. He'll hold on for the time being whilst we deal with this little problem, and O'Connor is a good, competent commander; he'll do the business alright."

Brooke pondered on that for a couple of moments.

"Sometimes it makes you wonder what kind of test God is setting us, doesn't it? Why is it that all of our trials seems to come at once?"

Dill considered the words for a moment.

"Perhaps they are just opportunities in disguise, Alan?"

Brooke smiled at that.

"Perhaps? But if not…well, we'll make our own."

He cleared his throat slightly, and shuffled to his feet.

"I have a favour to ask of you; before we brief Winston again."

Dill regarded him benignly.

"Anything I can do, Alan; as ever."

Brooke paced up and down for a few moments, then stopped abruptly and looked his old friend squarely in the eye.

"I think I have already seen an opportunity, John. I think Jerry has made a serious mistake and that he's going to stick his neck out just a little too far on this occasion. I have a feeling that we may be in a position to win a signal victory that will send a message to the rest of the world. I'm not entirely sure of my ground yet, but once we've had a chance to see what the enemy does tomorrow, I'm pretty confident that this time we'll be able to give him a taste of his own medicine and give him one back for Dunkirk."

Dill watched his friend carefully.

"I pray that it turns out so, Alan. Otherwise…" He pulled a face. "Britain is finished, and the war will be over by the end of the month."

Brooke returned his friends gaze without blinking.

"I understand that, John, which is why I am asking for your support when I make a proposition to the Prime Minister, this evening."

Dill spoke in a quiet, affable voice.

"What is the proposition?"

Brooke took a deep breath and spoke.

"I will know by tomorrow evening how I intend to deliver the fatal blow to the Germans. But if we fail…if *I* fail, and the Germans break out of Yorkshire, then I want permission to spray poison gas on them. I know that the RAF has squadrons prepared for the job if necessary."

There was a long silence between the two men. Eventually, Dill spoke.

"That is a proposition that will raise some eyebrows amongst our political masters."

He observed. "There is an air of distaste concerning chemical weapons following the Great War. And were we to use gas, there would be plenty of other countries queuing up to condemn us for doing so. Besides all that, it is a fact that there are many British civilians currently stuck within the German beach-head."

Brooke nodded.

"I am aware of that, John. You know that I am a religious man, and that I would not consider such a course of action lightly. But it may mean the difference between survival and utter destruction."

Dill returned the nod.

"You're absolutely right, Alan. I too, believe that in this situation, we must make preparations for every extremity. There will be no re-match if we fail this time. Defeat is not an option. I will support your recommendation, and I will ask the other Chiefs to do likewise."

Brooke smiled, thinly.

"Thank you, John."

A staff officer came into the room at that point, his face tired and strained but never-the-less, alert and full of urgency.

"Sorry, Sir…" He muttered when he saw the Chief of the Imperial General Staff.

"Don't mind me." Dill smiled, stepping aside. "You have much to do. Don't let me get in your way."

The colonel from Brooke's staff reddened slightly, then caught the C in C's eyes.

"We've literally just had a flash signal from Northern Command, Sir. HQ 2nd Division has managed to make contact with the brigade at Driffield, but carrier wave only."

Brooke straightened and threw a glance at Dill.

"Did they get anything from them?" He asked, looking back at the colonel.

The officer swallowed uncomfortably.

"They're still fighting at the moment, Sir." He began. "But the message said the brigade is down to twenty five percent strength and cut off in the centre of the town. It says they are being attacked by paratroopers, tanks, infantry and artillery. The airfield has fallen. They expect to hold out until midnight at the latest. The brigade commander will fight to the last man and the last bullet."

Brooke absorbed the information quietly. After a moment he spoke.

"That may just buy us enough time. It means the plan I have just discussed with General Adam should stand."

He looked briefly at Dill, then flicked his gaze back to the colonel.

"Was there anything else in the message?"

"Just one thing, Sir." Said the colonel. "The message ended…'God save the King.' "

ELMSWELL WOODS – WEST OF DRIFFIELD
SATURDAY 21ST SEPTEMBER 1940 – 1830 HOURS

Jackson held up his hand. Immediately, the file of men behind him came to a halt and stepped sideways into the hedgerow, as he'd briefed them to. They settled onto one knee, keeping their eyes peeled to the flanks and rear, glancing occasionally towards Jackson at the head of the line. Carefully, Jackson looked round the gate-post and scanned the road in either direction. The road was clear both ways, although the roofs of Little Driffield could just be seen above the substantial hedgerows to his east. Fortunately, it didn't appear as though the Germans in the village had a clear view of this particular crossing point. Away to the west, the York road disappeared around a bend, whilst the tiny hamlet of Elmswell was hidden by the woods that stretched across his front. The leaves on the trees were just starting to turn after a long and very hot summer. For perhaps the tenth time that day, Jackson thanked God for the late onset of the autumn and the resulting cover afforded by the hedgerows and trees.

Directly across the road was another gateway, which led onto a narrow farm track that disappeared into the closest finger of woodland. Just another two hundred yards and they would be in the trees. He turned back to face the others. Dutton was directly behind him now. The sergeant had positioned the young man there so that he could adapt his own pace to match the speed of the Home Guardsman with the badly blistered feet.

"Me and you will go over first and cover the other side." He murmured to the Home Guard private. "Once we're across, I want the others to come over in one go and spread out along that far hedgerow. Keep low all the way. We're barely two hundred yards from the village with the Jerries in. Pass it on."

Dutton turned and began passing the message to the others. Jackson waited impatiently while the instructions filtered down the line, then, taking a final look in either direction, he nodded to Dutton and the two of them leapt out of cover and crossed the road at the double. They settled down at the far side, with Dutton covering along the hedgerow towards the wood-line. Jackson quickly looked in both directions along the road, then waved the others to join him. They moved fast, bunching together as a group, and cleared the open tarmac in seconds.

"Spread out." Jackson ordered as they came past him. "Line out along the hedge."

As soon as they were shaken out in formation, Jackson moved to the head of the line again and waved his hand to indicate that they were moving off. At a crouch, he led them quickly along the edge of the field towards the cover of the trees. There were no ditches at this side of the road, but thankfully the hedge to their left was substantial, thickened by trees along its whole length, which gave them excellent cover from the enemy in the nearby village. With some relief, a minute or two later, Jackson led his men into the cover of the tree-line.

It was a thin strip-wood, perhaps thirty yards wide at this point, and curled around the edge of the next field like a hook, before heading westwards, around the back of Elmswell and towards open country. Jackson estimated that the airfield was barely half a mile away to their south, just beyond the next strip of trees. He scanned the ground and saw that they would have to follow the curling path of the wood-line until it brought them into the open fields well to the west of Driffield town. His deliberation was interrupted by a hiss behind him.

"Jerries!"

Jackson flattened immediately turning to look back northwards. To his horror, a German open-topped car was parked on the road, right in the gateway where they had assembled just minutes before. He could hear the engine running and watched as one of the men in the vehicle climbed out. Jackson held his breath and signalled to the others to keep low amongst the coarse grass and shrubbery that grew between the trees.

The German who had dismounted walked to the front of the vehicle and put a pair of binoculars to his eyes, apparently scanning directly in front of him, down the York road.

"He's being a bit bloody casual, isn't he?" Bishop whispered fiercely.

Jackson didn't reply. Instead, he indicated to Bishop to crawl backwards towards the far side of the tree-line. He then did the same to the others, and slowly, carefully, staying on their bellies, the group of British volunteers shuffled rearwards through the undergrowth until they were well out of sight. Jackson was the last to move. Before he followed the rest of his section, he saw the German climb back into his vehicle and disappear back towards Driffield.

With a sense of relief, Jackson signalled for his group to follow him, and one by one, crouching even lower now, they followed on after the Guardsman as he led them through the trees, tracing a path around the large field. Within five minutes, they had negotiated their way around the large meadow and were moving down the long stretch of narrow woodland, heading due west. The woodland was close in some places, yet with open spaces here and there, and Jackson worried that the wood was getting too thin to be of much use. Moments later however, the woodland thickened again and grew broader off to the right. They moved on rapidly, leaving the village of Little Driffield well behind them. Jackson could just see the tops of big green hangars in the distance to the south. Everything seemed quiet towards the airfield and he wondered, just for a second, if it was worth taking a closer look. Perhaps there were still British troops holding out there? As he dwelt on this, he looked right, trying to judge how close they were to the small settlement of Elmswell. It was then that he saw the German.

Jackson stopped dead in his tracks and stared in shock at the German soldier who was barely ten yards away from him. The blonde haired man, who was dressed in standard field grey uniform rather than parachutist garb, had been hidden from Jackson's view by a coppiced tree until the last moment. Bare-headed, and with no weapon evident, the young man was facing the tree, his feet spread wide apart, head back, eyes closed and a broad smile etched on his features. The German soldier appeared to be in ecstasy as his flaccid cock projected a steaming yellow arc of urine towards the tree. As Jackson gawped at the enemy soldier in disbelief, the German opened his eyes.

He looked, almost casually, towards Jackson, then away again. A split second later, his head snapped back in the direction of the tall British sergeant and his eyes bulged in fright, the spout of urine suddenly tailing away.

"Get your fucking hands up!" Jackson growled in a level voice, just loud enough for the man to hear, and reinforced the message by jerking the muzzle of his captured MP40 upwards at the same time. Whether the German understood him or not, Jackson never knew, because at that point, the man did something completely unexpected. He started screaming.

Like a terrified toddler confronted by a snarling dog, the young German let out a heart rending wail, turned, and then sprinted off into the trees, yelling hysterically as he went. Blinking in surprise, Jackson lifted his machine-pistol into the aim, but then lowered it again, with a curse.

"Bollocks!"

There was no point firing. Either way, the enemy knew they were here now.

"Run!" Jackson snarled over his shoulder at the others. "This way! Move it!"

He leapt forward and ran towards the southern edge of the strip wood. He came across a shallow stream that threaded its way through the trees and launched himself over it, barely breaking stride as he landed on the other side. His mind was racing as he pounded through the trees. Should he break out of the wood and cross the open field, in the hope of finding friendly forces at the airfield? Or, should he continue like this, keeping to the southern edge of the trees and by-pass Elmswell as best he could, before breaking out west at the end of the strip wood? He could see the far end of the wood now; perhaps three hundred and fifty yards away, maybe four hundred at a push? Just a few minutes and they would be past the enemy who were obviously somewhere off to their right in the trees, probably centred on the small hamlet that gave this wood its name.

He decided to go with the latter option and flung a look over his shoulder to see if the others were still with him. Bishop and Martlesham were close behind him, whilst Dutton had fallen back slightly. The remainder were close behind the limping Home Guardsman. Jackson looked back to his front and saw that he was heading straight for a thicket between two Ash trees. He brought up his arms and machine-pistol to shield his face and burst straight through the bushes, stumbling slightly as he did. Slowing at the other side in order to regain his balance, the Coldstream sergeant stared in shock at the three German soldiers standing only five paces away. The Germans were staring off towards the other side of the wood, listening intently to raised German voices coming from that direction, and they jumped in surprise as the tall khaki clad figure burst out of the undergrowth right next to them. One of the men was bare-chested and carried a shovel. The other two wore their field grey tunics with the sleeves rolled up, and one of them held a rifle.

Without a second thought, Jackson raised the muzzle of his weapon and squeezed the trigger. The skeleton-like machine-pistol chattered into life and the three Germans fell backwards immediately as if hit by some giant, unseen fist. As they toppled, Jackson saw the big red holes appear in the white flesh of the bare-chested German.

As the last body fell amongst the undergrowth and the echo of the gunfire faded, the sound of urgent shouting in German filled the wood to his right. At the same time, Jackson focussed his eyes on the other unusual items that filled the small clearing. A small anti-tank gun on wheels, about the size of a British 6 Pounder, was positioned against the edge of the wood-line, trained on the western edge of the airfield. A grey jacket hung from the barrel and various bits of equipment were laid out around the gun position. Off to his right, about fifteen yards away, Jackson saw a vehicle; one of the curious lorries with tracks at the rear and wheels at the front. As he took just a second to absorb the scene before him, another figure dressed in field grey stepped out from around the side of the vehicle. The German also held a machine-pistol, just like Jackson, and raised it ready to fire. As he did so, there was a thunderous roar near to Jackson and the unfortunate German was blown backwards against a sapling.

As the enemy soldier tumbled to the floor, his torso a mass of bloody holes, Jackson looked to his right and saw Bishop standing close by him, his shotgun held at waist height, its single barrel smoking from the discharge.

"That's for young Jack, you bastard!" The farmer snarled at the dead German.

Not far away in the wood, the angry German voices grew louder and random shots rang out, though no bullets came whipping through the trees in the direction of the British section.

"Run!" Jackson roared, waving an arm to indicate that they should keep going toward the western edge of the strip wood. "Get moving! Don't stop until you get to the far end!"

The group of Home Guardsmen and volunteers burst into action and began crashing through the undergrowth beyond the clearing, leaping over the fallen German bodies.

"Tom!" Jackson snapped as Martlesham ran past him. "Hold on, mate…help me cover the rear. Have you got any Jerry grenades?"

Martlesham swung round to face the sergeant, every sign of fatigue gone from his features; his eyes alert and set now. He stared at Jackson for a moment, but then his eyes widened suddenly in understanding.

"Yes!" He spluttered. "Yes, I've got two!"

"Good." Jackson barked, yanking out a captured enemy grenade from his own pouch. "Pull the cord when I say and drop it over the back of that half-track."

Martlesham dropped to one knee and propped the Lewis Gun against the back of the vehicle. Like a man possessed, he ripped his denim blouse open and plucked out one of the long handled German grenades. As he struggled with the hand held explosive, he heard the crash of undergrowth, and realised that more enemy were almost upon them.

"Get ready to run as soon as you lob it!" Jackson shouted behind him. "Stand by…"

The two men looked over their shoulders at each other and Martlesham saw that the sergeant was crouching over the breech of the anti-tank gun. He locked eyes with Jackson, and a moment later, the big Coldstreamer gave an emphatic nod. Together they yanked hard on the cords. Martlesham dropped his over the side of the enemy vehicle whilst Jackson jammed his underneath the breech of the gun.

"Fucking run!" Jackson hollered.

Martlesham grabbed his weighty machine gun and staggered away in the same direction as the others, his breathing rapid and heavy. As he ploughed through a low tangle of brambles, Jackson fell in beside him and loped off through the trees like an antelope being chased by a lion. As they broke out of the clearing, a flurry of shots sounded behind them and several bullets cracked through the wood, splintering trees as they flew past.

"Down!" Jackson roared, barely seconds after they had started running, and grabbed Martlesham's arm, pulling him to the floor.

The two men hit the ground and Martlesham felt the big ammunition drum of the Lewis Gun ram into his chest, winding him. He had no time to worry, for a split second later the two grenades exploded with a sickening crump, and a cloud of leaves, twigs, smoke and other detritus washed over them.

"Up!" Jackson shouted.

Even above the ringing in Martlesham's ears, the sergeant's command was like the crack of a whip, and the young man found himself staggering forwards a moment later, with Jackson by his side.

"Go to that log and turn about, Tom. Get down there and cover me as I come back."

The sergeant pointed through the trees in front of them to where a thick, fallen tree trunk formed a natural barrier about twenty yards further on.

"OK, Sarge…" Martlesham gasped, wondering what the NCO was going to do next.

The young Home Guardsman stumbled onwards towards the fallen tree. Beyond it, he could see the backs of their companions as they continued following the wood towards its western extremity. Jackson had fallen back from him now, out of his peripheral vision. The sound of German voices seemed to have fallen away somewhat too; the few voices he could hear sounding guarded and cautious now. He reached the tree trunk and threw himself over the moss covered obstacle, landing heavily on his side behind it. He pushed himself upright and peered over the top, just in time to see Jackson throw another grenade. Instantly Martlesham ducked behind the tree trunk and braced himself for the explosion. The few seconds that it took for the fuse to burn seemed endless, and during that lull, he remembered Jackson's instructions and grabbed hold of his Lewis Gun hurriedly. A split second before the grenade detonated, Martlesham heard the German voices again, calling out in alarm.

Crump!

Gritting his teeth, the young man reared up and slammed the Lewis Gun's tubular barrel sleeve across the trunk, pulling the butt back into his shoulder. To his surprise, Jackson was already sprinting back towards him. Something moved behind Jackson, way back in the trees, and Martlesham instinctively swung the gun barrel towards it. Aligning the weapon only roughly onto the target area, he squeezed the trigger.

Rat-tat-tat-tat-tat-tat-tat.

"Short bursts!" Jackson's powerful voice came to Martlesham, as the echo of the gun faded. "Short fucking bursts!"

"Sorry, Sarge!"

Rat-tat-tat-tat.

"Better!" Jackson snarled as he vaulted the tree trunk with a running jump. He landed next to Martlesham with a 'thump' and rolled over.

Cursing roundly, the sergeant struggled up into a kneeling position next to Martlesham.

"And stop calling me 'Sarge', Tom, for fuck's sake! It's Serg-*eant*."

Rat-tat-tat-tat.

"Half-left, Tom!" Jackson pointed through the trees to where there was movement. Martlesham swung round quickly, responding to the new threat. Rat-tat-tat-tat.

"That's enough, lad, well done. Let's go!"

The sergeant grabbed the young soldier's arm and pulled him to his feet. Together, they sprinted after their comrades, Jackson's hand clutching the sleeve of Martlesham's denim battledress, half dragging the younger man along.

They had gone perhaps another thirty yards when there was a flurry of gunfire some way in front of them. Instantly, Jackson let go of Martlesham's jacket sleeve, putting space between them.

"Keep going!" Snarled Jackson, his breathing heavy.

As they ploughed onwards, dodging between the trees and undergrowth, they heard a distinctive roar that could only be Bishop's shotgun. It was followed by several more shots and a burst of automatic fire, after which there was a sudden silence. Jackson slowed a touch and changed the magazine on his machine pistol as he advanced at a low crouch. Martlesham followed his lead and slowed, dipping his shoulders too.

They came across the rest of their group a moment later, in another clearing, and again surrounded by a dead German crew by a half-track and gun. As Jackson and Martlesham came into the clearing, Bishop turned, his face grim.

"These bastards heard us coming." He rumbled. "Dave's dead."

He waved a hand at a body on the floor, and Jackson saw that it was one of Bishop's friends from the village. As he glanced down at the bullet riddled corpse, laid sprawled in a bed of wilting nettles, Jackson realised he didn't even know the man's surname.

"We killed the rest of the Hun bastards though." Bishop added.

Further back in the wood, there was a whistle blast; then another. German voices were shouting orders.

"We've run into the middle of a whole bloody gun battery!" Jackson said aloud, the reality coming to him as he scanned the area. "That's the rest of 'em forming up. They're clearing the wood from one end to the other."

Bishop pointed to the north, through the trees.

"There's some kind of pond through there, about twenty metres in; long and thin by the looks of him."

He swung round and pointed westwards. "Not far until the end of the wood though, look."

Jackson needed no prompting.

"Tom? With me; same again. Search these buggers here for grenades, quickly. Bob? Keep going with the others. Looks as though we've gone right through them now, but keep your eyes peeled. Wait for us at the far edge of the wood. If we aren't with you in five minutes, break out over the fields and head west."

Martlesham was already frisking the dead Germans for ammunition. Bishop nodded his understanding and threw away his shotgun.

"That was my last cartridge. Suppose I'll have to use this new-fangled Hun machine-gun."

He dragged the MP40 off his shoulder and gave it a dubious look.

"Get going fellas." Jackson urged the others, accepting a German grenade from Martlesham. "Move fast; the bastards will be on us soon enough, and I don't want any of them getting in front of us and cutting us off."

Bishop nodded and growled at the other four men.

"Come on, lads. Shift your arses!"

With that, the burly farmer led the group off along the inside edge of the trees, moving flat out towards the far end of the finger of woodland.

Jackson turned back to Martlesham.

"Alright?" He asked the young man.

Martlesham nodded back, his eyes sharp; determined.

"Good lad." Jackson grinned. "Now, drop that grenade in the front cab this time; you'll stand more chance of immobilising the thing."

"I've got two grenades now, Sergeant." Replied the Home Guardsman. "I can put one each in both side s of the cab."

Jackson sucked his teeth thoughtfully.

"Okay, but be sharp about it. Don't be hanging around once that first one's gone in."

"I won't, Sergeant." Promised Martlesham.

The sound of more shouted commands, not far away, focussed both of their minds. The enemy were on the move again and closing fast. Splitting up to their positions, the two men looked in towards each other, in a repeat drill of their first, ad hoc demolition. Once more working on Jackson's nod, the two men yanked on the cords of their grenades, Martlesham working quickly to prime both of his and drop them deftly into the separate cabs of the armoured vehicle, before grabbing his Lewis Gun and bounding away. The two men broke through the undergrowth as they raced to put as much distance as possible between themselves and the gun position. Martlesham heard Jackson counting out loud.

"One…two…down!"

The two men threw themselves flat once more, this time into a shallow, yet convenient drainage channel.

Crump-crump.

The first two grenades detonated with their characteristic sharp bang.

Crump-booooom!

As the grenade that Martlesham had dropped into the passenger compartment exploded, it was followed immediately by a colossal, ear-splitting eruption that reminded them both of the impact of the big naval guns that had shelled them earlier in the day.

Both of the men cried out in alarm as the shock wave of the bigger blast passed over them, covering them in all kinds of debris and leaving them stunned and breathless. As the echo of the large explosion receded, there was a high-pitched tearing sound, and when Martlesham looked up, he saw a tree toppling over towards him. He scrambled sideways in a hurry, and the mature Ash tree crashed down across the drainage channel just a heart-beat later. Jackson, his face betraying complete and utter shock, raised his head and looked back towards the gun position. The gun itself was still there, its barrel depressed into the soil and its wrecked breach pointing upwards at an unnatural angle. Of the vehicle however, there was little left. The smoking wreck appeared to have been ripped to pieces from within.

"Fucking hell" Gasped Jackson. "You set off the ammo! It must have been piled up in the back!"

The two soldiers looked at each other dumbly for a moment, hardly able to believe the devastation they had wrought.

"Come on," Jackson said, his voice louder than it needed to be, due to the ringing in his ears, "let's go."

Up they got, seventeen year old Home Guard private and thirty year old Coldstream sergeant, and began tottering after their comrades once more. Whether the pursuit continued behind them, they had no idea, for their ears were buzzing from the explosion and they could barely hear their own foot steps.

They came to the end of the wood just a couple of minutes later. Several bursts of fire had come through the wood from behind them during their flight from the pursuing enemy, but the shots had all cracked well overhead and spun off in all directions, suggesting that the enemy were taking a more cautious approach now, and using searching fire, before advancing. Bishop was there at the wood's edge, silhouetted against the light brown earth of the field beyond where feint rays of weak sunshine illuminated the freshly turned earth. He waved them in.

"Looks clear. What shall we do? Follow the hedgerow round to the other side?"

Gasping for breath, Jackson shook his head.

"No…there's no time; we need to get across. Take Dutton and your two men…Get straight across there and give us fire support when we come over. Me, Tom and the lad with the big Jerry machine-gun will hold them off."

"Do you want me to stay here with you?"

"No." Jackson held up his hand. "Take them over and get them organised. You've done this before; you know what's needed. Now go, fast…"

Bishop needed no more urging. He barked out orders to the men concerned and led them straight out into the ploughed field, running clumsily over the clods of earth and heading for the hedgerow at the other side of the field. Jackson pushed Martlesham and the other Home Guardsman, a lad named Willis, down into position and gave them arcs of fire. Still gasping for breath, Martlesham removed his half-empty magazine from the Lewis and replaced it with the full one.

"Give us it here." Jackson said, indicating the half-full drum. "You keep your eyes on those trees."

Dropping low against the bank, he pulled one of his British .303 inch bandoliers around to the front of his body and dragged out two clips. With chafed and bleeding fingers, the Guards sergeant ripped the individual rounds out of the clips and began inserting them into the drum magazine with quick, practiced movements.

"Christ Almighty!" He breathed. "I'm hanging out of my arse here!"

Martlesham flung him an exhausted sideways glance and grinned.

"Jerries!" Willis hissed, and a second later, a volley of single shots rang out from inside the wood.

Crack, crack, crack. The shots flew overhead and onwards across the ploughed field. Rat-tat-tat-tat-tat-tat. Willis returned fire with the German light machine-gun. Crack, crack, crack. More German bullets snapped past them, including a burst of automatic fire. Martlesham ducked his head behind the sights of the Lewis Gun and opened fire. Jackson pushed the last round into the magazine and dropped it by Martlesham's right elbow, then rolled over into a position where he could use his own weapon. He cursed repeatedly as the ammunition bandolier, along with his slung Lee-Enfield, snagged on various bits of his equipment, causing him to struggle as he adopted a fire position.

He raised his MP40 and searched the trees to his front, looking for enemy movement.

Rat-tat-tat-tat-tat-tat-tat-tat-tat.

The German machine-gun operated by Willis spat its deadly metal slugs through the trees, shredding the undergrowth and ripping tree-bark from trunks as its fire raked the inside of the wood.

"Changing belts!" Willis shouted.

Rat-tat-tat-tat,

Martlesham covered the gap in fire.

Crack, crack, crack, crack.

Bullets came from behind them and off to a flank slightly, slicing through the woods. Jackson looked over his shoulder and saw the gun smoke by the far hedgerow. Bishop and the others had made it across and were giving them covering fire.

"Okay, fellas; let's go!" Jackson called to the other two men.

Grabbing their light machine-guns, Willis and Martlesham raised themselves into a crouch and turned towards the field. They paused as they saw several tracer rounds fly across the middle of the field in both directions.

"Straight over, move it!" Jackson shouted. "Come on, go!"

The two men jerked into life and set out into the plough furrows, whilst Jackson fired two quick bursts towards the spot where he'd seen movement amongst the trees just a second before. Pushing himself backwards and up, Jackson turned and followed after the two young Home Guardsmen, bending low as he ran. The other two were about ten or fifteen yards further on, and he could see their feet slipping and stumbling over the heavy clods of rich, brown earth. Within seconds, he too was feeling the effect of the ploughed soil on his legs. He felt as if he were wading through molten toffee, his hob-nailed boots picking up great lumps of the claggy earth with every step.

A burst of fire cracked past them at an angle that suggested the enemy were now on the wood line. Jackson glanced to his right and saw a tracer round flying towards them from several hundred yards away. A split second later, he caught sight of grey figures in the distant hedgerow by the York road. The Jerries were everywhere. Something cracked right past his ear and great spurts of earth erupted not far in front of him. Immediately, Willis staggered, then collapsed heavily, face down on top of his German light machine-gun. Martlesham pulled up sharply and stared down at his fallen friend.

"Mick?"

"Keep going!" Jackson roared at him.

The young Home Guardsman looked up in surprise.

"Keep going!" Jackson roared again, and this time Martlesham turned away and began running once more.

The sergeant was level with young Willis now and he slowed, reaching down for his arm and dragging the young man over onto his back. As the youngster flopped over, Jackson stared down into his smooth, handsome face and saw the wide staring eyes and the look of shock etched on the youthful features. A bloody coloured froth dribbled from the young man's mouth, and Jackson spotted the huge exit wound in the poor lad's chest. The teenager would be dead in seconds. A shot cracked by, so close to Jackson's head that he could have sworn he felt the rush of wind. In a pointless gesture of fury, he raised his machine-pistol with one hand and pulled the trigger. The automatic weapon lurched violently in his hand and spat its bullets in a wild arc towards the wood, from which they had just emerged. A second later, the small machine-pistol clicked on an empty breech and went silent.

Jackson threw the lightweight, metal weapon sideways contemptuously and grabbed hold of Willis' captured German machine-gun with both hands. With a cry of effort, the tall Guardsman staggered to his feet, lifting the MG34 with its trailing belt as he did so. As bullets flew past him in all directions, Jackson stumbled away from the dying Home Guardsman and began heading for the western hedgerow, which Martlesham had almost reached now. More earth spurted up near Jackson, but he kept on going, the muscles in his thighs protesting at the difficult ground. He snarled aloud at the pain in his taught muscles. His breathing was ragged now and he was unbearably hot, the sweat pouring down his face as he forced himself across the last twenty yards of open ground. He saw Martlesham crash through the hedgerow and dive head first over the fence. Bits of the hedge were literally disintegrating in front of Jackson's eyes, where Bishop and the others were blasting away with their weapons.

Moments later, Jackson reached the hedge. He saw a break in the foliage and went for it. At the last moment, he saw the barbed wire strands and threw himself over the thin cat-wire fence. He tumbled heavily over it and felt the painful scratch of a metal barb tear through his trouser leg and into his flesh. As he fell, head first into the grass at the far side, the metal barb dragged itself right across his outer thigh.

"Aaagh!" He winced as he felt the barb dig in.

His body finally cleared the fence and settled on the ground with a dull thud. He rolled over, gulping for breath like a drowning man and pushed the rim of his helmet up so he could see.

"Fucking.... hell!" He gasped, taking in great mouthfuls of air.

"Are you alright?"

It was Bishop's voice. The farmer was crouching next to him, staring at the regular soldier with concern. Jackson looked at him, straightening his spectacles as he did so.

"I...I can't slow my breathing down Bob...I think I'm going to shit myself!"

SEALION HEADQUARTERS – THE HAGUE, HOLLAND
SATURDAY 21ST SEPTEMBER – 1845 HOURS

"Still nothing?" Raeder stared at the commodore in exasperation.

"No, Sir," The commodore replied sheepishly, "nothing at all. The Luftwaffe say they've been overflying this part of the German Sea all afternoon but they've spotted nothing more than the few surviving British destroyers from the Tyne, which have pulled further east after taking a pounding from our big ships. Admiral Donitz has ordered the redeployment of U-Boats as instructed, and Admiral Lutjens has acknowledged our concerns about the carrier group. All major surface units have deployed to the northern and eastern flanks, less the Scheer, which is remaining on station off Flamborough Head whilst temporary repairs are conducted."

Raeder's fingers drummed the map table for a few moments.

"What about Prien?" He snapped irritably. "Has Donitz managed to get through to him?"

The commodore took a deep breath.

"He has, Sir. Prien insists that nothing has left Scapa Flow since his force has been on station. The other vessels in the force are all reporting the same too. They are adamant that nothing has slipped through the net."

Raeder stared hard at the commodore.

"And we have not missed any part of the anchorage with our photography? We are sure that the enemy ships are not secreted up some inlet?"

The commodore stiffened slightly.

"I'm absolutely positive, Admiral. The staff and I have put the photographs together and double checked them against the charts. We haven't missed a square metre of water. Those ships are not in Scapa Flow."

He paused, whilst Raeder brooded.

"And there has been no air-strike by carrier borne aircraft against the invasion fleet? No sign of those ridiculous bi-planes the Tommies are still using?"

"None, Sir." The commodore assured him.

The Grand Admiral brooded a moment longer, then thumped the table with a fist.

"Then where in the name of God are they?" He yelled, pushing back the chair and rising to his feet.

He stalked around the map table.

"Where are they?" He repeated quietly, his voice calming almost immediately after the short outburst.

The commodore watched him, aware of how much pressure the Grand Admiral was under. The plan to invade Britain had always been ambitious, and in the early days of the Fuhrers great dream, Raeder had done his best to dissuade him from even contemplating such a course of action. However, seeing that Hitler would not be swayed, and seeing too that the likes of Goering and Himmler would be constantly whispering their encouragement into the leader's ears, Raeder had gone out of his way to prepare for every eventuality and give the Kreigsmarine the best fighting chance. Even so, they were up against the most powerful navy in the world and Raeder knew that just one slight mistake could result in disaster. Losing all those destroyers in Norway hadn't helped their cause at all; but Hitler wouldn't listen to excuses like that.

"Might I make a suggestion, Sir?" The commodore asked politely.

Raeder looked across the table at him through knitted eyebrows.

"Go on."

The commodore cleared his throat.

"There is a possibility that the enemy ships slipped out of Scapa Flow yesterday afternoon, just after the first set of reconnaissance photographs were taken. Given that the enemy knew nothing of our plans, and given that as of yet, we haven't seen any indication that the carrier group is in the German Sea, there is a possibility that they may have been tasked to head around Scotland and pick up convoys coming out of Liverpool and Londonderry. We know that following their heavy shipping losses last month, the British have been bolstering their convoy escorts. That would explain the absence of the force from the picture so far."

Raeder thought on that for a while. He looked at the map and traced a route with his finger, around the north coast of Scotland, then followed the western coastline down towards the top of Ireland. After a moment, he flicked his gaze back up at the commodore.

"That's a possibility isn't it? But if it's correct, and if you were the Chief of Britain's Naval Staff, what would you do once you realised that an invasion was underway?"

The commodore shrugged.

"Recall them, Sir, I suppose; by the quickest possible route."

Raeder re-traced his finger back around the Scottish coast towards the Orkneys.

"So let's call it…say two hundred and fifty, maybe three hundred nautical miles?"

He looked up at the commodore, one eyebrow raised. The commodore nodded his agreement with the estimate.

Raeder straightened and looked squarely at his Head of Naval Operations.

"How long to cover that with a carrier and escorts? Fifteen hours from point of realisation?"

The commodore pursed his lips.

"I'd say ten if they made full steam, and assuming too that they hadn't got all the way round to the top of Ireland."

"Which means," Raeder went on, "that they would be due back in the vicinity of the Orkneys…"

The commodore finished the sentence for him.

"About now, Sir."

Raeder's face hardened.

"Get a signal off to Prien via Donitz. The previous instructions still stand, just in case we're wrong and the Luftwaffe's pilots are all blind. However, in addition, I want another third of Prien's force to fan out north-west of the Orkneys, covering all of the routes back around the top of Scotland. I want them moving within the next thirty minutes."

The commodore stood to attention and saluted.

"Yes, Admiral. I'll get the signal off immediately."

He turned on his heel and rushed off.

Raeder ran a hand over his face and took a deep breath. The operation was on a knife edge. The fleet carrying the Totenkopf Division was half way across the German Sea, escorted by surface units, a U-Boat, and aircraft. The empty transports were passing them in the other direction. The sea-lane that he had established was narrow and vulnerable and he dreaded the thought of the Royal Navy sailing right into the middle of it. By his reckoning there were still two hours of daylight left, before the night would give them some degree of safety again.

The sound of deep-bellied laughter rang through the vast hall that was filled with map tables and desks. Raeder looked up and saw a party of senior officers enter the room through the ornate double doors. All heads in the room turned momentarily to sneak a glance at the group huddled around the high-ranking visitor. Albert Kesselring was there, accompanied by Keitel, and several other senior members of the planning staff. In their midst was a fat, red-cheeked, jelly-jowled peacock, dressed in a pale blue uniform, hung with gold braid; a uniform that belonged in a fairy tale rather than a strategic headquarters. Herman Goering, Reichsmarshal and head of the Luftwaffe had arrived at Sealion Headquarters. Raeder groaned aloud.

"Jesus Christ!" The Grand Admiral murmured to himself in dismay. "What the hell is he doing here?"

GYPSEY HILL FARM COMPLEX – BY WOLD NEWTON
SATURDAY 21ST SEPTEMBER 1940 – 1900 HOURS

"Go, go, go!"

Hagen screamed out the order to Saltz from across the farm yard. In front of Saltz, Nuemark bent double and stepped sideways, exposing himself beyond the corner of the brick barn. He stuck his finger ends into his ears and grimaced as Bachman squeezed back on the trigger of the MG34.

Rat-tat-tat-tat-tat-tat-tat.

The machine-gun burst into noisy life, balanced across the squad corporal's back for stability, and spat its bullets towards the small, first floor windows of the farmhouse. Nuemark swore and brushed franticly at the hot, expended brass cartridge case that fell down the back of his collar.

"Ah! Fuck, fuck, fuck!"

Simultaneously, Saltz and the remainder of the squad burst out from the cover of the barn and clattered across the yard towards the doorway of the house. A bullet ricocheted off the cobbles in front of them with a spark and a whine. They ignored it and kept running. Another bullet bounced off the cobbles, and then they were against the wall, crouching in a line beneath a window, breathing heavily and preparing for the entry. Across the farmyard, Bachman slowed his rate of fire.

"Now!" Saltz snapped to the squad members next to him.

In a well practiced movement, one of the privates stood up, flattening his back against the wall to the side of the window. He swung his carbine to one side, and then brought it back round so that its metal butt plate smashed into the nearest window pane. Even as the glass shattered, a second soldier was reaching up with stick grenade in hand. He flicked his wrist and the grenade disappeared inside the building.

"Grenade!" Called the young private, as the whole assault group rapidly curled into balls on the floor.

Crump!

"Go, go, go!" Saltz was screaming, even as the shards of glass and bits of furniture flew over his head to rattle down across the cobbles of the farmyard.

Instead of using the door, they went through the window. Saltz sprayed the best part of a full magazine from his MP40 into the room, and a split second later, the first rifleman was diving head first over the lip of the shattered window. Another soldier followed and seconds later came the call from within.

"Room clear! Exit to hallway on left!"

Saltz jerked his head at the remaining two riflemen.

"In!"

Obediently, the two young soldiers threw themselves over the window ledge and disappeared. Saltz followed. As he entered the room and adjusted his eyes to the dim light, he saw the first assault pair already braced by the side of the doorway, grenades in hand. The second pair were crouching nearby, rifles at the ready. Saltz held up a warning hand.

"Save those grenades for a moment." He ordered the pair by the door, then to the others. "Straight through once I finish firing."

The men nodded their understanding and Saltz moved to the doorway. Tentatively, he poked the nose of the MP40 around the door frame and pressed the trigger. The remaining rounds in his magazine rattled off the plaster along the length of the inner passage. As his weapon clicked on an empty breech, he stepped back quickly and allowed the two riflemen of the second assault pair to barge past him. The following couple of minutes passed in a blur of explosions and gunshots as the small German squad cleared firstly the kitchen, and then the second room on the ground floor. It was done with a practiced ease, using techniques refined in Poland, Holland and France. Of the enemy however, there was no sign. The squad formed up quickly by the stairs and Saltz fell silent, using field signals to put the four riflemen into their assault positions. He signalled to the lead pair, and quietly, but quickly, they moved up the stairs to the halfway point; one covering forwards, one stepping backwards as he ascended.

There was a sudden thud of footsteps somewhere on the next floor and the soldiers reacted instinctively. They both fired single shots at the doorways they could see, then tumbled back down the stairs, the last man tossing a grenade as far down the upper landing as he could get it.

"Grenade!" He shouted, as the two of them literally fell off the bottom step and curled up in foetal positions in the hallway, realising that the blast might well bring part of the ceiling down.

The four seconds on the fuse seemed to take an age to elapse, and as the squad members silently counted the seconds off, they were aware of a scuffling noise, followed by something rolling, and then a heavy thud on the stairs. Saltz peeked up from beneath his arm that was covering his face and his eyes bulged in shock. The Tommies had kicked the grenade back down and the small explosive device was laying precariously on a step about halfway down the steps.

"Grenade! Get back!" He roared, throwing himself to one side and into one of the ground floor rooms. His riflemen hurled themselves the other way, tumbling over each other to get into the kitchen.

Crump!

It was a miracle that none of them were killed. As the thick smoke cleared through the hallway, Saltz, coughing on the dusty smoke, staggered out into the passage once more and looked into the kitchen. To his relief, he saw all of his men clambering to their feet, cursing roundly as they did so.

"Get lined out along here!" He roared at them, his shock turning to sudden rage. "Start firing through the fucking ceiling! Come on, move!"

His men stumbled into the hall again, raising their rifles. The first bark of a carbine rang out, and more plaster dust descended into the hall as the high velocity round went through the ceiling and into the upper landing. More shots sounded as the other privates followed suit, working the bolts of their rifles quickly in order to saturate the upper floor with bullets from below.

Without a word of explanation to his men, Saltz threw himself up the stairs, leaping over the middle section which had been ripped open by the blast of the grenade. He swung round as he came towards the top of the stairs, his finger already squeezing the trigger as he turned. The machine-pistol chattered into life and a hail of 9 mm slugs slapped into the walls of the upper landing, and anything else that was on it. That included the old long case clock and the grey-haired British Home Guardsman standing next to it. The old man in the greenish fatigue uniform, span around in a crazy pirouette as two of the heavy slugs ripped into his chest. The man was dead before he hit the floor, falling on top of his old fashioned rifle.

"Stop firing! Stop firing!" Yelled Saltz. "Follow me up! Landing clear! Let's go, come on!"

The unmistakable sound of boots on the stairs came to his ears, but his eyes were firmly fixed on the two doorways at the far end of the landing, one facing him and one off to the left. He lowered his machine-pistol slightly and fired several more rounds into the body laid in front of him, then brought the muzzle back up and advanced along the landing towards the two doorways. He heard the heavy breathing of his men close behind him, but kept his eyes on the two doorways.

"Both rooms together, stand by…" He ordered his men without looking back.

He flinched suddenly as a small object flew out of the doorway at chest height. He didn't have time to register what it was, but a split second later, the object shattered against the wall above the dead Tommy and, suddenly, a great fireball erupted in front of Saltz with a terrible whoosh.

"Whooaaa!"

With an unashamed cry of terror, the big German sergeant hurled himself backwards as the flames reared up before him. He barged into his leading rifleman and together they tumbled into a pile at the top of the staircase. Saltz could feel the intense heat on his back, neck and legs and his lungs felt as if they had been sucked empty of oxygen. A harsh odour came to his nostrils and he recognised the familiar smell of petrol. His men were shouting now; anger, terror, confusion, all mixed into a chorus of chaos. He heard the tinkle of shattering glass once more, followed by another great whoosh.

The heat was now so intense that it was painful, and both he and his men were scrabbling on all fours, trying to get away from the searing flames.

"What the fuck?" Gasped one of his men.

"What the fuck's going on?" Yelled another, coughing on the thick smoke that was rapidly filling the building.

"Get out!" Yelled Saltz, his voice coming out as a hoarse croak.

"Are they fucking mad?" Demanded the nearest private, staring in awe at the far end of the hall which was now ablaze from floor to ceiling.

Part of the banister and railing was also alight including the portion that ran over the stairwell.

Saltz swallowed painfully, trying to find his voice.

"They're absolutely fucking bonkers!" He forced his words out of a scorched throat. "They're gonna burn the place down with all of us inside!"

The private shook his head as he shuffled backwards, swinging his legs onto the staircase and trying to stand.

"What now, Sergeant?"

Saltz raised his voice as loud as he could and pushed the private into the other riflemen clustered by the top steps.

"What do *you* think? Get the fuck out of here…move!"

The five German infantrymen half slid, half tumbled down the stairs as the burning landing began to give way above them. Over the noise of the flames and collapsing woodwork, they heard a deranged voice shouting in English from somewhere above them.

"Welcome to England, Jerry! You're all going to burn in hell you Nazi bastards!"

The private in front of Saltz looked up angrily as he heard the voice begin to emit a chilling peal of laughter.

"What's that fucking island-monkey going on about?"

Saltz pushed the soldier downwards and into the lower hall, just as part of the landing collapsed sideways onto the stairs, leaving them with a fire-wreathed tunnel to run through in order to get to the door.

"Who cares?" Saltz barked, ducking low as a flaming plank of wood dropped past him onto the floor. "Just get the fuck out, man!"

BADGER'S HOLLOW COPSE – TWO MILES WEST OF RAF DRIFFIELD
SATURDAY 21ST SEPTEMBER 1940 – 1930 HOURS

"What do you lot think you're playing at?"

The angry demand made every one of the refugees from RAF Driffield look round in surprise. The fourteen individuals hiding in the small depression stared up with angst at the six heavily armed men, who glared back at them from the lip of the hollow. The tallest of them, a severe looking giant in Regular Army battledress and wearing spectacles, came wading through the beds of dying nettles towards them, casting his fierce eyes about at the disparate group, which included two WAAFs.

"And where are your bloody sentries?"

The grim looking soldier strode into the centre of the hollow, studying the group of RAF personnel intently, most of whom shrank away from him when they saw the large sergeant chevrons on his battledress sleeves.

Scotton averted his eyes as the soldier's gaze passed over him. He found himself looking into the eyes of Austin Bevan, who looked equally mortified. Their group had somehow managed to sneak out of RAF Driffield that morning as the battle had raged around them, led by one of the flying crew who hadn't been able to get to his plane in time to evacuate by air. They had stumbled haphazardly for several miles until they had found this useful piece of cover. There they had remained, completely unaware of what was happening; knowing only that a huge land and air battle was taking place around and above them, and that for the moment, they could play no useful part in it.

"That's all we need!" Scotton whispered quietly to Bevan. "Bloody Pongos!"

"Just as well we weren't Jerries wasn't it?" The Army sergeant's harsh voice cut in, making Scotton flinch. "Who's in charge here?"

One of the flying crew stepped forward and held out his hand.

"I'm the senior one mate. Sergeant Joe Hobley; air gunner."

The big Army sergeant looked down at Hobley's hand as if it were a poisonous snake, but after a moment, he took one hand from his weapon and shook with the other man. It was at that point that Scotton noticed the Army NCO was carrying a big German machine-gun.

"Sergeant Jackson, 2nd Battalion Coldstream Guards," The Army sergeant replied in a formal manner, "attached to the Filey Bay Home Guard. I'm assuming you lot are from Driffield? What happened at the airfield then?"

Hobley seemed to visibly shrink when Jackson told him who he was, but the RAF NCO somehow managed to produce a reply.

"Not sure to be honest, mate. We were all up and about, preparing the squadron for our mission over the Channel against the invasion fleet, when out of nowhere there's suddenly Jerry parachutists everywhere. Some landed on the airfield itself, and loads more came over the perimeter fence and right through the front gates of camp. That was about four o'clock. There was no sign of the local Army boys, and it was every man for himself. We managed to hold them for a bit, but most of the lads didn't have weapons to hand. We only just managed to get out of the place before it got overrun. We've been sitting tight all day just waiting for the Army to show up."

Jackson was frowning.

"Invasion fleet in the *Channel*? Are you sure about that?"

"Absolutely." Hobley replied. "We'd just had the briefing before the Jerry attack started. There are several invasion fleets off the south coast. We were meant to attack the eastern one, off Folkestone."

Jackson pulled a face.

"Well," He said after a pause, "I wouldn't worry about that for now, because the Jerries have landed for definite at Filey; thousands of the buggers."

"Filey?" Hobley gaped at him.

"Aye," Jackson said bleakly. "Me and some of these boys fought 'em on the beach until we ran out of ammunition." He jerked his thumb towards the other five men from his section.

"When we couldn't hold 'em off, we started fighting our way back here in order to link up with the local brigade. We've killed a few of the bastards on the way too. There's a pile of 'em just back there, in a wood that we came through an hour ago. You might have heard the shooting?"

Jackson paused briefly, as Hobley nodded affirmation that they had indeed heard the latest round of gunfire.

"The problem is," Jackson continued, "the local brigade seems to be shut up in Driffield town itself and surrounded by Jerries. They've got tanks there, lots of them; on the eastern side of the town. There's also a shit-load of Jerry infantry sealing up this side of the place, and those bastards we just came through were an anti-tank unit by the looks of 'em. All in all, it looks like 'round one' has gone to the Jerries."

The RAF personnel were intent now; listening to Jackson's every word. Hobley stared at him agape.

"Filey? Tanks? Bloody hell!"

Nearby, one of the WAAFs gave a small sob. Jackson's head snapped round instantly towards the young woman, who was sitting on a folded greatcoat beside the only other female of the group. For a second he furrowed his brow in agitation, but then relaxed slightly.

"You can pack that in, young lady." Jackson said firmly, but in a slightly gentler tone than was normal for him.

He flicked his gaze to the other woman, sitting beside her.

"And you can put that cigarette out. You can smell it from fifty yards away. That's how we found you lot. Besides, it'll be getting dark soon. No more naked lights until morning."

The WAAF blinked in surprise and stubbed out the cigarette. Around the hollow, some of the other airmen surreptitiously followed suit. Scotton and Bevan exchanged a look, and Scotton raised an eyebrow at his friend.

"What the hell do we do now, then?" Wondered Hobley aloud. "Sounds like the bastards are all around us!"

Jackson shook his head.

"No. I reckon you just got beyond their perimeter. It looks like they're settling in for the night where they are. Driffield must have been their main objective for the day. Judging by what we've seen over the last few hours, they're digging-in, ready for a counter-attack. Plus, it sounds as though they're still mopping-up in the town. We are in danger of being caught by one of their patrols mind you, so we need to sharpen up our act here a bit before we move off. There's barely an hour of full light left, so we'll get moving shortly, just after dark."

"Moving off?" Hobley frowned doubtfully." Where to?"

"Anywhere that has a formed British garrison that is prepared to fight. Then we can get back into this scrap and kill some more of the sausage-eating fuckers."

The sudden passion in Jackson's words took all of the RAF personnel by surprise, and the two WAAFs paled visibly at the comment.

"We thought we might try to head for RAF Leaconfield?" Hobley suggested, rather lamely. "It's just down the road there, before you get to Beverley."

Jackson cocked his head to one side slightly, considering the idea. After a while he shook it.

"I don't reckon that's a good idea, mate, to be honest. Leaconfield is the same distance from the coast as Driffield. The Jerries obviously wanted this airfield bad enough to drop parachutists right onto it, so I reckon the same thing's probably happened down there. I reckon we need to head south-west, on the Goole road. I know there's a major unit down that way, and we'll be heading towards the GHQ Line on the Ouse. It's a direct route and easy to follow, so we should be able to make plenty of distance, even in the dark. Hopefully we'll bump into our reserves coming the other way."

The RAF sergeant stared back Jackson wordlessly.

"Happy enough with that, mate?" Jackson prompted him. "We'll try and get you and the other aircrew back to an RAF station as soon as we bump into our blokes. The rest of us can tag onto whichever unit we come across."

Hobley looked unsure.

"I suppose…but we've only got a few rifles and a couple of revolvers between us."

Jackson nodded, understanding the reluctance to get into a fight without being properly armed.

"I know what you mean, but don't worry about that. Me and the boys have got plenty of weapons between us. We'll distribute them now and teach you how to use the German ones. We've even got a couple of German pistols that the girls can have."

He nodded in the direction of the two WAAFs.

Hobley smiled suddenly.

"Well that's a bonus at least, because they only got issued hockey sticks in the plotting room."

Jackson frowned and looked down at the two WAAFs. Indeed, there were two hockey sticks laid on the floor between them.

"Not enough weapons to go round on the station, see?" Hobley shrugged. "Even before the scrapping started."

Jackson shook his head in wonder.

"Jesus bloody Christ!" He swore under his breath.

Snapping his attention back to Hobley, Jackson straightened slightly and hefted his German machine-gun into a more comfortable position.

"Right," He said. "Can I ask for a couple of your lads with rifles to go on sentry while my boys get their weapons passed around? Once that's done we should be able to get moving; it's getting darker by the minute.

Hobley nodded.

"Yeah, sure, mate."

He turned and looked towards Scotton and Bevan.

"Billy? Austin? Can you two stand sentry for a few minutes? You've both got rifles haven't you?"

Jackson frowned slightly as the RAF sergeant openly used the airmens' first names in front of the others, but remained silent. Nodding, the two airmen climbed slowly to their feet, gathering their weapons as they did so. They stood quietly, looking from Hobley to Jackson, waiting for further instructions. Hobley looked as though he were reluctant to give them any orders. Jackson was eyeing them up darkly, taking in every aspect of their appearance. After a moment, he looked straight into Scotton's eyes and spoke.

"You, lad; get your helmet on straight. Where do you think you are, man?"

Scotton blinked several times and looked at Bevan. Bevan looked terrified. Scotton pulled his helmet straight and looked back at his friend who nodded that it was indeed sitting straight on his head, and not at its previous rakish angle.

"Martlesham? Take these two with you and put them out on sentry please?" The big Guards sergeant called up to one of the men in his group. "Spread 'em out and make sure they've got plenty of ammunition."

"Yes, Sergeant." Replied one of the men on the lip of the hollow, and beckoned to Scotton and Bevan.

The two airmen climbed the short slope to where the soldier in greenish-khaki fatigues waited for them. To their surprise, the man was wearing a Home Guard brassard and was obviously very young. He was carrying an old fashioned Lewis Gun; the kind that air gunners sometimes practiced on during their initial training, and his eyes were dark and brooding like those of his sergeant.

"Come on then." He mumbled, and turned towards the edge of the copse.

As they pushed their way through the brambles and thick nettle beds, Scotton tried to engage the young man in conversation.

"Does that sergeant treat all of you like children, then?"

The young Home Guardsman stopped abruptly and turned to stare at Scotton with hard, grey eyes.

"Sergeant Jackson doesn't treat anyone like children. He just treats everyone like soldiers. It's called discipline. If you want to live, get used to it."

The young man turned away from Scotton and walked on.

PART THREE

BREAKOUT

S +1
EARLY MORNING

OVER THE COAST OF YORKSHIRE
SUNDAY 22ND SEPTEMBER 1940 – 0030 HOURS

The flak took them all by surprise. It had been an easy trip thus far, heading along the guide-beam to cut the English coastline just above Hull. There was little anti-aircraft fire on the way in, the Tommies below being more pre-occupied with the Germans on the ground rather than the drone of unseen aircraft high above, and they had swung starboard onto their new course towards York without difficulty. To the north, many miles distant, they could see a lot of flak. Probably German guns, the crew assumed, engaging British bombers over the invasion area. The night was dark, with little moon remaining and the clouds getting ever thicker. The morning would prove to be grey and dreary, Gerring suspected. As for tonight, he was hoping for another good run. The planners had done a great job, laying a route down for them that circumnavigated the invasion area, in order to allow the fleet of Heinkels to stay clear of friendly flak, but not such a circuitous route as to take them over major enemy concentrations. All that had been fine until they got near to their target.

Due to the cloud, Gerring had ordered his pilot to drop lower so they could search for the thin silver thread in the darkness that would betray the line of the River Ouse to them. It took them just two minutes to spot the river, picking up the junction of the river where it joined the larger River Humber. A couple of minutes later, the first flak began to explode. Not much at first, just a dozen or so big explosions fired randomly into the air. Fortunately, the Tommies were expecting a higher level raid, so much of the flak went well above them. As they progressed up the river line, more flak came towards them, and this time, although the heavy guns were still firing high, the smaller ordance was reaching the right bracket and several air-bursts came uncomfortably close.

In front of them, Gerring's crew could see distant flames on the ground, further along their current course. That must be the target. They were the second squadron in the stream tonight, so they would have something to guide them in on this occasion. Because they were attacking a built up area tonight, every third bomber was dropping incendiaries.

"There you go, Gunther." Gerring pointed. "York. We're bang on course. Let's up the speed a touch more, because they'll know we're coming by now."

The pilot nodded and moments later, the aircraft began to hum a touch more urgently as the pilot gave her another fifteen knots, just short of top speed.

"Stand by, bombs." Gerring murmured.

"Right you are, Lieutenant." The bomb aimer replied, crawling into position.

It was just then that the first search lights came on. The half-dozen beams of light shot upwards suddenly, as if on queue, though they came from several different locations that must have been miles apart.

"Bloody hell, Lieutenant! I didn't expect that." Laughed the pilot nervously.

"Just keep going." Murmured Gerring as they passed through one of the beams.

York was closer now, perhaps ten miles at the most. Moments after the searchlights had cut through the night, more flak began to erupt around them, making the aircraft shudder. There was lots of it, including heavy stuff, and it was all in the right height bracket to be worrying.

"The bastards were waiting for us!" Cursed the bomb-aimer. "They must have every gun in England around this bloody town!"

"Heavier than Poland, I reckon." The pilot commented.

"And France." Gerring added. "And certainly as bad as London."

"Do you think they know we're after the railway?" Asked the pilot.

"Doesn't take the brains of a Reichsmarshal to work that out." Gerring murmured dryly.

"Didn't know they made Reichsmarschals with brains." Interjected the dorsal gunner.

"Watch it…" Gerring warned him gently, smiling all the same.

"Three miles to target, I reckon." Came the bomb-aimer's voice.

"Okay lads," Gerring said, "Let's stay sharp. Keep your eyes peeled for the railway line. Let's dump these bombs on target, and get the hell out of here. I don't want to make a second pass with all this shit flying about."

The crew peered intently below them, towards the ever brightening fires.

"See that bridge there, over the river; the thin one?" Cut in the bomb-aimer. "I reckon that's where the railway cuts the Ouse, just south of the town and the station."

Gerring murmured agreement.

"Reckon your right. Stand by to drop. Keep her steady Gunther; pass straight over the bridge. We'll drop shortly after that."

Crump!

A large fireball erupted worryingly close to port.

"Fuck me! That made me jump!" Swore the pilot.

"Steady Gunther, steady…" Gerring soothed him. "Stand by bombs, stand by…"

He held his breath, trying to judge the distance below. They were right over the bridge. He counted slowly.

"One, two, three…release now!"

"Bombs away." The bomb-aimer's voice sounded in Gerring's ear-piece. Then, seconds later. "Bombs gone."

"Okay Gunther." Gerring nudged the pilot. "Take us back up into the cloud, quickly, then bank thirty degrees to starboard and we'll get back over the sea sharpish. We don't need to hang around here anymore."

The pilot responded immediately, taking the machine up steeply as a searchlight beam came flicking towards them. For a few brief seconds, the cockpit was filled with dazzling light, but then it faded just as quickly as the plane was enveloped by thick cloud. Coming out above the cloud moments later, the pilot banked as ordered, until Gerring gave him the nod to level off and hold steady on that course. As the engines eased off slightly and the machine settled down to cruising speed with a comfortable hum, Gerring and the pilot exchanged relieved looks.

"Christ, Heinz!" Breathed the pilot. "That was a hairy one, tonight!"

"Certainly was." Gerring agreed, pulling his flying helmet aside slightly and wiping the sweat from the side of his skull. "I reckon we could be in for more of the same tomorrow, unless the Army boys make good speed and make their day two objectives on time."

He looked down between his legs towards the bomb aimer, who was paying attention to the forward machine-gun once more.

"How did that look Heigel?"

"Sweet Lieutenant; really sweet. I caught a quick look behind just before we went into the cloud and it looked like a nice neat stick, right over the target. We must have been bang on, near as dammit."

"Good stuff. Well done everyone. Now then, stay sharp until we get well out to sea. Another half an hour and we should be fairly safe."

"I can almost smell those sausages for breakfast." Said the bomb-aimer, and everyone chuckled.

They held their course for another ten minutes and picked up the guide-beam that would help them find their way back home. Bringing the plane onto the precise return course, Gerring sighed with a certain amount of relief. That really had been a surprisingly tough one, with several very near misses and two lock-ons from search lights. Just the long trip over the sea now; then breakfast and a welcome sleep in a nice warm bunk.

"Lieutenant. We've got an aircraft coming up behind us."

The voice of the dorsal gunner, who was sitting just to his rear, brought Gerring out of his reverie.

"One of ours?" Gerring demanded sharply.

"I think so. Hard to tell, but it's a twin engine job for sure, and I just caught a bit of moonlight reflecting off the nose; it's an all glass cockpit."

Gerring frowned. It was probably one of their own, given the intervals between aircraft in the stream. All the same, there were likely to be Tommy aircraft all over the place tonight. The enemy's own bombers would be trying to hit the German beach-head as hard as possible under the cover of darkness.

"Flash the recognition signal." Gerring ordered. "Once he sees it he should back off slightly."

The dorsal gunner never had the chance to reply, because at precisely that moment a long burst of automatic fire ripped through the fuselage of the Heinkel with a heart-lurching clatter. With a yelp of surprise, the pilot suddenly banked sharply to port, but as he did so, another long burst of machine-gun fire from the British Blenheim night-fighter slashed through their aircraft, raking along the starboard wing and into the engine. Even as the Heinkel flipped over and out of the enemy's cone of fire, the starboard engine burst into flames. The aircraft suddenly felt heavy and sluggish as the pilot tried to level off slightly and turn again. The controls were barely responding and Gerring saw that the starboard engine was completely out. Something wet was dripping down his neck and he raised a hand to wipe at it unconsciously. He pulled his hand away and in the glare of the flames he could see that it was blood. It was the blood of the dorsal gunner, who was slumped dead in his seat behind the aircraft's captain.

Another burst of fire suddenly cut through the aircraft from an angle, coming from the left this time. The British night-fighter was following them down, making sure of his kill.

"The controls aren't working, Heinz!" Yelled the pilot, his voice thick with terror. "I can't bring her up!"

Gerring's heart lurched. Suddenly his body felt terribly heavy and his mind was numb with the sudden fear that coursed through every inch of his being, starting from the stomach and rising up to his throat.

"Get out!" He barked, releasing his seat harness. "Bale out!"

THE LEVEL CROSSING – BY WETHERBY RACE COURSE SUNDAY 22ND SEPTEMBER 1940 – 0045 HOURS

"Is that York?"

Major Harold Watts of the 3rd Armoured Brigade, lead element of 1st Armoured Division, stared into the distance across dark fields. Many miles away, something big was on fire. The light from the blaze was widespread, and small onion shaped balls of orange flashed in the sky above. The noise of the bombardment came to his ears as a dull, constant rumble. Every now and then, he caught sight of what looked like a great tower of some kind, partially illuminated by the surrounding inferno. He guessed it might be the great Minster in the centre of the city.

"It certainly is." Replied the captain from the Royal Military Police. "I can see now why GHQ chose this little spot for the disembarkation area. I reckon half the city must be on fire by now."

"Poor buggers." Watts commented. "Still, thank God someone at the top is thinking straight. We've only got one chance at this; we can't afford to cock it up."

"Well, Sir, you're here now." Smiled the captain. "I reckon the Jerries are in for a shock before long."

"Hmm." Watts murmured thoughtfully.

He turned his full attention back to the Military Police officer.

"We shall see. Anyway, old chap; what's the drill?"

The captain indicated that they should walk along the line some way, and Watts fell in beside him, crunching over the gravel. They walked along the length of the train, the hulking silhouettes of the Matilda Mark 2 tanks looming above them as they progressed. Eventually, they came to the end of the train, the last truck of which was just yards away from the level crossing.

"Quite simple." The captain waved his hand towards the road. "Bring the tanks off here, making sure that all chocks and chains get deposited in these big bags here by the fence, then wheel right onto this small road. Follow it up for a few hundred yards and you'll be met by one of my sections. They'll direct you into a waiting area where you are to form up in line-ahead. You'll then be escorted to the divisional checkpoint where your own divisional staff will brief you and send you on your way. I gather you're going to circle the city to the north; they've been building engineer bridges over the Ouse, I've heard."

Watts expressed mild surprise, mixed with satisfaction.

"Crikey! It all sounds remarkably organised for once."

The captain laughed.

"Oh, it's organised alright, Sir. We've had very clear orders from Command HQ in York. There's to be no confusion; no delay. The whole route has been sign-posted and the RVs are all marked and manned. You shouldn't have any problems at all. Which reminds me; I've been told to inform each chalk commander that the time at the divisional checkpoint is limited to forty minutes, because we should have the next train along almost right behind yours. Orders are that when you get to the checkpoint, your lads need to prepare the vehicles for action. All initial running checks, valises removed from guns, the whole nine yards."

Watts nodded, his face serious. After a day of frustrated speculation on the train, it was all becoming real enough. They had left their barracks that morning after much rumour and several false starts. All they had been told was that the invasion was in Yorkshire and not on the south coast as first thought. Watts and the other squadron leaders had been briefed by their commanding officer that he would meet them somewhere near York; that they would be met and guided at the other end. Other than that, details had been few. Now however, looking through the September night towards a city in flames, Watts could pretty much guess most of it.

"Right then," He said firmly, "let's get on with it shall we?"

He plodded down the line towards the front of the train where he eventually met the squadron sergeant major, who had been herding the men together as they disgorged from the carriages into the pitch darkness. There was a delay of several minutes as every troop sergeant went through each of their crews by name, in order to ensure that all were present. As Watts waited impatiently for the roll call to finish, several of the men stood off to one side and urinated into the undergrowth by the edge of the line. Eventually, after some hissing and chasing by the sergeants, the squadron sergeant major reported that everyone was present, including the members of the Recce Troop who had accompanied them on this chalk. Watts briefed them quickly, and repeated the simple instructions. The squadron sergeant major said a few words afterwards, emphasising a couple of control measures, and then the men split off into the darkness to start upchucking their vehicles.

Watts and his sergeant major moved back down to the level crossing where the ramps had now been dropped from the rear truck of the train. He looked at his watch, peering at it closely in the darkness. Almost one in the morning. He wasn't tired. They had been lucky enough to receive more than fifteen hours of rest on the train. He was as awake and alert as he could be, and the tension was beginning to increase as each minute passed. Where would they be in the morning, he wondered? There was no point worrying. The night would pass quickly enough, and all of them were en route to meet their destiny, one way or the other. He listened to the subdued conversation of the crews as they prepared to offload their tanks, recognising individual voices of the squadron members he knew so well. Watts wondered how many of those men would still be alive, this time next week. He heard someone give a command, and a moment later, the engine of the first Matilda roared into life, filling the night air with the thick, distinctive smell of engine exhaust fumes.

Moments later, he and his sergeant major stepped back a couple of paces, as the young troop leader commanding the first vehicle, marshalled his driver forward and down the ramp. It was five minutes to one o'clock in the morning at Wetherby Racecourse as the first Matilda rolled onto tarmac. The First Armoured Division had arrived.

RAF DRIFFIELD
SUNDAY 22ND SEPTEMBER 1940 – 0100 HOURS

The three engined transport aircraft trundled along the ground, carefully following the lone torch of the marshal. Lieutenant General Richard Putzier watched the dark silhouette roll to a gentle halt and cut its engines. He heaved a great sigh; a rather impatient one. This was the ninth aircraft in the last hour. The most senior officer to have landed so far was a captain, but Putzier was impatient to speak with someone much more important. He vaguely registered that the door of the aircraft was open and that there was a conversation taking place between the occupants and the marshal.

Putzier was tired and agitated. He had been fighting hard since 0500 hours the previous morning, and hadn't slept for over thirty six hours. He had nearly been killed during the first few hours on the ground when his stick of patratroopers had landed right on top of an enemy anti-aircraft battery near Bridlington. Fortunately, the Tommies had been more surprised than the paratroopers, and after a short but fierce fight, several of the guns had been put out of action, though five of the paras had died in the process of destroying them. The rest of the day had been chaotic, and he had spent it desperately trying to put his dispersed paratroopers together into useable formations and despatch them to where they were needed. In the event, his 1st Regiment had achieved all of its objectives, with Bridlington harbour captured prior to the main amphibious landing, and several key points and villages secured by mid-morning, including the enemy radar station on Flamborough head. It had been achieved at a terrible cost however. He reckoned that the casualty rate was probably in the region of forty percent.

Not having time to worry about that, he had placed the 1st Regiment under the temporary command of Seventh Corps who were struggling to bolster the right flank after a near disaster at Scarborough. He had then sped inland on the back of one of 8th Panzers leading tanks to see how his 2nd Regiment had fared. Here too, he had discovered large scale casualties, the regiment having dropped right into the middle of a British brigade concentration area. Despite this, his hard-fighting paras had once more prevailed, capturing the airfield swiftly, causing substantial delay to enemy units trying to reach the coast, and bottling up the remnants of the British brigade in Driffield town.

Putzier glanced eastwards and saw that the town was still burning. He cursed inwardly. They needed to get those fires put out sharpish. It was those very flames that had guided the British bombers to the airfield just two hours ago. On reflection though, it had done the British little good. Their bombing had not been especially accurate, nor concentrated. Putzier reckoned that no more than ten bombs had landed within the airfield perimeter, and of those, only one had gone anywhere near the runway. Touch wood, the Tommy raid might have been a one off. Since then, the paras on Driffield aerodrome had been left alone, and it was just before midnight when the first Ju52 had droned in to make a bumpy, but safe landing on the former RAF base.

There was heavy anti-aircraft fire coming from the coast, which suggested that the enemy was concentrating his heavy bombers against the landing beaches. That was fine by him. Nearly two thirds of 8th Panzer Division was now stacked up around Driffield in a ring of steel, ready for the breakout at dawn. The Totenkopf would be pushing through behind them in the morning, and eventually the 35th Infantry would relieve the paras from their protection task here at Driffield. Then perhaps, he could reassemble his scattered division and take it into action as a complete formation.

His thoughts were interrupted as a file of soldiers in standard Army uniform filed past him in the dark towards the assembly area over by the big hangars. He was about to curse loudly, when two figures broke away from the file of soldiers and came over to where he stood with his personal command group. The two figures came up close and Putzier noticed that one of them was a paratrooper, the other dressed in Army uniform.

"General," began the paratrooper, "I have him here, Sir."

Putzier's pulse surged with excitement and he stepped forward to get a closer look at the man in the Army helmet. The figure was in the process of removing the steel headgear and gave a white toothed smile to the tired looking parachute general.

"Richard! How very nice of you to meet me!"

Lieutenant General Hans Graf von Sponeck held out a hand to his opposite number.

With a cry of delight, Putzier stepped in close and took von Sponeck's hand. The two generals shook hands vigorously, clapping each others arms in an unusual display of camaraderie for such senior officers.

"Hans, you old dog! Thank God you got here ok. Now I really do believe in miracles."

"Oh, you should never doubt the 22nd Richard, old boy." Replied the infantry general. "You glory boys might have all the fun with your parachutes and funny gear, but the professionals are here now so you can stop worrying."

"On the contrary." Retorted Putzier. "We've had to hide everything of value before your vagabonds turned up! Including the women from the Tommy air force who we captured!"

The two men laughed together for a moment.

"So, tell me Richard; are we all set up for receiving the division. There's Auntie Ju's strung out end to end right across the German Sea, so you'd best have a well oiled scheme for bringing them in and then turning them round again. I want to get both the 16th and the 47th Regiments in tonight, if I can."

Putzier nodded eagerly.

"Yes, Hans; don't you worry yourself old boy. We've got two runways operating and plenty of guides. We just need to hope that the Tommy air force stays away."

Von Sponeck glanced at his fellow general in the dark.

"Have there been any raids yet?"

"Just one." Putzier confirmed. "But it wasn't that bad and no real damage done. They seem to be concentrating on the beaches by the look."

Von Sponeck looked eastwards for a few seconds and nodded.

"Yes." He murmured. "I just pray they haven't got many night-fighters up over the sea. If they catch the Ju52 stream on the inbound leg, then my division will get decimated."

"Doesn't seem like the Tommies have got much left at all, Hans to be honest." Putzier pulled a thoughtful face.

"I expected a much bigger response; and faster too."

The infantry general frowned.

"Give them time, Richard. I think you managed to catch them by surprise today. This is England, remember? And there's nothing more dangerous than an Englishman with his back against the wall. We need to keep the pressure on. Did 8th Panzer make it?"

Putzier nodded.

"Yes. They got here about midday. It took a few hours to wheedle the last of their infantry out of the town but the place is more or less secure now. The panzer grenadier regiment is in the town itself, and there's a full panzer regiment spread out around the outskirts. There's also a panzer battalion back at Nafferton, ready to link up with you at first light. The battalion commander is waiting in the old Tommy headquarters to speak with you. We'll go and see him now."

"Excellent." Replied von Sponeck. "We'll need to get moving at first light. The rest of 8th Panzer's second panzer regiment is going to need space, and if the Totenkopf arrived on time, then they'll be pushing forward at first light too."

Putzier laughed suddenly.

"Christ on a bike, Hans, there's going to be a tank every five metres at this rate."

"Only for a couple of hours, old friend." Von Sponeck chuckled. "As soon as the 8th Panzer Division launches in the morning, the place will empty quickly enough. Doncaster in three days, Sheffield in four, England surrenders by day five; that's the plan. You'll get dizzy just watching the armoured vehicles go by."

As they walked across the grass towards the buildings of the former RAF station, a dark shadow passed by them with a throaty rumble, following the line of hooded torches that lined the runway.

"There's another one." Commented Putzier.

"Hmm." Von Sponeck mused. "If I were you, Richard, I'd start getting some of those aircraft back in the air and on their way home, otherwise it won't be just the tanks that are clogging the place up. You'll be up to your eyeballs in Junkers too, and you don't want them sitting all over your airfield if the Tommies do carry out another raid."

Somewhere, just a couple of miles eastwards, a stick of bombs landed randomly at the far side of town.

Putzier turned to look at his friend and fellow general.

"Speak of the Devil…" He said.

JUST WEST OF HUNMANBY VILLAGE
SUNDAY 22ND SEPTEMBER 1940 – 0115 HOURS

It was dangerous for Harper and McGinn to be abroad behind the German lines at this hour, but for all the wrong reasons. Sneaking out of the secret bunker just after midnight, their hope that the Germans might be distracted by the RAF bombing raid was proved correct. As they sat at the edge of the small wood, looking east towards the coast, the two men from the Filey Bay Auxiliary Unit were treated to a display that made the previous morning's events seem paltry. The whistle of bombs across the length of the bay seemed relentless, with bright flashes regularly throwing a brief light across the darkened landscape, to be followed by thunderous roars and earth tremors.

The invaders were adding to the cacophony with their anti-aircraft fire, which was extremely heavy, and the night sky was punctuated time after time by the orange fireballs of anti-aircraft shells detonating at their fuse-ceiling. Added to that were the endless streams of tracer that snaked up to the heavens like giant, luminous worms, before disappearing into the void. The problem for Harper and McGinn was that the RAF bombing did not appear to be particularly discriminate. Whether it was their plan to carpet-bomb the entire coastal strip, or whether their targets were obscured too much by the cloud, it was difficult to tell, but regardless, British bombs were falling over a wide area, both on land and out to sea, whilst Filey town itself was on fire.

The nearest miss for the two auxiliaries occurred when a whole stick of British bombs landed in a diagonal pattern, about three hundred yards away. The stick of four bombs crept ever closer to them, until the final explosive detonated just at the other side of the field, barely a hundred yards from their position. The impact of the bomb made them cringe and they felt their breath being literally sucked out of their lungs. Fortunately, the small rut in the ground where they flattened themselves hurriedly prevented them from taking too much of the direct blast, whilst the trees overhead took the sting out of the shrapnel and mud that was thrown through the night air.

Deciding that any move toward the beach would be too risky, the two men opted to sneak northwards, keeping well to the west of the coastal area that was taking the brunt of the British bombing. Their initial intention had been to try and reach the Filey to Malton road, assuming that the Germans would be using it as a main axis of advance. Once there, they could study the pattern of movement along the road and possibly identify an isolated vehicle to attack. Perhaps they might even find a useful culvert where they could plant some of their explosives and create a serious obstacle, as well as cause carnage amongst a German convoy? That plan had very quickly been scrapped, when a more obvious and immediate target presented itself.

They were in the process of moving cautiously over Muston Wold, when the sound of more aircraft came to their ears. The two men froze instantly and stared upwards in fear, half expecting to hear the whistle of bombs directly above them. The aircraft were certainly right overhead, and lower than the other bombers they had heard thus far.

"They sound bloody low!" Harper hissed, staring up into the cloudy blackness.

McGinn studied the sky for moment, his weathered features serious.

"Cloud must be getting worse." He murmured after a while. "They're losing height to get a better fix on their targets."

As McGinn spoke, there was a thunderous report of a large calibre weapon very close by, making both of the men jump.

The two middle aged auxiliaries pressed themselves flat and stared through the gaps in the hawthorn hedge, towards to crest of the Wold.

"What the bloody hell was that?" Harper gasped.

Another loud report, and this time the two men saw the bright flash, reaching skyward, from two fields away to their west.

"Anti-aircraft guns." McGinn observed calmly. "Big ones."

There was another gun flash, followed by two more in rapid succession, the noisy bark of their reports almost blending into one.

"Looks like a whole bloody battery!" Harper commented.

McGinn looked sideways at him.

"Looks like we just found our target, then?"

Harper realised that the question was rhetorical and shivered when he saw the gleam in McGinn's eye. Yet again, he found himself wondering what the old tramp's former occupation might have been.

He listened intently as McGinn outlined the initial plan. The pair of auxiliaries then spent several minutes making their final preparations, with McGinn expertly preparing the two small satchel charges, despite the darkness. Harper marvelled at the man's expertise and realised that he must have been trained for this kind of thing in secret. By whom, however, he had no idea. Harper was armed with his captured German automatic pistol and their section's Thompson sub machine-gun, along with a pouch full of hand grenades, whilst McGinn carried his revolver, the two satchels full of explosives, and a thin bladed but lethal looking dagger.

Once ready, the two British resistance fighters began to move cautiously towards the enemy gun position. Locating it was easy enough, as the German battery was now firing round after round at the rapid rate. A steady hail of shrapnel was pattering down around the surrounding fields as small fragments of exploding ordnance fell uselessly back to earth. Meanwhile, the latest wave of British bombers had begun to release its deadly cargo and both Harper and McGinn saw that the bombs were once again landing over a wide area, from Hunmanby, through Muston and towards Filey. Creeping cautiously along the hedgerow, they were now only one field away from the nearest enemy gun. Suddenly, even above the din of gunfire and bombing, a noise came to their ears that made them flatten themselves against the cold earth in alarm.

At first, it was hard to place the sound. Something like a cow in distress, merged with the noise of a protesting engine, thought Harper absurdly. The noise seemed to be all around them, and both Harper and McGinn turned their eyes skyward and back towards the east in an attempt to source the sudden burst of sound. They spotted it immediately. The British bomber came dipping out of the cloud in a wide flaming arc, its large, ungainly shape silhouetted perfectly against the backdrop of flames that had taken hold of its entire port wing and engine.

As the huge, fiery beast wheeled downwards and back on itself, towards the village of Hunmanby, the unholy moan of the stricken aircraft's surviving engine turned into a high pitched shriek. With a huge explosion, the bomber smashed into the field on the very outskirts of the village, missing the nearest houses by just a matter of yards. From above them on the wold, Harper and McGinn heard the cheers and shouts of delight, as the German gunners whooped and clapped, celebrating their kill. The fire created by the crash gave off an intense light and the two men pushed themselves even farther into the hedgerow in order to avoid being caught in the open whilst the surrounding area was illuminated.

They lay there, watching the remains of the plane burn, and listening to the excited chatter of the gun crews. It must have taken nearly ten minutes for the light to drop to the extent where it was safe to start moving again. By this time, the German voices had returned to more business-like conversation, the need for their guns still urgent, and the anti-aircraft bombardment continued unabated. Tentatively, Harper and McGinn moved along the hedgerow once more, until they came at last to the edge of the field where the nearest of the guns was located. Staring through the undergrowth, they immediately saw the big guns positioned at well spaced intervals across the level field, almost right on top of the wold. They reckoned that probably three of the guns were in this field with more in the field beyond, and began working out how to make their attack against such a well manned position.

"They don't look like they're expecting anything from the ground." McGinn observed. "I reckon we might stand a better chance if we just walked right up behind them from that side of the field, nice and casual. In the dark, they'll be more suspicious of a shadowy figure dashing about in a secretive manner, rather than someone just ambling through their position. Besides, most of them will be looking upwards."

Harper looked at his friend worriedly.

"Are you sure about that, Tommy?" He asked doubtfully.

McGinn smiled suddenly, surprising Harper.

"Ninety percent sure. Let's get round their rear and see, shall we?"

With that, he pushed past Harper and began following the boundary hedge towards the rear of the German position. Taking a deep breath, Harper followed him.

They continued to move cautiously at a crouch, until they reached the far corner of the field, so that they were just fifty yards or so from the nearest gun. From that position, they could see a number of vehicles parked up in another field, behind the gun line. In the area of the vehicles there was little sign of activity, although they did spot two dark figures carrying what appeared to be shells towards the gun line.

"We could do for their vehicles as well." Harper suggested, realising that the half-tracks were a bit of a sitting duck.

McGinn nodded, thoughtfully.

"Possibly." He agreed. "But guns first; they're the most important thing…"

He stopped abruptly and raised a finger to his lips, casting a warning look at Harper. A moment later, Harper heard the noise too.

Somebody was coming towards them.

The old soldier hefted his Tommy Gun and stared intently through the hedge and into the darkness, ready for the unidentified person whose footsteps were very close now. The sound of plodding feet on soil came distinctly to their ears and McGinn held up a warning hand to Harper, telling him not to fire. He pointed left. There was a small gap in the hedge at this corner of the field; not massive, but enough for a small tractor to pass through, and the two auxiliaries watched the opening expectantly. A moment later, the figure appeared. Tall, with a rifle slung over one shoulder, and his German pattern helmet clearly visible, the enemy sentry paused in the opening and gawped upwards towards where the balls of anti-aircraft fire continued to flash.

McGinn moved so quickly that Harper was taken completely by surprise. As the nearest anti-aircraft gun fired again, the old tramp launched himself upwards and into the hapless German, sending him sprawling backwards behind the hedge at the other side of the opening, landing right on top of him. Harper watched in shock as McGinn straddled the enemy soldier's chest and clamped a big hand over the winded German's mouth. He saw McGinn's arm come back slightly, and the glint of the thin, deadly blade. The next instant, McGinn's arm punched forward. The German's body went rigid and he emitted a low, strangled, choking sound. Seconds later, the German's limbs simply flopped idly and the choking noise stopped. Slowly, McGinn climbed to his feet. He turned away from the dead German and wiped his knife across his trouser leg. He stared at Harper for a moment, before jerking his head towards the gun-line.

"Come on, George." He murmured.

Harper stepped off hurriedly, following his companion, who had simply walked through the opening in the hedgerow and into the field where the enemy vehicles were situated. Catching up with McGinn, he fell in alongside him, glancing nervously towards the vehicles and around the field.

"We go for the first gun." The old tramp whispered harshly, and Harper noted that the man's accent had taken on that strange twang again, almost as if he were from a more well-bred background than one would imagine. "If we bump into anyone when we go past these vehicles, we'll have to kill them and go straight into the attack. The plan is quite simple. We walk up behind them. As soon as we are close enough, you shoot the entire crew and I place the charge. I've reduced the safety fuse so we'll have about a minute at the most to get away from the gun before it goes up. We'll run straight back across the field, away from this vehicle park area, then hop it as quickly as we can. We don't want to get cut off."

Harper, stunned by the speed at which events were suddenly developing, could only nod and murmur his understanding.

"Okay, Tommy." He said.

They were level with the nearest enemy vehicle and paused for just a moment to survey the area. There was nobody hanging around near the half-track that they could see, and the guns were still firing away to their right.

"Okay, George, let's do it." McGinn said, no longer trying to keep his voice down.

There was a gap in the hedgerow here, obviously recently cut by the Germans to allow easy passage to the gun-line. They went through it and began striding purposefully towards the German gun. As they tramped over the stubble, Harper's heart began to thump in his chest like a bass drum.

McGinn appeared utterly calm as he unslung one of his satchels. The German crew were serving their weapon in an urgent manner. To one side of the gun, somebody of rank was ordering adjustments to the lay of the weapon, and the rest of the crew were busy responding, whilst also feeding a new shell into the chamber at the same time. Off to their left, the neighbouring gun fired, causing Harper to flinch involuntarily. They were less than twenty yards away now and nobody had yet taken any notice of them. At the rear of the gun, two members of the crew were breaking open a long wooden crate. McGinn stopped five yards short of the two men by the crate and knelt down. He began fiddling with his satchel, and several moments later, just as the two Germans prized open the lid of the ammunition crate, there was a small spark in front of McGinn, which was followed by a whole series of sparks and a hissing noise. One of the Germans looked up towards Harper and McGinn as he pulled a long 88mm shell out of its container.

"Kill them, George." McGinn said calmly.

Harper squeezed the trigger of the Tommy Gun and held it tight into his body as the .45 inch bullets hammered out of the barrel and cut through the nearest two Germans, sending them careering backwards. Their arms and legs flailed wildly as the powerful slugs ripped through them, and several other members of the crew turned round in alarm. Harper raised the barrel and squeezed the trigger again. This time his burst was longer, and he traversed the weapon from left to right, cutting down the densely packed crew members at the rear of the gun. He saw the gun-layer topple sideways from his seat, but the gun's commander, who had been standing off to one side, suddenly began to run. There was a bark of a gun shot from Harper's right side and he saw the German commander stumble forwards, then collapse. Glancing down, he saw McGinn's arm was extended and holding a smouldering revolver.

"Start firing at the next crew." McGinn snapped.

Immediately, Harper swung around and faced left. Through the dark, he could hear the shouts of alarm from the next gun. Beyond it, another gun fired its shell skywards. He raised the butt of the Thompson into his shoulder now and aimed as best he could towards the dark bulk of the next enemy gun. He saw the dark figures clustered around it, and saw them start to move with urgency. He squeezed the trigger again, firing a short burst, and was rewarded with the sound of bullets whining off metal. McGinn was crouching underneath the trail of the German gun now, the hissing sparks of the fuse obvious in the dark. Harper fired again, then again. The Germans were shouting angrily now; urgently. A shot whizzed through the dark and cracked overhead, far too high to be of danger.

"Run!" McGinn shouted.

They ran. They ran as if the devil himself were after them. More shots and panic stricken shouting followed them through the darkness, although, and more rewardingly, the sound of anti-aircraft fire from the gun-line had ceased.

"How long have we got left, Tommy?" Harper gasped as they neared the hedgerow.

"Not long, old chum." McGinn replied, breathing heavily. "What are you like at the high jump?"

"Crap!" Harper shouted as he hurled himself over the thick hedgerow, from where they had first observed their target.

McGinn was with him, tumbling headfirst over the hedge and falling with an unceremonious thud onto the ground beyond.

"Stay down!" McGinn prompted.

His words were drowned out by the noise of the explosion. With a bright flash and a sickening crump, the satchel charge exploded where McGinn had jammed it, underneath the elevation gear of the German gun. Amongst the explosive din, there was an audible rending of metal.

"Christ almighty!" Harper swore.

"I reckon that makes us one-all." McGinn chirped.

"Fucking too right, it does!" His companion agreed.

"Now let's get out of here." McGinn suggested, climbing onto all fours. "Before a bunch of angry Jerries start claiming a penalty."

HEADQUARTERS NORTHERN COMMAND – YORK
SUNDAY 22ND SEPTEMBER 1940 – 0130 HOURS

"Alright then," Adam ran a hand over his tired face, pinching the bridge of his nose for a moment, "let's go through it, north to south and anti-clockwise."

He stared at the map which had been hung next to the bird table. Although the bird table remained the chief battle map, Adam wanted to go through his own dispositions in order to achieve clarity, so a brand new map with a reduced set of markings had been produced. He sat ready for the brief, his principal staff flanking him, whilst his Brigadier General Staff and the operations officer were both poised by the map itself. Thus prompted, the BGS began the commander's back-brief.

"In the north, Sir, 59 Div' has fully deployed and succeeded in holding Scarborough, sealing off the attempted breakout through Seamer. They have established a defensive line along the foot of the North Yorkshire Moors extending west to Pickering. Their frontage is strong, but there is little depth at the moment. By first light however, every Home Guard unit between 59 Div' and Guisborough will have been brought forward to thicken up the northern block. As instructed, the whole of the Derwent Valley is covered by interlocking machine-guns and anti-tank guns, and fully observed by artillery observation posts. The Catterick Garrison has occupied Malton and Norton and linked up with the 59 Div' flank at Pickering. The bridge at Malton is prepared for demolition, and once again, every Home Guard unit between Malton and Easingwold has been brought forward to give depth to the line.

Malton is being fortified, so even in the event of a breakthrough, it will become a self-sufficient defensive box. The Catterick Garrison has been placed under command of 59 Div'."

Adam looked at the dispositions indicated and nodded thoughtfully.

"How many guns can 59 Div' muster?"

The BGS consulted his notes before replying.

"They've got an under strength field regiment, Sir; two batteries of 18 Pounders, totalling 12 guns, and a battery of 25 Pounders which have been in action all day at Scarborough and running low on ammunition. That battery has five guns left in action."

The GOC Northern Command nodded in silence and thought for a moment.

"The Catterick Garrison came with no artillery, correct?"

"Correct, Sir." The BGS acknowledged.

Adam shifted in his seat for a moment and stroked his moustache in deliberation.

"Get onto the Middlesbrough and Teesside Garrison. I want every gun they've got that isn't concreted in, along with its crew, moved towards Pickering at best possible speed. 59 Div' will take them all aboard and deploy them as necessary to boost their artillery capacity. I want every square inch of the Derwent Valley covered by fire. It's one thing being able to see them coming, but we can't do anything about it if there aren't enough guns. In addition to that, I want the medium artillery regiment from Corps reserve moved to the area between Malton and Pickering to give direct support to the Malton box and the Catterick Garrison."

The operations officer began scribbling the orders down on his pad.

"Logistics?"

"Here, Sir."

"I want 25 Pounder ammunition despatched to 59 Div' immediately. Can we get it there before morning?"

"There's a large convoy of ammunition due to leave for 59 Div' echelon at Pickering around 0400 hours, Sir. I'll make sure it's on there."

Adam nodded, satisfied, and looked back at the BGS.

"Go on."

The officer's pointer traced a line from Malton down the River Derwent until it reached Stamford Bridge.

"This section between Malton and Stamford Bridge has been filled by three of the Corps machine-gun battalions, supported by Home Guard Units. We're bringing forward even more Home Guard to thicken the line, and the 24th Army Tank Brigade has now arrived in the area of Sand Hutton."

"Any anti-tank guns?" Adam demanded, as the BGS paused.

"Only a handful of Boys Rifles, Sir; nothing more."

Adam winced.

"This lot have been added onto 2 Div's strength haven't they?"

"That's right, Sir, and everything that 2 Div' has left is already deployed covering their main frontage, east of York."

Again, Adam paused for thought.

"Alright. Nothing we can do about that, other than make sure 2 Div' has spread its anti-tank guns out as much as possible. Stamford Bridge itself needs some coverage at least. Check on that, and while you're at it, get onto GHQ. We need more anti-tank guns. Every 2 Pounder they can plunder from every other command; we need them here, and we need them fast. Arrange an RV for all these reinforcements, and let's start making a priority list for who gets what first."

"Yes, Sir." Murmured the operations officer, writing speedily.

"The rest of 2 Div' then? What about them?"

The BGS took a deep breath.

"Well, Sir, as you know, we've essentially written off the Driffield brigade. What's left of them, mainly their echelon and a few stragglers, are concentrating at Holme on Spalding Moor, which we are turning into a defensive box. There are also a few stragglers reported as collecting at Fridaythorpe; another defensive box, which is currently being established by the Corps recce regiment."

Adam nodded, but said nothing. The BGS continued.

"The brigade at Beverley is in the process of falling back on Hull. The runway at RAF Leconfield was cratered just before midnight, and the brigade will begin to fall back sequentially, whilst conducting a delay operation. Once in Hull, the brigade will flick to command of 1 Div'. Meanwhile, as already mentioned, the remainder of 2 Div', including their other infantry brigade, is forming a defensive position along the Derwent from Stamford Bridge to Elvington, where the line then curves westwards to Wheldrake, through Deighton, to Naburn, where it meets the Ouse and the GHQ Line."

Adam smiled thinly.

"We are going to be in the thick of it here then, aren't we chaps?"

There was muted chuckling amongst the staff.

"As far as York is concerned, the population are now being evacuated to the west of the city, utilising church halls and the like. The City Home Guard is fully mobilised and placed under command of 2 Div'. All bridges have been prepared for demolition and now have demolition-guards in place. The engineers have begun the fortification plan as directed by you, Sir."

The GOC stared at the map for a moment, picturing the defensive measures that he had stipulated, then flicked his glance back to the BGS.

"Alright; I'm happy enough with all that. Now, what about our main worry; the Selby Gap?"

Once more, BGS dragged his pointer down the map, following the line of the River Ouse.

"44 Div' began arriving at 1800 hours. They've started to fortify Goole and Selby and the stretch in between. We've brought the South Yorkshire units of the Home Guard forward, from as far as Doncaster, in order to ensure we haven't missed a single gap along this complicated stretch. We've also ordered the 44th to cover the stretch from Selby, northwards, until they come to the junction of the Wharfe and the Ouse. They think it's a tall order, but will do their best for now. We've given them some of our Corps support units to assist, and GHQ has just confirmed that we're getting a Polish Battalion and the 3rd Machine Gun Brigade to assist us with securing the Ouse between York and Goole."

"Good." Adam sat up slightly. "That's very good indeed. What about the bridges? This whole stretch is littered with crossing points."

The BGS nodded and pointed to a series of small symbols on the map, each of them sitting at intervals along the blue line of the River Ouse.

"All bridges have been prepared for demolition and garrisoned, Sir. We've indented for additional mines from GHQ and they have promised that they will be with us just as soon as they can get them here. Most rail stock is currently being used to bring in the reserves."

Adam grunted acknowledgement.

"And then finally, Sir." The BGS went on. "1 Div' is now in place along the Humber, all the way to Cleethorpes. Also, the Lincolnshire Home Guard has been brought forward to the coast to provide depth to the Humber line. We've asked GHQ for another division to help cover this stretch, but we haven't heard who we'll get as of yet."

The GOC stood up and moved closer to the map, studying the detail.

"And Commander 1 Div' is happy that he is taking on Hull and the Beverley brigade from 2 Div'?"

"Absolutely, Sir." The BGS confirmed. "He's acknowledged the message and will assume command of them from 0600 hours."

Adam accepted the reassurance in silence and ran his eyes over the map searchingly. After long moments of study, he stepped away and took his seat once more.

"And how are we doing with the GHQ reserve?"

"So far, so good, Sir. I believe that lead elements of 1st Armoured have begun to arrive at Wetherby. The concentration area has been marked for them and the engineers have thrown two bridges across the Ouse north of York to allow for the passage of lines if required. In addition to that, the lead elements of 2nd Armoured have begun to arrive near their concentration area just south of Goole."

Adam's eyes lit up.

"Have they now? Well that's good. That's very good."

He sat back in his chair and thought for a while. After some deliberation, he spoke to the audience at large.

"Gentlemen, this morning we were caught on the hop, without a doubt. Once more, the enemy has proved to be resourceful and imaginative. However, despite his initial success in getting a substantial force ashore, we still have everything to play for. The 59th has done a sterling job at Scarborough, and even though it's under intense pressure, I feel that we have managed to put a very hard shoulder against the German door which he is unlikely to budge in the near future. We are not strong enough in that area to counter-attack yet, but we can hold him, and must continue to do so."

Adam stood suddenly and walked back over to the map. Turning to face the bulk of the staff, he jabbed a finger into the map at Driffield.

"*This* is the German centre of gravity. This is their pivot point. Which way they go next, nobody knows."

He looked around his staff, their faces serious and tired, yet expectant. They respected and trusted him. He was a straight laced, old fashioned general; but a fair one who paid attention to detail, and his staff had every confidence in his ability.

"So we must do everything to throw him off balance here. We must try to establish what he intends next whilst at the same time delaying him as much as possible, in order for the GHQ reserve to fully deploy and launch a coordinated counter-attack."

He smiled suddenly.

"So, to that end, we're going to lead Jerry a merry dance."

He jabbed his finger into the map again.

"These boxes we have mentioned; I want them reinforced tonight. Machine-guns, anti-tank guns, mines, obstacles, the whole nine yards. I want them ready to fight by first light, and let's keep pumping in resources until the last safe moment. I have permission to use one of the brigades from 2nd Armoured Division for delaying operations, as long as I don't get them decisively engaged..."

He looked at his BGS meaningfully.

"So, let's get the message to them. I want an armoured screen west of Driffield by day-break. Their job is to get a fix on exactly where the enemy is, what his strength is, and where he's going. They are to withdraw in front of an enemy push, but do their best to impose delay. Whilst all of this is going on, I want the boxes fortified and supplied. By the time 2nd Armoured withdraw back over the Ouse, I want to leave the enemy with a few prickly problems at his side of the river."

Some of Adam's staff were smiling now, absorbing the fighting spirit of their GOC. He poked his finger from point to point on the map.

"Fridaythorpe, Holme-on-Spalding Moor, Allerthorpe Common, Skipwith Common, Stamford Bridge. Let's make all these places into impregnable little fortresses that will force the enemy to make detours, or make them stop and deal with them."

He glanced at his BGS.

"Holme-on-Spalding Moor will be a vital bit of ground, so make sure we've got somebody reliable there. And all the while we strengthen this little net, into which the enemy has kindly placed himself."

Adam took a deep breath and gave a confident smile.

"It's been a rough day, gentlemen. Our plan, I think, remains good. Please see to the detail immediately and make sure we have no loose ends. I don't want ammunition sitting idle; get it to where it's needed. I don't want the GHQ reserve blundering around hopelessly when they arrive because there's nobody to point them in the right direction. The devil is in the detail, so make sure you dot every 'i' and cross every 't'."

Adam paced towards the staff, looking around the faces.

"Once you've done all that needs to be done, gentlemen, get some sleep. Yesterday was a busy day; today will be even busier."

He fixed his gaze on the Royal Air Force wing commander who was standing amongst the group.

"Michael? You'd best wait behind for a moment, please? We need to discuss what your boys can do for us come first light."

"Right-o, Sir."

Adam clapped his hands together suddenly.

"Alright gentlemen; let's back to the war."

S +1
DAYBREAK

U-47, 20 MILES SOUTH-EAST OF THE ORKNEYS
SUNDAY 22ND SEPTEMBER 1940 – 0540 HOURS

It was light enough to see a good distance, perhaps even call it 'dawn', but sunrise was still almost an hour away. Prien raised his binoculars and gazed towards the distant sky-line where the Orkneys lay. Nothing. A feint dark line showed where the nearest of the islands sat on the horizon, but other than that, nothing. No smoke, no flashes, no Royal Navy. They had been sitting on the doorstep of the great beast for over twenty four hours, ready to throw themselves into the fray in order to cripple the great British battle fleet before it could get clear of its harbour, but for reasons that were beyond Prien's comprehension, the Royal Navy had refused to come out.

They had been on the surface all night, expecting to see the enemy breaking out under cover of darkness, but the wait had proved fruitless. Not so much as a gunboat or armed trawler had emerged from Scapa Flow. And then there had been the signal from Fleet HQ. The high command wished to know if any British ships had been spotted leaving the anchorage, specifically, an aircraft carrier, two cruisers and a handful of destroyers. Prien's reply had been instant and quite clear. No. But the signal had come back again, stating that the ships mentioned had 'disappeared' from Scapa Flow within the last thirty six hours. The signal hinted that the ships might have left in the small window of time between the last reconnaissance flight and the insertion of the U-Boat screen. Even so, those ships would have had to sail right through the approaching U-Boats if they'd come south.

A flurry of signals had been sent between Prien and Fleet HQ, some of them heated, but eventually, the message had come back, flagged with Donitz's own name; release a third of the force to sweep south into the German Sea, and another third to cover the narrow gap between mainland Scotland and the Orkneys. HQ believed that the British carrier force had been despatched westwards to assist with convoy duty and that they would be subsequently recalled. Thus it was important to ambush the force as it returned. The logic was sound, Prien supposed, knowing how badly the British convoys had suffered over recent months.

Even so, he was uncomfortable with the fact that he now had just six boats to lock down the three main exits from Scapa Flow. Inside that vast anchorage, a place he had been just a year before when he achieved both fame and notoriety for sinking HMS Royal Oak, the great array of British capital ships sat waiting for their moment. Battleships, heavy cruisers, medium and light cruisers, destroyers, frigates and gunboats; the great naval base contained more ships than the entire German surface fleet could muster, and it was his task to keep that mighty force where it was, or sink it as it left.

And therein lay the frustration for Prien. The invasion was a day old. Twenty four hours had passed since the German army had spilled ashore onto the soil of England. Surely, even allowing for caution, the Royal Navy should have reacted by now? Surely, their fat, drunken Prime Minister, who talked a good fight on the radio, would be demanding that the Royal Navy was deployed to meet the threat? But nothing. Prien lowered the binoculars and took a drag on his cigar. There must be something he was missing.

His thoughts were interrupted by the shout of the sentry at the other side of the conning tower.

"Aircraft!"

"Where?" Prien swung round, suddenly alert.

"Not sure, Sir." The man replied, frowning into his own pair of binoculars. "I can hear him; I'm sure of it. Somewhere off to starboard."

Prien scanned the clouded sky with the naked eye but saw nothing. A small gust of sea breeze whispered past him and he caught the sound of an engine.

"I can hear him!" Prien acknowledged, stepping alongside the man.

"Prepare to dive." He snapped the order to another sailor, who ducked his head inside the hatch and relayed the message.

He was running his eyes across the flat grey sheet of the sky, desperately trying to locate the plane. It could be one of their own, perhaps? HQ had said that more reconnaissance flights over Scapa Flow had been scheduled to try and find out what the British were playing at.

"There!" The sentry suddenly pointed to the north-east, his arm almost level with the sea.

"Where?" Demanded Prien again.

"There, Captain; coming in low."

Prien stood behind the man's shoulders and followed the direction of his arm. Immediately, he spotted the black dot coming straight for them, still some miles out. Raising his binoculars, he tried to get a fix on the aircraft.

"He's bloody low isn't he?"

Prien swung the binoculars from side to side, then steadied himself as he found the target.

"Bollocks!" He cursed.

The plane was broad and fat, with high mounted wings and floats, quite unlike any German aircraft that he knew of, but exactly like the British aircraft that he feared so much.

"Everyone below! Prepare to dive! Prepare to dive! Enemy aircraft approaching!"

Prien was hollering the instructions as he followed the sentries through the hatch. As he dropped inside the confines of the submarine, he could hear the noise from the engines of the British plane as it closed on them. He saw the First Lieutenant looking at him for further instructions, whilst the crew were already busy preparing the boat for diving.

"Tommy plane." Prien snapped in explanation to the young officer. "Take her down."

The lieutenant needed no further urging and began rattling off instructions, as Prien strode to his usual position by the periscope.

"Twenty fathoms, Heini; straight away, then take us north-east for five miles before we come back up to periscope depth."

The lieutenant nodded and began relaying the instructions. As he did so, a whole series of loud metallic clangs sounded on the hull of the boat as machine-gun bullets struck her side. Even as the hatch was being secured, they all heard the roar as the big Tommy plane passed over them. There was a loud 'thunk' outside the boat, which made Prien stop and look upwards at the roof of the submarine.

"That was a bomb." He said in a clipped voice. "Get us under, and make it fast."

There was little else he could do now, other than watch the crew move with their characteristic speed to submerge the vessel. Never-the-less, he chivvied them up.

"Come on; faster! That plane will be turning for another pass."

He felt the familiar sensation as the submarine slid beneath the waves and he gave a small sigh of relief. It wasn't over yet though. They needed to get deep and move position. His location would be transmitted immediately by the aircraft, and there was no doubt that the pilot would be summoning other aircraft or ships to the area. Did this mean that the British were finally coming out?

They were going deeper now, and the sound of the aircraft was nothing more than an uncomfortable memory, although they did hear one small sound, which they assumed was another bomb being dropped. Prien paced the deck impatiently, waiting for the First Lieutenant to indicate that they had made sufficient distance and that it was time to bring the boat back up to periscope depth.

"Once we've made the distance, bring us back onto a north-westerly bearing before we go up again."

"Yes, Captain." The lieutenant acknowledged as he studied the gauges at one side of the compartment.

Prien was sweating. This was the moment they had been waiting for. He was sure of it. A shame he hadn't had the chance to warn off the other boats in the flotilla. Would the British come out of all three exits at once, or just come out of the main exit in a mass formation? His mind began to race with the possibilities. If it was the latter, he would have to summon more boats to reinforce him, and get a message off to Donitz too. That would mean surfacing again, albeit briefly. He would have to take the risk. He couldn't handle the entire British fleet with just his own and one other submarine.

"Sir?" His signals officer had appeared by his side, a worried look on his face.

Prien looked at him, a frown creasing his brow.

"What's wrong?"

The signals officer cleared his throat and handed a scrap of paper to Prien.

"This message had just come in when the alarm sounded, Sir. We've just decoded it."

Prien ran his eye over the message. It was from U-33. The message was not good.

Priority/U-33 under attack by torpedo armed aircraft/Stop/Boat has received one hit and sinking/Stop/Abandoning ship/Stop/Message ends

Prien looked up.

"U-33?" He wondered aloud.

"She's covering the western exit isn't she, Sir?" The First Lieutenant suggested, glancing over his shoulder at Prien.

"Yes." Prien confirmed. "She's been hit by planes carrying torpedoes."

Everybody in the cabin stopped and looked at him.

"Torpedoes?" The First Lieutenant frowned. "You don't attack submarines with torpedoes! What were they doing? The crew must have been half asleep!"

"Which Tommy planes carry torpedoes?"

The officers in the room exchanged troubled looks.

"I think they have some bi-planes that carry torpedoes." The signals officer suggested. "The planes they normally use on…"

"Aircraft carriers." Prien finished the sentence for him.

The silence in the control room was absolute. After a moment, Prien spoke.

"Take us up to periscope depth and make sure we've turned north-westerly again."

The crew jumped to it, and within minutes, the First Lieutenant gave the nod that they were in a position to use the vessel's viewing device. Prien hauled the periscope upwards and folded down the hand-grips. Jamming his eyes against the goggles, he quickly got his focus and bearings. He scanned the sea left and right. The sky was brightening slightly, but there was nothing of note as he stared towards the main exit from Scapa Flow. For long minutes he stared towards the distant horizon and began to feel a nag of doubt. With a snort, he swung the periscope around a full ninety degrees to scan the ocean in a north-easterly direction. He froze instantly, catching his breath.

"My God!" He whispered.

"Captain?" The First Lieutenant murmured.

Prien stepped back and waved a hand toward the periscope goggles.

"Take a look, Heini. Tell me what you think."

The First Lieutenant followed the instructions and bent his neck to gaze through the apparatus. He too caught his breath. There was no mistaking the black clouds of smoke that were spaced out at regular intervals along the horizon to the north-east.

"Ships. They're strung out in a line; as if they're…"

The lieutenant's voice trailed off.

"Sweeping?" Prien suggested.

The lieutenant glanced sideways at his captain and nodded.

Prien maintained a calm expression.

"What do you see beyond them?" He asked.

The lieutenant put his eyes back to the goggles.

"Another smudge of smoke…" He ventured after a while. "…a bigger one. Hard to tell what it is, but it must be something big. Something like…"

"A carrier." Prien supplied the logic again.

The First Lieutenant stood straight, a worried look on his face.

"But how did they get out of Scapa Flow without us spotting them? And why are they still here?"

Prien rubbed a hand across his stubbled face and thought for a moment.

"They've been somewhere." He said at length. "Somewhere that we've missed. And now they're back, sweeping a path clear, around the islands. That means that the British Home Fleet will be coming out behind them, whilst most of our submarines are sitting at the other side of Orkney, gawping westwards and in completely the wrong place to react! And the rest have been sent on a wild goose chase in the German Sea!"

He stalked around the control room for a few moments, the crew watching him closely.

"What do you want to do, Captain?" The First Lieutenant asked. "Attack them head on? We'll be able to get a couple of torpedoes off well before we're in range of their direction finding equipment."

Prien shook his head.

"No. We'll be lucky to get a hit, and then we'll have to run for it; and we can't outrun them underwater."

He turned away for a moment in order to hide his flustered expression.

"Fucking hell!" He whispered to himself. "The whole damned plan is falling to pieces!"

"Sorry, Sir?" The First Lieutenant spoke up. "I missed that."

Prien swung round.

"South-east. Change direction and go full out. We need to get a message back to Fleet HQ and we can only do that on the surface. In addition, I don't want to be caught in that drag-net. If we try to take the Tommies on frontally they'll just roll over us and eventually one of them will fix our position. Then we'll be fucked!"

He looked around the control room.

"Turn us around and let's get out of here. Head for deeper water and get us clear of the Orkneys. Otherwise, there'll be no schnapps and medals after this one."

On the surface of the North Sea, rounding the western edge of the Orkney Islands, the aircraft carrier, HMS Furious, preceded by her escorts and cruisers, was sweeping the coastal waters clear of submarines. The force was using the ancient but reliable Swordfish aircraft as an advance guard, along with the Sunderland flying boats from the shore based squadron on Orkney itself. The success against the enemy submarine had been unbelievably lucky. To catch a submarine so off-guard, whilst on the surface, was a pilot's dream come true, and to then hit such a small vessel with a torpedo of all things, made the whole episode worthy of legend.

In actual fact, an even greater legend was being created in the wake of the successful attack by the Swordfish, for behind the inexorable progress of the mother ship and her escorts, the frigates and destroyers of the Royal Navy were emerging from Scapa Flow to join the sweep, which would take them right round to the southern tip of the islands, from where the Home Fleet's battle squadrons were poised to break out into the open sea. Operation

Sealion was a day old. German troops were fighting on the soil of Britain. And the Royal Navy was coming out to fight.

NORTH DALTON – 5 MILES SOUTH-WEST OF DRIFFIELD SUNDAY 22ND SEPTEMBER 1940 – 0550 HOURS

"Bloody hell, Sergeant! We nearly brassed you up! Thought you were a Jerry patrol when we saw the blue uniforms. Just as well we spotted you at the last moment in your khaki gear." The young officer gazed down at Jackson from the turret of his Vickers VIB light tank with a look of relief.

Jackson pulled his feet in, automatically reverting to parade ground precision, and gave a butt salute to the officer with his captured German machine-gun.

"Sorry about that, Sir. We picked up a bunch of stragglers from RAF Driffield who managed to escape when the Jerries landed. I don't suppose it helps much either with us carrying all these Jerry weapons?"

The officer suddenly noticed the MG34 in the sergeant's hands and raised an eyebrow.

"Anyway, Sir, if it's Jerries you're looking for, you haven't got far to look. I'd watch yourself as you go forward, because there's a battery of enemy anti-tank guns in a wood line, just north of the aerodrome. They've got quite a good enfilade shoot down the western edge of the runway. And behind that, they've got a fortified position with infantry in the village of Little Driffield. I expect they're well dug-in on the airfield itself too. Also…" Jackson continued, "they've got a shit-load of tanks assembled at the far side of town. Looks like they've got a whole division queuing up there."

The officer's eyebrows rose even higher.

"Indeed? You seem to have conducted a very thorough reconnaissance? How on earth did you manage to get through that little lot."

Jackson quickly explained the complicated tale of the previous day's action. As he spoke, the officer's jaw dropped progressively lower, and the other members of the tank crew stuck their heads out of the hatches to listen. As the Coldstream sergeant was talking, the vehicle commander of another tank came running across to eavesdrop. Jackson noted absently that the man was a corporal.

After Jackson had finished speaking, there was a long silence as the tank crew absorbed the enormity of the previous day's events and the sergeant's part in them. The officer's face was serious now, the flippant, slightly jolly attitude gone completely.

"Crikey," Murmured the lieutenant, thoughtfully, "you have been through the mill, haven't you?"

He fidgeted in the turret slightly.

"Anyway, no need to worry about us running into those anti-tank guns; we're not going any further forward."

Jackson frowned.

"Why not, Sir? Aren't you putting in a counter attack?"

The lieutenant gave a grim smile.

"Not with just two squadrons of light tanks, we're not. We're just the screen force; the lead elements of the 2nd Armoured Division. We've just driven two hundred miles to get here and refuelled twice on the way. We only got here about an hour ago. The rest of the Division is concentrating west of the Ouse, behind Selby. We've been told to conduct a forward recce and give the 2nd Infantry Division chance to fall back to their defended localities."

Jackson was still frowning.

"So what's the plan then, Sir."

The officer laughed suddenly.

"Wish I knew, Sergeant, I really do. I gather that the general idea is to slow the Jerries down a bit whilst GHQ fortifies a line along the Ouse and gathers the general reserve on the western bank. Once we've got enough people assembled, then we'll be launching our counter-attack; but it won't be today. Most of the reserve is in the Midlands or the Home Counties. Moving that many people takes time, so we've just got to keep the Jerries busy for as long as we can."

Understanding dawned on Jackson's face.

"Right; where do you want us then, Sir?"

"Not here." The officer replied curtly. "We're going to be fighting a mobile action, and I'm afraid that you and your little band will just get lost in the chaos. We've been ordered to clear out all Home Guard units and all stragglers we find, and send them back down the road to Holme-on-Spalding Moor. There's a concentration area there where the 2nd Infantry Division is trying to sort out the muddle. If you go to the back of this village by the pub, as quick as you can, you might just catch the last transport. There's a staff sergeant back there, clearing the village of everything that might be useful for defending the box."

"The box?" Jackson frowned again, not understanding.

"Yes. Holme is going to be turned into a defensive box with the intention of holding out for a full week. The idea is to create these little boxes all over the eastern side of the Ouse which will act as thorns in the German side. We've been told that everyone we sweep up has to report to the nearest box."

Jackson nodded slowly, his mind trying to picture the map of Yorkshire and fit all the information together like a jigsaw puzzle. It sort of made sense to him. He turned round to gaze at his mixed group of soldiers, civilians and airmen and wondered how many of them would actually be any use in a fight. As he was turning the information over in his mind, the officer in the turret suddenly flinched, then put a hand over the ear-pieces of his headphones. He was listening intently to something being passed over the radio set. As Jackson watched the young man's face for clues, there was a distant rumble of gunfire somewhere behind him, towards the southern side of Driffield town. Mortars by the sound of it; possibly guns. There was a ripple of alarm amongst his disparate group.

"Calm down." He warned them. "It's miles away yet."

He looked back to the officer.

"That was the OC. Jerry armour's been spotted moving around the southern edge of Driffield on the Beverley road."

Jackson gave a low growl.

"Sounds like they're laying some kind of barrage too?" He said.

The young officer nodded his agreement.

"Well, Sergeant, you'd best get moving. I suspect it's probably going to hot up around here pretty soon. Remember, no matter what happens, head for Holme-on-Spalding Moor. Don't be tempted to wander off. The whole countryside is being stripped bare and pulled into the boxes. You won't be safe anywhere else."

"No dramas, Sir." Jackson acknowledged the advice. "We'll be off then. Best of luck to you. Oh, and remember, Sir; the Jerries move bloody fast and fight hard. Don't let the bastards get you fixed in one place. Once they've pinned you down, you're stuck."

The officer smiled.

"Thank you." He replied in a quiet voice. "And the best of luck to you, too."

Jackson braced his body up again, stiffening into the position of attention.

"May I have your permission to carry on, Sir, please?"

The officer and the dismounted corporal from the other tank exchanged surprised looks.

"Yes, please do…" The lieutenant replied, slightly bemused.

Jackson executed another butt salute on the machine-gun and carried out an immaculate right turn, thumping his ammunition boot into the heavy soil with a loud thud. Having done so, the sergeant looked across at his mixed group of followers and gave a jerk of his head.

"Alright, you lot, let's get going. Quick as you can. Martlesham? You bring up the rear."

The tank crew watched the group file past, noting with interest the myriad orders of dress and unusual mix of weaponry. As the last member of the group disappeared through the gap in the hedgerow and into the village, the corporal from the second tank looked up at his troop commander and shook his head in disbelief.

"Bloody Guardsmen!"

THE DRIFFIELD TO BRIDLINGTON ROAD – BY NAFFERTON SUNDAY 22ND SEPTEMBER 1940 – 0600 HOURS

Corporal Klaus Weisman of the 2nd Regiment, 7th Parachute Division, turned and waved his hand. Immediately, the twenty or so paratroopers under his command, most of them wounded, began ushering their prisoners onto the grass verge. In total, Weisman and his men had eighty three Tommy prisoners. They were the survivors of the Driffield garrison who were still fit to walk, and Weisman's battalion commander had been keen to get them out of town at the earliest opportunity. Driffield was now bursting at the seams with German troops and vehicles and every inch of space was needed. The only Tommies who had been kept back in the town, were the senior officers, who were being interrogated by the staff of the 8th Panzer Division. Thus, it had become Weisman's task, along with the other walking wounded from his battalion, to escort these prisoners the three kilometres or so to the prisoner collection point that the field police had established in a large farm complex on the eastern outskirts.

As the Tommy prisoners were herded onto the wide verge, Weisman turned back towards the approaching convoy that had prompted the move off the tarmac. It was just starting to get properly light, although the sun was unlikely to come up at all today he noted sourly, gazing up at the leaden grey sky. The vehicles travelled without their headlights on, though Weisman could tell from the revving of engines that the approaching vehicles were motoring at some speed. As they drew nearer, he saw that the convoy of lorries was being led by a halftrack.

He could understand the desire of the convoy commander to make best speed. With the onset of daylight, the Tommy fighters, if there were any left, would almost certainly be out hunting. Come to think of it, the sooner Weisman could get his prisoners offloaded, then find the shelter of a nice little wood or farm building, then the happier he would be. The vehicles were barely a hundred metres away now and he heard the grumble of the half-track's engine as it reduced speed, shifting down a gear. He stepped back to ensure that the vehicles would have a clear passage, and was joined on his left by Sepp Waldorf, another corporal from his battalion.

"More vehicles? They're going to be bumper to bumper in that town before long!" Waldorf observed.

"I think there'll be room enough soon." Weisman replied. "Hear that barrage a few minutes ago? I reckon that's 8th Panzer on the move."

Waldorf stared towards the half-track at the front of the column, which was slowing considerably, as if the driver meant to pull up alongside the two corporals.

"This must be the rest of 8th Panzer's grenadier regiment coming through, is it?"

Weisman was also staring at the halftrack, his eyes narrowing into a squint.

"Oh, for fuck's sake." He murmured.

Waldorf looked at his friend in surprise.

"What is it?"

Weisman's face was grim.

"It's not 8th Panzer." He answered, the bitterness obvious in his voice. "That's a deaths head badge on the front of that half-track. It's the Totenkopf."

Waldorf whistled.

"The Waffen SS? They didn't hang about getting here, did they?"

Weisman's face grew darker.

"I hate these bastards!" He growled.

The half-track rumbled to a standstill in front of them, and a haughty looking individual leaned over the side and looked down on them. The man was dressed in one of the strange looking mottled camouflage smocks that the SS liked to wear and Weisman saw that the insignia on the man's black collar indicated that he was a company commander. The SS officer gave them a cold look.

"Who are you?" He demanded in a sharp voice that betrayed a Berlin accent.

Wesiman returned the officer's look with a stony gaze of his own.

"Corporal Weisman, 7th Para Division. Who are you?"

It was an outrageous thing to say to an officer in one of the Fuhrer's pet units, but Weisman was extremely tired and didn't really care. He had nothing but contempt for these people, who he believed to be nothing more than uniformed thugs. The SS officer started at Weisman's reply and gave the corporal a severe look. For a second, he didn't respond, but then he seemed to give the paratrooper the benefit of the doubt, assuming that the corporal was like most paratroopers; tough but slow-witted.

"I am Hauptsturmfuhrer Merkal," he replied, gathering his poise again and speaking in a pompous tone, "of the SS Totenkopf Division."

Weisman continued to regard the officer with a blank stare.

"Morning, Captain." He said, deliberately using the equivalent military title, instead of the SS rank.

If the officer was irritated, he didn't show it. He glanced at the prisoners behind the two corporals for a moment, a look of distaste creeping over his features.

"Who are these scum?" He demanded.

A flicker of anger rose inside Weisman, but he fought it down.

"They're all that's left of the British garrison in Driffield, less some officers that are being interrogated by 8th Panzer. We've been told to hand them over to the field police at the prisoner collection point."

Merkal looked back at the corporal for a moment, then threw a glance over his shoulder.

"Ah, yes." He said, his voice mellowing slightly. "We have just passed them. The collection centre is about five hundred metres up there."

He jerked his head back in the direction of Bridlington. Looking back at the two corporals, he changed the topic of conversation.

"How far is Driffield?"

Waldorf jerked a thumb towards the town.

"Just up there, Sir; about two kilometres."

"There's a divisional checkpoint on the edge of town." Weisman elaborated, accepting that it was his duty to assist the SS, even if he didn't like them. "It's manned by the field police and some staff officers from 8th Panzer and 5th Corps."

Merkal nodded his understanding.

"Excellent." He snapped. Then, in his mellower voice, asked. "How was it? Did you have much trouble?"

The two paratroopers exchanged a look. It was Weisman who replied.

"It was pretty grim to be honest. We landed right in the middle of a Tommy regiment. They fought us till the very end."

Again, the SS officer appeared to bridle slightly at Weisman's reply.

"Well, they'll have something to think about now they've got the 8th Panzer and SS Totenkopf in their back-yard, won't they?"

Weisman bit back a sullen reply.

Merkal ran his eyes over the crowd of British soldiers on the verge again. After a while, he pointed towards a group of them.

"Who are they?" He asked, a dangerous tone creeping into his voice.

The two para corporals turned to follow the SS officer's gaze.

"Those ones there, in the greener coloured uniforms, with the grey hair? Who are they?"

Waldorf looked up at Merkal, his face bearing a puzzled expression.

"Part of the Tommy garrison, Sir; from Driffield."

Merkal was standing on top of the half-track's cab now, in order to get a better view.

"They are old men." He said, his voice sharp. "Their uniforms are not the same as the others. Those arm-bands they're wearing; what do they say?"

Realisation flooded across Waldorf's face.

"Oh, those ones?" He said. "They're some kind of volunteer force; a militia I think. I don't know what the exact translation is, but those arm-bands say 'peoples volunteers' or something like that".

Merkal looked at Waldorf with a hawkish look.

"So they're francs-tireurs?" He asked, his voice suddenly cold and somewhat quieter.

"They're brave men." Weisman piped up. "They fought well."

Merkal thought for a second.

"But they are francs-tireurs none-the-less." Merkal said again, calmly. "And you know what the orders are concerning them?"

Weisman began to feel a rising sense of unease.

"We've been ordered to take them to the prisoner collection point; nothing more."

He kept his voice as neutral as possible, sensing that the SS officer was trying to provoke him in some way.

Merkal smiled unexpectedly; something that made Weisman shiver.

"Yes, yes." Merkal said in a reasonable tone. "I'm sure your commander has been quite specific with you, but I'm assuming that you are aware of the Fuhrer's personal direction regarding the treatment of francs-tireurs?"

The alarm bells began ringing for the two para corporals. They had no idea what 'Fuhrer Order' the SS man was talking about but knew that it was foolish to start arguing the toss over such things.

"All the commanding officer said was…"

"Yes." Merkal cut Weisman short. "I'm sure he did. But your commanding officer has just fought a long, hard battle and I imagine that he is exhausted. He is unlikely to be troubling himself over the minute details of the operational orders. On the other hand, I am lucky enough to be well rested and I am fully familiar with the details concerning illegal combatants. I will take those men in the green uniforms off your hands."

Weisman felt an awful sense of dread wash over him.

"We can just hand them over to the field police…" He began, but Merkal cut him short once more.

"The field police deal with prisoners of war, Corporal. You will hand the regular soldiers over to them. I will deal with the terrorists."

Weisman was speechless. His stomach suddenly felt heavy, as if a huge stone had just landed right inside it. Merkal was turning and shouting instructions to the commander of the lorry behind him. Moments later, half a dozen SS men dismounted from the rear of the vehicle and came running up to stand by the half-track. Weisman looked over the squad with distaste. They were all tall men, with harsh, aggressive looking features; the party faithful of National Socialist Germany.

Within a heartbeat, Merkal had issued the instructions, and his squad were moving amongst the worried looking prisoners. One by one, the older looking Tommies in the fatigue style uniforms were dragged out of the main body and formed up as a small, separate group on the opposite verge. Weisman counted the men quickly. Fifteen. One of the Tommies in the small group had a defiant look on his face and was staring at the SS men with a look of pure hatred. Weisman noticed that the man wore a set of coloured ribbons on his breast pocket and surmised that he must be a veteran of the last war.

"You can go now."

Merkal's words snapped Weisman out of his private thoughts.

"Sorry, Sir?" He frowned, looking up at the SS company commander.

"You can go now." Merkal repeated, his face still etched with a smile. "Get that lot up to the collection point; off you go." The SS officer indicated the main body of British prisoners.

Weisman shot a questioning glance at Waldorf, who returned the look with a warning shake of his head. Reluctantly, Weisman turned back towards his own men.

"Right lads, get this lot moving. Bring 'em along this verge; straight up the road there."

He stepped back against the half-track to allow the prisoners to be herded past.

"Lead them on, Sepp, will you?" He said to Waldorf. "I'll follow on."

Waldorf nodded and stepped off at the head of the long column of prisoners. As the British soldiers passed by, Weisman avoided their eyes.

When the last of his men had gone past at the rear of the prisoners, Weisman fell in behind them and glanced back up at Merkal.

"Good day, Captain." He said bleakly.

Merkal smiled and tapped the peak of his cap with one hand.

Weisman followed his column past the line of SS lorries until they were clear of the convoy and able to move back onto the tarmac. He was brooding on what had just taken place. Inside, he was angry, yet he felt completely helpless. He couldn't stand up to an SS captain. He would really be in the shit if he tried to push things any further. On the other hand, he reflected, he could still go back and demand to see the Fuhrer Order that Merkal had mentioned. He walked past the remains of a Tommy personnel carrier that lay on its side by the grass verge. He noticed, absently, that there was a bomb crater hard by it; also that there were expended cartridge cases all over the road, and that the neighbouring field was black where the stubble had been on fire recently, the harsh smell of smoke still lingering in the morning air.

He physically jumped when he heard the machine-gun fire. With a curse, he stopped dead and whirled around to look back down the road towards the convoy. Several more bursts of fire rang out; the unmistakeable chatter of MP40s. He could see very little, only that there was a cluster of SS men crowding around something at the very front of the column of vehicles. Moments later, several single shots rang out; slow, deliberate, methodical.

"Wankers!" Weisman snarled to nobody in particular.

He turned back towards his own column and saw that everyone, German and British alike, was staring past him back towards the SS convoy. His fellow paratroopers were hollow-eyed and grim. The British were frightened, nervous looking, and talking urgently amongst themselves. He felt a sudden surge of anger. Not just anger, but shame too.

"Get fucking moving!" He shouted at his men. "Nobody told you to stop. Get these fuckers moving again."

He grabbed one of his men and dragged him along the road, forcing him to stop looking back at the SS convoy.

"Come, on, stop gawping! It's none of our business. Let's get these Tommies handed over so we can fuck off back to the battalion."

His men began pushing the Tommies along the road, forcing them to turn away from what was happening by the stationary column. Even as they did so, the sound of revving engines came from behind them, and Weisman glanced over his shoulder to see that the SS vehicles were already moving forward again.

When he looked back, he found one of his men pushing a lone Tommy, who was refusing to move, a look of unbelievable rage on the man's face.

The young paratrooper who was trying to chivvy him along was looking worried, and had his rifle levelled at the prisoner. Weisman rushed across.

"You…move…" He spoke in broken English, desperately trying to remember the small amount he had learned at school.

The prisoner shot him an angry glance and said something. Weisman missed the full sentence but recognised the first word as an obscenity.

"No worry…" Weisman tried again, waving a warning hand at the other paratrooper and trying to calm both men down. "You is safe…" He struggled to find the words in English. "They is SS…bastards. All bastards."

A brief flash of understanding appeared in the Tommy's eyes. Weisman saw that the man wore two white chevrons on his sleeve, which meant that, like the German NCO, the Tommy was also a corporal.

"You safe…move now."

The Tommy looked at Weisman, his breathing beginning to calm slightly. He flicked a look over Weisman's shoulder towards where the other group of Tommies had just been executed by the SS. Then, reluctantly, and with a suspicious look still etched on his face, the Tommy corporal turned away.

Heaving a sigh of relief, Weisman followed on behind the crowd of men. This had supposedly been a straight forward task, he reflected bitterly. Thanks to the SS, it had turned into a complete nightmare. If the Tommies were spooked anymore, they might make a break for it. He needed to get them into the collection centre and out of the way as soon as possible. Fighting down a rising tide of anger with the SS Totenkopf, Weisman began striding out towards the front of the column, overhauling the mass of prisoners and their guards. He would make sure that the field police knew exactly what had happened. He would report it to his own officers too. Perhaps he couldn't take on the SS himself, but he was sure that the higher ranks amongst the Luftwaffe and the Army would take a different attitude. He had plenty of witnesses. His boys would all stand by him; they hated the SS as much as he did.

Weisman looked up and saw a motorcycle combination parked by the gateway of a large farm complex, some way ahead. There were men standing around the entrance looking this way. He saw Waldorf walk up to them and engage in conversation. It was the collection centre at last, thank God, and the column of prisoners began to wheel left into the gateway. Weisman was still thanking God when the shouting started and the first enemy aircraft flipped into view and opened fire.

The Tommy aircraft pounced on them out of nowhere. Suddenly, Weisman was face down in the ditch at the side of the road, spitting out gob-fulls of stinking mud, as the roar of aircraft engines and panic stricken shouting filled the air. Over it all, came the continuous, deafening crack of multiple machine-guns, firing simultaneously in long bursts. High-pitched whines followed one after the other as bullets ricocheted off the tarmac and span crazily in all directions. Something thumped down next to him and Weisman looked up to see the body of a dead Tommy hanging over the edge of the ditch, the man's eyes wide and staring, a slow trickle of blood pouring from his open mouth. Weisman stared at the dead man's face and cursed his luck, yet again. It was barely dawn, and the Royal Air Force was back with a vengeance.

At the other side of the road from Weisman, Corporal Les Downey of the East Yorkshire Regiment pressed himself flat against the earth in the gateway of the field. Until just thirty six hours earlier, he had been relatively content with life. The job of defending the airfield at Driffield had seemed like a cushy number, especially as Downey was a local lad, from Pocklington. His life had been fairly comfortable, with only the one air-raid to spoil the balmy English summer and the endless nights of chatting up the WAAFs in the tea-rooms. Then the Germans had come and turned his world upside down.

Despite that, he had fought well, finally ending up in the town centre after being cut off during a failed counter-attack against the Germans attacking the airfield. He had fought on with one of the battalions from the resident brigade until they had finally run out of ammunition and surrendered the night before. As far as he knew, he was the only survivor of his company from the airfield. Surrender had brought a certain amount of relief. He reckoned he would live to see the end of the war, even if it was in a prisoner of war camp, but the massacre of the Home Guard boys just a few minutes earlier had changed all that. He had understood what the Jerry NCO in charge of their group was trying to say. He had tried to tell Downey that it was the SS who had murdered the old men from the Home Guard, and that he and the rest of the prisoners would be safe. It was obvious that the average German didn't like the SS.

But what if they bumped into more SS? He had heard about those bastards before. There were all kinds of tales about the atrocities committed by German troops during the British retreat to Dunkirk, and Downey didn't fancy having anything more to do with the SS if he could help it. He looked around the field in front of him. It was a big field; flat, surrounded by hedges, and empty of people. Another aircraft roared overhead and the deafening clatter of machine-gun fire assaulted his ears, and he cringed as the .303 inch bullets slammed into the road and nearby farm buildings. This was the icing on the cake, he decided; being shot-up by your own air force!

He looked around him. There were a number of bodies on the road; some German, some British. Most of the group had scattered into the ditches and farmyard at the far side of the road. The German motorcycle was on fire and belching thick black smoke. The nearest living German was face down in the bottom of the ditch on his side of the road, nearly twenty yards away. Downey looked back into the field. He knew this area like the back of his hand. He didn't want to end up being gunned down, either by the SS or the RAF. He made up his mind, forced himself into a standing position, and ran.

He ran faster and harder than he'd ever run before. Behind him, another aircraft roared down the length of the road, its guns chattering mercilessly. He sprinted along the side of the field, his eyes picking out the lowest point in the hedgerow at the far side of the meadow. His heart was beating in his chest like a bass drum and his breath was coming in huge gulps. No bullets cracked through the air beside him and he was barely thirty yards from the next field. He caught movement out of his eye corner and saw the silhouette of the single seat fighter banking sharply to the left over the fields at tree-top height. For a brief second, he caught sight of the green and brown camouflage pattern and the dark blue and crimson roundels on the wings.

"Go on fly-boys!" He gasped to himself as he pumped his arms and legs like steam-driven pistons. "You just keep firing for as long as you want!"

SEALION HEADQUARTERS – THE HAGUE, HOLLAND
SUNDAY 22ND SEPTEMBER 1940 – 0620 HOURS

The assembled German officers listened to the briefing with serious faces. It was early in the day for such a conference, but the German High Command had known from the outset that this operation would succeed or fail within the first five days, and thus they had resigned themselves to a busy week. Besides, the detailed reports that had been filtering in overnight demanded immediate attention. Once the service operations officers had each read through the various messages from the field commanders, Keitel stepped to the front of the room and asked for observations from the heads of service. Raeder was the first to contribute. He chose his words carefully, not wanting to worry the others, yet at the same time, needing to make them understand how critical the next twenty four hours would be for the Kreigsmarine.

"To some degree," he began, "the attack against the dummy fleet was very much what we were hoping for. I can't help feeling however, that we have missed an opportunity here. The losses were the ones we expected, with most of the skeleton crews being able to evacuate in good time, and all of the fighting ships making good their escape, however, our U-Boats were not as successful as we might have hoped, and the Luftwaffe were not able to give as much support as we expected. A much heavier attack on the enemy force was required…"

Kesselring bridled instantly.

"We cannot see in the dark and we cannot be everywhere at once!" He protested. "The crews are already exhausted. They are snatching just an hour or two of sleep between missions whilst their machines are refuelled and rearmed. In addition, we had an entire infantry division to move by air, railheads to bomb, top-cover missions for the Totenkopf convoy, whilst still maintaining a force ready to launch at first light to cover the breakout…"

He tailed off, not wanting to sound like a spoiled brat.

Raeder listened patiently to the protestations before going on in a quiet, measured voice.

"I am not criticising anyone." He soothed. "I am simply saying that we are now starting to see how thinly stretched our resources are. Getting the force ashore seems to have been the easy bit, but giving sufficient depth to the beach-head and keeping the Royal Navy and Royal Air Force at bay for another seventy two hours is going to be much more difficult. It was always difficult in theory; but in reality it is proving to be something of a trial."

He gave a deep sigh and rose to his feet, moving tiredly across to the map of the British Isles and the German Sea.

"The British destroyer force has succeeded in breaking up the dummy fleet with the loss of only one of their ships, and the surviving six are now steaming somewhere off to the south of the landing areas, probably in line with the Humber. Hopefully, the Luftwaffe's morning raiders will spot them and report their position soon enough. We have all the U-Boats south of the landing area searching for them. The Admiral Scheer, although damaged, has been ordered to take station to the south-east once more to guard this flank with several destroyers. The main reason for my concern isn't so much the presence of British destroyers, but the fact that somewhere along the line, this enemy flotilla has picked up an ageing battleship from God knows where. The reports say that the vessel is a vintage unit, but despite that, she mounts some pretty big guns and made short work of the dummy fleet. We cannot afford to let that beast get within range of the Bridlington beaches. Plus there are still two enemy cruisers at large somewhere, and they must be dealt with also."

Kesselring, slightly embarrassed by his earlier outburst in front of these senior officers, interjected.

"I will pass the message to all squadrons to keep alert for the enemy naval force, and re-task two squadrons of Bf110s to deal with them once they've been located. We need to try and sandwich them between the Scheer and the U-Boats, and then our fighter-bombers can go in and finish them."

Raeder nodded silently in grateful acknowledgement, before continuing.

"As for the landings themselves, we have succeeded in recovering the first wave and getting the second wave across to England without serious incident. The unloading overnight has proved to be difficult however. The sea state has worsened slightly; not too much, but enough to cause problems with landing equipment across the beaches. Bridlington harbour is now open and working to full capacity, and the sloped-landing at Filey is also proving useful, but trying to off-load straight onto the beaches in anything less than optimum conditions is a dangerous and time consuming business; hence the fact that only half the Totenkopf is ashore. We are really starting to feel the effects of the failure to secure Scarborough."

Von Brauchitsch cleared his throat.

"Any thought of capturing Scarborough now is just a fantasy, as you have heard from the reports."

"Indeed." Raeder allowed. "I am not suggesting that we sacrifice any more men trying to crack open a heavily fortified town. All I am saying is that the landing of the second wave, and all of the echelons and stores for the first wave, will be necessarily much slower than we allowed for. There will be competition for resources between formations, so it will be for the Army to decide where their priorities lie."

Raeder paused for a moment to let the information sink in.

Keitel and Von Brauchitsch exchanged glances, and then together looked at Kesselring.

"What is the forecast for the improvised airstrip?" Keitel asked without preamble.

Kesselring had the answer ready, for he had his own vested interest in the provision of airfields in England.

"The first site has been identified, right by the coast and just south of Bridlington, at a place called Lisset. I am told that the Army have moved well beyond this location already and that it is secure enough to begin work. Our engineers will be on the job already. I hope to be able to use it to bring in the rest of the 22nd Division tonight, and have it ready for use by combat aircraft by tomorrow morning."

"Good. That will take some pressure off the beaches in another twenty four hours." Keitel was scratching his chin thoughtfully. "For the time being however, we will have to take another look at the disembarkation plan and prioritise the landing of the follow-on stores and units, as the Grand Admiral rightly points out."

He looked back at Raeder.

The Grand Admiral took it as a signal to continue.

"Which brings us to the greatest threat facing the invasion force; the British Home Fleet. As you are aware, at some point just before Sealion North began, the British carrier, along with two cruisers and, we believe, three destroyers, quite literally disappeared from Scapa Flow. At the moment, we have absolutely no idea where this force has gone. We have searched extensively in the German Sea with a full third of our available U-Boat force and continuous sweeps by the Luftwaffe. So far, there is no sign of them. We are currently working on the theory that they were despatched to the west coast ports to pick up convoys heading across the Atlantic, and that they might be returning via the north coast of Scotland with best speed. To that end, we have further thinned our U-Boat screen off the Orkneys to cover that approach."

"What is the best case scenario?" Keitel asked.

Raeder looked surprised.

"Best case?" He took a deep breath. "I suppose the best case is that those ships are half way across the Atlantic and don't come back in time to have a decisive effect."

Keitel pursed his lips.

"And the worst?"

Raeder scanned the expectant faces in the room.

"You can take your pick. One option is that our main fleet is attacked by torpedo carrying aircraft from the carrier, followed up by attacks from shore based aircraft, after which the British cruisers and destroyers make a seaborne attack, joined by the surviving destroyers from the Tyne."

He saw the look of discomfort on the faces of the other senior officers. At last, probably too late, they were starting to realise the enormity of the task that the Kreigsmarine had been given. He went for the killer blow.

"And then…whilst we're using all of our major surface units to deal with a multi-pronged assault, the main battle squadrons of the British Home Fleet break out of Scapa Flow. Twenty four hours later, every Kreigsmarine surface ship in the German Sea gets sent to the bottom."

There was silence in the room. Keitel finally broke it.

"Nothing is more important than keeping the Royal Navy away from the landing areas."

He looked at Kesselring.

"The Condor squadrons are to patrol the northern part of the German Sea continuously. As soon as the British carrier group is spotted then you are to commit every resource available to destroy it, and the same goes for the main body of the Home Fleet should it break out successfully. You can keep your Ju88 and Bf110 squadrons assigned to ground support over England, but every Heinkel wants to be diverted against the Royal Navy when it comes out to play. I will speak to Goering for you, and request that your Air Fleet is further reinforced with Dornier Squadrons, now that Sealion South is complete."

The supreme head of the German armed forces then switched his gaze to Von Brauchitsch.

"And the heavy guns, when they finally get ashore, I want some of them positioned on the coast in order to give the fleet some close protection. We must work faster to get the echelons of the 8th Panzer, 12th Infantry and SS Totenkopf ashore as soon as possible. Then we can clear all unnecessary shipping from the coast and get it safely back in German waters."

The eyes flicked back to Kesselring again.

"The balance of the 22nd Division must be in England by tomorrow morning. Thereafter, the transport fleet must work round the clock to fly supplies across the German Sea. Get your new airfield up and running quickly. And keep Driffield safe. As soon as Leaconfield is in our hands, start using that too. We have perhaps three or four days of maximum effort to bring the Tommies to their knees. I know it is tiring, but the British are still reeling from Dunkirk. They *will* break first. They *must* break first."

Keitel's directives were coming thick and fast now.

"Speak to Donitz." He turned his attention back to Raeder.

"I want a carpet of U-Boats between the Orkneys and the invasion beaches. We cannot afford to go chasing ghosts. Just concentrate every U-Boat in the northern part of the German Sea, and sink anything British that comes near."

Raeder nodded and was about to respond, when one of his staff officers came rushing through the door of the briefing room. The man spotted the Grand Admiral amongst the group of senior officers and hurried across, a grave look on his face. Seeing the young officer's expression, Raeder called out to him whilst he was still halfway across the room.

"What is it?" He demanded sharply.

The officer came to a halt in the centre of the room, as the combined staff of the German armed forces turned as one to look at him.

"Grand Admiral..." He began hesitantly. "My apologies for interrupting, but there is a flash signal from Admiral Donitz, concerning Captain Prien at Scapa Flow..."

Raeder felt his pulse quicken.

"Go on." He said, evenly.

The officer gulped slightly at being under the scrutiny of so many senior officers.

"The British carrier group we've been searching for, Sir; it's arrived."

There was a collective murmur amongst the officers. Raeder felt the excitement rising inside. At last! Now they could take decisive action against the enemy force.

"Arrived back at the Orkneys?" Raeder queried. "Off the north coast of Scotland?"

The officer shook his head.

"No, Sir. The British ships have approached from the north-east. They have arrived in the rear of Captain Prien's force, and they are sweeping around the eastern and southern side of Scapa Flow in a broad screen. We have already lost one U-Boat. There is a report of British destroyers coming out of the eastern exit of Scapa Flow, behind the carrier group."

Raeder was speechless. The blood had drained from his face completely, leaving him pale and sickly looking.

"From the north-east?" He asked, shocked. "From Norway?"

"Yes, Sir." The naval officer confirmed.

There was a long silence, which was finally broken by the sound of more footsteps entering the room. Another harassed staff officer came through the doors, this time from the Luftwaffe. Seeing the assembly of silent, serious faced officers at the far side of the room, he skirted the wide table and came around it to stand in front of Kesselring.

"Yes?" The commander of the Sealion Air Fleet looked at the newcomer.

"General, a flash message from the group in Norway…" Whispered the officer.

"Read it aloud, please?" Kesselring asked, flicking his gaze around the other Generals in the room.

The staff officer hesitated for a moment, surprised at being asked to read a Luftwaffe signal out publicly, but non-the-less, he took a breath and began.

"We have just received this from the Norwegian based squadrons. At 0455 hours this morning, a Heinkel crew returning to Stavanger from a raid on Darlington sent a report back to their station. They reported seeing a force of six unidentified ships, three of them of substantial size, steaming south-west, approximately thirty miles north-east of the Orkneys. The crew were unsure who the ships belonged to, but shortly afterwards, they reported that they were being attacked by British Fighters. Since then, there has been no more contact with the aircraft.

The Luftwaffe officer's words were followed by another long silence as the German Generals came to terms with the seriousness of the unfolding drama. Eventually, it was Keitel who broke the spell.

"Well, at least we know what we are up against. Raeder? Get on to Donitz and get every U-Boat we have into the German Sea immediately. No questions from him; no complaints. Just get our submarines between Scapa Flow and the invasion force as fast as you can. Kesselring?"

Keitel looked towards the man who commanded the air power.

"Everything you've got spare Kesselring. Everything that's on its way to England, and everything that's ready to fly from Norway; get it up now, and get it over Scapa Flow, before this entire operation comes crashing down around our ears."

CABINET WAR ROOMS – STOREY'S GATE, LONDON
SUNDAY 22ND SEPTEMBER 1940 – 0630 HOURS

"Seelöwe?" Brooke fixed the Director of Military Intelligence with a searching look.

"Yes, Sir. It's German for 'sealion', and they are suffixing it with the words 'north' or 'south'. There is no doubt that this is the codename of the German operation, split into two distinct parts; one on the south coast, and one on the Yorkshire coast."

Brooke pursed his lips.

"And you are convinced that your earlier interpretation of German intentions from May and June is now correct, and that the air battles and naval movements of July and August were a diversion?"

The Director nodded.

"We are, Sir. There can be no doubt. The Director of Naval Intelligence has double checked every fact and figure, and studied the air photographs taken at last light over the French coast. The findings are pretty clear. Every single capital ship that the Germans have is now in the North Sea, whilst U-Boat attacks have virtually ceased in the Atlantic overnight. Not a single ship lost in the North Atlantic for six days. Given the losses over the summer, that is a startling development in itself. But add to that the fact that the harbours at Calais, Dunkirk, Boulogne, Dieppe and Le Havre are virtually empty of ships and boats, with no evidence of large concentrations of stores or troops or vehicles, and there can be only one conclusion."

The Director jabbed his finger at the map and tapped it repeatedly over the town of Bridlington.

"It's here. This is their main effort. This is where the war is going to be won or lost; in Yorkshire."

Brooke nodded.

"And we're not just making the facts fit our own opinions?"

"No, Sir." The Director's eyes never wavered as he returned his superior's gaze.

"Right then…" Brooke murmured thoughtfully, turning to his Logistics Officer. "Those plans we drew up about the movement of assets from the other commands; make it happen, immediately. I want every round of ammunition, every 2 and 25 Pounder, every mine and every roll of barbed wire, and I want it in Yorkshire by tonight. And the engineer bridges too; I want them transferred to Northern Command without delay. Derek?"

He flicked his gaze to another staff officer at the rear of the room.

"Give the Commando School at Achnacarry the warning order. I want them ready to move as soon as I get the Prime Minister's permission."

The two officers murmured their understanding and left the room. As they did so, a figure came in through the open door. Brooke raised a smile when he saw that it was his old friend, the Chief of the Imperial General Staff.

"Good morning, Alan." Smiled Dill, as he took in Brooke's tired looking face. "How are you doing? Did you manage to get some rest overnight?"

Brooke smiled weakly.

"A little." He said, but then instantly revised his answer. "Enough. I did with much less in Belgium and France back in May."

Dill stared at his friend for a moment, studying the man's dark features and sunken eyes, measuring the huge resolve that he knew lay beneath the surface. Satisfied, he removed his cap and joined Brooke and the Director by the map.

"Anything new?"

Brooke sighed.

"In terms of action, nothing significant yet, though our assumptions of yesterday have solidified into raw fact. I spoke to Adam a little while ago. There was a lot of action up here near Scarborough and Seamer last night. The 59th repelled a strong German attack, but then were roughly handled themselves when they tried to counter-attack. It looks like a bit of a stalemate and we suspect that the enemy has two full divisions covering this northern shoulder of their beach-head. The 59th are confident they can hold and have been resupplied with ammunition. Adam is also reinforcing them and extending the line westwards towards Pickering and Malton. As of yet though, there is no German heavy armour in this sector."

Dill studied the map and its complex markings, taking in the symbols and unit designations with a professional eye.

"It seems that the enemy is concentrating his main force on Driffield then, as we suspected yesterday? Any idea which way he will turn yet?"

Brooke shook his head.

"Not yet, though I suspect we will find out soon enough. There has been a lot of bombing in depth, especially in the Midlands. You can see that the enemy is trying to isolate this battlefield in his own way. You have to admire the thoroughness of it."

Dill gave a grunt of a laugh.

"Mmm. Efficiency is generally a given with the Germans. However, I have brought you some good news, you'll be pleased to hear."

Brooke raised his eyebrows.

"This early in the morning?"

Dill chuckled.

"Your experiences in France have made you cynical, Alan."

"I prefer to call it realistic."

Dill nodded, conceding the point.

"Anyway," Dill continued, "the first good news is that the Home Fleet appears to have successfully broken out of Scapa Flow. I just had word from the Chief of Naval Operations. The Furious Group arrived back at the Orkneys at first light and managed to sweep a clear lane for the fleet's destroyer flotillas to come out through. There are reports of a U-Boat being sunk. The entire destroyer force is now sweeping southwards and the battle squadrons are breaking out as we speak."

For the first time in thirty-six hours, Brooke gave a genuinely happy smile.

"That's marvellous news."

"Isn't it just? Pound and the Commander Home Fleet played that one nicely. I'm meeting with him later to discuss his plans for the Home Fleet, before we go and see the Prime Minister. Winston will undoubtedly have some scheme of his own in mind and we need to have our own plans and counter arguments prepared."

Brooke nodded enthusiastically.

"Yes, I can imagine. That's a wise move."

"There is a down side to all of this, however."

Brooke eyed his friend suspiciously.

"You will not be receiving quite as much air support as you have enjoyed over the last twenty four hours, Alan."

Dill caught the look of alarm in his friend's eyes, and went on quickly.

"Not the Air Striking Group." He elaborated quickly. "Newall has confirmed it will remain at your disposal. In fact, he has reinforced it with a Polish fighter squadron, another Blenheim squadron, and the Gladiator squadron which is fitted for using the gas dischargers. The latter of course, can only be used with Ministerial approval. Otherwise, the group is yours to use as you see fit. I understand however that they took a few casualties yesterday, so I would urge you to be careful where and when you use them. We can't really afford to lose them in penny packets, because once they're gone, they can't be replaced."

Brooke absorbed the information silently.

"The main change is going to be fighter cover, and the scope of bomber operations." Dill went on. "Essentially, Fighter Command is going to focus on three main tasks. A third of their force will be used to fly top-cover for the Home Fleet, now that it's broken out. Another third, based in the south, will fly long range sweeps out towards Holland, over the North Sea, in an attempt to cut the enemy air-bridge. What's left will be used to provide a back-stop over Yorkshire and the Midlands, in order to protect our railheads and concentration areas."

Brooke was nodding now.

"That all makes sense, actually. To be honest, I would have made a similar decision were it mine to make."

He looked at his friend, regarding him shrewdly.

"What about the bombing policy, then?"

Dill pursed his lips.

"You will need to be careful around Newall and Portal for a while. Bomber Command suffered heavily yesterday. The Germans may lack for fighter cover, but their anti-aircraft umbrella is pretty damned deadly. In addition, the accuracy of the bomber force is, by their own admission, not as good as it could be, especially at night. To that end, Newall is proposing a new strategy, which I have to say, I am in favour of."

Brooke's face was unreadable.

"Which is?" He enquired mildly.

Dill took a breath and ploughed on.

"There will be no more small raids. All targets will be hit from high-level, where the cloud allows. All raids will be conducted at a minimum of group level, so you're talking maybe sixty aircraft per raid, sometimes more."

Brooke made no response, so Dill continued.

"Essentially, Newall wants us to give him an update, every six hours, on what we see, at Army level, as the two most serious threats to us on the ground. These two targets will then be allocated to the bomber groups for their next strike. The strikes will not be precision by any means. Rather, anything that lies in the vicinity of the target will be obliterated by a carpet of bombs. He says that it's the only way to guarantee any real effect. The bonus for us is that since the Home Fleet is now out of Scapa Flow, there are no more plans to attack the German fleet off the coast. That means that we essentially have Bomber Command at our disposal, but we will have to be bloody careful about the targets we select."

Brooke thought on this for a moment.

"Do you have any targets in mind at this stage, Alan?" Dill asked.

The Commander Home Forces exchanged a look with the Director of Military Intelligence. Without saying anything, Brooke jabbed his finger at the map, pointing directly at the town of Driffield. Maintaining the silence, the Director saw the indication, looked back at Brooke, and nodded firmly. Brooke turned back to Dill.

"Driffield." He said. "And everything in a three mile radius of the town. That's our first priority; followed by the road between Driffield and Bridlington. I know the town is probably still crammed with civilians, but the fact is that we have a German head of steam building up there. Driffield must be hit hard, and hit fast."

A sad smiled crossed Dill's features.

"I thought that would be the case." He said quietly. "As did Newall. Two entire bomber groups are receiving their orders as we speak. There is a lot of cloud up north at the moment, but it is expected to clear mid-morning. I know that the Air Striking Group is already making low level sweeps over the town but, unless the Prime Minister forbids it at our 0730 hours meeting, then at 1000 hours this morning, nearly one hundred bombers will flatten Driffield town."

Brooke and the Director accepted the information wordlessly. After a while, the Commander Home Forces broke the silence.

"War is a terrible business. And sometimes, we must do terrible things for the greater good. We can only pray that God understands our reasons for such actions."

Before the Chief of the Imperial General Staff could reply to that, there was an urgent knock on the door, and one of Brooke's staff entered.

"Sirs," he began without preamble, "there are two flash signals from Northern Command."

Brooke nodded curtly at the officer.

"Go on, Jamie."

The staff officer raised the first signal.

"The brigade at Beverley reports that Leaconfield aerodrome has been successfully cratered, and that they are under pressure on a broad front from large formations of enemy infantry and light armoured cars, backed by artillery and mortars. They are withdrawing quickly in order to prevent being enveloped on either flank."

He paused, looking up for Brooke's reaction. Brooke turned the information over in his mind quickly, before replying.

"What's the second message?"

The officer flicked to another piece of paper.

"Lead elements of 2nd Armoured Division are now in a screen five miles south-west of Driffield. They report a column of tanks moving south out of Driffield on the Beverley road."

Brooke flicked a worried glance at Dill, then the same at the Director.

"They're going for Hull, after all." The Director murmured.

Brooke turned back to the staff officer.

"Draft a reply to Northern Command. I'll be there in a moment to check it over. Tell them to get that brigade back into Hull immediately and to ensure the city is fortified. Also, tell them to find another brigade and get it over the Humber and into Hull, quickly."

Brooke paused a moment, his mind working rapidly.

"In fact," he went on, "tell them to make it the Guards Brigade from 1 Div, and tell them to appoint the commander of the Guards Brigade as the Hull Garrison Commander. I want that city held at all costs. Do it now."

Thus dismissed, the staff officer hurried off. Brooke took a deep breath, casting a serious look at Sir John Dill.

"Tell Newall and the Prime Minister that I fully support the new bombing strategy. Tell them to flatten Driffield by all means; and the sooner the better."

S +1
AFTERNOON AND EVENING

HOLME-ON-SPALDING MOOR – EAST YORKSHIRE
SUNDAY 22ND SEPTEMBER 1940 – 1230 HOURS

"Who the fuck are you?"

Major Jack Tobin, Quartermaster of the 3rd Battalion Hallamshire Rifles, ran a withering gaze over the tall, bespectacled sergeant who was standing to attention in front of him. Actually, Tobin had a reasonably good idea who the sergeant might be, because the man had slammed-in his feet in a style that was only seen in one part of the British Army; the Foot Guards. And Major Jack Tobin hated Guardsmen.

Jackson stared back impassively, fixing his gaze an inch above the officer's eye-brows, in a manner that he always adopted when confronted by a senior rank with a hostile face. He recognised instantly what kind of a man he was faced with. This was an ex-ranker; a former warrant officer who had been granted a Quartermaster Commission at the end of a full career as an enlisted man. They generally came in two types, Jackson reflected. One was the wise, good humoured type. They knew their job inside out, were full of good advice, and always looked to see how they could best help those for whom they had a responsibility. The second type consisted of those who were, quite simply, complete and utter wankers. This individual, Jackson reflected, appeared to be one of the latter.

It had been a long morning for Jackson and his group. They had, as promised by the tank crew, found transport back to Holme-on-Spalding Moor at the rear of North Dalton, but it hadn't been a military vehicle. They had been herded onto a flat-bed farm trailer which was being towed by a tractor, both of the vehicles having being requisitioned by an enterprising staff sergeant from the Royal Army Service Corps. Then, for almost six hours, they had been driven, at a painfully slow pace, back along the main road towards Holme. The members of Jackson's little ad-hoc group had been enormously grateful however, finally having the chance to lie down and sleep as they trundled slowly back towards their own front-line.

Time and again, they had been forced to pull over to allow more British tanks and armoured vehicles to pass. The odd member of his group had managed to raise a cheer as the vehicles passed, but to Jackson's professional eye, there was little to cheer about. The vehicles that passed them were light tanks in the main, armed only with heavy machine guns. Of all the armour that they saw, only six of them were the heavier cruiser tanks mounting 2 Pounder guns. And of course, they had the air attacks to contend with.

There had been less than Jackson had expected, but even so, on no less than three occasions, he and the rest of his band had been forced to hastily abandon the trailer and dive into nearby woodland or ditches, as twin-engined enemy aircraft came screaming along the road, churning up the tarmac with their heavy canon shells. Amazingly, through all of the morning, their vehicle, and indeed every member of the group, had avoided damage or injury. The group was stronger by ten now. There had been a pair of private soldiers from the East Yorkshire Regiment in the village, escapees from

Driffield like their RAF colleagues. As well as that pair, Jackson had found an eight man section of Home Guard under a lance corporal and taken them under his wing. Now however, he was standing in front of the most senior officer present, at what was supposed to be a defensive box at Holme-on-Spalding Moor. To be truthful, the sprawling village looked very little like a defensive position, and more like a chaotic mass of vehicles, stores and waifs and strays.

Taking a deep breath, Jackson forced himself to remain calm.

"Sergeant Jackson, Sir, Coldstream Guards, temporarily attached as military instructor to the Filey Bay Home Guard."

"Oh, really?" Sneered the unpleasant looking quartermaster. "Cushy number gone bad, eh? So how did you end up here? Have *you* run away from the Germans too?"

Jackson flushed red and felt the anger rising. Again, he forced himself to stay calm.

As he looked back at the squat, swarthy looking officer, Jackson felt not just a sense of distaste, but a stab of recognition too. He was sure he had come across this man before. Suddenly, the officer's whole demeanour felt familiar, yet Jackson couldn't quite place him.

"No, Sir." Jackson replied, keeping his voice even. "We've spent the last thirty-six hours conducting a fighting withdrawal in the face of the German advance. On the way we've…"

"Yeah, yeah, alright!" Tobin interrupted him. "Don't give me any of your war stories. Looking at the state of you, you've been dragged through a hedge backwards. As if I didn't have enough to cope with, without having all the odds and sods in East Yorkshire dropped in my lap!"

Jackson fumed silently. He took his eyes away from the malicious looking quartermaster and focussed instead on a green staff car that was pulling into a lay-by just a few yards beyond the officer.

"If you're looking for a truck to the rear, you can think again." Tobin sneered. "Nobody's going anywhere unless I say so, and right now, I'm busy sorting out everyone else's problems, so you can keep out of my way until I get round to you."

Jackson tried again.

"We don't want any transport, Sir. We just need some more ammunition so we can fight the Jerries when they get here…"

"We?" Tobin demanded in a high pitched voice. "We? Who the fuck is '*we*'? And who the fuck do you think you are demanding ammunition off me?"

Jackson was becoming irate now and he was finding it difficult to maintain an impassive exterior. His natural urge was to punch this obnoxious little turd of a quartermaster into next week. Fortunately, he was spared the dilemma, because at that point the confrontation was interrupted.

"What's going on here? Who are you?"

Tobin turned to face the newcomer, another officer, who had just emerged from the staff car. Jackson remained at attention, and quickly ran his eyes over the new arrival. He saw instantly that the officer was a lieutenant colonel and unlike the quartermaster, he was dressed in fighting order; the only concession being that his steel helmet was strapped to his side-pack and he wore his more comfortable service dress cap on his head. Seeing the newcomer's rank, Tobin hurriedly threw a sloppy salute at him.

"Major Jack Tobin, Sir." Replied the quartermaster. "I'm the QM of the 3rd Hallamshires and the senior officer here."

To Jackson's amusement, the colonel gave Tobin an appraising look; one which didn't suggest he was impressed by what he saw.

"Not any more, you're not." Replied the colonel in a cool, urbane voice.

"My name is Ripley, from the divisional staff. With immediate effect, I'm the commanding officer of the Holme Box. How many men have you got?"

Tobin was visibly taken aback by the blunt questioning.

"Erm.., it's hard to say really because of all the comings and goings. We've got about a hundred or so from the brigade echelon, and then there are some RASC troops just…"

"Is the place ready for defence yet?" Ripley cut him short, impatiently.

For a second, Tobin was speechless. Eventually, he managed to find his voice.

"I've been trying to sort it all out, but there's a lot of confusion, no one really knows what's going on…"

"The bloody Germans are on their way! That's what's going on!" Ripley suddenly snapped at Tobin.

The quartermaster, who was carrying more weight around his belly than an infantry officer should, went bright red at the implied reprimand. He attempted a blustered defence of his inadequate response.

"Yeah, I know that, Sir, but it's all these waifs and strays that keep turning up and getting in the way!"

Jackson flicked his gaze off into the distance as he saw Ripley's eyes turn towards him. The lieutenant colonel stared at him for a moment.

"And you are?" Ripley asked, his voice cool again.

Jackson rattled off his details once more.

"Sergeant Jackson, Sir, Coldstream Guards, temporarily attached to the Filey Bay Home Guard as an instructor."

Ripley cocked his head slightly at Jackson's words.

"Coldstream Guards? Were you in France?"

"Yes, Sir?"

"Which battalion?"

"2nd Battalion, Sir; with the 1st Division."

A smile suddenly appeared on Ripley's face.

"Then I suspect that you and I have shared a few scraps, Sergeant. I was a company commander with the Hampshires."

Jackson relaxed slightly and allowed a feint smile to cross his face.

"Reckon we did, Sir."

Tobin was glaring at Jackson out of the corner of his eye.

Ripley continued to stare at the sergeant thoughtfully.

"Filey Bay Home Guard, eh? So how did you end up here then, Sergeant? And is that a *Jerry* machine-gun you've got there?"

Quickly, succinctly, Jackson explained the events of the last day and a half to Ripley, who listened intently to the story. When Jackson had finally finished, Ripley let out a long breath.

"Crikey, Sergeant! You've been having your own private war by the sounds of it! So what are you doing now?"

Jackson risked a glance at Tobin, who was giving him a dark, warning look.

"I was just asking the quartermaster for some ammunition, Sir; and finding out where our defensive positions are going to be."

Ripley looked at Tobin.

"Have you sorted that out yet?" He asked crisply.

"I…was just trying to find out how many blokes he has with him, Sir."

Ripley looked at Jackson and raised an eyebrow in query.

"Thirty including myself, Sir, but two of them are WAAFs, and three of them are aircrew who probably need to get back to an airfield. So call it twenty five, Sir; a fifty-fifty split of Home Guard and RAF with a couple of regulars. We've got a Lewis Gun, this Jerry machine-gun, two Boys Rifles and a whole load of pistols and rifles between us, Sir. Oh, yes, and some Jerry sub machine-guns, too."

Ripley was nodding now, impressed by the detailed and concise briefing.

"Good. Well done, Sergeant."

He looked at Tobin again.

"Get those aircrew and WAAFs sent to the rear and give this chap all the ammunition he needs; and anything else he's short of."

Tobin nodded sycophantically at the colonel.

"Yes, Sir; of course."

Ripley switched his gaze back to Jackson again and smiled.

"Get those non-combatants sent back, Sergeant, then draw your ammunition and start sorting your boys out. With immediate effect, they are No.1 Platoon of the Holme Garrison, and you are the platoon commander. Any questions?"

Jackson took a deep breath and braced his body up slightly.

"May I have your permission to carry on, Sir, please?"

"Bloody Guardsmen!" Laughed Ripley, raising his hand to his cap in salute. "Yes, please."

BY SLEDMERE – EAST YORKSHIRE
SUNDAY 22ND SEPTEMBER 1940 – 1245 HOURS

"It's these fucking Tommy farms!" Nuemark grumbled as he rested his legs on an ammunition box and massaged his arm. The flesh wound from the day before was still smarting, though it had been cleaned out again and re-bandaged by the medics in order that he could remain with his squad. "Each one is like a small fortress, with these bloody great walls, and big barns they've got. Half a dozen men can hold up a company for hours."

Saltz mumbled his agreement as he pushed another handful of 9mm rounds into his machine-pistol magazine.

"We could really do with the Stukas on this one, couldn't we? Hopefully they'll fly some in once they've got some airstrips sorted out."

"Amazing views over these hills though, don't you think, Sergeant?" Bachman looked up from where he was wiping his machine-gun bolt with a piece of oily rag.

Next to the young private, Nuemark scoffed.

"Amazing fucking killing-areas more like! I heard the First Battalion got cut up quite badly this morning in that last village. They took a couple of dozen casualties just trying to cross the open ground, before they even managed to break into the place."

"I heard that too, Corporal," Commented another soldier, "when I took the ammo state over to Company HQ. Captain Dullman was talking about it with the platoon commanders."

Nuemark adjusted his legs and slid another 7.92 mm round into an ammunition belt.

"We need tanks in this kind of terrain. We'll be here forever if we try to do it on foot. This ground is a defender's paradise."

Saltz looked up from his magazine-filling.

"The tanks are all going south-west, Martin. That's the main effort. All we're doing is keeping the flank secure for them. They haven't got enough shipping to bring more than a couple of panzer divisions over, so every armoured vehicle is being committed where the need is greatest. Look on the bright side; just a couple more days and the panzers will be into the industrial part of the country; then the Tommies will collapse in no time. Just think, in two days you'll be able to enjoy the delights of real English prostitutes in the back streets of York!"

There was a groan of longing from several of the men in the group, but Nuemark snorted in derision.

"Not if Bachman here is still alive, we won't. He'll be dragging us round all the Tommy churches to stare at the fucking architecture!"

The group erupted in laughter. Bachman, still cleaning the working parts of the MG34, turned red, but smiled at the corporal's jibe.

They were sitting around the yard in one of the high-walled British farms that had just been the subject of their discussion. The farm had fallen to them after a lengthy fight that morning, and had cost the company three dead and several more wounded. It had transpired that the enemy garrison had consisted of just half a dozen members of the uniformed Tommy militia, backed up by a couple of regular soldiers; all of them armed with nothing more than rifles. The platoon was tired and still slightly unnerved from the battle of the previous evening, where the Tommies had essentially committed suicide by setting the building they were defending on fire, once the Germans assault squad had gained entry. Saltz and a number of his men were still feeling the effects of the noxious smoke that had filled the building, not to mention the painful singe marks on their skin that had come from the falling timbers as they made their escape from the inferno.

After a dark and surprisingly peaceful night, the platoon, along with the rest of their battalion, had been moved onwards, heading sharply south-west and off their original axis of advance. The rumour was that their division had exploited too far over to the north during the struggle to form the beach-head. Apparently, the 7th Division didn't have enough room to manoeuvre, whilst a gap was opening between the 17th and 35th Divisions. Whatever the reason, they had marched over seven miles that morning before being pushed up as point-company, only to come under enemy fire shortly afterwards. Now they were taking some rest while the other companies in the battalion pushed through them on the new axis.

"It was a bit chilly last night, wasn't it?" Bachman commented to the squad at large.

"Fucking freezing is how I'd describe it!" Nuemark agreed. "When are our large-packs going to catch up? I could really do with my greatcoat tonight. Look at that sky; it's got some big fucking rain clouds in it."

Saltz leaned to one side and slid his re-filled magazine into a pouch.

"I suspect we'll be getting cold for another couple of nights, mate." Replied the squad sergeant. "There'll be nothing but ammunition and panzer fuel coming over those beaches at the moment. Remember the brief? We've got four days to finish this business and bring the Tommies to their knees; five at the most. Once we've done that, you'll be bedding down in a nice cosy English cottage, if you're not getting pissed on the local beer. They brew it strong here, you know?"

Nuemark looked beyond Saltz and frowned.

"Looks as though we might be getting closer to those pubs, then; here comes the boss."

Saltz looked around and saw Lieutenant Hagen striding towards them across the farm yard.

"Close in, men." He called to the collection of lounging soldiers as he made a direct line for Saltz.

Sensing that something was afoot, the members of the platoon climbed stiffly to their feet and shuffled in closer around Saltz's squad.

"Well done this morning, men." Hagen began. "Another pain-in-the-arse attack for just a handful of Tommies, I know, but you did a good job. The company commander is singing our praises."

Nuemark gave a cynical laugh.

"Do we get a prize then, Sir? Like some hot food perhaps?"

There was a smatter of tired laughter amongst the platoon.

"I'm afraid not, Corporal." Hagen smiled indulgently at the platoon joker. "We've got other things to worry about; we're on the move again."

This time the collective sound was of groaning.

"Are we making more room for the 7th Division then, Sir?" Asked Saltz.

Hagen pulled a face.

"Sort of. We are going south, but not just to give the 7th some elbow room. In fact, the news is entirely good. After chasing ghosts across these hills for the last twenty four hours, we've finally found a large bunch of Tommies who want a fight. There's a village a few miles from here, right on the flank of 8th Panzer and the 35th Division; a place called Fridaythorpe. There's at least a Tommy company holed up in the place and they've already shot up a recce call sign from the 35th. The village is placed within our new divisional boundary and the regiment has been tasked to go and take the place out. After that, we're keeping on south-west for a place called Pocklington, in order to guard the 8th Panzer's right flank."

This time there was no response from the assembly. Instead they just absorbed their platoon commander's words with serious, tired faces. Eventually, Saltz spoke.

"Well, at least we'll have a proper enemy to fight; instead of pissing around trying to clear old men out of farms. How long have we got before we move, Sir?"

Hagen glanced at his watch.

"Form up in twenty five minutes." The officer said. "Step off at quarter-past."

Saltz nodded his understanding.

"Okay fellas," He looked at the men from his own squad. "Get your weapons back together and take a quick shit if you need one. We've got a war to fight."

THE ARMOURED SCREEN – BY MIDDLETON-ON-THE-WOLDS SUNDAY 22ND SEPTEMBER 1940 – 1300 HOURS

"Back Higgins, back; quick as you can!"

Lieutenant Mark Longhurst of the Royal Middlesex Hussars began rotating his turret over the rear decks of the Vickers light tank, as the driver brought the vehicle around in a tight circle and began accelerating across the freshly turned furrows of the field. Somewhere off to the right, Longhurst caught the sharp report of a 2 Pounder gun on a cruiser tank and thanked his lucky stars that the two troops of medium tanks had caught up with them before the enemy thrust had gathered fresh momentum.

It had been a long morning. Having sent the collection of stragglers under command of the Guards sergeant on their way, Longhurst had taken his troop forward, keeping level with No.1 Troop on his right, edging carefully towards the village of Bainton. Having nudged into position without incident, he had spent another twenty minutes listening to the radio reports from other vehicles, who could see German armour pushing south from Driffield in the direction of Beverley. And then it had happened; so quickly they had almost been caught napping. The two German light tanks had poked their noses through the opposite hedgerow with little caution. They had paused just long enough to take in the terrain to their front before advancing further into the open field. That was when the first sounds of machine-gun fire had come to Longhurst's ears from the south. The gunfire was followed almost instantly by a contact report from No.1 Troop.

Without prompting, Longhurst's other two tanks had opened fire on the two enemy vehicles to their front. Just two hundred yards away, the German tanks had reacted aggressively, lurching forward in a sudden dash towards the British. In keeping with the squadron leader's direction, Longhurst had given the signal to withdraw to the troop's previous bound position. Over the air, he heard that No.1 Troop was conforming to their manoeuvre. In fact, it had surprised Longhurst how easy it was to lure the Germans on. He had expected them to be more cautious, and had anticipated having to exchange a considerable amount of fire with the enemy before they were drawn in.

But on they came; fast and aggressively. By the time Longhurst's troop was back at the next hedgerow, the two German tanks were already pushing through the undergrowth of the positions just abandoned by the British vehicles. Once again, the German vehicles had come straight on, their own machine-guns chattering loudly, and Longhurst had jumped involuntarily as a full burst of enemy bullets clanged off the hull of his tank. On came the Germans, as the last Vickers tank slipped behind cover. Longhurst ordered his driver to stop then put his eyes to the viewing aperture in the turret. He saw the clods of earth flying as the two German tanks came on, and then saw a third tank, and a fourth, push through the hedgerow behind them. And just at that point he heard the hammer-blow sound of the 2 Pounder anti-tank gun from the divisional anti-tank company as its crew sprang the ambush.

He had watched, horrified yet enthralled, as the first German tank literally stood on its nose from the impact of the powerful armour piercing shell. He watched the vehicle slam back down onto its tracks, and then suddenly erupt in flames; thick black smoke billowing out from underneath it, obscuring the hull and turret of the vehicle.

"Bingo!" Higgins had cheered excitedly.

What followed had been a classic anti-armour ambush. A second German light tank had brewed up moments later as the British dismounted 2 Pounder screen had ripped into the bold German advance guard.

Within a couple of minutes, it had finished. The German tanks had retired, leaving two burning vehicles in front of Longhurst's troop, and a third in front of No.1 Troop.

"Round one to us, Sir, eh?" Higgins, his driver had chuckled.

"They'll be back Higgins, don't you worry." Longhurst had cautioned the lance corporal, before ordering the troop to nudge forward again.

Indeed, he had been surprised yet again by the speed with which the Germans turned decision into action. Barely had his troop moved past the burning German vehicles, than the enemy tanks had reappeared. Only this time, there were more of them, and two of them were much bigger, heavier tanks.

On this occasion, his attempt to lure the Germans on had not been so much a deliberate act of tactical skill, as a desperate attempt to survive. There had been no less than five German tanks that time, and they had come on with all guns blazing; a heavy German shell missing Longhurst's vehicle by just yards. Pulling hurriedly back onto the 2 Pounder screen, the Vickers tanks had then broken left to guard the flank, as the enemy's light tanks began filtering round to try and roll up the British gun-line. Meanwhile, the heavy German tanks had paused in the far hedgerow, searching for targets. One of the German heavies paid the price for nosing too far through the hedgerow and had lost its track, a 2 Pounder shell slamming into the tank low down.

The 2 Pounders however, had come under pressure themselves. The gradually encroaching ring of German tanks had raked the British position with machine-gun fire and Longhurst had seen the gunners cowering behind the bullet catchers of their small compact guns. It was then, as Longhurst had wondered how he was going to extract both his own troop and the 2 Pounders from this predicament that salvation had arrived. At first the hollow boom had just sounded like the normal background noise of battle, but after a few moments Longhurst had realised that the ground under the vehicle was shaking, as if they were experiencing some kind of earth tremor. And then, as suddenly as they had come against them, the Germans had withdrawn out of sight once more.

It was the irrepressible Higgins who had pointed out the reason for the sudden break in the action.

"Christ almighty, Sir! Will you take a look at that?"

Perplexed by what he could see through the limited view of the observation slits, Longhurst had opened the hatch and cautiously peered out. And that was when he felt the intensity of the shock waves coming straight towards him from the direction of the enemy, and saw that the sky line to the east was literally black with smoke. The sounds of heavy explosions, perhaps a mile distant, were quite obvious now, as was the slightly more subdued drone of aircraft, passing somewhere overhead. Just in the nick of time, the RAF had arrived, and by the look of it, they were here in force. Whatever their intended target, it was getting hammered, and the enemy had gone to ground.

That had given their squadron the breathing space it needed, and on orders from the OC, the 2 Pounder screen had hooked up their guns to their carriers and moved back to the next stop-line. Once they had occupied their new positions, the British tank squadron itself had pulled back to join them. Thus had passed the first half of Longhurst's Sunday. They had been tasked to hold the German advance back from the edge of the Wolds until last light, and with around six and a half hours to go, the combined screen of armour and towed anti-tank guns was only four miles from its break-clean line.

And right now, Longhurst was wondering whether any of them would survive the day at all. The German thrust following the British air-raid had been instant, and powerful. It was clear that they were in no mood for delay, and that they were aiming to make up time. A short, but heavy artillery strike had descended upon the British stop-line; not a precision bombardment, but a creeping barrage. It had started five hundred yards to Longhurst's front and rolled inexorably towards him. The deluge of enemy shells had rumbled over them, knocking one of the dismounted 2 Pounders out of action nearby. Then, following the sharp artillery mission, the German armour had come forward once more, a full battalion of tanks this time. If the earlier action had been a close run thing, this action was on the verge of becoming a disaster. Trying to avoid becoming decisively engaged in the face of such overwhelming force was easier said than done.

The 2 Pounder crews had done a sterling job, courageously serving their guns in the face of the onslaught. One of the crews had paid the ultimate price however, when a German tank shell had smashed straight through the bullet catcher of their weapon, decapitating the loader and peppering the gun layer with shrapnel. Several bursts of machine-gun fire had quickly finished off the surviving crew, and so the 2 Pounder screen was down to just two fully crewed guns. The squadron leader had ordered the remaining guns back another bound before they were over run, and the light tanks were ordered to cover that withdrawal.

That had been the point where they had almost met their end. With the only weapons capable of penetrating German armour now moving rearwards, Longhurst and his men could do little to hold the Germans at bay. His three tanks had made a mad dash forwards, their .50 inch machine-guns hammering away in what was nothing more than a display of bravado. Corporal Brannigan's tank had been lost within seconds when a German shell had smashed into his tiny armoured vehicle, taking the turret clean off. In retaliation, Longhurst had laid his own heavy machine-gun onto the German vehicle responsible and opened fire. He had been rewarded by the sight of the enemy vehicle's track disintegrating, as the powerful .50 inch bullets cut through the links and track pads of the panzer. Despite that, the turret had turned menacingly in Longhurst's direction. He might have achieved a mobility kill, but the heavier German tank could still use its deadly main armament.

Taking evasive action, it was then that the young British officer had heard the squadron leader on the radio net, warning of the heavy friendly call signs coming across their front from the south. With a cry of relief, Longhurst had cheered as much as his crew, as the newly arrived cruiser tanks had burst through the hedgerow to his forward right and ploughed straight into the flank of the German armour. Those cruisers were now blasting away with vigour into the side armour of the enemy vehicles; the Germans struggling to respond to the new threat.

With his turret now fully to the rear, Longhurst could see several burning tanks, all of them German, except the smoking hulk of Corporal Brannigan's wrecked vehicle. He flicked open his hatch again to get a better orientation, and caught sight of the angular, sleek looking cruiser tanks dashing across the fields from right to left. There seemed to be a sudden lack of German vehicles, and he found himself breathing a huge sigh of relief as they broke clean from the enemy yet again.

"Hold on, Sir!"

Higgins' warning prompted Longhurst to grab onto the sides of the turret hatch, and a second later the vehicle lurched violently as it negotiated a small bank. As the vehicle dropped down over the small ridge, Longhurst glanced to his right and saw that one of the 2 Pounders was once again being set-up ready for action.

"That's us back with the 2 Pounders again, Sir." Higgins commented, spotting the gun crew himself.

"Roger that." Longhurst acknowledged. "Swing us back round quickly, and pull up by the gun for a moment. I want to speak to the gun controller."

Instantly, the driver brought the tank hard round and they rolled up to the 2 Pounder crew.

"How much ammunition have you got left?" Longhurst shouted down as the vehicle slid to a halt.

A corporal looked up from the back of the carrier that towed the gun.

"Twelve rounds and then we're out." He replied grimly.

The tank commander glanced at his watch. Ten past one in the afternoon. They really needed the Germans to hold off for a while.

Just at that point, the radio crackled into life again.

"Hello all stations, this is One. The heavy call signs will now hold the axis with the anti-tank assets. Our call sign complete will peel south-east and RV on the south side of the axis, in the first strip wood. One-Two, roger so far over?"

Longhurst pressed on the transmit button and smoke into his microphone.

"Roger, over."

A second later, the squadron leader's voice crackled over the airwaves again.

"Roger. We have an enemy column moving along the railway line in the low ground on our southern flank; several light tanks and some half-tracks. Looks like they're packed with infantry and they intend to roll us up from the south. One-One, roger so far."

Another voice came onto the air; Longhurst's opposite number in No.1 Troop.

"Roger. Confirm the 2 Pounders remain here with the heavy call signs, over?"

"Roger." The OC spoke again. "That is correct. One-One, remain in situ. One-Two, peel to your right now and meet me at One-One's location, out."

The message complete, Longhurst shouted down to the corporal again.

"We've got enemy tanks and infantry trying to outflank us on the right, down in the valley. We've been ordered to the south side of the road to ambush them. You're to stay here and work with the cruiser tanks."

The corporal stared up at him with serious eyes, an armour piercing shell cradled in his hands. He flicked a gaze eastwards towards the scene of their previous action, the smoke still billowing from the burning tank hulks.

"Are those cruisers coming back, then?" The corporal asked dubiously.

"Supposedly…" Longhurst shrugged, searching the distant fields himself in an attempt to spot the heavier British tanks.

He looked back at the NCO in charge of the anti-tank gun.

"Speak to the first tank commander who comes near you. Those cruisers have 2 Pounders as well. You might be able to scrounge some more ammo; I'm assuming it's the same stuff."

The corporal didn't reply.

"Good luck." Longhurst smiled weakly, feeling as if he was deserting the poor gunners.

The NCO just nodded at him, then went back to preparing his gun position.

"Okay, Higgins." Longhurst shouted down into the tank. "Let's get moving over the other side of the road, and keep your eyes peeled for the OC."

As the driver responded and the tank rumbled forward, Longhurst turned in the turret to beckon the other surviving vehicle from his troop. As he did so, he watched the anti-tank gunners settle into their positions on the weapon. Grim faced and silent, the four man crew peered through the viewing slots of the bullet catcher intently, staring into the distance, the anxiety etched taught on their features. As his vehicle rumbled onwards, leaving the 2 Pounder crew to their fate, Longhurst suddenly shuddered.

CHURCH HILL – HOLME-ON-SPALDING MOOR
SUNDAY 22ND SEPTEMBER 1345 HOURS

"It's called," Ripley fixed his audience with a hard look, "dispersed defence. Forget the concept of front-lines and all that stuff. The Germans don't fight that way, and neither shall we. In essence, each of those four farms will become self contained defensive islands. You'll each receive a 2 Pounder anti-tank gun, Boys rifles if you don't already have them, some engineers to help you with the wiring and mining, and a whole pile of ammunition."

The collection of officers and senior NCOs stared back at the lieutenant colonel with wide eyes.

"Make no mistake." He went on. "There will be no withdrawal from this position. We either hold out, or we die. The intention is to create chaos in the path of the German advance. Essentially, you need to barricade yourselves into those farms, ensure you can fight on a three hundred and sixty degree arc, and kill anything that looks German when it comes within range. As the Jerries try to by-pass you or outflank you, they'll run into another fortified location. It's a bit like the French cavalry riding around the British squares at Waterloo. And all the while, the troops in the main defensive position here on Church Hill, and at the rear, by the Hall, will be picking them off and providing you with mutual support."

The newly arrived garrison commander took a deep breath.

"It's going to be bloody, so prepare your men in advance. We need to hold out here for up to five days, in order to allow the GHQ Reserve to manoeuvre into a position to counter-attack. We *must* hold on at all costs. I have been promised that by this evening we will have a heavy machine-gun company from the Divisional Support Group. That equates to a couple of Vickers machine guns per position, so you'll have plenty of fire-power. The two remaining 2 Pounders and all the spare heavy machine guns will be here on this hill. In addition to all of that, we have radio contact with Div HQ, and we have the support of two batteries of 25 pounders which are situated at the other side of the Derwent. It's long range for them, but we can bring fire down as far forward as the main road between Pocklington and Market Weighton, so if anything comes near us, we can hammer it."

Ripley scanned the faces again.

"Gentlemen." His tone softened slightly. "This is going to be a tough show. Once the armoured screen has gone, we'll be in the front line. You can bet a year's wages that the Luftwaffe will be paying us a visit at some point, even though we've got pretty good air cover at the moment. There'll be mortars, artillery, and of course, tanks; lots of the buggers. So dig in deep, barricade strongly. Hit them hard, and hit them first."

He paused to allow his words to sink in.

Far off to the east, up on the Wolds, plumes of black smoke were rising. Every now and then, tiny black dots could be seen zipping amongst the tumble of grey clouds, but whether they were enemy or friendly, it was impossible to tell. The rumble of gunfire and bombs was a feint but constant reminder of the onslaught that was to come.

Sitting amongst the group of junior officers and senior NCOs, Jackson looked up at the garrison commander. He felt a flush of inspiration, and the rising excitement that came from the prospect of battle. The running was over at last. It was time to fight. Not only that, but it was time to fight under a man who knew his business. Like most of those who had fought the Germans on the continent, Ridley had obviously learned hard lessons, and now the results of those lessons were coming out. This was indeed a new kind of warfare and Jackson was warming to it. Ridley was everything that Jackson admired in an officer; business-like, efficient, polite where politeness was warranted, and professionally competent. Unusually for many officers, he seemed able to consider the broader strategy of the situation, whilst still maintaining an eye for essential detail.

Jackson's opinion was reinforced just a moment later.

"Now then, Quartermaster?" The colonel flicked his gaze to Major Tobin who was sitting to one side, looking sullen and worried. "These scratch platoons that are defending the farms need resourcing properly. The two Home Guard platoons will need every round of .30 inch ammunition we've got, as well as .303 inch for their Lewis Guns. The regulars from your echelon will be fine with their standard weaponry. Sergeant Jackson's platoon however, are to hand over any .30 inch weapons they have, and the ammunition with it. I want his group completely armed with .303 inch weaponry, although I'm happy for him to keep hold of his little Jerry arsenal. All of that needs sorting out straight after this; along with steel helmets, medical supplies, cold rations and water. You'll have plenty to keep you busy."

Tobin was nodding vigorously and fumbling for a note book.

"Yes, Sir; I'm already on that. It'll all be sorted."

Ripley gave him a suspicious look.

"Good." He commented dryly. "It will require your full attention."

The colonel turned away from the quartermaster and rattled out more instructions, allocating platoons to locations. He pointed towards the farm that sat furthest east, right by the side of the road that led up onto the Wolds.

"That place there," He said, "is the key to this position. If the enemy gets a clear run up that road, to this hill, then we're finished before we've even started. To that end, it must be held to the last extremity. Sergeant Jackson?"

"Here, Sir." The Coldstreamer piped up at the sound of his name.

Ripley fixed his eyes on Jackson and smiled.

"Your platoon will hold that position. Happy?"

Jackson nodded.

"Happy, Sir." He confirmed, his heartbeat suddenly picking up.

"All of these places will be given codenames for simplicity." Ripley warned them. "The main defensive position up here will be known as Waterloo. The farm to the south will be called Talavera. The farm to the rear will be Barossa, and the defensive position in the village will be called Corunna. The farm to the north will be known as Salamanca."

At this point, Ripley searched out Jackson once more, catching the sergeant's gaze.

"And for you Sergeant Jackson, down there, right at the forefront of the battle, we're going to call your farm 'Hougoumont'."

Jackson smiled, impressed by Ripley's knowledge of Coldstream history.

"That's a good name for a farm, Sir." The big sergeant replied.

"Yes, I thought you might like it." The colonel replied. "So make sure you don't lose the place, eh?"

HMS HOOD – 70 NAUTICAL MILES EAST OF ABERDEEN
SUNDAY 22ND SEPTEMBER 1940 – 1400 HOURS

She cut through the relatively calm waters at a stately twenty knots, all 46,000 tons of her. HMS Hood, widely regarded as the most powerful battleship afloat, was capable of shifting much faster, an impressive 29 knots at full tilt. Partly in concession to the older battleships however, and partly to allow the destroyers to keep up whilst still conducting anti-submarine sweeps to the rear of the fleet, she ploughed along at a steady pace in the centre of the ever swelling force of British ships.

On the bridge of the Hood, the Commander-in-Chief of the British Home Fleet, Admiral Sir Charles Forbes, looked to both port and starboard and felt a swell of pride; pride tinged with apprehension. This was the first time that the Royal Navy had sailed into battle with such a powerful fleet since

Jutland, and Forbes remembered that grim day all too well. He had never thought to see such carnage again, yet here he was, just three months from retirement, leading the Home Fleet on a collision course with the Nazi German Navy which he knew was waiting for them, expectantly, not far off the coast of Yorkshire. Allowing for the ships that were, by necessity, away on convoy duty or with Cunningham in the Mediterranean, they were all here; the carrier Furious, the battle-wagons like Valiant and Renown, the cruisers Newcastle, Berwick and Norfolk, amongst a whole range of destroyers. And once Rodney managed to join them, steaming rapidly from Rosythe after a successful breakout there, her three triple batteries of sixteen inch guns would really give them some extra punch.

It would take them another five hours, once they had changed course, to reach the enemy fleet. Prior to that, fingers crossed, there would be a concentrated air strike against the enemy's heavy ships, in order to distract them as the Home Fleet arrived from the north to give them a good pounding prior to nightfall. After that, the plan was to haul off to the west and RV with the survivors of the Tyne flotilla in the vicinity of Dogger Bank, before launching a final, crushing attack against the enemy fleet on the following day. At the same time, Furious, with a destroyer escort, would patrol the centre of the North Sea and attempt to locate and destroy the enemy transport convoys as they crossed from mainland Europe to the invasion beach-head.

All of this sounded simple of course, but he knew that they would be under attack all the way. The break-out from Scapa Flow had been carefully orchestrated in the knowledge that there was undoubtedly a whole string of U-Boats lurking in the vicinity. Thus far, they had succeeded in running down and sinking two of the enemy submarines, yet despite that, one of their destroyers had suffered serious damage from a torpedo strike and been forced to pull back on Scapa Flow before it sank. That was why it was essential to proceed at this measured pace; so that the fleet could stay together, properly covered on every side by the destroyer screen, and with reconnaissance aircraft flying constant missions ahead of them, to pinpoint and attack submarines that might be lying in wait on the surface.

And of course, there was the enemy air force. The Luftwaffe, he was sure, would make an appearance sooner or later. There was an RAF fighter squadron flying top-cover just off to the west, but he knew how stretched Fighter Command already was. That was the other reason for the concentrated formation. If the Luftwaffe arrived, they would be greeted by a devastating umbrella of anti aircraft fire. Forbes drew in a deep breath and turned all these facts over in his mind. Three months to retirement and faced with the biggest challenge of his lifetime! The weight of responsibility that had suddenly been placed on his shoulders was so huge he could hardly come to terms with it, for the outcome of this battle would decide the fate of Britain. Within less than forty eight hours, he knew, he would be either a national hero, or a reviled failure. The thought made him shiver, and he suddenly felt a pang of sympathy for his old commander, Admiral Jelicoe; the man who had fought the Germans at Jutland.

His thoughts were interrupted by the sound of a klaxon. Suddenly, the bridge was alive with activity, and the guns of the ship's anti-aircraft batteries were swinging to port. The ship's Captain came across to him and gave a cheerful smile.

"Signal from Furious, Sir. One of her aircraft has spotted a large enemy bomber formation approaching from the north-east; forty plus. She's launching her remaining fighters to intercept. Looks like we're about to have a busy afternoon!"

Forbes smiled back.

"Yes, quite so."

The Captain turned away, pulling off his cap and replacing it with a steel helmet. Forbes glanced down at his own helmet and wondered if it was the done thing for an Admiral of the Home Fleet to wear a helmet in the face of the enemy. Would the men think less of him for wearing one? Would they actually notice the fact in the thick of battle? And of course, what would happen in the event that Forbes became a casualty.

Taking another deep breath, the Commander-in-Chief of the British Home Fleet decided that with the fate of Britain at stake, he was in no position to be taking unnecessary risks, just for the sake of vanity. Setting his face and bracing himself for the impending engagement, he reached for his helmet.

CABINET WAR ROOMS – STOREY'S GATE, LONDON
SUNDAY 22ND SEPTEMBER 1940 HOURS – 1820 HOURS

The Prime Minister allowed himself one of his trademark rumbles, which could indicate anything from intense anger, to deep satisfaction. When he spoke however, his tone lay somewhere between those two emotions.

"So, all in all," He cast his gaze around the combined Chiefs of Staff, "a better day for us than yesterday? Still a situation of mortal peril, but allowing that we now have at least an even chance? From the Royal Navy and Royal Air Force perspective, would that be an accurate summary?"

Pound and Newall exchanged a look before murmuring their agreement.

"That is the case, Prime Minister." Pound replied. "The Home Fleet is now in open water. We are now trying to concentrate them in order to deliver a killer blow to the German fleet. The newly reorganised Furious group should be able to have an effect almost instantly on any German sea lanes, given that their main surface units are already fully engaged with our battle squadrons off Whitby. The survivors of the Tyne flotilla have now joined the battle squadrons, whilst the survivors of the Harwich Flotilla will continue to operate independently to the south of the invasion area, assuming that the news about the Scheer is correct."

Churchill nodded sagely.

"If the Scheer is indeed nothing more than a floating wreck, and the other capital ships of the enemy fleet are already engaged, then we may at last be able to open up their southern flank with a small but fast flotilla."

He pouted briefly.

"A shame about the Erebus, though. Her sacrifice may well have turned the tables for us however."

Pound nodded in agreement.

"She did us a great service before she went down. To inflict so much damage to a modern ship like the Scheer was no mean achievement for such an old ship, manned by a crew that was still in training."

Churchill was nodding vigorously now, his imagination captured by the valiant stand of the Erebus in the unequal battle with the German pocket battleship.

"And so your forecast for the next twenty four hours is what, first Sea Lord?"

Pound considered his words carefully.

"We have not achieved enough speed in order to engage the enemy fleet decisively this evening. There is barely two hours of light left, and the battle squadrons have only just sighted the enemy ships. That of course, is due to the constant air attacks they have suffered for the last few hours. Therefore, I am hoping that this evening we can at least cause some damage to the enemy's capital ships, after which the battle squadrons will haul off to the east, ready to return en-mass at first light. The enemy has no alternative but to stand and fight. If they don't, then they abandon their beach-head to its fate. If they do stand, then we have them pinned between our fleet and the coast. The only way they could possibly get away with anything less than total destruction, is if they make exceptional use of their submarines, and continue with huge air attacks against our ships."

Churchill immediately switched his gaze to Newall.

"But we have now taken precautions to minimise that risk, have we not Chief Air?"

"Yes, Sir." Newall answered in his clipped tone. "Our wide ranging fighter sweeps with the 'Big Wings' from 12 Group have seriously hampered German fighter operations over our coastline today, and that has allowed 13 Group to have some success against the enemy bomber formations coming from Norway, Denmark and Germany. I am hoping that the Army found their ability to cope vastly improved during the course of today?" He threw a questioning glance at Dill and Brooke.

Dill answered for them both.

"It has been a better day today." He admitted. "The main formations allocated to the GHQ Line are now in position and preparing it for defence. The bridges over the Derwent south of Elvington will have been blown by midnight once the armoured screen has withdrawn, and all defensive boxes have now been established along the Derwent and to its east. Furthermore, we believe that we now have the measure of the enemy's intentions."

Churchill looked at the CIGS from under knitted brows.

"We do?"

"Yes, Sir." Dill continued. "Initially, from first light until around midday, we believed that the main enemy thrust was going for Hull, via Beverley. However, since then, the enemy pressure in this area has reduced. We still believe that the Hull Garrison will find itself facing at least two enemy infantry divisions in due course, but it does appear that all the enemy's armour and hard hitting assets are now being channelled south-west, towards Selby and Goole, via the Holme-on-Spalding Moor box. The armoured screen covering that axis has had a hard day, but as we speak, they should be disengaging and pulling back with all speed to the line of the Derwent. We expect the Holme box to be in contact with the enemy before midnight. The German front is starting to develop a 'finger' if you like, and that finger is indeed pointing straight towards the industrial Midlands and the South Yorkshire coal-field."

Churchill shifted in agitation and gave another deep rumble. This time, his eyes fell on Brooke.

"And are you ready for the coming battle, General Brooke? Are you all set to take the full force of the enemy? More importantly, when do *we* attack? I would like to be able to give the American President some reassurance that we are not about to roll over and die. He is having real problems with the 'isolationist' lobby over there, you know? I want to give him some dead Germans to talk about on Capitol Hill."

Brooke, in his usual manner, took Churchill's question in silence, and spent a moment or two considering his answer, holding the Prime Minister's gaze without flinching.

"The Seventh Corps has arrived at York and is moving into its concentration area. The Fourth Corps too, is rapidly assembling north of York. The Guards Armoured Division is still assembling at Harrogate and is awaiting its skeleton headquarters, which I have stripped out of Southern Command in its entirety. We could attempt an attack now, but, like the attempt at Arras back in May, it would be a hastily planned and half-cocked effort. Against such competent soldiers as the Germans, we would be risking our only chance of success."

Churchill gave the C in C Home Forces a belligerent glare.

"Who will command the Guards Armoured Division?"

"Montgomery," Brooke answered with a wry smile, "He will be in situ at York by midday tomorrow… with me."

The Prime Minister raised an eyebrow.

"Montgomery?" He grunted. "He's the fellow who upset the Chaplain General in France, is he not?"

"He is indeed, Sir." Brooke remained calm. "But of all the senior officers I worked with in France, he was the one most able to handle chaotic situations and maintain order amongst his command. I trust him entirely."

Churchill didn't answer for a moment, taking the time to suck on his smouldering cigar before he did so.

"A good choice General Brooke; I agree with your selection. And I assume you are going forward to command the counter-attack forces personally?"

Brooke nodded.

As he was prone to do, Churchill changed tack without warning, thumping his hand down on the table.

"So, back to my original question; when do we attack?"

Brooke took his time to answer, and when he spoke, his voice was matter of fact; perfectly calm.

"Not before last light tomorrow; and only once I have the German main thrust where I want it. In short, I will attack once I have allowed the German spearhead to cross the River Ouse. That is when I will deliver the killer blow and give you a decisive victory to wave in both Roosevelt's and Hitler's faces."

There was utter silence in the room. Churchill's eyes were bulging. Every staff officer around the table, less Dill, had turned to look at the Commander in Chief Home Forces as if he had gone mad.

"The River Ouse," Churchill spoke slowly, frowning as he did so, "is the GHQ Line. It is our last stand position."

Brooke allowed a brief pause before replying.
"It is indeed, Prime Minister." He said quietly. "You are quite correct."

'HOUGOUMONT' FARM – BY HOLME-ON-SPALDING MOOR SUNDAY 22ND SEPTEMBER 1940 – 1830 HOURS

"Come on, dig faster." Jackson chivvied the crew of the 2 Pounder. "Hear those explosions? The Jerries will be on our doorstep before long. I want this position ready to go in the next thirty minutes."

The crew of the 2 Pounder, all Regular Army men including a sergeant, made no reply. Instead they bent their backs to the task and increased the speed with which they were filling the draws of the sideboard with earth. They had learned within minutes of arrival at the position that the tall Guards sergeant was not to be argued with, and so they continued to work liked Trojans in order to complete their reinforced gun pit at the northern corner of the farmyard within the specified time-frame. If Jackson's severe features and sharp tongue were not enough to keep them hard at it, the ever increasing sound of battle was. They knew that the 2nd Armoured Division was bleeding itself dry, attempting to hold back the enemy tanks until dusk, in order to allow the Holme-on-Spalding Moor box to be as well prepared for the coming onslaught as possible.

Jackson left the 2 Pounder crew to their work and stalked off towards where the farmyard came closest to the main road. As he neared the far corner of the yard, he saw that the two RAF men he had assigned to this position had almost completed their improvised bunker. He ducked down to gaze underneath the door which had been placed horizontally on pillars of brick and reinforced with packed earth.

"Well done you two." He barked at the dark figures within. "This is looking quite good."

"Cheers Sarge…I mean, Sergeant." Bevan called from the shadowy interior.

"Once you've stacked that ammo, get this roof camouflaged," Jackson instructed the pair of airmen, "and then give a hand with the barricades at the gate."

"No dramas, Sergeant." Bevan acknowledged cheerfully.

The tall Sergeant walked on, towards where the sappers were putting the finishing touches to the string of obstacles on the main road. That young airman, Bevan, was really up for it, he reflected; unlike his sullen mate, Scotton. Still, this was what war did to people. It brought out the true character of the individual. He was still thinking on this when he arrived at the main road, via the farm's wide gateway.

"Nearly done, Sergeant." He was greeted by the full corporal who commanded the half-dozen sappers. The NCO was busily engaged in windlassing the last few strands of barbed wire that had been erected as an obstacle curtain on either side of the main road. The road block itself was a mix of everyday items requisitioned from the farm. An overturned tractor, drained of its fuel, was surrounded by earth-filled oil drums and boxes, which had been erected behind three huge craters in the tarmac. It wasn't ideal, but it would slow up a tank and make the route impassable to wheeled vehicles.

"Are the mines in place?" Jackson asked, surveying the belt of defences.

"Oh, aye." The corporal replied enthusiastically. "They're all in position at the far side of the wire there, on both sides of the road. So, no more movement forward of the wire, please?"

Jackson nodded.

"I'll pass the word. Have you got any mines left?"

The engineer corporal thought for a moment.

"I think we might have four or five perhaps? Do you want me to put some further across towards the gateway there?"

"No." Jackson turned and pointed to the far side of the farm. "About two hundred yards in front of the 2 Pounder position, there's a thick hedgerow that can be approached from that small wood beyond, quite easily. I reckon that if the Jerries try to get round our flank, that's where they might try to launch from; maybe even bring a tank up to knock out the 2 Pounder. Do you reckon you can lay some kind of trap behind that hedgerow to catch them out?"

The corporal from the Royal Engineers tied off the last bit of wire and glanced down at his watch.

"We've still got about an hour of daylight." He said, sucking his cheeks in thoughtfully. "I'll go do that straight away for you, Sergeant; then I'll get the boys into the buildings to start reinforcing the fire positions."

Jackson smiled, impressed by the sapper NCO's positive attitude and industrious nature.

"Good man..." He said, then broke off as the sound of an approaching vehicle came to him.

Along with the engineers, he looked up in alarm, thinking for one horrible moment that the Germans had broken through the armoured screen already.

"It's alright, it's one of ours." Called Dutton, who was acting as the forward sentry by the barricade.

Gingerly, his blisters still hurting him, the young Home Guardsman climbed up onto the barricade and began flagging the vehicle down. Jackson saw that it was a strange looking armoured car, the name of which eluded him. The drab-green vehicle slowed to a stop, just before it reached the craters, and the vehicle commander hailed them from across the rubble.

"Got a straggler here for you. Best give him a rifle and take him on board. We'll be pulling back shortly."

As the officer shouted to them over the noise of the engine, Jackson saw a man climbing down from the vehicle. He was a big man, much like Jackson, and was dressed in khaki battledress, adorned with two chevrons.

"How's it going up there, Sir?" Jackson enquired.

"It's bloody awful!" The armoured car commander shouted back. "Thank God it's nearly dark. We've lost over half the squadron and all the 2 Pounders in our group. We'll have to pull off soon; then they'll be all yours. I hope you're ready for them."

Jackson grimaced at the casualty state of the armoured screen.

"We're almost there, Sir, thank you. Best of luck.

"And you lot." The officer waved in acknowledgement. "You'll need it!"

With that, the vehicle engaged its reverse gear and began executing a turn. The man who had dismounted was being guided across the obstacle by Dutton, who warned him where not to walk, lest he wanted to activate a land-mine.

Jackson went to meet the man, and as the new arrival descended the obstacle, Jackson saw that the man was wearing a grim look on his features.

"Where are you from, son?" The sergeant asked.

The corporal gave Jackson an appraising look, before speaking in a local accent.

"B Company, 3rd East Yorkshires. We were the garrison at RAF Driffield. I'm the only survivor."

Jackson shook his head.

"Not quite lad, we've got a couple of your blokes here. You can go see them in a moment. Where's your rifle?"

The corporal bridled for a moment, but managed to remain calm.

"It was taken off me by the Jerries when I was captured." He replied, his voice sullen.

"You were a prisoner, were you?" Jackson raised an eyebrow in mild surprise. "How did you get away?"

The young man considered his answer for a moment, noting that he was being watched by the whole group at the obstacle.

"I ran off when our column was strafed by an RAF fighter. Everyone dived for cover and I legged it over the fields. I circled round Driffield, dodging the world's supply of Jerries, then kept on running until I bumped into our tankies back there."

Jackson was impressed.

"That's some risk you took, young fellah."

The look on the corporal's face grew darker.

"Yeah…well, there was no way I was staying around when I saw what happened to the Home Guard boys."

Jackson frowned.

"What do you mean?"

The corporal glanced around him and saw that Dutton was wearing the Home Guard uniform. He continued his story, his voice bubbling with barely suppressed anger.

"They marched us out of Driffield at first light this morning, guarded by some Jerry parachutists. Then this column of trucks pulls up; full of those SS bastards."

"SS?" Jackson's own face hardened.

"Aye." The corporal continued. "They separated the Home Guard boys from us regulars; about a dozen or so. Then, they sent us on with the parachutists. As we marched on, they gunned down the Home Guard boys in cold blood by the side of the road; just murdered 'em!"

There was silence amongst the soldiers by the barricade.

"I won't forget the bastard who done it, though." The corporal was almost spitting with rage. "If I ever see the fucker again, I'll give him what for!"

Jackson glanced at Dutton and saw that the young man had gone pale.

"Right," Jackson said, wanting to get things moving again, "we'll make sure that all of that gets reported up. In the meantime, corporal, we'll go and get you a weapon so you can start paying those Jerries back straight away. Welcome to Holme-on-Spalding Moor; you just became a part of the garrison."

S +2
THE THIRD DAY

BY REIGHTON VILLAGE – EAST YORKSHIRE
MONDAY 23RD SEPTEMBER 1940 – 0300 HOURS

"It's a big set-up. What do you reckon they're up to, Tommy?"

Harper glanced through the gloom at the man who commanded his auxiliary unit. McGinn was peering intently through the darkness, towards the large farm complex tucked against the side of the railway.

"That's a headquarters." He said, confidently. "A big one. At least a division I'd say; possibly a corps."

Harper frowned at his companion.

"Do you reckon? A big HQ like that stuck out here in a farm? Surely they'd be tucked up in the town at Filey or Brid; maybe even Hunmanby?"

McGinn turned towards Harper and murmured quietly into his ear.

"That's exactly what you *would* expect; which is precisely why they aren't doing it. Think about it George; what would be an easier target for the RAF? A big fat juicy town, sat right on the coast by a prominent headland, or a non-descript farmhouse a few miles inland?"

Harper did think about it and instantly saw the sense.

"Aye, suppose your right there." He allowed. "But maybe it's just a storage area or something. We don't *know* it's a headquarters for sure."

"Oh, yes we do." McGinn smiled through the darkness. "Look over there, right at the top of the farmhouse, just by the chimney stack."

Harper followed McGinn's direction and strained his eyes to study the roof.

"Use your peripheral vision." McGinn advised him. "Cock your head to one side and look out your eye-corner. Can you see anything unusual on the roof?"

Harper did as instructed and scanned the rooftop.

"Hmm." He pulled a face. "It looks like there's two or three long sticks poking out of the roof. My eyes are going all funny."

McGinn shook his head.

"Nothing wrong with your eyes, George. Those 'sticks' are there all right; only they're not sticks, they're antennas."

"Antennas?" Harper looked at his friend sharply.

"Yes, old boy; antennas. The Huns have got their wireless sets up there in the attic and they've removed the tiles so they can pop their antennas out. It gives them a better range, see?"

Harper looked at his companion in surprise. He had learned more about the old tinker over the last two days, than during the many years of their acquaintance thus far.

"Tommy..." Harper ventured. "I'm not being funny mate, but you seem to know an awful lot about these things for a tinker. And you've suddenly developed a funny accent."

McGinn was silent for a moment, before replying in a voice that was tinged with sadness.

"Yes...strange how it all comes back to you when the situation requires."

Harper frowned.

"Funny how *what* comes back to you?"

Again there was a protracted silence, but eventually, McGinn spoke again.

"I haven't always been a tinker, you know? I was in the last war too."

Harper didn't reply. He was fascinated by the sudden change in McGinn's voice. The strange twang that he had noticed over the last couple of days was now the dominant part of the man's accent. It was a well-spoken accent; some might say upper class.

"I was in the infantry; the 4th Battalion the Mercian Volunteers. I went all the way through..."

McGinn paused again, a slight hesitance in his voice, so Harper prompted him to continue, his curiosity fully aroused now.

"What did you do, mate? Signaller?"

"No..." McGinn's voice was barely a whisper now. "I was the Commanding Officer."

Harper almost fell backwards in surprise.

"What?" Was all he could manage to say.

"I was the Commanding Officer. I fought the battalion right through from 1914 until the battle of Cambrai, all without a scratch. I got wounded at Cambrai. Not too seriously mind you, so they ended up putting me on the divisional staff for the rest of the war while I mended properly."

He flashed a sudden smile at Harper.

"So, you see George, I really do know a thing or two about headquarters."

For long moments, Harper was speechless. Eventually, he found his voice.

"But...how did you...I mean, how..."

"How did I end up as a tramp?" McGinn finished the question for him. "Quite simple really. I went back home after the war and took over the family business. Tried to get over the misery of the war by drinking a lot, doing lots of parties and such like…a lot of gambling too. Didn't take care of the family business. By 1924 my wife had seen the writing on the wall and walked out, taking the children with her. Didn't take long for the business to go under then…So I went out for a walk one day, and I never went back."

Harper was completely stunned. He just sat there watching McGinn, who looked almost relieved that he had told Harper his story. They sat in an uncomfortable silence for long moments. Eventually, McGinn forced a sad smile.

"Out of everybody in the country, I'm probably the only person glad of this war. At last I get to have another chance at something I'm good at."

He clapped Harper lightly on the arm.

"Come on, old boy; let's go back to the others. We need to make a plan. Tomorrow night we're going to blow this place to kingdom come."

'HOUGOUMONT' FARM – HOLME-ON-SPALDING MOOR
MONDAY 23RD SEPTEMBER 1940 – 0450 HOURS

"Stop firing! Stop firing!" Jackson roared at the top of his voice across the darkened farmyard.

Eventually, the sound of gunfire petered out, and the last shots faded into echoes on the still night air. He grabbed hold of Corporal Downey, the straggler from the East Yorkshires, by the arm.

"Corporal D, get over there and calm that bloody lot down, mate. Stay with them until I'm sure it's all over."

"Righto, Sarge." Downey replied.

The corporal, now equipped with rifle and steel helmet once more, and with several bandoliers of ammunition slung over his shoulders, doubled off into the night towards the heavy machine-gun position. Jackson winced at the use of the word 'Sarge' but let it go. There were other things to worry about at the moment.

He ran across to where the firing had first started, by the rifle pits covering the road block. As he went, he resolved to speak to the commander of the section from the divisional machine-gun battalion. They were a welcome asset, but obviously inexperienced. He reckoned they must have gone through at least a couple of hundred rounds during the brief alarm, and he suspected that they were probably diring blindly into the night. He reached the small bunker in the corner of the farmyard that housed two of the RAF personnel and knelt down at the rear, peering inside.

"What's going on?" He demanded.

A white blob of a face peered out.

"Not really sure, Sergeant." Came Bevan's voice. "We heard people talking over by the road block, then the sentry over to our right shouted a challenge. Next thing we knew, there was gunfire all over the place. I think it was a Jerry attack."

The silence that now hung over the farm and surrounding fields suggested otherwise.

"More likely a patrol, scouting ahead before daylight." Jackson suggested the most likely explanation.

It would make sense. The armoured screen had done their job well and held the Germans back on the edge of the Wolds until night had fallen. The defenders of the farm had listened to the surviving British tanks circumnavigating their box in the darkness, as a large RAF bombing raid had taken place towards Driffield, a few miles to the east. Presumably, thought Jackson, the raid had taken place to allow the British armour the opportunity to break clean. Whatever the reasons, the hours following the withdrawal of the 2nd Armoured Division units had been extremely quiet; eerily so. By the time it had reached midnight, a strange calm had descended on this part of Yorkshire, as if both sides had, by mutual agreement, taken a breather. Jackson had taken the opportunity to get some much needed sleep, taking it in turns with Corporal Downey to monitor the sentries throughout the night. He'd managed to get three and a half hours; his first sleep in two days. It was barely enough to scratch the surface of his exhaustion, but better than nothing, and woken suddenly by the flurry of gunfire, Jackson was fully alert once more.

He moved to the bunker by the gate which covered the road block. On arrival he found Dutton, armed with the Boys Rifle, along with one of the civilians from Burton Fleming, carrying a Lee Enfield.

"What happened?" Jackson snapped.

"Jerries, Sergeant." Dutton replied in an unusually calm voice. "No mistake. We heard their accents plain as day. They were at the far side of the road block. One of them climbed onto the top, so we took a couple of shots. He disappeared and then there was some shouting and lots of gunfire. Then the Vickers from the far corner of the farm opened up, right across our front."

Jackson nodded, instantly understanding what was going on.

"What was the explosion?"

"We think it was a Jerry grenade. It wasn't one of the mines. It exploded on this side of the barricade, right in the centre of the road."

Jackson sucked in his cheeks thoughtfully.

"I reckon you're right, Dutton lad. They probably used it to give them some time to make a break for it. Well done, fellahs. Glad to see you're both alert."

He took a deep breath.

"Problem is though, all that bloody machine-gun fire and shouting over there has given the game away. The Jerries'll know this is a major position now. I think we can stand by for a slightly noisier visit before long as a result."

Jackson glanced eastwards at the dark sky. The shifting, patchy cloud of the day before was thickening as dawn approached, threatening rain. Dawn might be delayed slightly this morning, and perhaps that might delay the first German thrust. One thing was for sure however; the Germans were coming. It was only a matter of how long it would take them, but they were coming alright. He looked back down at the two men in the bunker.

"I'll pass the word around. We're going to stand-to early, as of now. Everyone awake and ready to go. It won't be long now lads. It won't be long at all."

HMS HOOD – IN THE VICINITY OF DOGGER BANK
MONDAY 23RD SEPTEMBER 1940 – 0600 HOURS

Sir Charles Forbes had not expected this. Having fought all the previous afternoon to ward off the continuous air attacks, he had finally made contact with the enemy's capital ships about an hour before last light. By his reckoning, he had been faced by the Hipper, Gneisnau, Scharnhorst, Nurnberg and Koln, backed by around five destroyers. His own force of ten destroyers, five cruisers, four battleships and an aircraft carrier should have been an easy match, but the Germans had been waiting and their gunnery had been very impressive. More than that however, they were being far from defensive. The Germans had attacked the British as soon as they had sighted them, making full steam for the Home Fleet. Having finally beaten off the last enemy aircraft, the British ships had been forced to deploy into line of battle rapidly. Then the first U-Boat had struck. One of the British destroyers, perhaps getting careless, had been hit from the rear port side by two torpedoes and sunk.

With night falling, the German fleet closing rapidly, and U-Boats harassing the Home Fleet's rear, Forbes had pulled off to the east as planned, heading for the rendezvous with the survivors of the Tyne flotilla. It hadn't been the simple job he had anticipated however, for the German surface units had followed him. It defied belief, but the inferior enemy force had pursued him in the dark, engaging the Home Fleet using radar controlled gunnery throughout the night. Now as daylight broke, the Germans were there, ready for a full scale encounter, and the British ships had been saved the job of closing on the Yorkshire coast. As the British capital ships heeled over into line of battle, the first salvoes from the German heavies came whistling towards them, ploughing into the dark, murky waters of the North Sea and sending up huge spouts of water.

"Doesn't look as though they're going to take it lying down, Sir, eh?" The Captain of the Hood grinned at the Commander in Chief.

"It certainly doesn't." Forbes agreed grimly.

His mind was racing. He had a number of options now. He could keep his whole force here, less the carrier group which was already detached, and engage the enemy until he had achieved a decisive victory over their biggest surface units, or he could split his force. He could keep his own battle squadrons here with a destroyer escort, whilst the remaining destroyers, probably the entire 20th Flotilla, went hell for leather towards the coast to attack the German landing force.

Destroying the German landing force would end their invasion almost instantly. With their sea lane cut, they would have to rely on air supply, and he doubted if even the Germans could keep that up for long. But having said that, to detach so many destroyers at this point, with a huge submarine threat on the periphery of the fleet, was also a massive risk. What if one or two of his big ships were sunk by torpedoes? The dual between the big ships would then be much more even. What if the U-Boats were able to concentrate in such force that he lost his entire fleet to torpedoes, rather than to enemy gunnery? He stared out of the bridge at the grey sea and the grey sky. At least the weather helped. Perhaps the Luftwaffe would not be too much of a problem today? He already had three ships damaged by bombs from yesterday's raids. Could the British Army hang on for one more day? If they could, then he was sure that with maximum resources, he could utterly destroy the enemy's major surface units before nightfall. Once they were taken care of, he could deal with the landing fleet and beach-head at his leisure.

Forbes made his decision. This would not be another Jutland. Today, he would force an outcome, and that outcome would be a victory for the Royal Navy. The destroyers would stay to guard his flanks. He turned to his Flag Lieutenant.

"Pass this message to the fleet. Battle Squadrons are to engage with enemy capital ships as already directed. 20th Flotilla is to conduct anti-submarine sweeps on all flanks throughout and act as anti-aircraft screen. The Tyne group is to take station to the north of the Battle Squadrons and be prepared to exploit success as directed. They are to guard against enemy destroyer sorties in addition."

The Flag Officer jotted down the notes quickly, before glancing back up at his commander.

"Is that all, Sir?" He asked.

Forbes paused for barely a heartbeat.

"Tell the Battle Squadrons to open fire."

SEALION HEADQUARTERS – THE HAGUE, HOLLAND
MONDAY 23RD SEPTEMBER 1940 – 0800 HOURS

"Gentlemen, the situation is critical." Keitel threw his harsh glare around the room. "Speak to your staff; this is no time for excuses or weakness. The operation is now at the point of make or break. We have the entire Home Fleet at large in the middle of the German Sea, thick cloud over most of England, large formations of enemy fighters sweeping well out to sea and interdicting our air corridor, a sea state which has worsened overnight, and two major rivers to cross before we reach our primary objective. Raeder?"

He looked towards the Grand Admiral.

"The orders have been given?"

"They have." Raeder confirmed, grimly. "The landing force, everything that is still necessary, has closed on the coast as far as possible. All spare shipping is on its way back to European ports as we speak. The entire U-Boat force is now concentrating in the German Sea. They will provide a fall back net behind our surface units and on the flanks of the British fleet. We need to be careful about where we deploy them, as the enemy is currently steaming off Dogger Bank, which is treacherous for all ships, but especially for submarines. That said, our major surface units have managed to keep the enemy's main force at bay over night and I believe we may be able to continue that well into daylight."

"It must be all day." Keitel cut in. "We need another twenty four hours, which means that your big ships need to keep the Royal Navy away from the coast until last light as a minimum. If the ships need to be sacrificed, then so be it."

Raeder's face paled. Keitel saw it and pressed on.

"The Fuhrer has been quite clear. This is all or nothing. We must break England in the next forty-eight hours, or else never. Is the Scheer still afloat."

"Beached." Grunted Raeder. "Just off Bridlington. But she still has two gun turrets working. And the Emden and Schleisen are still with the landing force."

"Good." Keitel snapped. "Then we are where we are. Speak to Lutjens and Donitz. Make them aware of the requirements. At least another twenty four hours. We fight to the last ship."

Raeder stared bleakly at the head of the German High Command. 'We', he thought?

The Grand Admiral had no further chance to discuss the unfolding drama, as Keitel, reverting to the traditional Prussian autocratic manner, was already switching to Kesselring.

"The 22nd are complete in England"

"They are." Kesselring nodded. "Though we lost over twenty aircraft to enemy night-fighters. On a positive note, we managed to get a squadron of Stukas into Lisset just before first light, with eleven of the twelve arriving safely and fully bombed up. There'll be a squadron of 110s coming in there as we speak. They will be under direct command of Busch for Army co-operation."

"Is that all we can get?" Von Brauchitsch asked.

"For the time being." Kesselring nodded curtly. "Everything else is being launched to cover the Kreigsmarine and the beach-head. Besides, the cloud won't allow us to achieve much over England today. It may frustrate us yet over the German Sea."

"Then so be it." Keitel intervened. "You know what to do, Kesselring. I know your crews are tired, but there must be one last effort. I have spoken to Goering. The other Air Fleets have been placed under your full command now. You do not need to *ask* their commanders anymore; you *order* them. Take what you need. Give the Kreigsmarine everything you can spare. The beach-head must hold out for at least another twenty four hours."

Kesselring gave another curt nod, his arms folded tightly across his chest.

"Understood." He said.

Finally, Keitel turned to Von Brauchitsch.

"You have spoken to the Army Commander?"

"I have." The Chief of the Army Staff replied. "Busch is clear what is needed. The push is already underway. The 1st Mountain Division and the 7th Infantry, reinforced by the Parachute Division, are aware that there is to be no more offensive action in their sector. The 17th are being moved south-west in order to protect the flank of the main effort whilst making a feint towards

York. The 12th and the 22nd have been told to seal off Hull and then go firm. The 8th Panzer and the Totenkopf are going full ahead for the Derwent and the Ouse, with the 35th coming up behind them to deal with any pockets of resistance."

Keitel appeared satisfied with the report.

"Good. And do we think that we have encountered the enemy's main force yet?"

Von Brauchitsch pulled a face.

"Hard to say. We've come up against a very strong infantry based defence in the north which explains why the Scarborough operation came to grief. The only Tommy armour we've come across is on our own main effort, and although it held us up a bit yesterday, it was completely incapable of stopping our own armoured forces. It looks as though the Tommies really did leave everything behind at Dunkirk. I am confident that we can beat their Army hands down, provided we can keep the RAF off our backs. Their bombers have been systematically knocking the hell out of Driffield and all the feeder routes into it for the last twenty four hours."

"Tell Busch to live with it." Keitel snapped, his voice taking on a ruthless tone. "And tell him that I want him over the Derwent by last-light; over the Ouse by dawn. Then, once he's over, I want every tank and half-track he's got smashing the enemy coal fields to pieces. Forget capturing things intact; we just need to make sure that the continuation of the war will be impossible for the British, so destroy everything. Understood?"

Brauchitsch took a deep breath.

"I'll tell Busch."

THE FRIDAYTHORPE BOX
MONDAY 23RD SEPTEMBER 1940 – 0900 HOURS

"Come on! Keep fucking going!"

Saltz was exhausted by the crawling, yet still found the breath to snarl over his shoulder at the members of his squad, who were following him along the hedgerow.

It was chaos. Complete and utter, deadly, bloody chaos. The Second Battalion had been cut up badly as they attacked down-slope towards the eastern end of the village. The wide, freshly turned over fields had allowed the Tommies excellent lines of fire, and the hedgerows and ditches that bordered those fields had been cleverly prepared by their attackers with mines, barbed wire and booby traps of all kinds. It had taken them nearly two and a half hours just to get onto the forward edge of the village, and still they hadn't captured any of the buildings. So it was that the reserve battalion, with Saltz's company leading, had been brought up and pushed into the assault.

The problem was, he and his men were still some distance from their final assault position, which lay a hundred metres away at the far side of the field.

"Keep moving!" Saltz yelled over his shoulder breathlessly, as he forced his aching limbs to propel his body forward, keeping as low to the ground as he could.

He came across a dead soldier from the Second Battalion lying right in his path, a large red hole in the man's chest and a gob of blood spread over his mouth and chin. Ignoring the corpse, he crawled over it as several shots cracked past him. Having negotiated the body, he found two separate machine-gun teams blocking his way. They were laid in the prone position, blasting away, the muzzles of their weapons poking through the thick hawthorn bushes towards the village. The No.2s of each gun were sprawled flat next to their gunners, busily replenishing the links of the ammunition belts. Saltz crawled around their legs and forced himself on, his body protesting at the torturous pace.

Something ripped through the hedge to his left and struck the soil just in front of him, sending a spurt of heavy brown soil into his eyes.

"Ah, fuck!" Saltz rubbed furiously at his eyes, with the back of his hand.

"Are you alright, Sergeant?" Came the voice of the man behind him.

"I'm fine." Saltz snapped, blinking the last grains of earth from his eyes as he started forward again, pulling himself along with his elbows.

There were two officers holding a heated conversation a little way ahead.

"So where's the fucking fire mission, then?" One was screaming at the other.

"It'll be coming down soon!" Protested the other. "We sent a runner!"

Saltz crawled past the two men.

"Who the fuck are you?" Demanded one of the officers, who Saltz suddenly realised was the commanding officer of the Second Battalion.

"First Battalion, Sir, lead assault company." Saltz answered, not bothering to stop.

"Thank fuck for that!" The major called out as Saltz crawled by. "Turn left at the next hedgerow and follow it down; that's the best way into the village."

Saltz already knew that. He kept on crawling.

There was a sudden 'whoosh' over Saltz's head and he looked left, freezing in position and pressing himself closer to the earth.

Crump! Crump! Crump!

Three mortar bombs landed on the forward edge of the village, making the ground shudder beneath the sergeant.

"That's our mortars coming in now!" He heard the other officer shouting.

Instantly, Saltz clambered to his knees and looked back at his squad.

"On your feet! Those are our mortars! Let's get moving while we can!"

He forced himself up, and with a sense of relief, began running at a low crouch along the hedgerow. He glanced back and saw the rest of his squad, and indeed the whole platoon following suit.

He came across a line of riflemen, lining the hedge. Some of them were engaging the enemy; one of them was dead, whilst another was trying to bandage his shattered hand. Saltz leapt over the prone soldiers from the Second Battalion and ran on towards the corner of the field, followed by his men. As he arrived at the corner, he found a large Tommy shell scrape, reinforced with logs and sandbags. The position had been cleverly dug on the junction of four hedgerows, thus giving its occupants an all round view and field of fire. As he jumped across the hole and turned towards the village, he saw two khaki clad bodies in the bottom of the pit, whilst another German machine-gun team was using the captured trench for their own benefit. He caught a glimpse of hundreds of expended cartridge cases glistening in the bottom of the body strewn pit, just before he landed at the other side and ran on.

"Second Battalion coming through!" He announced to the soldiers in the area, in order to ensure they didn't shoot his ankles away by mistake as he made the forward passage of lines.

Around him, the weapons fell silent as first Saltz, then the rest of his squad and platoon, pounded past, all of them breathing like asthmatics.

Crump! Crump! Crump!

Three more rounds from their own mortars landed on the village, and Saltz registered the hissing sound of a piece of red hot shrapnel whizzing past his ear.

"Keep going! Nearly there!" He roared above the cacophony.

His legs felt like they were on fire from the exertion of the last half an hour, but the big sergeant forced himself on. A bullet cracked overhead, but he ducked lower and ran even faster.

At last, he reached the point where the hedge met a garden fence and he slowed as he approached it. The house beyond the garden fence had just been hit by a mortar bomb and smoke was billowing from the shattered windows. Trying desperately to slow his breathing, Saltz eased his pace to a fast walk, still keeping low as he came to the fence. Suddenly, the wooden panels of the fence erupted in a shower of splinters as several bullets smashed straight through it, one of them missing him by inches.

"Take cover!" He yelled, throwing himself to one side and peering desperately through the fence for the enemy.

Another bullet hit the fence just above his head, making him wince at the noise, but then he saw a small skein of wispy grey smoke and spotted the enemy position beyond the cottage, concealed amongst a thick flower bed.

A rifleman flopped down next to him.

"Enemy in the flower bed…straight in front…" Saltz could barely issue the target indication he was breathing that heavily. "Put some fire down…I'll grenade him…then we go for him."

The neighbouring soldier fired instantly then worked the bolt of his rifle to recock it.

"Spread out!" Saltz yelled as he sensed, rather than saw, the rest of his squad crowding in behind him.

Crack!

"Ugh!" One of Saltz'z riflemen collapsed back into the hedge as a powerful .303 inch round went straight through his shoulder.

"Fucking spread out! Keep low!" Saltz was roaring as he yanked the lanyard on his stick grenade.

He rose to his knees and hurled the explosive device with every ounce of energy he could muster, before dropping back to the earth again quickly.

"Grenade!"

Crump! The explosion sent clods of earth and flowers sailing into the air and a small cloud of dark grey smoke rolled across the lawn of the cottage.

"Gooooo!"

Saltz was already on his feet, bringing up his machine-pistol. It was mid morning at the Fridaythorpe Box, and the killing had begun.

'HOUGOUMONT' FARM – HOLME-ON-SPALDING MOOR MONDAY 23RD SEPTEMBER 1940 – 1030 HOURS

"You alright, bonny lad?"

Jackson looked on impassively as the old farmer and his wife attempted to tie the strip of table-cloth around Scotton's calf. The surly RAF airman had taken several small mortar fragments during the bombardment that morning, just before the first enemy attack. Unable to do anything about it, the airman had fought on at the bunker covering the road block until he had collapsed through loss of blood and shock. He was conscious again now, but looked decidedly pale.

"I think I'll be alright, Sergeant. I need a cup of tea or something, then I'll go back and join Austin."

Jackson nodded. The poor chap was still out of it.

"Good lad. I'll get one of the boys to give you a hand to walk back over."

With that, he turned and left the farmhouse kitchen and doubled quickly across the yard to the barn. Entering the building, he climbed the ladders to the hay loft where he found Martlesham scanning the distant hedgerows with his binoculars. Next to him, an airman was filling one of the Lewis Gun drums with fresh ammunition.

"Anything yet, Tom?"

"Nothing too close to us, Sergeant." The young Home Guardsman replied, keeping his eyes glued to the binoculars. "But there's lots of vehicle movement up on the high ground."

Jackson cleared his throat and spat a pile of mucus into the straw.

"That'll be their tanks. That first lot was just their recce group; like the one we brassed up in Burton Fleming. We're really in for a proper fight before long."

The airman looked up at Jackson with a worried expression, and the sergeant caught the look.

"So, more Jerries for us to kill, eh?" The Coldstreamer said, brightly.

The airman managed a weak smile. Jackson noticed that the young lad's hands were trembling as he placed each new round into the magazine.

"A bit chilly this morning, too." The airman commented in a shaky voice. "You can tell autumn's nearly here."

The airman was trying to put a brave face on, but wasn't being very successful. Jackson actually felt for the poor bloke. The lad hadn't been trained for this kind of business.

"Aye," Jackson replied gently, "but look on the bright side…it's nearly Christmas."

The airman's face dropped, and Jackson decided to give it up as a bad job.

"Keep your eyes peeled, Tom." He clapped the Home Guardsman on the shoulder as he stood up. "Shout out when you see anything coming towards us."

As he stood, Jackson caught a brief glimpse of the aftermath of the attack through the hole in the roof. The enemy armoured car beyond the road block was still burning, as was the light tank at the far side of the field, both victims of the 2 Pounder. The disabled half-track sat further back along the road, its engine block punctured and smashed to pieces by the heavy slug from the Boys Rifle. He could also make out several bodies strewn across the tarmac. The sight gave him a deep sense of satisfaction, but he knew that the worst was yet to come. Descending the ladder, he left the barn and went around to the front of the farm, where his platoon's forward positions were located.

As he crossed the rough, earthen pad of the farmyard, he saw Corporal Downey moving between the various bunkers and shell scrapes, checking the ammunition state of his section.

"All well?" Jackson asked as he closed the gap.

Downey looked over.

"Not too bad, Sarge; could have been worse. One of the RAF boys has taken some shrapnel to his back, but it's not bad. We've patched him up and he can still fire his rifle."

Jackson absorbed the information quietly, looking over to where the 2 Pounder crew were hastily reinforcing their position. Downey caught the look and grinned. It was the first time Jackson had seen the man smile since his arrival.

"They took a near miss from that Jerry tank." He chuckled. "It shook 'em up good and proper!"

"I bet it did; and there'll be more of that to come. They did well though; a tank and an armoured car. Those 2 Pounders are proper little killers, aren't they?"

Downey didn't have a chance to reply. Their conversation was interrupted by a shout of alarm from across the yard.

"Aircraft! Don't know who's but they're coming our way!"

The two NCOs turned towards where one of the civilians from Burton Fleming was waving vaguely into the distance. They followed the indication and quickly picked up the black dots in the leaden sky. The drone of their engines was increasing steadily in volume, and as they broke through a patch of cloud, Jackson felt a prickle of alarm.

"They've got to be Jerries." He said, almost to himself.

"Typical." Downey grunted. "Where's our bloody air force gone then?"

Jackson was squinting behind his spectacles now, trying to focus on the dark blobs that were on course to pass them by, several miles to the south.

"They're Stukas!" One of the RAF men from Downey's section called out suddenly.

"Don't be daft, Ronnie!" Said another. "Stukas aint got the range to get this far."

Just at that point, the leading aircraft tipped its wings, banked steeply to starboard, and began to drop at a rapid rate towards the cluster of farms around the hill and village of Holme-on-Spalding Moor. The other aircraft in the formation followed suit, peeling off in a well practiced fashion. As they did so, the pitch of their engines suddenly changed to a high pitched whine.

"Fuck me, they *are* Stukas!" Downey swore.

Jackson suddenly found the memories of the beach at Dunkirk flooding back into his mind. He felt a rising sense of panic as he watched the leading aircraft, with its crooked shaped wings, loom larger and larger as it dived down towards them.

"Take cover!" He screamed at the top of his voice and began running for the gun pit that held the 2 Pounder. A second later, just as the Coldstream sergeant landed heavily on top of the gun-layer, the first German dive-bomber released its deadly cargo…

FLAMINGO 'B' FOR BERTIE – OVER NORTHAMPTONSHIRE MONDAY 23RD SEPTEMBER 1940 – 1045 HOURS

"You'll have the 20th and 24th Guards Brigades, along with the 21st and 23rd Army Tank Brigades, reinforced by the divisional artillery from the 35th and some engineers from the Ripon Garrison. This division is going to be used for a short period only, so your staff is nothing more than a skeleton crew. There will be no time for excessive staff work, so you'll have to run this like you did the withdrawal through Belgium and France; simple orders and tight control of your brigades."

Brooke looked across the aircraft's cabin at Major General Bernard Montgomery, to gauge his response. Montgomery nodded in approval.

"They're all good units, from what I hear." He replied in his clipped voice. "What do you want me to do with them?"

Brooke pointed at the small scale map of Yorkshire.

"Full orders will be given at 1800 hours tonight, at York Racecourse, once I've had a chance to speak with Adam. Essentially, the plan is this…"

He quickly outlined his general strategic intent, mentioning that for the purposes of this operation, all defensive forces under Adam were to be designated as the 1st Army, whilst the two and a half corps being mustered under Brooke for the counter-attack were to be referred to as the 2nd Army. He explained how Montgomery would have the key role of flank protection for the Fourth and Seventh Corps, whilst at the same time steam-rollering into the second echelon of the German spearhead and establishing a pivot-point for the rest of the Army. Finally, he explained the probable timing of the counter-attack.

Of all those privy to Brooke's plan thus far, Montgomery was the only one who had not made some facial expression that betrayed surprise or shock. Instead, he simply continued to stare intently at the map in Brooke's hands.

"I understand that it's something of a risk, allowing them to get across the Ouse…" Brooke said, hoping to prompt his old subordinate into a response.

Montgomery flicked his gaze up to meet the eyes of his Commander in Chief.

"It's a good plan." He said in his tight, clipped voice. "I would do something similar if it were my decision. War is full of risks, and I think that on this occasion we have no option but to take them. I like this plan. I only have one question…"

Brooke returned Montgomery's gaze.

"Which is?"

"What if the Germans break through the pocket, or if they somehow get across the Ouse south of Selby?"

Brooke took a deep breath.

"There is nothing for them to break through. Instead of a line, we have started to construct a deeply layered defence all the way back to Nottingham. Once they get across this river, they will find themselves slogging away endlessly, as if they were wading through mud. I would like to keep them all tied up neatly here in this pocket, but if they don't take the bait, well…we'll attack anyway."

Montgomery smiled.

"When do we start?"

"Not before 0600 hours tomorrow; probably later, depending on how quickly the Germans push."

"And we're confident that they'll reach the Ouse by last light today?"

Brooke nodded.

"Unless they run out of fuel, they'll probably be knocking on our door by the time we begin orders this evening."

Montgomery's smile broadened.

"Best keep the orders short then, Sir, eh?"

'HOUGOUMONT' FARM – HOLME-ON-SPALDING MOOR
MONDAY 23RD SEPTEMBER 1940 – 1115 HOURS

"Get back to your positions! Stop gawping! Get back and cover your bloody arcs!"

Jackson ran across the farmyard, waving his arm franticly and snarling at the collection of men who were staring, half dazed, toward the collapsed barn. At another time he could have sympathised with them, for he understood the mind-numbing terror of a Stuka attack, but right now all he could think of was what was about to happen. He had no idea how the Germans had managed to get Stukas in the skies over Yorkshire, but he knew that something would be following them on the ground, for that was how the German war machine worked.

"That was just the preparatory bombardment! The Jerries will be coming soon; now get back into your fucking shell scrapes!"

He grabbed the arm of one the civilians from Burton Fleming, span him around and pushed him back towards his position.

"You two, get back in your bunker!" Jackson bawled at the two airmen known as Bevan and Scottton.

The latter pointed at the barn.

"There are people in there!" He protested.

Jackson bared his teeth at him.

"I know that, and I'll sort it out. You concentrate on the bloody division of panzers that's about to come across those fields! Now, get back into your bunker and observe your arcs…*move*!"

Still glancing over their shoulders at the partially collapsed building, the two airmen reluctantly turned back towards their fighting position. Jackson noted that Scotton was limping badly on his injured leg.

The sound of Downey's voice came to Jackson's ears. The corporal was engaged in the same activity as the sergeant; swearing and cursing at the shocked defenders, trying to snap them out of their dazed state in preparation for the inevitable attack.

"Corporal 'D'?" Jackson hollered through the drifting smoke that was slowly dissipating on the still air.

"Yeah? Over here!"

Jackson looked around and caught sight of the NCO coming towards him from the direction of the 2 Pounder pit.

"Any casualties over there?" Jackson demanded.

"No; everyone's okay, although that last bomb scared the shit out of them. It was a *bit* fucking close, mind you!"

"There'll be worse to come soon." Jackson snorted, looking around the farmyard. "You go round the front of the position and make sure these bastards are all in their trenches and watching their arcs. You can bet your arse the Jerries will be coming at us again soon. I'm going to get a couple of blokes to check through the barn and see if Martlesham and that RAF gadgie are still in one piece."

"I'm on it." Downey snapped an obedient reply and rushed off.

Jackson turned and ran around the huge pile of rubble and timber that had once been a part of the barn.

"Tom?" He yelled up at the surviving part of the building. "Tom? Martlesham? Are you up there?"

"Here, Sergeant!" A feint, yet recognisable voice drifted down to him from the ruined loft.

"Are you aright, Tom?" Jackson shouted back up.

"Yeah..., I'm okay, but that RAF fellah has disappeared. He went through the floor when that side of the building collapsed. I think he's under that pile of bricks."

A white face appeared in the dark shadows of the exposed loft, and Jackson felt a sigh of relief as he looked up and saw that the young Home Guardsman was still in one piece.

The dive-bombing attack had been a huge shock to the defenders. The German aircraft had pounced down on the British positions at Holme-on-Spalding Moor like birds of prey, swooping in for the kill. Jackson, having been on the receiving end of Stukas before, was feeling remarkably lucky. Their position had only taken one direct hit, and that appeared to have done nothing more than bring down one end of the great barn. He reckoned that the poor airman was probably dead; buried underneath several tons of rubble. Despite that, he found it hard to believe that they hadn't incurred more casualties. From beyond the farm, up on the hill, he could see over half a dozen drifting clouds of grey smoke, where the main position had been heavily pounded by the enemy aircraft.

"We'll have to look for him later." Jackson hollered up to the young man. "Get back into your position and shout out if you spot the Jerries moving."

The young Home Guard private gave the sergeant a thumbs-up and disappeared back into the gloom. Seeing him disappear, Jackson moved beyond the rubble and ran past the farm-house at the far side of the inner courtyard. Arriving at the rear of the farm, he found more shocked and disoriented defenders.

"Get back into your positions. Everything's okay. That was just a near miss; there's no serious damage. Keep your eyes peeled on your arcs, because the Jerries will be on their way again soon. Stand-by for them to try an outflanking manoeuvre."

Slowly, their eyes still displaying the shock from the sudden bombing attack, the men defending the rear of the farm began returning to their stand-to positions.

Bishop appeared at Jackson's left shoulder.

"Bloody hell, lad! I haven't been as close to a bang as big as that for over twenty years!"

Jackson clapped the middle-aged farmer on the shoulder reassuringly.

"You know the score, Bob; they always sound worse than they are. Now then, I need you to get the boys back into position and keep them on their toes. The Jerries will be back again soon. They don't hang about, you know?"

"Aye." Bishop nodded, grimly. "I'll do that. Bloody Huns! Just you wait till they show their faces in front of me!"

He had barely spoken when the sound of machine-gun fire erupted from the front of the farm.

"That's ours." Bishop observed, looking sharply towards the east. "It's the Lewis Gun."

"Stand-to!" Jackson bellowed instantly. "Stand-to!"

He loped off across the courtyard, bawling the order to stand-to as he went.

Jackson was level with the still smouldering ruin of the great barn when the first mortar bomb landed about fifty yards away to his left, just beyond the northern extremity of the farm. He dropped flat amongst the rubble, skinning his knees and elbows on jagged brickwork as he did so. He kept his head low until he was sure the last of the shrapnel had zipped by then looked up, yelling toward the loft.

"Tom? Tom? What is it? Tom?"

For a moment, there was no reply, but then the young man's voice came to him as another mortar bomb landed some twenty yards in front of the 2 Pounder position.

"Sergeant Jackson! The Jerries are going around us!"

"What?"

"The Jerries are going around us!" The voice came again. "There are two groups of them coming around on the left. There's a column of tanks going wide to the north, about six hundred yards or more, and another column of armoured cars and half-tracks about three hundred yards out. They're curling round…, no, wait…they're turning towards us!"

Crump! Crump!

A pair of mortar bombs landed behind Jackson somewhere and he pushed himself down into the brickwork.

"Tom, what are they doing?" Jackson yelled up again, once the blast had passed over him.

This time, Martlesham's voice was panic stricken when he replied.

"They're coming straight for us, Sergeant! Straight towards the 2 Pounder; towards the corner of the farmyard, by the haystack. They're fanning out; there's loads of 'em!"

"How many, Tom? What are they?"

"Infantry and armour; tanks as well. They're fanning out…"

The young man's voice faltered and a second later, a long burst of fire from the Lewis Gun erupted from the loft, where the young man was watching the approaching enemy.

"Jesus fucking wept!" Jackson cursed.

Forcing himself up, he sprinted across the open ground towards the 2 Pounder pit. More German mortar rounds hit the ground behind him and several pieces of shrapnel whizzed past his shoulder as he pounded at full pelt across the muddy yard towards the heavily camouflaged and protected anti-tank gun.

"Corporal Downey!" He bellowed. "Enemy tanks and infantry coming from half left, straight towards the 2 Pounder! Stand-by; here we fucking go!"

He leapt over the large wooden posts that had been laid flat around the lip of the 2 Pounder pit and landed with a grunt amongst the crew.

"What's going on, mate?" The pale-faced sergeant commanding the anti-tank gun asked.

Jackson regained his balance and pushed the rim of his helmet up so he could see the gun commander's face.

"You've got Jerry tanks coming straight for you, right through that hedgerow there!" He pointed across the field to where the sounds of multiple engines were now unmistakable. "Infantry too. Here we go, boys. Here we fucking go!"

"Tank action!" The gun layer screamed suddenly, and began moving the gun using the course-scale traverse gear.

Jackson and the gun commander looked across the field and spotted the vehicle straight away. A German tank, dark and menacing, was just visible beyond the hedgerow at the far side of the ploughed field. A machine-gun in the vehicle's turret crackled into life and a stream of bullets passed high above their heads and slammed into the remains of the damaged barn.

Instantly, the crew went into action.

"We've already got one up the spout." The commander reminded the gun-layer. "Tell us when you're on."

"Lock!" Yelled the layer, and the No.2 snapped the traverse gear locking lever shut.

"Nearly there, stand-by…" Murmured the layer as he pressed his eye to the sight and turned the fine scale drums.

"Stand-by…"

Boom!

"What the fuck..?"

The German vehicle erupted in a gout of flame and black smoke, even without the 2 Pounder firing.

"Who did that?" Demanded the gun commander, perplexed.

Something suddenly occurred to Jackson.

"The mines!" He said. "The engineers had some mines left over. I asked them to lay some along that hedgerow. They must have run over one."

"Bonus!" Grunted the gun-layer, and then straight afterwards screamed out the prescribed orders as another enemy vehicle poked its nose through the hedgerow.

"Tank-action! Unlock!"

Jackson tapped the gun commander on the arm.

"I'll leave you to it; good shooting. I'll be in that nearest shell scrape."

With that, the Coldstream sergeant scrambled out of the gun pit and ran at a crouch towards the nearby rifle-pit.

He dropped into the hole and found an elderly Home Guardsman and one of the privates from the East Yorkshires. As he did so, the first cracks of rifle fire sounded from the positions covering the road block.

"Here we go, lads!" Jackson announced as he dropped down next to the two men and slid his rifle over the front lip of the shell scrape.

"Take your time and make every shot count; this is going to be a big one!"

Across the field, the distinctive shapes of German halftracks burst through the hedgerow, machine-guns clattering away from above the grey-coloured cabs. The enemy bullets began cracking overhead in a constant, deafening stream, and Jackson had to use every ounce of air in his lungs to make himself heard to his two companions.

"Go for the gunners and commanders…Fire!"

Jackson was the first to shoot.

He dropped his foresight blade onto the thin, indistinct shape of the man behind the machine-gun in one of the enemy half-tracks and squeezed the trigger. Allowing only a fraction of a second for the follow through, Jackson didn't wait to see if he'd hit his target. Instead, he worked the bolt of his rifle feverishly and brought the sight back up to his eye again, searching for another target. The other two men were firing now, and the loud bark of their rifles was sending painful shockwaves into Jackson's left ear. He ignored the pain and searched for a target. The half-track in front of him was suddenly hit from the side by something. Parts of track and running gear span off into the air. The vehicle swerved to one side, and men began jumping from the vehicle into the heavy brown furrows of the field. Panzer grenadiers.

The Coldstream sergeant picked a man in field grey carrying a machine-pistol, and began tracking him with his foresight. He saw the man waving and shouting at his comrades.

"Commander." Jackson whispered to himself, allowing his foresight to drift a hair's breadth in front of the running man.

He squeezed the trigger and the Lee-Enfield lurched violently in his hands. Jackson held his breath for a moment as he followed through the shot once more, and saw the enemy soldier suddenly drop to the ground. With a grunt of satisfaction, Jackson worked the bolt again.

There was a loud roar to his left as the 2 Pounder fired, and Jackson caught the whiff of the shell fumes as the breech clinked open a split second later.

"Reload!" He heard the gun commander screaming franticly.

Suddenly, something slammed into the dirt, right in front of the shell scrape, sending heavy brown soil and stones into the faces of the three British defenders. It was followed by another impact, and another. Jackson pressed himself as flat as he could, ramming the bolt of his rifle closed as he did so. He looked around and saw that his two companions were unhurt, so he came back up and continued to fire.

"Half-track, over there!" The private from the East Yorkshires shouted.

Jackson looked half-right and saw that one of the enemy half-tracks was speeding towards the farm and would crash through the hedge beside them in just a few seconds. Before Jackson could react, the private was on his feet and fumbling with a grenade.

"Keep low!" Jackson warned him.

The young man ignored him and yanked the pin free from the grenade, before lobbing it towards the vehicle and dropping quickly back into the pit.

Jackson watched the small round object land in the thick plough, several yards in front of the vehicle. A second later it exploded; too early. As the clods of earth and smoke settled, the enemy vehicle roared over the seat of the explosion and smashed into the hedgerow to their right.

Jackson clambered to his knees and swung his rifle round to face the enemy vehicle. Beside him, the young private was already pulling the pin from another grenade. The vehicle had skidded to a halt just after ramming its way through the farm's boundary hedge. Instantly, a group of half a dozen grey clad figures popped up from within. The British private lobbed his second grenade. One of the Germans saw the movement and swung his machine-pistol round, squeezing the trigger and letting rip with a long burst. The British private took several rounds straight through his chest and toppled backwards over the Home Guardsman. His throw had been good however, and the deadly green egg-shaped grenade landed inside the rear compartment of the open topped vehicle with a loud clang.

The Germans let out a collective cry of alarm and began leaping over the side of the half-track. A split second later, the grenade detonated with a loud metallic boom. Bodies and bits of equipment flew through the air above Jackson as the vehicle erupted in a thick black cloud of smoke. Dropping sideways into the shell scrape, Jackson cursed out loud as the ear splitting sound of the explosion assailed his ear drums. Still cursing, he yanked the captured German parachutist's pistol out of his gas-mask satchel and popped his head above the lip of the shell-scrape again. A hail of machine-gun fire slapped into the smouldering vehicle and the surrounding earth, as Martlesham raked the enemy with fire from his vantage point in the barn. Above the crack of bullets Jackson heard a grunt, and a second later, a German soldier collapsed onto his knees, appearing suddenly on the edge of the smoke cloud that billowed from the ruined half-track.

The German, clasping a rifle with one hand and holding his shoulder with the other, looked up and spotted Jackson in the shell scrape. For a brief instant, their eyes met, and then Jackson fired the pistol and shot the man through the chest. The enemy soldier flipped backwards without a sound and lay still. Jackson pushed himself up and clambered out of the shell-scrape. He staggered across to the burning vehicle and walked around it, carefully, watching out for any surviving enemy. He found only one; a man who was wounded in both shoulders, sitting in the driver's cab. Jackson saw the man fidgeting through the observation panel at the front of the vehicle. Not hesitating in the slightest, the sergeant poked his pistol through the observation slit and fired three times. He saw the driver slump sideways.

Machine-gun bullets cracked through the air around Jackson, and another mortar round landed over to his right near the road block. He looked around and saw that the battle was fully joined. The crew of the 2 Pounder were working their gun furiously, and the Home Guardsman in the shell scrape was already firing out into the field once more. Jackson suddenly realised that this was the big one; this was the fight of his life. There was nothing left to do but fight on, as hard as he could, until it was over, one way or the other. Taking a deep breath, and ignoring the pain in his ears, the sergeant shoved the pistol back into his haversack and took hold of his rifle with both hands again. He ducked down and jumped back into the shell scrape, next to the old man from the Home Guard. There were still more Germans to kill.

HMS HOOD – 70 NAUTICAL MILES OFF THE YORKSHIRE COAST MONDAY 23RD SEPTEMBER 1940 – 1400 HOURS

"Message from Rear-Admiral Destroyers, Sir." The officer approached Forbes on the bridge of the British Flagship.

"What is it?" Forbes asked, taking his eyes away from his binoculars.

"He reports three ASDIC contacts, Sir. He believes the enemy has got a pack of U-Boats trying to come in behind us. He's requesting permission to break off and deal with them."

Forbes' reply was instant, his mind working at full tilt, his senses sharpened by the pressure of battle.

"Detach the Tyne Flotilla. The others will maintain the close screen behind us and on the flanks while we pursue the enemy ships."

"Aye, aye, Sir." Acknowledged the Lieutenant-Commander.

"Admiral Forbes, Sir?"

The C in C Home Fleet turned to face the First Lieutenant of the Hood.

"We've got two large ships at red one sixty, Sir; range 24,000 yards. Looks like what's left of the Humber Squadron. We're checking now, Sir."

Forbes nodded curtly.

"Good. Get that identification immediately. Two more cruisers will do us very nicely I think."

The First Lieutenant knuckled his cap and turned away, moving straight for the Petty Officer of Signals.

Forbes removed his helmet for a moment and rubbed a hand over his face. It had been a long night and even longer morning. Despite that, thus far, the results had been satisfactory, if not conclusive. The enemy had lost two of their five big ships. The Koln and the Gneisnau had been sunk during the lengthy engagement just after dawn, with the Koln literally exploding after an entire broadside from the Renown. The Hipper too, was burning and badly damaged, but along with the Scharnhorst and Nurnberg, it was running for the coast, its speed apparently unaffected. It hadn't been a one-sided fight however, for HMS Berwick was also a burning wreck and had been left to fend for herself with just one destroyer to cover her back. The Home Fleet had also lost two destroyers; one to a U-Boat and another to an air attack that had caught them unawares during the height of the sea battle.

That had been the tricky moment; trying to engage the enemy's biggest and most deadly ships, whilst fending off several waves of Junkers 88 at the same time. The cloud was definitely helping them, forcing the enemy to come in much lower than they would normally, and Forbes suspected that there were more enemy bombers out there who simply couldn't find them under the blanket of cloud. Even so, it had been an uncomfortable morning. It had been shortly after the last bomber had disappeared when the Renown had finished the Koln, and that had been the point when the Germans had turned and run. Forbes now sensed that the climax of the battle wasn't far away. If indeed, the two ships approaching from the south were the survivors of the Humber Squadron, then victory was becoming increasingly likely this day; provided of course, that the Luftwaffe stayed away.

"Enemy's turning, Sir!"

The announcement from the Hood's Captain, brought Forbes back to the present.

"Turning?" Forbes looked up.

"Aye, Sir; Scharnhorst and Nurnberg turning broadside to fire, along with escorts. Hipper looks as though it's keeping on for the coast."

"The buggers are trying to delay us, aren't they?" Forbes frowned. "I wouldn't be surprised if we had another visit from the Luftwaffe before long. And there's no doubt they're trying to hem us in with their U-Boats. We need to keep that destroyer screen in tight."

"Admiral Forbes, Sir? Identification confirmed; those two cruisers are ours. It's the Humber Squadron alright, Sir!"

Forbes glanced at the First Lieutenant.

"Very well, signal them to move onto the southern flank of the German ships and engage them when in range. We'll try and take them from two sides at once."

He turned back to the Captain.

"Signal to the rest of the fleet; squadrons back into line and engage immediately. Let's finish this thing, shall we?"

PART FOUR

DECISION

S +3
EARLY MORNING

'HOUGOUMONT' FARM – HOLME-ON-SPALDING MOOR
TUESDAY 24TH SEPTEMBER 1940 – 0330 HOURS

"Watch and shoot!" Jackson hollered across the darkened farmyard. The barn was burning now, and a scorched Martlesham was beside him in the shell scrape, still manning the Lewis Gun. The farm-house, completely burnt out, was still smouldering. The smell of smoke clung to the cold morning air and the fleeting fog that it created gave the remains of the farm a surreal appearance. The latest bombardment had finished abruptly just a minute ago, and somewhere in the darkness Jackson knew, there were enemy.

They had survived the previous morning's attack by the vehicle-borne panzer grenadiers and tanks by the skin of their teeth. The 2 Pounder had done great work, slicing through the German tanks that had poked their noses through the distant hedgerows. In addition, the 2 Pounders that were sited on Church Hill and in the neighbouring farms had provided a deadly cross-fire that had torn into the German attack from several directions. The Vickers machine-guns, similarly deployed, had cut through the groups of panzer grenadiers as they had tried to storm the farm, and finally, the artillery barrage that had been brought down, presumably by Colonel Ripley, had broken up the combined armoured and infantry attack in the fields directly east of 'Hougoumont'.

It had been achieved at some cost however. Five of the farm's defenders, including the airman buried under the rubble, had been killed during the fierce battle, and another four had been wounded, one seriously. Almost a third of the farm's defenders were out of action, and Jackson had dreaded the next onslaught. That onslaught however, had never come. Instead, 'Hougoumont', along with Church Hill and the other defended farms, had been subjected to a constant barrage. Initially, the barrage had consisted of a fresh deluge of mortar bombs, but after a while they had given way to much bigger, and much more accurate artillery shells.

It was during those long hours of bombardment that the runner had arrived from Church Hill, with a message from Colonel Ripley. The Germans it seemed, were by-passing them. Long columns of tanks were moving north and south of the Holme Box, the northern column swinging back onto the Selby road, whilst the southern column was following the Goole road. The

German intentions were reinforced when the Stukas returned in the afternoon. Instead of diving down upon the little defensive box at Holme, the ugly little dive-bombers had flown on past them, cruising westwards towards the Derwent and the Ouse.

In short, the Holme Box was well and truly surrounded. At first, the enemy bombardment had appeared to be a distraction, deliberately instigated whilst the by-passing manoeuvre was executed, but as the day wore on, it became apparent that the bombardment was just the start of a long artillery preparation. When the great barn took another direct hit, and the farmhouse took three more, Jackson had ordered the buildings to be evacuated. The defenders now skulked inside their shell scrapes and bunkers, taking what shelter they could, and awaited the Germans' next move. And it seemed that their next move was about to begin.

Jackson had gone beyond exhaustion now. His senses were numb and he was functioning from habit only. After the long hours of shelling, the sudden quiet was ominous. It wasn't truly silent, for somewhere behind the defenders, well to the west, the sound of fierce battle continued. Despite that, in the dark arena of Holme-on-Spalding Moor, everything was still and tense. Then it happened.

The streams of tracer arced lazily towards them before seeming to pick up speed, dropping onto the defenders with an ear-splitting series of cracks. Orange tracer rounds bounced off the ruins of the farm and the courtyard, hurtling off in all directions. Jackson peered into the darkness, towards where the fire was coming from. It was intense and constant. He reckoned there was a platoon's worth of machine-guns lining the distant hedge at the far side of the field. He strained his eyes to see if he could pick out the dark shapes of enemy soldiers advancing, but other than the squat black silhouettes of the wrecked tanks and half-tracks, he could see nothing in the field itself.

"Come on you bastards!" Jackson murmured to himself. "Where are you?"

Next to him, Martlesham and the older Home Guardsman were also staring through the shredded hedge, desperately searching for targets. They could see none. Instead, burst after burst of enemy gunfire slapped into the brickwork of the half-demolished barn behind them, whilst yet more bullets thudded into the soil in front of them.

"What the fuck are they playing at?" Jackson fidgeted with the chin-strap on his helmet.

"Perhaps they're just trying to put the wind up us, Sergeant?" Martlesham suggested.

"The buggers are up to something!" Commented the other Home Guardsman.

Then the whistles began; their piercing calls audible over the gunfire. All three men in the shell scrape turned their heads towards the north.

"What's that?" Martlesham wondered nervously.

"Whistles." Jackson grimaced. "Over to the north. They're coming from the flank. This is just a diversion, or their fire support group."

He got to his knees.

"Stay here. I'm going to take a look."

"Keep your head down..." Martlesham urged him.

Jackson was already moving. He ran as fast as he could, bending almost double.

He came past the rear of the 2 Pounder pit and saw the surviving members of the crew huddling behind the gun.

"Jack', what's going on?" The gun commander called from the gun-layer's seat, the gun-layer himself having been killed the previous evening, his head taken clean off by a large fragment of shrapnel.

"Looks like a flank attack." Jackson paused by the gun position, dropping onto all fours. "If there are no tanks, stand-by with your rifles."

There was a sudden eruption of gunfire from the northern boundary of the farm and a moment later a yellow flare sailed high above the surrounding fields, bathing the countryside in its garish light.

Chaos ensued. The whistle blasts grew even more frantic and there was shouting now, in both German and English. Bullets cracked through the air in every direction and for a moment, Jackson thought his senses would be overwhelmed. Leaving the gun crew, he crawled along the hedgerow that bounded the northern side of the farm and came to the first position. There was a lone airman in the pit, blasting away with his Lee-Enfield.

"What's going on?" Jackson demanded, dropping into the pit beside the young man.

"Jerries over there; in that hedgerow that comes hard up against the back of the farm!"

The airman never looked at Jackson. He simply shouted the answer as he emptied round after round in the direction of the enemy.

Jackson looked through the hedge and saw that there were indeed enemy close to the farm; less than a hundred yards away in fact. The dark figures moved rapidly along a hedgerow that joined the farm's boundary hedge at its north-western corner, and out in the middle of the field there were long lines of enemy, dashing forward in short, fast bounds.

"Bloody hell!" Jackson breathed in awe.

There must have been at least two companies of men out there.

"Martlesham! Get over here with that Lewis Gun! Move it!" Jackson roared back across the farmyard.

He jumped up and ran back towards the 2 Pounder pit.

"Keep firing!" He yelled over his shoulder at the airman as he left the pit.

His heart pounding, the sergeant ran back along the eastern boundary of the farm, telling the 2 Pounder crew to start using their rifles on their left of arc. Next he came to his own shell scrape.

"You stay here!" He ordered the older man. "Tom, get over to the shell scrape beyond the 2 Pounder and get that gun going; there's bloody hundreds of 'em coming across the field!"

Martlesham nodded and swept up his spare magazine and bandoliers, then clambered out of the pit.

Jackson ran on along the hedgerow. He came to another position, this one with a door covering it, topped with soil. He recognised the position instantly and ducked his head inside, conscious of the bullets filling the air around him.

"Bevan? Scotton? You in there?"

"Yes, Sergeant." The two voices chorused in reply.

"Scotton, stay here; Bevan, with me, there's a load of Jerries hitting us from the north."

As Bevan began scrambling out of the improvised bunker, Jackson ran on to the gateway of the farm. He found the three defenders in the next position looking north, worried looks on their faces.

"You, and you…" He pointed to Dutton and another man. Stay here and watch that road block, for fucks sake! You…" He pointed at another of the stragglers from the East Yorkshires. " With me. Bring that Jerry machine-pistol."

He turned and ran back along the hedge, picking up Bevan as he went.

"Get your bayonet on!" Yelled the sergeant, dragging his own heavy blade out of its scabbard as he ran.

The sound of gunfire and shouting from the far side of the farm was even louder now. Jackson veered across the farmyard towards the rubble of the great barn, in order to cut the corner; Bevan and the other man hard on his heels.

"What's going on?" A voice came to him.

Jackson saw the corporal from the Royal Engineers with two of his sappers, running towards him from the rear of the farm.

"Jerries on the northern side…" Jackson gasped as he jumped a pile of rubble. "Follow me…all of you!"

They cleared the rubble and emerged into the courtyard. In front of them was the northern boundary, a combination of thick hedge and several small brick storage barns. Bullets were cracking through the night, the tracer flashing past like angry fire-flies. Jackson could hear the chatter of German machine-guns, mixed with the slower chug of a Vickers and a Lewis Gun. The light faded slightly then brightened again as another flare sailed into the night sky. All along the boundary hedge he could see flashes of gunfire as the handful of defenders on this side blasted away at the assaulting Germans. Quickly getting his bearings, Jackson led his group towards the far corner of the farm yard where the Vickers machine-gun was positioned, next to a dung heap.

Crump! Crump!

Before he was halfway there, two small explosions occurred right on the point for which he was aiming. The sound of the Vickers stopped. There was a brief lull in gunfire, and then the sound of multiple German voices, screaming orders with great urgency punctuated the night. And then they were there, right in front of him. The cluster of German infantrymen in their distinctive helmets and high-leg boots burst through the large gap in the hedgerow, firing their weapons down into the pit where the Vickers crew lay dead or dying by the wreckage of their weapon. Several loud shots rang out from along the northern boundary and one of the Germans flopped backwards like a toppling scarecrow. His comrades looked up, searching for the danger, and they saw Jackson and his followers pounding across the cobbles towards them.

"Chaaarge!" Screamed Jackson for want of something better to shout.

The flare died out above them and the yard descended into relative darkness once more. Several shots rang out from the Germans, followed by a burst of fire from a machine-pistol.

Jackson felt bullets crack dangerously by and heard a grunt of pain behind him. He kept going, his Lee-Enfield levelled with its bayonet reaching wickedly for a target. Another flare burst overhead and Jackson found himself barely two long strides from a German soldier. The enemy infantryman, working his rifle bolt in a standing crouch, looked up in terror as the tall, khaki clad figure loomed up before him. Jackson saw the man's eyes widen and his lips part in the beginning of an appeal. A split second later, Jackson's bayonet punctured the man's chest as the huge Coldstreamer slammed into him at full tilt, rifle and bayonet braced for the impact. The force of the strike threw the enemy soldier backwards into the shattered machine-gun position. As the German flipped backwards, spread-eagled, Jackson drove his bayonet deeper and howled a war cry that was enough to curdle the blood. The other Germans shrank back around him, and brought up their weapons.

He caught their movements in his peripheral vision and knew he was just seconds from death. Stamping his boot onto the belly of the dying German, he twisted his bayonet and dragged it free of the body. He registered a German rifle pointing straight towards his head from the right hand side. Before he had a chance to react, a stocky figure in civilian clothes and wearing a steel helmet loomed up behind the German and brought a large shovel down on the back of the man's neck. Without a sound, the German collapsed heavily onto his knees. Jackson recognised the figure of Bob Bishop taking a second swing with the shovel. It connected with the pole-axed German's head and he toppled forwards, face down in the machine-gun pit. Gunshots sounded by Jackson's ear, and he swung back to the left. There were people all around him, shooting, hacking and stabbing.

The airman called Bevan barged past him and at point blank range, shot a German who appeared from behind the hedgerow. Another German, half dazed on all fours by Bevan's feet, gave a moan. Without hesitation, the airman slammed the brass butt of his rifle down onto the man's helmet, knocking him unconscious. The sappers were there now, tearing into the surviving pair of enemy infantrymen.

"Spread out!" Roared Jackson. "Spread out and get down! There'll be more coming along that hedge!"

Even as he spoke, the chatter of a machine-pistol kicked in from several yards along the hedgerow. Bevan span around with a grunt, then staggered and fell. Jackson instinctively grabbed the man's shoulder and pulled him down into the body filled pit.

"Grenade the fuckers!" He yelled to the men around him. "Someone fucking grenade that hedge!"

Jackson glanced down at the wounded airman who was leaning heavily against him. He turned the man as best he could and looked into his face. Bevan's eyes were dilated and filled with shock. Blood was pouring from his mouth in a great dark wave. It was still two hours before dawn, and the last stand at 'Hougoumont' had begun.

HMS HOOD – 45 NAUTICAL MILES OFF THE YORKSHIRE COAST TUESDAY 24TH SEPTEMBER 1940 – 0400 HOURS

"Signal from Norfolk, Sir; the Captain's given the order to abandon ship. She's going down."

Forbes was glad of the darkness. Despite the years of maintaining such a calm façade, it was hard to conceal the pain he felt at the loss of another ship to one of the dreaded German submarines; especially one of his precious cruisers. She had over 800 men aboard. Trying to rescue them in the darkness would prove troublesome, especially with a whole bunch of U-Boats on the prowl. He had lost a destroyer too, just after midnight. Forbes tried to console himself with the fact that they had sunk both the Scharnhorst and Nurnberg the previous afternoon, along with no less than three U-Boats. Even so, the enemy ships had done considerable damage to some of the British battleships and cruisers during the long engagement. That left the enemy, to his knowledge, with the Hipper and Scheer, both of them heavily damaged, along with the Emden and a whole range of destroyers, mine-sweepers and patrol boats.

He was confident now however, that the enemy was finished. He had no doubt that their rear would be harassed by U-Boats relentlessly during the coming twenty four hours, or that the Luftwaffe would return to make life difficult, but they had the enemy against the coast, and all of the biggest German ships were now at the bottom of the ocean. Just an hour or two, he realised, and the final act of this great drama would begin. Forbes addressed his Flag-Lieutenant.

"Tell Rear Admiral Destroyers to detach two ships to pick-up survivors with another pair as protection. Then, tell him to keep that screen tight up to the main fleet. We can't afford to lose anymore ships like this. And pass the word to the entire fleet to prepare for air attacks as we get closer to dawn. The cloud's thinning out rapidly. Looks like it's going to be a lovely day; just what we don't need."

"Aye, aye, Sir." The officer acknowledged and turned away.

Forbes looked at the Captain of the Hood.

"Poor old Norfolk. Roll on dawn; then we can finish this business once and for all. I was hoping we'd have got it done by last night..."

The Captain of the Hood gave a wry smile.

"Jerries put up a real fight, Sir, eh? Those were bloody good ships they had."

"Good crews, too." Forbes murmured. "And they had no other option. Their backs are against the wall. They've got no option but to stand and fight for as long as they can."

The Captain didn't reply for a moment.

"Any idea how the Army's doing on land, Sir?"

Forbes shrugged.

"Not entirely sure. I know they were caught out by the rapidity of the German advance on the first day, and that they've been trying to slow them down while they move up the general reserve from the south. Other than that, I've got little idea of how it's going. Churchill won't give up easily though. He's a real fighter."

There were several sudden bright flashes in the distance which made both men look up.

"What was that?" Forbes snapped.

The answer came seconds later as the unmistakable sound of incoming shells split the air. The shells passed close to the Hood, but were not of immediate threat. More flashes of light punctuated the darkness and one of the Hood's officers on watch turned towards his Captain and the C in C.

"Message from the radar room, Sir. Enemy ships moving fast on a bearing of 49 degrees. At least two big ones and more than a dozen smaller vessels."

Forbes shot a look at the Captain.

"They're trying to break out." The Captain frowned. "Are they mad?"

"No." Forbes shook his head. "They're German. Like I said, they've got no other option. They're not going to take this lying down by any means!"

Forbes strode across the bridge and looked out of the window. The night sky was peppered with flashes, the sound of distant heavy gunfire rumbling ominously across the waves.

"Well, let's get on with it then, shall we? Signal to Rear Admiral Destroyers and Commander Cruisers; half the destroyer force to the Cruiser Squadron, the remainder with the Battle Squadron. Cruiser Squadron to swing south, then conduct sharp turn to north, and begin a trawl up the coast. Tell them to sink everything in their path. The Battle Squadron will move due north and attempt to block the enemy breakout."

He turned and looked at the Captain of the Hood.

"They're heading for Denmark or Norway. Get a signal of to the Furious Group and let them know. I want to make damn sure they never get there."

CAWOOD – ON THE RIVER OUSE
TUESDAY 24TH SEPTEMBER 1940 – 0415 HOURS

SS Oberscharfuhrer Ernst Feisler was struggling with the current of the river. He hadn't realised quite how strong it would be and as a result, he and his small storm group were being dragged closer and closer towards the small village with its swing bridge. He grunted with the effort of fighting the current using just one arm, whilst trying to hold his MP-40 above the water using the other. Countless times, his chin dipped below the water line and he found himself spluttering a mouthful of dirty river water. There were twelve of them; the strongest swimmers in the company. It was a drastic course of action, swimming the river, but the orders had been quite clear. Cross the Ouse before daybreak at all costs.

Not far away to the south, he could hear the fierce gunfire from the town of Selby, where a full regiment from the Totenkopf was trying to force its way through the industrial part of the town towards the bridge over the River Ouse. That battle, he knew, wasn't going well. Nor for that matter, was the one taking place even further south, towards Goole, where 8th Panzer was desperately trying to batter its way over the river. The Tommies had finally decided to make a stand, and the entire river line was covered with machine-guns, anti-tanks guns, mines and pre-registered artillery. In addition to that, the enemy's air force had finally appeared below the clouds and conducted large scale bombing raids, all along the east bank of the Ouse, making life very unpleasant for them. Their own Luftwaffe they were told, was having difficulty getting through, although a squadron of Stukas and another of 110s had managed to stage forward to one of the captured airfields and were now able to fly close support missions for the two lead divisions.

Feisler's company, the reconnaissance company from his battalion, had slowly been pushing northwards, trying to find a weak spot in the defences. There was always a weak spot in a defensive line, just as there had been on the Meuse and the Dyle, back in May; and they had found it here now, on the Ouse. The previous river hadn't bothered them the day before. The Derwent was a cinch for the well-practiced German engineers to bridge, especially with little resistance coming from the far bank.

This river, the Ouse, was different though. It was wider, deeper, and even faster flowing. But they had found the weak spot all the same. The Tommies had thought that by winding the swing bridge to their side of the river, they could deny the enemy a passage, but they had reckoned without German ingenuity and drive. What's more, the stretch of river by the village of Cawood wasn't subject to the heavy artillery cover that was the case further south. Even better, the defenders on the far bank were thin on the ground. Feisler suspected that this was a unit boundary. Those were always the weakest spots in any line of defence, because the adjoining units often neglected to tie up the details of who was covering the key bits of ground.

He was only fifteen metres from the far bank when the first shots rang out. They weren't especially accurate shots, and they were nothing more than sporadic rifle fire, but even so, it meant they had been rumbled. A bullet sliced into the river to his left and he felt the splash of water on his face.

"Faster!" He called over his shoulder, redoubling his efforts, as the current pushed him level with the first terrace of houses in the village. "Get to the bank, quickly!"

A burst of slow machine-gun fire hit the water nearby, and he heard one of his men give a startled cry.

"Keep going!" He was shouting now.

From the west bank of the river, a sudden eruption of fire startled him. Just as quickly, relief washed over him as he realised it was the remainder of his own company letting rip at the Tommies on the far bank. His feet suddenly touched the muddy floor of the river bank and he half-walked, half-slipped the last couple of metres into the reeds at the very edge of the river. He was there. Struggling against the mud and the thick reeds, he dragged himself out of the water and onto firmer ground. He felt heavy and ungainly, his uniform sodden and spilling water. His feet, devoid of boots, stepped on sharp stones, broken twigs and reeds, but he ignored the minor pain and clambered up the bank. Pausing just below the lip, he slung his grenade satchel over his shoulder and grasped his machine-pistol with both hands. His limbs were screaming in protest at the recent physical exertion of swimming the river with weapon and ammunition elevated.

The noise was terrific now and bright tracer was zipping almost directly overhead, mainly from the German side towards the British, but even so, bullets continued to slap into the water, and he saw one of his men suddenly fall back under the surface of the river and disappear. Several others were across now and they too were staggering up the muddy bank, fighting through the undergrowth and trying to maintain their balance. He reached down, offering a hand to the nearest man, who took it gratefully, clambering up beside his commander. Within a couple of minutes, there were ten of them assembled.

"We're already in the village," Feisler snapped, starting to feel the cold, "so no fucking about. We're going straight down this lane towards the bridge. Kill anything in your way, but don't stop no matter what. Schwarz? Are you here?"

"Here." The sergeant from the engineers confirmed.

"Good. You stay close to me. As soon as we reach the bridge, you get to work; understand?"

"Got it." The engineer replied, still breathing heavily.

"Okay, let's go." Feisler ordered, and clambered over the top of the river bank.

They were greeted with fire immediately. Bullets cracked past their ears and bounced off the tarmac as they ran at full pelt along the side of the houses. As they ran, some of the SS men blasted away at the windows of the houses with their machine-pistols. One of them, for no particular reason, lobbed a stick grenade through the ground floor window of one of the houses. The glass shattered noisily and then, several seconds later, there was a dull crump, and a cloud of dark smoke spewed out into the street.

The covering fire from their own men was dangerously close now, and Feisler began blowing his whistle as he ran.

"Feisler! Feisler!" He called out his name over and over. "Feisler! Feisler!"

After a few moments the friendly fire began to switch further down the road, and the Oberscharfuhrer led his small group onwards. A sudden burst of machine-gun fire from some unseen Tommy position ripped straight through the centre of the squad and two of the SS men tumbled across the cobbles. Their comrades didn't even hesitate; they just ran on, pounding down the tarmac for the bridge.

They could see the winding house now, and the curve of the bridge's superstructure where it sat parallel with the bank, just thirty metres ahead. Feisler barked out instructions.

"Okay, that's it! Clear the junction and give Schwarz some cover… Move!"

The SS men burst onto the junction with a roar of defiance. They found a small, concrete pillbox that had been built against the end of the terraced houses. Its only occupant was so busy engaging the enemy across the river that he never saw the SS men coming from his left. Within seconds, he was dead and the pill-box was gushing smoke from the grenade that had been dropped through one of the firing ports. The house on the opposite corner was also occupied and a burst of machine-gun fire slammed into the ground around the ruined pill-box. Feisler returned fire with a full magazine, then ordered another man to engage the house whilst he reloaded.

"Feisler! Feisler!" He continued to shout his identity back across the river, terrified that his small group would be riddled by friendly fire.

"Feisler! Is that you?" A familiar voice carried across the river above the gunfire.

"Yes!" He shouted back. "We're by the pill-box on the right of the junction. The enemy are in the top floor of the house on the left of the junction. I'm sending the engineer into the winding house. Did you get that?"

"Got it!" The voice of his company commander replied.

Within seconds, the entire weight of covering fire from across the river began to converge on the house across the road, and the sound of bullets slapping into brickwork and shattering glass became relentless.

"Okay Schwarz, get into that winding house! Get that fucking bridge back over the river! Move!"

The engineer sergeant lurched off towards the small cabin.

"Watch the rear!" Feisler ordered one of his men. "There are still Tommies back down the way we came. I don't want them getting up our arse!"

He looked around the corner of the pill-box and saw the flash of several rifles in the dark. Quickly, he pulled his head back into cover. He dragged out a stick grenade from his satchel, unscrewed the cap, yanked on the lanyard, then lobbed it around the corner with all the force he could muster.

Crump!

The grenade exploded, and the enemy fire from the main street slackened a touch. Feisler looked back across to the winding house. He could see the dark shape of Schwarz and one of the SS men working furiously away inside the half-wooden, half-glass shed.

"Come on, come on!" Feisler murmured to himself.

He looked down at his watch. It was heading rapidly towards dawn. He had just eight men with him, two of whom were struggling with the bridge. He had to hold out for just a few minutes; just long enough to get the bridge back in position. It didn't matter if they all died; they were Hitler's chosen, the Waffen SS. They did the jobs that the Army baulked at. Casualties weren't important, but results were. And if Feisler and his men got this bridge back over the river, the Waffen SS would pour across it and onto the west bank of the Ouse. Then, for Britain, it would be the end…

BY REIGHTON VILLAGE – EAST YORKSHIRE
TUESDAY 24th SEPTEMBER 1940 – 0430 HOURS

"Move!"

McGinn opened fire with the Thompson sub-machine-gun, using short, controlled bursts to spray the hedgerow at the far side of the field. To his forward right, Harper sprang up from the grass and began doubling back towards him. He pounded past the commander of the auxiliary unit and, after running a few more yards, turned and dropped onto his belly against the small embankment. Instantly, he opened fire with his rifle, working the bolt rapidly after each shot.

"Move!" He screamed at the top of his voice to McGinn.

The older man jumped up and began running for the cover of the embankment too.

It was all going wrong. They had expected to get in fairly close to the enemy HQ; certainly close enough to be able to shoot up the building and lob their grenades and satchel charges amongst the collection of vehicles parked outside, if not through the windows of the building itself. The enemy HQ however, was far bigger, and more heavily manned than they had anticipated. McGinn had sent the other pair round to the western side of the farm, whilst he and Harper had approached from the north. The idea was that McGinn and Harper would get in close and cause the necessary destruction with explosives and grenades, whilst the other two would then open fire from a distance and create a diversion, in order to allow the two older men to make a hasty withdrawal. But the plan had come to grief early, thanks entirely to the dogs.

On their previous recce of the farm, the two auxiliaries hadn't seen or heard any evidence of dogs, but on this occasion, there had been several animals in the farmyard, and before McGinn and Harper had even got within a hundred yards of the place, the hounds had begun barking. It was immediately apparent that the dogs were not your average farmyard mutt. Within moments, urgent sounding German voices were calling to each other amongst the collection of buildings and vehicles. And then, quite unexpectedly, a patrol of three Germans had emerged to the immediate right of the two British attackers. There had been a challenge, a pause, a hail of gunfire, and then the night had descended into chaos. The farm and the surrounding area came alive with Germans. Flares sailed into the night and the sound of the dogs grew louder and more frantic. They were guard dogs; of that there was no doubt. McGinn and Harper had run.

Harper was down to the last three rounds in his magazine as Tommy McGinn ran the last few paces towards the cover of the embankment. Bullets cracked through the night and the barking of the dogs continued unabated. He had no idea where the other pair of auxiliaries were, or what their fate had been. If they had escaped from the vicinity of the farm, then they would RV back at the bunker. As Harper chambered a new round, he saw McGinn stagger slightly. At first, he thought that the older man had simply stumbled over a hummock of grass, but then he saw his friend slow down and begin to walk as if drunk.

"Tommy! Are you alright?" Harper barked as he closed the bolt and fired another round in the direction of the muzzle flashes.

His companion reached the edge of the embankment and literally toppled over it.

"Tommy!"

Harper dropped down the embankment and grabbed hold of McGinn, who had collapsed face down on the reverse slope. With a grunt, Harper heaved the man over. An awful smell came to Harper's nostrils and McGinn gave a terrible groan.

"I'm hit George. Leave me." The older man gasped, his voice filled with pain and shock.

"What? Where?" Harper demanded, desperately searching his friend's body in the darkness for signs of an injury.

Then he saw it, and the source of the smell became obvious. Harper felt as if a stone had just dropped inside his stomach.

McGinn had been shot through the lower back, the heavy calibre bullet exiting through his abdomen and taking half of the man's guts with it. To Harper's horror, he saw a long, glistening snake-like organ slide out of the injured man's gaping wound.

"Oh, Jesus!" Harper swore.

He had seen these kinds of injuries many times during the Great War and had never expected to see anything like it again; until the Germans had come back to haunt him that is. He knew what the injury meant.

"Go!" McGinn rasped again.

"Tommy, let me help you…"

"No!" McGinn's voice snapped through the darkness with sudden intensity. "I'm dying. Save yourself…but don't let them take me alive."

Harper knelt there and looked into the fierce eyes of his friend.

"Tommy, I…"

"Do it." McGinn snapped again. "Shoot me; then go. Do it quickly. They can't take me alive George."

Harper bit his lip, biting back the emotion that was suddenly threatening to overwhelm him. He shook his head and tried to find the words, but nothing would come. Not far away, the sound of German voices and the bark of their dogs grew louder.

"Do it, man!" McGinn's voice had lost all vestiges of country twang now. He was the well-bred colonel again; his voice clipped, precise, ruthless.

Harper just stared at his wounded friend and felt the first tears prick at the corner of his eyes.

"Please, George." McGinn begged him, his voice softening.

As if in a dream, Harper reached into his satchel and felt for the captured German pistol. He dragged it free and released McGinn, allowing his friend to roll onto his front again. His hand trembling, he pushed the muzzle of the pistol against the back of his friend's head, then closed his eyes.

"Thank you, George." He heard McGinn say.

Bang!

The sound of the gunshot made Harper jump, even though he knew it was coming. As the echo of the shot died away, he let out a huge sob. He twisted away from McGinn's lifeless body before opening his eyes. Another sob came, then another, and he couldn't stop. He was crying like a heart broken child as he scrabbled for McGinn's sub-machine gun.

He found the weapon in the dark and lifted it, along with his rifle and the German pistol. Nearby, the German voices sounded urgent and vengeful. Their dogs were snarling and snapping in the darkness, demanding to be let off their leashes so they could lurch after their prey. Sobbing like a baby, Harper dragged himself to his feet and stumbled off across the next field. Several bullets followed him, snapping close past his ears. Somehow, he managed to cross the hundred and fifty yard stretch without being hit and threw himself at the hedge.

He collapsed heavily onto all fours in the field beyond, allowing his weapons to spill onto the grass. He wasn't a young man anymore and he was literally retching now with the physical effort of the chase. Between the huge gulps for breath, the old soldier continued to emit pitiful sobs for the act he had just been forced to commit.

"It's not fair!" He spluttered to himself, giving in to the despair of the moment. "It's not fucking fair! Fucking, bastard Germans!"

He sat back on his haunches. In an instant, the despair turned to anger. More than anger; a bloody rage that began to feed off his hate for the people who had brought him to this place, this time, this predicament.

"Fucking Germans!" He screamed into the night.

A sudden change in the noise of the dogs suggested that they had, at long last, been unleashed.

"Fuck it!" Snarled Harper, his voice calmer now but the tone still fierce.

He stuffed a hand into his satchel and pulled out a grenade, then grabbed hold of the German automatic pistol. Turning, he pushed his head through the hedge, staring back across the field towards his pursuers. He could hear the pant of the snarling canines as they raced towards him in the dark. Behind them, he could hear the triumphant voices of the Germans as they found McGinn's dead body. He took a deep breath and brought up the pistol.

"Right, you fuckers!" He spat the words out. "It's time to fucking pay!"

S +3
DAYBREAK

HEADQUARTERS GERMAN 41ST ARMY CORPS – BUBWITH TUESDAY 24TH SEPTEMBER 1940 – 0530 HOURS

General of Panzers Georg Reinhardt was a man under pressure, and the news he had just been given wasn't helping.

"They're doing what?" He asked his chief of staff in disbelief.

The colonel took a deep breath and repeated the news that had just come through from 16th Army Headquarters near Reighton.

"The fleet is breaking out?" Reinhardt repeated the information, his face betraying the shock. "They're abandoning us?"

"Not according to Army HQ, General." The colonel tried to soothe his commander. "They say it is a tactical manoeuvre in order to avoid the British Navy trapping them against the coast."

"And how are we supposed to fight a war with no supplies?" Reinhardt exploded.

The colonel remained calm.

"The corps has two days of supplies left, Sir. And I have checked with Army HQ; there is another two days of supply in Army reserve. The air bridge is to be used to bring in all future supplies until we force the British to surrender."

Reinhardt regarded his chief of staff with a sceptical look.

"Ah, yes." He said, his voice calming slightly. "I was forgetting. Once we are over the river, the British will surrender and all will be well; according to OKW and their crystal ball."

His chief of staff allowed himself a smile.

"We already have a power station and a coal mine at this side of the river, Sir. Army Intelligence says that there is a huge coal field and industrial area at the far side. Once we get into that, Sir, we'll cripple the British war effort. We're almost there."

Reinhardt raised an eyebrow.

"I have read the orders, you know Knopfler."

"Of course, General." The colonel replied, blushing. "My apologies."

"Don't apologise." Reinhardt grunted. "Someone's got to be an optimist. Have we burned that power station yet?"

"The orders have gone out to 8th Panzer already, General. They should be on it now."

Reinhardt nodded.

"See that they are."

The General leaned forward and shone his torch on the map-board which was strapped to the side of the half-track's rear compartment.

"So how are we going to get across this river, then? The reports are saying that Goole and Selby are a no-go; heavy fighting, lots of roadblocks and mines; no go good for tanks. And I gather that the whole river line is well covered, all the way down towards Hull. Forcing our way over this little obstacle is going to be difficult."

The chief of staff leaned in close to his commander, pointing at the map.

"I've got the Totenkopf probing further north, towards York. The river gets narrower as it gets closer to the city. We'll see if we can find a weak spot there maybe?"

Reinhardt ran his eyes along the line of the river on the map.

"Mmm. The problem is, if we go too far north before we cross, we'll have to swing very wide, before turning south. We may even find ourselves with this other little river to cross, here; the Wharfe. That could put another day or two on our timeline, and we don't have the supplies to risk that…"

"General? General Reinhardt, Sir?"

Reinhardt looked up with a flicker of annoyance at the staff captain who had hailed him from the rear of the next half-track.

"Is it urgent, Jurgens?"

The captain was wild-eyed with excitement.

"The Totenkopf are over the river, Sir!"

Reinhardt narrowed his eyes, suspiciously.

"What?"

"The Totenkopf are over the Ouse, Sir! They've got a storming party over the river at a place called Cawood. They've managed to wind a swing-bridge back over the river and get a full company across. They're clearing the village on the west bank now."

Reinhardt pointed his torch back at the map.

"Where's Cawood?"

His chief of staff found the small village and jabbed his pencil at it.

"Here, Sir, just below the junction with the Wharfe; a few miles above Selby."

Reinhardt shook his head.

"Are the Tommies mad? Why didn't they blow the bloody thing? Don't they think we can swim?"

The general quickly studied the map and traced his finger along the main routes out of Cawood and southwards.

"Well done the Totenkopf." He murmured. "If we go over there, we take Selby from the north, we capture this airfield here at Church Fenton, and we're just a few miles from the main road south. In addition, we have all these lovely power stations and coal-mines in our grasp."

The general looked sideways at his chief of staff.

"Bloody hell, Knopfler; I think we might just pull this off."

Reinhardt sat up and looked back across at the staff captain.

"Jurgens? Get onto the Totenkopf. Tell that thug Eicke to get his entire division over that bridge... now. I want him to leave a strong battalion covering Selby, and tell him to shell the shit out of the place, just so the Tommies don't get suspicious. I want a solid bridge-head as soon as possible."

"Yes, General." The captain turned to his signaller and immediately began relaying the instructions.

"Knopfler?" Reinhardt turned back to the chief of staff. "Tell 8th Panzer to abandon the push on Goole. I want a regiment of tanks over the bridge at Cawood by mid-morning. The rest of the division should prepare to follow it on orders. Get onto the 35th Infantry too. Tell them to leave a covering force at the Tommy pocket around Holme, then move everything else to relieve 8th Panzer in front of Goole."

The chief of staff was nodding vigorously as he reached out to tap his signaller on the shoulder.

"Immediately General. I'll get onto the Luftwaffe at Army HQ too, and get their forward squadrons to switch onto the Cawood axis."

Reinhardt bent his head to study the map again.

"Oh, and Knopfler; tell the 35th to get moving straight away, they've got a lot of marching to do."

BISHOP WOOD – THE SELBY POCKET
TUESDAY 24TH SEPTEMBER – 0730 HOURS

Lance Corporal Jack Woods was working as fast as he could. His finger ends were cut and bleeding from the constant repetition of ramming round after round into the Bren magazines. Crouching in the bottom of his trench, his boots crunched on a sea of empty brass cartridge cases. Pushing the last round into position, he placed the magazine onto the parapet above him, then grabbed another empty one.

"Everything still clear up there, Chalky?"

"Yes mate." Private 'Chalky' White replied, staring intently across the wide, level fields towards Cawood and Wistow. "I wish those bloody mortars would pack it in though."

White ducked a moment later as yet another mortar round dropped through the tree canopy and exploded somewhere in the wood. The tortuous creak of tree-trunks and branches being ripped apart came to them as the echo of the explosion faded. With an improvised roof of logs, reinforced with packed earth, their position was relatively well protected from the bombardment however.

"It's when the mortars stop that you need to start worrying, mate." Woods replied as he pulled a handful of rounds out of a clip and began feeding them into the magazine. "You can bet your arse they'll be back soon."

Their battalion was dug-in along the apex of Bishop Wood, covering the southern side of the Cawood Pocket, with arcs facing straight towards Cawood village itself, and due east towards the coal mine and the fortified village of Wistow beyond it. The Germans had appeared just after dawn, but the British had known they were coming. The gunfire from Cawood had alerted them that the enemy was taking the bait, and just after first light, the first German vehicles had come trundling cautiously down the road. The first German vehicle, a kind of armoured car, had been hit by a 2 Pounder when it was still four hundred yards from the front edge of the wood. The armoured vehicle had been literally ripped apart by the anti-tank gun, and moments later, the heavy Vickers machine-guns covering the same arc had riddled the remaining soft skinned vehicles with fire, immobilising the small staff car and one of the lorries. The few Germans who had escaped were mown down quickly and everything had gone quiet once more. And then, ten minutes later, the attack had begun.

The mortar and artillery bombardment had been short but heavy, and behind the curtain of explosions, a mass of enemy infantry, backed up by armoured cars and machine-guns mounted on motorcycle combinations, had surged along the road and the neighbouring hedgerows towards the wood line and the farm buildings in the open ground to the east. It was a quick, hastily prepared attack, with the intention of concentrating huge force at one point as quickly as possible in order to smash through the British line. It had failed signally. The British position was not a line at all, but an extensive series of fortified positions and obstacles designed to absorb and entangle the enemy in pre-arranged killing areas.

The enemy, dressed in unusual grey-green mottled smocks, had charged straight into the trap. At four hundred metres, the 2 Pounders and heavy machine-guns had done their deadly work. Then as the enemy fought their way forwards, still unsure as to where the main British position was, they had been riddled by small arms fire from Bren Guns and rifles. Coming up against the widespread wire entanglements, road-blocks and minefields, the German attack had bogged down. That was the point when the British artillery had come into play. Two square miles of farmland and roads were systematically bombarded by two entire regiments of artillery. The 18 and 25 Pounder shells had burst amongst the ploughed fields and hawthorn hedges, leaving the stalled German troops stunned and incapable of further offensive action. All the while, White had blasted away with his light machine-gun, engaging the fleeing enemy soldiers as they desperately tried to extricate themselves.

As his gun controller, Woods had been given little chance to issue fire-control orders. The targets were self evident and the amount of defensive fire so immense, that the lance corporal had found himself with no other role, than to keep re-filling the never ending stream of empty magazines. His only respite was for a few seconds every couple of minutes as he changed the barrel on the light machine-gun. Having filled the last magazine, Woods placed it on the parapet and stood up once more.

"Have you managed to clean those gas parts yet?" He asked the gunner.

White shook his head.

"No mate, sorry. They're still red hot."

"Okay." Woods allowed, seeing that indeed, the spare barrel was still steaming in the damp morning air. "We'll give it another five minutes."

The sound of explosions suddenly stopped. As the echoes died away, an unusual and slightly creepy silence fell over the shattered woodland. Woods and White exchanged a worried glance.

"Looks like we might have to clean them later?" White said.

Then they heard the engines. They snapped their attention back to the fields beyond the wood line, and the stretch of road that passed across their front at a diagonal, heading towards Sherburn-in-Elmet.

"Those engines sound a bit different." Woods was frowning.

"All engines sound the same to me." White pulled a face.

Woods was shaking his head.

"No, mate; I'm telling you, that's not a normal engine. Definitely not a motorbike or one of those trucks."

Just then, the first burst of machine-gun fire came rattling towards the wood. The two British infantrymen from the 44th Division heard the series of sharp cracks pass to their left. More bursts of fire cracked through the trees. Then came a bigger, more shocking crack; followed by a loud explosion.

"Tanks!" Woods exclaimed as the first of the dark, squat, metal monsters pushed its way past a burning armoured car.

"They're over to the right, as well!" White shouted, pointing.

Wood looked across to the right and saw a line of the metal beasts rolling forwards towards where the neighbouring battalion was holding the coal mine, about six hundred yards away to his east.

Behind the tanks, more groups of infantry were running forward again, trying to keep up with the advancing panzers.

"Bloody hell, Chalky! Here we go son; this is the big one!"

The private hauled the Bren Gun up into his shoulder and ducked his head down to look through the rear sight.

"You aint kidding there, mate!" Replied the gunner. "Just keep those magazines coming!"

HQ NORTHERN COMMAND – YORK
TUESDAY 24TH SEPTEMBER 1940 – 0800 HOURS

The HQ was packed. Brooke and his small staff had filled up what room was left in the already busy rooms of the building. It was necessary though. The timing of the counter-attack with the hastily formed 1st Army needed to be timed perfectly, and the only way for Brooke to get a proper feel for that was to sit on the shoulder of Adam and his staff as they co-ordinated the defensive battle.

"So they're definitely across?" The C in C Home Forces queried Adam's Brigadier General Staff.

"They are, Sir. No doubt about it. The 44th Division say their brigade covering the southern edge of the Cawood Pocket have been in contact for a couple of hours now. They repelled the first attack quite convincingly. They also report that a second attack towards Selby is developing, supported by armour. The enemy axis appears to be south, south-east, through Wistow."

Brooke studied the map with Adam.

"But they're holding it?" Adam questioned the BGS.

"They are, Sir." The brigadier replied.

Brooke studied the map a moment longer.

"If I know the Germans, they'll be pushing west towards Church Fenton before long. They won't let themselves get bogged down; not with so much at stake."

Adam nodded his agreement.

"I think you're right. It won't be long before the whole pocket is under pressure. Now they're across the river they'll push everything they can over that bridge. The big question is, how long will it take them?"

Brooke pulled a face.

"It won't be long. They may be moving west even now. They are unbelievably fast at exploiting success. I think we'd better start queuing things up, don't you?"

Adam pulled a face.

"Do you think we might give the game away if we go too early?"

Brooke glanced at his watch.

"Even if we give the word to bomber command now, it will be at least an hour before the first squadrons can be airborne and over the targets." Brooke looked round for the Air Liaison Officer and caught his eye. "Don't you think?"

The RAF officer nodded.

"That's about right for No.4 Group, Sir. You're looking at between 90 minutes to a couple of hours for the others."

Brooke exchanged a quick glance with Adam, before looking back at the RAF officer.

"Do it. Everything as originally requested. Ask Bomber Command to start lifting now."

The RAF man acknowledged the order and rushed away to the telephone.

Looking back towards the map, Brooke fretted a little more.

"What about the Air Striking Group? A bit early for them though, wouldn't you agree?"

Adam murmured his agreement. A voice came from behind them. It was the Wing Commander in operational command of the group.

"They can be over the target within forty minutes, Sir, from the moment you give the word. I would just remind you though, Sir, that the group has suffered nearly fifty percent casualties already. I suspect that you'll get one last mission out of them before they need some serious reorganisation."

Brooke and Adam mulled over the statement, remaining quiet. Eventually, Brooke spoke.

"Yes. We've really got to make this one count haven't we? We wait then. But…"

At this he turned to the Army colonel who was acting as his own operations officer. "The time is rapidly approaching for the ground attack. Send the order to all corps and divisions of 1st Army; all units to come to five minutes notice to move by 0830 hours."

The colonel acknowledged and turned away. Brooke looked back at Adam.

"Everything else still quiet? Up by Malton and Stamford Bridge? Nothing developing in front of Hull?"

Adam shook his head.

"Nothing apart from patrol activity and some exchange of artillery. It's as though the enemy is putting everything he's got into this thrust over the Ouse."

Brooke thought on that for a moment.

"I hope to God that's the case Ronald, because this is going to take some careful timing."

THE BRIDGE – CAWOOD
TUESDAY 24TH SEPTEMBER 1940 – 0830 HOURS

SS Grupenfuhrer Theodor Eicke turned and glared at the half-track as it slid in next to his staff car, sending muddy splashes over the side of the open topped vehicle and onto the seat beside him. He raised his chin, ready to deliver an obscenity filled rebuke to the commander, but checked himself when he saw the heavy-jowled face of Lieutenant General Adolf Kuntzen, commander of the 8th Panzer Division, looking down at him.

"Morning Theo." Kuntzen barked at his SS contemporary. "Started your own private little war, have you? Well done, old boy!"

Eicke stood upright and reached out for the side of the half-track. With a grunt, the big SS officer dragged himself up the side of the armoured vehicle and over into the rear compartment.

"Have you got the rest of your panzers with you?" Eicke asked without pre-amble.

"Certainly have. I've got the rest of the lead regiment behind me. The other regiment is on its way and the panzer grenadiers will follow once they've been relieved by the 35th. You should have seen our lead company already?"

Eicke grunted an acknowledgement.

"Yes, they've arrived. I just sent them forward with our lead regiment to force a way through to Selby from the north. I had a battalion cut to pieces first thing this morning when we tried it, and the rest of the regiment along with your panzer company have just taken a pounding too."

The SS Gruppenfuhrer flipped open his map and jabbed a thick, sausage like finger towards it. The enemy have got a line of heavily fortified positions along this line here, north of Selby. Now you've brought up a full regiment of tanks, we'll be able to break through no problem. I've been onto Corps HQ and asked for the Stukas, too. Fuck knows where they are! They should be right up the front with us."

He spat over the side of the vehicle and clamped his pipe between his teeth. Kuntzen meanwhile was frowning at the map.

"If you've been spanked twice already trying to get through here, then I reckon it's time to try something different Theo." He ventured.

"Once your panzers batter their way through, we'll have Selby." Replied the SS officer grumpily.

Kuntzen was shaking his head.

"I don't think so, old boy. That shitty little town has got nothing of real value. Everything we want is right behind it; the coal-fields and the industrial areas. Why throw ourselves into the jaws of a waiting lion? I propose to go due west."

He jabbed his own finger at Eicke's map and indicated the direction.

"We go west, hard and fast, take out this airfield, then swing sharp south towards the main highway. By doing that, we envelope Selby anyway, and take a short cut to our main target area. I saw big chimneys in the distance on the far side of the river as we motored up. We're almost there now, so no point wasting time trying to winkle a bunch of Tommies out of the town. I say we go hard and fast around them so we can rip the heart out of their war effort; that's what will hurt them the most."

Eicke glowered at his opposite number with jealousy. Eicke was a fighter, a brawler; a man who brooked no argument and who believed that blunt and overwhelming force was the solution to everything. Kuntzen however, was one of Guderian's brood; a panzer general, well educated, clever and incisive, with a flair for grand strategy. Hearing Kuntzen's words, he realised that the man was talking sense. Even so, Eicke was resentful that he had not thought of the idea himself.

"I suppose it could work." He grunted, reluctantly.

"Good. Then we are agreed." Kuntzen nodded, satisfied. "I'll get onto Corps HQ too, and reinforce your request for the Stuka squadron."

The panzer general looked back over his shoulder suddenly, staring north.

"York is up that way, isn't it? What have you got covering the flank?"

Eicke chewed his pipe in annoyance. He didn't like being questioned by anybody.

"I've put a couple of companies up there, and an anti-tank screen."

Kuntzen looked back at Eicke with shrewd eyes.

"You've only got the 37's haven't you?"

Eicke nodded.

"I'll drop off a couple of batteries of 88's for you as the division comes through." Kuntzen promised his opposite number. "You can keep hold of them until the 17th Infantry come up on our right and seal off York."

Eicke mumbled his grudging thanks.

"Right then, Theo," Kuntzen grinned at his fellow divisional commander, "let's go win this war, shall we?"

MAIN STREET WEST – BARMBY MOOR
TUESDAY 24TH SEPTEMBER 1940 – 0900 HOURS

"Right lads, get your weapons cleaned. By the time that's done, we should have some food on the position. Lieutenant Hagen just came back from Company HQ. There's going to be no move before midday. We've been told to go firm and hold the northern flank of the main spearhead. Apparently they're going over a big river this morning, and everything is being concentrated for that. Once we've cleaned weapons, had some scoff and prepared some shell scrapes, you'll be able to get into some routine and get your heads down again."

Saltz's instructions were greeted with a collective, tired cheer, which somehow sounded more like a groan. The squad, now an amalgamation of First and Second Squads due to casualties, had arrived in the little village just before dawn after an exhausting night march.

They had been given a substantial house to occupy at the west end of the village, and the family of Tommies that had been cowering in the pantry had been moved out and sent into the village to stay with friends. The exhausted soldiers had been allowed just three hours of sleep before Saltz had kicked them all awake, even though the squad sergeant was just as tired as his men. The battle to clear Fridaythorpe the day before had been long and bitter, with the enemy fighting to the last man. Saltz's entire regiment had been sucked into the battle in the end, suffering almost two hundred casualties in the process. It had been a bloody day's work.

Then had come the long night march to Pocklington. They had reached the small town only to find that they were required to march an extra mile or two, until they reached an outlying village to the west. Like all night marches, it had been stop-start, with the soldiers literally falling asleep as they walked, bumping into the man in front whenever the column stopped unexpectedly. But here they were at last, after four days of relentless marching and fighting, with an opportunity to take a proper rest and sort themselves out before the next phase of the operation. Even better, the thick cloud and on-off rain of the day before had dissipated overnight, and although there were still patches of cloud in the sky, a surprisingly strong sun was breaking through them, revealing a wonderful blue vista beyond.

By the window of the main room, Bachman and Nuemark looked tiredly over their shoulders at Saltz.

"I hope the cooks have organised something good; that Tommy town must be full of lovely grub." Nuemark licked his dry lips as he imagined the smell of freshly fried sausages.

Next to him, Bachman began poking his ears, an irritated look on his face.

"What's up Bachman?" Nuemark glanced at him with dark, sunken eyes. "Your ears still giving you shit from all those shells yesterday?"

The young machine-gunner nodded.

"I can't get rid of this damned buzzing! It keeps coming back every few hours."

Nuemark opened his mouth to reply, then stopped, his mouth hanging open. His eyes swivelled in their sockets as he looked upwards, out of the shattered window, and into the sky above.

"Fuck me!" He whispered.

He looked back at Bachman.

"That's not your ears, mate."

He switched his gaze to Saltz.

"Jo', I think we might have a problem."

Saltz was already striding across to the window. He could hear the noise himself now. He leaned over Bachman and Nuemark, resting a hand on the window ledge and stared up into the clearing skies. He caught his breath immediately. Right above them, thousands of feet up, were aircraft. Lots of aircraft. Big aircraft. Bombers. They were in close formation, one wave after another.

"Are they ours, Sarge?" Bachman asked.

The sound of anti-aircraft fire sounded from the direction of Pocklington.

"I don't think so, somehow." Saltz replied, as he watched them pass overhead, flying eastwards.

And then the first little specks appeared underneath the bombers, tumbling like tiny black droplets towards them. Saltz heard the whistle as the first bombs came rushing towards the ground. He tore himself away from the window in panic.

"Take cover!"

S +3
MID-MORNING

NEAR MEEKE WOOD – THE CAWOOD POCKET
SATURDAY 24TH SEPTEMBER 1940 – 1030 HOURS

"The Tommy bastards are everywhere!"

Captain Helmut Grindt of the 3rd Panzer Company swore into his microphone in frustration as he watched another of the light Panzer II tanks erupt in a spout of flame and smoke.

"Where did that come from?"

His driver's voice came up to him.

"I think it came from the left, Sir; from over by those farm buildings."

Grindt looked towards the cluster of buildings that lay several hundred metres to his immediate left and swore.

"Right, ignore the fuckers and go straight on. We'll leave them for the Totenkopf to deal with."

He clicked down the pressel-switch of his wireless set and snapped out a series of quick orders.

"All call signs, all call signs; be aware, we have Tommy guns to our left in the farm. Keep moving at best speed, due west. We need to get past this anti-tank screen quickly. Everyone follow me. Move now."

He released the pressel and yelled to his driver.

"Come on then, Mueller, let's go!"

The engine of the powerful Panzer III roared into life and the tank lurched forward again. As it did so, a bright flash caught Grindt's eye through the periscope and he only just managed to brace himself before the shell struck them a glancing blow across the back decks.

The whole vehicle shuddered violently and there was a massive, metallic thud, as the Tommy shell scraped the top of the tank's rear and exploded harmlessly. The gunner swore loudly and looked around him in panic, expecting to see the turret erupt in flames. Grindt calmed him with a reassuring smile.

"Steady down, man, it was only a near miss. You just keep your eyes peeled to the front. And Mueller?"

"Yes, Sir?"

"Don't stop the tank again unless I tell you to. We're a sitting duck if you do. Just keep on moving her backwards and forwards if need be. Don't stay still again, whatever you do."

"Right, Sir."

Grindt began to think quickly. The enemy anti-tank screen was more extensive than he had first thought. He had little room for manoeuvre to his right as the Third, Heavy Tank Company was rolling across the open ground to the north, heading straight for the airfield. His own company had intended to turn the Tommy line, but it was proving difficult to find a gap, and so he had no choice but to plough on further west before turning sharply to the south and into the enemy rear. He was still considering his options when the tank slewed to a halt, throwing him against the rear of the main gun.

"Ahh! Fucking hell, Mueller! What are you doing man?"

"Anti-tank ditch, Sir; we won't get over that."

Grindt jammed his eyes to the periscope and cursed.

The Tommies had excavated an existing ditch and stream so that it now presented a wide, deep obstacle that his tank would not be able to negotiate. He ran his eyes along the ditch and saw that it extended out of sight to the left. On the right, it extended towards the village of Church Fenton.

He gave a snort of frustration. It wasn't ideal getting mixed up in a built up area without infantry support, but there would be more chance of finding a way over or around the obstacle nearer the village.

"Okay, go hard right. Follow it towards the village."

He clicked on the wireless set again and repeated his instructions to the rest of the company. He was getting hot now, closed down inside the sweaty confines of the tank, and his temper was beginning to fray accordingly. The company was already out of formation and he needed to impose some kind of order again. They were passing a small wood to their right when Grindt spotted the opportunity. An old farm track over a culvert for the original stream had been left intact, just a hundred metres to his front. He was about to instruct his gunner to put some bursts of machine-gun fire onto the bridge and track in order to search for mines, when a voice crackled in his ear piece.

"Karl Zero, Karl Zero, this is Karl Three; there's a bridge over the ditch opposite the small copse. I'm going over."

Grindt pressed down the switch on his pressel box and was about to tell the platoon commander of his Third Platoon not to go over until he'd checked that the bridge was clear, but as he opened his mouth to speak, a Panzer II cut in front of his vehicle and rolled over the culvert.

"No!" Grindt shouted desperately over the wireless, but barely a second later, the Panzer II reared up in a cloud of black smoke, just as it cleared the bridge and moved onto the track beyond.

"For fuck's sake!" Grindt thumped his fist against the inside of the turret. "Mueller, take us over that bridge and push that bloody wreck out of the way!"

Within a few seconds the driver was swinging the metal beast carefully onto the narrow bridge. He lined the tracks up and shouted a warning to the rest of the crew.

"Hang on tight, lads!"

With an angry roar, the Panzer III surged forwards over the bridge and shunted the smaller tank up its rear end. Inside the turret, Grindt and his gunner held onto the various instruments with white-knuckled hands, as Mueller forced the tank forwards. The burning hulk began to move, and Mueller shunted the vehicle once more. The wrecked Panzer II slid forwards and veered off to one side of the track. As it did so, it hit another mine hidden somewhere in the verge, and the huge explosion sent a tremor through Grindt's tank.

As the blast subsided and the swearing in Grindt's tank eased, he saw that the wrecked Panzer II had been flipped onto its side by the explosion. Through the billowing smoke, the captain could see the first farm buildings on the outskirts of Church Fenton, perhaps a kilometre to his front.

"There's the village; let's go; straight forwards."

"What about the mines, Sir?" His gunner asked worriedly.

Grindt gave him a wink.

"We'll just have to take our chances, won't we? Mueller…drive!"

THE TREE LINE – BY NABURN WOOD
TUESDAY 24TH SEPTEMBER 1940 – 1050 HOURS

Second Lieutenant Will Parsons nodded to the squadron sergeant major in acknowledgement of the signal. It had been passed by hand because they were still on radio silence. Parsons and his gunner dropped inside the turret of the heavy Matilda II Infantry Tank and battened-down the hatches.

"Okay, Jennings. Start her up."

With a splutter, then a roar, the compact but heavy metal beast came to life. Their regiment was lucky. It had taken delivery of the much sought after Mark II tanks only a fortnight before; two per troop. It wasn't ideal, but better than nothing. Not only did these 25 ton monsters have three inches of armour plate, they also boasted 2 Pounder guns with an impressive muzzle velocity. As a tank man through and through, Parsons was disappointed at the relatively slow speed of the tank, but, as his superiors kept reminding him, the Matilda was an Infantry Tank; designed for close cooperation with men on foot.

They would have that cooperation today. Their entire brigade was concentrated over a frontage of just two miles, whilst the division's other brigade was at the far side of the Selby road and ranged across a three mile front. The division was essentially a solid wall of armour and stacking up behind it was the best part of two full divisions of Canadian and New Zealand infantry. The Seventh Corps was the most completely equipped and powerfully armed in Britain, and soon, that power would be unleashed onto the German flank. It couldn't be long now, surely? Not now they were battened down.

This would be his first action, having joined the regiment just after Dunkirk. As a new boy, he had tried to get his hands on every report he could about the fighting in France, and he had relentlessly pestered the more senior chaps in the Mess for their war stories, so eager was he to prepare himself for his own blooding.

And now that time was near. His hands were sweating, and he suddenly needed a piss. Too late. Somewhere outside, a distant, continuous rumble began that could be heard above the engine.

"That's the guns opening up." He said aloud, and tried to imagine what it would be like to be on the end of six full regiments of field artillery.

Each Canadian division owned two of them, and the Corps had its own pair of field artillery regiments too. Parsons listened to the hammering of the guns as they loosed off salvo after salvo from their gun-lines by Naburn village and Crockey Hill.

"Won't be long now." Parsons fidgeted in his seat.

He glanced at the breech of the 2 Pounder.

"Have we got one up the spout?"

Next to him, the loader shook his head.

"No, Sir." The private drawled laconically in his cockney accent. "Do you think we should stick one up?"

"What?" Parsons looked at the loader in surprise?

The gunner and loader instantly burst into fits of laughter.

"Bloody hell, Sir! How many times have you asked us that in the last hour? Of course we've got one up the spout! You didn't think we were going to spit at the Jerries did you?"

Parsons felt his face redden.

"Bloody hell, Dawkins…"

The radio crackled into life.

"All stations, this is Zero. Radio silence is lifted. Stand-by…"

The clipped, precise voice of Major Watts, the squadron leader, was unmistakable. The gunner and loader instantly fell silent and looked at Parsons, their faces suddenly serious. Outside, the rumble of the artillery barrage continued like an endless thunder storm. A few moments later, the squadron leader's voice came through the ear-piece once more.

"All stations, this is Zero. Stand-by. H-Hour in five, four, three, two, one…go, go, go; tally-ho, tally-ho!"

All along a five mile frontage, just south of the city of York, more than two hundred tanks from the British 1st Armoured Division broke cover and began rumbling forwards across their start-line. The British counter-attack had begun…

THE RIDGE – STILLINGFLEET
TUESDAY 24TH SEPTEMBER 1940 – 1115 HOURS

Merkal hated being on the flank. He had two main reasons for that; the first being that by sitting on the flank, he wasn't in the thick of the action with the rest of his unit and the tanks from 8th Panzer. If he was ever going to stand a chance of winning the Knight's Cross, he needed to be up front, where the action was. The other reason, quite simply, was fear.

He had been on a flank before; just a few months earlier in mid-May, in a small village near Arras. It was during those heady days of the rush to the Channel, when the German offensive had been less than two weeks old, and they had swept everyone before them with contempt; the Dutch, the Belgians, the French and the British. But then, on that warm May morning in the village square, as he and his company took some rest and awaited the call forward, the British tanks had pounced on them.

The small, noisy vehicles had clattered into the village at speed, taking Merkal and his men completely by surprise. Within seconds, it had been carnage. The Tommy machine-guns had raked the SS trucks with fire, chopping down man after man as the vehicle drivers attempted to escape from the square in blind panic. Merkal had been lucky enough to be the first one out of the village, and hadn't stopped driving until he ran into none other than the commander of the 7th Panzer Division, a general by the name of Rommel.

It was Rommel himself who quickly deployed the big 88 mm guns into a rough screen and began picking off the Tommy tanks one by one, as they pursued Merkal's fleeing column of trucks. For over an hour, Merkal had lay hidden with his driver in a sunken lane, while a general and a handful of gunners stemmed the tide of the British counter-attack. The memory of the event still brought terrible memories back for Merkal; memories of anger, and memories of shame.

That said, he had gained his revenge several days later, when his company had taken almost a hundred British soldiers prisoner, following a particularly vicious battle, which had left over thirty more SS men from his regiment dead. Having rounded the Tommies up, he had marched them into a field and lined them up against a barn, before machine-gunning the lot of them. The Army Corps to which they were attached had asked disapproving questions afterwards, but his divisional commander, Theodor Eicke had made the problem go away without too much fuss. Merkal was sure that his beloved commander would do the same again if anyone raised a question over the death of the Tommy militia members that he had gunned down outside Driffield the other day.

All these things ran through Merkal's mind as he dragged himself out from underneath his half-track. The air-raid had been something of a shock when it had begun just an hour and a half ago, although they were lucky enough to be on the periphery of the huge aerial bombardment. The artillery barrage that had followed the bombing was the real surprise though. It had descended on them like a tidal wave, but instead of passing over them in a rush, it had crept painfully slowly through their defensive screen, with shell after shell slamming into the ridge and the nearby village. The wheel of the half-track he had been sheltering under had been taken off by a large chunk of shell case that had narrowly missed his head. All around the hillside, Merkal could here moaning and shocked voices calling out to one another. His own ears were buzzing from the terrific noise of the barrage, and his arms and legs were more than a little shaky. And then he heard something that made his entire body suddenly feel as though it were made of jelly.

"Tanks!"

Hardly daring to believe his ears, the SS company commander hauled himself upright and staggered up the slope towards the crest of the ridge. A whistle was blowing somewhere off to his left, sounding the stand-to. He could hear the voices of the gunners from the anti-tank platoon that he had managed to secure for his position.

"Which one?" Screamed one voice.

"The closest one! There!" Screamed another.

Woomf!

The sound of the PAK 37 anti-tank gun barking into life was unmistakable. Merkal stumbled on towards the gun position.

As he gained the crest and dropped in behind the low silhouette of the gun, Merkal's mouth dropped open in shock, and a small cry of dread escaped from him involuntarily. There were tanks everywhere. Tommy tanks. As far as the eye could see, from left to right, there was a line of armoured vehicles, heading steadily up the gentle slope towards them from the mass of woods and hedgerows to the north. Behind the first wave, another line of tanks was emerging from the trees. One of the tanks was already on fire and as Merkal watched, the other PAK 37 over to his right fired too. He watched in fascination as the armour-piercing shell slammed into the front of one of the leading tanks, making it rear up like a startled horse. As the metal beast crashed back down onto shattered tracks, it began to burn. Thank God he had anti-tank guns with him!

"Come on!" Merkal suddenly yelled at the sergeant commanding the gun to his front. "Fire again, quickly!"

Woomf! The gun lurched as it spat another round out towards the approaching wave of armour.

"What does it fucking look like we're doing?" The sergeant swore at him without even looking to see who had made the comment.

Shocked at the response, Merkal could only watch as the gun crew ejected the spent shell case from the breech and replaced it with a fresh round.

"They're peeling off left and right!" Shouted the gun-layer.

The sergeant poked his head up and, like Merkal, saw that the first line of enemy tanks was parting in the middle.

"They're going round the flanks!" The gun-layer shouted again.

"Don't worry." The sergeant responded. "They'll run into the section in the village and the section by the road junction. We'll catch 'em in a cross fire."

The gun commander tapped the gun-layer's shoulder and pointed towards the second wave of British armour, which was now level with the pair of burning tanks from the first wave.

"There you go; hit that bastard there!"

Another Tommy tank was trundling through the smoke of the burning wrecks and coming straight towards them. This tank was different to the others. Although not much bigger, it seemed squatter, and more solid looking, though its speed was unusually slow.

Merkal watched, unable to offer any practical advice, while the gun team laid their weapon onto the new target. Several moments later, the gun lurched again as the crew released yet another shell. Merkal watched the bright blur of the armour piercing round arc through the air towards the lumbering Tommy tank, seeming to take an age to reach its intended target. But the crew were good and the gun-layer was spot on. The round suddenly zipped down towards the British tank, slamming into the turret of the vehicle, just above the gun…and bounced off.

"What the fuck?" Cursed the sergeant.

"What happened?" Demanded the gun-layer, dragging his eyes from the sight and looking over the gun-shield.

"It fucking bounced off!" The sergeant said, visibly shaken.

Merkal felt the panic rise inside him. It might be moving slowly, but the Tommy tank, along with its neighbours, was coming inexorably closer.

"Fire at it again! Quickly!" Merkal screamed at the gun crew from behind.

This time there was no answer from the sergeant. Instead, the crew jerked into action, and repeated the well practiced routine of reloading and re-laying the gun. As they did so, a streak of light came from their right hand side, and Merkal watched a shell from the flanking 37mm anti-tank gun slash across the field and slam into the side of the same Tommy tank that had already survived one hit. To his disbelief, the shell exploded with a bright flash and metallic boom, and yet the enemy vehicle continued to roll forward without pausing. In fact the vehicle had barely shuddered under the impact of the shell.

"Firing now!" Shouted the sergeant, and the gun in front of Merkal barked in anger once more.

Again, both he and the crew watched the shell cut through the air towards the target, and smash into the enemy vehicle. This time, there was a bright flash and a boom. They watched in fascination as the smoke cleared.

"It's stopping!" Yelled the gun-layer.

"Yes!" The sergeant slammed his hand against the breach in exultation.

Merkal let out a sigh of relief. It was short lived.

"It's not dead!"

Merkal heard the gun-layer's words and caught his breath, snapping his attention back to the tank. The vehicle sat like some huge, powerful bull in the middle of the distant field some three hundred yards away, and the SS officer fought down a groan as he saw the tank's turret begin to move. The slim looking gun slowly turned off to an angle then stopped. A second later there was a brief flash from the muzzle of the tank's gun, and then Merkal was staring in horrid fascination as a speck of light seemed to dart across the slope at an unbelievable speed, heading straight towards the PAK 37 to his right.

He heard the results before he saw them; the sound of a sickening impact against sheet metal, followed by the sharp explosion of the shell. He swung his gaze over his right shoulder and saw, to his horror, the neighbouring gun literally standing on its trails, its barrel pointing at an acute angle skywards, whilst from within the cloud of smoke, bits of human body parts began emerging, completely divorced from their owners. An arm, the grey sleeve of which bore the distinctive black Totenkopf wrist band, curled through the air in a ridiculously lazy fashion and then thudded down into a furrow of earth, barely ten metres from Merkal.

"Get down!"

The sound of the gun commander's voice brought Merkal back to reality with a shock. Instinctively, he dropped flat on his belly, and it wasn't a moment too soon, as a hail of heavy calibre machine-gun bullets slapped into the shield of the gun, whilst yet more cracked close overhead or slammed into the soil around them. Without a sound, the gun-layer toppled sideways, half of his head shot away. The loader, crouching behind the dead layer, began crying out in disgust as he wiped furiously at the bloody brains and jelly that had spattered across his face and chest.

"It's moving again!" The sergeant was shouting hysterically. " It's coming for us! We can't stop the fucking things!"

Merkal felt his bowels loosen in fear, a sensation that was enhanced by the memory of his previous encounter with British tanks. He remembered now, that even with the big 88 mm guns, General Rommel had been pushed to stop some of the enemy tanks. And Merkal didn't have any 88s. Suddenly, the feeling of panic overwhelmed the SS officer, and despite his desire to be a hero of the Third Reich, and much to his shame, he heard himself screaming out the same words over and over again.

"Pull back! Pull back!"

CHURCH FENTON RAILWAY JUNCTION – THE CAWOOD POCKET
TUESDAY 24TH SEPTEMBER 1940 – 1145 HOURS

"Engels? What the fuck's going on?"

Captain Klaus Becker of the Third Panzer Grenadier Battalion dodged through the trees and threw himself down next to the Lieutenant who was cowering behind a tree-trunk.

"We can't get into the hotel, Sir!" The Lieutenant grimaced. "The Tommies have got us pinned down from three sides and I lost the whole First Squad when we tried to storm the place! There's no way into the village this way!"

Becker looked around him in despair. It was a disaster. They had been called forward to support the leading panzer companies, as they tried to break through or turn the Tommy line. Thus far, that had proved impossible, and Becker was just starting to understand the trap that they had been lured into. Having by-passed a fully committed Totenkopf Division who were desperately trying to force their way south into Selby, Becker and his men had followed in the tracks of the forward left panzer company. On one side, they had been heavily engaged by the defenders of Church Fenton, whilst from the other, round after round from cleverly hidden anti-tank guns and hails of machine gun fire had prevented them from turning south and breaking out into more open country. Steadily, they had pushed on westwards, desperately trying to find the gap in the enemy defences; a weak spot or overlooked boundary. Instead they had been sucked deeper and deeper into a maze of tank traps, ditches, road-blocks and mine-fields, all of them covered by anti-tank guns and small arms fire.

Finally, in one last attempt to find an opening, both he and the panzer company commander had opted to punch hard for the railway station that lay at the western end of Church Fenton. According to the radio, another battle group was heavily engaged on the north-eastern side of the village by the airfield. If they could just break through, they would be able to isolate the village and use it as a springboard to punch deep into the enemy's rear. But it just wasn't happening.

Behind Becker, the wide open fields to the south of the railway station were littered with burning panzers and half tracks. Half his company was stalled on the railway lines as they attempted to dislodge the stubborn defenders of the houses that sat right on the apex of the railway junction. The other half was pinned down here in the small copse of trees, right next to the railway bridge. Across the road, a heavily fortified British pub was alive with enemy, and the pavement and road outside it was littered with dead panzer grenadiers.

"They've got the whole place sewn up!" Becker murmured to himself through gritted teeth as he surveyed the scene of devastation. Over by the railway lines, where some of his men were lining the track and blasting away furiously at the cluster of houses, Becker suddenly heard a loud whine, followed by a 'crump'. The ground trembled beneath him and he looked beyond the trees towards the source of the noise.

"Fucking hell! Not again!"

Another artillery bombardment descended on his men by the rail tracks. The enemy observer must be extremely good, for the shells were smacking right into where his men were stacking up, ready to assault the buildings, whilst keeping clear of the fortified houses.

"Where's the fucking Luftwaffe?" Becker suddenly shouted in frustration. "What's happened to the Stuka squadron?"

What Becker didn't realise was that neither the Stukas, nor the squadron of 110s that had been forward-based on the improvised airstrip at Lisset, would be arriving to give them any kind of help. Both squadrons had been caught shortly after take off by a large group of Hurricanes, flying advance guard for the British bomber force. In a fierce air battle over Holme-on-Spalding Moor, that was actually more of a slaughter, the two squadrons of German ground attack aircraft had been torn to pieces. It was a similar story over the North Sea, where every spare fighter that the British could muster had intercepted the German long range bomber forces as they flew west to help their ground forces deliver the killer blow, and attack the British Home Fleet. German air power over Yorkshire was now nothing more than history.

The British bombardment ended as abruptly as it started. For long moments the battlefield was unusually quiet as both sides allowed the echoes to fade and raised their heads ready for the next onslaught. Becker's mind was working furiously to come up with a solution. His messages back to the battalion commander were being fended off with orders to 'wait' and he had lost communications with the commander of the panzers. He needed to do something quickly before this predicament became a defeat. Any hope of sorting out the mess ended just moments later.

At first, the sound of the aircraft engines made Becker's heart leap with renewed hope, but then he glanced up and saw the bright blue and red symbols on the dark shapes that roared low overhead. A split second later, the whistling began, and then, just a heartbeat further on, the first British bomb exploded amongst the surviving panzers to the south of the village. The Royal Air Force was back with a vengeance.

S +3
MIDDAY

THE BIG HOUSE – BARMBY MOOR
TUESDAY 24TH SEPTEMBER 1940 – 1230 HOURS

"Shut the fucking door! They're coming round the back!" Dullman screamed down the stairs of the big, manorial looking farm house.

Nuemark, the last member of the platoon to enter the house, turned and ran back along the hallway towards the big, sturdy oak door.

The counter-attack had come as a shock. Although the Germans had expected some kind of British riposte, they hadn't believed that the Tommies were capable of such a huge, powerful, and sudden offensive. It had burst on the men of the 17th Infantry Division like a storm. The high-level aerial bombing had been nothing more than a warmer into the bank. To the slight surprise of the Germans, the vast majority of British bombs had landed outside the villages of Barmby Moor, Pocklington and Market Weighton. Instead, the huge weight of ordnance had been deposited on the woods and copses that surrounded the built up areas and it had been a long while before the penny had dropped with Captain Dullman.

"The bastards are picking off the anti-tank screens!" He had rumbled ominously, several minutes after the last waves of bombers had departed. "They don't know where they are, so they're systematically bombing every piece of cover they can find!"

And it was during that moment of realisation that the attack had begun. The Tommy artillery had laid a carpet of explosions right up to the village's western edge, and emerging out of the smoke behind the last of the explosions was the mass of tanks and men. So used to seeing small pockets of enemy resistance had Dullman become, that at first he could only stare in shock towards the fields to the north and west of his position, as a solid wall of men and vehicles advanced towards his company at speed.

The Tommy assault had been swift, bold, and terrifying. Big, solid looking tanks that seemed impervious to the battalion's 37mm anti-tank screen had smashed through the perimeter posts and begun machine-gunning every building in site. Behind those tanks, squad after squad of tall, powerfully built enemy infantry had smashed their way into the first buildings in the village, howling war cries that were enough to freeze the blood.

And so here Dullman was, trapped in the big house behind the church, with only the survivors of Hagen's platoon and his own tactical headquarters for company. The house's moat, far from proving an obstacle, had become a useful aid to the Tommies, who had set up a group of light-machine guns along its lip and were now saturating the windows of the house with fire. Somewhere out on the streets of the village, Dullman could hear the metallic clatter of tank tracks on tarmac. Meanwhile, the sound of angry, urgent British voices told him that their house was about to be assaulted.

"Shut the fucking door and barricade it!" He screamed down the stairs once more.

Nuemark was already there, slamming the heavy door shut. The corporal turned around, his back to the door and snarled at two nearby soldiers.

"Get some fucking furniture over here, quickly!"

The corporal reached out for a small wooden trunk that sat to one side of the doorway, and began dragging it towards him. As he bent forward, the doorway above his head splintered noisily and two heavy bullets exploded through the wood and into the hallway. A moment later, the large door burst open, propelling Nuemark forwards and face down on the floor.

In the open doorway, two huge figures in khaki appeared. One of them held a revolver and shot a nearby German private straight through the chest. The Tommy's companion swatted aside the rifle of the other German soldier and rammed his long bayonet deep into the man's stomach. The German gave a pitiful scream as the Tommy forced him backwards onto the floor, forcing the bayonet deeper into his guts. With an exclamation of both fear and anger, Dullman, still at the top of the stairs, squeezed the trigger of his machine-pistol and let rip with a full magazine. The two Tommies toppled sideways against the wall and collapsed amongst the other bodies in the hallway.

His weapon empty, Dullman pounded down the wide staircase and threw himself at the wooden door, slamming it shut again. He saw a key in the lock and turned it, feeling the heavy mechanism click shut.

"Get this fucking door barricaded!" He bawled.

Another private was at his shoulder already, and he recognised the young machine-gunner called Bachman from Hagen's platoon. The soldier was dragging a heavy side table into position behind the door, and having positioned it, he used his boot to push the abandoned wooden trunk under it.

Dullman turned around and surveyed the carnage in the hallway. The German soldier with the bayonet in his guts was whimpering into the lap of one of his squad mates. Saltz was hauling the stunned and winded Nuemark to his feet. Beyond them, Hagen was blasting away with his machine-pistol out of a shattered window in the next room. The captain looked around the bodies on the floor. The Tommy with the rifle and bayonet was clearly dead, his body peppered with ragged holes. The dead Tommy had been a giant of a man however and Dullman stared in disbelief at the size of the man's heavy, studded boots. The other Tommy had a little brass star on either of his epaulettes and Dullman realised he was an officer. To his surprise, the blood stained enemy officer suddenly coughed and moved an arm.

Dullman stepped over to him and knelt down by the dying man. He grabbed the young Tommy's collar and gently turned his head so that he could look at the man in the eyes. Saltz, Nuemark and Bachman looked on as the company commander spoke to the wounded Tommy in English, his voice surprisingly soft.

"Who are you, boy? What unit? What's going on? How many are you?"

For a long moment the dying youngster didn't reply, but eventually he managed to whisper an answer through lips that were bubbling with blood.

"Scot's Guards, old boy…" Gasped the wounded British officer.

"What?" Dullman asked again, his voice sharper now. "What did you say?"

The British officer smiled weakly as a rivulet of blood trickled down his cheek and onto his shoulder.

"Scots Guards…" The youngster managed to say weakly. Then with a smile, he said, "You're fighting the Brigade of Guards, Jerry…"

A moment later, the young man died.

Dullman stood and turned towards the others in the hall. Hagen had come to stand by the doorway of the next room and was looking on whilst he changed the magazine on his weapon. Dullman's face was dark and worried. None of his men had ever seen him look so pensive.

"We're in big fucking trouble." The captain said ominously.

There was silence in the hallway for a while.

"What did he say, Captain?" Saltz finally asked.

Dullman took a deep breath.

"He said he was from the Brigade of Guards. I've fought them before in Belgium, when I was with the 7th Division. They're the British King's personal bodyguard troops."

Hagen walked into the hallway some more.

"What does that mean, Sir?" He asked.

Dullman scanned the faces in the hallway, and the look on his face chilled them to the bone.

"It means they won't stop fighting until they're all dead…or until we are."

KELFIELD – 1 MILE EAST OF CAWOOD
TUESDAY 24TH SEPTEMBER 1940 – 1245 HOURS

Parsons couldn't believe it. He had come through his first action without a scratch, despite having taken no less than five direct hits. Three of those had come from the small anti-tank guns on the Stillingfleet ridge, whilst the other two hits had been sustained not long after they had rolled over the enemy guns, machine-gunning the fleeing infantry as they did so. It was as the British came down the southern slope of the ridge that they were engaged from the forward left by something bigger, probably the dreaded 88 mm flak guns. It looked as though the guns were situated off to one flank, somewhere in the direction of Ricall, but he had been unable to spot them.

He had winced in anticipation as two big shells slammed into his Matilda II from the left; one hitting the rear deck of the tank and the other catching the turret. The second round had made one hell of a noise and for just a moment or two, he had watched in horror as the inside of the turret glowed red where the armour piercing shell fought to penetrate. The noise and vibration caused by the hit had made his nose bleed, but despite this, the red glow on the turret had faded and his tank remained one hundred percent intact. It was then the squadron leader had come on the radio and informed them that the neighbouring squadron was wheeling left to attack the new threat, whilst their own squadron was to plough straight on for the Ricall-Cawood road. For about the tenth time in as many minutes, Parsons thanked God for giving him a Matilda Mark II.

Now, as Parsons fought to get his bearings through the telescope, he suddenly caught his breath. Right in front of him was what seemed like half the German Army queued up in one great column, and completely unprepared to deal with the sudden appearance of British tanks on their flank.

"Bloody hell, Sir! Where do we start?" Breathed Warner, his gunner.

"Shoot anything with a gun first." Parsons responded, surprised at how calm his own voice sounded. "Then machine-gun the infantry when there's nothing left to blow up."

"Sir! Jerry tanks on the edge of the trees to our right."

Parsons looked in the direction indicated and saw the group of vehicles parked alongside the small wood. He could see one big tank with a large gun, two smaller tanks, and several wheeled vehicles. The enemy were side on to them but desperately traversing their guns onto the British armour.

"Incoming!" He yelled as he saw the big vehicle fire. "Traverse right, Warner!"

Clang-boom! The German shell hit them with a noise similar to that of the big anti-tank gun from earlier. This time however, there was no red glow, and the vehicle hardly gave a shudder. Warner didn't even pause in his traversing.

"I've got him; stop the tank!"

The driver slammed on the brakes at the gunner's direction. As soon as the vehicle settled, Warner began turning the fine adjustment gears of the gun.

"Quick as you can, Warner, before those others lay onto us!"

"Nearly there!" The gunner assured his commander.

Clang! A small shell bounced off the Matilda; then a second shell from the other German light tank came in low and slammed into the soil, fifteen yards short of the British armoured vehicle.

"Come on, Warner!" Parsons urged.

"On!" Warner yelled, locking the adjusting gears. "Firing now!"

Woomf!

The 2 Pounder gun roared into life. Even before the echo had dissipated, the gunner had opened the breech and the loader was extracting the empty shell case. Through their periscopes, Warner and Parsons watched the brief swirl of their shell speed towards the centre, and biggest, of the three German tanks. The aim was true and the shell hit the German vehicle just below its main gun. There was a flash, a cloud of black smoke, and then bits of metal shot skywards. A split second later there was another explosion, much bigger, which lifted the turret clean off the German tank.

"Bloody hell!" Parsons exclaimed.

"Christ almighty, it went right through the bugger!" Warner gave a whistle.

Jennings, barely able to see the enemy vehicles from his driver's seat, gave a whoop of joy.

"You little dancer!" He shouted up to the turret crew.

"Reloaded!" Yelled Dawkins.

"Take out the right hand tank of those two little ones!" Parsons ordered.

Within seconds, Warner had unlocked the gun and re-laid it onto the new target.

"Firing now!"

Again the gun barked; and again, the crew watched in amazement as the shell sliced straight through the target. The remaining German vehicles didn't wait to contest their wood any longer; they ran for it.

Just at that point, the radio crackled into life.

"All stations, this is Zero, keep moving, keep moving. We've got them against the river. All heavies go for the tanks; light vehicles go for the infantry and guns. Shoot everything. If you run out of bullets, run the bastards over! Out!"

Parsons shouted to the rest of the crew.

"You heard him, lads; let's go! Straight for them. Warner, let's have some more good shooting!"

With a roar, the Matilda juddered forwards again, trundling down-slope towards the distant column of enemy vehicles and men.

Over a thousand German troops, along with dozens of tanks and vehicles, were hurriedly attempting to turn and face the sudden threat from the north;

pinned as they were against the bend of the River Ouse. As they did so, the British artillery's forward observation officer watched in satisfaction as another barrage came screaming down amongst the packed German column. The German flank was wide open. The British Army's most powerful armoured formation was upon them; and the slaughter was about to begin.

PARADISE WOOD – THE CAWOOD POCKET
TUESDAY 24TH SEPTEMBER 1940 – 1300 HOURS

Clunk.

The breech of the 2 Pounder opened and the No.2 on the gun flicked out the empty shell case. Immediately, the loader thrust a new shell into the still smoking chamber then pulled his hands away sharply before the No.2 slammed the breech shut once more.

"Reloaded!"

The gun-layer was already on his desired target. Their first shell had crippled the heavy German tank which had come trundling back eastwards through the smoke and chaos of the battlefield. Perhaps forgetting the carnage that the defenders of the wood had caused them on their initial thrust for the airfield, the Germans had withdrawn right back into the field of fire of the British infantry company and the section of 2 Pounders attached to it.

Having adjusted the fine elevation of the gun, the gun-layer yanked his head away from the sight.

"On!"

The gun-commander, bleeding from a bullet wound to his shoulder, didn't even pause.

"Fire!"

The squat gun spat a small dart of flame from its muzzle as it propelled another armour piercing shell towards the immobile German tank. The high velocity shell slammed squarely into the turret of the beast, just above where the first shell had destroyed the tank's running gear just moments before. Smoke began billowing from the vehicle as the explosion subsided and a figure clambered out of the hatch at the front of the tank. He was alone. No one else exited the burning tank, and the sole survivor of the crew dropped onto the ground and began crawling away on all fours towards a nearby hedge.

The fields surrounding the wood were littered with burning vehicles and dozens of dead bodies, virtually all of them German. There was little small arms fire from the infantrymen who lined the perimeter of the wood, protecting the three 2 Pounders, for the last German infantry attack had fizzled out over forty minutes ago. Many of the enemy vehicles had simply ignored the flanking fire from the wood and sped past, heading deeper into the trap that had been laid for them, but even so, the defenders had been subjected to several furious assaults, firstly by vehicle-borne panzer grenadiers, and then by a horde of strangely uniformed SS troops. Now, Major Claude Banford, officer commanding 'C' Company, The Royal Elmet Rifles, stared across the smoke covered battlefield and dared to hope that the worst was over.

He looked toward the 2 Pounder which had just destroyed the German tank and shouted his congratulations to the crew.

"Well done, you lot! How much ammunition have you got left?"

The gun-commander turned to see who was calling them and, seeing the company commander, held up his good arm and flashed his fingers open twice.

"Down to the last ten rounds, Sir."

Banford gave a thumbs-up in acknowledgement.

"Roger. Keep your eyes peeled then and try to keep it to just one round per target. Easier said than done, I know…"

He smiled at the gun-commander to show that he was not ignorant of the difficulties of hitting a moving tank.

The sound of aircraft engines roared overhead, and Banford glanced up to see a flight of three Blenheims flying unbelievably low over the fields to the north, heading towards Cawood. As they passed, their machine-guns chattered into life, raining death upon some unseen target to the east of the railway line. Banford shook his head in wonder at how his company had managed to survive under so much enemy pressure. In truth, when he had first been given his mission, he'd suspected that his company was being deliberately sacrificed and that they would all die. Now however, he found himself feeling admiration for whoever had devised such a cunning defensive plan.

Throughout the battle, whenever the Germans had attempted to destroy Banford's annoying little pocket of resistance, they had found themselves caught from several different angles. In addition to the defenders of Paradise Wood, the enemy had also taken fire from another company dug-in by the village of Ryther. At the same time, the observers on the Towton ridge were continuously bringing barrage after barrage down amongst the German formations as they rolled across the open ground. That open ground had been heavily prepared with all manner of obstacles, including the mining of the two railway lines that ran north to south through the pocket. As the German armoured thrust and follow-up infantry had struggled to negotiate these obstacles and react to the flanking fire of the fortified posts, the RAF had come in low, between artillery bombardments, to strafe the exposed enemy time and again.

"Major Banford, Sir?"

He turned at the sound of his name being called and spotted Sergeant Lawson running towards him through the shattered wood at a low crouch. The sergeant had become the acting company sergeant major when the original holder of that post had been killed during the first German infantry attack.

"Over here!" Banford raised his hand and waved a revolver towards the NCO.

The sergeant veered towards him and skidded to a halt, coming to rest in a kneeling position by Banford's shell scrape.

"What is it, Sergeant Lawson?" Banford asked, seeing the man's excited look.

"The Jerries, Sir. They're surrendering!"

"What?" Banford asked incredulously.

"Not all of them, Sir." Lawson cautioned him. "They've got vehicles and tanks moving back towards Cawood, but there's a group of about fifteen infantry that we've had pinned down for an hour or so on the south side of the wood. They've just put a white flag up and come out into the open; straight after that last barrage."

Banford was starting to feel the first tingle of exultation as he listened to the sergeant's words. His day had started with a sense of grim resignation. That had developed into one of cold fury as he had fought the enemy hard throughout the course of the morning, resolved that he would make the Germans pay dearly for the destruction of his company. For the first time however, he was beginning to sense that perhaps there was going to be a completely unexpected outcome to this situation. Unbelievably, Banford thought he could smell the tantalising scent of victory.

S +3
THE AFTERNOON

500 YARDS NORTH-WEST OF 'HOUGOUMONT FARM'
TUESDAY 24TH SEPTEMBER 1940 – 1415 HOURS

The burst of machine-gun fire slammed into the body of the truck with a metallic hammering noise.

"More Tommy tanks! Go right at this junction then head towards that high ground. Our troops must be in that direction."

Merkal was terrified. The last few hours had become a living nightmare. It was like Arras all over again, only twenty times worse, and he felt as if the entire British Army was out to get him personally.

Back at Stillingfleet Ridge, Merkal had managed to get to one of the few lorries left intact after the huge Tommy bombardment. Without waiting to give any firm direction to his dispersed company, or attempting to warn the German troops massing around Cawood or Kelfield, Merkal had ordered his driver to head directly for the village of Ricall. Even in the heat of the moment and with his judgement clouded by fear, the SS officer realised that if he didn't get to Ricall then the Tommy armour would trap him against the River Ouse, along with the rest of his division and a large portion of 8th Panzer.

Arriving at Ricall, chased all the way by bursts of machine-gun fire, Merkal had enjoyed just a brief flicker of hope when he found two full batteries of 88 mm guns ranged in a wide screen at the northern end of the village. That hope had died quickly enough. Although the first Tommy tanks to appear were quickly despatched by the mighty 88's, the lightly armoured vehicles were again followed closely by the slow, lumbering, heavy tanks that had proved impervious to the shells from the PAK 37s. Yet again, these squat British monsters had rolled inexorably forwards, seemingly oblivious to the impact of the 88 mm shells that hit them. Within minutes, a large percentage of the 88 mm crews had been gunned down, whilst some of the guns themselves had been shattered by heavy shells. As the thickly armoured tanks had rolled over the remains of the 88 mm screen, their lightly armoured companions had reappeared, speeding back into the fray from the flanks, to chase down and slaughter any surviving Germans.

Watching all this from half a kilometre behind the anti-tank screen, Merkal had begun to experience a rising sense of horror at the inability of the German guns to stop the Tommy armour. Rommel had managed to do it at Arras, so why wasn't it possible here? Even the last minute arrival of a tank battalion from 8th Panzer, punching north through Ricall on its way to the bridge at Cawood was insufficient to stem the British tide. The German tanks had driven straight into the fray, attempting to deploy into extended order, but the lead vehicles had been torn apart by the British tank guns, and then, whilst still only half deployed, a second line of British tanks had come onto the German flank from the north-east. Within a short while, the northern fringes of Ricall had become a scene of utter destruction, with burning German tanks littering the expanse of freshly ploughed countryside.

It had been enough for Merkal. Without a hint of shame, he had snapped out the orders to his driver and roared off due east, towards the temporary sanctuary of the distant woods at Skipwith. More by luck than judgement, Merkal had found his way through the sprawling woodland using old tracks, before finally exiting on the eastern edge of the small forest. During his journey, Merkal had come across a battalion of infantry from the 35th Division, who were halfway through clearing the woodland. He had paused only long enough to warn them about the tanks before speeding off again, claiming to be on his way to Corps HQ with an important message.

He had then crossed the River Derwent using one of the small pontoon bridges that 8th Panzer had thrown across the river just twenty four hours before, again insisting to the field police sentries that he was carrying vital information to Corps HQ. He had only just managed to persuade them to allow him access to the bridge, when the Tommy attack caught up with them. More tanks, again preceded by a fierce bombardment, came rolling across the water meadows on the western bank of the river, sending the German troops in the area into a flat panic. Merkal had forced his vehicle onto the bridge, even as the first PAK 37s from the 35th Infantry vainly began engaging the enemy armour.

And it wasn't over yet. He was somewhere just to the north of where the British had made a stand the day before. He recognised the wide, muddy tracks through the fields that had effectively become a by-pass around the Tommy position for the 8th Panzer and Totenkopf spearhead. The burst of fire that had just slammed into his truck had taken the SS officer by surprise, for he hadn't thought for a moment that the British could possibly have been on this side of the Derwent yet. But here they were. Over to his forward left, a group of British light tanks were churning across the fields, at an angle that would surely cut him off; their machine-guns spitting fire as they came.

"Go right! Go right!" He yelled at his driver, repeatedly.

Their lorry was just coming to a tarmac road, when the first Tommy tanks burst out of cover on their flank. With a squeal of brakes and a growl from the engine, the driver managed to turn the ungainly vehicle a full 90 degrees at the last moment, changing direction southwards. As the lorry's wheels gripped the solid tarmac, the driver put his foot down once more and accelerated away, heading southwards toward the not too distant hill that was crowned by shattered trees and a ruined church.

"We'll outrun them on the tarmac!" Merkal shouted above the roar of the engine, although in truth, he had no idea where he was going or what he was going to do next.

He didn't have time to think on it, for as their lorry rounded a bend in the road, the driver suddenly slammed the brakes on, and Merkal was catapulted into the windscreen as the vehicle screeched to a halt.

"What the fuck..." Cried the SS officer in shock as he slammed against the front of the cab.

"Sorry, Sir." The driver apologised quickly. "Roadblock ahead. What now?"

Pushing himself back onto the seat, Merkal saw that in front of them was a wide crater in the road. Beyond it was an improvised barricade made from telegraph poles, furniture, rubble and all manner of battlefield detritus. The whole obstacle was draped with barbed wire that ran off over the flanking hedgerows and into the fields.

"Shit!" Merkal exclaimed.

Just at that point, the vehicle seemed to rear up underneath them as something big and heavy smashed through the cab and into the engine. The vehicle immediately stalled, and Merkal glanced sideways at the driver who was screaming in agony. The man's legs were covered in blood and a long thin sliver of metal was sticking into the side of the driver's calf.

"Fucking hell! Where did that come from?" Merkal wailed, the feeling of terror beginning to overwhelm his senses.

The windscreen of the vehicle suddenly shattered as a hail of bullets smashed into the vehicle from some unseen enemy. The driver went silent instantly as his head was split in two by a bullet, showering Merkal with blood and brains. The SS officer was too terrified to notice however, and with his arms covering his face, he kicked open the door of the truck and tumbled out onto the tarmac, crying out as his knees hit the rough road surface. Even as he hit the floor, he realised that his machine-pistol was still in the cab, but another burst of gunfire slamming into the vehicle was enough to tell him that it would have to stay there.

Several more bursts of fire hammered into the vehicle and he saw that it was starting to smoke. Something, somewhere on the lorry, was burning. Desperate not to be near the vehicle when the fuel tank exploded, Merkal crawled desperately across the road towards the ditch by the hedgerow. He dragged himself over the lip of the ditch and slid sideways into the foot or so of filthy water and sludge that covered the bottom. He could hear a tank engine somewhere, but it sounded quite a way off. Then he heard the voices; British voices. He hauled himself up against the bank and stared through the roots of the hedgerow into the field beyond...then caught his breath.

Across the corner of the field, barely a hundred and fifty metres away, was a heavily damaged farm house, surrounded by equally bombed-out barns and sheds. The field between him and the buildings was littered with German corpses, and even further across the field, he could see burnt out half-tracks. Most shockingly of all, coming across the field towards him, were a group of men. They were dressed in a variety of uniforms but their weapons, with the long, wicked looking bayonets attached to them were unmistakable. He was trapped, and the British were coming for him…

MOBILE HEADQUARTERS – 1ST CANADIAN INFANTRY DIVISION
TUESDAY 24TH SEPTEMBER 1940 – 1420 HOURS

The villages of Cawood, Stillingfleet and Ricall formed a geographic triangle. On two sides of that triangle, the land was hemmed in by the eastern bank of the River Ouse. The axis of advance for the British Seventh Corps effectively closed the door on the third side of that triangle and the parcel of land thus enclosed was a scene of utter devastation. Standing atop the cab of his headquarters radio truck, Acting Lieutenant General Andrew McNaughton, the commander of the Canadian contingent and, for the purposes of the British counter-attack, the commander of the Seventh Corps, shook his head with a mix of exultation, awe and disgust.

The men from his 1st Canadian Infantry Division were securing the area of Cawood and establishing a heavy defensive screen around the village, in order to prevent the escape of any German forces who had crossed onto the west bank of the Ouse. Those not involved with that blocking operation were busy rounding up the survivors of the German column that had been caught hard against the river on a narrow country road, without any room for manoeuvre. All around him, the land was half-obscured by the drifting smoke from dozens of still burning vehicles. Tanks, half-tracks, lorries, staff cars and motor-cycles, they were everywhere. When the massed tanks of the 3rd Armoured Brigade had crested the ridge at Stillingfleet, they had been presented with a gift of a target. Halting some five hundred yards short of the milling Germans, the British armour had begun lashing into their enemy with a vengeance. Within a short time, the tanks had been joined by their supporting anti-tank guns, and the slaughter had intensified.

By the time the 3rd Armoured Brigade had wheeled eastwards to follow on the remainder of 1st Armoured Division, there had been little left for the Canadian infantry to do, other than round up the bewildered survivors and block the bridge at Cawood. This was war at its ugliest; ugly, but absolutely necessary. There was no time for mercy or restraint on this occasion. The British and Commonwealth forces had one chance to strike a death blow to the German invasion, and there was no room for failure.

"Sweet Jesus!" McNaughton curled his nose at the smell of burning flesh that came from several nearby tank hulks. "I guess the Germans just got their own little taste of Dunkirk?"

His Brigadier General Staff looked up at him with a broad grin.

"Didn't know what hit them, Sir! Same thing happened over at Ricall too. 2nd Armoured Brigade has reached the village of Bubwith, with 2nd Infantry close behind them. They've detached the New Zealand Brigade to clear the woods at Skipwith."

McNaughton glanced at his map.

"Exactly as we planned it." He murmured. "But now for the difficult bit. Has the 2nd Armoured and 2nd Infantry been reminded not to exploit beyond Bubwith until they receive orders?"

"Yes, General; and 3rd Armoured Brigade is preparing to wheel south-east towards Howden. They're just waiting for the 1st Infantry to catch up."

McNaughton looked about him once more, a grimace on his thin, shrewd face.

"Okay, get a message to 1st Infantry. I want a brigade to stay here and secure Cawood and block any escape from the pocket. Tell them to get their other brigades moving straight away. They are to be prepared to clear the outskirts of Selby if any Germans have managed to hole up there. Clear?"

"Absolutely, Sir." The Brigadier General Staff responded.

McNaughton clambered down from the truck and slapped his senior staff officer on the shoulder.

"Let's get the men going then. We've got no time to enjoy the spectacle. I want to be in spitting distance of Hull before last light."

'HOUGOUMONT FARM' – HOME-ON-SPALDING MOOR
TUESDAY 24TH SEPTEMBER 1940 – 1425 HOURS

"Are you sure they're British?"

Jackson eyed the young private soldier with disbelief.

"Yes, Sarge." The private grinned back at him. "The Colonel is positive. He say's there's at least a dozen Vickers tanks, plus some big infantry tanks too. He says there's a horde of infantry in khaki coming up behind 'em; should be with us shortly."

Jackson looked around the shattered farm, surveying the ruined buildings and sprawled bodies; most of which were German. His small force had held onto the farm by their finger-tips during the night. Over half his men were dead or seriously wounded, and he had been forced to shrink his perimeter in the last hours before dawn.

No more German attacks had materialised however. Instead, he and his men had been subjected to almost constant mortar and artillery fire, until just an hour ago. Now, unbelievably, a runner had arrived from Colonel Ridley on Church Hill, informing him that a major British counter-attack force was coming straight towards them from the north. More than that, the runner had also informed him that there was heavy fighting everywhere to the west, and signs of panic amongst the distant German columns that had been by-passing them throughout the night. That there was heavy fighting, Jackson had no doubt. He had been listening to it for the last few hours, and had witnessed the RAF dropping hundreds, if not thousands of bombs, in a long carpet to their north and west.

"The Colonel said to be sure not to engage our own blokes, Sarge."

The private's voice snapped Jackson out of his thoughts. He nodded.

"We'll be careful. Now get yourself back up the hill and tell the Colonel that I've got fourteen men left who are fit to fight and I'm running low on all natures of ammunition. I've also got seven men seriously wounded. They'll need a doctor soon or they'll die."

The excited looking private nodded and made to head off.

"And big lad?" Jackson called after him.

The private stopped in his tracks and glanced back at the big Coldstreamer.

"What's your name?"

"Private McWilliams, Sarge." The soldier replied.

Jackson regarded the man as a school master would an ignorant pupil.

"There's an E-N-T on the end of Sarge, young McWilliams; make sure you use it."

The young soldier looked stunned at the reproach, but before he had a chance to acknowledge in any way, a flurry of gunfire sounded from the other side of the ruined farm.

"What the bloody hell was that?" Jackson asked rhetorically breaking into a run. He lurched through the rubble of the derelict barns towards the northern perimeter, moving as quickly as he could. In truth he was physically and mentally exhausted, like a punch-drunk boxer, after five days of marching and fighting with little sleep, food or water. As he stumbled through the chaotic ruins of the farm complex, he began to fear that his men had already sighted the approaching British troops and fired on them by mistake. There were several more bursts of gunfire, but by the time he had made his way to the back of the farm, the shooting had ceased.

"What's going on?" Jackson demanded of nobody in particular.

Downey appeared out of a shell-scrape to Jackson's right.

"Jerry truck just came up to the rear-road block. We hit it with the Boys Rifle and brassed it up with the Lewis. Tom Bishop's just gone forward with Martlesham and a couple of other Home Guard lads to check it out. We saw one of 'em drop out the vehicle."

Jackson frowned.

"Are you sure it was German? I've just had word that our boys are counter-attacking from the north. There's a big column of British tanks and infantry coming straight for us at this side."

Downey shook his head.

"Definitely a Jerry truck; no mistake."

No sooner had the corporal made the statement, than Bishop and his group pushed through the corner of the hedgerow with a German in their midst. The enemy soldier was dressed in field-grey trousers and jack-boots, whilst his upper body was garbed in a multi-coloured baggy smock of mottled pattern. The German was helmetless and as he was pushed across the farmyard, he looked up from underneath a cropped mop of blonde hair and threw a look of disdain towards Jackson. The big sergeant walked across to meet the group and returned the German's baleful look with tired, emotionless eyes. After a couple of moments of mutual study, Jackson reached out a hand and pulled the collar of the German's smock aside.

For a moment the prisoner tried to resist, but Jackson cuffed him around the ear with one of his shovel like hands and the German staggered under the blow, a look of utter outrage on his dour face.

"Stand still Jerry or I'll kick your fucking head in!" Bishop snarled from behind the prisoner.

Whether the prisoner understood the words or not was unclear, but he certainly understood the meaning. He remained motionless as Jackson pulled the smock open and searched him roughly.

Satisfied that the man was unarmed, Jackson's eyes narrowed as he studied the silver runes that glistened on the black collar boards of the tunic that the German wore beneath the smock. The sergeant's eyes flicked up to meet those of Bishop.

"This bastard's in the SS." He growled. "Looks like an officer to me. Take him into the bit of the farm house that's still standing and keep him in the parlour. Watch the bastard like a hawk; I want to have a word with him."

Bishop grinned wickedly.

"SS, eh? I've heard about those buggers. I do hope he needs some encouragement to join in the chat."

The burly farmer gave the prisoner a push.

"Come on, Hun. Let's find you somewhere cosy, shall we?"

As the prisoner was led away, Jackson turned back to Downey.

"Corporal 'D', get round the boys please and let them know we're expecting company from a relief column. Tell them not to fire at anything unless they can guarantee that it's German."

The corporal, a deep frown etched on his face, was watching the group with the prisoner as they pushed him towards the farmhouse. He glanced at Jackson.

"Sergeant, that Jerry…"

Jackson interrupted him.

"In a minute Les; please? I need you to get round the lads first and warn them. I don't want anyone brassing up our own boys."

The corporal hesitated for a moment before nodding curtly and turning away to get on with his task. Jackson turned and followed the group with the captured German.

By the time Downey rejoined him, Jackson was getting pretty annoyed with the prisoner. The German would say nothing, and the nearest they had got to a response from him was when he had spat on the floor in front of the oldest of the three Home Guardsmen and Bishop. That had earned the prisoner a cut above his right eye from Martlesham who, quite unexpectedly, had swung the heavy butt of his Lewis Gun at the German's head, sending him sprawling back against the corner of the room.

"Sergeant Jackson?"

The Coldstream sergeant glanced over his shoulder at Downey as he appeared in the doorway. The corporal was looking towards the prisoner with fierce interest.

"I need a word with you; it's urgent."

Without a word, Jackson turned away from the prisoner and went over to the doorway.

"What is it?" Jackson grunted as he left the room and moved into the partially collapsed hallway of the farmhouse.

Downey leaned in close to Jackson, his eyes serious and his voice low.

"He's the bastard who murdered our lads outside Driffield."

Jackson looked up sharply.

"What?"

"You remember what I told you about those SS fuckers, separating the Home Guard boys and gunning them down? Well, he was the one in charge; he gave the orders."

Jackson squinted, as if experiencing some kind of pain.

"Are you sure?"

Downey nodded vigorously.

"Absolutely; no mistake. I was only yards away from the bastard when he stopped our column. It's him; I'm telling you."

Jackson began nodding, thoughtfully.

"No mistake?" He asked again.

"No mistake." Downey assured him.

Jackson turned and stepped back into the room.

"Come with me."

The two NCOs walked into the centre of the room and looked down at the sullen faced SS officer. The prisoner, holding a hand to his injury, stared back up at them suspiciously. Jackson addressed the man.

"Two days ago, you ordered the murder of a group of British soldiers outside Driffield. They were members of the Driffield Home Guard."

Jackson saw the man's eyes widen. In the corner of the room, the two older Home Guardsmen, both from the Driffield area, muttered something angrily. The prisoner darted his eyes around the room at the angry British faces, then spoke.

"I am a member of the German armed forces and I am a prisoner of war. I am protected by the Geneva Convention."

The German's English was good; heavily accented perhaps, but precise and clear, all the same.

A wicked grin appeared on Jackson's haggard face. He pointed to Downey.

"This man watched you do it. He saw everything. He saw you separate them from a column of prisoners and then gun them down."

The German's eyes were becoming more and more frightened now, and his gaze was flickering around the room in fear as he attempted to push himself further into the corner.

"And these men here…" Jackson pointed to the Home Guardsmen from the Driffield area. "…are the friends of the men you murdered."

"I demand to be treated in accordance with the Geneva Convention!" Spluttered the German.

"Sergeant Jackson?"

Another of the farm's defenders shoved his head around the door.

"We've got British tanks coming over the field. They've got infantry on the backs of them. It's the relief column, Sergeant!"

"I'm on my way." Jackson dismissed the man without looking round.

The Coldstream NCO was still staring hard at the prisoner. When the messenger had disappeared again, Jackson spoke once more.

"Oh, fucking really?" He literally spat the words at the man in the corner. "Well, listen to me you box-head bastard; I'm going to see to some business and I'll be gone for a while. If you so much as move a muscle while I'm gone, these boys here will be forced to give you a taste of your own medicine. And when I come back, I'll be wanting some answers; so you'd best find your voice while I'm away."

With that, Jackson turned and left the room, leaving Hauptsturmfuhrer Merkal of the SS Division Totenkopf staring in terror at the five angry looking Tommies who remained.

When Jackson left the ruined building, he stopped dead amongst the debris of battle that littered the farmyard. Parked in the gap of the hedgerow where last night's climactic struggle had taken place, was a British tank. It was one of the big cruiser tanks, and in addition to the commander and gunner, the vehicle was festooned with khaki clad infantrymen, hanging off the sides and rear decks. They were talking excitedly to a handful of the farm's defenders, who were gathered about the armoured vehicle, laughing like children. Hardly daring to believe his eyes, Jackson walked at a measured pace across to the tank.

Halting in front of the metal beast, Jackson looked up at an infantry corporal standing on the front deck of the vehicle and hailed him.

"Nice to see you, bonny-lad; I'm Sergeant Jackson of the Coldstream Guards. I'm the commander of the farm's garrison. Who are you?"

The smiling corporal hesitated then suddenly stood to attention with difficulty atop the tank. Behind him, his men clambered quickly to their feet.

"Guards Armoured Division, Sergeant." The young NCO said in a respectful Scouse accent.

Jackson blinked in surprise.

"The Guards what?" He asked incredulously.

The corporal repeated the term then allowed himself a broad grin.

"Sounds odd, Sergeant, doesn't it? We only got formed two days ago. The tanks are from an Independent Armoured Brigade and we're from 1st Battalion Irish Guards, part of 20th Guards Brigade. We just came through the Jerries like a dose of salts back there! Got the bastards back for Boulogne, sure enough!"

The Coldstream Sergeant ran his eye across the Liverpudlian Lance Corporal and his men. They were all big lads, with their buttons fastened and their web equipment properly fitted; smart and efficient looking. Jackson knew the Irish Guards well, and the smart appearance of this bunch belied the savage fighting spirit which he knew lay beneath the surface. For the first time in many days, Jackson allowed himself a genuine smile.

"Good old Micks!" He laughed.

His laughter was interrupted by the sound of an agonised scream that suddenly cut the air from within the farmhouse. At the sound of the terrible wail, Jackson swung around. The scream was cut short abruptly. Jackson began striding quickly towards the farmhouse, bringing his rifle back into the shoulder, ready to fire if required. He was barely halfway across the yard when the five men emerged from the building. He slowed his pace. They were all his men; Bishop, Downey, Martlesham, and the two older Home Guardsmen. Jackson stopped, fixing them with a dark look. Every one of the five men looked back at him impassively. The sergeant's eyes quickly took in the fresh blood on the bayonets of four of the men and he knitted his eyebrows in quiet disapproval.

"What happened?" He asked, his voice taught with anticipation.

For a moment, nobody spoke, but then Downey answered, his voice almost conversational.

"He tried to escape, Sergeant. We had no choice but to stop him…with our bayonets."

S +6
THE END OF A LONG WEEK

RAF CHURCH FENTON – NORTH YORKSHIRE
FRIDAY 27TH SEPTEMBER 1940 – 0700 HOURS

The aircraft landed very early that morning. Within seconds of the plane taxiing to a halt, the Prime Minister and Dill were clambering down the steps onto the tarmac. Brooke and Adam saw that Churchill was dressed as formally as ever, with his bowler hat, walking stick and greatcoat. Dill, ever the professional, looked serious and business-like, whilst Churchill was grinning from ear-to-ear, like a ten year old who had just bunked off school for the day. After warm greetings all round, and a brief opportunity for the VIPs to meet with the commanders of the 2nd and 44th Infantry Divisions, Brooke ushered his visitors into the waiting vehicles; Dill climbing into one car with Adam, whilst Brooke and the Prime Minister took the other. In a third vehicle, Brendan Bracken, Churchill's Private Secretary, travelled with Pug Ismay and Barney Charlesworth.

Once they were mounted, the small cavalcade pulled away and fell in with its escort; no less than four cruiser tanks, four Bren Carriers and two truck loads of Canadian infantry. The entire column was preceded and followed by military police outriders. The precaution was absolutely necessary, for the final German resistance around Bridlington and Driffield had only crumbled the previous afternoon, and Brooke had yet to be sure that every single wood, valley and remote barn in the East Riding of Yorkshire was properly cleared of rogue Germans. He had tried to persuade the Prime Minister to put off the visit until after the weekend, but Churchill was not to be argued with on this occasion. Britain had defeated the Nazi invader and he was determined to see the grisly results of the recent battle himself, preferably with plenty of cameramen on hand to capture the moment. If nothing else, this trip would give him enormous clout with the Americans, who were still cautious in their support for Britain.

They didn't have to go far to their first stop. Just before they reached the village of Cawood, the column halted and Churchill insisted on being given a detailed account of how the German spearhead had been trapped in the Cawood Pocket and systematically destroyed by a combination of anti-tanks guns, heavy artillery and air-strikes. The rotund politician could have spent all day walking from one blackened tank hulk to another, tapping each one experimentally with his walking stick, had Brooke not promised him more interesting fare. And so, just a few miles further on, over the much contested swing bridge, Churchill was presented with a scene that might have come from the Book of Revelation.

Even Churchill, alive with fighting spirit, fell silent at the sight of dozens of burnt out tanks and vehicles, stuck end to end on the narrow road between Selby and Ricall. Many of the vehicles still housed charred corpses that had yet to be buried and the whole area still reeked like a charnel house. After long minutes of staring silently at the scene of destruction, the Prime Minister turned to Brooke and Adam.

"How did we do such a thing to them? Our bombers?"

"No, Sir." Brooke shook his head. "This was mainly the result of our Matildas and the 25 Pounder regiments."

Churchill's eyes widened.

"Our tanks did this?"

"Yes, Prime Minister; mostly anyway. Although the Mark II Infantry Tanks have shown themselves to be slow and occasionally temperamental, the Germans have found it extremely hard to penetrate their armour, and the 2 Pounder guns they carry can slice through most German tanks without difficulty."

Churchill nodded soberly as he listened to Brooke's explanation, never once taking his eyes off the acres of wrecked vehicles that lay before him. After a while, he spoke; his voice low and full of gravity.

"And now the Nazis will realise, that the wages of sin really *are* death."

They moved on, heading east through yet more fields strewn with wrecked German armour and all manner of other vehicles. Here and there, they came across knocked out British tanks, but the vast majority of hulks were those bearing the German cross.

After an hour or so of steady driving and much discussion, they arrived at Holme-on-Spalding Moore, where they walked to the top of Church Hill for a commanding view of the country side. This defensive box had been on the main axis of the German advance, slowing the enemy considerably, and taking much of the impact out of the enemy Blitzkrieg tactics. On the crest of the heavily cratered hill, the commander of the garrison, a lieutenant colonel from the Hampshires, succinctly described the preparations for defence and the subsequent battle for the Holme Box, including how a lone sergeant from the Coldstream Guards, with a collection of waifs and strays, had managed to hold the most exposed part of the position despite ferocious German assaults.

All of what was said pleased Churchill. He spent a long while surveying the countryside with binoculars, and listened intently as Brooke explained how the counter-attack by the Guards Armoured Division had thrust south-eastwards from Elvington and Kexby and caught the enemy right on a divisional boundary. After many questions and answers, the group of VIPs took their leave of the colonel and walked back down the slope to the waiting cars. As they went, Churchill threw a meaningful look towards Brooke and Dill.

"Good man that young half-colonel, eh? Knows how to fight. He should be a brigadier before long, don't you think?"

Brooke agreed that indeed the lieutenant-colonel had conducted an impressive defensive battle, and that given a fair wind, he would probably skip through the rank of full colonel pretty quickly before being assigned to command his own brigade in due course.

The journey went on. As the convoy nudged past a column of Canadian infantry, the Commonwealth soldiers recognised the squat figure of Churchill inside his car, and within moments, hundreds of voices were cheering as if they were at a football match. The delighted Canadians held up their fingers in the 'V' for victory sign and waved their helmets as the vehicles trundled by. Churchill of course, was beaming like a child who had just won first prize in some boyish game or other, and he waved back at them, returning the 'V' sign as he went.

Further along, they came upon the rear of a column of troops from the 20th Guards Brigade, marching eastwards along the main road to Driffield. At the rear of the column, a towering, scar-faced warrant officer saw the approach of the convoy and recognised that it was somebody very important. He bawled some instructions to the front of his company, and the column of Guardsmen wheeled left into a lay-by, halting smartly, turning sharply to their right then bringing their rifles into the slope. As the staff cars neared the stationary unit of soldiers, a major standing at the front centre of the formation barked out an order. Then, with a flash of precision that was typical of the British Foot Guards, the entire company brought their rifles down into the present arms stance, their heavy ammunition boots thumping down in one, thunderous crash on the gravel.

Churchill ordered the driver to stop in front of the major, who was saluting smartly with his hand. The Prime Minister wound down the window of the car and stuck out his head, a broad grin creasing his granite-like features.

"Good morning, the Brigade of Guards!" He called loudly.

"Good morning, Sir." The major replied in a dignified voice. "No.3 Company, 1st Battalion Welsh Guards, and all's well, Sir."

Churchill laughed out loud.

"Marvellous! Absolutely marvellous! Well done men, all of you; you're the pride of Britain!"

The major spoke again.

"Leave to carry on, Sir, please?"

"Yes, please." Churchill waved his hat towards the company of Guardsmen. "Thank you very much indeed."

They drove on, and Churchill sat back, chuckling away to himself.

"Excellent soldiers, aren't they? The Guards? Don't know what we would do without them." He chuckled again "Leave to carry on, Sir, please? What's that all about? Reminds me of when I was with the Grenadiers in the First War."

Brooke smiled indulgently. The Guards did have their detractors within the Army, but he was not one of them. He had seen them perform feats of soldiering during his career that few other units could hope to replicate.

"They had a hard fight getting over the Wolds, Prime Minister, but they did a sterling job; absolutely sterling."

Churchill grunted.

"I was thinking, General Brooke; perhaps this idea of a Guards Armoured Division could become a permanent thing?"

Sensing that Churchill was about to discover a new hobby-horse, Brooke murmured a response that was suitably non-committal.

Their next stop was Driffield. They didn't stop long. The town was a pile of ruins. It had been the centre of gravity for the whole invasion since day one, and had suffered accordingly. Not only had the British and Germans fought ferociously over the town twice, but the RAF had bombarded the town and its feeder routes remorselessly throughout those first critical days. Looking at the shapeless ruins of the ancient market town, Churchill mumbled a question to Brooke.

"How many civilians died here?"

Brooke cleared his throat.

"We don't have exact figures yet, Prime Minister, but I am led to believe that there are several hundred civilian dead and wounded."

Churchill became melancholy.

"This is one of the few things that my conscience will find difficult to bear, General Brooke. I did this."

"No, Sir." Brooke disagreed with the Prime Minister in a calm voice. "We all had a part in this. I wanted this area targeted by the RAF. It was a necessary evil for the greater good."

Churchill pulled a sour face.

"No." He snapped. "This is all my doing. I am the one who told the British public to stay where they were in the event of an invasion. I promised them that by doing so they would be assisting in their own subsequent liberation. Instead, I have visited nothing but utter destruction upon them."

Brooke studied Churchill's face for a moment. The feisty politician was truly upset by the fate that had befallen the population of this quiet little market town in Yorkshire.

"You did what any person in your position would have done, Sir. There is only one person to blame for what happened here, and he lives in Berlin."

Churchill regarded the general for long moments, before allowing a sad smile to ease the pained look on his face.

"Thank you, General Brooke, for your kind words. Could we move on though, please? I feel the presence of the old 'black dog'. Let us be gone from here."

Brooke gave the order to the driver and they moved on.

They arrived at Bridlington a little after midday, where they met up with Montgomery and McNaughton at the ruined harbour. Following a lengthy chat, the VIPs moved along the sea front a little, in order to get a good look at the Admiral Scheer. The heavily damaged battle-cruiser was beached about half a mile out from the shore, and had tilted over to starboard somewhat over the course of the last few days. The sight of the shattered wreck of the once formidable German ship put Churchill in an ecstatic mood. If an example of Hitler's folly were needed for all the world to see, this was it, and Churchill insisted on being photographed with his generals there and then, with the dark hulk of the abandoned warship as a backdrop.

From there, they drove over to Filey Bay to view the biggest of the German landing beaches, and dismounted by the cliff-tops that overlooked a narrow draw in the coastline. Adam took the lead here, explaining the topography to the visitors, and pointing out various items of interest. Brooke, already fairly familiar with the details, took the opportunity to wander off from the main group and halted by an abandoned trench that overlooked the wide beach. He glanced down with interest at the trench. It was British, evidently, and was well made. The location of the trench gave it a commanding view across the beach and the entrance to the draw in the cliff. It had once been mutually supporting with the demolished pill-box at the far side of the draw, which, he remembered, was known locally as Hunmanby Gap. Around the lip of the trench, and covering the whole floor of it, were dozens of empty brass cartridge cases. Somebody had put up fierce resistance here at some point he realised.

"Hard to believe isn't it?"

Brooke looked round in surprise at the sound of Churchill's voice. The Prime Minister was only a couple of feet to his left, having approached quietly. The remainder of the group were still standing some twenty yards away, deep in discussion.

"This time last week we had no idea where or when the Germans would strike; yet now our greatest trial seems to be over."

Brooke looked out across the rolling waves to where the pale blue sky met the horizon. There were ships there; big, Royal Navy ships, and plenty of them.

"Yes. Almost impossible to accept isn't it?" Brooke replied mildly. "That so much could have taken place in less than a week."

The two men were silent for a while, but after a moment or two, Churchill spoke again.

"If this doesn't convince the Americans that we're not a lost cause, then nothing will."

Brooke glanced at him.

"You think they'll come in with us?"

Churchill shrugged.

"Perhaps? Not this year though. Roosevelt has an election to fight, and there are plenty of people in America with no stomach for a war in Europe. He's taking a big gamble, going for re-election. If he's successful though, I think he might be persuaded to join us."

Brooke pondered that for a while.

"Will the war still be going by the time he decides?" Brooke wondered aloud. "Perhaps after this..." He waved his cane at the numerous broken hulks of invasion barges that littered the wide bay, "...Hitler might sue for peace."

The Prime Minister gave one of his characteristic rumbles.

"We have saved our country, General Brooke, but we have not saved Europe. The Nazi shadow will continue to blight the Continent for some time. We will not be able to remove that shadow on our own. We need the Americans. For the sake of the entire world, we need the Americans; which is why I intend to send a military envoy to Washington."

Brooke felt his curiosity rise. Churchill was leading him somewhere.

"We need a voice there." Churchill went on. "A man with diplomacy and tact. A man who can speak to both the politicians and the military men. A man like Sir John Dill."

Brooke raised an eyebrow.

"You can't send General Dill Prime Minister!" He exclaimed.

Churchill eyed the Commander in Chief Home Forces with mild amusement.

"You don't think Sir John is a suitable envoy?" He queried.

"On the contrary." Brooke said curtly. "I can think of no-one more able, but General Dill is the Chief of the Imperial General Staff; you can't send him to America."

Churchill was still regarding Brooke with that disconcerting look that was half appraising, half mischievous.

"I could send him if I found a new CIGS." The politician countered.

Brooke scoffed.

"And where would you find anyone capable of taking his place as CIGS in the current environment? There is no-one capable enough to replace him! We are struggling to find suitable commanders for our Corps and Divisions as it is!"

Churchill fixed Brooke with a shrewd look.

"There is one man." He said.

"Who?" Demanded Brooke.

Churchill jabbed his walking stick towards the general. "There is General Alan Brooke, the saviour of Britain."

Brooke was speechless. He opened his mouth to reply, but then closed it again, not sure what to say. Churchill waited patiently for his response.

"I will not be a part of any plan to remove General Dill from post." Brooke said at last, his voice tight and controlled.

"You won't have to." Churchill grunted. "Sir John has already volunteered for the Washington job, and he recommended you as his successor."

For the second time in as many moments, Brooke was lost for words.

"He did?"

Churchill nodded.

"This war has plenty of time left to run General Brooke, and we shall all end up in very different places to whence we began. Sir John has already seen his destiny. Now it is time for you to realise yours."

The Prime Minister took a deep breath of the fresh sea air.

"You don't need to panic though, General. The move won't happen this side of Christmas. I expect it would be spring next year at the earliest. There is much clearing up to be done after all this; and Home Forces still need a bit more of your attention before they are good and ready to take the war back across the Channel. Besides, we still need to see who the next occupant of the White House is going to be, before we make any firm decisions."

He turned to look at Brooke again.

"Why don't you think on it for a while? I'll let you know when I need an answer. In the meantime..." He nodded down towards the water's edge. " General Adam has promised to show me this Nazi landing craft. Perhaps we might learn some lessons from them, eh?"

With that, the Prime Minister turned away and began walking back over to the others.

"Join us when you are ready, General Brooke; no hurry." He called over his shoulder as he went.

Brooke watched the group of generals and politicians, along with their dismounted escorts, wander off into the depression that led down to the break in the cliffs. Once the last member of the party had disappeared through the hedgerow, the Commander in Chief of British Home Forces knelt down on the rear parapet of the trench, and began to pray.

He was unsure how long he stayed there. He prayed for the deliverance of the nation, for his wife and children, and for the countless men and women who had given their lives so far in this great endeavour. He prayed also for the strength to see him through whatever this war would next throw in his direction. After a while, feeling much more clear minded, Brooke climbed to his feet. He raised his binoculars and scanned with them, back and forth, trying to imagine the scene that must have presented itself to the occupants of this trench on that fateful morning, when the might of the German Third Reich descended on this beautiful section of coastline. As he swung his binoculars along the shore line, he caught a glimpse of the Prime Minister's party, and focussed the field glasses onto the knot of people by the barge.

Brooke frowned as he studied the group. They were all there; the men in uniform, along with the tall, bespectacled figure of Brendan Bracken, standing in a line by the ruined enemy vessel that boasted the designation 'P4' on its hull. Strangely however, they were all standing with their backs to the boat, whilst Churchill, his outline obvious even at this distance, was standing on the deck of the wrecked landing craft. For a moment, Brooke couldn't understand what was going on, but then, with a sense of disbelief he saw precisely what was occurring.

Whilst his senior officers and assistants politely turned their backs, the Prime Minister of Great Britain was urinating on the remains of the German invasion barge. Even from this distance, Brooke felt sure that Churchill's face was a picture of childish glee.

"Now wouldn't that make a good picture to flash around the world?" Brooke wondered aloud.

He lowered the binoculars and shook his head. Churchill could be infuriating at times, but by God, you couldn't help love the man for his wondrous spirit. A gull cried overhead and Brooke, ever the bird-lover, automatically glanced up to locate the creature.

He saw the bird instantly. It was nothing special, just a common gull; the kind that fed off the waste washed up on the shore. It hovered there, balancing on the thermals that flowed invisibly over these high cliffs. Brooke had seen thousands of birds like this in his lifetime and, like many folk, would hardly give them a second glance. Despite that, on this glorious September evening, with a warm sun falling gently in the western sky behind him, General Sir Alan Brooke, Commander in Chief British Home Forces smiled broadly as a single tear left his eye and trickled down his cheek. Then, for some reason he could not fathom, he began to laugh.

Lightning Source UK Ltd.
Milton Keynes UK
11 February 2010

149937UK00001B/6/P

9 781907 294389